The Rock House

The Rock House

Delana Jensen Close

ISBN-13: 9781978340602
ISBN-10: 1978340605
Library of Congress Control Number: 2017916188
CreateSpace Independent Publishing Platform
North Charleston, South Carolina

Prologue

Welcome to Rockville
God lives here
And so does the devil.

Noah Edwards reads the sign and then looks around him and wonders why anyone would choose to live here, especially God—or the devil. Shimmering heat waves pulsate across a dried-up hayfield and fade into the horizon; tiger-striped monarch and swallowtail butterflies glide above purple thistles and brilliantly yellow mustard weeds. Honeybees circle a precariously leaning beehive, two rectangular wooden boxes one atop another, and in the shade of a willow tree, a half dozen milk cows huddle together near a sagging wire fence, lazily switching horseflies from their backs with stained, ropy tails. Brassy-faced sunflowers follow the sun, and the only sound is the incessant shrill of insects. Turning back, he gives his full attention to the sign God lives here painted in black across a weathered signboard and to the retort crudely carved, scraped, and scratched into the paint beneath the eccentric proclamation: AND SO DOES THE DEVIL.

Climbing back into his buggy, Noah sits slapping a stick into his left palm while he studies the two small arrow-shaped signboards nailed to a post at the junction of the road. The arrow pointing south reads JOHNSTOWN, 18 MI. The other, pointing west, reads ROCKVILLE, 1 MI. Unable to decide between Rockville, with God and the devil, or eighteen more miles of dust and heat, he removes a pocketknife from his pants pocket and sets to work whittling a point onto one end of the stick. He tosses the stick into the air and watches noncommittally as it falls to earth amid a little stir of dust.

A flip of his wrist sends ribbons of leather rippling along the back of the horse. "Giddy up, Miss Molly," he says to his mare. "It looks like we're going to Rockville."

Part 1

CHAPTER 1

June 1902

THE SMALL MIDWESTERN TOWN OF Rockville lay at the foot of a mountain: a solid, comforting mass of earth, rock, and vegetation not native to the state or even the country, pushed there eons ago by ice-age glaciers. A giant russet-colored boulder, jutting out from its resting place halfway down the mountainside, dominated the view. The townspeople called it the Rock House.

The same dusty road that had led Noah to the railroad station soon became Rockville's Main Street, where, in summer months, oil was laid down to settle the dust and lumber planks put down at street corners when it rained. The place was as quiet and deserted as the countryside he had been driving through all morning. Noah tied his horse with the buggy to the hitching rail in an alley separating the Parlett Hotel from the barbershop.

Sudden laughter from the shop interrupted the stillness of the late afternoon, drawing Noah to the sound. As he opened the door, he glanced at the florid black and gold lettering on the plate-glass window: MA'S BARBERSHOP. JOHN MURPHY, PROPRIETOR. When he entered, the laughter abruptly stopped.

A man who resembled a heavyweight boxer wearing a white collarless waistcoat and black bowtie, his red hair glossed with brilliantine and parted in the middle, greeted him with a broad smile and a show of teeth, of which the two front ones were gold. "Can I help you, mister?"

"Do you barber this late in the day?" Noah asked, removing his hat and revealing flaxen hair in need of a trim.

"I barber sixteen hours a day, six days a week," the barber said, flicking hair from one of the four barber chairs not covered with a sheet. He gestured for Noah to sit down.

The barber hadn't finished with Noah's tonsorial when a black man cradling a white poodle in his arms entered the shop. "Mister," the man said to Noah, "will you be staying at the hotel?"

"Yes, sir," Noah answered. "I believe I will." His reply brought snickers from the men loafing in the shop.

"And will you be wanting supper?"

"Right again."

"Then I'll take your bags to your room and stable your horse. What's her name?"

"Miss Molly." Noah waited for the snickers and was not disappointed.

"That's a fine name for a mare," the man said. "You can check in with Mrs. Parlett. If you don't find her in the hotel lobby, look for her in the dining room or clerking in the store."

Noah, along with the two traveling drummers he had seen in the barbershop earlier, and Mr. Goldman, a seller of fine jewelry, were the only guests in the hotel's dining room for dinner that evening. Later the two young salesmen quickly returned to the pool hall, while Mr. Parlett and the jewelry salesman fell into a discussion of business conditions elsewhere in the state. Noah, feeling bored, decided to work off the dulling effects of his daylong buggy ride by taking a walk. Leaving the hotel by the lobby entrance, he glanced up at the balcony and saw Mrs. Parlett quietly rocking and fanning herself. He touched the brim of his cap in deference to her. The hotel was built over the general store, of which the Parletts' home consisted of the two center-front rooms.

Noah turned to his right and strolled past the Rockville Repository, the Farmers Co-op, and the United States post office with its traditional flagpole, the flag removed for the night. A large maple tree stood on the sidewalk close to the street, the only maple on the otherwise elm-lined street. Crossing over, Noah could see on the far side of the block a white clapboard church with a faded red roof and a bronze bell hanging in the cupola. So far, it was the only church he'd seen.

It was the first Saturday evening of summer, and the air bristled with expectancy. Up and down the tree-lined streets, screen doors slammed open and shut, porch swings creaked, and neighbors called to one another across hedges and fences. Sounds of youthful voices pierced the night, calling "Olly olly oxen free!" Housewives hurried through their final readying-up activities. Men took their weekly baths, and young children were pummeled into their bedtime rituals by fretting mothers. Young ladies dressed for their beaus, and the young men horsed around outside the pool hall, waiting for the time to go calling. A cooling breeze flowing down the mountainside closed the flowers for the night, and, from the darkening gardens, fireflies flickered into view. Noah returned to the center of town, and the barbershop.

John, the owner, did not seem surprised when the young blond-haired man showed up at Ma's, but he did wonder what he was doing in town. In Rockville, the only thing to do on a Saturday night was to hang out at Ma's; even men who abstained during the week would down a short one. As for the rest of the time, except for getting a haircut, most gentlemen shied away from his place. John Murphy never advertised that his establishment contained a stand-up bar with a brass foot railing and an oil painting of a nude woman hanging on the back bar—the best-kept secret in Rockville. He didn't have to. The place had liquor and beer for anyone who wanted a drink, but it had to be consumed in the narrow barroom, out of sight of the barbershop and pool tables. John served as bartender and sometimes bouncer. From his vantage point at the end of the bar, he could keep track of the activities of his enterprise. He could tend to his bar customers and keep tabs on the two pool tables and the men sitting on benches surrounding the perimeter of the room talking crops, politics, and weather, leaving the area devoted to his barbering trade in the shadows and off limits. Everyone accepted this arrangement—except cattle rancher Chance Collins.

Somehow John was not surprised when Noah appeared. Finding an empty stool at the bar, John motioned to him. He set a mug of foaming beer in front of him and said, “It’s on the house.”

During the evening, men drifted in and out or moved on to new groups. Eventually time slowed, talk lagged, and, with no more arguments or laughter for time-worn jokes, men yawned. Someone said, “I expect it’s time to go home.”

John Murphy sighed. “It’s looking to be one of those Saturday nights when everyone goes home early,” he said to Noah. Then, a young man, his face flushed and lively, entered Ma’s and, making his way to the bar, ordered a beer and a short one and said to John, “Guess who’s having a baby?”

John paused, not sure he wanted to know. “Who?” he asked with a grunt.

"Abigail Langley, that's who," the man said, looking as if he'd just sold a prize heifer at the county fair.

"Gus, she's just a kid. Are you sure you know what you're talking about?"

"Damned but I do. Ma stopped over there earlier this evening, and she said every pot on the kitchen stove had water boiling in it. I went over there myself—not to the house, mind you, just to the gate—and Brother Griggsby comes walking out of there all in a huff. I said, 'What's goin' on in there, Brother Griggsby?' And he said, without even slowing his pace or looking at me, 'A whore's having a baby.'"

"It can't be a baby," John said to Gus. "It must be some other kind of sickness."

"She's awfully young to be having a baby, isn't she?" an older man said.

"Does Abigail Langley have a beau?" John asked.

"She ain't never had a beau that I knowed of," said the white-haired and white-bearded Dell Tate.

"We're goin' up there and nosin' around," a young man said as he playfully boxed his buddy's shoulder.

"You do that, but don't let anyone catch you poking around," John said with a wink at the marshal. "They might take one of you for the father." He roguishly twirled the ends of his red mustache between his fingers.

Chance, dressed in his customary black twill pants and shirt, cattleman's boots, and a leather belt fastened with a hammered-silver buckle, was feeling his oats. "That preacher would call the mother of Jesus a whore!" he said when he heard the gossip.

Scraping his thumbnail along his forehead, he pushed his black, broad-brimmed hat to the back of his head, exposing the purplish needle-pocked scar on the right side of his face. The white upper forehead common to all farmers in summer was not seen on Chance's swarthy skin. From behind the bar, John observed him and wondered if it was the scar that made Chance the mean bastard he was.

The scar, the result of a mule kick when Chance was a kid, extended from his temple to the corner of his mouth and turned his upper lip into a permanent sneer. The gash had been stitched together with a needle used to sew up horseflesh; whenever John shaved him, which was daily (except for the Sabbath), the scar reminded him of a badly darned sock.

Straightening out his right leg, Chance removed a knife and a plug of tobacco from his pants pocket and commenced to cut off a chew. With a yellow-stained finger he worked the tobacco into his cheek and then set about cleaning his nails. When he looked up, the man he called Blackie was staring at him. Chance belligerently shot a wad of brown tobacco juice in the direction of the brass spittoon but missed it. He motioned with his pocketknife until he got the attention of Ross Taylor, a skinny cowpoke who worked cattle for Chance. Moving with haste, the cowpoke shifted the spittoon in the direction in which Chance was pointing.

Chance narrowed his eyes and leered at the black man, his scarred smirk exposing teeth with gold fillings, gold caps, and pond-scum-green remnants of tooth enamel.

"Someday, Blackie, I'm going to whup you good," he said. "Thinks he belongs," he said to Ross with a sneer.

A low, melodious laugh came from the throat of the tall, dark figure leaning against the jamb of the front door. "Anytime you say, Mistuh Collins," he said, stroking the head of the white poodle he held cradled in his left arm. "Just you name the day."

Chance scowled at the poodle. "That ain't no dog, it's a goddamn rat." He spat tobacco juice into the spittoon hard enough to cause the brass to ping.

The dairyman, Gus Wilson, now with too many short ones under his belt, called out to a white-faced, simple-minded youth in the room, "Hey, Pie Face, you the father of Abigail Langley's baby?"

Pie Face drooled and blinked and sucked in air while he laughed, vigorously nodding his head up and down.

Chance scoffed at the idiot before turning his attention to the stranger, who had left his seat at the bar and now stood, hands deep in the pockets of his blue-and-white-striped seersucker jacket, watching a pool game.

Chance studied the stranger while scratching at the scar on his face. He found physical perfection in a man to be repulsive. Shoving the Bull Durham pouch back in his shirt pocket, he stepped from the barber chair. "I'm Chance Collins," he said as he extended his hand.

Noah's blue eyes sparkled as he took the proffered hand. "Noah Edwards," he said, but his smile quickly faded when a stab of pain raced up his arm to his shoulder. The scar-faced man kept on smiling but didn't loosen the grasp of his handshake.

"You ain't been in town before, have ya?" Chance asked, his gold teeth glimmering in the harsh light. "Say, maybe nine months ago?"

"Certainly not," Noah answered as he tried to free his hand.

"Anytime a man rides into town in a buggy, it's fer a funeral or to stay," Chance said in a drawl.

"I didn't come for a funeral," Noah said angrily. His hand felt numb.

"Well, you don't look like no farmer, and we don't need no schoolteachers."

Noah's Nordic blue eyes turned to ice. "I'm a music teacher and a minister," he said, wondering if he could knock the guy down with a left-handed punch. Trying not to attract attention to what must have looked like a friendly handshake, Noah again attempted to pull his hand away from the man's bear-trap grip.

"Well, I sincerely hope you don't play the pie-ano," Chance said sarcastically. Then, quickly releasing the stranger's hand as if it was something too hot to handle, he stepped away and said in a voice loud enough to get everyone's attention, "Well, I'll be damned, folks, but I think we got ourselves a music teacher. That's just what this town needs." He pointed his nose in the air and imitated a snob playing piano. Leaning into Noah, he said in a mock whisper, "Let me give you a bit of advice, mister. Don't get married, 'cause your wife and kids are gonna starve to death." Then, feeling pleased with himself, Chance looked to his cohorts to join him in his hilarity.

The tension in the air dissipated when the two young men who had left Ma's earlier came bursting through the open door, full up with their own importance.

"It's true! Abigail Langley's having a baby. We couldn't see anything, but Mrs. Langley came out the kitchen door and threw a pail of water on the lawn, so it ain't her what's sick. We could hear noises in that downstairs bedroom, and Doc's horse and buggy is hitched to the gatepost."

"Must be serious if they called in Doc Townsend," John said.

The pronouncement caused much agitation and a lot of nudging and bumping of one another among the men in the barbershop. The married men wanted to go home and tell their wives the latest gossip but were reluctant to leave. Amid short barks of laughter, too loud and too frequent, men nervously juggled the contents of their pockets: knives, coins, nails, wheat chaff, sulfur matches. Tonight, more men than usual were slipping into the dark, narrow room behind the pool tables with its stand-up bar and brass foot rail.

Noah remained in the barbershop until he was no longer amused by the antics of the Saturday night crowd, and left for his hotel room.

He stretched out on the bed by the open window and soon fell asleep, only to be awakened by someone singing in a beautiful baritone voice a song of golden shores and marble halls. It was ten thirty and closing time at Ma's, and each Saturday night, seated in the doorway of the barbershop, Harlan Jones, the man they called Blackie, sang. He sang happy songs and sad songs, everyone's favorite hymns, and songs with strange rhythms, sometimes clapping his hands and snapping his fingers for accompaniment. Now and then, hypnotized by the summer night and the music, folks would stroll downtown and sit on the store steps and listen to him. But this was late on Saturday night, and he sang only to the regulars at Ma's, ending as he always did with an old familiar hymn. People living nearby, either sitting on their porches or preparing for bed, sang the hymn along with him; it seemed a fitting thing to do at the end of a long week.

"Goodnight, Harlan, thanks for the singing," said the barber, holding the screen door open while Chance Collins and three other men made their way out.

"He sure can sing," said one of the farmers.

"Hell, Frank, all niggers can sing. If you was a nigger, you could sing, too," Chance said. They laughed.

Noah sat massaging his hand and watching the men below mount their horses. John had cautioned Noah not to tie his horse anywhere near Chance's. "His horse is as ornery as he is," he had told him. The lights suddenly blazed bright inside Ma's, and from his hotel window, Noah could see Harlan at work cleaning up the place.

"Horse's ass," Noah muttered as Chance Collins rode out of the alleyway on his big black stallion. It was then when he remembered the sign at the crossroads from that morning: GOD LIVES HERE, AND SO DOES THE DEVIL.

Well, I've met the devil; now I wonder who God is?

At midnight the streetlamps went out, and Noah, lying in total darkness, thought about the young woman who'd had a baby but not a husband. He hoped her fall from grace had been an act of love.

CHAPTER 2

Early Saturday evening

ABIGAIL LANGLEY WAS INDEED HAVING a baby, and under the most trying of circumstances. By refusing to give up the name of the father of her baby, she had exasperated the hard-shelled Baptist preacher Brother Griggsby of Old Church to the point that he had lost his temper. But he wasn't the only one in a bad humor. The unmarried, fifteen-year-old Abby was livid. She was hot. She was in pain, and she wanted nothing more than to kick off the bed covers and rip off her clothes. Scrubbing at her forehead with both palms, she pushed back the heavy tangle of auburn hair plastered to her face and shoulders, which proved to be as suffocating as the room she was lying in. She'd like to chop it off. All of it.

What Abby had succeeded in doing was to put the brother's reputation as keeper of the morals of his congregation of Old Church to the test. She had refuted his astuteness in ferreting out unseemly and untoward conduct by any member of his church before it got out of hand. But, for the most part, the brother was grievously troubled because the young woman was denying him the gratification of bringing her back to Jesus. What he wanted from the unfortunate girl was a soul-searching, heartrending, tell-all confession followed by a hallelujah-filled, tub-thumping, God-be-praised unbosoming of her transgression before the members of his belief.

Another round of racking pain rolled over her, causing her to suck in her breath and close her eyes. The brother quickly lifted the sheet and was ogling the heaving abdomen when Abigail screamed and lashed out at him with a bared leg.

Covering herself, she raised herself to her elbows; narrowing her eyes into green slits, she made eye contact with the lecherous, aging preacher. "Get out of this room!" she said in a low, threatening voice. "I don't want you in here."

"Then give us the name of the father," the enraged Brother Griggsby shot back.

"Never! I will never name him, and especially to you! I will take his name with me to my grave."

"To your grave and straight to hell!" he said explosively.

"Oh!" she cried, as much from the conjured pictures of hellfire tormenting her mind as from the actual hell tormenting her body.

Abby, feeling alone in her purgatory, the pillow beneath her head wet with perspiration, locked her jaws to the moans and cries of labor and stared with loathing toward the brother whose voice, with a dreary edge of petulance, was droning on.

"I won't let Aunt Em help you until you name the father," Griggsby said, nodding toward the midwife standing nearby. Abby glanced at Aunt Em and could tell by the look on her face that she was fit to be tied. He added, "You let us know who the man is, and we'll bring him here—right now, tonight—and have you married and saved in no time at all, and all done in the name of Jesus. Just name the man!"

The preacher's righteous outburst had left him thirsty. Moving to the walnut chifforobe, he picked up the pink-glass carafe, placed there for his convenience, and poured himself a glass of water. While he drank, he examined his silver-haired reflection in the mirror on the chest of drawers. He jutted his jaw forward and tightened the skin on his neck; he turned his large head from side to side admiring his looks, which he considered saintly. At the same time, the godly man was observing with prurient interest the reflection of the writhing girl on the tousled bed. Brother Griggsby was counting on the repentance of this woman to realize his own dream: the validation of himself as the moral disciple of God embraced by a larger community, far beyond the narrow boundaries of this country parsonage.

With this in mind, he stationed himself at the girl's bedside and bore down with a vengeance on forcing a confession from her. "Girls who have their babies out of wedlock have a harder time in labor," he said. "I've seen it before. I saw one woman die in childbirth without repenting, and she and her baby are now damned to the fires of hell for all eternity."

A great crushing wave of pain rolled over Abby, draining the blood from her face. She grasped the brass rail behind of her head and allowed the first moan to escape her lips.

The midwife rushed toward the bed, but Brother Griggsby turned and, stretching out his arms, blocked her way. "She doesn't need your help, Aunt Em," he said, his voice vibrating with emotion. "She needs God's help. Girls like her need to get down on their knees and beg God's forgiveness."

"She's in no condition to get down on her knees, Brother Griggsby," Aunt Em snapped. Her hazel eyes flashed, and her cheeks warmed to a deep red as she flung the towel she was holding onto a chair and abruptly left the room and the house.

With Aunt Em gone, Abby pulled the sheet over her head; then, turning her face to the wall, she pushed a corner of the sheet into her bloodied mouth and ground at it with her teeth. She was not about to give Brother Griggsby the satisfaction of hearing her scream.

Abby's mother, the widowed Nita Langley—a once-pretty woman grown old and bitter after the untimely death of her husband, long before the unseemly pregnancy of her daughter—made one of her many trips to the bedroom, this time bringing with her a white porcelain pitcher filled with hot water. With each entrance, she kept her eyes averted from her daughter.

Nita Langley's dark eyes, pale skin, and black hair, upon her marriage to a redheaded, blue-eyed Irishman, had combined to give the couple's only child dark-green eyes, silky and deep-auburn hair, and creamy skin with the warmth of summer.

On her mother's next trip into the room, she brought Brother Griggsby a tray of refreshments: tea and a plate of cookies. Abby found the smell of the hot tea nauseating.

Smiling with difficulty, her mother placed the tray on a small table beside the overstuffed chair where Brother Griggsby was seated. Tonight, in the unflattering lamplight, the lines in her mother's face were etched long and deep.

Abby, suddenly experiencing the worst of her labor pains, panted and groaned and grabbed onto the head rail and broke into a profuse sweat. Knowing that Aunt Em was not there, both women started to panic.

Nita wrung out a towel in warm water and wiped Abby's face and neck, plumped up her pillows, wrung out the towel again, this time in cold water, and left it on Abby's forehead, partially covering her eyes. The contraction subsided, and Mrs. Langley left the room.

Abby peeked from beneath the towel and watched the brother spoon sugar into his teacup, stir, taste, and add more sugar before lifting the cup to his thick lips. Evidently satisfied, he set the heavily sugared tea aside and, with a pudgy hand, lifted the dainty flowered dessert plate from the tray; his thickset fingers plucked up the first of the cookies.

During Brother Griggsby's act of reaching for the cookies, Abby glimpsed a mended, still-fraying shirt cuff. She found secret satisfaction in the preacher's grimace as he tugged on his coat sleeve in an effort to hide his wife's graceless patchwork.

As he poured more tea, the preacher wondered if it was too soon to remind the elders of his congregation, again, of the miserly stipend they paid their clergyman; maybe he would just send all five of his offspring to church in their bare feet.

A long shadow fell over Brother Griggsby in his sugary bliss, and he looked toward the bedroom door. There, silhouetted by the light from the gas lamp in the living room, stood Dr. John Townsend, a black medical bag in one hand and Aunt Em standing at his other hand. The doctor, an impressive figure of a man, was made more so by the tall black silk hat he always wore.

"That'll be all for tonight, Brother Griggsby," the doctor said, his voice as cold and harsh as his face. "Your presence here is no longer required." The doctor, known for the bluntness of his tongue, held the bedroom door open and waited for the preacher to exit.

Brother Griggsby, with ill-concealed anger, rose from his chair and left the room.

Dr. Townsend closed the door behind him and hung his hat on the newel post of the bed, as was his custom. He said, "Now, Abigail, let's have that baby."

He poured water from the white ceramic pitcher sitting on the dresser into the matching ceramic basin;

then, using the soap and brush he carried in his satchel, he washed his hands and dried them on a hand-embroidered white linen towel offered to him by Mrs. Langley. He removed a stethoscope from his bag and listened to the baby's heartbeat; placing a hand on Abby's abdomen, he immediately felt the strength of the long, hard contraction.

"It isn't going to be easy, Abby, but if you listen to Aunt Em and obey her instructions, everything will be just fine." He patted her shoulder. "I'm here to help."

Emma Townsend, the doctor's second wife and one of two midwives in town, was the one who most often delivered the town's babies. But "Aunt Em," the name she was known by, did more than deliver babies; she also attended to the many physical needs of the town, from being born to dying. A blessed feeling of love and healing flowed from her to those who were ailing; just knowing that she was on her way was the perfect tonic for whatever ailed a sick person.

Children claimed that the nasty medicines they were forced to take tasted better when Aunt Em administered them. And, best of all, if she accidentally broke her fever thermometer, she would put the silvery-looking liquid into a pie pan and let them play with the magical blob, rolling it around in the pan or on the palms of their hands. She left the bone settings, operations, and more serious afflictions with complications to her husband.

Aunt Em leaned over the bed, murmuring comforting words of encouragement to Abby while wiping perspiration from her neck and face. "He's gone," she whispered to her. "That old brother's gone, and you can yell and scream all you want. It helps, God bless you." She turned and said to her husband, "You should attend to all the women when their time comes and scare away that preacher. Lordy, but he's a caution."

The doctor, reacting to Aunt Em's deep, infectious laugh, also laughed. "He sure took off, didn't he?" When John Townsend smiled, his face relaxed, which made him appear quite handsome and years younger.

"Her contractions are getting closer together," Aunt Em said. "I think getting mad at that old Griggsby speeded you up," she said with a chuckle to the mother-to-be.

Abigail could feel hands on her body and hands rubbing her back, orders given, and crying and hoarse screaming, all of it dreamlike. *They're so far away*, she thought. *Everything in the room looks so far away.* And then her mother was there, bathing her, changing her gown, rolling her from side to side. Aunt Em's mouth was moving, but Abigail could no longer hear or understand what she was saying.

She was in a strange new world with a sky of brilliant blue; she carried a heavy bundle and was climbing the steps of a great white marble stairway that stretched up and up and finally disappeared into the heavens. Her arms ached, and she was weary all over, but she was unable to put the burden down or stop climbing. The bundle grew larger and heavier, and the stairs went on and on.

Aunt Em, preparing the newborn, was cooing and talking baby talk. "Isn't he a fine boy?" she was saying. "Isn't he a big, pretty boy?" After wrapping the baby in a blanket and pulling a corner of it beneath his tiny chin, she presented the baby to Mrs. Langley. "Look, Grandmother, look what a handsome grandchild you have."

Mrs. Langley, expecting the infant to look familiar, took a peek, forgetting that all newborns look alike. "Humph," she said.

"Abby. Abby!" It was Aunt Em's husky voice calling her. Opening her eyes, she saw Aunt Em holding the bundle from her dream.

"It's a boy," she said, placing the bundle in her arms and laughing in that deep way she had. "A nice healthy boy, and one of the prettiest babies I've ever seen." The doctor was gone, having left women's work to the women.

Abby gazed into her baby's face, and when she did, all the pain and humiliation she had endured faded away. "Oh, my love, we have a son," she whispered, kissing her baby's head.

CHAPTER 3

WITH BABY RONNIE ASLEEP IN the cradle beside her, Abby relaxed into the pillows on the daybed in the living room, taking pleasure in the warmth of the sun on her face and the comfort of the presence of grace she felt on Sunday mornings that was absent other days of the week.

Humming along with the clarion bells, Abby told herself that if she could forget her mother's unhappiness, the threats of damnation from Brother Griggsby, and the unrelenting pain of small-town gossip, she would be happy.

Aunt Em was there at sunup, her enthusiasm as invigorating as the spring day. She had examined and bathed both mother and newborn; as she rushed off to her next patient, she left them to continue becoming acquainted with each other.

Abby's mother, after silently serving her daughter breakfast in bed, putting diapers to soak, and cleaning the kitchen, was spending Sunday morning in her room.

Noah Edwards, dressing in his hotel room, was listening to the ringing of the nine-thirty bell coming from the downtown church he had seen on his walk last night. It was a reminder that half an hour remained before Sunday services began. Men in their barns, women in their kitchens, and children playing outside and trying not to get dirty all knew that at the sounding of the "half bell," it was time to leave for church.

Noah read the slate hanging beside the double-door entrance to Old Church. It made known the subject of the morning's sermon: THE SEVENTH COMMANDMENT: "THOU SHALT NOT COMMIT ADULTERY."

Oh boy.

Noah placed his stiff-brimmed straw hat on the floor beneath the bench on which he sat. Wearing white pants with a blue blazer, he stood out in the somber-clad congregation—like a "green corn worm on a red apple" was the way Perthy Prettyman, the town busybody, described him.

Young ladies seated on the left side of the aisle peeked around the shoulders of mothers, aunts, and grandmothers to get a better look at the tall, handsome stranger sitting with the men on the right side of the aisle. The singing, without accompaniment, had Noah tapping his toes and urged the singers along.

When the prayers were said, the hymns sung, and the sacraments taken, Brother Griggsby stepped to the lectern. The preacher, his voice low and intimate, spoke to them with a clannish, we're-all-in-this-together solemnity. "By now you all know what took place in our little village last night. Something foul and evil happened here," he said with a wrinkle of his nose. "The odious actions of a lady member of our very own faith have shamed us all. Every man, woman, and child in this dear little town of ours has been disgraced by this woman's immoral conduct. A woman who leads a man to lust deserves our scorn, and until Abigail Langley confesses her terrible sin, names the man who shares her guilt, and begs forgiveness from God, from her minister, and from this morally upright congregation, she will be denied the sanctity of this church. Nevertheless, along with her repentance, she will be taken back into our fold, and her terrible sin against God made as white as snow. We are willing and waiting to forgive."

After a long and uncomfortable pause, Brother Griggsby struck the lectern with his fist, causing some in the congregation to jump. "God lives here!" he shouted. "His spirit is our spirit. He lives in our hearts. He lives in our minds. He lives in our fields and in our streets. He watches our every move, and when He does His bookkeeping in His big black book up there in heaven, what kind of mark will He put down after your name? Will it be a good mark—or will it be a bad mark? Remember, on God's pencil, there is no eraser." His voice trembling, he added, "And the devil lives here, too. Oh yes. He lives here, and he is devilishly happy today because he has added another misbegotten soul to his army of sinners. The devil loves evil. He lurks about waiting to catch us in our moments of weakness. We learned last night what can happen when we leave the path of righteousness and take the path of transgression."

His voice grew plaintive. "The passion of the flesh is fleeting, my friends, but burning in hell is forever. It's God's forgiveness that is eternal. In sin you were born, in sin you were conceived, and in sin you will die and suffer the consequences of hell's damnation—unless you repent and accept Jesus as your savior, while there's still time."

Noah stopped listening. This was the same hellfire-and-damnation sermon he had heard during all his childhood years. He thought, *What an enormous confidence you must have in us, God, to entrust us with this earth, with one another, and most of all with ourselves.*

CHAPTER 4

ON MONDAY MORNING, NOAH ENTERED the dining room of the Parlett Hotel in the attire of an English gentleman dressed for a day of horseback riding. He was welcomed by Mrs. Parlett, who seated him before a bank of floor-to-ceiling arched windows glowing in the morning sun. Boston ferns and houseplants overflowed their ornate plant stands, and vividly flowered fabric covered the seats of the dark wicker chairs. The tinkling music of glass wind chimes, put in motion by the soft breeze coming through the open transoms, fell soothingly on his ears.

He smiled up at Betsy, an appealing young woman with light-brown hair and a ready smile, as she greeted him with a cup of coffee. A white apron covered her long black skirt and white shirtwaist. After serving Noah his breakfast—a bowl of oatmeal followed by potatoes, biscuits, hotcakes and a breakfast steak topped with two fried eggs—she helped the older waitress, a buxom, graying widow, clear the dishes from the table next to Noah's.

Glancing toward the hotel kitchen, where Nita Langley was the cook, Betsy lowered her voice before asking the older waitress, "Who do you think the father of Abigail Langley's baby is?"

"I don't know, but I do know I wouldn't let a man deliver for me," the widow said in a clipped, hushed tone. "I don't care if Dr. Townsend *is* a doctor—he should take care of the broken bones and leave the babies to Aunt Em."

"Aunt Em's going around town today proud as a peacock," Betsy said. "She says it's the prettiest baby she's ever seen. Just as if the baby had a father and everything's as right as rain."

"Aunt Em ought not to say that about a child born on the wrong side of the blanket," the widowed waitress said, briskly scraping and stacking dirty dishes. "It ain't proper."

"Mrs. Langley would never let Abby work at the hotel," Betsy said, "because she didn't trust the salesmen."

"Maybe it's her daughter she shouldn't trust."

"She's always tried to keep her looking plain as buttermilk."

"Well, it's hard to hide a swan in a henhouse," the older waitress said with a sniff.

Upon hearing the swan comment, Noah's eyebrows rose. He sat sipping his second cup of coffee and perusing a sign used to prop open the door to the large salesroom on the ground floor of the hotel that was called the Annex:

Dr. Thomas H. Veering, D.D.S.
Tooth extraction
Gold or silver fillings
Gold teeth
Care for bleeding gums
Gum boils
Halitosis (bad breath)
All mouth discomforts
Chloroform upon request
Open from eight to eight
Very reasonable costs

After finishing his coffee, Noah sauntered into the Annex. Dr. Veering, an itinerant dentist, was the occupant of the Annex for the month of June. The rent of the Annex included a discount on his hotel room and food. He was seated in his dental chair reading from the *Hub*, Rockville's only newspaper.

"How's business?" Noah asked.

The tall, loose-limbed man sprang from the chair. "Not bad," he said, buttoning his coat. The men introduced themselves and shook hands. "I come through here once a year and pick up a few customers. It takes them a while to get up nerve enough to come in and see me. I always attract a crowd, though," he said with a nod at the large display window. "Especially when I'm extracting teeth," he added with a wink and a smile.

Noah said goodbye to the dentist and stepped out of the Annex's street entrance and onto the sidewalk; as he passed the hotel lobby, he took a quick look inside. The little white poodle he'd seen earlier was napping in the sun on the window's ledge; he saw its owner mopping the lobby floor.

The emporium's specials for the day were promoted in green watercolor paint on one of the store's windows: EGGS 12¢/DOZ. COFFEE 25¢/LB. SUGAR 16¢/LB. Fragments of conversation between two women who stood on the emporium's steps leading to the store's front doors flowed past him like currents in a stream.

"But Abigail was always such a nice, quiet little girl," a woman who looked like a schoolmistress was saying.

"Still water runs deep," Ethel White, a descendant of the *Mayflower* Whites, crisply replied. Her disapproval of the subject of their conversation showed in her pale-blue eyes.

Noah passed the hitching rails and horseshoe pits in the alley and entered the shop for a morning shave.

John Murphy motioned Noah to an empty chair, tucked a white apron across his chest, and continued to listen to what the customer he was finishing up with was saying.

"My wife said Brother Griggsby told one of the ladies from her Tuesday sewing circle that Abigail bared a naked limb to the brother. Kicked him with it, he claims."

"I'd like to have seen old Griggsby's face when he saw a bare leg," the barber said, laughing as he lathered Noah's face.

"Well, he got even with her yesterday in church," the customer said. "Excommunicated her, he did—kicked her right out of his Garden of Eden."

After his shave, Noah thanked the barber and walked to the livery stable. He had Miss Molly saddled and checked on, his buggy packed with his personal belongings for his journey east to Cambridge, Massachusetts. He was to finish his education at Harvard University, where, if all went as planned, he'd receive his doctor's degree in theology. Noah wanted the degree, the title, the experience, and the education a major liberal university could provide him.

He had spent two years at Cambridge University in England, but he missed home, and when his grandfather had died and Noah had returned for his funeral, he decided to finish his education at an American school.

He rubbed his fingers across the small engraved brass plate attached to the side of his carriage: HOWARD EDWARDS, BUGGY WORKS. His grandfather had owned two buggy companies, one in Chicago and another in Saint Louis. Noah, as his only living relative, had sold the companies and set out on his search for enlightenment.

Noah's intention for the day was to tour Rockville on horseback and then climb the mountain to the giant rock he'd seen on his way into town and take in the view from there.

This being Monday and wash day, the glider swings and rocking chairs on front porches were all empty. The women of Rockville washed clothes on every back porch, and on every kitchen stove, a pot of bean soup simmered.

Even though the laundry activity was taking place in people's backyards, Noah still felt himself being watched. He was, after all, someone new in town.

It was noon when Noah, coming by way of the Italian immigrant quarry town of Saint Margaret's and the town's cemetery on Stony Creek Road, dismounted Molly at the town park on Main Street. Leaving the horse at the watering trough, he entered the grounds through the turnstile gate.

Across the street, a woman wearing a man's straw hat abandoned her laundering chores and came to stand near the white picket fence in her front yard. Noah raised his hat to acknowledge her interest in him.

Noah was more than surprised when he discovered a beautiful little garden separated from the grandstand and the remnants of what once had been a baseball field by an ornate iron fence. A fountain, topped by two marble swans spouting water into three graduated and scalloped cream-colored marble tiers, was the garden's centerpiece. The place was named Fountain Park, he noticed.

Selma Ward, the woman whose interest Noah had piqued, was responsible for the park. Selma's one-woman crusade to beautify Rockville had made the park a reality, and she was the park's sole caretaker. To date, getting the marble fountain had been her most difficult undertaking. The all-male town council had been determined not to let "ol' Selmy" get her way on this one. "We don't need no high-falutin' fountain," a council member argued.

"Yeah," another one said, "it's money over the dam."

But in the end, Selma had worn them down.

Two boys were sailing miniature boats made of sticks and leaves in the lowest tier of the fountain. Upon seeing

Noah, the oldest boy ducked behind a shade tree. Noah recognized the younger one as the pale-faced lad whom he had seen in the barbershop Saturday night.

"Hello, son," Noah said. The boy stared up at him.

The other lad, tossing a stone from hand to hand, ventured from his hiding place and, after ambling around the fountain, stood facing Noah. "That's Pie Face," he said, keeping his hand close to his hip and using his thumb to point toward the other boy.

The strip of hair from the boy's Apache haircut had been reduced to stubble, and the near baldness of his scalp accentuated the roundness of his face and the whiteness of his skin. Noah now understood why they called him Pie Face. Nodding toward the mountain, Noah asked the older boy, "What's the big rock up there?"

"That's the Rock House," the boy said, not turning around to look. "It's not a real house; it's just a big old rock. The drummers who come to town call it a tombstone. They say Rockville and everyone in it is dead and buried, and that's our tombstone. See that house over there?" he said, pointing to the distance. "The girl who lives there had a baby, and she's got no husband." He ended this bit of gossip with a downward, no-nonsense nod of his head.

On this extraordinarily beautiful day, Noah was thinking, the townspeople's thoughts, even those of the kids, were on an illegitimate baby and the washing of clothes. To Noah, gazing toward the mountain, the giant slab of rock looked more like a great all-seeing eye than a tombstone. He mounted his horse and headed west toward the mountain, keenly aware that the woman behind the picket fence was still watching him.

He kept his horse to a slow walk as he sauntered past a faded pastel-blue house on a corner lot with gingerbread woodwork on the front porch and the upper balcony painted a pristine white. A small sign hung on a wire fence near the gate: MRS. NITA LANGLEY, DRESSMAKER.

The pleasurable scent of roses floated from the colorful garden to the street. Noah was certain this was the home of the young woman who had been ridiculed, relentlessly gossiped about, and excommunicated from her church. He suddenly felt an overwhelming sadness for her and in his heart silently offered up a prayer.

From her daybed, Abby watched a handsome stranger, dressed in an English riding habit like the men in the English novels she loved to read, ride by on horseback. Bright sunlight glinted gold on the man's blond hair, showing beneath his bowler hat. She knelt on the bed and pressed her forehead to the window pane; she watched until he was around the bend in the road.

"There's a new man in town," she said, dropping back onto the bed and fluffing her pillows. The pillowcases, which she had embroidered for her hope chest when she was nine years old, were embroidered with an image of a calico kitten chasing an unwinding ball of blue yarn.

"You're moving around too much," Aunt Em said. Aunt Em was holding Ronnie on a towel spread across her lap and was showing Abby how to bathe a newborn.

"If I don't belong to a church," Abby said to Aunt Em, keeping her eyes averted from hers by watching Ronnie clumsily trying to get his thumb into his mouth, "how will my baby be baptized?" The state of her baby's immortal soul was uppermost on her mind.

Aunt Em, gently pulling baby Ronnie's thumb from his mouth and laughing at the face he made, said, "Well, we have us a baby—we can start our own religion."

The door between the living room and the kitchen slammed shut.

Aunt Em drew in a deep breath and let it out in a long sigh. "I'm afraid growing up in an orphanage left your mother without a sense of humor. Don't worry about it, Abby. I was never baptized, and it's never bothered me."

Abby's eyes grew large. "Really, Aunt Em, you're not just saying that? Everybody's baptized. Aren't they?"

"I figure God knows what He's doing," Aunt Em said as she placed the baby in Abby's arms.

"I hope so," Abby said nervously as she put her lover's child to her breast.

CHAPTER 5

NOAH RODE TO THE END of Main Street, where the stone bridge arching over Stony Creek gave way to a handsome driveway and the mansion of Dr. John Townsend. The doctor had made his fortune from proprietary medicines compounded to his formulas. One of them became an astonishingly popular cure-all liquid patent medicine called "Survivall" sold in pharmacies and mail-order catalogs and ads in newspapers and magazines. No one knew what the doctor's fortune amounted to, but they knew it was considerable. The doctor caught the 6:30 train every Monday morning to oversee his pharmaceutical empire in the city and returned on the 4:10 every Friday evening. When his son Adam turned six, the boy accompanied his father to attend a boys' academy in the city.

The Townsend mansion, built on a knoll with a view of the town, overlooked Stony Creek, which today reflected the calmness of the sky. Large shade trees and terraced gardens graced the gentle slope of the lawn, with stone steps leading from one garden to the next until they reached the white gazebo at the water's edge.

Several Italian immigrants from Saint Margaret's, who loved the life-giving feel of soil more than the hard stone of their town's quarry, kept the grounds of the mansion in immaculate condition, while their wives carried out the housecleaning chores.

Noah tethered Miss Molly upstream from the bridge, where the horse could drink and graze in the shade of the trees growing along its bank. Through the trees he could make out what looked to be an abandoned icehouse. It was almost hidden from view by willow and sycamore trees and overgrown underbrush. From here, Noah began his climb to the Rock House.

A path was not discernible, so Noah selected the best footing he could find among rocks, shrubs, hardy flowering bushes, and small trees as he steadily wound his way upward. Trees and the cover of vegetation made it easy to lose sight of the rock. When at last the Rock House came into view, Noah was surprised to have climbed beyond it; he found that he was now looking down on the large stone slab. *It really is the size of a house*, he thought.

The long climb during the warmest part of the day had left him hot and thirsty. Peeling off his shirt and undershirt, he stretched out on the flat rock. A cooling breeze flowing down the mountainside felt refreshingly invigorating on his bare skin.

He rested his head on his folded arms and gazed in wonder over the valley below him: to the south lay outlying farms, and beyond them stretched great forests of hardwood trees. At the foot of the mountain, he could see Stony Creek shining like a dazzling silver stream of light as here and there the sun dappled the rapidly moving water on its journey to the sea.

He stood to get a better view. Most of the houses in town were too small to be visible, or they were hidden by trees, but he could make out the stores on Main Street, the white clapboard church with its red roof, the school, the glint of gold from the cross on the Catholic chapel in the village of Saint Margaret's, and the post office where Old Glory with her forty-five stars hung serenely in the midday air.

Something out of kilter with the landscape drew his attention. Far to the south side of town, he could see amid a stand of trees an object that strangely resembled a very large boat. The town seen in miniature looked idyllic and peaceful—maybe too peaceful. *Yet Rockville could be the ideal place to begin my ministry,* he thought. *Too bad they're so set in their ways.* He combed his fingers through his hair and said aloud, "I wonder if I could convert them into believing in the Golden Rule and forgetting the burning-in-hell and the eye-for-an-eye vindictiveness of the Old Testament."

Standing there on the Rock House and looking down on the little town, Noah felt a kinship with the place. He spread his arms wide and shouted, "You're mine! Do you hear? I'm coming back to raise you from the dead. Me. Noah Edwards." Noah picked up his shirts and, laughing and shouting, stumbling and sliding, descended the mountain.

During his weeklong stay in Rockville, Noah had explored the creek, visited the lumber mills and grist mills, descended into the stone quarry and coal mines, observed the men at work, rode out to the farms, and talked to farmers and mill hands. Now, with his possessions packed into his buggy, he was on his way out of town. But he had one curiosity he needed to satisfy: the object he had seen from the Rock House in a grove of cottonwood trees that looked so incredibly like a large boat. He headed south.

After following the sound of wood chopping, Noah came upon an elderly man wielding an ax. The man eyed him with suspicion without lowering the ax.

"My name is Noah," he said as he cautiously offered his hand to the man with the ax.

"Ya. Well, in that case, I been a-waiting for you."

Both men laughed as they shook hands, and Noah gazed in wonder—at an ark.

Lars Larson, the ark builder, sinewy and rawboned, with long, flowing white hair and beard, looked to Noah like the biblical Noah might have looked. "Why," Noah asked, "would you build a boat miles from a large body of water, and why an ark? Is another flood coming?"

"I don't know about no flood," Lars said with a chuckle. "God hasn't let me in on that one. I just wanted to do it, daggamit. It's an ache inside me that wants to build the daggum thing."

"How long have you been working on it?"

Lars scratched his head. "Twenty-some years, I reckon," he said, spitting tobacco juice onto a pile of wood shavings. "T'isn't one of them things you finish. It just goes on and on."

"Would you show me your ark?" Noah asked.

"I will indeed," Lars said proudly.

Lars lifted a door located midway on the starboard side, and they entered a large empty space. They climbed a stairwell in a rear alcove of the boat and ascended to the upper deck, where Noah saw that a spacious cabin the size of a comfortable apartment had been erected. Back on the ground, Noah walked around the ark again, slower this time, admiring the craftsmanship and the dimensions of the boat. Returning to Lars, he said, "You're quite a builder, Mr. Larson. I wonder—would you consider selling it?"

Lars grabbed his chest and stepped back as if dealt a blow. "Yesus! Vhy, vhy," he stammered, trying to catch his breath, "vhy, nobody ever asked me that before."

Noah placed his hand on the elderly man's shoulder. "There's no need to tell me now; just consider it. You see, I'm on my way to divinity school, and when I graduate, I'll be a bona fide preacher, and I'm going to need a church, and I've decided I'd like it to be right here in Rockville."

"Well, I never," Lars said, letting out his breath. "A preacher!" He was pleased that someone liked the end result of his obsession—someone who didn't think he was crazy. "I will consider it, by dangie, I will, yes, sir." He shook Noah's hand and patted him on the back. "I surely will."

Noah settled himself in his buggy and, giving the horse a smart slap on her rump, sent them on their way.

"A church in an ark, Miss Molly, now what do you think of that?"

CHAPTER 6

ABBY'S MOTHER WAS BAKING BREAD. The homey aroma brought tears to Abby's eyes. Her mother had been kneading bread dough the day Abby had first told her about her condition. That had been last January.

"How long since your monthly sickness?" her mother had asked.

"Five months," Abby replied.

Her mother put one hand across her bosom and, after catching her breath, demanded, "Who is he?"

"I don't know," Abby lied. For the first time in Abby's life, her mother struck her. She slapped her with her flour-covered hand and began sobbing. Abby felt the life drain from her face and silent tears run down her own cold cheeks—two pasty-faced women weeping into their hands in the lonely remorse of their secret torments.

After the slap, Abby and her mother lived like strangers, never speaking, always cooking their own meals, cleaning up their own messes and simply waiting for the inevitable.

Later that same month, Grandmother Langley arrived from the ranch to spend a few days with them. They were in the kitchen when Grandma, eyeing Abby suspiciously, bluntly asked, "Are you fixin' to have a baby?"

Abby's mother began banging pots and pans around. Grandma turned around and glared at her. "If it's a baby, it's a comin', and ain't nothin' can be done about it," she said. "Only the good Lord can do that." She turned back to Abby. "Are you fixin' to get married?"

All Abby could do was shake her head no.

After an uncomfortable silence, they moved out of the hot kitchen and into the front room, each choosing one of three rocking chairs to sit in. Grandma picked up the sewing basket she'd brought with her, a round, flat-bottomed reed basket that fit comfortably in her lap. Deep in her own thoughts, she sorted through the socks, choosing a pair to darn that already matched the thread in the big-eyed darning needle.

Abby's mother sat disconsolate, her head bowed and her hands resting in her lap. A large ball of colorful fabric strips for weaving into rag rugs lay on the floor at her feet. A strip of cloth torn from scraps of an old dress was draped across her lap, ready to be sewn onto the next strip that made up the ball. Her needle remained idle in her fingers.

None of them felt comfortable enough to rock.

"I've heard about homes where girls can go and have their babies," Grandmother said, keeping her eyes on her darning, "and afterward the home arranges for the child to be adopted."

"I'm keeping my baby," Abby said.

Her mother leaned forward in her chair. "And do what?" she said, her voice demeaning.

Abby was too scared to do anything; she didn't know what she would do. She just kept daydreaming and praying that her baby's father would somehow make everything right.

"Then come to the ranch," Grandma said.

But Abby didn't want to go anywhere. She just wanted to hide—or die.

From the living room window, she watched her twin cousins, Corvus and Cetus, as they trudged up the sidewalk. Now that the twins were nine years old, it was their turn to stop at their aunt's house after school and do light chores. Their teenage brothers, Orion and Aries, picked them up when high school was over for the day and gave them a ride home on the backs of their horses.

Corvus and Cetus went around to the kitchen door and knocked. Abby's mother sighed and, rousing herself from her stupor, left the living room for the kitchen to let them in. Abby knew her grandma was not in the mood for the antics of Abby's twin cousins today.

"It'll all work out," Grandma said, putting an arm around her shoulders.

Abby told her how sorry she was. Grandma embraced her and kissed her on the cheek. "Things have a way of working out for the best," she said. "You'll see. We'll all get through this in our own way. A woman having a baby is the most natural thing in the world. But in the meantime..." Her voice trailed off, and she lowered her head and looked up at Abby in a confidential way. "But in the meantime," she repeated, "your ma's gonna be as cross as two crossed sticks."

Abby and her mother followed her into the kitchen, where the twins were shrugging out of their winter coats, exposing pieces of paper pinned to their clothing in the process.

"Land sakes, what's that stuck all over you?" Grandma asked with a laugh.

"It's Tag Day at school," the twins said simultaneously.

"Oh, I remember that," Abby said, smiling at her young cousins and trying to behave as though her world had not turned upside down and caved in on her.

"It's embarrassing. What tag is it today?"

"It's 'Ing Day.'"

"What in the world is 'Ing Day'?" Grandma asked.

"When you don't pronounce the 'ing' sound at the end of a word, the teacher writes it on a piece of paper and pins it to your clothing," Abby explained.

"And if she thinks you're doing it on purpose—" Corvus began.

"—she sticks you with the pin," Cetus said, finishing the sentence for him.

"Well, you look like molting chickens. Come over here and let me have a look at you," Grandma said as she adjusted her spectacles.

The boys sat at the kitchen table, drinking glasses of milk and enjoying warm bread spread with thick cream and sprinkled with a generous layer of sugar, while Grandma read aloud from the scraps of paper.

"Singing, reading, licking," she read, alarmed. "You boys been fighting at school again?"

"Licking," Corvus said, demonstrating the word by sticking out his tongue and licking sugar from his fingers.

"Well, it tastes better when you say *lickin'*, don't it?" Grandma said. "And here it says, *eating* in big letters."

"That's 'cause we said *et.* Miss Simms hates *et* almost as much as she hates *ain't,*" Corvus said.

"She says when she hears the word *ain't,* it gives her a headache," Cetus added.

"My word, she must have a delicate constitution," Grandma said. "And what's wrong with *et,* anyway?"

"*Et* ain't a word, Grandma," the twins said, giggling.

"You funnin' me?" she said huffily. "And whatever happened to readin', 'ritin', and 'rithmitic?"

"You dropped your 'ings,' Grandma." Laughing hilariously and jiggling around on their chairs, the boys managed to tip over a glass of milk.

"Are you in this year's spelling bee?" Abby asked, wiping up the spilled milk with a dishcloth and glad for any subject, or task, that would take her mother's mind off her predicament. She remained stoic, however, even when serving another glass of milk to the playful boys.

"Uh huh, for our fourth-grade class, along with those stuck-up Davis twins," Cetus said. Both boys made faces, since the Davis twins were girls.

"The best speller in the whole school is Sherman Jackson McCoy," Corvus said.

"He comes to school in his bare feet," Cetus said.

"Yeah," Corvus said. "His dad was killed by a Hatfield."

"Don't repeat gossip," Grandma said.

It was then when Abby felt her baby's first stirring: a twisting movement like it was turning over. She clutched at her abdomen, let out a cry, and fell into a kitchen chair, the twins staring at her wide-eyed. Grandma pressed Abby's head to her bosom and began massaging her back, while Abby's mother, appalled, yanked the milk-soaked dishcloth from her daughter's clenched fist and threw it into the sink.

"Your cousin Abby has a sore back," Grandma said to the startled boys.

Remembering the scene, Abby smiled through her tears as the smell of baking bread brought her back to the present. She wondered if her mother smiled when she thought about it.

CHAPTER 7

September 1902

SUMMER WAS PASSING, AND IT was harvest time on the many farms surrounding Rockville. Grains were being harvested, dumped into burlap sacks, and stockpiled into granary bins. Farm boys spent their days trampling down cornstalks in the brick silos, their heads popping out of the various dumping doors in the tall cylindrical structures as the level of silage grew skyward. Vegetables and fruits were "put up"—canned, pickled, dried, and stored. It was the getting-ready period for what was to come. Threshers and hay men had to be fed, and the job of cooking, serving, and washing dishes was a never-ending cycle. The unseasonably hot autumn, combined with the wood-burning stove in the kitchen that was fired up all day, made a house unbearably hot. For everyone in the household, the day began before morning light and ended with everyone bone weary after nightfall.

With the cooling of the weather came the butchering of hogs, the making of sausage, and the frightful job of keeping inquisitive children away from the making of soap, which included the rendering of lard by boiling strips of pork fat and the adding of skin-eating lye.

Along the perimeter of the fields, the tall white Queen Anne's lace, now faded to gray, was giving way to the brilliant red of the sumac and to fall.

Handmade posters announcing a cake contest, with time and rules printed on them, appeared in store windows and were nailed to the big "Poster Tree" in front of the post office. The contest was to be held at Old Church on the coming Friday night.

In fact, it was a surprise birthday party for Aunt Em. Bernice Johnson, Emma Snow, and Jane Caldwell, the three women in charge of the event, called at the home of Aunt Em and Dr. Townsend and invited them to judge the cake contest, thus making sure they would be in attendance.

"Lordy yes, I'd love to," Aunt Em said of the invitation. "Sounds like fun." She chattered on in her husky voice, laughter bubbling to the surface as she ushered the committee of three into a combination living room and kitchen in the back of the house. A small fire burned in the kitchen fireplace because the mansion, built of granite from the quarry, was always cool.

When the doctor's first wife and mother of their son Adam, then four, had died before the house had been completed, many of the rooms were closed off and never lived in or furnished. Aunt Em's informality did not require a big house built for entertaining and show, but the few rooms they did reside in were unmistakably hers. The large kitchen was pleasant and comfortable, and tonight a warm, spicy odor scented the air.

The doctor, seated at a desk in a corner of the kitchen, rose to greet the women. Always formally solemn, he made them uneasy, but Aunt Em's good humor made up for what seemed to be a lack of warmth in the doctor.

Aunt Em was not stylish. She kept her dark-brown hair cut short and her skirts above her ankles. She didn't have time for fussing or tripping. She had never been called pretty, not even good-looking. She had been called a "nice" girl, a "friendly" girl, a "smart" girl, but never a pretty one. Aunt Em had sparkling hazel-green eyes, and after years spent looking into mouths with decayed or missing teeth, she considered her large healthy white teeth her best asset, beautiful in their soundness.

"It will be an honor," the doctor said with a flourish when asked to judge the cake contest.

Aunt Em served the guests gingerbread, warm from the oven, and hot cocoa. She said, "Can you remember when we used to have fun in Rockville? When we were girls, we always had hayrides and dances to go to. You remember, Bernice? Whatever happened to change all that?"

"We can serve the Lord better without frivolity."

"Oh now, Bernice, I don't think the good Lord meant for us to spend all our time worshiping Him," Aunt Em said. "After all, when He created the world, He set aside one day for rest."

Later, after the women had left and Aunt Em had set the kitchen right, the doctor put aside the book he was reading and joined her on the sofa before the dying fire. Looking at her thoughtfully, he said, "Aunt Em, I've decided to build the people of Rockville an opera house, a gift from you and me."

For a moment she was speechless.

"Well," she said at last, "God bless you, Doctor."

"Now, Aunt Em."

"Well, He can bless you, too," Aunt Em said to her irreverent husband. The laughter came back into her voice. "I think that's wonderful. It's time the people in Rockville found something to do besides go to church."

"We'll have a fight on our hands," the doctor said.

"It's one you've always wanted."

"It'll give that so-called preacher new material for his sermons," the doctor said, followed by one of his rare laughs.

"Just what does one do in an opera house, anyway?" Aunt Em asked.

"Have a good time," he said and laughed again.

When Dr. Townsend and Aunt Em arrived at Old Church for the cake contest on Saturday night, sunshine was streaming from its tall, narrow, unadorned windows. In the early days of Rockville's history, the large building had been the meetinghouse for the whole community, and over the years it had been home to many Protestant denominations. No matter the sect, however, Sundays were devoted to the Lord, and on that day the children went to Sunday school in the schoolhouse, while the congregation went to church in the church house—three times.

Every event in the town had been held in the meetinghouse, including dances, until Brother Griggsby, a hard-shelled Baptist preacher, descended on the oldest church in town and, like a bolt out of the blue, expounded hell-fire and damnation and convinced one and all of his worshippers that they were sinners in dire need of saving.

"There will be no dancing in the house of the Lord!" he declared.

"Then where will we dance?" several members of the congregation asked in dismay.

"You won't," the new minister replied. "Dancing is a sin; all that touching and holding causes impure thoughts. And no musical instruments—musical instruments are inventions of the devil. Singing, yes; music, no."

And so, the longer the preacher was in Rockville teaching the horrors of hell to the happy, folksy congregation, the more pious and dour they became. He also declared that the building housing the church would no longer be called the meetinghouse. The new brother liked Old Church for a name. "Old" was good, mature, wise, and traditional, not like that upstart Presbyterian church. So the meetinghouse became Old Church, and the new Presbyterian church was soon called New Church.

That was twelve years ago, and Old Church's ostracized organ still stood in a dark corner of the stage covered with a quilt of a crazy-work design, a stark reminder of their once-wicked ways. New Church set the social standards, but Old Church was everyone's conscience. The portly, middle-aged brother had arrived in Rockville with a new bride, his first wife having duly expired, and the children from that union now grown and living elsewhere. Soon after the arrival of the new wife—an awkward, socially inept young woman with plump rosacea-red cheeks and chin—she was marked, like Cain, by the ominous piece of information that she, the wife of Brother Griggsby, had been caught indulging in an afternoon nap.

With a burst of bright colors and smiling faces and a roar of "Happy birthday, Aunt Em," the doors of Old Church swung open to greet the doctor and his wife. No one could recall seeing Aunt Em so surprised. And cakes! Cakes were everywhere. Chocolate cakes and white cakes, yellow cakes and pink cakes, angel's food and devil's food, long ones and tall ones, big ones and little ones, plain ones and fancy ones, sunk in the middle or sloped to the side; one even had a piece missing.

Each family brought a cake, and all the families were there. Whether they were Old Church, New Church, home churched, or no church, they were there to celebrate Aunt Em.

Aunt Em shook hands with the men and hugged the women and children—although many men hugged her in return.

"God bless you. God love you," she said to each.

Old Church appeared almost pretty, its starkness relieved today by colored streamers of crepe paper tacked into each corner of the large room, coming together in the center of the ceiling in a mass of paper flowers.

It was announced that Aunt Em and Dr. Townsend, as the judges, would choose one cake as the winning entry. The winner was to receive a blue ribbon and a silver dollar. For the women present, the dollar would mean a new dress.

Aunt Em and the doctor walked up and down the rows of tables. With so many entries to choose from, the cakes would have to be judged on looks. "I wish I could give each one of you a ribbon," she said.

"Only one, Aunt Em!" several voices in the crowd called back.

One cake stood out: a round, two-layer, yellow-frosted cake beautifully decorated with real purple violets, the violets' small, delicate beauty crystallized to resemble flowers in snow. Grape leaves, treated to the same frosty look, formed a garland on top of the cake and encircled the words "Happy Birthday, Aunt Em" in a graceful script of green icing.

Aunt Em and the doctor, after viewing all the cakes, stood by the cake decorated with the violets and held a whispered consultation.

"Well," Aunt Em finally announced, "if we must choose just one, I guess it'll have to be this one."

A murmur of approval came from the crowd. All the women present were curious as to who had baked the winning cake. No one knew. No one would hazard a guess.

Each woman, before bringing her cake to the church, had attached to the bottom of the plate, with a paste made of flour and water, a slip of paper with her name on it. The doctor held the plate aloft, and Aunt Em removed the slip.

"Abigail Langley!" she announced to a stunned crowd. No one applauded. People scanned the crowd looking for Abigail, and although they knew she wasn't present, they wondered aloud how the cake had arrived there.

Aunt Em, delighted, pocketed the blue ribbon and the silver dollar. "I'll give the prize to her myself," she said. "Why, bless her heart, her cake is just as pretty as she is."

"Pretty is as pretty does," whispered Perthy Prettyman.

They sampled the many varieties of cakes and drank cold lemonade, the ice for the occasion donated by part-time undertaker Bill Tibbits. The drink was made doubly refreshing by the fact that no one had died that week, which meant a corpse hadn't been kept on the undertaker's ice.

The women (and some of the men), upon tasting the cake, begrudgingly admitted that the Langley woman's cake was delicious as well as attractive. Everyone's spirits were restored, and they forgot, for the moment, their disappointment that the disgraced and excommunicated Abigail Langley had won the cake contest, and the dollar.

CHAPTER 8

WITH THE BIRTH OF HER daughter's illegitimate child, Mrs. Langley's sewing business ceased, and she was forced to take full-time work at the Parlett Hotel. She ate her meals at the hotel and did her sewing and laundry there as well. The daylong separation was easier on both mother and daughter. Abigail's world consisted of her, baby Ronnie, and Aunt Em, who stopped in almost daily to bring news of the town and to teach Abigail how to take care of an infant. If Aunt Em was attending someone who had something "catching," then Abby and Ronnie did not see her.

At three months, Ronnie recognized the affectionate Aunt Em. He would squeal with delight as soon as he heard her cheerful voice, his little arms reaching out and his feet kicking up and down on the pad of his cradle. Abby, heeding Aunt Em's advice to get out of the house, retrieved the wicker buggy from the attic that had been hers when she was a baby and made preparations for Ronnie's first outing.

"Just hold your head high," Aunt Em had told Abby, "and smile at everyone. Look them right in the eye and don't back down."

On a bright late-summer's day with honeybees humming, the corn showing tawny tassels, sweet-smelling sweet peas climbing wire fences, and pink hollyhocks disguising not-so-sweet-smelling privies, Abigail proudly pushed the baby carriage, with Ronnie in his best dress and crocheted cap, down Main Street past homes and businesses to the Parlett Emporium.

By the time she reached the store, Ronnie was sleeping. She turned the carriage's parasol at an angle to keep the sun from shinning on his face, parked it on the sidewalk, and set the brake. A small boy, overly dressed for a hot September day, was sitting on the cement steps in the shade provided by the hotel's second-floor semicircular balcony and became totally absorbed in Abby's maneuvering of the buggy.

Abigail entered the store, and with a weak smile and trembling legs moved to greet the only women customers in the store, Mrs. Letty Peacock and her daughter Maureen, who was the same age as Abigail. The two women, mouths agape, watched Abby approaching and grabbed for their skirts and hiked them above their ankles. They backed away from her as though something horrible were drawing near them, stopping only when they bumped into a glass display case and set the articles in the case to vibrating.

Mr. Peacock, the only man in the store, was trying on reading glasses from the showcase and gawked bug-eyed at Abigail through the magnified spectacles, while his Adam's apple, rising from his faded gray work shirt, bobbed up and down in his reedy neck, giving the impression that he was about to cackle.

Abigail whirled about and was rushing toward the screen door when Mrs. Parlett's friendly greeting stopped her short.

"Why, Abigail," she said, "how nice to see you. May I help you?"

Defiantly, Abigail faced her, but she saw only kindness in Mrs. Parlett's blue eyes. Stammering and unable to find her voice, she thrust her shopping list into Mrs. Parlett's hand. Behind her, Abby heard the slap of the screen door closing and Mrs. Peacock's shrill voice shrieking at her grandson, who had been left sitting on the steps.

"Markey, get away from that—that nasty baby." The words bled into the simple day like dogs yelping at a cornered rabbit.

Terrified, Abigail rushed to the door in time to see Maureen's little three-year-old boy standing on tiptoe, with both hands grasping the edge of Ronnie's buggy as he peeked inside at the sleeping baby boy.

Maureen rushed from the store and, snatching her son away from the buggy, dragged him by one arm to the hitching rail, where the Peacocks' horse and buggy waited. When all were on board, the family fled from the alley as if they were being pursued by Lucifer himself.

With face burning, Abigail returned to Mrs. Parlett, who had the goods from Abby's list assembled on the counter. Abby hurriedly placed them in her crocheted shopping bag. "Please put them on my mother's bill," she said, and left.

Two women who were climbing the emporium's steps and observing Abby's hurried flight from the store stopped in the middle of the steps and, unabashedly looking her up and down, showed their disapproval with their tightly puckered mouths.

Abigail was at the turnstile gate at the park before she was finally able to raise her head, and when she did, she saw Grandma Langley's wagon and team of horses parked at the side gate to her house and her sixteen-year old cousin Orion carrying baskets of peaches into her kitchen.

Abigail had not seen her cousin since he had taken her cake to the cake contest for Aunt Em's birthday. He gave her a quick hug before he left to water the horses. As soon as Orion was out of hearing, Abby broke into a gale of wild sobbing. She held on to her grandmother and did not stop her pent-up hysterics until the baby's cries had grown louder than her own.

"My land sakes, girl, what happened to you?" Grandma asked. She disentangled herself from her granddaughter's grasp and tried to quiet the baby.

"I'll never go downtown again as long as I live. I hate them. I hate all of them!" Abby threw herself onto a kitchen chair and dropped her head onto her folded arms; she continued her crying, explaining between sobs what a humiliating experience Ronnie's first excursion to town had been.

"To heck with them," Grandma said. "Leave here and come and live at the ranch with me and Uncle Pete."

In the midst of this scene, Aunt Em came bursting into the kitchen. Snatching her sunbonnet from her head, she fanned herself with it as she headed for the water tap. She stopped short when she saw Abigail's red eyes and both mother and baby's wet faces. "What happened?"

Grandma repeated the story. Aunt Em jerked the bonnet back onto her head, unceremoniously snapped the ties into a bow beneath her chin, and stamped toward the door.

"Why are you leaving?" Grandma asked of Aunt Em's retreating back. "You better stay out of the sun, or you're going to have sunstroke."

"I'm fixing to give that Letty Peacock a stroke. 'Nasty baby' indeed!" she said as the screen door banged shut behind her.

CHAPTER 9

June 1903

ABBY CELEBRATED RONNIE'S FIRST BIRTHDAY with a cake and party, a sad little affair with Aunt Em as the only guest. It was during his first year when she came to realize that the small dividend she received from her father's insurance would not cover the expense of raising a child, and so, with the coming of spring, she obtained a temporary job at Seth Owens's farm.

"Oh, I'm all thumbs this morning," Abby said to her reflection in the chifforobe mirror as she tried again to set the black hat with a striped grosgrain hatband in shades of pink, blue, and lavender squarely on her head. Although she had been excommunicated from her church, working on the Sabbath still had an unsettling effect on her.

The job, which she did six days a week, required helping Mrs. Owens with the cooking for family and hired farmworkers as well as sewing school clothes for their teenage daughters, Betty and Ruth.

Seth Owens was not a religious man and seldom attended church, but he did acknowledge the Sabbath by working no more than half a day, and on that day Abby came to work so that his wife could also enjoy a morning of rest. Abby enjoyed working for the Owenses. They treated her and Ronnie like family, even insisting that she take her meals with them. They wouldn't hear of her waiting on them while they ate.

Ronnie, sitting on the floor beside her, was tugging on her skirt and making unhappy sounds.

"Ronnie, please don't fuss. I know you don't like your cap." From beneath his blue wool cap and arrow-straight black brows, Ronnie's dark eyes scowled up at her. "We're going bye-bye with the horsy. You'll like that," she said consolingly as she hurried about gathering up the things they would need for a daylong stay. She carried Ronnie outside and sat him on the lawn by the kitchen gate, where he could watch for the buggy.

Melburn Owens, the oldest of the family's five sons, arrived at the Langleys' kitchen gate promptly at six o'clock, as he did every morning. Getting out of the wagon, he picked up Ronnie and helped Abby into the buggy. Melburn held Ronnie on his lap, and the child clutched the leather reins in a fierce little grip.

As they rode through the early-morning streets, Abby wondered what the town was saying about her now. She scrutinized Melburn from the corner of her eye. He had been afflicted with a bone infection from smallpox when he was a baby; the point of his right jawbone was missing, and the skin of his face was stretched tight over the absent bone. He tended to draw attention away from the deformity by ducking his head toward his right shoulder when anyone looked at him from that side. He was thin, had brown hair, was of medium height, and was seven years older than Abby.

"It's a beautiful morning," she said.

Melburn, a man of few words, acknowledged her statement by pulling on the brim of his hat before hiding his misshapen jaw in his turned-up coat collar. Abby looked away; if there were to be conversations on these daily journeys, it would be up to her to initiate them, she knew. She thought, *But do I want to encourage him?*

When Abby entered the kitchen, she knew that Mrs. Owens would remain in bed until eight; she found bickering children and everyone hungry. After the two Owens sisters covered their good Sunday clothes with aprons made from bleached flour sacks, she put them to work getting the youngest boy, Peter, ready for church and stacking the dirty dishes. She fried up a stack of hotcakes for everyone who would be attending church: Mrs. Owens, the girls, the two teenage boys, nine-year-old Peter, and Melburn.

Abby went to the Owenses' bedroom and tapped on the door. Mrs. Owens opened the door, and Abby knew at once what was holding her up: she had something on her head resembling a toadstool. "Wait one moment, Mrs. Owens, please. You're going to church, but not with that monstrosity on your head." She returned with the new hat she had worn for the first time that morning. Holding forth the hat, she said, "It's yours for being so nice to me." Her voice wavered, and she stopped trying to say anything.

Mrs. Owens's chin quivered as she sat down and succumbed to the hat. In one short morning, Abby had become very dear to her.

When Mrs. Owens appeared in the kitchen wearing the hat, everyone (including Mr. Owens) stopped eating and stared. She looked amazing. Mr. Owens jumped up from the table and held the chair for her, and one and all put on their best table manners.

After they loaded up the surrey and set off for Old Church, Abby attacked the dirty kitchen while Ronnie attacked his high chair with much kicking and squealing. Mr. Owens came in with Ronnie's coat and bonnet.

"He hates his bonnet," Abby said.

"Of course he does. He's a big lad," Mr. Owens said to Ronnie as he put one of Peter's caps on his head. "We men have work to do," he said to Ronnie as he picked him up, "and right now we're going out to the corral and tend to the lambs and chickens."

"I'll need eggs," Abby said as she waved goodbye to Ronnie and his new companion.

Later, Abby stirred up batter for the strawberry shortcake she was planning for dinner—something other than the usual biscuits. She was using a recipe she'd found in last month's *Ladies Home Companion.* Abby had slid the roasting pan onto the oven door and was basting the beef roast when Mrs. Owens came into the kitchen, followed by the rest of the churchgoers.

Mrs. Owens immediately set Betty and Ruth to work hulling strawberries. Taking the spoon from Abby's hand, she said apologetically, "I don't like having you working on Sundays, Abby."

"I don't mind," she said. "I can't go to church anyway. I've thought about attending New Church, but I don't think they want us, either." She took a quick look across the kitchen, where Ronnie sat in a highchair. Not going to church was a thorn in her side, and she worried constantly about where and when Ronnie would be baptized.

Ronnie, not liking the confinement of the highchair now that he had been outside, was throwing everything the young Owens brothers gave him to play with as far as he could, which delighted the boys.

Mrs. Owens gave Abby's hand a quick squeeze and, lowering her voice, said, "If today wasn't the Sabbath, I'd tell you what I think of Brother Griggsby."

"There's just one thing about strawberries I don't like," Betty said from the kitchen table where the sisters sat hulling berries. "They remind me of Brother Griggsby," she said as she held up a plump red berry.

"Oh, did you have to say that?" her sister Ruth said, making a sour face. "Do you think they'll show up for dinner today?"

Abby felt a jolt of ice water shoot through her veins. Alarmed, she turned to Betty. "Do you mean that Brother Griggsby's coming here for dinner?"

"They never miss the first Sunday of strawberry season," Betty said, checking her nails while looking at her red-stained fingers. "This, after we've done all the work, and we don't have enough berries to go round, and then we have to eat canned peaches and watch the Griggsbys eating our strawberries." She picked up a red berry, gave it a vicious squeeze, then quickly licked at the ripe juice as it ran down the side of her hand, after which she gave a fat berry to each of her little brothers and held one to Ronnie's mouth for him to taste.

"How do you think Brother Griggsby knows when we're having the first shortcake of the season?" Ruth asked her mother.

"I think God tells him," the youngest boy said.

"Shame on you, Peter Owens," his mother said, removing the shortcakes from the oven and using the crook of her elbow to wipe perspiration from her brow. "You mustn't talk that way about the Lord."

"Well, just the same, someone must tell him," Ruth said, talking above the noise Ronnie was making by pounding his bite of berry to a pulp on the tray of his highchair, apparently not caring for the taste of strawberries.

"If they do show up today," their mother said, a warning tone in her voice, "I don't want you boys 'accidentally' pushing Johnny Griggsby into the watering trough again." Peter giggled. "I mean it," she said, sounding out of sorts. Brother Griggsby and his brood took Sunday dinner at the Owenses' house twice a year. Because it was a long walk from town, they avoided the winter months and the hot summer Sundays and showed up at strawberry time in the spring and harvest time in the late fall.

Peter, looking out of the window, excitedly shouted, "Uh oh! Here they come! Here comes Brother Griggsby."

"Oh darn," the girls said.

"Hush," Mrs. Owens said. "They'll hear you. And come away from the window." Then she, too, peeked out from behind the curtain, just to make sure. Abby, clearly distressed and standing behind Mrs. Owens, also peeked. They could see Brother Griggsby, his wife, and their five offspring plodding up the dusty lane leading to the house.

"Pa," they could hear little Johnny saying, "I think I smell strawberries," and his family all quickened their pace. Inside the Owenses' kitchen, the children were coaxing their mother into saving the shortcake for them. "Please?" they all pleaded.

"I couldn't do that," Mrs. Owens said, wringing her hands. "It just wouldn't be right."

"Please?" they pleaded again.

Mrs. Owens, holding open the screen door while shooing away flies with a dish towel, seemed happy to see their Sunday guests and greeted them warmly. "I do hope you haven't eaten," she said. "We're just about ready to sit down to dinner. Won't you join us?"

"If you're sure it isn't too much bother, Sister Owens," Mrs. Griggsby said. She liked calling members of Old

Church "brother" and "sister," a holdover from her Quaker upbringing. Mrs. Owens assured her that it was no bother at all and ushered them into the parlor, where they settled down to await Sunday dinner.

The uninvited dinner guests sat at the hastily extended dining room table rapturously sniffing the air; mingled with the heavier smells of Sunday dinner were the mouthwatering aroma of strawberries and the sweet delicate scent of Abby's shortcake cooling on the sideboard.

Seth Owens and his three older sons then came in from the field, where they had been laboring since sunrise. The girls carried buckets of warm water outside and set them down in the shade of the big oak tree near the kitchen door. A wooden crate propped against the tree held a chipped blue-enamel basin and, in a saucer, a chunk of homemade lye soap.

The men took turns washing up, and each man threw his used water onto the lawn. A cracked mirror in a bent tin frame hung from a nail on the trunk of the tree, and worn towels and a comb lay on the seat of an old chair next to the crate. After the men were presentable, they entered the house, with Melburn going to his room to put on a clean shirt, tie, and jacket.

In order to accommodate sixteen people, a table from the parlor was added to the length of the dining table, which now extended into the living room.

Seth Owens's jaw muscles tightened as he entered the room and was confronted by the Griggsby family, who were already seated for dinner. He greeted them, but not as graciously as he had his wife. After everyone was seated, Seth looked around the table for Abby. Mrs. Owens, with a shake of her head, was warning her husband to keep quiet.

With a look of understanding, Seth addressed the preacher. "Would you kindly offer up a short blessing, Brother?" he asked, pointedly stressing the word "short."

Murmurs of appreciation greeted the steaming platters and bowls of roast beef, baked ham, fried chicken, mashed potatoes, glazed parsnips, creamed peas with carrots, and dried corn creamed with thick heavy cream. Applesauce, pickles, pickle relish, fresh-baked rolls, newly churned butter, and a variety of jams and jellies were passed around, and plates were heaped to overflowing.

From where he was seated, with his end of the table partially in the living room, Brother Griggsby was surprised to get a glimpse of Abigail Langley in the kitchen tending to her child. She was wiping the baby's hands and face with a cloth, and when the child pushed his fingers into his mother's mouth, she nibbled on them, which made the boy laugh.

Brother Griggsby had heard that Abigail was an admirable cook and was working as a hired girl at one of the farmhouses, but he hadn't known she was working for the Owenses. He soon saw her with the tot in her arms as she walked down the long hallway. By craning his neck he was able to discern, by the closing of the door, which bedroom she had entered.

After a second helping of everything, the preacher addressed Mr. Owens. "I see you're still breaking the Sabbath, Brother Owens."

"No, just making an honest living."

"Remember the Sabbath to keep it holy," Brother Griggsby intoned. "'Be not deceived, God is not mocked, for whatsoever a man soweth, that shall he also reap.' Galatians chapter six, verse seven."

"That's exactly what I do, Brother," Seth said, looking him straight in the eye, "sow and reap. I don't bother Him, and He don't bother me."

"'What shall it profit a man, if he shall gain the whole world, and lose his own soul?' Mark nine, verse thirty-six."

The Owens women, in an attempt to interrupt the flow of the conversation, began to noisily clear the table. While Brother Griggsby relaxed in his chair and waited for dessert, he noticed that the door to the room Abigail had entered had come ajar. It was open just enough for him to see the woman sitting on the side of the bed, her back to the door. She seemed to be nursing her child, for he could see the top of the baby's head in the crook of her arm.

Watching her, Brother Griggsby felt a rush of heat settle in his groin; he whipped away the napkin tucked beneath his chin and dropped it into his lap. Then, moving about uncomfortably on the wooden chair, he picked up a spoon and put it back, coughed into his napkin, and dabbed sweat from his forehead.

But no matter how hard he tried, no amount of distraction could keep his eyes from straying to the beckoning door. The partial scene of a mother nursing her child had taken possession of him. The shameless hussy—only a wicked woman could make a man feel this way.

"Brother," Seth Owens said, "I hope the food you're eating today isn't giving you a bellyache, because a lot of it was put in the earth on a Sunday and taken up on a Sunday."

Their father's frankness made the girls blush.

The preacher, caught up in his own frustration, let the remark pass. He was thinking that any woman who could stir a man to the brink of humiliating himself in public was a whore and an unfit mother.

Once the table was cleared, Mrs. Owens and her two daughters carried in dishes of peaches, placing one on the table before each person before passing around a platter of cookies. The preacher's children looked at the peaches and then at their pa.

Brother Griggsby, still incensed by the depraved feelings the woman had aroused in him, stabbed at the unwanted dessert. The fruit was Mrs. Owens's prize peaches, those she had won blue ribbons for at the state fair and served only on special occasions. Still, canned peaches you could have anytime. The members of the two families avoided looking at one another, and the rest of the meal was consumed in silence.

Seth Owens's Sunday dinner set hard on his stomach. He had been ridiculed in his own home, at his own table, and he didn't like it. He had planned on resting for the remainder of the day, but now, with a curt excuse, he left the table.

Melburn entered the kitchen, where Abby was cleaning up; his mother and sisters were entertaining the Griggsby women in the parlor. He placed a small train engine he had carved for Ronnie into the boy's hands as he sat in his highchair and then approached Abigail. She stood at the sink attacking a mountain of dirty dishes.

"I'm going to drive the Griggsbys home, and then I'll be back for you," he said.

She thanked him for Ronnie's toy. She knew Melburn liked her, even though he never looked directly at her when they spoke. She was embarrassed and yet pleased that he had taken to wearing a jacket when in her presence. For his part, Melburn, always feeling inept and clumsy, was annoyed with his family for teasing him about the jacket.

After a respectful length of time had passed, Seth Owens went to work in the south field near the lane leading to the house, where Brother Griggsby would clearly see him when he left for home. Johnny Griggsby would also have a chance to dry out after being dunked in the watering trough for a remark the boy had made about having canned peaches for dessert.

As Seth worked, a plan began to form in his head. If he planted wheat today, he could call it his Sunday Crop: planted on Sunday, cared for on Sunday, and taken up on Sunday. He went to the toolshed and found a board and nailed it to a fence post facing the road where it could be seen by all passersby. With a can of red paint and a brush, he made a sign: SETH OWENS'S SUNDAY CROP.

Seth removed his hat and waved to his boys lounging on the front porch, and motioned for them to come to the fence. "Get out the drill," he said. "We're going to plant wheat!"

"Today?" the two young men said as one.

He pointed to the sign, and they took turns climbing on a fence post to read it. "Aw, Pop, not today. We're tired! We're supposed to rest on the Sabbath." But they both knew that once their father had set his mind to something, there would be no getting out of it.

That evening, the Owens family had strawberry shortcake for supper, all but hidden in fluffy clouds of fresh whipped cream. And yet, when Mrs. Owens took a taste of hers, she burst into tears.

"I did a mean and spiteful thing today," she said through tears, "but I just can't stand the way Brother Griggsby eats up our food and then criticizes your pa."

"That preacher is the one who's mean and spiteful, Ma, not you," Melburn said in a sudden burst of passion, surprising his family. He was still seething about the comments Brother Griggsby had made when Melburn had driven him and his family home: "Abigail Langley is an unfit mother," Brother Griggsby had said. "A woman cannot lay with a man before marriage, have a child from that illicit union, and be a fit mother."

"In my opinion, sir, Miss Langley is a very fit mother," Melburn said in retaliation.

The fool, the preacher thought to himself. *He is besotted with the hussy.* And Brother Griggsby's unyielding dislike for Abby intensified.

THE ROCKVILLE HUB
June 26, 1903

The main topic of conversation this summer in Rockville has been Seth Owens's "Sunday Crop." The citizenry here have gone out of their way to ride by Seth's farm and, after having done so, have remarked that they cannot remember seeing a better crop of wheat. Seth plans on harvesting his Sunday Crop of wheat on the third Sunday of August.

Seth recently purchased a new grain binder. The contrivance, while being pulled across the field by a team of horses, can in one operation cut the wheat and tie it into bundles. The machine uses twine in place of wire. The bundles are then stacked upright, tripod fashion, by the field hands to dry until threshing time.

Although pleasure rides on Sundays are considered to be a breaking of the Sabbath, many people plan on riding out to the Owenses' farm to watch the new machine in action.

Some folks are planning on having a picnic and taking baskets of food for an outing at the quarry lake.

We wish you the best of luck, Seth, on your Sunday Crop and your new binding machine.

CHAPTER 10

August 1903

ON THE THIRD SUNDAY MORNING of August, Chance Collins, astride his horse Demon, rode to Bobby Lee Preston's place to buy a rabbit. The men sat at the kitchen table in the drooping fabric-ceilinged room drinking coffee that Bobby Lee's wife, Agnes, poured from a blue-enameled pot into chipped cups.

Bobby Lee was explaining to Chance his latest idea for a money-making invention and was sketching a picture of it onto the cracked and yellowed oilcloth table cover. Eight-year-old Amy sat at the opposite end of the table holding two-year-old Billy on her lap while spooning oatmeal into the squirming child's mouth. Her other brothers were playing on the bare wooden floor of the small kitchen, rolling a sock ball back and forth, and their mother was trying to maneuver around them in the crowded kitchen.

Agnes said to the girl, "Precious Amy, please take your little brothers and go in the front room." The townsfolk had scoffed at naming a baby Precious, as she had done. The women's sentiments were that "if I don't call my own children 'Precious,' why would I call someone else's child that?" So the little girl was Amy to everyone except her mother, who called her Precious Amy.

Chance drew his feet back toward his chair to make room for Agnes when she refilled his coffee cup. He couldn't remember seeing her when she wasn't pregnant. He smiled up at her with his scarred smile, but his eyes remained indifferent. The big-bellied woman made him thankful he was single. Feeling generous, Chance gave BJ, the nickname for Bobby Junior, a quarter and told him to pick out a rabbit and stow it in his saddlebag.

"Mum's making rabbit stew for Sunday dinner," Chance said, referring to the name everyone in town called his mother. "While it's cooking, I'm going over to Seth's and have a look at that new machine of his."

"Go on now," Agnes was saying to the boys as she made moving motions with her hands. Reluctantly, the kids moved to the cot in the living room. The cot provided the family, or anyone who happened to call on them, a place to sit and at night served as a bed for Precious Amy and young Billy.

Narrow, steep stairs in a corner of the room led to the attic through an opening in the ceiling. The upstairs room held a white wrought-iron bed for Bobby Lee and Agnes, a cradle for the baby, and straw ticks scattered about the floor for the other children.

Riding home from Bobby Lee's, Chance passed Seth's farm and for about the hundredth time read the "Sunday Crop" sign. He was sick of looking at the sign and doubly sick of hearing about the damned Sunday Crop. That was all anybody wanted to talk about, and down at Ma's, John was taking bets on how many bushels Seth's damn Sunday Crop would yield. "Well," he chuckled, "just what if there ain't no Sunday Crop to collect on?"

When he arrived home, Chance pulled the rabbit from the saddlebag and carried it into a work shed. He secured the animal, its heart beating violently, between his legs while he tied a strip of burlap rag he'd doused with kerosene around the body of the wretched animal.

Holding the rabbit by its ears and shaking it to keep it from scratching his arm, he walked to the fire barrier of barren earth that separated his field from Seth Owens's field and, striking a match, touched it to the strip of burlap. Swinging the flaming rabbit in circles above his head, he released it into the "Sunday" wheat field. "Run, you damn little birthday cake!" he yelled as he watched the rabbit fall to earth and scramble away and, doubling over with laughter, he struck at his thighs with his big callused hands.

"What 'ere you doing, Chancellor?" his mother called to him. Mrs. Collins had come to this country as a bride from England and had retained her Cockney accent. She stood on the kitchen stoop, a fleshy woman wearing a dress printed with small pink-and-blue flowers, a broach haphazardly pinned at the neck of the lace collar, and her hair a white topsy-turvy bird's nest atop her head.

She had pale milky-blue eyes and saw everything through the twilight of her own coming night.

"I'm helping Mr. Owens harvest his crop, Mum," Chance replied.

"That's a nice laddie," she said with a trill.

Chance had kept his Cockney accent until his first year of school, at which point it had been taunted, mimicked, ridiculed, and beaten out of him. Wanting to fit in, young Chance gladly obliged his schoolmates by dumping his mother's accent and replacing it with the crudest of American English.

As he returned from taking his horse to the watering trough, Chance saw Marshal McCombs riding by. Chance walked to the gate, and the marshal got off his horse and joined him there. The marshal removed his hat and was swiping a handkerchief across his brow when he pulled himself up and, stretching his neck, looked over Chance's shoulder.

"What you looking at?"

"Smoke," the marshal replied. Deep wrinkles rayed across his temples as he squinted into the bright day. "By God, I believe Seth Owens's field's on fire!" Hurtling himself back onto his horse, the marshal raced toward Seth's house.

On the same third Sunday morning in August, Nita Langley went to church. She still had the sympathy of everyone at Old Church. Her daughter's shameful transgression had endeared her to their hearts. They also hoped, as her friends, that she just might reveal to them who the father of her daughter's illegitimate baby might be. Surely she knew.

Grandma Langley had come to town and was staying with them. She said she wouldn't go anywhere in which a member of her family was not welcomed. Besides, she didn't much care for Brother Griggsby, or a church without a piano. "And," she added, "that wife of his who leads the singing? She couldn't carry a tune in a gunnysack."

Shortly before noon on that same day, the bell at Old Church, joined a few minutes later by the school bell, began a frantic tolling signaling disaster—and that usually meant fire.

Grandma and Abby, the latter holding her baby, stood by the front gate looking in all directions, and then they saw it: southeast of town, a curtain of smoke hanging in the air like an approaching storm. At that distance they couldn't tell whose farm it was coming from.

The doctor in his buggy, with Aunt Em beside him, came trotting by and slowed down enough to call out, "It's Seth Owens's wheat field!"

"Oh," Abby said. "Oh, that's terrible!"

Well-dressed churchgoers riding in their smart carriages coming from the direction of New Church, with their well-groomed horses stepping lively, fell in behind Dr. Townsend's carriage, all on their way to the fire. People driving past the house who saw Abby at the gate with her baby stared at her as much as they did the big cloud of smoke in the distance. Grandma and Abby were still lingering at the gate watching the smoke when Nita arrived home from church.

"It's Seth Owens's wheat field," Grandma informed her.

"Yes. I know. It's his Sunday Crop," Nita said, disdain chafing her voice. "Melburn Owens came to the church house begging us for our help."

"Oh, but Nita, a farm, that's a hard one to take," Grandma said with a sad shake of her head.

"Someone must be hurt, or the doctor wouldn't be going," Abigail said, clearly distraught.

Also on the same third Sunday morning in August, as the congregation of Old Church streamed outside following the morning service, they were stunned to see a cloud of blue-black smoke spiraling into the sky on the southeastern horizon and Melburn Owens riding his horse right up to the double doors. He yelled inside to the remaining congregation, "Pa's wheat field's on fire! Marshal McCombs wants the water wagon and a bucket brigade!" Then, turning his horse around, he raced for home.

"Hell bent for leather, he wuz," Tate Morgan reported the next day to the regulars at Ma's.

The church bell clanged its urgent message to the rest of the town: "Fire! Fire!"

An exodus of people made their way to the Owenses' farm on foot, horseback, and buggy. None of the men were empty-handed; each carried a wooden or metal bucket.

Seth Owens's Sunday Crop was in flames. The men formed a line from the watering trough to the field, passing buckets of water from hand to hand, flinging the emptied ones behind them. Young boys picking up the buckets raced back to the trough, where another group of volunteers manned the pump.

The new fire wagon was set up between the burning field and the house and farm buildings to put out any sparks that might ignite there. Its newly trained fire brigade was painfully uncoordinated, given that this was their first real fire.

Mrs. Owens sat on the front porch with a blanket wrapped around her, even though it was a hot August day, and wept hysterically. Aunt Em sat in a rocker next to her, watching for signs of shock.

"The Lord is punishing us for working on the Sabbath," Mrs. Owens cried out.

The women in attendance understood, and they agreed with her. But some of her ramblings didn't make sense to them, especially the ones concerning strawberries. God is punishing us for working on Sundays—this they understood—but what did God have to do with strawberry shortcake?

Chance Collins was there helping to put out the fire right alongside the other men, proving he was a good neighbor.

The wheat field was destroyed. During the height of the fire, Seth attempted to knock down the Sunday Crop sign from the fence, but the fire was too hot for him to get close enough to do so.

Retrieving a pole from the woodpile, he tried to push the sign into the fire, but it remained steadfast; although other fence posts were burning, it remained intact. The fire destroyed the wheat crop, one shed, the south fence, and the new binder. The sign was the last thing to burn. The red letters of the public statement curled, writhed, and slowly turned black as the crowd watched and read for the last time, "Seth Owens's Sunday Crop."

CHAPTER 11

SETH'S SUNDAY CROP WAS THE main topic of conversation in Rockville that summer until the covers had been thrown back from Bobby Lee's abode and all the heartache and poverty that took place in the little house shamefully exposed.

Agnes Preston was awake early. It wasn't daybreak, but in the purple-gray light filtering into the attic room, she could see the emporium's calendar hanging from a nail on the bare wall and could make out the date and the store's motto: "We sell everything from needles to threshing machines." It was the twenty-eighth. She was eight weeks past due. *I'm only twenty-five years old,* she thought, *and I have six children.*

Quietly, and without a sound, the tears began. She looked at her husband, arms and legs stretched out and taking up most of the bed, the soft light of early morning reflecting on his face. No marks of time or worry shown on the youthful face of Bobby Lee Preston. He still looked as young as when she first met him—a barefoot country girl come to town to live with the Prestons and attend school.

She'd paid for her room and board by doing light housework that over time turned out to be hard work, including barnyard chores. As a result, she didn't get to school very often and by spring was in love and pregnant.

The baby whimpered. She reached out and rocked the cradle until he quieted, then she left the bed, carefully stepping over little sleeping bodies on the attic floor.

Without stirring, BJ watched his mother wipe away her tears. When he was ten years old and had finished fourth grade, he could quit school and get a job. He knew it was expected of ten-year-old boys. He looked at his dad, who quickly took up the whole bed and was on his back and snoring. His pa was a dreamer, he knew, and nothing was expected of him.

Downstairs, Agnes studied her daughter asleep on the cot, a baby brother snuggled in the curl of her body. Precious Amy had never slept alone. When Agnes had the next baby, this one would move to a straw tick on the floor upstairs, and the one in the cradle next to her bed would join Amy on the cot.

Unlike the boys, Precious Amy did not inherit her father's good looks. She was plain like her mother, with pale skin and straight brown hair. She did have her father's blue eyes and long black lashes, but her eyes were set too far apart in her face to be attractive, and at times she was shy to the point of seeming stupid. Still, at the age of eight, you could see signs of the woman she was destined to become.

The boys, on the other hand, were always into things, up to boyish pranks. Their mother's anxieties and fears had not translated to them, only to Amy.

The children knew their mother cried because of her red eyes and blotchy face, but they never actually saw her cry. Their father cried, however. He would sit at the kitchen table or on the cot and cry just like they did when they were hurt or hungry.

Agnes had a dream, just one: a better life for her Precious Amy. Her dream was to see her daughter married and living in a nice house with billowing white lace curtains at the windows. She wished she could have time to teach Amy to embroider, but it was mending that was needed in this house. So, Amy was often found sitting on the cot and sewing patches on worn-out clothing by the dim light coming in from the small window overhead.

Agnes sat at the kitchen table as she waited for the fire to get hot enough to boil the chestnuts in the coffeepot. She struggled with her dilemma, her cracked red fingers tracing the holes in the oilcloth covering. When new, it had been white with red geraniums and had sat on her mother-in-law's kitchen table. Now it was yellow, the geraniums faded to a sickly pink.

By the time the coffee was perking, Agnes had made up her mind. She got to her feet and, taking a paring knife from a kitchen drawer, stepped outside. She cut a willowy branch from the tamarack tree that grew close to the outhouse; she grasped the slender tip of it in her left hand and, with her right thumb and forefinger, stripped the feathery green leaves from the length of the stem and returned to the house.

Before she drew the faded cretonne curtain across the bailing twine that stretched between the doorjambs, she again observed the children and made sure they were sleeping. Hiking up her nightgown and squatting, she separated the lips of her vagina; holding them open with one hand, she fed the limb into her body cavity until she felt pressure from it. Gritting her teeth, she made several jabs at whatever was preventing the branch from going in deeper.

Somewhere a child cried. Agnes rose, took a clean dish towel from a drawer of the cupboard, and pushed it between her legs. She put on an old wraparound apron hanging from a nail beside the door over her gown, built up the fire, and fed the bloody stick into the flames. Upstairs, the crying baby began to wail.

Amy pushed back the curtain and stood rubbing her eyes, one bare foot scratching at the top of the other. She said sleepily, "The baby needs fed."

"Oh!" Agnes cried. She bent over, a terrible cramp tearing through her abdomen.

"Mama, Mama!" Amy cried, holding onto her mother. "What's the matter, what is it?"

"Get everyone up and down here," Agnes said.

Agnes never went to bed that day. But after feeding her family flapjacks from the last of the flour, frying up one with a strip of fatback folded inside for Bobby Lee's lunch pail, and seeing him off to a one-day job at the Harrisons' farm, she went to bed.

At noon, she called Amy and told her in a weak voice to bring her a jar of water and to bring the quilts up from the cot down below. Agnes was cold. Even though the covers from the children's straw pads were piled on top of her, she was cold and abnormally thirsty.

BJ, the oldest boy, was worried. He had gone to the attic to see his mother. Her naturally pale skin was bleached to whiteness, and her eyes, with their dark circles beneath them, seemed to be buried in her face. The younger boys were too scared to cry for their mother and remained on the couch; they weren't fighting, for a change.

BJ went to his grandma Preston's house and told her their ma was sick. She told him she was busy and eventually sent him home with a loaf of bread and a pail of milk, but first she made him remain long enough to chop wood and stack it on the kitchen stoop. Mrs. Preston didn't like her daughter-in-law. She claimed Agnes had tricked her son into marriage and was a lazy, uneducated girl.

Amy returned to the attic after feeding her brothers bowls of bread and milk. When Agnes saw the tired little girl, she tried to get out of bed but was too feeble to do so. She asked for clean towels and a bucket of water.

Amy, thinking her mother was going to wash, brought warm water and a towel, but she cowered when her mother dropped a blood-soaked towel into the washbasin and watched with horror as swirls of dark-red clots roiled the clear water.

"Amy, you have to go and fetch Aunt Em," her mother said. Amy shrank from the request by backing away. Her mother's voice, slurred and difficult to understand, commanded her, "Amy, this is no time to be scared. Go get Aunt Em."

Aunt Em was not at home, so Amy returned with Dr. Townsend.

CHAPTER 12

THE FIRST THING THAT ASSAILED the doctor's senses was the metallic odor of blood, followed by the strong ammonia smell of diapers that had been dried and used a second and even a third time without washing. Five or more boys were piled on top of a cot positioned against a wall, all of them big eyed and silent.

The girl climbed the wobbly stairs to the attic, with the doctor following. A woman was lying in a white iron bed and was so pallid of face that his heart skipped a beat.

Upon seeing her mother, Amy became even more frightened. Making tight little fists of her hands, she pushed them against her mouth and, squeezing her eyes closed, she all but fell into the rocking chair. Her mother appeared to be dead, and the doctor seemed almost certain she was.

"God, what have you done this time?" Dr. Townsend said, looking to the ceiling. "Amy," he said, gently shaking her, wanting to make sure she was all right. "Can you follow directions? Can you go downstairs and build up the fire in the kitchen stove and heat the flatirons? Can you do that?" He patted her shoulder. "And when they're hot, bring one up here. Have BJ help you."

As soon as Amy left the attic, the doctor went to work, first hanging his hat on the bedpost. A chain was also hanging from the post, secured by an iron ring with some kind of stovepipe contraption on the end of it. With the tip of his boot, Dr. Townsend moved aside a loose floorboard and looked straight down on a potbellied stove. He figured this must be one of Bobby Lee's labor-saving devices he'd heard about, one that required a hole in the floor. He was able to stoke the stove in the room below without leaving his bed in the room above. The doctor shook his head in awe of the man's ingenuity, and his laziness.

He replaced the board and shoved the bed away. Drawing aside the multiple layers of covers, he began his examination of the woman where she lay on a blood-soaked mattress. When he pushed back her eyelids, he didn't note any response to the light, although he did feel a faint pulse in her neck. It would be a terrible fright for the children to see her like this, he knew, but he had to think of the patient first, and she was too feeble to move or clean up. The thin little blankets covering the pile of quilts on top of her were free of stains, so he covered over the signs of blood the best he could.

"God! God!" he implored as he went downstairs and confronted the bewildered faces of the children trying to cope with a fearfully ill mother. The older ones were sitting on the cot, with the younger ones seated on the floor at their feet. He knew Agnes was bled out, but when he looked into their eyes, all pleading with him to take care of their mother, he was willing to try anything. "Who's the oldest one here?" he asked. Bobby Lee Jr. stood up. He was a tall boy for his age. "Can you ride a horse?"

"Yes, sir."

"Do you know where 'Batman' lives?" The doctor was quite sure every kid in town knew Ole Olsen by his nickname and where he lived.

"Yes, sir."

"All right, come with me," the doctor said.

Outside, he unhitched the horse from the carriage and told the boy to ride out to Batman's place and tell him that Dr. Townsend required his services. "Then, on your way back," he said, "stop by my house and see if Aunt Em's there; if she is, tell her I need her."

Ole Olsen and his brother Els, when they were eighteen and twenty years of age, respectively, had made their way from Norway to America in 1872 and then to a place near Rockville where their father had settled. They found Papa dead, and they found the place where he had lived: a dugout that was half cave and half log cabin and was full of bats. Ole celebrated the killing of the bats by attaching one to the hatband on his cap, and forever after he was known as Batman.

When Amy returned to the attic with a hot iron wrapped in an old blanket, she found the doctor sitting in a rocking chair by her mother's bed, holding her hand. He got up and held the bundle, warming his own hands before placing the bundle under the covers by Agnes's feet. He then massaged her hands with his warm ones.

Responding to the warmth, Agnes rolled her head and muttered, "Don't wan' a baby."

After hearing her response, the doctor lifted her head and spooned some of his Survivall medicine into her mouth. The medicine, when sold to the public, was 20 percent alcohol; the one he carried in his satchel was 40 percent.

She opened her eyes and, not recognizing him, said, "Am I in hell?"

"Good God almighty, woman, no, you are not!" Catching himself, he finished in a soothing tone. "Agnes, any woman who has borne a child has earned her place in heaven. You'll go to heaven," he said reassuringly as he smoothed back her hair from her forehead. "Try not to worry about it. Agnes," he added, "you terminated your pregnancy this morning. What did you use?"

"Stick," she slurred. "Don't wan' 'nother baby, I don't..." Her voice faded.

"When, Agnes, when did you use the stick?"

"Before breakfast," she said, her breath hissing through her labored breathing. "I'm tired—please let me sleep."

A patient pleading for sleep gave the doctor a new motivation to do something. She turned to Amy. "Where's your father?"

"I don't know," she answered as she twisted a lock of straight hair between her fingers. "He was s'ppost to work at the Harrisons' today." Her thin little chest heaved as she tried to control a sob. Amy's shyness kept her from speaking up, and he strained to hear her.

"Well, you better try the pool hall," the doctor said in exasperation, "and wherever you find him, tell him to come home quickly."

Amy almost fell down the steep steps in her rush to find her father. The children were still huddled on the cot and cried when Amy said, "No, you can't see Mama."

Batman soon arrived on his big gray horse, with BJ riding beside him on the doctor's horse. While Batman examined Agnes, the doctor took BJ aside. "Did you find my wife?"

"Yes, sir, I did. She's at Abigail Langley's house. Baby Ronnie's sick, and Abby is sick herself from worry. Aunt Em said for you to 'carry on, you're the doctor.'

"Did she laugh?"

"Yes, sir, I believe she did."

"Was she making soup?"

"Yes, sir," he said quietly, a look of helplessness crossing his face.

"You're a fine young man, BJ. In a few days, you come up to my office and see me."

Ole Olsen was passing his hands lightly over Agnes's body, and then in his Norwegian accent, he said to the doctor, "It is too late. She has lost so much blood, so much. Her ghost has left her body. It will be floating around for a while." He looked about the room. "Sometimes it is very hard for the spirit to leave. Her strong will to live is holding it back, you see."

The doctor settled in a chair at Agnes's bedside. Ole, on leaving, gave him a sympathetic pat on his back, and the doctor was very much aware of Ole's energy passing into him. Batman's presence in the house intimidated the children. Downstairs, Ole handed a bag containing hard candy to BJ, who was feeling cocky because he was the one who had gone to fetch him. The children were not as interested in the contents of the bag as they were in the dead bat on the man's hat. Ole removed his hat to let them get a better look. The bat's head was fastened to the front of the hat, and the wings were spread around to the back. The boys pointed to the bat's beady black eyes and the little sharp teeth protruding from its dried-up mouth. They touched its mouselike body; as they relaxed, he pat each one on his head.

Ole also possessed strange powers, and this, along with the bat on his hat, made the townsfolk leery of him. He could blow away heat from burns and rid a person of warts by counting them in his native tongue. He could stop bleeding in man or beast when nothing or no one else could. He was the weathervane for unnatural events. He would show up in town, where folks could attest to his being among them, before any calamity had taken place. They loved his practical jokes and funny stories, especially ones at their own expense. In the old country, Ole's gift for healing had been used in place of a doctor.

Dr. Townsend found Amy in the kitchen huddled on the floor back of the stove. Unable to find her father, she had returned home and had added wood to the stove and water to the teakettle. Her head was on her knees, and her arms were wrapped around her legs. One of the toddlers was leaning against her. "Amy," the doctor said, "it's time we say goodbye to your mother." Together they took the children upstairs, Amy carrying the sleeping Wesley. They stood around their mother's bed, and when Agnes opened her eyes and saw Amy caring for the baby, her eyes filled with tears.

The doctor sat by the bed with Billy in his lap, Agnes's hand in his. The teakettle whistled, and after a while it didn't whistle any more. Agnes made gargling noises in her throat and then was quiet. The doctor pulled the blanket up to her chin and folded her hands on her chest. The day faded, and the shadows grew long.

Bobby Lee's head appeared at the top of the attic steps, soon followed by the rest of him. His face turned chalk white when he saw his wife lying abed during daylight hours with her children huddled about her and the doctor sitting beside her holding a sleeping child. "What's the matter?" Bobby Lee asked, his voice breaking.

"Your wife's dead." The doctor said the words quietly, but somehow they grew loud and filled the room.

Billy woke up. "Papa, I'm hungry," he said, and he began to cry.

Then Bobby Lee began to cry, and he sounded just like Billy.

CHAPTER 13

September 1903

WORKING FOR THE OWENSES HAD been a pleasant experience, but Abby's next job as hired girl turned into an ordeal. Ethel Eugenia White, of the *Mayflower* Whites, was unpleasant to her from the beginning of her employment with her family. Mrs. White constantly sniffed her disapproval of every household task Abby performed. She found fault with her cooking, although she consumed every bite. She found fault with her dishwashing, complaining of bits of food stuck on the dishes; she even found fault with her dusting, saying the furniture lacked a shine. Abby was constantly on call to wait on the family but was never invited to eat at the family table as she had been at the Owenses' farm—not that she wanted to.

Mrs. White, now that she had the chance to do so, took every opportunity to scrutinize Abby's baby. She had to admit that he was a beautiful child, but where did his looks come from? Rockville did not have many dark-haired and dark-eyed residents.

"We are a fair-skinned, fair-eyed people," she acknowledged, with smugness. "Of course, there's the grandmother; I've never been quite sure what nationality she is. Some kind of foreigner, I suspect." And to add to Abigail's misery, on her first week of working for the Whites, Brother Griggsby had shown up one afternoon and had taken tea with Mrs. White. She first glimpsed them sitting side by side in the parlor. Brother Griggsby was making a crucial point of the story he was telling by tapping his forefinger on his knee. After Griggsby left that day, Abby always received hostile stares from Mrs. White; whenever Abby was present, Mrs. White kept a vigilant eye on her eighteen-year-old son, Teddy.

Abby knew that Mr. and Mrs. White tittle-tattled about her, and after Brother Griggsby's visit, the whispering, head shaking, and sidelong glances became more frequent. But she was acquiring a thick skin.

Saturday evening, after completing her third week of work at the Whites' place, Abby had had enough and gave notice that she would not be returning. The expression on Mrs. White's face was well worth missing the extra week's pay.

The afternoon of the following day, Melburn Owens called on her. The visit was agonizingly awkward. He brought a toy boxcar he had carved from a tree branch for the train engine he had previously given Ronnie, and then he took the boy for a ride on his horse.

"You men must be thirsty," Abby said to them when they returned. She served tea on the front porch, giving Ronnie apple juice in a tin cup. Each time she spoke to

Melburn, he blushed. She talked about the weather, and he blushed. She asked about the Owenses' crops, and he blushed. Upon his departure, her mother came to the screen door. "Melburn Owens is a good man," she said, approval honeying her voice.

Abby headed for her rose garden and strode about talking to the roses. "I can't," she said to a sweet-smelling yellow rose. "Of course he's a good man," she said to a luscious pink one in the height of its bloom, "but not for me. Ronnie's father will always be the only man for me." She picked a red rose and began the wistful litany: "He loves me, he loves me not…"

After she gave her notice, Abby escaped the gossip about her by packing up Ronnie and going to the ranch in the wagon with Grandma and spending six weeks with her and Uncle Pete.

On her first morning back, Aunt Em came bustling up the walk and into the house. Aunt Em never knocked on any door, and whatever she found inside people's homes never shocked her. "Where's my baby? Where's my big boy?" she called out. Ronnie hadn't forgotten the sound of her voice, and he was kicking and squealing. Aunt Em was always full of the town's goings-on and knew most of the stories firsthand. "Agnes Preston died: she aborted herself with a tamarack stick and bled to death. Doctor couldn't do a thing for her. He even sent for Ole Olsen and his laying-on-of-hands to stop the bleeding, but by then she had lost too much blood to stay alive. And all those little ones," Aunt Em said, "the oldest boy's only seven, and the youngest one's still nursing. I declare, she got in a family way at the drop of a hat."

Abby turned her head, hiding a guilty blush.

Aunt Em continued. "After I left here that day, I went out to Sedon's. He shot himself in the foot. I swear that man is the clumsiest human being on the face of the earth. I couldn't find the doctor, and he couldn't find me. But oh, when I finally showed up at Bobby Lee's"—she shook her head in dismay—"it was about the saddest sight I ever saw. There was not a thing to eat in that whole blessed house. Well, they're all at Bobby Lee's place today. The Benevolent Society from Old Church, and the Guild from New Church, and that mother of Bobby Lee's, are all there trying to outdo each other. God bless them all." She cooed into Ronnie's face and patty-caked with his hands. Then she added casually, "I heard Melburn rode out to the ranch to see you and Ronnie."

Abby knew people were talking about her. She could see it in people's faces and feel it in the prickling of her skin when she was in the company of others. The talk was about Melburn Owens calling on her and of Brother Griggsby's righteous indignation that she had "led the man astray."

"You don't have to take just anybody, Abby."

"It's not as if I have a lot of choices," Abby said.

"I believe Melburn would make a good father," Aunt Em said humbly.

Abby tipped her head back and stared at the ceiling, blotting out the image.

CHAPTER 14

January 1904

The year 1904 was a time of uncommon events. The people of Rockville referred to it as "the hot summer "or "the coughing winter." Someone would ask years later, "Remember that hot summer when those two boys drowned in a pond on their pa's farm trying to keep cool?" And they would nod, all-wise and all-knowing.

The citizens of Rockville referred to the year as one with two seasons: the bad winter and the bad summer. The winter had seen the deaths of fourteen babies, all whooping to their deaths in a matter of two weeks.

In early January, Abby awoke to a blinding light tormenting her eyes. Swinging open her bedroom door onto the small balcony, she looked out in amazement upon a dazzlingly bright winter landscape. Deep, undisturbed snow covered the ground and was piled high on trees, shrubberies, fences, and fence posts. Nowhere did she see man, animal, or bird.

She propped Ronnie up in his highchair by the kitchen window, where he could watch her as she attempted to shovel a path to the root cellar. The snow was so deep she could only skim the surface with the heavy metal shovel. At the cellar door, she dug down to the bare ground in order to pry open the heavy door. Leaving the door open, she entered the cavern-like room; from a box of matches she kept in a closed mason jar on the nearest shelf, she lighted the hanging lantern.

Once inside, she breathed in the agreeable aroma of the cool clean mushroom smell of the dirt floor and the cornucopia of harvest riches: fruits and vegetables stored in separate bins. She found enjoyment in the row upon row of glass jars with their fruits of summer's treasures gleaming jewellike from the shadowed shelves. A cured ham hung in a sack from a hook in the ceiling. The apple peeler mounted on a tree stump in the middle of the room stood ready for the next harvest.

She gathered up potatoes and apples and a jar of cherry preserves and placed them in a basket to take with her to the house. All of it brought home at Thanksgiving time from Grandma Langley's, the rewards of their labors of last fall.

Abby was grateful she did not have to dig a path to the outhouse. Her father, on one of his trips home, had installed a bathroom in the house, taking the necessary space from the oversize country kitchen.

She made a little snowman for Ronnie and set it on the window ledge. Ronnie was squealing and wriggling and trying to climb out of his chair. An unusually warm spell in January quickly disposed of the snow and brought about a profusion of illnesses. The adage "An early thaw in the new year, a full cemetery I fear" was fulfilling its prophecy. All over town, quarantine flags torn from lengths of red cloth were nailed to gate posts warning people of the dreaded whooping cough. As a result of the epidemic, Abby and Ronnie never saw Aunt Em. She waved to them when she passed by the house and blew them kisses. Abby missed her terribly.

The winter was lonely, and she saw no one. Aunt Em stopped once but kept a safe distance by remaining on the porch. She told Abby that, if she needed her, she should tie a colored cloth to the balcony railing.

Aunt Em reported that Abby's mother was confined to her bed at the hotel, as were Mr. and Mrs. Parlett; she said that it seemed to her "the whole town is sick abed." In a hushed voice, she confided, "Eleven little children have died from whooping cough. Mrs. Simon lost two on the same day: one in the morning and one in the afternoon. Poor thing, it's done something to her mind. She keeps calling out their names and searching for them."

Aunt Em said her "God bless you," but not in her usual jovial manner. She looked wan and tired. "Stay inside," she warned, "and don't let anyone come in the house or get near the baby." Aunt Em hesitated, wondering if she should tell Abby that Brother Griggsby was spreading rumors about her and calling her an unfit mother, but then she thought better of it. The young mother had enough worries without adding that one.

Abby spent the long winter days in bed, with Ronnie beside her. Except for taking care of his needs, she didn't have any reason to get out of bed. The inertia of solitude had robbed her of the will to care about her personal appearance. During the day she wore an old blue plaid flannel robe that had belonged to her father that she now found comfort sleeping in it at night. She never coifed her hair, just tied it back and out of the way with a ribbon. Sometimes she thought of her lover; the pain and humiliation of being forsaken by him were mostly gone, and an uncaring numbness had filled the void. She could not see a future for herself or Ronnie; she could not even think of one. *You don't deserve a child. You are an unfit mother. Brother Griggsby has said so.* Becoming even more despondent, she would cry and feel utterly worthless.

The faraway sound of bells interrupted Abigail's long respite from her terrible insomnia and hellish nightmares, and in a deep, coma-like sleep, she struggled to hear them. No. Not bells—cries. The sounds of crying.

She woke cold, cramped, and disoriented, her mouth so dry she couldn't move her tongue. Through a fog, she could see Ronnie standing in his crib, his arms stretched out to her and tears streaming down his face. She made an effort to stand but fell to the floor, her legs too numb to hold her up.

She looked about, stunned. They were downstairs; everything of Ronnie's was downstairs. The crib! How did the crib get downstairs? She couldn't think. She didn't know where time had gone or how much time had passed. She didn't even know what day it was, and she started to fear for her sanity. What if she ended up in the state lunatic asylum? What would become of Ronnie? Would her mother care for him? But her mother hated Ronnie.

She strained to pull him over the crib railing. He was freezing cold and soaking wet and clung to her neck sobbing brokenly and wouldn't let her put him down. She stripped his wet clothes from his chilled little body and wrapping him in a blanket, made a fire in the cold fireplace, then put him to her breast.

She had lost her milk.

CHAPTER 15

March 1904

ON A BLUSTERY MARCH DAY with a mixture of rain, sun, and snow, Abby heard a knock on her front door. Disheveled and apprehensive, she cautiously peeked out from behind the living room draperies. Her mother stood there with five men and two women. Abby recognized them as members of Old Church who were ordained to call on people whom they perceived were breaking the ordinances of the church. The seven were chosen for their peerless piety and their success in setting sinners back on the straight and narrow path of righteousness. A visit by the seven was a dreaded and feared occasion and a source of great humiliation. Some likened it to a visit by medieval inquisitors, which prompted the townsfolk to refer to them as the Unholy Seven. Much to her relief, Abby saw that Brother Griggsby was not among them. But John and Ethel White, newly appointed to the group, were.

They stood like a covey of blackbirds: black-hatted and black-robed figures, black-gloved hands gripping black umbrellas. Abby couldn't speak, her body sagged, and she held onto the opened door stricken with terror and a terrible foreboding. She did not want them in her home, but it was also her mother's, her father having left the property to both of them from his insurance policy.

Her mother entered the house, followed by the seven men and women; she turned her head sharply upon seeing the crib in the living room with a sleeping Ronnie in it. She looked doubly annoyed when she noticed a coal-oil lamp carelessly left on the dining room table, its smoke-blackened chimney in need of a good washing, and a layer of dust covering the tabletop. *What will people think?* "Let's go into the parlor," she said, leading the way, with Abby obediently following after them.

Even in winter, the scent of dying roses filled the room. August was the month her father had died six summers ago. Roses had been plentiful when he'd returned ill from the Spanish-American War. Roses filled baskets, vases, and mason jars, decorated tables, and surrounded the coffin to lift the spirits of the bereaved and to mask the smell of death. In Abby's memory, the scent of roses still perfumed the sunless room—the sad room. *I need you, Daddy,* she thought.

Her mother raised a window shade to lighten the room, which caused Abby to feel shame about her slovenly appearance. Late afternoon, and she was still barefoot and in her nightgown, wearing her father's old blue bathrobe. She sank onto the chair with the matching floral needlepoint-covered footstool and tried to hide her bare feet beneath it.

John White, an excessively devout man, as Abby knew from the weeks she had worked for the Whites, avoided eye contact with her as he nervously shifted his weight about in search of a comfortable position on the small rosewood chair he had chosen to sit on.

Mr. Johnson, seated next to him, removed his hat and placed it on his knee. He was a small man who was losing his hair and combed what was left crosswise over his balding pate. He was dressed in his Sunday meeting suit, as were the others, which signified the seriousness of their calling here today.

Mr. White cleared his throat—a call for the opening of the meeting. "The greatest blessing that can befall a child," he said, "is to be born into a good Christian home." They all nodded in agreement. The blood drummed in Abby's head. *What do they want?*

His reproachful eyes bore into hers. "We are here to thrash out the welfare of your child."

Who is moaning? She wondered. *Someone is moaning.*

"Your worthiness as a mother has been brought to our attention," Mr. White said.

Mr. Dinwoody nervously added, "We are very concerned about the religious instruction your child will receive."

The exceedingly religious and very deaf Mr. Wallace, a hard-faced man with weather-darkened skin, barked at her, "Are you seeking God's counsel concerning your son's eternal soul?"

Mr. Miller asked, "What kind of sinful life is this fatherless boy exposed to, living alone with an unwed mother?"

Mrs. White, seated with Mrs. Dinwoody on the couch, asked in her twittering voice, "What kind of man will he grow up to be?"

Thinking of Ronnie as a man was frightening. *What kind of a man will he be?* Abby wondered. She was overwhelmed from everyone talking at once. She couldn't think clearly and could barely follow the dialogue.

"We only want what is best for the child," Mrs. White said with a sniff, nervously fingering the mourning broach on her black silk bodice made by a jeweler in Saint Louis who specialized in making mourning jewelry from the hair of the deceased. "The broach," she would tell people, "is made from the precious hair of my dear departed mother."

"Mrs. White, you know I'm a good mother," Abby said pleadingly. "You watched me care for Ronnie when I was working for you." She heard the moaning once more and again asked herself where it was coming from.

"You live a very secluded existence here, and under certain circumstances, it could be a cause for clandestine meetings."

Abby's jaw dropped.

"Is that good for a child?" Mr. Johnson asked.

Before Abby could reply to his innuendos, Mrs. White spoke up. "Do you know Sam and Rachel Nelson?" she asked in a patronizing voice.

Abby nodded, numbly wondering why Mrs. White was asking her about the Nelsons. *What do the Nelsons have to do with me and Ronnie?*

"They are looking to adopt a child," she said, sounding pleased. The moaning became louder.

Abby found her voice at last. "Is Ronald going to hell? If he's baptized, will he go to hell?"

"Not if you name the father!" old Mr. Wallace snapped, pinching his dry lips together between thumb and a gnarly forefinger into a vinegary pout. The man was known to ask a blessing at his dinner table in a babble that lasted as long as half an hour, during which time food turned cold and bellies rumbled while he beseeched God for blessings and atonements from sin.

"Name the father!" he demanded in his raspy, parched voice.

"I can't," Abby said, moaning; then she realized that she was the one who was moaning.

"Not even to save your own son from burning in hell?" he asked in a thunderous tone.

Abigail crossed the floor and dropped to her knees in front of the elderly man. The faded blue ribbon holding back her hair had come untied and fallen to the floor, leaving her unruly auburn hair cascading about her shoulders. The belt of her father's blue plaid robe had also come undone, and the contour of her body was visible through the material of the nightgown she wore beneath it.

"If I tell you who the father is, will Ronnie be spared from going to hell?"

A prolonged silence followed her question. As she watched them, she grew cunning: *What if I joined New Church? Would they let Ronnie be baptized and saved, or will they demand the same of me—the name of his father?* Thinking of her lover made her angry. *We should both burn in hell. We're both sinners.* Still on her knees with her back to the women, she moved to the chair next to where Mr. White sat. The women for the first time saw her bare feet and recoiled in their chairs as if to distance themselves from the taint of her flesh.

"Ronnie's innocent," she said, attempting to appeal to the unyielding Mr. White. "Why should he be made to suffer for my sin? I'm the sinner. I'm the bad person. I'm the one who should burn in hell." Her voice was ragged and her lovely face racked with pain.

"Then tell us who the father is," John White wearily repeated.

She would not allow herself to name the man she loved. She could not even say his name aloud. Her shoulders slumped and, hiding her face in her hands, she wept. She knew she would go to her grave, silent and without remorse, still loving him with all her heart.

"Abigail, get up," her mother said, leaning over her. With one hand holding Abby's hand and her arm around her waist, she helped her daughter to her feet and across the room to the settee, where she had been seated. Their eyes met, and Abby for the first time saw genuine concern in her mother's face. They sat together, side by side, and Abby let her head fall onto her mother's shoulder. But her mother said, “Sit up. Sit up.” The annoyance in her voice quickly pushed her daughter away from the longed-for comfort.

Mrs. Langley smoothed her dress over her knees and, not looking at Abby, spoke out in an unnaturally high voice. “I am speaking as a mother and a grandmother, and I’m saying what I think is best for the child. He needs a father—and a mother. He needs a lawful birthright and a happy future. I think the child should be adopted.”

Bit by bloody bit, Abby’s life trickled from her mother’s mouth while the heads of the religious do-gooders bobbed up and down in righteous agreement.

“Mother, how could you?” Abby asked in a shocked whisper. “I know you don’t love us, but you are Ronnie’s grandmother.” As if to remind his grandmother, the baby began to cry. Her mother’s arm was still around her shoulder, but Abby shrugged it away and stood up to face her. “Leave us alone,” she said to her mother. And, turning to the others, she said, “Please. All of you just leave us alone.” Then she ran from the room.

The following week the seven called on her again, this time with the Nelsons in tow. Again they sat in the parlor, the men with long, pious faces and steepled fingers tapping at their chins, and the women’s intolerant faces trying to show sincere concern.

Abby, drawn and listless, short of sleep, poorly nourished, and robbed of vitality, was seated in a chair, where she held Ronnie on her lap. Gone was the radiance that was so much a part of who she was. *It's like a dream,* she thought, *when demons pursue you and you can't move.*

"He will have a good home," Mr. Miller said.

"He has a good home," Abby countered.

Her mother approached and placed a hand on her shoulder. Abby shrugged it away. "Abigail, I think it's best for Ronnie, or I wouldn't be here. He needs to be with other children. What will happen to him when he begins school? He'll be a laughingstock."

"No!" Abby cried, holding her baby close to her bosom and trembling with emotion. Ronnie, seeming to sense his mother's agitation, began to whimper.

"He's never been baptized," her mother whispered as she returned to her seat. The two virtuous, black-shrouded women shook their heads, tsk-tsking each other.

Mrs. Nelson, smiling timidly, drew close to Abby. She was young and pretty and looked at Abby with extraordinary kindness in her blue eyes. "We've wanted a baby for ever so long," she said sweetly, "and I would be very good to him—" She choked up and couldn't continue with what she was about to say.

Mr. Nelson came to her rescue. Taking his wife's hand in his, they stood before Abby, hands clasped.

Ronnie, with his thumb in his mouth, was rubbing a corner of his favorite baby blanket back and forth across his nose. Mrs. Langley, catching her daughter's eye, glared her disapproval of the blanket and the thumb-sucking.

"We dearly want a child," Mr. Nelson said, "but God in His infinite wisdom has deemed not to bless us with one of our own. We're prepared to provide a child with a good home, a good Christian upbringing, and a fine education, and we will love and cherish him as our very own."

Mrs. Nelson, during her husband's petition, was bestowing loving glances on Ronnie. Ronnie, usually shy around people (having known so few), was fascinated by Mrs. Nelson and stared up at her wide-eyed.

"We are moving from Rockville to Portertown," Mr. Nelson said. "We've bought a house there next door to my sister, who has three small children."

Ronnie has never seen another child, Abby thought.

Unexpectedly, Mrs. Nelson began to cry, burying her face in her husband's shoulder and crying with heart-wrenching sobs. Mr. Nelson wrapped his arms around his wife in a protective embrace and tenderly led her through the parlor door and out onto the privacy of the front porch.

Ronnie, sliding from his mother's lap and dropping his baby blanket, crawled to the door from which the couple had disappeared.

The loving tableau of husband and wife embracing tore at Abby's heart. She was stunned by the sight and forced into thinking about a mother and a father for Ronnie. "If he doesn't belong to me, will he go to heaven and not hell?"

Abby's words, bled of all passion, were as cold as river stones in winter, and just as heavy in her heart.

CHAPTER 16

June 1905

The Rockville Hub
June 9, 1905

Don't scare the horses

Dr. Noah Edwards, doctor of divinity, graduate of Harvard University magna cum laude, visited our fair town a few years back and has now returned to begin his ministry with us.

Dr. Edwards has purchased the replica of the ark built by Lars Larson in which to house his church. He is moving the ark to a lot on Main Street, which he has also purchased.

> This momentous event will take place tomorrow, June 10th. A map of the route is printed on page two of The Hub. The rules for watching the event are as follows:
>
> No cheering. No whistling. No whooping. No hollering. No clapping of hands or stomping of feet. Stay off the designated streets and on the sidewalks. Leave all dogs at home, penned up or tied up. We all know that a fleet of horses working as one pair will be as jittery as Mexican jumping beans on a hot day.

It had taken a full month of negotiations before Noah was given permission by the Rockville town council to move the ark. During that time he held meetings with the council, with people who owned homes along the route, and with men who offered teams of horses for the occasion. It seemed everyone wanted to be a part of this extraordinary event and therefore donated their time, horses, and expertise.

The logistics of moving a structure fifty feet long, thirty feet wide, and twenty-four feet high seemed impossible. Surprisingly, the most enterprising man was Chance Collins, who volunteered to organize the men and choose the horses. The ingenious Lars Larson, with his Norwegian cousin, Ole Olsen, built a sled with a ramp attached on which to transport the ark.

By sunrise on Saturday morning, a crowd of townspeople was already standing alongside the selected route; by midmorning, the crowd was spilling over the sidewalks and onto private property. Marshal McCombs and his deputy, Bob Hansen, both grim and official looking, appeared on horseback wearing gun belts, weapons exposed, each patrolling a side of the street and intermittently scowling at anyone who stepped out of bounds or acted rowdily.

It was noon before the ark was maneuvered onto the sled, the horses hitched up, and the procession set in motion. Chance Collins and his pair of horses were in the lead, preceding six teams of horses, two abreast. Three street corners needed to be negotiated, followed by the most crucial move: transferring the ark onto its foundation.

Lars Larson stood at the helm of the ark looking for all the world like a biblical Noah with white hair flowing, long beard glistening against the black of his coat, eyes transfixed and gazing straight ahead. What did he see? An ocean? Ancient seas? The Flood?

The crowd did not disperse during the afternoon break. None of the onlookers wanted to lose their places along the route. There was much waving back and forth between bystanders on opposite sides of the street and by those who wished others to see them and acknowledge that they, too, were in attendance and a part of the historic occasion. Will Stanton, an enterprising dairyman, showed up along the route with milk cans containing lemonade and sold drinks for a nickel a cup from the back of his farm wagon.

After the men and horses reached their destination and the ark was successfully anchored onto its foundation, everyone in town was in a festive mood. Some of the more sedate people in the crowd (but who still wanted to celebrate in some way) sat demurely on the steps of the emporium and sang song after song, young and old together. Ma's, in contrast, was filled to capacity, the revelers inside noisy and rambunctious.

The horsemen who had provided and steered the teams of horses were the heroes of the day, Chance Collins being the biggest hero among them. Everyone congratulated Chance on his skill with horses and complimented the marshal and his deputy on their crowd-control abilities.

"Hey, Marshal, would you really have shot us if we'd scared the horses?"

"You wouldn't be in here tonight drinking beer if ya had," the marshal boasted.

Chance, seated in the barber chair and feeling his drinks, yelled out above the din, "I smell a rat! Ratsy McGillicuddy, what little mousehole you holed up in?" Chance, shading his eyes from the gaslight hanging over one of the pool tables, peered into the darkened corners. "John, bring me a piece of cheese," he said cunningly. "I got to coax that little rodent out of its hiding place." Chance left the barber chair in search of his quarry, pushing well-wishers aside when they patted him on the back.

Noah, after having a beer with the merrymakers in the pool hall and singing a song with the songsters sitting on the store steps, spent the rest of the evening getting acquainted with his new domain. He inspected bedroom, bath, and kitchen, living and dining areas, envisioning the way he wanted each room. Lars had fancied up the ship's cabin with a Victorian gingerbread porch, and Noah knew he wanted a glider.

The following Saturday evening, Noah left his quarters on the deck of the ark and went below to the chapel. The pews were installed, the small organ set in place, and the chandeliers hung. He ran his hands over the silent keys of the organ and then, hearing an odd sound, did so again. He definitely was hearing something: a shuffling sound coming from the body of the church. Standing very quietly, he listened with unwavering attention. The noise was coming from beneath him.

Quietly descending the two steps of the platform, he paused again; the unusual sound was coming from the storage space beneath the pulpit. Noah, kneeling, cautiously opened the long narrow door and peered into the darkness. Closing the door, he went to his quarters and returned with a lantern and shone it into the dark space beneath the pulpit. The light picked out something, an animal maybe, and then he saw the bare foot.

"Come on out of there!" he said in a commanding voice. Silence. "What are you doing in there?" No answer. The best place to find Marshal McCombs or learn of his whereabouts was at the pool hall, and that was where Noah went to look for him.

Upon their return, the two men approached the pulpit; the marshal bent over and flung the door wide and stepped back. He waited a time before stooping and shining a light inside. A fearful whimpering sound was coming from the hollow space beneath the platform.

McCombs crawled inside and disappeared for a while before squirming back out and dragging a body, clasped by the ankles, with him. Noah instantly recognized the white-faced boy who had been sobbing and clinging to the door; when Marshal McCombs loosened his grip on him, the boy quickly scampered back inside.

"It's Pie Face," the marshal said, shaking his head. "It'll take something sweet to draw him out and calm him down. His ma, and a new baby brother, died over there today." He nodded his head in the direction of their house.

Noah returned, accompanied by his housekeeper, Rosie Kandel, bearing a plate of still-warm honey candy. The taffy was pulled, twisted, and broken into pieces until it no longer resembled the tawny color of dawn but the white glare of an arctic noon.

The marshal lured Pie Face out of his hiding place with the promise of a treat. Once he was out of the storage space, the boy snatched at the bait with both hands.

"He'd plumb follow you over the mountain for a piece of candy," Rosie said. "It takes sweets to calm him down. Something in his constitution needs sugar."

"His parents are Lon and Mary Swazey. She died in childbirth early this morning, and the baby, too," the marshal said, trying to explain the boy's unusual conduct. "There's so many kids at that house, if one or two come up missing, no one takes notice. Pie Face has always been left to wander on his own; the whole town feeds him like a stray dog."

"What's his given name?" Noah asked.

The marshal scratched his head. "I'm darned if I know." He looked to Rosie for an answer, but she shrugged as well. She was watching the kid, though, and she followed him to the prow of the ark, not knowing if it was the boy or the plate she was keeping her eye on.

The marshal looked about the chapel. "I haven't been in here since the day we moved it."

"I'll show you around," Noah said enthusiastically.

Marshal McCombs was duly impressed with the ingenuity Lars had applied in finishing the ark. The tour ended in the kitchen, where Rosie waited for them with cake and strong coffee.

"Pie Face won't come away from the prow of the ark," she explained. "He understands it's a boat, and he's waiting for it to move. He'll have sticky fingerprints all over the place," she said, fussing.

At one time, the Lon Swazey place had been an impressive piece of property, but it was now showing serious signs of neglect. Marshal McCombs knocked on the door, which was opened by a nervous, pink-faced, and red-eyed man. The marshal and Noah removed their hats, each keeping a hand on the elusive prey.

Mr. Swazey stood blinking at his son as he silently ran through a mental ladder of the names of his children. "Oh, ah, Pie Face," he stammered, not coming up with a name. "Has he been giving you trouble?"

"No, not really," the marshal said. "Just needed some candy." He patted Lon's shoulder and offered his condolences on the passing of his wife. Then he introduced Noah. "This here's the new minister in town, Noah Edwards. Has his church in an ark."

The man, while shaking hands with Noah, suddenly became agitated. "I don't belong to a church no more, but I want her to have a decent funeral. She was a good Christian woman." Still pumping Noah's hand, he asked, "Would you do it? Would you hold a funeral for her?"

Joe and Rose Langley, on their way to Mary Swazey's funeral—the first service to be held in the ark—stopped to pick up Nita. Abby had fresh roses waiting in a mason jar for them to take to the funeral and later leave at the cemetery. Sadness clouded her aunt Rose's face as she looked at her niece. "Why don't you come with us, Abigail?" she asked.

"I'm not allowed in church, remember?"

"But the service is being held at the ark, and Dr. Edwards is a very nice man. I think you'll like him. Going to church would give you a chance to sing again," she said in a lighter tone.

Abby glanced at her mother's unforgiving face and saw only disapproval. "Not today," she said. "Maybe another time." Abby was surprised her mother had agreed to attending a church other than her own, even for a funeral. *I guess curiosity got the better of her.*

This was Mary's day.

The memory of her, like a gray thread, was woven into the fabric of the day as the townspeople hurried through their morning chores in preparation for her funeral. The women who lived on Mary's street were busy making their best dishes: cakes, pies, meat roasts, and potato and cabbage salads. The food was to be left in Mary's kitchen for the family and out-of-town mourners to consume later. The women remained long enough to pay their last respects and to take a final look at Mary's earthly remains.

On funeral days, farmers came in early from the fields, the miners from the mines, and children remained close to home. Storekeepers prodded lingering customers into leaving their shops so that they, too, could attend the funeral, for all businesses would be closed during the hours of the service.

The absence of Mary was bewildering to her family as they, too, prepared for the burial. This required tiptoeing in and out of the darkened parlor by the older sisters, who furtively glanced to the far side of the room where their mother, with their tiny infant brother embraced in one of her arms, lay in a coffin supported on two chairs.

The daughters searched the oak chifforobe for clothing to wear to their mother's funeral. This was something their mother used to do. The chifforobe sat in a corner of the room, a brightly colored velvet scarf with a long silken fringe draped over it. A wedding tintype of a young Mary and her bridegroom, Lon, was displayed on the top of the chest, along with a cut-glass vase holding red crepe-paper roses.

Soon Mary's family would sit in this room on stiff dining room chairs dressed in their Sunday best, and the townspeople would file past the coffin and gaze upon their mother and the stillborn child. They would dutifully comment on how natural they looked, "just like they're sleeping," cluck their tongues and shake their heads, pat the younger children on the head, and murmur condolences to the husband. They would gather in clusters in the front yard and converse in whispers until the half bell sounded. Slow and mournful would be the tolling of the bell that day until the horse-drawn hearse reached the church, followed by the mourners, most of them in carriages, some on foot, and a few in farm wagons.

At the sounding of the bell, anyone who was not a relative left the parlor, and only the immediate family remained. Dr. Edwards ushered them to the casket for a final goodbye. The crying began again as he offered a prayer for acceptance to an anticipated heaven before he escorted them outside.

The room was empty, waiting for undertaker Tibbits to come in and close the casket. Pie Face stepped from behind the parlor door of the "company room," open that day for the viewing. His mother, whenever he was frightened or bewildered, used to bring him into this seldom-used room, away from the prying eyes of others. She would draw him into the corner of the room, where the parlor door—if opened inwardly and pulled close to the wall—concealed them in a little secret hideaway. When fully hidden, she would unbutton her dress, exposing a breast that was always with milk, and, holding him tight, would stroke his head while he nursed. Once he again felt secure, they would remove themselves from their hiding place.

He crept out now from back of the door and nudged his mother's shoulder where she lay in the box. She didn't open her eyes, and with tears trickling down his white pudgy cheeks, he proceeded to pull the baby from his mother's arm and lay it at her feet.

Undertaker Tibbits entered the room. Everyone, including the family, had forgotten Pie Face. His heart went out to the childlike young man bending over his mother's corpse. His head reclined on her breast, and the rigid circle of her arm, free of the baby, rested coldly upon his shoulder. Mr. Tibbits placed a sympathetic hand on the boy's back and then with horror pushed him away from the casket.

Clumsily, but with great haste, he buttoned the starched white shirtwaist of the deceased woman and hurriedly locked the casket, not remembering until evening that he had forgotten to place the dead baby back in his mother's arms.

So in death, Mary finally escaped the burden of caring for a child. The last fleeting look at her was a work-worn hand, fragile in its lifelessness, seemingly waving goodbye as the lid closed on her with a soft final thud.

THE ROCKVILLE HUB
June 16, 1905

ARK DOCKS ON MAIN STREET

Saturday past, amid a sea of spectators, Noah's Ark came to rest on our very own Main Street. The people of Rockville, in a display of convivial enthusiasm, symbolically extended an olive branch to its young helmsman by earnestly wishing the modern-day Noah, and his Chapel of the Ark, a long and successful tenure.

> Exploring the Ark is a religious experience. The stained-glass windows, the golden oakwood of the walls, floors, and pews, and the tranquil atmosphere of the building combine in a medley of serenity. The beautiful new church, being non-denominational, is open to one and all.

The newspaper contained one obituary:

> Robert Gilbert Jr., 29 years of age, beloved son of Robert and Eleanor Gilbert, died from an apparent suicide late Saturday night by means of rat poisoning. Robert, who was sometimes called "Ratsy" by friends and acquaintances...

CHAPTER 17

August 1905

RETURNING FROM A MORNING RIDE on his recently purchased mare—a feisty strawberry roan with black mane and tail—Noah stomped up the outside-rear staircase of the ark to his living quarters. Removing his black cap and the black jacket he wore over his tan riding breeches, he threw them onto a bench. Scowling and slapping his riding crop against his English boots, he strode back and forth across the deck.

The town baffled him. Had he made a mistake in coming to Rockville? He leaned over the railing. "How am I going to raise you from the dead?" he yelled at the town below.

Rockville was a good town, a prosperous, growing town, and the citizens as a whole were an industrious people—and religious. But just how religious? He knew they had few resources with which to express themselves. Sports of any kind were prohibited, and of course dancing was absolutely forbidden. Apart from enjoying themselves, the people of Rockville seemed to have everything they needed—with the exception of a good time.

The only entertainment the young people indulged in that Old Church did not forbid was meeting on the steps of the Parlett Emporium on Sunday nights and singing. But Noah had soon learned after moving to Rockville that Old Church and Brother Griggsby ran the town.

On a Sunday evening not long after he first came to town, Noah joined the young singers on the steps of the emporium and engaged them in conversation. He wanted to find out what they enjoyed doing other than singing.

"We liked Aunt Em's birthday party, and the day the ark was moved to Main Street," one of the young men said.

"We like it when the whole town gets together—not just Old Church or New Church, but everyone together having a good time," Orion Langley added.

Noah ran his fingers through his hair. There had to be more for young people to do than sit on a step once a week and sing. *What can I do?* he thought. What did other towns have that everyone enjoyed, something that gave them pride?

Baseball. Baseball?

"Baseball!" he shouted from the deck of the ark, making a triumphant swinging motion with his riding crop at an imaginary ball.

Noah searched the town for a baseball and bat and found neither. "Try the Langley lumber mill," Lars

Larson suggested. "They play ball out there. Joe Langley has enough sons for a team of his own."

"Shucks, Preach," said the twenty-year-old redheaded "Sags" (short for Sagittarius), the grin on his freckled face full of mischief, "why didn't you tell us you wanted a baseball?"

Each Langley child was named in honor of a constellation, astronomy being a passion of their father's. Leo, Sagittarius, and Andromeda ("Andy") had been borne by Joe's first wife; their only daughter, two-year-old "Peggy" (Pegasus), had died during a cholera epidemic.

"We've even got a bat!" the usually inhibited twenty-two-year-old Andy said from where he sat on the corral fence. They all laughed.

Leo, the oldest brother and business head of the Langley enterprises, said, "We've always played ball here at River's Bend. Years ago, Dad made his living playing ball."

"Yeah," Joe Langley said in a drawl. "When I was a young man, there was nothing I'd rather do than swat those balls, but I gave it up to stay home with my boys. Can't take a family with you when you're barnstorming around the country and the pay's so poor. Orion there," Mr. Langley said, nodding toward a handsome young man with black curly hair and blue eyes filled with intelligence and good humor, "is a natural-born, all-around athlete. Heck, they're all good ballplayers," he said, "except for our fiddle player here."

He put his arm around fifteen-year-old Aries, a romantically poetic young man with long, wavy, black hair who raised dark, languorous eyes to Noah. "Someday he's going to be a famous violinist," Joe said. He dropped his arm. "But you don't play ball in Rockville, and I guess it's just as well."

Noah asked, "If you like the game so much, Mr. Langley, then why do you say that?"

"Well, most people—and I'm talking about the rest of the country now as well—think baseball players are bums who're too lazy to work a regular job."

As they talked, Joe was steering Noah toward a shed near the barn. Mr. Langley opened the shed door and motioned for Noah to step inside.

Bats! Baseball bats! More bats than Noah had ever seen hung from the rafters. "We're always on the lookout for good hardwood to make bats—any wood that's really primed. Old trees, old logs, old fence posts, old wagon tongues we turn in the furniture shop. My wife makes most of the balls. She's the best wrapper and stitcher there is."

Leo, looking around, said, "Where's the twins?"

After getting shoulder shrugs from his brothers, he nodded to six-year-old "Percy" (Perseus). After he gave Percy a leg up to a rafter, the boy untied a bat and handed it down to him. Leo, expressing pride, dusted off the bat before handing it off to Noah. Percy jumped from the rafter, and they moved outside.

Noah, approving of the smooth grain and heft of the bat, rotated his shoulders a couple of times and, stepping away from the others, took a few practice swings and then made a powerful, beautiful cut.

"Hey, you've played some baseball in your time," Leo said, impressed.

"That I did. My junior year at Harvard, I made the varsity team."

"From the looks of that swing, you could've made it in a professional ball club."

"Baseball's not my calling," Noah said.

"You've got the knack, Doctor," Joe said. He also was impressed.

"And that's why I'm here today, Mr. Langley. I want to organize a baseball club in Rockville, and I'll need you and your boys to help me."

The young men grew quiet and cautiously eyed their father while they waited. Finally, after thinking it over, Joe wiped his hand on his pants leg and, reaching out to Noah, said, "We'll do it. By golly, it's about time we played baseball again in this here town." While the men shook on it, the boys were slapping one another's backs and hooting and laughing.

Mr. Langley removed his hat, wiped sweat from his forehead with the crook of his arm, and pointed the hat in the direction of the house. A woman who was propping the screen door open with one hip was stepping from a doorway and onto the porch. Two of the boys sprinted to her side and took a tray holding a pitcher of lemonade and glasses from her.

"Come and join us," Mr. Langley said, "and meet the missus."

Rose Langley was a tall, attractive woman with black, wavy hair and a smile that made you feel welcome. Women kept pouring out of the house and onto the wide wraparound porch. Joe introduced Noah to his sisters-in-law: "Camellia, Hyacinth, Violet, Lily, Iris, and Zinnia, and this lovely lady is my mother-in-law, Ivy Mosley."

Mr. Langley bowed deeply before his mother-in-law seated in a rocking chair, and she in turn swatted him on the shoulder with a string fly swatter. "So you're going to play ball," she said. "Well, you better take my girls with you, 'cause they can play your pants off any day in the week." Everyone laughed.

"That's the truth," Mr. Langley said to Noah. "You're staying for supper?" he said as he put his hat on his head and left to feed and corral his horse.

The great room of the Langley home extended the length of the house and had a solid look of strength and comfort. One end of the large room was taken up with the kitchen, and the other boasted a rock fireplace made of boulders removed from the earth when the land was cleared for building the house and the furniture factory.

On either side of the fireplace were built-in cases holding books as well as an impressive display of Indian artifacts excavated from the earth along with the boulders. Shelves and window ledges overflowed with books.

A chandelier made from the horns of stags hung above the table. Cups carved from bone cradled the candles and were attached to the antlers with leather thongs. The large light was held aloft by ropes and was raised and lowered by a pulley.

When Rose and her six sisters were joined by their six husbands, supper turned into a liberation party celebrating the return of baseball to Rockville.

"Old Griggsby's not going to like getting his toes stepped on!" someone said.

"Well, Noah's got big feet," Joe Langley said. Everyone laughed and looked toward Noah's shoes.

CHAPTER 18

When Abby saw the men enter the ballpark, she stopped weeding her vegetable garden, stripped the leather work gloves from her hands, and, untying the heavy apron from around her waist, bunched it into a ball and tossed it onto the porch. She rolled down the sleeves of her pale-blue blouse, tucked stray wisps of hair into the bun on the back of her neck, and then leisurely strolled along the path of her rose garden, finding enjoyment in the beauty of the roses and their romantic fragrance.

If Orion stops by after ball practice today, she thought, *I'll send a bouquet of flowers home with him for Aunt Rose.* Orion was her favorite cousin, as close to her as a brother. As she neared the fence, she looked again at the crowd now gathered in the park. She sighed; even women were present. She would have to relinquish the pleasure of her garden for the smothering solitude of her house. Her appearance on her front porch inspired too much curiosity.

Selma Ward, looking over her picket fence from across the street, saw Abby standing at her gate but gave her no sign of recognition. Instead she nodded her approval of the properly dressed ladies occupying the little park today. They were gathered around the fountain, pretending they hadn't a notion in their heads that young men would be present.

Only last summer, the same girls had been jumping rope, playing in stacks of hay, nursing skinned knees, pushing one another in barn swings, and wearing shapeless dresses with unkempt hair whipping about their newly budding bodies. This summer, immaculately feminine, with the wholesomeness of newly laundered linens dried in the sun, they were consumed in the art of attracting beaus.

Their thick, shining hair was caught up in huge white bows at the napes of their necks, and straw hats with flat brims and ribbons adorned their heads. Gracefully swanlike, they glided about the garden in boned chin-high lace collars with white, puffy-sleeved bodices and twenty-inch waists encased in white linen skirts and bespoke femininity in both dress and manner.

"Their mating instincts will bring them to the park" was Noah's answer to shocked mothers when they asked him what the girls would be doing while the boys played ball.

Noah knew the town was waiting for him to show an interest in someone. As yet, however, no one woman had attracted him. Young ladies with parents in tow were showing up for his Sunday morning services at the ark, which made him assess his every word and gesture. Noah suspected they were more interested in him as an available bachelor than as a minister.

The two closest of friends among the group of newly matured ninth-grade girls assembled in the park today were inseparable: Jennifer Jeanne Oberlander, the banker's daughter, and Susan Millicent Leffler, whose father was president of the stone quarry. Susan was as brunette in hair and eye coloring as Jennie Jeanne was fair. Every mother wanted her teenage daughter to be best friends with the popular Oberlander and Leffler girls, or at the very least to belong to their circle of friends.

The Rockville quarry was mined entirely by Italian immigrants living in the quaint little mining village of Saint Margaret's, where they had their own church and school. Their Catholic priest conducted church services in Italian and taught their children reading, writing, and arithmetic in both English and Italian in a one-room schoolhouse. The owners of the stone quarry, including Mr. Leffler and the officials of the mine, being Anglo-Saxon and Protestants, lived in big stone houses on Stony Creek Road, and their children attended the town school.

A practice ball flew over the fence and came to rest close to where the girls were sitting. Orion Langley, running while keeping his eye on the ball, hit the fence full force, knocking the wind out of him. Susan recovered the ball and tossed it back to Orion, who, when catching it, looked not at her but at blond and dimpled Jennie Jeanne, who lowered her eyes and did not look at him in return. All the girls watched the good-looking young man as he returned to the practice game.

"I wish I could play ball," Susan said. "I wish I could run—just run and run like a wild horse." Grabbing the loose ends of her dark hair, she lifted her arms high and rocked her head back and forth, imitating a horse.

"Girls mustn't exercise too much," the plump, motherly Sadie said. Everything about Sadie was motherly, which made her appear older than she was. "We have to conserve our strength for when we get—well, you know."

"Climb the hill?" freckle-faced Annie said, using a local expression that meant a woman was pregnant. Annie hid her blushing face in her hands, and they all giggled—all but Sadie, that is, who never made light of women's duties.

"It's a woman's burden to bear children," Sadie said with self-assurance. The girls could not imagine themselves ever being in a climb-the-hill condition.

A billowing white cloud passed overhead momentarily, casting a shadow over the little park. Elizabeth Johnson, tall and dignified, and Alice Mills, barely measuring five feet, left the group and, sauntering over to the west fence, stared at the Langley house.

"Can you see her?" Alice whispered.

"No," Elizabeth whispered back, "the honeysuckle vines are too thick. I think she's there, though, watching us. She watches everything we do. It's the only way she has of having any fun."

"She gave her baby away," Alice said. The two girls grew quiet. "My mother calls it a 'love baby.' She says she must have loved it very much to give it away so it could be raised by an unsullied woman."

"She'll probably go crazy and end up in the state asylum. All for love," Alice said with a sigh.

"They say she walks the streets at night so people can't stare at her."

"I hope we never have to walk in her shoes."

"Oh! We never will," the stately Elizabeth said indignantly.

"Let's go to the drugstore and cool off," Sadie said, fanning herself with an embroidered white handkerchief. "Maybe Mr. Stevens will give us a cardboard fan."

"Or a Coca-Cola fan with a picture of a pretty lady on it," Jennie Jeanne said, her blue eyes smiling and her dimples deepening.

At the Stevens Drugstore, the girls sat at the marble-top counter sipping ice-cooled sodas. High above their heads, a fan hanging from the white-embellished tin ceiling droned lazily, swirling the air with a lemon-vanilla-root beer breeze.

Before long, the young men from the ballpark, sweaty and noisy, swaggered into the store, taking up the remaining counter stools or sitting at the small round tables on dainty black chairs with wire heart-shaped backs. Hot and thirsty and buoyed from ball practice, they boisterously called out to one another, ignoring the girls. After settling down, some of them approached the counter where the girls were seated. Orion stood behind Jennie Jeanne and stared at her image in the mirror until she looked up and met his gaze. She locked eyes with him for a second before returning to her soda. As she sipped nervously, the liquid in the soda glass made a bubbling noise that made her blush and embarrassed her too much to meet his gaze again.

"Singing tonight?" a bass voice asked.

"Yeah! Yeah!" were the masculine replies, accompanied by backslapping and shoving. The girls responded with giggles. Leaning close to Jennie Jeanne's ear, Orion whispered, "Will you be going to the sing-along tonight?"

A butterfly took flight from her stomach and caught in her throat. In Rockville, the rite of passage from grade school to high school was to turn old enough to join in the singing on the steps of the Parlett store. The steps were the preferred gathering place for young people and afforded them the opportunity to get together with others their own age—or with one person in particular—without chaperones. Jennie Jeanne whispered, "Yes," still not looking at him.

In the lightness of the mountain air, the voices of the young singers carried easily to the listeners at home, reminding them that all was right with the world, everything safe and sound and orderly. "Just a Song at Twilight" they sang, and "My Sweetheart's the Man in the Moon," and "Casey Would Waltz with a Strawberry Blonde." On and on until it was time to go home.

At ten o'clock, the crowd on the store steps dispersed, and the young people drifted away in various directions, Jennie Jeanne, Susan, and Alice to the big stone houses on Stony Creek Road. The Langley brothers, living at the end of Stony Creek Road and beyond, did not mount their horses but walked side by side with the girls, their horses following behind them. Orion walked between Jennie Jeanne and Susie. Sags walked with Alice and was teasing her.

"You'll soon be old enough to go on dates," he said.

"I'll never be that old!" she said, giggling.

Out of the blackness of night, a lone figure emerged. Walking briskly in the middle of the road was Aunt Em, on her way home from attending the sick. "Who's there?" she called out, laughing. "Some of my babies, I declare?" They gathered around her, the girls giving her hugs, and Aunt Em returned them. "God bless you," she said in her throaty voice. "Old Mother Carrie passed away tonight. Tell your folks. Funeral's on Tuesday."

"We'll walk you home, Aunt Em," Orion offered.

"Land sakes, no," she replied. "I've got eyes like a cat. You walk the young ladies home. Go on now. I expect the doctor to be along any minute." She shooed them away with a brisk movement of her hands and, still chuckling, disappeared into the dark.

Orion escorted Jennie Jeanne to her front door. "If you come to ball practice on Saturday, I'll treat you to a soda afterward." Then, tipping his hat, he ran to his horse and jumped onto its rear end and into the saddle. He caught up with his brothers as they raced toward home, all of them teasing Orion about being "sweet on a girl."

Abby, brushing her hair and listening to the singing from the balcony of her bedroom, remembered when she was part of a group. She missed singing almost as much as she missed her friends. Now those friends were married, most of them with children. *Will I ever be married and have another child, and sing again just from sheer happiness?* She slapped at her damp cheeks. "You cry too much," she scolded herself.

CHAPTER 19

THE CARD PLAYERS—HENRI AND Francoise Parlett; George Leffler, the successful, self-made, self-educated quarry owner and his wife, Wanda; the druggist Richard Stevens and his charming and affable wife, Barbara Stevens—were gathered at the home of banker Leon Oberlander and his wife, Lottie. All were members of New Church and, within the dictates of their religion, believed a game of cards was only a sin when played on Sunday or for money.

The couples sat talking in the parlor awaiting Dr. Townsend. Upon his arrival, the husbands excused themselves and retired to the library, where they talked politics, drank imported liquor, and (without their wives' knowledge) gambled for high stakes, each of them being a man of affluence. The ladies played bridge in the parlor, drank tea or homemade root beer, and gossiped. When the men again joined the ladies, refreshments were served.

Jennie Jeanne entered the parlor of her parents' home smiling and displaying captivating small dimples at the corners of her mouth. She said hello to her mother's guests, adding a bow. Jennie Jeanne, as her mother had been in her day, was now considered the prettiest girl in town. Her long blond curls bounced, and when she smiled, her blue eyes slanted upward, giving her an elfin appearance. She was young and happy and in love. Lottie, however, believed she was still the reigning beauty of the town, as did Mr. Oberlander. But tart-tongued Perthy Prettyman had recently been overheard saying that "Lottie Oberlander's no longer a spring chicken, and she has the neck to prove it."

When it came to deciding who deserved to be called the town beauty, the quintessential loveliness of the immoral Abigail Langley was never taken into consideration.

Jennie Jeanne knew she was too old to curtsy, but she knew it would please her mother, and she did want a favor. Mrs. Oberlander puzzled over the request her daughter had just asked of her. "If you are quite sure it is all right with the other mothers, then it is quite all right with me," her mother said in her precise musical voice, which she had developed while faithfully practicing piano scales. "They want to sleep outside on the lawn," Mrs. Oberlander explained to her guests. "Bring your little friends into the parlor to say hello to everyone," she said to her daughter, who quickly hugged her mother.

Susan, Anna, and Alice—all fourteen years of age, awkward and graceful, teetering between child and woman—entered the room. The men came into the parlor to rejoin the women. Mr. Oberlander kissed his daughter's forehead and asked, "What are you doing up so late, young lady?"

"We were downtown singing on the store steps," she said, glancing over at Mr. Parlett for approval because they were his steps.

"Everyone was there," Susan said, blushing and giggling. "Everyone" to them meant boys, and to Jennie Jeanne it meant Orion Langley.

"Well, stay, by all means, and have something to eat with us," said Mr. Oberlander.

"Oh, may we, Mother?" Jennie Jeanne asked.

"Let them stay, Lottie," the ageless and dignified Mrs. Parlett said. "I like having young people around me."

"I tell you, the young people in this town never have any fun." This was one of Dr. Townsend's favorite themes when he wasn't deriding religion. "Inactivity isn't healthy, and young girls especially need exercise as much as boys. They should be dancing and skating and playing ball and swimming, yes, and attending the theater."

The girls whispered to one another. "I'd love to dance with a boy," Jennie Jeanne said, making an unhappy face because the girls often danced with one another, one of them taking the lead.

"It will never happen here," said Mr. Leffler, Susan's father.

"Why shouldn't it happen here?" the forward-thinking Mrs. Leffler asked her husband. Susan, frowning, looked anxiously from one parent to the other.

"It *can* happen here," the doctor said. "We can make it happen here."

The girls retired to their slumber party on the lawn wearing white cotton gowns and snuggling into a bed made of quilts brought from the house. Too excited to sleep after listening to Dr. Townsend's ideas, they talked of dances, party dresses, and young men.

Inside the house, the Saturday night get-together lasted until after midnight. Being up that late was unheard of for the card players—or, for that matter, anyone who lived in Rockville.

"We tried dancing at Jennie Jeanne's birthday party last year," Lottie Oberlander said. "The children didn't know how to dance, and the boys wouldn't even try, so the girls were made to dance with one another. Then, the following Sunday…" she said, glancing out of the open window to the lawn, making sure her conversation wouldn't be overheard by innocent ears. Lowering her voice, she said, "That awful Brother Griggsby gave a sermon to his parishioners. He said women touching men and men touching women while dancing causes lust and was created by the devil for that very purpose. The children were the laughingstock of the entire town. I don't know why it was any concern of his, when all the children present were members of our own church."

Barbara Stevens added, "Some of the members of New Church are just as prejudiced against anything that's fun as those from Old Church. I myself would like to be given the choice to dance or not to dance."

"Well, I won't try it again," said Lottie. "This year, for Jennifer Jeanne's birthday, we're going to Camp Chautauqua in Logan for a week."

"Lottie, you haven't told me this," said Mrs. Parlett.

"Why don't you come with us, Francoise?" Lottie said to Mrs. Parlett, giving the French name the same deep-in-the-throat pronunciation that her husband, Henri Parlett, did. "And you, too, Wanda and Barbara." The women became girlishly excited, and while they made plans, the doctor was appealing to the men.

"Chautauqua once a year is not enough culture and entertainment to sustain growing children until the following year. I'm telling you, we can have Chautauqua right here in Rockville the year round."

"How?" Mr. Leffler asked.

"I want to build an opera house as a gift from me and Aunt Em, but to do so, I'll need your support." The room fell silent, each envisioning an opera house.

Wanda touched Mrs. Parlett's arm, almost reverently. "Oh, Fran"—not for her the fancy pronunciation—"remember the opera we attended when we were in Chicago for the fair?"

Mrs. Parlett, rocking in the small rocking chair, her thoughts far away, nodded agreeably.

The men were also silent; they, too, were remembering the gaiety of the Chicago Auditorium with the fashionable men and women all exhibiting a visible show of wealth.

"It's human nature to want to have a good time and to better oneself," the doctor said. "If we begin this, I believe most of the town will join in. America is an affluent country today, and we're in the dawn of a new century. We want entertainment and enlightenment."

"There's a lot of money right here in Rockville," said the banker, "and it ought to be put to use—circulated, so to speak," he said, smoothing his thinning, graying hair. "After all, it takes money to make money." He pried his gold watch from the watch pocket in his too-tight vest.

"The five of us right here could build an opera house," said Mr. Leffler. "We could support it ourselves if we had to. Of course," he said with a chuckle, "the price of admission might be a little steep."

"It would be worth it," said Mr. Parlett. "Bring in one of those Swedish Nightingales, the one in a gilded cage. I'd like to see her again."

"Oh, Henri," Mrs. Parlett scolded, playfully shaking his arm.

The following day, Dr. Townsend and the banker were seen looking at the vacated Fuller property on Main Street, where the almost-blind, and for many years widowed, John Fuller had lived before his demise. The property was situated between the school and the Wallace house.

Everyone in town was speculating as to what was going on. Members of Old Church said that members of New Church were building a burlesque house and that naked women would perform in it. This made the strait-laced members of New Church indignant, and for a time they did not speak to the more sophisticated members of their own sect. Old Church members were snubbing New Church members, and relations between friends and neighbors became tense.

CHAPTER 20

September 1905

"Play ball!"

FOR THE FIRST TIME IN ten years, baseball was being played in Rockville.

Late Saturday afternoon, a lumber wagon with nine young men aboard rolled into town, and, after surveying the stores along Main Street, the men entered the emporium. They inquired of Mr. Parlett if the town had a baseball team. If so, they said they were the Roseville Roses and would like to challenge them to a game.

Mr. Parlett lit up; he loved baseball. But because it was too late for a game that day, and because sports of any kind would never be played in Rockville on a Sunday, he promised free meals to the Roseville team if they would remain in town for a game on the following Saturday.

The Roseville team camped out at the park and during the week played two practice games with the Rockville team. The only announcement for the practice game on Monday, besides word of mouth, was a hurriedly scribbled notice nailed to the Poster Tree. Still, the game had a fair turnout for a Monday. Most of the town's business leaders were in attendance, and some of the stores closed early.

Mr. Parlett was there, seated in the grandstand behind the rusted chicken-wire fence, alongside Oberlander the banker and Dr. Townsend. The fence had been installed years before, when baseball had been a big part of the summer's entertainment in Rockville; this was before Brother Griggsby came to town and convinced them they were sinners.

The Roses were young men from a small town just like Rockville. For the big game on Saturday, however, they showed up wearing uniforms: white pants with red pin stripes, red caps, red and white socks, and their team's name emblazoned in red on their white shirtfronts.

Mr. Parlett, as he watched the hometown team for the first time, liked what he saw. He was impressed by Orion's fastball and natural grace as a pitcher, and he chuckled with good humor each time Lester Dinwoody came up to bat. Lester's father, Hyrum, had told him not to bother coming home if he played ball; the young man informed his dad, "Come hell or high water, Pa, I'm playing baseball."

Joe Langley, feeling responsible for the break between father and son, had taken Lester in and given him a job at the mill. He figured the boy needed something to make him feel like a competent man more than he needed a heckling father. But, more important, the lad possessed a great arm and a fast pair of legs.

The home team had a poor showing and lost 1–7. Still, Mr. Parlett bet Oberlander that if the two teams played again, Rockville would win. Oberlander took the bet, saying the hometown team was too inexperienced, but Parlett liked the hometown team's enthusiasm.

"We need us a name," Leo said at the supper table that night.

"The Rockville Roses," his brother Sag said in a falsetto voice while pretending to smell a bouquet of flowers.

"The Rockville Rocks," said Corvus and Cetus.

"Rockville Rockets," said Aries.

All the brothers turned toward the one nonathletic brother, a look of awe on their faces. "The Rockville Rockets!" they said in unison.

Rose, with her mother and sisters, worked late into the night appliquéing "Rockville Rockets" in a royal-blue fabric onto nine new pale-blue cotton work shirts.

The mayor declared Saturday to be a holiday. The stores closed at two o'clock, and an all-seats-taken crowd was in the park to watch the game. It would be unseemly for unescorted ladies to be seated in the grandstand for a ball game, so the young ladies of the town were seated on the benches in Fountain Park or sat on the grass, their full skirts spread around them like flowers strewn about the lawn.

Orion, having seen Jennie Jeanne in the group, purposely missed a warm-up ball thrown by Sag and let it hit the fence, which gave him the chance for Jennie Jeanne to notice him. This maneuver did not go unnoticed by Leo, nor did the fact that Orion was all fired up and soon helped win the ball game.

At the end of the game, a jubilant crowd of well-wishers swarmed onto the field. The people were so happy—not just in their team winning a ball game but in seeing one at all—that they included the losers in their rousing congratulations as well.

Dr. Noah Edwards had a power swing that had everyone watching him. "That new preacher seems to be an all-around admirable fellow," Dr. Townsend said to Oberlander.

"And he has money, too," the banker said in an aside to Parlett.

John Saunders, the Rockets' first baseman, with his sister Eloise in tow, cornered Noah after the game and introduced the two. Noah observed that the very sedate sister had very flirtatious eyes.

While acknowledging the introduction, Noah was looking over Eloise's shoulder, where the enigmatic woman he'd noticed earlier had appeared on the upstairs balcony of the Langley residence. She was removing a quilt from the railing, and the sunlight glistened enticingly on her auburn hair. Noah kept his eyes on her until she entered the house, all the while listening to Eloise gush over his sermon of the Sunday past. He wondered if, from the advantageous view of the balcony, the redheaded woman had watched the game.

After their successful showing against the Roseville Roses, the Rockville Rockets played a ball game every Saturday afternoon. Rockville had enough players for an opposing team plus an old timers team made up of men who had played years ago and were still tough competitors.

Men who made it known they were interested in getting into the game sat on benches near the diamond. And men who wanted to play, but for one reason or another were not asked to join the team, sat the farthest away from the action. One of them was Harlan.

Chance Collins did not want to play—he wanted to umpire. After much discussion between Joe Langley, Noah, and Leo, the team accepted his offer.

Each game day, the crowd in the grandstand increased. The Italian Catholics from Saint Margaret's fielded a team of their own named the Saints.

At the first game the Rockets played in competition with the Saints, the flamboyant Flora Maria Brocoloni sang the "Star-Spangled Banner." The townswomen who attended the game begrudgingly admired the singer's strong operatic voice, which everyone present could clearly hear.

"I'm not sure I-talians should be singing our national anthem," Perthy Prettyman sniffed. "I'm not sure they're even Americans."

It was an incident that occurred during the game with Saint Margaret's in which Harlan was drafted onto the Rockets. Harlan was seated, as usual, on the farthest spectators' bench, but still close to the action, with three of Chance's cronies.

It was the top of the ninth, Orion was at bat, and Sags was dancing off second. The Saints' left fielder fell as he ran to catch Leo's fly ball, knocking the wind out of him and the ball from his hand. He lay on the ground grimacing with pain as he watched the ball bounce away from him. The outfielder knew from the two distinct roars that came from the grandstand that he didn't have to retrieve the ball. Sag was home safe, and Orion, the next hitter up, had crossed the plate for a home run. The game was over, with the Saints scoreless and the happy Rockville fans pouring onto the field. The ball hopped, skidded, and rolled to the far corner of the park, where Harlan recovered it.

Mr. Langley, always on the lookout for lost balls, motioned for Harlan to throw him the ball. Harlan tossed the ball up and down in his right hand, testing the feel and weight of it. He noted the flat side and the worn stitches before throwing the ball hard, fast, and accurate from the far field to Mr. Langley, standing on the pitcher's mound. The ballplayers watched openmouthed. Mr. Langley, making a sweeping gesture with his right arm and jabbing a forefinger toward his feet, shouted to Harlan, "Get over here!"

Whenever one of the townsfolk asked Mr. Langley about having a black man playing on the team, he responded with an emotional rebuke. "Good God, man, this ain't about black and white, this is about baseball, and yes, damn it, winning."

Harlan played his first game with the Rockets, in left field, the following Saturday. When it was his turn at bat, he looked to umpire Chance Collins. His eyes and facial expression asked Chance, *What are you going to do?*

Chance said in a low growl, "I don't like you, Blackie, but I want this to be the best damn ball team in the county—hell, in six counties. I'll do right by you, boy. I'll be fair. We'll settle our score another time." Their eyes locked in icy emotions, flamed hot, and then cooled.

At the plate, Harlan dug his heels into the ground, swallowed the hate bile that had erupted into his throat, and, with all his stored-up wrath, swung at the first pitch, knocking the deformed, leaden ball far into right field, where it came to rest behind the outhouses. He sprinted for home—a hometown hero.

"Well, hell!" said a rejoicing Mr. Langley, with a stranglehold on Leo's neck. "He can hit, too!"

"We live by the Bible," Brother Griggsby said from his pulpit. "We abide by the Bible. We die by the Bible."

He was overreacting and showing his apprehension, and he knew it. The old rapport between minister and congregation was not there. At one time he had held them captive in the palm of his hand. His word was the law; they were one and the same. Today this was not so. His congregation was spiritually separate from him: aloof and cold.

"Beware of heathens coming into our midst and preaching false gospels. They will turn son against father and father against son. They will make us worship false idols and kneel down to false gods, all the while doing evil work in His name. What will happen to our holiest day of the week when we play ball on the Sabbath, like they do in the big heathen cities? Are we to forsake our churches for a ballpark? What will become of our young men and women? Who's going to work while the men are off hitting a ball with a stick and running around in circles? Our women? Who will watch and care for the children? Man was made to work and to worship, not to play games, and you don't play baseball, or any other game, on Sunday—not even checkers! Sunday is the Lord's day!"

"No one, as yet, has desecrated the Sabbath," the bored, stony-faced congregation wanted to say to their brother.

I have lost my flock, he thought. A sob of frustration issued from Brother Griggsby's wet lips, and with it all restraint. He wept unashamedly. In the past when he had cried, his parishioners cried with him. Today, they looked away, dry-eyed and embarrassed.

CHAPTER 21

October 1905

The burgeoning ripeness of autumn lay wantonly upon the land. Rosy plump cherub pumpkins, freed of their withered intertwining shackles, lazed languidly upon the spent earth. Papery sylph cornstalks, pillaged by man of their seed, stood wigwam-style in the brown fields, and the winy aroma of fallen apples fermenting in the heat of Indian summer intoxicated the senses. Ashes, oaks, and maples, never shy, flaunted their fall robes before shedding them one by one to scamper across browning lawns and sidewalks. Autumn goes not quietly to its winter slumber; it parties, parades, boasts, and cajoles, giving up its abundance in a riot of pleasurable smells and sensuous colors.

It was fall in Rockville, and that meant deer-hunting season. Men with guns swaggered about the town, confident in the Old Testament's promise of man's dominion over the fish of the sea, the fowl of the air, and over every living thing that moved, proclaiming by their arrogant bearing that to stalk and to kill is man's God-given right.

Each year, Mr. Parlett sponsored a Hunter's Ball at his hotel. The ball was the only dance still held in Rockville after Brother Griggsby had appropriated control of the customs as well as the morals of the town. Those friends of Francoise and Henri Parlett who enjoyed parties and dancing would attend, but mostly, the ball was for the hunters from the big cities and the few men who brought women with them. The hunters came by train, wagon, and horseback, all there to bag something, anything: deer, bear, rabbits, wild turkeys, and wild pigs.

Each fall a local farmer would comment that he "hoped the city slickers had sense enough to recognize a cow when they saw one and not shoot it."

At the end of the monthlong event, Mr. Parlett awarded a hundred dollars in gold to the man who brought down the biggest deer. He could afford to be generous, given that his hotel and emporium during the hunting season did a land-office business, selling everything from guns and ammunition to camping equipment and provisions. Like the store's motto boasted, "We sell everything from needles to thresher machines."

Mrs. Parlett hired Abby to arrange flowers and to bake and decorate the cake for the 1905 fall ritual.

"Your daughter is a real artist," Mr. Parlett said to Nita Langley when he entered the hotel's kitchen and saw the cake. Frosting in the colors and shapes of fall leaves outlined the large sheet cake, and an image of a buck with a magnificent mantel of antlers was pictured in the center of the cake, all created from a palette of icing.

Mr. Parlett left the kitchen in search of Abby, whom he found in the hotel lobby arranging a large dramatic bouquet of flowers in a hammered-brass container. The display was made up of flowers from Abby's garden, with sprays of red and yellow autumn leaves, wildflowers, and peacock and pheasant feathers brought by her grandmother from her ranch. Abby placed it on the lobby table below the mounted head of a deer with giant antlers. A brass plate attached to the walnut panel read:

WINNER OF THE FIRST DEER-HUNTING AWARD
CLEM MORTENSEN
OCT. 31, 1882

Abby stepped back to appraise her handiwork. Mr. and Mrs. Parlett, looking at her with new respect, applauded the display.

Embarrassed by their praise, Abby said, "It needs a bow. If I may, I'll get some ribbon from the store."

"You get anything from the store you want," Mr. Parlett told her.

Not everyone who came to Rockville was there to hunt. The boardinghouses were full, and townsfolk hosted relatives and friends. Countless people were there to attend one or more of the many family reunions that took place in Rockville every year at this time. Grandma Langley drove into town in the buckboard and stayed with Abby, where she helped her with preparations for the two hunters' celebrations taking place on the same evening: the ball at the hotel and the shindig at River's Bend.

On Saturday afternoon, Grandma drove the wagon to River's Bend. Abby, sitting beside her, held a replica of the cake she had made for the hotel ball. Orion and Sags met the wagon at the front gate; Orion took the cake from Abby, and Sagittarius helped the women from the wagon before driving it to the hitching rail. Orion took Abby and the cake to the springhouse. Not wanting to get her shoes wet, Abby didn't enter, but she held the door open for Orion.

That task done, she turned in the direction of the grove of trees that harbored the Langley cemetery and the grave with the white tombstone of an angel spreading its wings adorning the top of it. "Peggy" Pegasus, only daughter of Rose and Joe…

"Not today," Orion said, taking Abby firmly by the elbow and steering her away from the little grave and toward the house.

"Today is happy time," he said, striking an Indian pose and thumping his chest. "Big chief say, 'Today is happy day.'" He flashed a smile that was so cheerful it startled her.

Orion was the happiest person she knew. She gazed up at him. "I'll try, Riney."

Her beautiful face and sad eyes clutched at his heart. "I promise I won't let the witches and goblins get you."

Abby, in a gesture of fondness, placed her hand in his.

The large veranda swarmed with people, and Abby knew that the house would be chaotic with merriment. Relatives on both sides of the family tree loved parties and dancing and thrived on noise, overcrowding, and a raucous good time: everything that was frowned on in town.

Abby pressed closer to Orion. "Please don't leave me," she pleaded.

He gave her hand a reassuring squeeze.

When twilight gave way to dusk and everyone was satiated with food, the tables were removed from the veranda, and the piano was pushed from the living room onto the porch. Candles—in Japanese paper lanterns strung across the veranda and in carved jack-o'-lanterns exhibited on tables and fence posts—were lighted and carefully watched throughout the evening.

In the east, the hunter's moon rose full and mysterious, haughty in its autumn beauty and the power it cast on man's earthly desires. "Shine on, shine on, harvest moon," sang the merrymakers standing in a line across the porch with their arms wrapped around one another's waists, all swaying from side to side as they serenaded the great orange globe.

Grandpa Mosley, Rose's father, wearing a coonskin cap, finished tuning his fiddle; after the singers were through serenading the moon, he played the Stephen Foster song "Oh! Susanna." Aries, wearing a white shirt with full sleeves and a black, flowing tie, joined him, also playing fiddle. Where Orion was handsome, Aries was beautiful. His shoulder-length hair was blacker, his eloquent eyes bluer, and his long, thick lashes curled upward; his fair skin was flawless.

Rose played piano in the Langley family band. Leo drummed, and Aunt Lily's husband, Wilber Miller, played saxophone. The dancing began with a reel, everyone stomping and moving to the song "He Played All Night by the Light of the Moon, but He Couldn't Play Anything but 'Old Zip Coon.'" They waltzed, they do-si-doed, they clogged and reeled. The men at the party kept a hot trail going from the house to the barn, where hard cider and harder liquor quenched their thirst and renewed their high spirits.

Leo's Italian girlfriend, the exotic Flora Maria Brocoloni, whose father was foreman and spokesman for the Italian immigrants at the stone quarry, sang a romantic ballad, with Aries accompanying her on piano. Her father (and singing coach) was Aries's music teacher. She possessed great confidence in her ability as a singer and herself as a young woman. Her vivacious friendliness almost made people forget that she was "I-talian" and Catholic and to accept her for who she was, with only a few "Let's wait and see" attitudes prevailing.

Flora Maria's large golden hoop earrings, dazzling in the candlelight, drew everyone's attention, and when she mentioned that tiny gold earrings had been secured in her earlobes when she was a baby to protect her against deafness, the women present raised their eyebrows at one another.

Whenever Leo danced with Flora Maria, which was often, Orion took over the drumming. Flora Maria was never without a dance partner, and Sags, the clown, while dancing with her and feeling envious, couldn't resist teasing her. Pursing his lips and kissing his bunched-up fingertips, he imitated the Italian quarry workers' broken English. "Flora Maria, your name is like a creama puffa ona my lips."

For the first time in two years, Abby was happy. Her melancholia lifted, and for a while she forgot the son who was forever lost to her. She danced with her cousins and sang a duet with Orion called "I'll Take You Home Again, Kathleen," and she was coaxed into competing in the clogging contest with Grandpa Mosley. He always won, somehow clogging and playing fiddle at the same time.

As she rode home in the buggy after the party, Abby's remorse set in. "It's the whispering I can't stand," she said to her grandmother. "It's like a currycomb scraping down my back. And they're right: I shouldn't be out dancing and singing and having a good time."

Grandma Langley put an arm around her granddaughter's shoulder and gave her a hug. "It's all right to have a good time, Abby; you don't have to feel guilty every minute of every day."

"Oh, but I do feel guilty every minute of every day. I cry myself to sleep every night. I cry for Ronnie; I miss him terribly. I'm so lonely, Grandma. It's awful."

"You know what I hate most about this whole affair with you?" Grandma said, slapping the reins along the horse's back. "It's that you lost your spunk. You always had sass and gumption. Even when you were a baby, no one got the better of you. You were always so cocksure of yourself. That's the second biggest thing that was taken away from you. And I hope you're not crying for that good-for-nothing man, whoever he is. Good riddance, is what I say. I surely hope he's out of your life for good."

Her grandmother's condemnation of the man she loved, would always love, would love forever, and then forever more, upset her further. "He is out of my life," Abby said, her voice breaking.

"But not your heart?"

"No, never, or Ronnie."

CHAPTER 22

November 1905

THE HOTEL REMAINED BUSY AFTER the hunting season was over. Mr. Parlett, who appreciated Abby's work ethic, asked her to stay on and help with the preparation of food as well as the serving of meals in the hotel's dining room. The relationship between mother and daughter was still strained, but they managed a cordial work relationship.

Abby liked working at the hotel. She appreciated the compliments from strangers, who, not knowing her past, left her bigger tips than they did Betsy or Gladys, the regular waitresses.

A. B. Caldwell, inventor of farm machinery and proprietor of the ABC Farm Equipment Company, was a successful widowed older man who was staying at the hotel for two weeks and had taken a shine to Abby. Each evening, rather than rushing off to the pool hall, he lingered over his meal and finally asked Abby if he might call on her. Abby's distress at his request was so apparent that he refrained from talking to her for the rest of his stay and eventually inquired about her at the barbershop.

Gossip about Abby, because someone had shown an interest in her, was again resurrected, and it intensified in the days to come. The Parletts had been aware of the talk but had chosen to disregard it. The time came, however, when they could no longer ignore the gossip.

A traveling drummer named Carney, who had sleeked-down hair and wore loud checkered suits, upon his next arrival at the hotel approached Mr. Parlett in the lobby; he shook his hand and congratulated him for "offering the convenience of a woman for your male guests."

"What are you talking about?" Mr. Parlett shouted.

Carney paled from the intensity of Mr. Parlett's unexpected anger. "Why—why, I heard on the train that a woman was available at your hotel."

Mr. Parlett grew apoplectic; a vein throbbed on his forehead, and he shoved the cocky drummer backward. "Never!" he said, raising his forefinger and shaking it in the man's face. "Never in this establishment will there be a woman for a man's convenience!"

The following morning, Mr. Parlett went to John Murphy's barbershop for his daily shave. When John finished him off with a brisk patting of bay rum on his face, Mr. Parlett asked the barber if he could have a word with him in private. They crossed the alley to the hitching post, where John planted his back against the iron rail rubbed smooth from years of chafing from leather reins. He rested his elbows on the rail.

"Has there been talk in the barbershop about Abigail?" Mr. Parlett asked him.

"Yes, there has. They all know she's had a baby out of wedlock, and that makes her an easy target for gossip. They all seem to like her, and they think she's a fine looker. But," he said, grimacing and raising his shoulders, "there's the usual bragging and rough talk that goes on between men. It's mostly harmless."

Mr. Parlett grunted. "I like Abigail. She's pleasant to have around and she's a darn good worker."

"The talk will die down. It always does. I'll try to put a damper on it."

"I'd be much obliged, John." The two shook hands. Mr. Parlett, hands clasped behind him and deep in thought, walked slowly back to the hotel.

When Abby arrived at the hotel for work, Betsy told her that Mr. Parlett wanted to see her in his office. The office was a corner room in the rear of the store. Abby climbed the six-step staircase that joined the dining room to the store. The office door was ajar, and she tapped on it before looking in. She was all smiles, because she liked Mr. Parlett and was expecting good news and a word of praise.

"Abigail," Mr. Parlett said, looking at her from over the frame of his gold-rimmed glasses. "Come in and close the door." He did not ask her to be seated, so she stood like a schoolgirl in front of his desk. He cleared his throat. "I'm sorry, Abigail, but business in the hotel has slowed down now that the hunting season is over, and we find we no longer need extra help. You've been an excellent employee, and when things pick up, I fully intend to call on you again."

He handed her an envelope, and Abby knew it contained her final pay at the hotel. It took her a moment to accept what was happening. She'd heard the commotion in the lobby the day before and was sure it'd had something to do with her. Also, her mother was back to banging pots and pans and not speaking to her.

Abby left the premises behind a facade of ladylike composure, but inwardly she was seething with indignation. She crossed the street to the school, where she could walk on the deserted sidewalk, only to suffer the stares and whistles of the men who were clearing the grounds of the old Fuller place for the Townsend Opera House. The town gossips and the attention she garnered from men were going to keep her in quarantine for the rest of her life, she thought in response to the workers' reaction to her.

As she passed the Fuller place and approached the Wallace property, she stopped and stared across the street at Frieda Johnson's boardinghouse. She realized now how much she was going to miss her job—and the people.

She was uncertain what she wanted to do, but she knew she didn't want to go home to an empty house. Just then, she heard the sounds of yelling and the breaking of glass coming from inside the Wallace home. Pie Face, his arms hugging his head, came stumbling out the front door and onto the porch. Behind him, beating on Pie Face's back with a broom, was old Mrs. Wallace, screeching hysterically in a high-pitched voice. "Get out! Scat! You liked to have sceered the living daylights out of me. Git!"

Pie Face tumbled down the wooden steps and fell into the yard among the chickens, which sent them to squawking and hopping about in a cloud of dust. Mrs. Wallace, still in pursuit of her unwelcome intruder, limped down the steps and continued shooing and pushing him with her broom, right out of her front gate.

Abby, as confused as the chickens, remained stationary while Mrs. Wallace spilled out her tale of woe to her. "I was canning applesauce and went into the front room to close the door against the noonday sun and found him hiding back of it." A shiver passed over her body. "I swear I thought I was seeing a ghost. Why, that white face of his is enough to give a person a heart attack."

Her voice quivered, and she set to briskly fanning herself with her apron, stopping short when she seemed to realize it was Abigail Langley she was baring her soul to. Gasping, she turned and, with surprising agility, hobbled back up the steps and into the house, peeking from the curtained window in the door to see if Abby was still standing there at her gate; then she furtively peered up and down the sidewalk to see who, if anyone, had seen her talking to the town adulteress. All she saw was a group of boys holding grasshoppers by their spindly insect legs and commanding them to "Spit tobacco. Spit. Spit."

Screams like Mrs. Wallace's, coming from one house or another, had become a common occurrence since the death of Pie's mother, and the town soon learned to pay little heed to them. The community knew by the timbre of the scream that another unsuspecting housewife had found Pie Face hiding back of an inside door. In fact, they gave the yell a name: the Pie Scream.

Abby was upset by the Pie incident, but that was not why she was gazing across the street at Frieda Johnson's boardinghouse—all the time knowing full well that Mrs. Wallace, from behind her ecru lace parlor curtains, was watching her every move.

Marshal McCombs, riding by on his horse and noticing Abby's indecision, politely tipped his hat to her. "The boy's harmless," he said.

The boy isn't why I'm upset, Abby wanted to tell him; instead she smiled and thanked him.

Frieda Johnson opened her door and, after taking one look at Abby's face, wrapped her long thin arms around her in a compassionate embrace. "I saw him," she said. "He's going to scare us all to an early grave."

I think I'll begin locking my doors, Abby was thinking.

Taking Abby's hands in hers, Frieda drew her into the parlor room of the home she shared with three unattached female schoolteachers. "Make yourself at home, Abby, while I fix us some tea," Frieda said. Once a piano teacher—in fact, she had taught Abby to play—Frieda was striving for a carefulness of speech that came from the lasting effects of losing her hearing after a bout of influenza with an abnormally high fever.

While she waited for Frieda, Abby was drawn to the piano in the window alcove of the parlor, curious to see if the photo of her father, taken on a hunting trip to Africa, was still there. Sure enough, the photo of him with his dynamic smile, wearing a safari hat with a zebra-skin band, was there in a silver frame on the polished top of the baby grand piano.

Frieda had been a good friend of Abby's father, and the sympathetic expression on Frieda's face when she opened her door to Abby told her that she would be her friend, too. Whenever her father had come home from his journeys, Frieda had been a frequent guest at the Langley home. She was enthralled with Ronald Langley's pictures of his travels and his tales of faraway places, much more than his wife was. Frieda Johnson's cross to bear was being born a woman in a man's world; Frieda's lifelong dream was to travel.

Sitting on the piano stool, Abby played a one-finger melody of "La Paloma," her father's favorite song. Abby sighed and thought, *Maybe if I had been a boy instead of a girl, he would have stayed home...*

"I miss him, too," Frieda said, setting down a tray with tea things arranged on it.

Abby turned around on the swivel stool and, facing her, said, "I lost my job."

"Pooh," Frieda said, waving her hand as if brushing away a fly. "Another one will come along."

"But I loved my job," Abby said, her voice cracking.

"It's better not to love anything too much."

CHAPTER 23

December 1905

On the first Saturday in December, the sky was blue, the air cold, and on the ground a brittle crust of snow had formed. Downtown, the stores were ready for Christmas and were enjoying brisk early holiday business. The Farmers Co-op windows had a showing of farm toys, some carved by Ole Olsen, while the Goody Shoppe enticed shoppers with plates of sugared green and red cookies; the windows of Stevens Drugstore offered perfumes, toiletries, and a new Coca-Cola display. At lunchtime, after school, and all day Saturday, eager young faces were pressed against icicle-cold windowpanes.

The alcove windows on either side of the entrance to Parlett's Emporium overflowed with samples of available Christmas merchandise. The window on the left had a display of toys for girls: play dishes, music boxes, storybooks, and coloring books. Victorian dolls with porcelain heads wearing gay-nineties hats were displayed sitting at a dolls' table set with china teacups and saucers, while soft-bodied dolls slept in Victorian doll carriages.

The boys' alcove had tin soldiers marching around the window's edge as well as sleds, skates, a bicycle, puzzles, books, balls, and a train set. Tissue-paper cutouts of snowflakes hung from the ceiling of each alcove. Inside the store, multipaned doors protected the merchandise in the alcoves. The doors were opened only by Mr. and Mrs. Parlett or their handsome "catch of the county" son, Pierre, whom everyone in town called Perry.

And lucky indeed were the children who had a penny or an egg to spend. They could enter the store without adult supervision and see the Christmas merchandise from a new angle before suffering the long, tormented minutes agonizing over the sweet they most coveted in the glass candy case.

It was on that first December Saturday when Dr. Noah Edwards met young Mary Louise. Bumping into each other, they came toe to toe in the crowded emporium. She stood, head tilted back and looking straight up into his face, and her insouciance touched his heart.

"And who are you?" Noah asked, laughing.

A woman's voice, coming from behind Noah, surprised him. "She's poor little Mary, my granddaughter." The woman moved around Noah and stood behind the girl, one hand on each shoulder.

"Is 'Poor Little Mary' her given name?" Noah asked, knowing given names could be tricky.

"Land sakes, no," the woman replied. "Her name is Mary Louise."

Noah bent over and, taking the girl's mittened hand in his, said, "Hello, Mary Louise, I'm very happy to make your acquaintance."

She had a pert little mouth in a heart-shaped face, and ringlets of brown hair fell from beneath the red knit-wool toboggan she wore on her head, a sprig of green holly pinned to the upturned cuff. "I'm blind," she said, smiling at him in artless innocence.

"I'm sorry," Noah said. Her confession had caught him by surprise. Straightening, he introduced himself to the grandmother. "I'm Dr. Noah Edwards," he said.

"Oh, shaw, I knowed who you was. You've got that church on a boat."

"Ark," Noah said.

Shoppers milled around them, greeting Grandma Richards and saying "Hello, poor little Mary" to the blind girl.

The following Sunday morning, Grandma and Mary Louise, wearing the red cap with a fresh sprig of holly berry, arrived for Sunday morning worship at the ark. They were seated in the fifth row, behind Lars Larson and his family and Ole Olsen and his. The Langleys, Joe and Rose, and their eight sons took up the first two rows. The tranquil smile never left the girl's face, nor did her attention stray from the sound of Noah's voice.

"Ask, and ye shall receive; seek, and ye shall find; knock, and it shall be opened." Noah, his blond, blue-eyed handsomeness enhanced by a black clerical robe with a front panel of blue silk, began his Sunday morning sermon. "Ask in sincerity and seek in the solitude of prayer, believing the door will open. In this season of giving and receiving, it is befitting that we dwell upon the gifts we seek from our Savior and to know that the gifts you seek from Him are made possible through faith. Faith is a gift. Faith is a gift you give yourself and cannot receive in any other way.

"Believing beyond a shadow of a doubt is the key that opens the gift of faith. The faith of our fathers moved mountains, parted the Red Sea, and delivered Daniel from the lion's den and Jonah from the whale. Turning the key requires that kind of faith. Allow yourself to believe. Give yourself permission to believe. The gift you desire is made possible through believing and is as simple as asking, already believing it is yours. Ye shall receive." Leaning forward and placing his folded arms on the lectern, he spoke to them in a manner of confidence. "The gift you see in your mind is real. The gift you desire in your heart of hearts is real and is yours for the taking. See it. Feel it. Want it. Taste it. Desire it. Believe it. Trust it. Have faith in it. Have faith in yourself. Ask, and ye shall receive; seek, and ye shall find; knock, and it shall be opened. Illness is not a visitation inflicted upon us by a jealous God, but it is something we can inflict upon ourselves. Sickness can infiltrate our bodies from our own thoughts. Our own thoughts can make us sick."

As Noah continued his sermon, he reflected on each person in his small group of worshipers—the Larsons, Olsens, and Langleys, and now Mary Louise and her grandmother were here helping to fill the pews, along with two newly devout, marriageable-age women complete with the obligatory escorts.

"The light of Jesus is within you. Each and every one of you has the light and the gift of the magi. All that is required is faith. Faith as tiny as a mustard seed can move a mountain or cure a pain. We have the freedom of choice: we can choose to be sick, or we can choose to be well. The choice is ours.

"Learn to let go of bad thoughts. Bad thoughts are poisonous, and just as surely as you would die from drinking strychnine, so can your innermost thoughts poison and sicken you. But good thoughts can heal. Good thoughts can raise you from the dead. They can raise you from sickness, from pain, from despair, and, yes, from blindness. Believe, as a child believes," he said, looking at Mary Louise, "and ye shall receive as a child receives." He paused a moment and added, "Our Bible lesson this morning will be read to us by Orion Langley."

Orion made his way to the podium. Opening his Bible, he placed it on the stand. "Our lesson today is from Matthew chapter seventeen, verses fourteen through twenty-two." Orion recited the lesson of faith and the grain of mustard seed without referring to the text, his voice firm and sincere. Since falling in love with Jennie Jeanne and knowing that someday he would be a husband and a father, the head of a household like his father and his father before him, he had taken on a new maturity and was expressing it in every facet of his young life.

With their newly found faith directed toward the blind girl, the congregation rose and sang heartily from their hymnals:

Amazing grace, how sweet the sound
That saved a wretch like me!
I once was lost, but now am found,
Was blind, but now I see.
'Twas grace that taught my heart to fear,
And grace my fears relieved;
How precious did that grace appear,
The hour I first believed!

"Thank you," Noah said. "My closing prayer today is for a healing to take place in the body and soul of Mary Louise. I ask each of you to silently offer up your own healing prayer for her in your prayers, wherever and whenever you pray in the days ahead. May grace dwell in your hearts and in your lives. Amen."

Dr. Edwards's sermons always made the members of his congregation feel good and gave them food for thought, but they were left with a lingering feeling of uneasiness for not having been chastised into repentance by a sermon of hellfire and damnation.

Each Sunday after the church service, Noah invited different parishioners to join him for dinner on his rooftop home, and today he invited Mary Louise and her grandmother. His housekeeper, Rosie Kandel, did not much take to one or two people for Sunday dinner; she preferred a crowd and a party-like atmosphere. After a pot roast dinner followed by a moist, yellow black-walnut cake, Rosie entertained Mary Louise, while Grandma Richards told Noah the story of "poor little Mary."

"Mary Louise is ten now, but she was six when she lost her sight. Lordy me, like to have scared me to death. I was a-killing a chicken, you see, it was November, and there was snow on the ground. I chopped off its head, and it was running and flopping around, you know how they do? Blood was splattering all over the place, and some of it got on the little white apron Mary Louise was wearing. She starts to screaming, wouldn't stop, and wouldn't let me anywheres near her. Then she fell down and just laid there stiff as a board. I sent a neighbor for Aunt Em, and Dr. Townsend comes, too. We get her into bed, and she 'ppeared to be just fine, but the next morning she woke up blind."

Noah asked, "What did Dr. Townsend have to say about it?"

"He said it was 'his-toe-ree-ah.' He said something bothering her mind could make her blind. I don't know anything about that, but that's what he told me." She stretched both hands toward Noah, palms up, like she was handing him the explanation on a platter.

Noah explained to the grandmother the importance that faith and prayer had in effecting a healing. He encouraged her to tell Mary Louise bedtime stories, stories where she was no longer blind. "If we can get her to want to see badly enough, she will see."

Later in the week, Noah paid a visit to Dr. Townsend, who told him all he knew of Mary Louise's blindness. "Her mother died in childbirth. No, no," he said, gesturing and moving his hands back and forth. "She was not my patient. Her husband didn't trust doctors—just the Lord." He lowered his head and, leveling his eyes at Noah, waited for his reaction.

Noah only smiled.

"The girl was very young when her mother died," Dr. Townsend said. "I don't think she remembers it, but I believe something brought it to mind when she saw the chicken blood. I sent her and Mrs. Richards to a specialist in Saint Louis, but he didn't find anything wrong with her eyes, so my prognosis is hysteria. The mind can do strange things to the body."

"Is there a chance that, after four years, her sight could return?" Noah asked.

"Well, in my professional opinion, I don't think it's likely—possible, maybe, but not likely."

"Would you mind if I tried?"

"What do you have in mind?" the doctor asked.

"Faith."

The doctor's eyebrows shot up. "A dose of religion, huh? Sure, go ahead—it can't hurt," he said with a shrug of his shoulders.

"A dose of believing," Noah countered. "I am not a charismatic healer, nor is the ark a Pentecostal church, but I'd like to try. She is so serene in her blindness."

"Ah, yes," the doctor said, "serene indifference. Her visual problem is not physiological, and it isn't the result of a 'wandering womb,' as the Greeks believed hysteria to be. My son writes me from Austria that a Dr. Freud is saying that all hysteria in women is sexual in nature. I don't hold with that, either. I think there are times when the mind can be overwhelmed by human conflicts, and the body reacts. Sometimes the body overcomes the ordeal, and sometimes not. No, young man, I do not object. By all means, do whatever you can for her. Now, let's find out if Aunt Em's home. If she is, she'll want to see you."

Noah stayed for supper, served Aunt Em–style at the kitchen table.

"Have you had a healing before?" the doctor asked Noah.

"Not of my own accord, but I can bear witness to many of them. My grandmother, who raised me, was a Christian Science practitioner. She enjoined many cures during her lifetime through prayer, including mine."

The doctor leaned forward in his chair. "Tell me about it."

"Not unlike Mary Louise, at some point after my mother died, I lost my ability to walk. My father couldn't cope with the loss of his wife and the rearing of a crippled son, so my maternal grandparents took me into their home to raise. My Christian Scientist grandmother had prayer circles all over the country praying for me to get well. Every night she prayed at my bedside, but she added storytelling to the bedtime ritual as well. She told me stories about what I would do when I was walking again: play ball, and win the ball game. She would tell it so vividly that I could see myself running around the bases and scoring home runs. Stories about me winning a bicycle race on the Fourth of July, or climbing a mountain to save a friend who was in need of rescuing. In every story, I was using my legs. She told the stories in such a way—and I could see the pictures so clearly in my mind—that they had to come true."

"We all know the power of the mind," the doctor said. "We experience it daily just by making up our minds to do something and then putting our backs to it."

"Well, she instilled in me the blessed gift of believing, and in a year's time I was walking."

"Did you have a calling to enter the religious life?"

"No. I had a wanting inside of me to do something for humanity."

Aunt Em broke in. "Mary Louise is reminded daily that she is poor and blind. First her mother died, and everyone shook their heads and said 'poor little Mary.' Then that scoundrel of a father deserted them, and again everyone said 'poor little Mary.' Then she lost her sight, and 'poor little Mary' became her name."

Noah spent two evenings a week reading to Mary Louise and Grandma Richards. He told stories of a blind girl who, once she believed, was given back her sight. Noah prayed, Grandma prayed, the small group of believers at the Wednesday night prayer meetings at the ark prayed, but Mary Louise's condition did not change.

CHAPTER 24

Early summer 1906

FROM FAR AWAY, THE TINKLING of chimes and the ringing of bells could be heard on little gusts of wind before the earth echoed the plodding of hooves and the turning of wheels, announcing the arrival of the olive-skinned people. Like the swallows of Capistrano, the Gypsies had returned to Rockville. Stores and houses emptied, and people lined Main Street to watch the colorful parade of gaily dressed travelers in twelve horse-drawn wagons. Flowers and ribbons festooned the horses' manes and harnesses, and bells jangled from their bridles.

Each caravan was decorated, from the humblest—a small, two-wheeled cart belonging to young newlyweds with an arch of bent twigs over the wagon bed covered with brightly patched canvas and pulled by a donkey—to the lavishly carved barrel-top *vardo* drawn by a team of white horses. The vardo displayed a Dutch door, with curtained windows and yellow sunflowers painted on the wooden panels on either side of the door. Carved and brilliantly colored birds and butterflies filled the arch over the door and reappeared on the wagon tongue.

The citizens of Rockville viewed the parade with mixed emotions: excitement, of course, but also distrust and superstition. There would be horse races and horse trading; the buying, bartering, and selling of goods; fortunes told and deep-lined palms crossed with coin; and singing, dancing, and thievery.

The flamboyant Meiko Toma—showman, horseman extraordinaire, flamenco dancer, and connoisseur of women and horses—audacious in the expertise of his attributes, pranced alongside the caravan on a golden palomino with a flowing, cream-colored mane and tail. He wore tight-fitting black pants, and his dark, curly hair hung over the collar of his red satin shirt. A pencil-thin mustache, not the bushy, drooping ones many of the other men in town wore, enhanced the magnetism of his face. He possessed the grace of a dancer, with the self-assurance of a well-coordinated man, rather than that of an effeminate one; a man with a foreign accent and a voice as smooth as silk; a man who was at peace with himself. The Gypsy's expressive eyes, their extraordinary blue color enigmatically changing with his emotions, skillfully appraised the bystanders.

Men vacated the pool hall and smithy and stood on the street to get a better look at rider and horse. They knew Meiko from his previous trips to town, and they knew that whatever horse he rode in on would soon be sold at auction.

"I heerd'a palomineeys, but I ain't nefer seed one afore," said Tate Morgan.

Others were less charitable. "Yeah, wonder who he stole it from?"

"If he rode into town on a horse, he'll ride out of town on a horse—you can bet on that."

The men watching the parade sneaked nervous glances toward their horses tethered to the hitching rails.

The town's children lost their fear of the strangers long enough to take a peek at a brown bear in a wagon cage. The Gypsy children and the organ-grinder's little monkey, riding in the music makers' wagon, peeked back at them.

Marshal McCombs rode alongside the lead wagon, conversing with the driver while escorting the caravan to the campground at the town park. The Gypsies would set up their carnival in the park and remain for several days—or until the money no longer flowed.

The carnival was the only entertainment Brother Griggsby never railed against from his pulpit, and he had little to say about it outside his church, which made the townspeople feel free to enjoy themselves without having to worry about their immortal souls.

Abby and Frieda sat side by side on Abby's front-porch glider. From there they could see and, in a vicarious way, experience the excitement of the carnival. Abby remembered the enchantment she'd felt as a child when she and her father had gone to see the Gypsies. She wished she and Frieda could attend the festival, but Frieda hated crowds, and loud noises hurt her ears. So

Abby sat, resigned. She wondered if Ronnie had seen the Gypsies and if his new mommy and daddy had taken him to the carnival. Placing her hand on her chest, she pressed hard where pain like a double-edged sword was piercing her heart.

A buggy drove up to the front gate and stopped. Abby recognized it as the Owenses' horse and buggy and knew the driver was Melburn. He had stopped at her gate several times since she'd lost Ronnie, but he'd never come to the door. Both women sat very still until at last he drove on.

Good, she thought. *If he never calls on me, then I'll never have to decide if I could accept him for a husband.* He was another painful reminder of her son.

From inside the screen door, her mother said, "Melburn Owens is a good man," her approval softening her usually sharp tone.

"He is a very good man," Abby said tartly, "and someday I hope he finds himself a very good wife." *I'm beginning to sound like my mother,* she thought, and was instantly sorry for her reply. She sat studying the patient aloneness of Frieda, a woman like herself, without man or child. Blinking unwanted tears from her eyes, she touched one foot to the floorboards and resumed the calming motion of the glider.

By nightfall, the town park was a lively place, a cacophony of alien noises and astonishing colors. The townspeople, starved for entertainment, flocked to the park. They spent money to see the dancing bear, tossed pennies into the tin cup of the begging monkey, nodded their heads and tapped their toes to the carefree music of the concertina, and dared to have their palms read. Two rows of wagons, each side facing the other, formed the midway. Colorful cloth fabric, draped between the wagons from the side of one wagon to the next, created canopies under which the Gypsies displayed their goods.

One such shop sold bottles of healing potions, dried medicinal herbs, and charms to ward off evil spirits. Sags Langley—always willing to try anything—and his friends purchased bottles of a liquid medicine from one such vendor, who claimed it was made from an old Gypsy formula and was guaranteed to make you "feel like a man." The young men concealed the bottles in their jacket pockets, sneaking swigs from the concoction whenever possible. To Sags, the "old Gypsy formula" tasted like a watered-down version of Dr. Townsend's very popular patent medicine, Survivall, from which the doctor had made his fortune.

Joe Langley bought a watering trough carved from poplar logs by two of the more industrious travelers; the Gypsy tinkerer soldered handles and spouts back on tin pots brought to them from the kitchens of the townswomen and repaired tin toys belonging to their children.

The printed sign hanging from one of the wagons announced MADAM CHERVOSKY—PALM READER. The old woman saw something special, or lucky, in each palm she read. For the young women, she hinted that a young man was interested in them. "You set his heart aflame," she would rasp. The seeker, her upturned palm indecent in its nakedness, would look away, shielding her innermost secrets from the Gypsy's unsympathetic gaze.

Jennie Jeanne waited nervously behind the Gypsy woman's wagon for her friend, and when Susan climbed down the wagon's shaky steps, blushing, giggling, and feeling superior, she urged Jennie Jeanne to hurry and get her palm read. "It was amazing," a wide-eyed Susan said. "She knows everything!"

Her heart racing, Jennie Jeanne climbed the steps and entered the Gypsy's wagon. When Jennie Jeanne reappeared, she was white faced and looking scared; when Susan inquired about what had happened, she said the Gypsy woman's wagon had been too hot and had made her feel faint. Jennie Jeanne was relieved when, after her own experience with the fortune-teller, Susan became entranced with a basket maker who sat on a low stool outside the fortune-teller's stall, deftly entwining delicate reeds into artistic containers. It would keep her from asking questions about Jennie Jeanne's fortune.

The two friends chose small baskets from the vendor. Tiny bells attached to ribbons dangled from the rims and made cheerful sounds. They wore them on their wrists, like purses, as they strolled along the midway. When they met up with Orion and his friend George Spencer, the girls flirtatiously shook the reed baskets into their faces. The four quickly became pairs. Jennie Jeanne strolled along with Orion, both nibbling on pieces of sticky candy and laughing delightedly when a stolen sugary kiss momentarily bonded their lips.

The Gypsy newlyweds had painted their little donkey with white stripes to resemble a zebra. A sign hanging from the animal's neck advised: RUP HIS NOSE FOR GOOT LUCK. The smiling, winsome bridegroom, with his thirteen-year-old bride holding a basket and sitting on the donkey, led them through the crowd. The bride's large dark eyes, made even larger and blacker by kohl paint, shone as brightly as her golden hoop earrings. Yellow and purple field flowers were tucked into her long black hair, and her angelic, pouting mouth glistened with red pomade. The beguiling child-woman offered her flowered basket to the townsfolk, who, succumbing to her charms, readily dropped coins into it.

When darkness fell, lantern light inside the makeshift shops, with their colorful, fabric-covered tops, gleamed in the night like Arabian jewels. Flaming oil-dipped torches bathed the grounds in light. The fire walkers' shallow, four-by-thirty-foot pit, located in front of the grandstand, glowed with red-hot coals; with the coming of night, the pit added an excitable urgency to the atmosphere.

Deputized marshal Al Sorensen stood guard at the shell game, watching the bean and the walnut shells as they were moved rapidly about on an upturned wooden crate. The hand-is-quicker-than-the-eye game was a big moneymaker for the Gypsies, but it left many of the men of the town disgruntled.

The organ-grinder strolled through the crowd, cranking out music on a concertina. His monkey, its round, beady eyes staring up at the strangers from beneath a tiny sombrero, danced in time to the music before begging coins with a tin cup clasped in its small, furry hand.

Noah arrived with Grandma Richards and Mary Louise. He patiently explained the sights and sounds to the blind girl. When Mary Louise leaned over to pet the monkey, it snatched the bonnet from her head, and Noah had to wrest it from the frisky little beast. Despite the excitement, Noah found himself watching the overflowing throng in the hope of seeing a certain redheaded woman.

The brown bear always drew a crowd, and when the circle around the laconic beast grew large enough to satisfy the trainer—a dark little man with tobacco-stained fingers—he shook out a rhythm on a tambourine. The bear, wearing a short pink net skirt, rose up on his hind legs and performed a dance by lumbering from one foot to the other while turning about. The caretaker was careful not to perform near the fire pit, because the bear had learned to dance by having his paws burned and had been known to run amok if he reacted to fire. After the performance, the trainer passed his tambourine around for an offering.

Hidden away from the main thoroughfare, a fat little man stood by the entrance of his makeshift theater mindlessly tapping the tiny brass cymbals on his fingers while his indolent eyes glided over the men as they read his sign: WORLD-FAMOUS BELLY DANCER. A chalkboard sketch of a woman wearing a head-to-toe veil, her eyes uncovered and downcast, arms bare and seductively curved over her head, readily caught the attention of the men attending the carnival. Under the cover of darkness, men slipped into the theater tent to see the belly dancer; Andy Langley and young Lester Dinwoody were among the shamefaced crowd. They stood huddled with farmers, businessmen, and strangers, married and single, in the small enclosure, all of them pulling their hats lower on their already-lowered heads.

When no more customers could crowd inside, the tent flap was closed. Someone began strumming and thumping a tune on a guitar, and, from the back of the dimly lit room, a figure appeared wearing a robe. After stepping onto the platform, the robe was removed, revealing a man dressed in black tights with a sizeable tattoo of a nude woman covering his bared chest and abdomen.

Embarrassed and deceived, the conned men, grumbling, began to leave but were soon caught up in the gyrations of a man moving his arms gracefully above his head while his body swayed erotically to the rhythm of the music. The woman captured in ink on his torso writhed seductively, her ample hips moving around in figure eights as her body undulated to the throb of the compelling music; in the heat and haziness of the tent, the men soon forgot that that which they lusted after was the tattooed belly of a fat Gypsy man.

On the midway, another trumpet fanfare sounded, and a wooden platform was soon carried into the crowd of curious bystanders. Gypsy musicians strumming guitars strolled to the stage, while others cupped their hands and clapped, making sharp staccato sounds to the beat of the music. Meiko Toma and a woman emerged, both dressed in the traditional costumes of flamenco dancers. With gallant panache, Meiko kissed her hand before helping her onto the stage.

The woman, her black hair pulled into a chignon on the back of her neck, her cheeks bright with color, and her mouth a cruel red slash, sang a lusty ballad in a strange tongue, performing the song with fervor. Raising her arms above her head and stamping her black leather-strapped shoes against the wooden floor, she began the dance; deftly snapping the castanets on her fingers sharply together, she clacked out the rhythm. She caught up her skirt, and, swishing it from side to side, revealed a glimpse of a slim ankle and the flash of a leg, defined by the red ruffles lining the inside of her black-and-white polka-dotted dress. The suppleness of her shapely body was a jarring contrast to her hardened, deeply lined face. After bowing amiably to the applause of the audience, she gracefully stretched an arm toward Meiko.

Meiko Toma jumped onto the stage smiling as someone born to applause. Majestically moving about, he absorbed the hum of anticipation and waited for the right moment of hushed expectancy. Flinging his arms above his head and clapping his hands to the slow, steady beat of the music, he began the execution of the Spanish flamenco, building in emotion, rhythm, and intensity into a skillful display of intricate footwork. With his shoulders flung back and his hands pulling on the bottom of his short bolero jacket, he strutted and tapped, his face molded into fiery passion as the dance grew in power and excitement to its dramatic climax. In the last prolonged spin of the mesmerizing dance, hot, wet droplets clinging to strands of his tangled black hair spun off into the night.

Meiko acknowledged the wild ovation by accepting the audience's adoration with a deep bow and by going down on one knee. When he finally looked up, his roving eye encountered the heart and soul of Flora Maria Brocoloni, her expressive face unashamedly revealing the spell that the dance, the music, and the man had cast. Her dark eyes glistening with emotion, she grasped Leo's hand; pressing it to her bosom, she said, "Oh, Leo, I must sing on a stage. I must perform for people—many people." Leo, unaccustomed to such raw emotion, withdrew his hand and looked away, embarrassed.

After the dance performance, the rope stretching between two wagons and preventing access to the fire pit was removed, revealing the white ash that covered the red-hot coals. The eager crowd made its way to the grandstand, while others, wanting to be closer to the entertainment, gathered near the pit. Marshal McCombs and his deputies helped the Gypsies push the crowd into an ever-larger circle so that everyone could see the grand finale of the evening: the fire walkers.

Two dark-haired young men with red bandanas wrapped and tied around their heads, their torsos and feet bared and pants rolled up to their knees, held their hands close to the coals, testing the heat. The self-assured fire walkers motioned to the crowd, inviting them to walk through the fire; breathless, the onlookers shook their heads. After a loud drumroll, the two Gypsy men slapped at the soles of their naked feet and wiggled their bare toes. The drumming grew quieter, but the rhythm intensified as the first man walked deliberately, sedately, and unfazed over the path of burning coals, followed by the second fire walker. They finished to a burst of drumrolls, whistles, and wild applause.

The carnival was over.

The happy crowd sauntered slowly from the park, reluctant to lose the spell and the magic of a perfect summer evening. The young high school–age attendees left in a group, Orion and Jennie Jeanne among them, walking side by side and holding hands.

"Can you find the North Star?" Orion asked her. Jennie Jeanne's eyes swept the sky. Quickly locating the stars that formed the Big Dipper, she followed the handle of the constellation and pointed to Polaris. Orion, looking about, gave her cheek a quick kiss.

"You are my North Star, Riney," she said with somber sincerity, her enchanting face upturned to his.

The magnetism between Orion and Jennie Jeanne had always been there. Even in grade school, Orion, like a big brother, had been guardian to the captivating little girl. As they grew older, other girls tried to tempt the popular Orion away from Jennie Jeanne, but they never succeeded. She had always been Orion's girl. Loving and protecting her came naturally to him—a responsibility he accepted and never questioned, even when his brothers teased him about having an old sweetheart. Jennie Jeanne was six months older than Orion, and a girl being older than a boy was frowned upon, even when the difference was only a few days.

Jennie Jeanne did not sleep well that night. She was unable to shake from her thoughts the warning she had received from the fortune-teller. The old Gypsy woman, grasping her hands and looking defiantly into her face, had frightened her.

"What they say about you, it is no true," she had said after looking at Jennie Jeanne's palms and furiously shaking her head. She dragged down the corners of her mouth and shrugged as if to say, *But it is none of my business.* "Unfortunately, you will never know the truth," she said lamely, her mouth scornful.

What in the world had she meant? Jennie Jeanne wondered later. She didn't think she could tell anyone—certainly not Orion, or even her best friend—because the woman's warning just didn't make sense.

The horse auction, where farmers, herdsmen, cattlemen, and Gypsies all traded and sold horses, took place at Chance Collins's farm the same time every year as the carnival. This year it was Dr. Townsend who bid top dollar for Apollo, the golden palomino Meiko Toma had offered for sale.

The day after the Gypsy caravan departed, Meiko's ornate vardo could be seen parked in the backyard of the doctor's mansion. The Gypsy was now in the employ of the doctor.

CHAPTER 25

June 1906

ONE BY ONE, STICK BY stick, piece by piece, everything—the crib, the highchair, the baby quilt, the carved wooden toys, his little fingerprints, every living trace of him—was destroyed, the house wiped clean of her son.

The first star of the evening appeared. She began to make a wish but then stopped. Her wish was never going to come true.

Hidden from view by the darkness of night and the honeysuckle vines, Abby was once again listening to, and watching, life being lived. Somewhere, a man attending to late milking chores was singing, a cluster of rowdy boys were playing marbles underneath a streetlamp, and three women walking home from choir practice at New Church appeared momentarily in the light from the gas streetlamp before being swallowed up again by darkness, their voices calling "good night" as they parted, two walking on together, the steps of one going on alone.

"Good night," Abby said, not audibly enough to be heard. "It's my son's birthday today. He's three years old." Her fingers wiped at a tear, and she was reminded of Ronnie's soft baby hands caressing her cheeks and the baby touching his forehead to hers and looking into her eyes and laughing his giggling baby laugh.

It was only when she awoke in that darkest hour before dawn—the hour when one comes face to face with one's soul—that she allowed herself to remember him and the days they had shared together. She shook her head, annoyed with herself for thinking of him now. "Stop it. Stop it."

A farmer drove by with a load of hay, its sweet, newly mown fragrance scenting the summer evening. The driver's shadowy figure, perched high atop the wagon, was silhouetted against the sky, his deep, sleepy voice urging the tired horses to "giddy up."

"Giddy up," Abby quietly mimicked as he passed.

She rocked, listening to the crickets fiddling and frogs croaking, one frog not too far away, another in a deep bass answering from a distance. She wondered what they were saying.

"*Croak*, croak, *croak*, croak," one after the other said.

Maybe they're having a lover's quarrel, she thought. "My son is three years old today," she told them.

"*Croak*, croak, *croak*, croak," they answered.

"Soon the town will sleep," she told the frogs out loud, "and then I'll walk. When I walk in the daytime, I don't feel real; no one ever looks at me. They turn away, or they look through me. It's as if I don't exist. I'd like to shout at them: 'Look at me! I'm alive! Let me see your faces. Let me hear your voices. Somebody touch me.'"

"Cheater!" one of the marble players said. "You know that's my best shooter."

The boys were on their feet. "You knew we were playing for keeps!" a juvenile voice said in retaliation.

"I was playing for keeps," Abby whispered. "Why weren't you? Why didn't you come back to me?" She rocked and moaned, a despairing singsong humming, as tears ran down her face.

Another figure appeared under the streetlamp. Nita Langley was coming home from her day's work at the hotel. Crossing the street and unlatching the front gate, she approached the house, her footsteps sounding hollow on the sidewalk as she continued on around the porch and let herself in the kitchen door. She didn't give any indication of whether or not she had seen her daughter sitting there alone in the June night.

A gleam of light from a gas lamp came from somewhere within the house, a pale-yellow square that reflected onto the front lawn, and, like a projection of a woman from a lantern slide show, a shadowy image of Mrs. Langley flickered upon the drawn window shades as she moved about the living room. The light went out, and all was dark.

"It's your grandson's birthday today, Mother," Abby said, speaking in a normal voice. Why not? There wasn't anyone around to hear her, only the frogs and cicadas and other nocturnal creatures like her, singing out their mating calls; she was the only one without a song.

The town slept.

Is this emptiness all there is? she thought. *Is this all there will ever be?* A cold, hard lump formed in her chest and pushed against her ribs. Abruptly she stopped rocking. Racked with pain, she tilted her head to one side as though listening to something, or someone, and gazed into the blackness of the night.

CHAPTER 26

"LORD, WHEN I CONSIDER YOUR heavens, the work of your fingers, the moon and the stars, which you have set in place, what is man that you are mindful of him, the son of man that you care for him?"

Noah sat on the bank of Stony Creek, his back propped against the trunk of a sycamore tree, enjoying the summer evening as he contemplated the night, the stars, the peace he felt within, and the eighth psalm. Muscles sore, limbs aching, palms blistered, he was dead tired, but it was a tiredness that had come from a job well done.

A pond on Dr. Townsend's property near the old icehouse, adjoining Stony Creek, had that day been widened, deepened, and dredged of rocks, roots, and debris. It was to be a place where the young men of the town could swim. The agnostic Dr. Townsend got a kick out of the fact that Brother Griggsby, in one of his Sunday sermons, had vehemently condemned the swimming hole as a device of the devil intended to lure boys away from their Christian duties.

Late that afternoon, after the dredging was completed, Noah had stripped down to his underpants and gone for a swim. The men he had worked with all day apprehensively watched him from the bank before finally stripping down to their summer long johns, drawers, or nothing at all (as was the case with one man) and, joining him in the stream, splashing one another and cavorting about like young boys. To Noah's surprise, none of the men knew how to swim. Young and energetic eighteen-year-old George Spencer, after a few instructions, was in no time swimming back and forth across the pond.

Noah climbed the skeleton of the old icehouse. From an opening in the second-floor loft, where he had nailed a newly milled plank earlier that day (thinking at the time that it could be used later as a diving board), dived into the deep end.

The older men shook their heads as if to say "not me," but George said, "Would you do that again?" Noah, grinning, climbed to the loft and this time did a back flip off the board.

"Could I do that, Dr. Edwards? Could I dive from up there?"

"Sure you can, George, maybe by the end of summer. You can also call me Noah. Here, we'll practice from the bank. Keep your head down and your legs straight, then spring and jump." George disappeared under the water for what seemed an unusually long time. The men standing on the bank peered into the water, watching and waiting, and when George's hand, holding a rock, broke the surface, followed by his grinning face, the worried men cheered.

George threw the rock to Noah, who caught it and threw it back. George sprang from the water and easily palmed it. *A natural athlete,* Noah thought. *Tomorrow I'll bring a ball and a bat.* He was still looking for players for his baseball club.

At sunset, the men dressed and left for town in Ralph Cox's wagon, still behaving like boys playing hooky from school.

Noah's enthusiasm was contagious. He made people feel good by encouraging them to have fun, something that was new for them. They had been taught that play was for children and laggards, and if you weren't hard at work, then you were a ne'er-do-well and an offense unto God.

Noah liked to help out by showing up at sites where he thought people could use an extra hand and pitching in. He was easygoing and likable, with a surprising wit for a clergyman, so the laborers soon accepted him as one of them and not as the "new preacher."

Feeling hungry and tired but wanting to prolong the euphoria of the day, he stretched out on the bank with his head resting on his crossed arms and watched the sky as it changed from the blue of late day to pink, to wine, to deep purple. He was waiting for it to be dark enough to see the wonder of the Milky Way and a sky full of stars.

Noah opened his eyes and for a moment wondered where he was. The woodsy smell of the newly milled lumber mingling with the roiled smell of the fast-moving water soon reminded him. He rose and stretched and, dusting himself off, made his way to the old icehouse, where Miss Molly stood patiently waiting. As he led her to the pond for a drink, the lateness of the hour made him wish he had gone back to town with the others. He was stiff from the day's work, and the coolness of the night caused his muscles to ache.

He was walking her back into the icehouse when he heard a sound that sent sleeping birds fluttering from their roosts and a cold chill racing down his spine. A woman's angry voice was shrieking: "I want to talk to you!"

Noah looked around. Was she addressing him?

"I hate you! I hate you!" The words, screamed with passion, reverberated along the creek. Noah remained motionless, listening for the sound of the voice. He was leery about overhearing what sounded like a private quarrel. Then, hearing the splashing of water, he felt his skin prickle and made his way back to the stream. With the light from the stars, he could make out the figure of a woman wading in the stream, her angry voice soaring heavenward.

"Do you hear me? I am sick of living!" Her arms flailed at the heavens. "I am sick of you." Her fist jabbed at the sky. "You don't exist. I hate you!"

Noah, recognizing in her words a plea for survival, shouted at her, "What are you doing out there?"

The woman screamed again, a long, hysterical keening, before she disappeared beneath the surface of the water.

"Can you swim?" Noah shouted. She reappeared, coughing and sputtering. "Get out of there!" he yelled, the anger in his voice belying his fear. The weight of her wet clothes, along with the swift undertow of the water, was pulling her toward the icehouse and the deeply dredged end of the swimming hole meant for diving.

Noah yanked off his shoes and coat and jumped into the water. He swam to the middle of the stream and grasped her by her shoulders. She struck at him with both hands.

"Leave me alone. I want to die. Oh, please don't stop me. I want to die!"

The woman's constant struggling hampered Noah's attempts to get a good grip on her as she unknowingly drifted nearer the deep end of the pool. He would seize hold of her and begin swimming toward the shore, but each time, the woman, in her furious attempt at self-destruction, managed to break free from him. Finally they both went under, and when they surfaced, she had a stranglehold on his neck. She gasped, coughed up water, and had a look of surprised panic on her face. Her long skirts entangled his legs, and her heavy wet hair sweeping across his face was blinding as well as suffocating. *Dear God, help us,* he prayed as he fought to free himself from her terrified grasp.

His hand struck the underpinnings of the icehouse. Swinging one arm up, he grasped a protruding board, another new one he had nailed there that afternoon when he was teaching George how to dive. Hanging by one hand from the board, he managed to break the death grip she had on his neck and kick free of her skirts. He wrapped his legs around her body and, with a hand on either side of the plank, he moved one hand and then the other along the board until he reached the frame of the icehouse. With a last burst of strength, he expelled himself from the water, dragging her with him onto the bank.

He unceremoniously flipped her onto her stomach and fell across her, knowing that, as worn out as she must have been with her struggle to end her life, she could not possibly escape the weight of his body. They lay gasping, throats sore, muscles weak, belching water, heads throbbing. *Lord,* he thought, *I don't know when I've ever been so tired, or so cold.*

Noah slid off the woman and onto his side and lay there numbly studying her until his breathing grew normal. She lay sobbing, one fist feebly pounding the ground close to her face, her wet clothes clinging to her body, and, with each new coughing spell, water spewed from her nose and mouth.

She lay disillusioned, defeated, and empty.

When she saw him looking at her, she said, forcing the rasping words from her tortured throat, "You had no right to interfere!"

"You changed your mind, lady," he said defensively, then with great exasperation asked, "Who are you?"

"No-b-body," she said, hiccupping.

"Do you think if I built a fire, the natives will come running with their buckets?"

"It's y-your reputation, not m-mine," she retorted, still hiccupping.

He struggled to his feet and stood staring down at her. *I'm too blamed tired to save her a second time,* he thought. "Will you stay put?" he asked, his voice harsh.

Wearily she acquiesced.

Retrieving his coat and shoes and finding matches in his jacket pocket, he searched the icehouse for wood shavings and scraps of lumber. He made a pile of his findings on the dirt floor in the middle of the icehouse and touched a match to the shavings. When the fire caught, he brought the woman inside and, after helping her onto a pile of loose straw, draped Molly's horse blanket across her quaking shoulders.

Hot flames spiked the fire, and shadows danced on the silvered boards of the old icehouse. She sat huddled under the heavy blanket, wearily wringing water from the sodden mass of her skirt. When the heat from the blaze reached her, she leaned into its warmth and, after sitting and staring dejectedly into the fire, began to pull leaves and twigs from the matted mass of her hair, darkened to blackness from its soaking wetness. As her hair dried, she fanned out the tangled strands, letting them fall loosely onto her shoulders.

Kind of pretty, Noah thought as he watched her in the firelight and added another stick of wood to the flames. She had not offered him an explanation for her suicide attempt, nor an apology. "Who are you?" he asked again.

"Abigail Langley," she said. "Your housekeeper's Rosie Kandel, so I'm sure you've heard of me."

Just then, he saw the deep-red glow coming from her drying hair. "Oh!" Noah said, realizing he was face to face with his mystery woman.

Abby, interpreting his explosive recognition of her as a condemnation, shot him a hostile look. But what Noah was remembering was the gossip in the barbershop from his first night in Rockville, so long ago, and the excommunication sermon he'd heard at Old Church the following Sunday morning—not anything Rosie may have said to him.

Occasionally, in the years he'd been away at school, something would trigger a memory of the girl who had borne the illegitimate child and would make him wonder what had happened to her.

"It's my son's birthday today. He's three years old."

Noah was aghast. "Why would you want to kill yourself on your son's birthday?"

"I gave him away." The awful confession brought on a fresh outbreak of the keening cry.

Searching for something, anything, to say, Noah said, "I thought about you when I was away at school."

"You thought about me?" The crying stopped, and just the hiccups remained.

"I was here in Rockville three years ago today."

She began to rock back and forth. "I don't want to live. I don't want to live."

Noah sat down beside her, and, placing an arm across her blanketed shoulders, rocked with her. Her soggy clothing made a squishing sound, and her drying hair gave off the musty, wormy smell of pond water.

"It's all right," he whispered. "Shhh! It's all right." Her body remained rigid.

She finally quieted and said between gasping sighs, "You're the new minister, aren't you?"

"Yes. I'm Dr. Noah Edwards."

"Aunt Em has told me about you. I've seen the ark."

For the first time, Noah heard the pleasantness of her natural voice. "Have you been inside the ark?" he asked.

"Oh no. I don't go to church. I no longer believe in God."

"Is He who your quarrel is with?"

"The reason I gave away my son was to keep him from suffering hell's damnation, then I hated God because He is a terrible God, and then I hated myself. I don't believe in anything or anyone anymore." Her body slumped. "I have no one," she said, and began quietly weeping.

"You have yourself. Believe in yourself. We each have our own private quarrel with God, and our first vengeful act when we think He has forsaken us is to deny Him. But ceaselessly, deep down in our soul, something instinctively tells us there is a God."

"I'm unclean," she blurted out.

"In what way?" Noah asked, surprised.

"I'm—not clean."

Deciding on which tack to take, he looked for a long time at her bowed head. "What do you mean? Do you not bathe?"

The question seemed to embarrass her, and she answered without looking at him. "Of course I do."

"Do you clean your teeth?"

Again a whispered, agitated, "Yes."

"Do you think unclean thoughts?"

"Certainly not!"

Good. She's on the defensive, he thought. "Do you wear grubby clothes?"

Looking down at her dress caked with drying mud, Abby smiled wanly. "Not usually."

"In God's eyes, we are all perfect. We can lose our way, but we are still His perfect creations. Do you think we could be unclean if He created us in His image?"

"The elders of the church think so. They convinced me I was a terrible woman, and therefore a terrible mother, and so I let him go—my baby."

Suddenly, and with great compassion, he asked, "Where is your son?"

"He was adopted by a couple who live elsewhere," she said, looking everywhere except at his eyes. "You know, you're the first person to ask about him? In all this time, you're the only person who's talked to me about him. Sometimes I get scared." She dared to look into his eyes. "I'm afraid I'll forget how to speak. It's hard being shunned."

"You can always pray."

"I used to pray, and do you know what I prayed for? Not forgiveness, because I haven't repented; I loved my son—and his father." Her voice quavered. "I prayed for a friend. One friend," she said, her words ringed with tears. "Before the baby, I had friends, but I knew after Ronnie was born that their parents wouldn't let them associate with me. One day, I was sitting on our front porch, and my best friend walked up to the gate, and we just looked at each other, then she walked away, almost running. I wanted to run after her. I wanted to hold on to her and beg her to talk to me. I wanted to tell her everything. I wanted to say..." Her words trailed off.

"At first there was the baby and Aunt Em. He couldn't talk, but he could make noises." She smiled at the memory. "And I could hold him, and love him. Human beings have to have someone to love, or we aren't human beings," she said, shaking with emotion.

She was talking to Noah as she'd never talked to anyone before. The cover of night and the reckless attempt at her own destruction had made her bold. And Noah was listening, knowing that confession is catharsis for the soul.

"My mother hates me, and I don't know why," she said wearily. "She says she always knew I would come to no good, and I don't know why she would've said that." She looked down at her empty hands.

"Have you told Aunt Em how you feel? How unhappy you are?"

"No. I don't want to burden her." Abby inhaled a deep, ragged breath. "When I gave up my baby, I think she felt it as much as I did. The memory of what I did is so unrelenting that sometimes I think I'm crazy and don't know it."

"You're not crazy, but I think you are very lonely, and you're punishing yourself for something you did that was very noble on your part. You need something to fill the void. You don't want an act from your past to be the sum total of your life, do you? You can start over, you know. What do you want? What is it you want from life?"

She leaned into him, feeling gratitude in his touch.

Deep in their own thoughts, they both gazed out from the open space that once had been a door at the path of golden ripples reflecting across the creek from a late-rising moon. Tomorrow, the same water, purified of the life-and-death struggle that had taken place here tonight, would be far away.

"Why don't you leave Rockville?" Noah asked. "It would be an opportunity for you to become a whole new person."

She stared at him in astonishment. "I couldn't. Oh, I couldn't." She covered her face and began the rocking again.

Noah pulled her hands away from her face and forced her to look at him. "What is it you're so afraid of?"

"Nothing. Everything." She thought of her father. "Of never being loved by anyone again."

Noah moved his body around so he was facing her. "To some," he said, "the unshakable belief that love will come to us in all its joys and promises of fulfillment is enough to keep us strong—and alive. Maybe you'll have to be strong enough to make your own happiness. Don't let them keep you down," he said, nodding toward the town. "And don't keep yourself down. Those are good people, and they'll forgive you. Your trespass is like a deformity; they have to get used to it before they can accept it, or you. Take one step at a time—walk to the post office and back."

"I can't," she whispered, recalling the bitter excursion to the emporium when Ronnie had been a baby.

"God doesn't work for us; He works through us. If you can't run, walk; if you can't walk, crawl; and if you can't crawl, then lie there. When you can't move at all, pray. How we see ourselves in our own minds is who we really are. Tell yourself you deserve happiness, and then expect it. God can only exist through you. He needs you to exist. God is not able to express His powers to you, only *through* you. When you're ready for change, the change will come."

All at once, becoming embarrassingly aware of the intimacy of their closeness, she rose; she removed the horse blanket from around her shoulders and handed it to him. "I'm going home," she said.

"I'll take you home."

"You don't have to. I'll be all right."

"I want to. We'll both have to ride old Molly, though, or we'll never get out of these brambles. Here, hold out your hand." He placed five sulfur matches with a small rough rock on her palm. "Now go over there and sit on the bank, and give the name of each one of your problems to a match. Acknowledge each one—mourn it, hate it, curse it, love it—whatever it takes. Light and burn each match and toss it into the water, and your guilt with it." He placed one more match on her palm. "This one is for you," he said, closing her fingers over them. "It's time to put an end to your sorrow, Abigail."

It was the first time he had spoken her name, and she found she liked the way he said it.

Noah carried water from the stream in a lunch pail someone had left behind, doused the remaining embers, and threw dirt on what was left of the steaming pile to make sure the remnants of the fire were out and covered. At the same time, he kept an anxious eye on the devastatingly tragic woman who stood at the water's edge; he watched as, every few minutes, a flame arched from her fingertips into the night like a falling star.

When they later reached Abby's kitchen gate, he helped her down from the horse. Shaking her head, she said, "I—I can't thank you for saving my life, but thanks for seeing me home."

"Someday, I believe you'll thank me. Learn to expect happiness, Abigail, and it will come."

Nita Langley stood at the window of the darkened living room and watched as a man helped her daughter from his horse. In the light coming from the lamppost from across the street, she could see that Abby looked disgraceful. Her hair was loose and hanging down, and her dress was clinging to her body. Mrs. Langley's face ignited with shame. She knew they had come from the direction of Stony Creek Bridge, but it was too dark for her to recognize the man, or the horse.

"So that's where the little Jezebel meets them," she muttered to herself as her daughter quietly let herself in the kitchen door and the unidentified man rode on toward the center of town.

CHAPTER 27

THE FOLLOWING DAY, NOAH LEFT his mare tied to the hitching rail at the town park, crossed the road to the Langley home, and was unlatching the front gate when he hesitated, not knowing in what state of mind he would find the woman he had saved from drowning the night before. He looked toward the house with trepidation. Perhaps she had concluded her act of annihilation or had further retreated from the world of reality. He was wondering if he should even be calling on her when the door to the house opened, and she appeared on the porch.

She smiled as she walked toward him, meeting him halfway. The sun, catching her in its benevolent light, glistened in her auburn hair, warmed her skin to an apricot glow, and dappled her large green eyes with golden light. Her gaze was bright and unfaltering as she reached out both hands and greeted him with a warm and vibrant hello. He stared in awe at the woman she was meant to be.

When the Maker looked upon this wonderful creation of His, He must have shouted hallelujah, he thought. "Your parents should have named you Gloria," he said, feeling self-conscious in his outright admiration of her. *She fair takes my breath away.*

"I feel glorious," she said, radiating self-confidence, a smile showing a dimple in each cheek. She linked her arm through his and walked with him to the porch.

But where was the wretched despair of the night before? Noah was confused as he tried to compare the total eclipse of her life last night to the brilliant illumination of it today.

She sat on the porch glider, with Noah on the railing facing her. "I slept last night, yes I did," she said, smiling broadly. "Probably from exhaustion, but my last thought before I fell asleep was what you said about expecting happiness. I awoke this morning with a great lightness inside of me, a feeling of being reborn." She laughed. "I know this will sound silly after last night, but I truly feel like I've been baptized and my sins washed away." Her cheeks colored. "I feel that, last night, I truly left my childhood behind me and became an adult."

"Baptism is a rebirth of the spirit," he said.

She rose and walked to the porch railing. "At daybreak this morning, I stood on my balcony looking out on a beautiful day. Rockville is so pretty. 'Rock-ville's a pretty little town,'" she sang, mimicking the birdsong all schoolchildren liked to sing. "It looked to me the way it did when I was a child, and I realized I wanted to live—not just be alive, but live—and right here in Rockville." Then, turning and facing him, she very simply said, "Will you help me?"

Noah was ecstatic; he wanted to jump fences, turn handsprings, shout. Instead he dropped to one knee and, taking her hands in his, said, "I promise to help you and never forsake you." With Abby's confession and her plea for help, Noah felt his ministry had begun.

Abigail Langley was cleaning house. Windows and doors were open. The carpets hanging outside on the clothesline had been beaten dustless with wire paddles, and the windows upstairs and down gleamed. Floors scrubbed, wallpaper sponged clean, every dish in every cupboard washed, furniture rearranged, cobwebs wiped away from corners, and the door knocker on the front door wiped clean and the brass polished. Once, cobwebs on the door knocker—a sure sign of her empty life—would have made her cry, but today she laughed, and she laughed again when she retold the story to Aunt Em.

Aunt Em had stopped in on the third day of Abby's housecleaning purge, and they now sat on the porch glider. Aunt Em, as usual, was full of news. "When Bobby Lee's parents bought him a new suit of clothes—after Agnes had died from aborting herself with a tamarack stick—and watched after his kids while he went traipsing off to the capital to look for work, they never had a notion of what a shock they'd be in for. Bobby Lee's back in town, and with a new wife—calls herself Velvet. She has the reddest hair you've ever seen; looks like her head's on fire. And when she dresses up to go to town, Lordy me, she looks like Cinderella going to the ball.

"Poor Agnes died because she didn't want another mouth to feed. When a woman says 'enough,' God, or her man, ought to listen. Well, Bobby Lee's new wife has a boy: skinniest, most scared little thing you've ever seen. God bless him," she said with a shake of her head. "Bobby Lee's a fine looker, but he's got absolutely no get-up-and-go, just a headful of dreams." Throughout her reporting of the latest news, Aunt Em had been eyeing Abby. She now said, "Something's come over you, Abby, and for the better, I dare say."

"I've found a new appreciation for life."

"Well, whatever you've found, don't let it slip away—grab it, and hold on," she said, making one of her deep, throaty chuckles. "By the way, I ran into that new preacher," Aunt Em said cheerfully. "He's a very likable young man. He's just what this town needs: someone to rile up the people, and that old Brother Griggsby, and get the town moving again. Now there's a man you ought to meet."

Aunt Em did not miss the rush of scarlet to Abby's cheeks. She thought, *Now, where did she meet the new preacher?* "You know, Abby, it's time for you to find yourself a beau, settle down, get married, and have a family. Make your own happiness."

Abby gasped a short little gasp—this was the same advice Noah had given her. "But Ronnie was my happiness."

"I know. I know it still hurts," Aunt Em said, patting her arm, "but you can have a normal life right here in Rockville: a husband, and another baby…lots of babies. You'd make a good mother, Abby. Find a way to be needed. If they need you, they'll respect you."

Aunt Em should have been a preacher.

CHAPTER 28

A SUBTLE WAVE OF PARLOR curtains—the most advantageous place in the house to see without being seen—rippled open and shut along the length of Elm Street. The attraction was a woman shading herself with a black lace parasol and a seductive swaying of hips as she carefully picked her way along the earthen sidewalk that ran in front of the homes on Elm Street.

She was being watched in secret, and then in shock, when she was seen to raise the skirt of her purple taffeta gown to cross the dusty street, daringly showing a hint of ankle encased in leather, but a show of ankle just the same. Done up with paint, powder, and a beauty mark, red hair aflame in the noonday sun, floating in an aura of imitation-French perfume, Velvet Preston sashayed down Elm Street and through the doorway of the Parlett Emporium.

In a matter of minutes, a small knot of women and men had gathered in the store, which was surprising because it was noon, the hour in which everyone in Rockville ate dinner. From a distance, and around and over the pickle barrel, the salt barrel, the sugar barrel, the flour barrel, the cold cast-iron stove, and a counter piled high with men's work clothes, the townsfolk watched Velvet Preston's every move. They knew each item she purchased and, right down to the penny, how much she had paid for it. They watched, entranced, as her slender gloved hand dipped into the beaded purse dangling from a chain on her wrist, with strings of glistening, jet-black beads attached to the bottom of the bag undulating with her every move.

Mr. Parlett, gaping with the others, paraphrased a Bible quote to Mrs. Parlett: "She doesn't hide her light under a basket, does she?"

By evening, the debut of Bobby Lee Preston's new wife to the town had been told and retold. The small amount of money she had spent now amounted to many dollars, and the purple dress, in the telling and retelling, had gone through many color changes until it finally emerged scarlet as sin.

The rumors about Bobby Lee and his new wife were rampant: She was a rich widow who was taking Bobby Lee and his children back to the city, where they would live in a big, fine house. She was divorced, they whispered. She was buying the Townsend mansion, where they were going to live. She was a stage actress. Tsk! Tsk! Tsk! She was rich, she was poor, she was humble, she was proud, but in her rainbow assortment of gowns, Velvet Preston was never an ordinary sight in the little borough of Rockville.

Mrs. White, of the *Mayflower* Whites, was heard to imply that "she's all icing and no cake."

"Oh, she's a fine feather," Perthy Prettyman said in agreement. "But when it comes time to scratch, can she do it?"

Bobby Lee's good looks, along with a new suit of clothes ordered from the Sears, Roebuck & Co. catalog and a little spending money in his pocket, had fooled Velvet into thinking he was rich. In the city she had made a fancy living as a fancy lady, but the time came when she wanted respectability and had looked on Bobby Lee as her salvation.

In the meantime, Bobby Lee had become somewhat of a celebrity in his own hometown. Which social obligations should be extended to Bobby Lee and his new bride was the topic of conversation at both the meeting of Old Church's Tuesday Benevolent Society and the Thursday Social Guild meeting of New Church.

"You mark my words: only Jezebels paint their faces and paste those little black patches on their cheeks," Brother Griggsby confided to the ladies at the Tuesday Benevolent Society meeting. The ladies secretly wondered how their good brother knew about those little black cheek patches when they didn't even know about them themselves.

The rumor that Velvet was rich stopped the day she asked for credit at the emporium store, as did the courtesy the town had previously shown to her. Nevertheless,

Bobby Lee remained a celebrity at Ma's and was the butt of many good-humored jokes.

"By hell, Bobby Lee, you're just plain lucky," Chance said, chiding him. "You go to the city and come back married to that pretty little filly. Why, they ain't a man alive who wouldn't be damn glad to put his brand on her every night," he said amid knowing winks and elbow jabs. "The last time I went to the city, the only thing I could find to poke was some little street beggar, but she squealed like a stuck pig and hollered for joy." Chance swung himself around in the barber chair. "You make them squeal, Blackie? You make them li'l ol' nigger gals yell for more?"

Harlan went on with his janitor work. Cleaning the barbershop was his second job of the day, the narrowing of his eyes the only discernible sign he was angry.

To the rest of the town, Bobby Lee's station in life had not altered; he still had a family he couldn't support and two more hungry mouths to feed.

CHAPTER 29

July 1906

ON MONDAY MORNING, WHEN THE women of the town were at home washing clothes, Abby began her new routine: walking to the post office twice a week. She walked past the ballpark, the yellow-brick schoolhouse, the drugstore, and the Goody Shoppe before crossing the street to the post office, thus avoiding the barbershop and hotel.

Today she found a letter from the president of the bank in her mailbox. She waited until she was home and on her own front porch before she opened the letter. The formal note was from Mr. Oberlander himself, who wished to have a meeting with her. She couldn't imagine why the president of the bank would want to see her, although she did know one thing for certain: the appointment was for her twentieth birthday.

Promptly at 1:30 p.m. on her birthday, Abby, wearing a tan suit and hat with a fan of peacock feathers on the crown, entered the bank. She could remember coming here as a small girl with her father. And there sat Miss

Stone, the bank owner's secretary, on her high stool at the high desk, just as she had been sitting all those many years ago. Her back was still ramrod straight; her once-dark hair, now with wings of gray, was still pulled into a severe knot on the top of her head; her color was still the paleness of someone who spends her days indoors. It was Abby's first confrontation with anyone in town since she'd made the decision to change her life by becoming a viable part of the community.

Miss Stone was completely caught off guard. Seeing Abigail Langley in the hallowed institution of the Rockville Repository was as sacrilegious as seeing her in church. Miss Stone compressed her thin, judgmental mouth so tight her lips disappeared.

When Abigail recognized the better-than-thou expression on Miss Stone's face, she felt defenseless, but only for a second. Setting her back as straight as Miss Stone's and lifting her head a little higher, she said, "I have an appointment with Mr. Oberlander."

Before Miss Stone could reply, Mr. Oberlander himself appeared in the doorway to his private office. "Good afternoon, Miss Langley," he said, all cordiality and smiles as he escorted her inside his inner sanctum. Mr. Oberlander held a chair for her; once she was comfortably seated, he sat down opposite her in his leather desk chair. "Happy birthday," he said.

Abby was more than a little bit uneasy, sitting there in a dark-red leather chair with Mr. Oberlander behind his massive mahogany desk wishing her a happy birthday. *Maybe he does this with all the bank's customers,* she thought.

"You are twenty years old today, correct?"

"Yes." Her back wasn't quite as straight as it was when she had confronted Miss Stone, but her voice was clear and firm.

"Well, Miss Langley, I have some very pleasant news for you. Your father, when he was alive—a good man, a very good man, a fine gentleman," Mr. Oberlander said, looking at her and nodding his head up and down to emphasize his point, "your father had a trust fund set up for you in the way of stocks in railroads and gas and oil fields. All very wise investments, with the proviso that the stocks' and monies' accumulated interests were to be given to you on your twentieth birthday. Happy birthday," he said, handing her a paper with dates and columns of figures written in a fine Spencerian hand. The final tally at the bottom of the sheet amounted to thousands of dollars.

Abigail was stunned. While she tried to gain control of her senses, she sat with her lower lip caught between her teeth, trembling as if with a chill. Mr. Oberlander quickly poured a glass of water from a cut-glass decanter and slid it across the polished desktop to her. Not trusting her shaking hands to pick up the crystal glass, she licked at her lips with the tip of her tongue. With her face burning and her mouth so dry she could only whisper, she finally managed to say, "Mr. Oberlander, did you think about this accumulation of money when I had my child? Could I have been given my inheritance then?"

"My dear young woman, I did think about it—I certainly did. But I have learned through experience that conditions, when left alone, have a way of working themselves out in their own good time, and for the best. I don't believe the courts"—he cleared his throat—"even under the circumstances, would have changed the will, so I abided by the stipulations your father had set forth." The banker poured himself a glass of water, his face flushing from the allusion to her immorality.

Does he think losing one's child is a way of working things out? she thought.

Recovering from the indelicate turn the conversation had taken, Oberlander ceremoniously handed her another document, yellowed with age and in her father's handwriting, and pointed to the last paragraph for her to read: "If I am not present on this, my daughter Abigail's 20th birthday, June 8, 1906, whoever is the president of this institution shall purchase a gift (not to exceed $50) befitting a young lady of twenty, and present it to her on my behalf. Signed, Ronald Langley."

Through her tears, she saw the courtly banker extending a small gift-wrapped package to her. "Open it. Open it," he said brusquely, self-consciously moving things about on his desk.

With cold fingers, she untied the bow, careful not to tear the wrapping paper, and uncovered a black-velvet case. The case held a golden locket on a golden chain, intricately engraved with hearts and flowers and with two heart-shaped openings for pictures. The inscription on the inside of the locket read, "My Abigail, love Daddy."

As she reverently fastened it around her neck, Abby thanked Mr. Oberlander. "It's lovely, and I'm certain it's just what my father would have chosen." Then she added, "But what about my mother? Is there anything in the will for her?"

"The will states that the property and the house belong to both you and your mother, and, upon her demise, it will revert entirely to you. Mrs. Langley was amply provided for upon her husband's death, and the money still rests here in this bank, untouched. In fact, you are both women of very substantial means."

She signed more papers and thanked him again. He stood back of her chair, holding it for her while she rose, and led her to the door. With his hand on the brass doorknob, he hesitated. "I know this is not the time, nor maybe the place," Mr. Oberlander said, "but may I ask you what may seem like a very impertinent question? You needn't answer if you don't wish," he said in a rush of words.

"I'll answer anything I can."

"You know, Mrs. Oberlander and Jennie Jeanne both love beautiful clothes, and I merely wondered where you purchased the charming hat you are wearing. If you will forgive me for being forward, it is most becoming."

"Oh," she said in surprise, "I made it." She placed a hand on her hat and felt her cheeks growing warm. "And the suit, too," she added, looking down at the skirt in an attempt to hide her embarrassment.

Mr. Oberlander lost some of his aplomb. "You did! Well, that's very admirable, ah, yes indeed, very admirable."

Abby stood on the sidewalk in front of the bank, inattentively reading the sign displayed in the empty Goody Shoppe window across the street: MOVED TO A LARGER LOCATION ON 2ND STREET. The clock inside the bank read 2:00 p.m., and she thought, *Half my life has been compressed into one hour.*

Walking slowly toward the hotel, Abby was thinking clearly and honestly about her relationship with her mother. Other than the fact that her mother had stopped speaking to her, their relationship hadn't really changed that much from how it had been before Ronnie was born. *All these years,* she thought, *my mother has been financially secure, and yet she chose to work rather than stay home with me.*

Abby knew nothing of her mother's life before she'd come to Rockville as a schoolteacher and married Ronald Langley, except for the knowledge that her mother had been brought up in an orphanage, an unfortunate circumstance her mother never spoke of or explained.

Abby walked to the rear entrance of the hotel and entered the kitchen. Her mother was standing at the restaurant-size iron stove, stirring something in a large black kettle with a long wooden spoon. The kitchen was hot, and her mother's face appeared damp; her hair was stringing out from the bun on the nape of her neck. Her mother's moody disposition made her unpredictable, and she was often cross. She gave her daughter a quick disapproving look—a look that Abby had come to expect over the years.

"Do you know what day this is?" Abby said to her mother, making her voice sound as gay as she had felt in the bank. Her mother didn't answer. Abby drew a few steps closer. "Why don't you like me? My father loved me, but you never did, and I think I deserve to know why." Her happy feeling had dissipated fast, and her heart was beating rapidly.

"Don't you mention your father to me." They were her mother's first words to her in months, and they were spoken in anger.

"I *will* mention my father. He is my father, and I am his flesh and blood." Abby tapped her fingers on the locket. "He loved me." Her voice quivered uncontrollably. "Why don't you? What did I do to make you hate me?"

Her mother's eyes flared in a flash of jealousy as she glanced at the gold locket. "The only thing your father ever did for you was to spoil you rotten." Mrs. Langley slapped the dish towel she was holding across her shoulder. "I should've let him take you back to Texas with him when he wanted to, so he could spoil you even more, no doubt. You were always too uppity for your own good. It was my place to unspoil you, Little Miss Princess," she said, placing her hands on her hips and swaying her shoulders back and forth, "and bring you down to size."

"I've just come from the bank," Abby said. "In all these years, you didn't have to work. You could've stayed home with me, and we could've made a life together. If you had loved me, even a little bit, perhaps I never would have gotten pregnant."

"Hush," her mother said, her eyes darting toward the dining room door. "Don't say that word," she hissed. "Someone might hear you."

"Not saying the word doesn't change the truth, Mother," she said with a trace of sarcasm. "If you had been a real mother, you would have helped me when I needed help. You would have made it possible for me to keep my child. We could have left Rockville and made a new life for ourselves somewhere other than here, the three of us, but no, you wouldn't even talk about it. I would like to know how you could have been so indifferent to your own flesh and blood."

Abby was too angry to cry, but she desperately wanted to. She wanted a mother who would take her in her arms and hold her while she cried, cried for all the years of loneliness and all the unjustified hurts she had endured.

"You're the kind of woman who comes between a man and a decent woman," her mother said.

Abby gasped. "What do you mean? What kind of woman?"

"The kind of woman who throws herself at a married man," her mother said, looking her daughter up and down, disapproval showing in every nuance of her face. "Indecency leaches out of you like poison from nightshade."

Abby placed her hand on her chest as she tried to still the shock of her mother's words. "It's because I won't give you his name, isn't it?" she asked. Abby was more upset than she had been in her entire life. "You and everybody else in this damn town—all you ever wanted was his name!" she said, shaking in anger.

"Don't you use profanity in my presence, missy!"

"I'm not going to use any words in your presence," Abby shot back. "I'm not even going to look at you in your presence."

Her mother gave a short snort and, turning her back on her daughter, moved the soup kettle to the far side of the stove, whipped the towel from her shoulder, and, in a ritual of finality, wiped her hands on it. Then, hanging the towel on the handle of the oven door, she left the room.

I guess her responsibility to me is over, and with it, my devotion to her, Abby thought as she exited the back entrance to the kitchen, slamming the door behind her.

That night sleep toyed with Abby, coming and going in fitful spasms. She speculated about what she should do with the money. Late into the night, she could hear her mother moving about in her room and in other rooms of the house. During the wakeful minutes, Abby fondled the gift from her father where it lay in its velvet case on the empty pillow beside her. The news that her father had wanted to take her back to Texas with him was something she had not known until today. She thought, *He wanted me and not my mother?* She mulled this knowledge over in her mind, troubling how she might mend the bitterness between them. And did she want to?

Sleep had no sooner caught up with her than she was suddenly wide awake, sitting bolt upright in bed and very excited. Two events of the day had merged in her mind: the empty storeroom vacated by the Goody Shoppe, and Mr. Oberlander's complimenting her on the hat she'd been wearing and his very obvious surprise that she had made it herself.

She was still awake when morning came. It was one of those rare Rockville mornings when the sun rising over the stone quarry painted the town—and anyone out and about at that time of day—a luminous golden hue of molten amber and made of them, for a moment in time, idols more precious than rubies and more treasured than gold.

Abby, burnished in the aura from the sunrise coming through the window of her balcony door, watched her mother leave the house at six o'clock. She was still awake when her mother returned a short time later, riding with Harlan in the Parletts' grocery wagon.

Abby's mother and Harlan made several trips in and out of the house, each carrying parcels to the wagon as well as a straw suitcase, boxes, and finally her mother's trunk. *OK*, Abby thought as they drove away, *it doesn't matter. I've always been alone anyway.* "Expect happiness, Abby, expect happiness." She kept repeating Noah's words to her like a mantra, and then she remembered Aunt Em's admonition to "make them need you."

On the kitchen table she found a note held in place by the key to the house, although homes in Rockville were seldom locked, she knew. The note read, "The house is yours." Her mother had moved lock, stock, and barrel to the hotel.

At one o'clock that afternoon, Abby was dressed and on her way to the bank. In Mr. Oberlander's office, she revealed to him her plan: a millinery store!

Mr. Oberlander and Abby, along with Miss Stone, crossed the street to the storeroom and together explored the rooms. Abby couldn't hide her excitement of owning her own business.

The look of disapproval was still on Miss Stone's face, but gradually, grudgingly, she had to admit that the hat Abigail wore was very becoming. And wouldn't it be nice to have a hat store in town? It would mean not having to wait for a whole year to pass before you could buy a hat from the drummer who set up shop in the hotel's Annex. His hats were always picked over and out of style by the time he arrived in Rockville. And the hats he brought with him were mostly black and drab, in view of the fact that his customers were mainly from Old Church.

The stylish members of New Church made regular shopping trips to the state capital, but not everyone could afford to spend a day in the city, and if they did—people would gossip.

Miss Stone, taking notes, looked over the top of her spectacles to where Abby stood at the window, discussing details with Mr. Oberlander, and moved a little nearer to them. Would she dare buy a hat from Abigail Langley? A little tremor ran through her body.

In the back corner of the display window, thought to be inconspicuous, sheets of honey-colored flypaper, black with dead flies, lay curling in the sun. Abby made a mental note of how to protect the merchandise from the southern exposure and how to tastefully take care of any future flies.

The trio moved outside. Mr. Oberlander, tipping his hat to Abigail, said he would see her in one week at the same time of day, by which time he'd have all the details worked out for her approval.

Abby knew exactly how she wanted to proceed. For years she had yearned, dreamed, of going to the Fashion Institute of Chicago. She had pored over their ads in *Collier's* and the *Ladies' Home Journal*, had even sent away for brochures, and now, she thought with pride, she had the means to do so. But could she go alone?

CHAPTER 30

On the eve of the Fourth of July, 1906, Rockville's Main Street was unusually busy. The stores were open late, and out-of-town visitors—there for the ball game between Johnstown and Rockville the next day—along with many of the townsfolk, were downtown, some making purchases, others just out for a stroll.

Patriotic banners hung from lampposts, and red, white, and blue swags fluttered from front porches. Visitors walked the length of Main Street, all of them marveling at the Chapel of the Ark, and some, on a dare, actually stepping inside and looking around. Entering a church not of one's own persuasion was not forbidden, but it just wasn't done, so the act in itself was brazen.

That evening, the young people of Rockville staged a sing-along on the steps of the emporium. Band members and ballplayers from Rockville and Johnstown, and some of the young married couples from town, joined in. When the later-than-usual sing-along came to an end, Orion walked Jennie Jeanne home, where they lingered at her gate.

"Cat got your tongue?" Orion asked her, almost tongue-tied himself.

Jennie Jeanne did not look at him; she looked at the ground and answered him by shyly rolling her head back and forth. The faint popping of firecrackers could be heard in the distance.

"Penny for your thoughts," he said. This time she tilted her face up to his, and the glow from the lamppost by the gate made her face luminous. Her blue eyes, the pupils large and black, gazed into his. Orion slipped his arms around her waist and, gently pulling her to him, kissed her, their first real kiss. Jennie Jeanne did not resist.

Dropping his arms, Orion took a step back. "I'm sorry," he stammered.

Jennie Jeanne demurely looked up into his face and said, "I'm not." Then, putting her arms around his neck, she returned his kiss.

Orion, feeling the litheness of her young body pressed against the length of his, held her in a long embrace. "I love you, Jennie Jeanne," he whispered in her ear. Looking down at her, he said, "I love you with all my heart." He held her hand in his and walked her to her front door, where he quickly kissed her again. "I'm going to win that ball game tomorrow, just for you."

"I know you will, Riney," she said, her voice and heart quivering.

The morning of the Fourth dawned on a progressive, enlightened, and lighthearted America. The nation had recovered from the tragic San Francisco earthquake and fire and was enjoying the leadership of the most robust and youngest president in its history.

President Theodore Roosevelt, born into wealth in New York City (not in a log cabin, unlike many of our presidents), had brought new vigor and excitement to the country. As a child, the president had struggled with illness, and now, energetically healthy, he was a strong advocate for the strenuous life—enough so that the Rockville School Board was following the president's penchant for exercise by permitting the young men in the upper grades to play basketball in the coming school year.

As a result of this decision, the young women of the town petitioned the board, and especially the young women's parents, for the girls in Rockville to catch up with the young women throughout the rest of the county by having their own basketball team. The ark, and Dr. Edwards in particular, had given the young people of Rockville new hope for a more up-to-date town and a voice in the events that took place there.

Abby, wearing a white straw hat with a flat brim and a red and blue hatband, a white skirt, and a shirtwaist with puffy, elbow-length sleeves, entered the hotel lobby and climbed the stairs to Judge Andrews's law office. His was the first room on the second floor, and, like the Parletts' suite, it faced Main Street. She was nervous, but the excitement of the new life she envisioned for herself bolstered her courage.

Although it was the Fourth of July, it was still a weekday, and the door to the judge's office was open. Abby remained standing in the doorway until the judge, looking up from his desk and seeing a woman, scrambled to his feet, fanning away cigar smoke and quickly buttoning his jacket.

Abigail raised her voice in order to be heard above the din of people gathered on the sidewalks of the downtown business section to watch the parade.

"I'm Abigail Langley," she said.

"Uh," the judge said hesitantly before recognition brightened his face. "Ah, yes. Miss Langley. Come in, come in," he said, at once noticing that Abigail had about her the ambiance of a very sophisticated young woman. Moving from behind his desk and positioning a chair for her, his pulse quickened, and he was sorry the room smelled of tobacco smoke. "What can I do for you?" he asked, seating himself across from her.

Abby spoke quickly and decisively. "I'm planning on opening a millinery store in the Goody Shoppe's old location, and I wish for you to make all legal arrangements. I don't want the town council to turn me down because I'm a woman." *A fallen woman,* she thought, and she was sure the judge was thinking the same thing. "I wish for you to intercede on my behalf. I want as little gossip as possible. In other words, I don't wish to have my character attacked," she said, looking with unwavering candor into his eyes.

He nodded; both of them were very much aware of the conditions in which she would have to operate. She added, "I need you to find a carpenter who will work for me, someone who can paint and hang wallpaper; a person who is above reproach."

Henri Parlett appeared in the attorney's doorway. "Oh, Judge," he said, showing surprise. "I didn't realize you were conducting business today." Upon recognizing Abigail, he smiled and nodded to her. Although he had fired Abigail, he still felt a great deal of respect and admiration for her. "I came to invite you to view the parade from our balcony," he said to the judge, "and you, too, Abigail. Come along." The visiting Johnstown band began to play the patriotic march "Stars and Stripes Forever" loud enough to interrupt what he was saying. "Come along," Parlett almost shouted as he excitedly ushered them into his family's private quarters and onto the curved balcony overlooking Main Street.

"Sit here by me," Mrs. Parlett said, raising her voice and motioning Abby to a chair by the balcony railing.

They could see the formation of the entire parade in the street below. People stood four or five deep on each side of Main Street. Those who'd arrived early had been rewarded with seats in the shade on the steps of the emporium.

Abby could see Noah, who was standing in front of the empty storeroom across the street that would soon be her place of business. He looked very dapper in his white slacks, stiff, straw-brimmed hat, and a jacket as blue as she remembered his eyes being. She had not seen him since he had vowed never to forsake her. A lump of disappointment caught in her throat.

Leading off the parade was "The Spirit of '76." The subject of the famous painting by Archibald M. Willard today was being portrayed by three members of the Langley clan: Grandpa Mosley, his white hair flowing, beat out the rhythm to a Sousa march on a snare drum; Percy, dressed as a little drummer boy in a Revolutionary War jacket and tricorn hat, drummed on a toy drum; and mischievous Sags, his forehead bandaged and bloodied with beet juice, limped along playing on a fife he had whittled from a tree branch. Following them was a wagon wrapped with red, white, and blue bunting that transported the town's three remaining Civil War veterans, one wearing his faded Union uniform, and all of them proudly displaying medals on their diminishing chests. Marching behind them were fourteen veterans from the Philippine-American War and the Spanish-American War, the war during which Theodore Roosevelt had been assistant secretary of the navy.

The much-envied Johnstown band, dressed in white pants and shirts and red vests, stepped along smartly in time with the popular march, followed by floats sponsored by the town's merchants.

Eloise Saunders, this year's Miss Liberty, was draped in a white flowing robe, wore a silver tinsel crown, and held aloft a golden scepter; she and her attendants, two lively eighteen-year-old girls, graced the Parlett Emporium float. From her lofty position on the float, the lovely brunette waved to Noah, who raised his hat to her before she turned her attention to the balcony of the hotel and smartly saluted her sponsors, Mr. and Mrs. Parlett.

Noah followed Eloise's gaze to the balcony, and when he saw Abby, his heart began to race. She had been very much on his mind, but he was undecided as to what part he wanted to play in her life. If he offered her guidance, would his meaning be misunderstood? And what kind of guidance should he offer—spiritual or personal?

After the parade passed, Noah made his way across the street, where he met Abby as she was exiting the hotel lobby. He gallantly presented her with his miniature American flag the merchants had supplied to everyone along the parade route. The look in his eyes made her wonder if he was comparing her to the ogress she must have looked like the night he had rescued her from the creek.

"Are you going to the park?" he asked.

"Yes, but I'm picking up my friend Frieda on the way."

"In that case, if I may, I'll escort both of you ladies to the afternoon festivities," he said, smiling broadly and touching his hand to his hat brim in a spirited gesture.

They stood on the crowded sidewalk, an island unto themselves, with a stream of people flowing around them, each lost in the delight of seeing one another again. Their ordeal of the night at the creek had given the two of them an informality with each other that normally would have taken months to acquire.

At the grandstand, they sat decorously apart, with Frieda between them. Abby's meeting with Judge Andrews, her determination to succeed in her plan for a new life, and, of course, the inheritance from her father, had all given her a new sense of self-confidence. She had come out of hiding from the safety of the honeysuckle vines on her front porch, and here she was, sitting in the middle of the grandstand at the town park on the Fourth of July under the scrutiny of everyone present. Only Frieda separated her from a man handsome enough to turn heads—a man whom she had met less than a month before—and he had already given her reason to feel like a Fourth of July sparkler.

This was the second summer for the playing of baseball in Rockville, and this year the happy boosters overflowed the grandstand, filled the new bleachers and benches, sat on the grass in Fountain Park, and milled about the ballpark.

Brother Griggsby delivered the recitation of the Declaration of Independence, as he did every Fourth of July. Only his deep, resonant voice could do it justice. Many in the audience, Noah among them, quietly mouthed the words along with him. "When in the course of human events, it becomes necessary for one people to dissolve the political bonds which have connected them with another..." Before Brother Griggsby ended the reading, a faint humming noise could be heard. People anxiously looked about them.

"What is it?" Abby whispered to Noah. The whispering coming from others also swelled with the same question and rippled through the crowd like dry, rustling leaves.

"It's an aer-i-o-plane!" a man shouted from the playing field, pointing to the sky. The spectators on the field, turning as one, faced the sound. The grandstand emptied, and everyone poured onto the field. Noah and Abby, shading their eyes, mouths open in astonishment, were unaware that they were holding hands as the shadow of the giant bird passed over them. The plane was so close to the earth that patches on the underside of the fabric-covered wings were plainly visible. People waved and shouted, and the pilot rocked his plane from side to side.

Awestruck, the crowd watched the aircraft until it vanished from sight, remaining motionless for some time as they stared at the exact spot where the airplane had disappeared from view. Men coughed, blew their noses, and shook their heads, women dried their eyes, children were unnaturally quiet, and everyone was visibly shaken.

The band members, still holding their instruments, played a faltering, unrehearsed rendition of "Nearer My God to Thee," and the wavering voices of an emotion-filled crowd sang along with them.

After the excitement of seeing an airplane for the first time had died down, Noah treated Abby and Frieda to the Johnson Dairy's homemade ice cream, dipped from hand-cranked freezers, and escorted them back to their seats in the grandstand before excusing himself to play ball. "I'll see you at the fireworks tonight," he said to Abby. "You, too, Frieda." He tipped his hat and was gone.

Abby and Frieda, licking away at dripping vanilla ice cream cones, laughed merrily as they watched the children, arranged in age groups, competing for pennies or candy. Kids in gunnysacks hopped, stumbled, and fell toward the finish line. Children holding spoons with a potato balanced in the bowl carefully raced to the goal line, usually arriving with an empty spoon. Boys in pairs ran wheelbarrow races, and the youngest children tottered to a row of tin cans to find a penny hidden under each one.

The most anticipated contest of the day, and the one with the most enthusiastic supporters, was the footrace among the married women for the empty three-gallon wooden pail that had contained the hard candies given out as prizes to the children. The families and friends of the contenders rowdily cheered and encouraged the runners.

The widow McCoy had won the race for the coveted bucket two years in a row. She ran like a shameless hoyden, with her skirts pulled high above her ankles, titillating the men and shocking the women. It was widely known that the widow kept her money in a rolled, twisted, tight little wad in one of her black knee stockings, and the men were anticipating a peek at the wad—or, better still, a bare knee. In the bosom of each woman who entered the race today burned the desire, not for the wooden bucket, but to beat the widow.

The husband-calling contest followed the hog-calling contest, and this year the committee disqualified the widow McCoy because she didn't have a husband. It was rumored that her husband, after he hadn't returned from a trip to visit his mother in West Virginia, had been killed by a Hatfield. The widow was miffed by her elimination, yet she had in her possession another wooden candy bucket.

The great horse-pulling contest, with a cash prize of twenty dollars, was the only big-money event of the day. Wherever the men congregated—at the horse-pulling contest, the horse races, the horseshoe-pitching competition, or the calf roping—they speculated on who would win the ball game, with none of them expressing much confidence in the inexperienced Rockville team. The married women, as they supervised the children's games, wondered if it would be proper for them to remain, since they had never attended a ball game before.

Abby paid earnest attention to the game and had the feeling that Noah, who was playing second base, was performing for her benefit. Superbly athletic, he made running catches, diving catches, and leaping catches, and he made a throw to third base on his knees on a ground ball. And Jennie Jeanne, sitting with her friends in Fountain Park, watched as Orion, buoyed by his confession of love to her the night before, dazzled the crowd with his good looks, stunning smile, blazing fastball, and power pitching. Orion was a crowd favorite.

The Rockville Rockets, to the enthusiastic applause and cheering of the home crowd, won the baseball game against the Johnstown team, 5–2. After the game, the Johnstown team, in step with the band, good-naturedly put on a show of bravado as they marched to the train station, proving they were good losers; they vowed to beat the Rockets the next time the two teams met. The Rockville Rockets, joined by a jubilant crowd of local citizens, escorted them to the station.

Before they boarded the train, the Johnstown band was playing a spirited rendition of the "America Forever March" when, much to the amazement of those gathered on the train platform, a groggy, slightly disheveled William Jennings Bryan appeared.

The great orator and Democratic candidate for the 1907 presidential election against William Howard Taft was on his way to his second Fourth of July celebration and his second political address of the day. He had been catching a nap. Thinking the gathering was in his honor, and much to the astonishment of the crowd, Mr. Bryan delivered a rousing patriotic speech. His eyes, traveling over the crowd, found Abby's, and she felt what he was saying was meant for her.

"Destiny is no matter of chance," he said. "It is a matter of choice. It is not a thing to be waited for; it is a thing to be achieved."

The tired but jubilant people of Rockville set off for home. They needed rest and food, and they had a day's worth of chores to be done before the evening fireworks began: a cold supper to prepare, wood chopped, cows milked, and animals fed. What other surprises lay in store for them for the coming evening, no one dared contemplate.

That evening, Abby saw Noah before he saw her. He was talking to Eloise, who was still wearing her Miss Liberty robe and tinsel tiara and gazing rapturously up into his face. The two attendants who had shared the float with her were also paying him captivated attention. Then they all broke into laughter at something he had said, but when Noah saw Abby, he left the trio of young women and joined her and Frieda.

After the fireworks, under an obsidian sky with its own celestial fireworks, Noah escorted Abby and Frieda to their homes. He was feeling giddy after playing in a winning ball game and spending the evening in the presence of a woman who excited him.

"It's been a truly grand and glorious Fourth of July," he said.

"I'll bet no one in America had a Fourth of July as good as ours," Frieda said.

"Everyone should be grateful to Marshal McCombs for the fireworks exploding over the park, and not in someone's hayfield," Noah said.

"Two years ago, one landed in Mr. Johnson's field and burned up his haystack," Abby said.

"And an airplane! Can you beat that?" Frieda added.

"I never imagined I would live long enough to see a flying machine," Noah said.

"I never want to fly in one," Abby said. "I'm still shaking just from seeing it."

In the darkness of the night, Noah daringly put an arm around her shoulders and gave her a hug.

"No one lost fingers from holding onto lit fireworks," he said, pressing her fingers with his.

"And we saw William Jennings Bryan!" Abby said, sighing with pleasure.

"No one's haystack or barn caught on fire," Noah said.

"Oh my, and isn't Mr. Bryan handsome for a man of forty-eight?" Abby said with another sigh.

Noah looked down at her, and the look in his eyes made her giggle.

They parted company at Abby's front gate, both knowing he could not be seen escorting her to her front door.

CHAPTER 31

We hate whiskey
We hate rum
You can put them on the run.
Do it now!

Lizzie Doyle's Sunday school class of ten-year-old boys stood in front of Stevens Drugstore chanting the "We Hate Rum" pledge. Abby, Judge Andrews, and Bill Tibbits—carpenter, cabinetmaker, and part-time mortician—circled around the dedicated boy evangelists so that they could enter the vacant storeroom next door.

Inside the empty room, Abby unrolled her plans for the millinery store and placed them on the platform of the display window. She had completed the plans in watercolor; she showed them the design of the shop, the size and arrangements of cabinets and dresser, and the exact colors of the wallpaper and paint she wanted. She surprised both men with her eye for detail.

"Mr. Tibbits," she said, "I will be in Chicago for three weeks. Can the store be ready when I return?"

A pained expression spread over his face. Mr. Tibbits was listening to Abby as well as the boys trying to persuade the men of Rockville to give up drinking.

We hate liquor
We hate booze
You can choose
Choose not to booze!

Mr. Tibbits was wondering if, in his wife's opinion, working for Abigail Langley would be on par with drinking. Maybe he should consult with her before accepting the job offer, he thought. But when he saw the excitement on Abby's face, he felt a softening in his heart for this charming and much-maligned woman.

"Yes, it can be ready," he said with sudden enthusiasm.

"Good," she said, shaking hands with both of them. "Judge Andrews will handle the finances. Ask him for anything you need. I do wish for what's happening here to be kept secret," she confided to them with an engaging smile. "I want my shop to come as a surprise for the town."

At that moment, both men would have walked on hot coals rather than reveal her plans.

"Onward Christian soldiers, marching as to war!" sang the ten-year-old temperance workers as they marched across the street to Ma's Barbershop and Pool

Hall for the finale of their long, strenuous day. Abby and the men waited for the "demon rum" drive to disperse before they left the storeroom.

Hoarse, exhausted, and debilitated, Lizzie Doyle was also waiting for the drive to end. She wanted to send her rambunctious wards home and make her way to the office of Dr. Townsend, where he administered a once-a-year tonic to her—a tonic he poured from an unmarked bottle into a small, bell-shaped glass. Anything that nasty had to be good for her, or so Lizzie thought.

The golden liquid restored her spirits and sent her on her way, spiritually and physically renewing her until the following year, when another group of ten-year-old boys would suffer through the demon rum drive, and Lizzie would again receive transcendence through Dr. Townsend's magic potion.

CHAPTER 32

September 1906

THE DAY AFTER LABOR DAY, Abby opened her shop for business: Le Bon Marché. She had chosen the name and the décor—a new word in Rockville's lexicon—as carefully as she had chosen the merchandise. The door of the shop was painted olive green, and the velvet drapery in the large display window was of the same green color and was lined in a dusty rose taffeta. The cherrywood dressing table featured a folding triple mirror, rose-pink skirt, and a vanity bench upholstered in green velvet.

A stunningly beautiful hat was on display in the window, one that Abby had painstakingly created to showcase her skill and artistry as a milliner. The hat was her pièce de résistance, her coup, her be-all and end-all.

The French-style chapeau resided on a tall hatstand covered with a pastel coral-colored chiffon scarf. The scarf, pictured in the latest women's magazines, was designed for motoring—although no one in Rockville, as yet, had an automobile. Still, the filmy scarf, when covering a woman's hat and crisscrossing beneath her chin, with the ends flowing back of either shoulder, was a most flattering style for any woman.

Abigail had dyed the materials used in the decorating of the hat and had fashioned them into flowers. This included the large spiky Chinese mums in luscious fall colors of mauve, pumpkin, and russet that adorned the crown and spilled over onto the wide brim of the hat as well as smaller flowers in complementary shades. Intricate silk ribbon designs completed the hat, which was of cocoa-brown silk. The hat brim swept up on one side to frame a woman's profile, then dipped coquettishly low on the other.

Abby looked over her shop. Did it look too intimate, too frilly, too colorful, too much like a boudoir? Well, if it did, it certainly wasn't your typical Rockville bedroom; likewise, Le Bon Marché was not your typical store. It was a shop for women, a place where they would feel pampered. She loved it.

She stepped outside to appraise the overall effect. Feeling satisfied, she turned from the window and faced the town, silently pleading, *Please welcome me as one of your own.*

Farmers on their way to work slowed their horses and stared at the window, and shopkeepers, before opening their stores, stopped by for a look-see. Mr. Oberlander crossed the street from his bank and, after viewing the bonnet, gallantly tipped his hat to the lovely chapeau. No one entered.

Tuesday was the Benevolent Society's sewing-circle day, and although the starting time was two o'clock, the club women began drifting downtown early. They casually strolled past the new store and cast furtive peeks into the windows. Lone women did not pause, but if accompanied by another, they would stop and, after glancing about to see if anyone was watching them, peer into the window.

Some of the women, on the pretense of making a "very necessary" purchase, had congregated by the alcove windows inside the Parlett store; from there they could see across the street and grudgingly admire the distinctiveness of the new shop.

The sign hanging above the green-and-white-striped awning read: LE BON MARCHÉ, and, beneath the name, in small letters, "A Boutique for Ladies' Hats and Couture Dressmaking."

"Well! La-ti-da and hoity-toi," Perthy Prettyman said, mocking the name.

Abby's mother hated the name as well. "What will people think?" she complained to her reflection in the window of the hotel lobby. "That my daughter is putting on airs—that's what they'll think."

The gossip around town was that Abby had sold her baby to obtain the money to open her fancy store. But everyone knew the couple who'd adopted her baby didn't have that kind of money; besides, the Nelsons never would have stooped to buying a baby. The rumor soon died out.

Still, rumor or not, the women's fingers itched to examine the merchandise and the workmanship, but no one wanted to be the first to enter a store belonging to, of all people, Abigail Langley.

The first day passed without a sound coming from the dainty tinkling doorbell that would signal the arrival of a customer. The first week ended without the ringing of the bell or the showing of a customer at Le Bon Marché.

Abby spent Sunday at home, where she saw no one (as usual) and was in a terrible state of dread for the upcoming week. She had counted on two people coming into the store to wish her well: Aunt Em and Dr. Noah Edwards. For the time being, Aunt Em was in constant attendance on the elderly Martha Blackburn, who had fallen and broken her hip and now had pneumonia and was not expected to pull through, and Noah was on tour with the baseball club.

The second week went by with one caller, Sam Morris, from the *Hub.* Sam wanted to know if she wished to make any changes in the advertisement she was running in his newspaper. She hesitated before telling him, "No, it's fine the way it is." *As if anything was fine!* she wanted to scream.

In the third week of her opening, her mother crossed the street and entered the store. She did not show any interest in the shop whatsoever but just said to her daughter, "For heaven's sakes, Abigail, quit. Give it up. Haven't people made it perfectly clear what they think of you? They don't want you here. Go home."

With the feeling that she was fighting for her very existence, Abby confronted her. "When I was a little girl, I'd say, 'Mother, I can't do that,' and you'd say, 'Yes, you can.' You'd say, 'Make soup,' and I'd say, 'I can't,' and you'd say, 'Yes, you can.' And sometimes, in exasperation, you'd say, 'Oh, Abigail, just do it!' That is what I need to hear from you now. Please, Mother," Abby pleaded, "tell me I can do it. I need you to say I can do it."

"Oh, for heaven's sakes, Abigail," her mother said, as if anything she had said once to a child was important. "Haven't you humiliated us enough? Sell it. Burn it. I don't care what you do with it, but go home." She left the store.

Abby retreated to the far corner of the workroom, where she sought warmth from the cold potbellied stove and wept. After the cry, she was sitting and looking around her as she tried to decide what to move first when the little doorbell tinkled.

My mother, again? she wondered. She peeked into the shop. Dr. John Townsend was standing there in the middle of her store, and, as Abby hesitantly appeared from behind the curtain, he removed his tall silk hat.

It was obvious to the doctor that she'd been crying, which made him unsure if he had come to the right person for what he had in mind. With both of them feeling uneasy, the doctor put on a show of bravado. Placing his hat on the glass display case and striking his hands together, he said, "I'm taking Aunt Em to Arizona for the winter, and I want you to put together a wardrobe for her. I plan on leaving at Thanksgiving time, and the cost for her wardrobe is of no consequence, young lady. I want it to be the best. Top-notch." He was suddenly very animated. "I believe spending time away from Rockville, with a long rest in the clean air and sunshine for which the state is famous, will restore Aunt Em to her old self."

It was the noon hour in Rockville, the time everyone went home to eat dinner, so downtown was quiet when the doctor retrieved Aunt Em from the buggy where he had left her waiting; he had not yet told her of his plans.

Aunt Em, in her usual whirlwind state, rushed in and hugged Abby to her; then, holding the young woman's face in both her hands, she said, "I've heard so much about the hat, I had to come in and see it for myself."

Aunt Em's hands on Abby's cheeks felt hot to her, not the cool, soothing touch she remembered from her childhood. Abby, as she looked into Aunt Em's hazel eyes, knew the hat would be flattering on her, but somehow, hats never seemed to sit right on Aunt Em. And, just as disappointing, style didn't seem to interest her, either. It was like putting dazzling plumage on a brown sparrow that had not one whit of desire to be a songbird.

The colors brought out the green in Aunt Em's eyes, but they also showed up the sallowness of her skin. She had lost weight during the winter of the big snow and whooping-cough outbreak and had never regained the lost pounds or her old stamina. Seeing the careworn face beneath the glamorous hat made Abby's heart ache;

nevertheless, the hat definitely propelled Aunt Em into high society.

Mrs. Parlett joined her husband at the window of the store alcove, and she, too, stood looking across the street at the spurned store.

"Do you like the name?" he asked her.

Mrs. Parlett smiled. "Oui," she answered, in a voice that still retained a French accent. "And why not? Now we have a bit of Paree right here in Rockville, and it suits her. Abby is not an ordinary woman, you know."

Henri reached for the coin purse he carried in his pants pocket and handed his wife a twenty-dollar gold piece. "Francoise, ma chérie, would you like to buy yourself a new chapeau?"

Later that afternoon, Mrs. Parlett left the emporium, crossed the street, and opened the green door. The little bell jingled, and, in a short period of time, the hat disappeared from the window.

Francoise Parlett sat at the rose-skirted dressing table, and Abby placed the hat on her head. With her proud carriage and still-lovely face, Mrs. Parlett looked fabulous.

"It's the most beautiful hat I've ever seen," she said. "Abigail, you truly are a very remarkable young woman." Mrs. Parlett sat pensively studying her triple reflection. "You know," she said slowly, "this hat is the best advertising you'll ever have; therefore, I'm not going to buy it. It belongs in the window," she said, smiling. "Show me another one."

Disappointment showed on Abby's face, and Mrs. Parlett reached out to her and took her hand in hers. "Every woman who's come into the emporium for the last three weeks has been dying to try on this hat—oh, they haven't said so, but I know women, and sooner or later, they'll all be over here." She gave Abby's hand a squeeze of encouragement. "Don't lose heart," she added. Glancing out the window, she said, "Oh, look! Here they come now."

Mrs. Stanton and Mrs. White had left the emporium and were crossing the street, each trying to outdistance the other. Mrs. Parlett opened the door to them and called out, "Come in, Bertha, Ethel." Still wearing Abby's creation, she turned slowly about, modeling it for them. "Isn't it the most beautiful hat you've ever seen?"

Mrs. White sat before the mirror, ignoring Abigail's eyes as she placed the hat on her head. The hat performed its sorcery. In the mirror was reflected, not just the countenance of Ethel White, *Mayflower* descendent, but that of a celebrated woman. Reluctantly removing the hat, Mrs. White passed it on to her companion.

Soon the shop was full of women, all vying to try on the hat; each time one of them sat before the mirror with the hat adorning her head, she saw herself as she might be (or dared to be in daydreams): a younger, prettier, supremely sophisticated other self.

Lottie Oberlander almost flew through the door after she'd heard from her husband when he closed the bank at noon and partook of dinner at home. "Lottie," he'd said, "you should give the new store some business; it's good for the economy of the town—and the bank."

"If you think I should, Mr. Oberlander," Lottie said, putting on her hat and taking up her purse.

The hat again performed its magic. Mrs. Oberlander appeared ten years younger, and, wearing the hat, she could still be called Rockville's "reigning beauty."

Mrs. Parlett explained to her friend, as she had to the others, why she should not buy the hat, so Mrs. Oberlander bought a different one, all the time enviously eyeing the showpiece hat.

Abby had a look of current stylishness about her that gave women confidence in her taste. The women snapped up the hats and small items: the lavender-scented soap wrapped in lavender paper and tied with purple ribbons, and the small imported English tins decorated with a picture of a Victorian girl smelling a pink rose that contained rose-flavored cachous to sweeten the breath.

In celebration of the opening of the store, Abby gave each customer a small gift bottle of Grandma Langley's lavender lotion.

Later, the women of Rockville, while they were admiring their purchases, would wonder about the propriety of doing business with Abigail Langley, a woman who had been excommunicated from her church and had given away her baby. And again they would speculate, as they often did, on just who was the father of her illegitimate baby, anyway.

For the rest of the month, the curious, the buyers, and the "just looking" continued to come into Le Bon Marché—all except the women schoolteachers, whom the school board had banned from patronizing Abby's store after taking into consideration the type of shop it was, and her reputation. This ban placed Le Bon Marché in the same category as Ma's Barbershop and Pool Hall. The county school board's rules for women teachers for the year 1906 stipulated:

> Women teachers may not enter a place of ill repute.
>
> Women teachers may not loiter in the downtown stores.
>
> Women teachers may not marry during the teaching year.
>
> Women teachers may not be seen in the company of a man who is not a close relative.
>
> Women teachers must be home between the hours of 8:00 p.m. and 6:00 a.m., unless at a school or church function, or with permission of the superintendent to attend a non-school or church event.
>
> Women teachers must wear two petticoats, and their skirts must conceal their ankles.
>
> Women teachers may not wear bright colors or dye their hair.

> Teachers must keep the classroom clean: they must sweep it once a day and mop it once a week.

It was humiliating, but it certainly wasn't the first invisible hair shirt Abby, or the female teachers, had been made to wear.

Mrs. Parlett became Abby's biggest booster; she reminded the women who came into the emporium, "Be sure to stop in the new store while you're downtown. Le Bon Marché is a better millinery store than any I've seen in the state capital, and we should be proud to have it right here in Rockville." On occasion she would say to the men customers, "Tell your wives to visit the new store and try on the hat, just to see how young and pretty they can be." The men were skeptical about telling their wives anything that would encourage them to spend money, especially on tomfoolery.

Women who had once been Abby's friends also frequented the store. With toddlers in hand and babies left sleeping in carriages on the sidewalk, they obligingly congratulated Abby. While covetously appraising the busy store and its fashionable merchandise, they shyly initiated conversation and spoke of husbands who were also old schoolmates of Abby's.

On Saturdays, when the families came to town from the outlying farms and small settlements to do their weekly shopping, the hat was constantly out of the display window. By closing time of the fourth week, nearly every woman in Rockville and vicinity had tried on the hat.

Everyone except my mother, Abby thought wryly. She had, now and then during the week, caught glimpses of her mother standing in the hotel lobby, observing the commerce being conducted across the street at her daughter's store.

It took a while for the town to become accustomed to the new store with the French name, but in so doing, they anglicized the Le in the name of the store to "The" Bon Marché. Making this small adjustment seemed to satisfy them.

Although many women desired the hat, the elegant chapeau had become as controversial as the owner of the Bon Marché herself and a conversation piece no one dared own. Brother Griggsby had also labeled the beautiful hat "sinful."

CHAPTER 33

Mr. Parlett had grave doubts about sending Harlan Jones on the road tour with the Rockets, although he did finally send him off, with the admonition: "You be careful, hear? And come back."

During the summer, teams from other towns had come through Rockville looking to play the Rockets and had left with "their noses rubbed in it." The Rockets, riding high, discussed making a career of playing ball for a living, but the wise judgment of Mr. Langley prevailed when he persuaded them to take a road trip. "Travel from town to town and get a feel for it first, and then decide."

At the last minute, Noah surprised everyone by deciding to tour with the team. Also touring with the team was Princess, Harlan's little white poodle. Leo, the manager, had hesitated when Harlan asked for permission to bring a dog on tour, but then he said, "Sure, bring her along. She can be the team's mascot."

Various mothers' and daughters' pursuit of Noah had intensified after he was seen in the company of Abigail

Langley at the Fourth of July celebration, and he felt he could not face another dinner hosted by a family with a marriageable daughter. He liked the sweet-natured Eloise, but since the Fourth, her pursuit of him had become relentless.

"Dr. Edwards will come to his senses and realize that preachers can't marry Jezebels," Eloise's mother had advised her daughter. "In the meantime, don't give him a chance to be alone with that woman."

In one of Noah's classes at Harvard, the professor had briefly touched on the subject of the desirability of unwed ministers with a degree attached to their names. But the professor had failed to warn the young men of how persistent the pursuit would be. The crush that the teenage Susan Leffler had on him was more embarrassing than problematic. Noah was glad that between the two friends, it was the timid Susan, and not her friend Jennie Jeanne, who had the crush on him. The attention of that little charmer could definitely turn into a prickly dilemma for any man.

And Abby—what about Abby? He felt responsible for Abby, but what else he was feeling for her, he didn't know. Did he want to keep company with a shunned woman? Did a woman fit into his plans? He had, after all, dedicated himself to God, and to the service of mankind. So, at the last minute, Noah had thrown in the towel, left his church in the care of the Olsen brothers, and gone on tour with the Rockets.

The team consisted of Noah Edwards, George Spencer, Lester Dinwoody, and Harlan Jones; Leo,

Orion, and Sags Langley; Walt Eggers, from the hard-scrabble town of Shantyville; and Ed Kowalski, the only old-timer on the team. Ed worked at the Langley mills, where every good-weather day, the men played ball on their lunch breaks and after work. Kowalski had played in the minor leagues when he was young and was tough and knowledgeable about the game. For the duration of the trip, he took Joe Langley's place as team coach; he also took a ribbing for his Polish accent.

The ten men set off on their ball-playing tour in the Langley mill's lumber wagon, pulled by a team of horses. Leo, as player and manager, had been counseled by his father: "Keep an eye on them. Keep them in check and out of trouble, and win a ball game now and then." They left town with three dozen bats from the supply at River's Bend, stored in the wooden box that was the driver's seat, to sell or barter along the way.

The team played in small towns—some of them with grandstands smaller than Rockville's, and sometimes with cow pastures for fields—and in the first week of their tour won all of their games and again discussed making a career of playing ball. For the time being, however, their ambition was to get paid enough to stop having to pass the hat so they could have something to eat. Most days, if they were lucky, they collected enough in small change to pay for their supper, which consisted of steaks and baked potatoes. For a buck and a half, they could buy potatoes and twelve pounds of beef; they cooked the steaks on the camp stove and the potatoes in the campfire ashes.

They laughed over how fat Princess was getting from chewing on steak bones every day. "She'll soon be fat enough to eat!" they joked. The little white poodle had become everyone's pet.

Sitting around the campfire at night, after winning another ball game that day, the same question always came up: "How good are we, anyway?"

"It's time we found out," Leo said.

They were near Logan, a city with a population of over forty thousand and a team that got paid to play ball. Logan also had a sports store, where the Rockets intended to barter the bats they had brought with them for athletic shoes.

The Rockville Rockets drove the lumber wagon into the Logan sports stadium, the first one they had ever seen. The size and the round shape of it were intimidating. A practice game was in progress, and a handful of men sitting in the grandstand watched with indifference as Leo approached them. "I'd like to talk to the manager," Leo said.

"About what, lumber?" one of the men asked.

"We'd like to play you a game."

"Why, you a ball team?"

Leo clenched his jaw and said nothing.

"They look more like pea pickers to me!" someone called from the players' bench.

Lester drew their attention as he climbed down from the wagon.

"Hey, shorty, what position do you play?" someone called out.

"Shortstop, silly!" one of the players replied.

The player who was up at bat turned away from the pitcher and faced Orion, who was standing near the bleachers. Taking the ball from the catcher's hand, the player tossed it into the air and hit it with bullet speed in Orion's direction. Orion, with effortless grace, ran a few paces, jumped into the air, grabbed the ball, and, in the same easy motion, threw it toward Harlan, who, waiting with bat in hand, connected and blasted the ball into the top tier of seats.

It was their first real ballpark. Their first stadium. Their biggest crowd. And it was Sunday. Sunday was not a day for playing ball—or enjoying oneself in general—and it gave them an uneasy feeling.

Because of the Sunday blue laws, ballplayers in Nebraska, for one, had been incarcerated for up to ten days for playing baseball on Sunday. The blue laws in most of the forty-five states did not permit sports, entertainment, or commerce in any form to take place on the Sabbath.

Noah had held a church service that morning, as he had every Sunday morning of their tour. This Sunday he was trying hard to assure the team that it was all right to play ball on the Sabbath. "Baseball is played in other cities and towns on Sundays; it's just not played in Rockville. For many religions, and many people in the world, the day of worship is on Saturday. In a democracy like ours, state laws, or the laws of the municipality, supersede religious laws. Here in Logan, the law says that baseball can be played between the hours of two and five on Sunday afternoons. And that, gentlemen, is what we're going to do—play ball. Jesus has confidence in us; now let's have confidence in ourselves."

After Noah's pep talk and a sermon about Jesus on the mount, the players, strengthened in spirit, felt mitigated.

It was the top of the ninth and the final inning of a doubleheader with the Logan team. The Rockets had played well, and the score was tied 3–3. Sags was on first, and George on third. Before the pitcher began his windup, Sags flashed a sign to George to try for a double steal, meaning that Sags would take off for second on the next pitch, and, when the catcher threw the ball to second, George, on third, would try for home. The pitcher threw the ball, and Sags took off for second, but the catcher held onto the ball and refused to throw to second, knowing George would score.

On the next pitch, Sags yelled, "Try it again!" He reversed himself and ran back to first base from second. Sags figured the pitcher might throw to first, and then George would score. But nothing happened—there was Sags running like a blue streak from second back to first. The umpire, just as flabbergasted as everyone else, let the play stand. On the next pitch, Sags again took off for second, and the pitcher threw the ball to the second baseman so hard it looked like he was trying to kill him. George took off for home, making the game one up.

The angry home crowd threw rotting vegetables at the Rockets and yelled, swore, and shook their fists at them and the umpire. A police escort had to lead the Rockets from the park. The following day, the lead story on the sports page of the Logan newspaper read:

WE WUZ ROBBED.

How a good ballplayer like our own Charley Smith could shift his batting position and run to third base instead of first can only be explained by the fact that he was confused, as was everyone, by the shenanigans of the Rockville Rockets in a play they pulled off right before he came to bat.

I, for one, as editor and sports writer for this paper, intend to find out if there is a ruling on a player running from second base back to first, or running back from any base. If there is not a ruling, then I will see to it that one to that effect is drawn up immediately.

The Rockville Rockets, triumphant after winning a game against a semipro team, continued to travel through the state in a southerly direction. None of them had been this far south before. They were nearing the river, and the weather had turned hot and humid. This part of the state looked different to them. The people were different. They spoke differently, with a southern drawl; mostly, because of Harlan, wherever the team went, they were eyed suspiciously.

The river town of Bethel had a semipro team, and when Leo approached them about playing a game, their manager, wearing a grimy, sweat-stained red bandanna around his neck, said, "We all heard of y'all. Y'all pulled a fast one on them sissies up in Logan, but not with us'n y'all won't." With a look of satisfactory bravado on his pink, peeling face, he hooked his thumbs under his suspenders, stretching them out and back.

The Bethel ball team, the Bandoleers, were nicknamed the "Rednecks" because of the red kerchiefs they wore tied around their necks when they played ball. The men in the town, to show their support and loyalty for the home team, strutted about during the baseball season also wearing red bandannas.

Bethel was an excessively avid baseball town and didn't take kindly to losing.

When the Rockets appeared on the field for the second game of a doubleheader, the Bandoleers were playing that day; the Rockets faced a sea of waving red bandannas mixed with hoots and catcalls from the stands. None of the Bandoleer supporters took the "hick" team seriously, so their intention was to have fun with them.

Leo cautioned his players, "Stay calm, and play smart."

The stadium's infield was smooth, free of debris and weeds, but the outfield was uneven, with patchy grass and litter strewn across it, which made it easy to lose a ball.

During the game, when Harlan was running for a fly ball, someone ran out onto the field dressed in a white sheet, KKK fashion, with a red bandanna tied around his neck. The specter ran straight for Harlan, flapping the sheet, moving his arms around like a big bird, and shrieking like a banshee. Their joke caused Harlan to miss the fly ball. Those in the grandstand laughed, waved their arms, and made wailing noises. "Whooo!" they wailed. The umpires laughed along with the crowd, and the game remained a tie, with the visiting team up.

The Rockets, their anger tinged with fear, played cautiously, heeding Leo's advice to "play smart." Leo, catching Sags's eyes, warned his hotheaded brother with a sharp shake of his head.

Orion, who was gaining a reputation as a young "smoke baller," liked to come out of the dugout with guns blazing. Today on the mound he was poised, confident, and in command of his pitches. He was throwing the ball in and out and changing speeds, and he struck out the first eight batters he faced, which had a bile-rising, stomach-clawing effect on the Bethel crowd.

The Bandoleers pitcher, the fire-breathing Big Bull Gainey, with a reputation for eating hitters alive, was throwing knuckleballs and leaning back so far his upper body was parallel to the ground. Lester bunted a pop-up ball, and Bull Gainey, not used to bunters, in his scramble to recover the ball stumbled over his own feet, which got Lester to first base. Sags, next up, hit a line drive, but a double play by the Bandoleers got him out at first and Lester out at second.

Harlan was next at bat. In the outfield, a Bandoleers player was yelling and holding aloft a ball. He pointed to the ball, then back to the ground, intimating it had come from there. A planted ball in the outfield? Everyone in the grandstand knew that that's where the black man was playing left field. The anger coming from both teams, and the crowd, was palpable. The spectators in the grandstand began to make their weird "whooo" noises again and flapping their arms.

The umpire called for the ball, examined it, and tossed it to the pitcher. He had gone along with the sheeted disturbance earlier, but this time suspected, and rightly so, that the ball had been dropped by the same Bandoleer outfielder who had found it.

"Play ball!" he shouted.

The grandstand erupted in boos and catcalls, and debris was thrown onto the field.

"Kill the nigger! Kill the nigger!" the crowd chanted.

Harlan, with an iron grip on the bat and perspiration pouring from his scalp, shook his head to clear his eyes.

Whump! The ball soared high and toward the spectators standing in the outfield. Two of the outfielders, running toward each other with their eyes on the ball, were both seeing a different object; when one of them caught what he had his eye on, he found himself holding a wad of unwinding string, and the other player had the ball cover. The Bandoleers' right fielder viciously tore the trailing string from the ball and the cover from the other player's hand, and, jamming one into the other, threw it toward home plate to keep the ball in play.

Harlan, making sure he touched all the bases, galloped across home plate like a thoroughbred, ahead of the wobbling, string-trailing wad, and won the game by one. Again the team had to be escorted from the ballpark and given protection from the angry crowd.

"Tomorrow," Leo said, "we're going to hightail it for home."

Back at their campsite, they talked about packing up and leaving for home that night, but it had been a long, draining day, both physically and emotionally, and it was already twilight.

Leo was the first to hear a noise, and he nudged Sags awake. Quietly they alerted the others. "Who's out there?" Leo yelled.

"We don't want no trouble. Just give up the nigger!" a gravelly voice yelled back.

"We got to teach you folks from up north how to show respect," another querulous voice drawled.

Clouds sailing past the half moon created periods of light and temporarily turned the bodiless voices into shapes. A group of men stood near a row of poplar trees about thirty yards from the camp. The drifting light from the moon warned the men in the wagon of the rabble-rousers' position and told them about how many there were.

"Get the ball bats," Leo whispered. Sags, like a cat, sprang onto the box seat and beat at the peg holding the latch in place. Throwing open the lid, he passed out the bats.

"You stay out of this, Rion," Leo said to his young brother. Everyone was protective of Orion, sensing in the young man something out of the ordinary. "If anything happens to you, Dad will kill me."

"No," Orion answered. "It's my fight, too." He stood on the wagon back to back with Lester.

Harlan handed Princess to Sags, who dropped the barking poodle into the box seat and closed the lid. The rest of the team jumped down from the wagon, with George and the two farmers from Shantyville crawling out from their beds beneath the wagon, and together they met the rush of angry men armed with pitchforks and cudgels.

The sound of gunshots heard above the melee of pounding, kicking, swearing, and yelling startled both sides, causing them to stop in midfight and wonder who had been shot and who was doing the shooting. The Bethel marshal, along with six deputies on horseback, rode into the makeshift camp and rounded up everyone who remained at the scene. Most of the attackers had fled, leaving behind two bodies discernible in the waning light, writhing and moaning. Orion looked at them and said, "Not ours."

The marshal and his men persuaded the Rockets, for their own protection, to go to jail. "You'll be safe there," the marshal promised. "If you're behind bars, they won't get at you."

Leo agreed, on the condition he would be allowed to send a wire to his dad in Rockville. The other men were hesitant, suspecting an ambush.

Sags was badly hurt: blood was gushing from a cut on his head, and he was cradling his right arm. "I can still fight," he boasted.

"I give you my word," the marshal said. "I'm here to protect you." In a flash of moonlight, the gleaming silver star on his chest allayed their fears and made them trust him.

Joe Langley and Marshal McCombs caught the 4:10 out of Rockville the following day and arrived late in the evening in Bethel. At the jail, Mr. Langley tried to wrap his arms around all of his sons, with Lester squeezed into the middle and Sags gasping, "Watch the arm! Watch the arm!"

The marshal and Joe spent the night, along with the team, in jail as guests of the city. Sags had a bandaged head and an arm in a cast. "I got too close to the enemy," he bragged to his father, "and they beaned me. I just wish it had been daylight. I swear I could hear heads cracking." His blue eyes danced as he gave his father his "devil take the hindmost" grin.

"That was your own hot head cracking," Leo said.

In the recounting of the event to Marshal McCombs and Joe Langley, everyone was laughing, some wiping tears from their eyes, with Ed Kowalski the brunt of their jokes. Ed, a deep sleeper, had been the last one to awake and, with no time left to put on his pants, he had fought in his long johns. During the course of the fight, the back flap on his underwear had come unbuttoned and hung down to his knees.

"I thought I was seeing two moons—one up there," Leo said to Joe and the marshal with a nod, "and one in the middle of the brawl. When it was over and Harlan let Princess out of the box, she attacked Ed and bit him on his backside." They laughed wildly, with Princess barking and running from one to the other.

"Yeah, well…" Ed said. Then, shaking his finger at the dog, he added in his broken English, "No more porterhouse steak for you, little sister."

Noah, who was helping the doctor, had an angry, swollen bruise on his own cheek, a black eye, and a bandaged cut on his forehead. He chuckled as he listened to the laughter coming from the front yard outside the doctor's window.

"You should have been a real doctor, Noah. You're pretty good at this healing stuff," George said.

"What I know about medicine I learned from my grandmother," Noah said. "She said that if you put lard on it, sooner or later you're going to heal something."

The Bethel doctor, as he put a splint on George's broken finger, laughed. "And that's about what it adds up to, young fella."

Noah added, "There are times when I wish I'd gone to medical school. I think I could've made a bigger difference in people's lives by healing their broken bodies. Maybe I could've left their souls to others."

"Now, preacher," Leo said, putting a hand on Noah's shoulder, "we like you just the way you are."

The Bethel marshal told the Rockets that they'd put two of the town's troublemakers in the hospital. "So, I guess that makes you the winners of the fracas," he said.

The team returned home by train, and the townspeople turned up at the depot to welcome their heroes home and to parade with them up Main Street to the newspaper office. The whole team was herded into the small lobby of the *Hub*, where Sam took down the accounts of the game, and the fight, from each player.

The following day, a special edition of the paper, a keepsake copy, was given out free at the *Hub* office with a copy of it on display in the window: ROCKETS WALLOP REDNECKS—TWICE.

CHAPTER 34

Phoebe Griggsby, Brother Griggsby's wife, had walked past the Bon Marché many times during the first weeks of the store's opening but had never entered. At closing time on the fourth Saturday of its opening, she paused near the door and, seeing no one in the shop, darted inside.

"Sister Abigail," she said breathlessly, "if you please, would it be all right if I tried on the hat?" She looked about nervously and added, "Somewhere I can't be seen. The good brother would never forgive such vainglory."

Abby removed the hat from the window and retired to the workroom with Phoebe, along with the coral silk chiffon scarf that had covered the display stand. After drawing the curtain separating the two rooms, Abby had Mrs. Griggsby sit down facing the long mirror that hung on the wall of the workroom. Abby stood in front of the mirror and draped the silk fabric across Phoebe's shoulders and bosom, concealing the unbecoming dress she was wearing.

She picked up the large bottle of her grandmother's lavender lotion she kept in the workroom for her own use and patted some on Mrs. Griggsby's cheeks and chin, smoothing it onto her skin. Next she sprinkled talcum on a puff and lightly powdered Phoebe's face, expertly hiding the ruddiness of her rosacea and giving her instead the blush of youth. She then arranged the stylish hat on Mrs. Griggsby's head, tucked in stray wisps of graying hair, and stepped away from the mirror.

The preacher's wife gasped in disbelief. Surely, this was not she, not Phoebe Griggsby, gaping back at her. She took the ivory hand mirror Abby was offering and, smiling, turned her head from side to side, eyes transfixed on her reflection. Soon the lovely expression faded from her face and, with shoulders drooping, she handed the mirror back to Abby. "Thank you," she whispered, not looking at her. Her ruddy, sandpapery hands made little rasping sounds on the silk scarf as she pulled it from her shoulders and handed it, and the hat, to Abby.

"Wait," Abby said, placing a restraining hand on her arm. "Everyone who comes into the shop during my grand opening receives a gift." She picked up the large bottle of lotion and pressed it into the woman's hands. "I'm afraid I've run out of gift bottles," Abby said as a way of explaining the size and plainness of the container. The startled woman placed the gift in her string bag and left the store.

Abby remained in the workroom after Mrs. Griggsby's departure. Draping the silk scarf around her neck, she held the hat high above her head, rapturously arched and stretched her back, and rotated her shoulders to relieve her tired muscles. Swaying back and forth and looking up at the hat, she reflected on all the women who had tried on the hat since she'd first opened her store. After taking them all into consideration, she wished Mrs. Griggsby could have owned the hat. *But nothing this frivolous would ever be seen on the head of our good preacher's wife,* she thought.

"Put it on," a voice commanded her.

Abby whirled about.

Noah stood in the doorway of her workroom, grinning at her.

"Noah Edwards, you about scared me half to death!"

Noah, dusty and disheveled and face streaked with dirt, with a black eye, a bruise on his cheek, and a bandage on his forehead, his blond hair sweat-pressed to his head from the cap he now held in his hand, had just finished his account of the Rockets' baseball tour to the *Hub* newspaper editor. "Put it on," he said again, in a teasing tone this time.

Abby shook her head.

"Please?"

Abby, her heart racing, hesitated. She very much wanted Noah to see her in the hat. With much fortitude of character, she thought, she resisted the act of vainglory that Mrs. Griggsby could not and carried the hat into the shop, with Noah following.

"It's merchandise and not to be worn by the help."

"Not even when the help is the owner?"

"*Especially* when the help is the owner," she said, placing the hat in the window. "And why did you stop by?" she asked in a bantering tone of voice. "To try on the hat?"

"No, to see you in it," Noah said, his blue eyes sparkling as he flashed a boyishly charming smile at her. "If you won't model the hat for me, will you at least have a soda with me next door at the drugstore?"

Abby, happy to see him, and in high spirits from her success of the past week, readily accepted his invitation.

CHAPTER 35

IN THE INTIMATE DARKNESS OF late Saturday night, after the streetlights had been extinguished, the Bon Marché had its last window shopper. A man stood before the display window, running his tongue back and forth across his lower lip while contemplating the hat. A dull glimmer in the corner of the window caught his attention. He looked slyly about before striking a match. The light revealed a small gold easel holding a dainty, hand-painted sign that read EAR PIERCING PERFORMED IN PRIVACY. Pressing his forehead to the glass and cupping his eyes with his hands, he strained to see into the interior of the store. A rose from his heavy breathing bloomed on the cool windowpane.

The man began to tremble. Perspiration beaded his brow, and soon his whole body was shaking as his hands squeaked down the glass, leaving behind two smears of sweaty tracks.

Brother Griggsby pushed himself away from the window and, with unsteady steps, disappeared into the night.

When he reached home, he took up a lighted kerosene lamp and peered into the bedroom at his sleeping wife, who was lying on her back, mouth open, while emitting snoring sounds. He could see that her eyelids and cheeks bore crusted tearstains. Quietly closing the door, he climbed the narrow stairway to the attic.

The attic served as a study for Brother Griggsby when he desired peace and a hideaway when he needed escape. The alcove room housed mementos, books, religious pamphlets, packing cartons, and a table, chair, and cot. He retrieved a flat-topped trunk from beneath a pile of books. He dragged it into the lamp's circle of light and unlocked it with a key he kept on his watch fob.

The soft lamplight played on the trunk's contents: silks and laces, gossamer dresses of delicately colored chiffons. Corsets, lace, and beribboned corset covers, black lisle hose, flowery satin wrappers, and flowing nightgowns. His fleshy hands rippled through the apparel and, with senses exalted, he fondled the accoutrements. Greedily he breathed in the musky, womanly scent and thrilled to the luxurious feel and smell of each piece, trailing it across his face before dropping them one by one onto the cot.

At the bottom of the trunk, hidden beneath a piece of cardboard, rested his treasure trove of pictures: pictures of women's hats trimmed in flowers, feathers, and ribbons, and images of corsets and shoes. An advertisement, torn from a magazine cover, showed a woman in corset and slip with an abundance of supple bosom; the ad guaranteed that, if used faithfully, the balm would enlarge a woman's breasts in two to six months. A cracked and worn tintype showed two men dressed in women's lingerie. After carefully perusing the pictures, Brother Griggsby placed them back in the trunk and once again tried the attic door, making doubly sure it was locked and bolted.

Quickly undressing, he donned a woman's corset, excited fingers fastidiously fastening each tiny hook. He pulled on black lisle hose, securing them with blue satin garters, and he slipped his feet into red slippers with black dragons embroidered on the toes. He dabbed daintily at his full lips and plump cheeks with the remains of a ruby-red balm, extracted with the tip of his little finger from a small glass jar. Stepping back, he rubbed his lips together and looked with admiration at the coy image reflected back at him in the large, cracked wall mirror.

Encouraged, he placed a bandeau with varied-colored rhinestones on a black satin ribbon on his head, a white plume of feathers protruding upright from its center. His toilette completed, he minced about the room before sitting on the cot and languidly fanning himself with a white lace fan with a broken rib. Finally, extinguishing the lamp, he lay down. After he'd covered himself with his cherished collection of ladies' garments, a low, ecstatic moan escaped from his throat and into the dark, airless room.

At daybreak Brother Griggsby rose and, with a sense of immediacy, threw the garments into the trunk, tearing at the ones on his body as if entrapped in some loathsome net. In the innocence of the early-morning light, the tawdriness of the clothes was discernible to him: it was merely a pile of threadbare, soiled, perspiration-stained, worn-out, and outmoded clothing that was forced on every parsonage by virtuous church members seeking a dumping ground for their castoffs.

The brother checked behind the cot and under it, making sure he'd overlooked nothing before he slammed the trunk shut and locked it. From a carton on the floor, he brought forth a bottle whose label read ELIXIR OF FIGS.

"One dose and your system will be purged of all impurities," the label on the bottle promised. "Why suffer from gastritis, bloating, heartburn, nervousness, nausea, headache, upset stomach, and constipation, when one tablespoon of Elixir of Figs will relieve you of these symptoms?"

Tipping back his head, the good brother drained the bottle.

CHAPTER 36

EACH SUNDAY MORNING, BEFORE THE beginning of the church service, Noah presented an organ recital. The worshipers who packed his small church sat quietly, heads bowed, while the music soothed their minds and filled them with peace. On this particular Sunday morning, men with bandaged arms and fingers—along with bruises, bumps, and black eyes—could be seen among the parishioners; their minister was one of them.

In general, Noah never looked up during the quarter hour of playing. Sometimes he brought to mind his sermon, sometimes he prayed, or, as on this morning, he rewarded himself with the spell of the music.

Today, when the last strains of the organ drifted away, he raised his head and saw—the hat. She sat ever so demurely, head bowed, gloved hands folded in her lap. *Ah, woman, the loveliest of all God's creations,* he thought.

Abby raised her head, and her eyes met his subtle look of approval. *I wore the hat just for you,* her expression implied.

Noah, remembering yesterday, was thinking that she wouldn't wear the hat in her little shop when the two of them had been alone, but she could sit there in his church on a Sunday morning, more captivating than she'd ever been, and tantalize him while he preached a sermon. *Vanity, thy name is Abigail,* he thought, *and I fear I'm falling in love with you.*

Lars Larson gave the opening prayer, the congregation sang, and Noah, leaving his sermon notes on the organ, approached the podium. Today's sermon would be extemporaneous.

"This morning I'm going to speak to you on the subject of beauty—the beauty of our love for God, and the beauty of God's love for us. The beauty of the world He has given us. The beauty of the love a man has for a woman, a woman for her child, and children for their parents; the beauty of friendship, family, and home. I may even touch on women's bonnets."

The last remark induced gentle chuckling and amiable smiles from his congregation.

Here and there in the otherwise colorless surroundings of Old Church, flowers beautified the hats some of the women wore. Although the decorated hats were sparse, they bloomed prettily in the drab hall like a promise of spring. The congregation buoyantly sang the opening song; the usually dull Sabbath was close to one of gaiety.

Brother Griggsby stepped to the lectern. He appeared wan, his face drawn, and whenever he made a sudden movement, he seemed to wince in pain. In a ponderous voice of doom, he began the morning service.

"Wo-man—thy name is ev-il," he said, separating each syllable for emphasis. "The word *ev-il* originated with her, that first woman in the Garden of Eden. Eve was not the child of God. No! That first woman was carved from the rib of man and shaped to corrupt. She was brought into being with the cunning to entice man from his Godly state. Forged from an earthly bone, what did she remember of the glories of heaven? She listened to snakes and vipers. She conspired with snakes and vipers, and because of her, because of woman, the world knows sin, and wickedness, and lust, and shame, and vanity, and ev-il."

Nodding his head in a foreboding motion, his piercing eyes surveyed the decorated hats. "Clothes are to cover your nakedness, not to excite men to lust. Hats are to keep your heads warm in winter and cool in summer and to hide you from His eyes in His house. His house is a place of worship, not a showplace for women's finery!"

He was ranting, his fingers jabbing at them, his face an enraged red. "God created woman to serve man, to be man's perfect mate. Woman's duty is to keep her body perfect for him. Your body is not for mutilating. It is not for piercing." He tugged at his earlobe as he recalled the little sign in the window of the Bon Marché. "Anything done to decorate your bodies that can't be performed in public, or spoken of in public, or even thought about in public, is a sin." He leaned over the pulpit, enunciating each word. "Sin and vanity will lead you on the path straight to hell."

The flowers on the hats of the women in his congregation appeared to be wilting. This phenomenon, however, came from the wearers shrinking in their seats in order to avoid the condemnation of Brother Griggsby and the disapproval of the ladies of the flowerless hats.

Following the service at Old Church, the congregation gravitated to the center of town. The women of the flowered hats, their self-esteem flayed to chaff by their minister's rebuke, surreptitiously glanced toward the window of the Bon Marché, expecting to see the errant hat that had led to their fall from grace. But today, in place of the sinful hat, a lovely bouquet of flowers greeted their grievous stares.

At the Chapel of the Ark on this lovely day, Dr. Noah Edwards was concluding his sermon. "Woman, mother of the universe, thou art beauty. Thou art good, and merciful, and charitable, and yes, at times, stubborn, and illogical, and exasperating." Faces beamed and heads bobbed in agreement. "And pure, and modest, and faithful, and just. As you are God's helpmate in heaven, so you are man's helpmate here on earth. Woman—thy name is sacred."

CHAPTER 37

October 1906

Dr. Townsend was delighted with the notoriety the new store was causing. He had heard about the hat sermons and was hoping that, as the first customer of the Bon Marché, he had added to the debate and to the misery the store had caused Brother Griggsby. It also made the doctor supremely secure in his choice of Abigail as the dressmaker for Aunt Em's Arizona wardrobe.

During the first week of November, Abby was at the mansion for the final fitting of Aunt Em's traveling suit. Even after several fittings and visits, she was still reticent about entering the very private bedroom of Aunt Em and Dr. Townsend. Today the masculine room—with its dark carved furniture and high, canopied bed—still held vestiges of the doctor's morning toilette: a basin of soapy water on the shaving stand, soiled towels, and the lingering masculine scent of bay rum and talcum powder. The pink-marble fireplace, with carved nude goddesses entwined in grapevines holding aloft the stone mantel, contained the dying embers of the early-morning fire, now covered in gray ash.

A tintype of the first Mrs. Townsend, seated and with a young boy standing beside her chair, was displayed in a silver frame on a corner table next to a large brown leather Morris recliner.

Aunt Em, still as slim as an adolescent girl, was at last getting excited about the trip and pranced about in her lingerie without any outward sign of embarrassment, accustomed as she was to seeing humans in all stages of undress.

Abby grimaced at the sight of the large scar on Aunt Em's upper-left arm, from a smallpox vaccination done by an application of serum from a real pox that was scratched into her skin with a piece of broken glass when she was a child. It made Abby thankful the scar was trivial.

Aunt Em, seemingly aware of Abby's anxiety, rubbed her fingers over the shiny pink skin covering the large scar. "I've seen worse scars than mine—some the size of my hand, and others with lumps on them as big as boils. The outcome depends on the skill of the person who's doing the scratching, but it beats having the pox." She laughed and added, "I've never in my life had silk underwear. I hope the doctor likes them."

"Well, he ordered them," Abby said. "He came into the store with his list made out and knew exactly what he wanted."

"This hat is just not me," Aunt Em said, planting the hat on her head.

Abby had designed the hat to match the green gabardine traveling suit. The hat was trimmed in fur that matched the chinchilla cape and muff that lay on the bed next to the fancy box from the Marshall Field's store in Chicago, the one the furs and pieces of pelts had arrived in.

Abby rubbed her hand over the fur cape. "It's beautiful!" she said reverently.

"Try it on," Aunt Em said.

"Oh, I couldn't."

"Of course you can. I want to see what kind of an impression I'm going to make at that fancy resort the doctor's taking me to."

Abby removed the hat from Aunt Em's head and, after carefully arranging it on her own head, wrapped herself in the cool lushness of the cape and stood before the mirror, enraptured. She pushed her hands into the pockets of the luxurious fur and posed, turning left and right, then walked about the room, delighting in the effect.

"You're a sight for sore eyes," Aunt Em said.

Abby glided across the room and positioned the hat, just so, on Aunt Em's head. They were both laughing, confidentially, like best friends. Abby grew quiet, the laughter dying on her lips. She wanted Aunt Em to know. She wanted to share her deepest, darkest secret with her. Looking into her eyes, she said, "There is something I want to tell you."

Aunt Em made a negative motion with her head and, placing her fingers over Abby's mouth, tapped on her lips like she was sealing them shut, terminating for all time the confession.

Abby was hurt and disappointed, and the intimacy of the morning was broken. Did Aunt Em suspect what she was going to say, and, if so, why had she stopped her? Why couldn't she tell her best friend, her second mother, her secret—the name of the father of her child?

It was a week before the Thanksgiving holiday. Dr. Townsend, with Aunt Em in the cab of the carriage, rode to the station followed by Meiko Toma in the Survivall wagon loaded with steamer trunks, cases, and hatboxes. It was a cold, rainy November day, yet the train station and the depot yard were filled with well-wishers, all there to wish Aunt Em a speedy recovery and to wave them off. No one could remember seeing Aunt Em looking so worldly, and they became shy in her presence.

Aunt Em was at last in style, dressed in a slim tight skirt and a small neat jacket cropped at the waist. The matching hat, sitting properly on her head, enhanced the green in her hazel eyes, which today had their old sparkle to them. The traveling suit Abby had made for her was of a lightweight bottle-green wool gabardine in the very latest style—new to Aunt Em because it covered her ankles. The fur cape hung nonchalantly from her shoulders, with the muff dangling from her wrist, and small diamonds shone from her earlobes. It was one of the few times when the town had been made privy, in some small measure, to the extent of Dr. Townsend's wealth.

CHAPTER 38

December 1906

IT WAS CHRISTMAS, AND "HARK! The Herald Angels Sing" could be heard on the streets of Rockville. Two new stores had opened in town since Christmas last: just east of the *Hub* newspaper, the Music Arcade, owned by an entertaining young married couple, Donald and Dovie Vaughn, newcomers to town, and a men's haberdashery store called Andre Fontell Clothiers, Esq., located across the street. The Carlton Real Estate Company, with headquarters in the capital city, had opened a branch in Rockville and had purchased from Old Church the church's frontage on Main Street. The company's plan was to line the block with new businesses. Rockville was on the move, and its big-city expansion endowed everyone who lived there with an air of importance.

The Music Arcade sold phonographs and records, pianos and sheet music. The Vaughns both played piano, and the lively sounds of the latest hit music could be heard coming from the new store almost any hour of the day. A nickelodeon theater located in a back room of the Arcade seated twelve customers. For the price of a nickel, customers could sit on a stiff-backed chair, choose from a selection of a dozen films of real events (such as the Great San Francisco Earthquake of 1906), and watch one that ran for two minutes. For a dime, they could watch a thrilling, twelve-minute moving picture show such as *The Great Train Robbery*.

Noah picked up a new tailored suit from Fontell Clothiers and stopped by the Music Arcade to purchase a few phonograph records. Singing along with the Christmas music coming from the Arcade, Noah paused at the window of the Bon Marché, where a porcelain figurine displayed in the window caught his eye. He went inside to investigate.

Inside, Abby removed the eight-inch statuette of a young woman from the window and placed it in his hands. The model was a replica of a southern belle wearing a dress of blue ruffles and a straw bonnet with a blue ribbon tied beneath her chin. A collie was at her side.

"I'd like to give this to a young lady for Christmas," he said as he handed it back to her. The blissful expression on the face of the sculpture reminded him of the blind Mary Louise.

Abby bent to the task of wrapping the figurine in Christmas paper and tying the package with a red bow. Noah sat on the vanity seat admiring the gracefulness of Abby's movements and the beautiful cameo image of her head rising above the high collar of the filmy rose-chiffon blouse she was wearing with a dark-green skirt.

His eyes, tracing the tiny row of buttons extending from waist to neck along the curve of her back, caused a pleasurable awakening in his loins.

While watching her, Noah took into account what Abby's life would be like if she hadn't had a child. She would in all probability be married, he thought, and automatically he began to match her up with the eligible men of the town; he soon concluded that none of them were good enough for her. He was surprised to find that admitting this made his heart beat faster, and he found himself overcome with a feeling of proprietorship.

As Abby worked, she rebuked herself for the stab of jealousy she had felt when Noah had admitted that he wished to purchase the figurine as a gift for a young woman. She reminded herself that they were friends, nothing more. Dr. Edwards could never be interested in her in a sentimental way, she knew.

"Will you join me for Christmas dinner at the ark?" he suddenly asked.

Happily surprised but still smarting with the knowledge that he was purchasing a gift for a young lady, Abby nonetheless accepted his invitation. "Only if you will let me bring something. Dessert? I love to make desserts." Her raised brows arched charmingly over her dark-green eyes, which were large in anticipation of making a dessert for someone she admired. "Or, let me help Rosie cook. Please, I love to cook, and I never get to do it—well, not for someone else, anyway." Embarrassed by acknowledging the solitude of her life, she turned away.

"I'll do better than that," he said, placing his hands on her shoulders and turning her to face him. "I'll let you cook the whole dinner. Rosie's going out of town, and she's driving me loco from worrying about me."

The warmth flaming in Abby's cheeks flooded into her eyes.

That evening, Noah delivered the doll to Mary Louise. Her little hands felt all around the figure. She knew it was a woman in a long dress. "What color is her dress?" she asked him.

"You tell me," Noah said.

Mary Louise laughed, tipping her head sideways, and said, "You know I can't do that."

"Of course you can. If you want to badly enough, you can."

"But I'm blind!" She was unaccustomed to being denied anything; her voice quivered, and for once she was not smiling. With lowered head, she traced the outline of the doll with her fingers. "What is the little animal standing at her side?" she said with a sniffle.

"Someday you'll tell me, Mary Louise," Noah said with assurance.

She brightened. "I think it's Mary and her little lamb!"

"Or maybe it's Little Red Riding Hood and a big bad wolf," Noah said, joking along with her.

"Or Goldie Locks and the big bad bear," Grandma chimed in.

Thinking of all the possibilities, Mary Louise issued a long, sighing "Oh," and, trying to see through her blindness, stared very hard at the doll. For the first time since Noah had known her, Mary Louise wept.

"Ah," Grandma said with compassion, but Noah, moving his hands back and forth, mouthed the word "Good" and nodded his encouragement. Holding her hands in his, Noah sat beside the unhappy girl. "Do you want to see the doll with all your heart, Mary Louise?"

"Yes, with all my heart," she answered in a timorous voice.

"It will be hard work, but I believe you can do it."

Noah told her that the doll was to sit on the dresser in her bedroom, and every night, she was to look in the direction of the doll and pray to Jesus. "Tell Him that the first thing you want to see when you wake up in the morning is the doll. It will take time and will depend on how badly you want to see for yourself the color of her dress and what kind of animal is at her side." He then added for Grandma's benefit, "And Grandma can't help you."

He lifted the girl onto his lap. "Your eyes are perfect, Mary Louise, because God made them so. God gave you the gift of sight, and with your unwavering faith in Him, He will return the gift to you. Your desire to see the doll will make it so. You must go to bed every night believing that when you awaken in the morning, you will see the doll. Will you do that, Mary Louise?"

She sat glumly, not answering.

"Will you do it for me?"

The little coquette in Mary Louise returned. Looking up at him through wet lashes, her lips in a pout, she said, "Yes. I'll do it for you."

On Christmas night, Noah and Abby stood on the deck of his rooftop home, a couple bidding their guests good night. Abby was still glowing from the compliments she had received on her dinner. Frieda had lavishly praised her flaming plum pudding, and Mary Louise had been delighted with the description and taste of the jewellike fruit gelatin—a commercial dessert so new that most people had not tried it. Donald Vaughn, the only male guest, could not say enough about the tenderness of the standing rib roast, and Dovie said Abby should give cooking lessons. Grandma Richards, squeezing Abby's hand, said her rolls were better than any she could have "boughten in a bakery."

Each guest received a sugar cookie with his or her name written on it in colored frosting. The cookies hung from the scented branches of the fir Christmas tree, which Noah had chopped down the previous day and dragged home by a rope tied to his saddle horn, to be set up in the living room.

Big flakes of snow, made colorful by the lights from inside Noah's home, fell softly on them as they watched Donald tuck a fur robe around the three women in the back seat of his sleigh before climbing into the front seat beside Dovie and jingling away into the night.

Noah and Abby remained on the deck viewing the town through the snow. Noah, after nobly draping his coat around Abby, casually left his arm across her shoulders. "I can't thank you enough for giving me such a perfect Christmas Day," he said, close to her ear.

"You mustn't thank me. I should be the one thanking you," she said, turning her head to look up at him, his lips almost brushing her cheek. "Truly, I enjoyed doing it."

Reluctantly surrendering to the cold, they went inside. Abby held her hands out to the warmth of the stove, and Noah fed another lump of coal into the stove's round belly.

So great was her relief in knowing who had received the gift of the doll he had purchased from her store that she chided him with her knowledge. "Mary Louise confided in me that you gave her the little figurine, and she says she is not to play with it."

"I'm trying to build enough confidence in her, and I hope enough faith, to see again."

"Well, if anyone can build confidence in a girl, you certainly can," Abby said, feeling a bubbling sensation stirring within her. "Look what you did for me." Spreading her arms wide and smiling triumphantly, she twirled away from the stove.

So rapidly did he cover the space between them that it took them both by surprise. Taking her in his arms, he kissed her long and ardently, with her mouth answering his in return. To conceal their embarrassment in the passion of the unexpected kiss, they both began to clear dishes from the dining room table.

"After the ball is over, after the break of morn..." Noah sang, a towel tucked into the waistband of his trousers. He dried the dishes as Abby washed them.

"After the break of day," she added.

Noah, surprised by the melodious sound of her voice, wondered if there was anything she couldn't do. Then, remembering her moral transgression, he abruptly stopped singing and said with exaggerated firmness, "I've got to get you home, young lady."

They rode home in the buggy by way of Elm Street, where parlor windows gleaming with Christmas candles shone brightly into the darkness of the night. At her door they held hands, both effusively thanking each other again.

They did not share a good-night kiss.

In the kitchen, Abby lit a coal-oil lamp to illuminate her way up the stairs. In her bedroom, knowing she was too elated to sleep, she removed a quilt from the top of the hope chest forlornly stationed at the foot of her bed. She set the lamp on a chair beside her and, kneeling, opened the chest.

Inside the trunk of dreams were household linens, all made by her in the hope of someday proudly sharing them with a husband. She removed each piece, exquisitely embroidered and hemmed with fine lace, and laid them neatly in a pile beside her until she reached the very first entry in the chest: a set of embroidered dish towels she'd made when she was eight years old. She wept into her childhood dream: tears for old dreams, and tears for ones she dared not even give consideration to. For the first time since the birth of her baby, she had not thought of him or his father.

CHAPTER 39

February 1907

On a cloudless day in late February, once the country roads were clear of snow, Noah drove Abby the fifteen miles to the Langley ranch to visit her grandmother and her uncle Pete. Noah's housekeeper's twelve-year-old niece, Mary Lou, had been pressed into serving as chaperone for Noah and Abby when, at the last minute, Rosie was needed elsewhere.

Grandma welcomed them at the front door. Stepping outside onto the porch, she removed her apron and threw it over a hen roosting there on a cane-bottomed chair. She picked up the chicken, still covered with her apron, and carried it to the woodpile, where she chopped off its head. Later in the day, Abby, Noah, and their chaperone were treated to a Sunday dinner of chicken and dumplings.

Arthritic Uncle Pete, from the confines of his invalid's chair, showed Noah some of the intricate wood carvings he had once made; he insisted on giving Noah a miniature replica of the biblical ark he had made, along with several pairs of animals to go with it. The young chaperone spent the day playing with the ark and pairing the carved animals.

Uncle Pete, being hard of hearing, said loudly to Noah, "I ain't through with the animals yet. I aims to have two of every living critter before I'm finished. When the weather's hot and dry, my old hands can carve, but it tain't often."

"Els Olsen carves, too," Noah said, raising his voice so Pete could hear him.

"Yeah, Els is a good whittler. Him and Ole stops out here from time to time. Ole does a layin' on of hands fer me. It rids me of pain and lasts a pretty fair time, too." The loud talk and long conversation soon winded him, and he lay his head back on the pillow.

Grandma brewed one of her pain-relieving herb teas for him, and he sat sipping the tea while his deformed hands absorbed the comfort of the heat emanating from the large cup.

Grandma was so pleased that Abby had a beau that she was smiling and hugging her granddaughter the whole of the afternoon. Delighted with the matchup, she later confided to Pete, "The man's got religion, but he's nobody's fool, and he's a college graduate, to boot."

Noah invited them to the Easter celebration he was planning: an all-day outing to take place lakeside at an old abandoned stone quarry. "We'll have a sunrise service, followed by a picnic, and then we'll fly kites."

Abby stared at him wide-eyed. Noah laughed. “I was keeping it as a surprise.”

“I’ve heard of sunrise services,” Grandma said, “but I don’t know about flying kites.”

“Why not?” Noah said. “I think Jesus meant for us to enjoy ourselves. Maybe, when God rested on the seventh day, He flew a kite or played ball.”

It was after dark when Noah escorted Abby to her front door. “I won’t come in,” he said.

“I know—you have to get our chaperone home,” she said teasingly, smiling and nodding toward the sleeping girl. She touched his cheek with her fingertips, and he caught her hand, pressing it against his lips and kissing her fingers.

After the people of Rockville had enjoyed a balmy February, March came in with heavy snow and high winds before calming to its storied “come in like a lion and go out like a lamb”. The *Old Farmer’s Almanac* had forecast bright sun and gentle breezes for the last day of the month, which bode well for the kite fliers.

Abby, enraptured with the whole idea of spending Easter out of doors, went all out with decorated cakes, eggs painted in intricate designs, and a new hat befitting the occasion.

It was still dark when Orion and Sags, along with the twins, stopped to pick up Abby in the surrey wagon.

Aunt Rose and Uncle Joe followed in the lumber wagon with Aries and Percy and Grandma and Grandpa Mosley. All of the brothers had kites with them and were taking excessive care not to entangle the tails and strings or puncture the delicate paper bodies made from tissue paper or newsprint.

The twins, already pushing and shoving each other, grew even grumpier when they had to squeeze together to make room for Frieda Johnson and her bowl of potato salad.

Noah met the wagon with Abby in it and, looking at her with affection, encircled her waist with his hands and lifted her over the wagon wheel.

Sawhorse tables, hauled in from the lumber mill and set up the day before, were covered with white tablecloths and secured with rocks at the corners until laden with food, when the rocks were no longer needed.

By the time all the members of the Chapel of the Ark had arrived at the quarry and assembled at the water's edge, the sky had lightened. As the group waited in the eerie stillness of the predawn light for the sun to rise, a mysterious cloud of vapor, bright and dense as quicksilver, rose from the lake and, moving onto the shore, soon engulfed them.

The cloud, as heavy as mourning, shrouded the ghostly sycamores, wept with the willows, and filled each person with a terrible longing. Grouped together, yet separate from one another, they apprehensively breathed the damp air and nervously waited for the bewildering haze to lift.

From out of the dark, Noah's disembodied voice came to them.

"Let not your heart be troubled, neither let it be afraid."

After what seemed an eternity, a gossamer shade of lavender appeared in the mist, followed by iridescent lights of purple, rose, and gold. In a triumphant burst of blazing color, the rising sun rolled away the cloud of darkness, and the shining splendor of Easter morn was upon them.

Noah stood a few paces apart from the group, head bowed. Rays of the early sun stealing through the branches of the sycamore trees dappled his blond hair with gold and shone with tenderness upon the faces of his worshipers. When Noah turned toward them, his eyes were damp.

Following a moment of compelling silence, he called them to the morning devotional. "Lord of all that is glorious, this morning, in a very dramatic way, we, too, have experienced the darkness and the silence of Jesus's tomb and, in the rolling away of the cloud, have borne witness to the blessed miracle of life everlasting. Through your agony, Jesus, we have learned forgiveness; in your death, we have learned serenity; and in your resurrection, we have learned to believe."

Noah was looking at Abby, but his eyes were not focused on her; instead, he appeared to be aware of something at a great distance.

Noah's sunrise sermon that Easter morning was the story of the resurrection of Jesus told to the people in Noah's own words. He told of the darkness of the tomb and the rolling away of the stone at the mouth of the cave and the coming of the light of Jesus unto the world.

"Let us raise our voices," he said, leading them in the hymn "Come, Christians, Join to Sing."

Later, considering the mystical happening of the early morning, Noah was in a jovial mood. He sat for a short time at each picnic table and on the ground with those who had spread quilts on the grass. He ate of the many different foods—keeping an eye to Rosie Kandel, who could be jealous of others' cooking—and praised the weather, the bonnets, and the dyed eggs.

Before they had finished eating, young people from the other churches in town, their Easter services over for the day, began to arrive—young women because they were interested in one or another of the Langley brothers, and young men because they wanted to fly kites.

Nearly everyone present was new at kite flying, and a few people had early disappointments, but the Olsen brothers, Els and Ole, entertained everyone with their expertise at keeping the kites in the air and gave each child the thrill of holding onto an airborne kite. The kites, made during classes held at the ark by the Olsens each Saturday morning in March, glided gracefully, sometimes erratically or comically, as they swooped over the cavernous yawn of the quarry.

Noah helped Abby fly the kite he had made, telling her when to pull it in and when to let it soar. The congregation knew their pastor was sweet on Abby, so they watched the couple's conduct as much as the kites.

Surprising the Easter revelers, Dr. Townsend showed up at the celebration and delighted everyone when he helped a sprightly Aunt Em from his carriage. Aunt Em appeared in good health and was as jolly as ever, although she was forbidden, at this time, to attend to the ills of the town. Now the people would have to depend on Dr. Townsend alone to treat them.

The Arizona travelers had returned to town two days earlier. No one had been at the station to welcome them because only Meiko Toma had been informed of their return. Now, seeing their beloved Aunt Em for the first time since Thanksgiving, they all crowded around the chair provided for her. When it came Abby's turn to greet her, Aunt Em reached out her arms to her and, giving her a big hug, whispered into her ear, "Bless you, Abby; thanks to you, I was the most stylish woman in all of Arizona."

Ole Olsen gave Aunt Em a kite to fly, and younger children made her gifts of their most-prized eggs. The women forced plates of food on her and were disappointed when they saw how picky her appetite was—in their opinion, she looked poorly. "Nothing but skin and bones," they whispered.

The following week, Lars Larson and Noah were preparing the chapel for Sunday service when Noah stopped. Facing Lars, he said, "What's bothering you, Lars? Something is, so let's have out with it."

"I think it's none of my business, but I think I'll make it my business." He flicked his polishing cloth at the bench he was dusting.

The small muscles on either side of Noah's mouth tightened to whiteness. "Say it."

"I think, lad, it's not wise to be seen with Abigail Langley, not a man in your position." He lowered his eyes.

"The people in this town are better at producing gossip than they are children," Noah said, "and that's pretty darn prolific." Noah did have to wonder, however, about the propriety of flaunting a woman with an invisible scarlet letter on her bosom before his congregation.

"Well, they gossiping aplenty, all right," Lars concluded in his singsong dialect.

The gossip of a possible affair between Abby and Noah had caused business to fall off at the Bon Marché, but looking at hats was something women couldn't resist for too long. What's more, to everyone's chagrin, women from the city were coming to town just to purchase hats from the Bon Marché. This turned out to be good for the town, and since the women shoppers had to spend the night somewhere, it made for good business and a lively dinner hour at the Parlett Hotel.

The ark's flock did not grow smaller, but it did become quieter. The Langleys were noncommittal, and the Scandinavians were not their usual happy selves.

The townswomen, no matter what sect they belonged to, couldn't understand why Noah Edwards and Leo Langley, the two most eligible bachelors in town, preferred the company of questionable women: the town adulteress and an Italian singer.

"Abby is going to church regularly," someone said at the Tuesday Benevolent Society meeting.

"Well, if just going to church sanctified us, we'd all be as pure as the driven snow," Perthy Prettyman declared.

A few teens whose parents preferred they not attend Noah's church missed the Friday night gatherings at the ark, and the remaining teenagers showed an unaccustomed restraint toward their popular minister.

"He won't marry Abigail Langley," one of the young girls said.

"Why not?"

"You know, she's an adulteress," the girl whispered.

"Says who?"

"My mother. She says everyone knows it."

"Knows what?"

"You know," she said, grimacing and hunching her shoulders, "she did it with a married man."

CHAPTER 40

April 1907

THE FOLLOWING WEEK, REGARDLESS OF the gossip about its minister, the ark's Wednesday night prayer meeting went on as usual. Little blind Mary Louise was there and shared a poem she had composed with the group. Dressed in a black jumper with a pink ruffled blouse and pink bows in her hair, she stood in the middle of the prayer circle and recited her poem. "My poem is titled 'In His Garden,'" she said.

> I am just a little flower,
> One who cannot see,
> But with every sunbeam's kiss,
> I feel His love for me.
> It's love that fills His garden
> And makes the rain to fall.
> It's love that paints the rainbows,
> And makes the songbirds call.

His love does not play favorites;
It shines on one and all.

It was an early-spring morning in May when Mary Louise, with faithful expectations, turned her eyes toward the doll, as she did every day, and saw a faint haziness. "I can see!" she excitedly called out to her grandmother. When her grandmother entered the room, Mary Louise said, "I can see the doll, and you, and the room." She was kneeling on the bed and flinging her arms about her, laughing and quickly opening and closing her eyes.

On Tuesday night, when Noah arrived at Grandma Richards's house for his hour of reading to them from the novel *Little Women*, followed by prayers and meditations, Mary Louise was not seated in her usual place on the sofa, and Grandma, her cheeks a bright pink, looked flustered.

Noah was laying his outer coat on the back of the sofa when he heard Mary Louise's shy little voice coming from behind him. "Dr. Edwards, it's blue. The lady's dress is blue!"

Noah turned. Mary Louise, in an aura of radiant sweetness and holding the little figurine before her, stood on the braided-rag rug in the middle of the living room floor. She wore an identical blue ruffled dress, and her brown hair fell in ringlets from a look-alike bonnet, all of which Grandma Richards had painstakingly made in preparation for this day.

Noah stumbled backward, and when the back of his knees hit the couch, he dropped down on it and began to stammer. "Y-y-you can s-see?"

"Why are you so surprised?" Grandma asked. "You was the one who knowed it would happen. It was your faith in the good Lord what made her see."

Word of the miraculous healing spread like wildfire through the town, and the recounting of the story appeared in Friday's edition of the *Hub*.

Mary Louise Richards, a.k.a. Poor Little Mary, can now be called Rich Little Mary. She is rich in the blessing of a miracle that restored her sight.

Mary Louise's mother, Martha Richards Cleary, died when Mary Louise was five years old. Her father, Henry Cleary, a short time later, departed for parts unknown, never to be heard from again.

Mary Louise was raised by her grandmother, Mrs. Nelly Richards. Mary Louise lost her sense of sight one day while watching her grandmother behead a chicken.

Dr. Noah Edwards, doctor of divinity and pastor of the Chapel of the Ark, said it was Mary Louise's desire to see the doll

> that set in motion the faith she needed to regain her sight. He helped her to visualize herself as a seeing person through prayer and mental exercises.
>
> Dr. Edwards has most emphatically said that it was Mary Louise's deep desire to see again that made the miracle possible, not the doll.
>
> "The doll was only a means to an end, an exercise," he says.
>
> The small sculpture, purchased at the Bon Marché and given to the little blind girl as a Christmas present by Dr. Edwards, is a likeness of a young woman wearing a blue ruffled dress, often depicted in the dress styles of southern belles. A collie is standing at the figurine's side.

At Old Church, Brother Griggsby was overreacting and showing his apprehension, and he knew it. The old rapport between him and his congregation was no longer there. Once he had held them in the palm of his hand. His word had been law; they had been one and the same. Today that was not so. They were separate from him, aloof and cold, as he spoke.

"Thou shalt not make for thyself a graven image, or any likeness of anything that is in the heavens above, or that is in the earth beneath, or that is in the water under the earth; thou shalt not bow down to them or serve them; for I the Lord your God am a jealous God, visiting the iniquity of the fathers upon the children to the third and fourth generation of those who hate me, but showing steadfast love to thousands of those who love me and keep my Commandments.

"And the children of Israel did secretly those things that were not right against the Lord their God, and they built them high places in all their cities, from the tower of the watchmen to the fenced city. And they set them up images and groves in every high hill, and under every green tree. And there they burnt incense in all the high places, as did the heathen whom the Lord carried away before them, and wrought wicked things to provoke the Lord to anger. For they served idols, whereof the Lord had said unto them, 'Ye shalt not do this thing.'"

Brother Griggsby pounded his fist to bring home his point, his face a dangerous apoplectic red. "We, my brethren and sistern, do not pray to idols. We do not worship dolls and figurines. We do not believe in their healing powers. Only God can heal. I have been in the churches of the infidels—the Lutherans, the Episcopalians, and the papists, with their incense, idols, stained glass, and false gods—all of them the work of Satan. Satan can work miracles, too, you know, false and demonic miracles. We do not dwell in a dark, heathen European country that suffers under the spell of a pope. We are God-fearing, freedom-loving, flag-waving, sovereign Americans, and we do not pray to idols. We are the worshipers of the one true church and the one true God. Thou shalt not make unto thyself idols—or dolls.

"Who is this new minister who has come into our midst, snaked his way into our lives? What do we know about him? He says his church is nondenominational. Well, that means it could be anything. He has dolls restoring sight. Is the doll an idol, or is it witchcraft? Only God can restore sight, not man. And you know from which shop the doll was sold?"

He let the words hang in the air like a noose.

Even though the women of Old Church's Benevolent Society sat through a Sunday sermon blasted at them from the pulpit on the gravity of breaking the first commandment, they were nonetheless busily needlepointing and embroidering Mary Louise's little poem on pillows, tea towels, and white linen fabric to be preserved under glass and hung on the wall as a work of art.

The members of New Church's Thursday Sewing Guild were doing the same. "After all," one of their members reasoned as she diligently embroidered the prayer onto a parlor pillow, "Mary Louise belongs to all of us—not just the Chapel of the Ark."

The following Tuesday, at the Benevolent Society's meeting at the home of Perthy Prettyman, any items with the little poem embroidered on them were whisked out of sight and into sewing satchels and baskets before the already-riled Brother Griggsby arrived in time to partake of refreshments.

CHAPTER 41

May 1907

"I WANT TO BUY ONE a them dolls," a masculine voice said. Shading his eyes, Noah looked toward the door of the ark. A tall, thin man stood in the open doorway, the late-afternoon sun at his back. Stepping inside, the man removed his hat. The bony knobs of his wrists jutted out from the too-short sleeves of his faded shirt as he smoothed down his thinning hair. Respectfully he approached the pulpit, where Noah was seated at the organ.

"I want to buy one a them dolls," he repeated. "I got a sick boy."

Fierceness burned in his eyes, and when he jammed a hand into his pants pocket, the intensity of the act startled Noah. After all, it had been a crazed man reaching into his pants pocket at the Pan-American Exposition in Buffalo, New York, in 1901 who had produced a gun and shot and killed President McKinley. The man withdrew his hand and released the contents of his pocket onto one of the small round lamp stands located above the keys on either side of the organ.

Noah's alert mind counted one dollar and thirty-seven cents in coins.

"It isn't the doll that heals—it's faith," Noah said, speaking slowly.

"And how do you get that?"

The brevity of time he had in which to describe the spiritual state of grace that scholars had pondered through the ages startled Noah anew. He looked at the weary, unworldly farmer in his patched and faded clothes and asked, "What's ailing your boy?"

"He can't walk."

Noah rose from the bench and held out his hand. "I'm Dr. Edwards."

The man responded by first wiping his right hand on his pants leg, a long-time habit. "I'm Tom Brown." Some of the fire left his eyes.

Noah brought a chair from backstage and, setting it down next to the organ, invited the man to be seated. Noah took a deep breath and explained to him the process that had healed Mary Louise and why people were calling it a miracle. He began, "Faith is when we want something so badly, and we believe in it so much, that it manifests itself in the way of a miracle.

"It was prayers, and the intensity of the prayers, and Mary Louise's expectations, that made her see again, not the doll. I told her what to expect, and she believed me. When you plant a kernel of corn in the ground,

Mr. Brown, you expect it to grow, and you know in your mind, without any doubt whatsoever, that it will become a stalk of corn. You see it in your mind. You know it in your heart. You believe it. It's believing beyond a shadow of a doubt that your son will walk again that will make it so. Just like knowing the kernel of corn you plant will become a stalk of corn. That is faith. And faith can make you see again, or walk again—or grow corn."

Tom Brown's eyes had a skeptical look in them as they searched Noah's face. "If'n it rains, it'll grow," he said, leaning into the organ and pushing the little pile of coins closer to Noah.

Noah sighed. The farmer hadn't come to him to hear a lecture on how to grow corn. He already knew how to grow corn better than Noah ever would. What Tom Brown wanted was a miracle, a miracle of old, a miracle of the prophets. He wanted divination, saintly healings, the magic of wizards and soothsayers. He wanted results!

"I'll come by and see your boy," Noah said.

Noah went in search of Aunt Em and found her in the emporium purchasing the makings for soup. Although Aunt Em was no longer allowed to nurse folks, she could still make soup for them. Before her illness, Aunt Em had spent as much time cooking and cleaning for the sick as she had in nursing them.

Noah found her placing cans of tomatoes in her straw bag, which contained a paper-wrapped soupbone from the butcher shop. "What is wrong with Tom Brown's boy?" Noah asked her.

"His father's stiff neck," was her snappish reply. "The boy was born with rickets. All Tom's children have rickets, except for the two first-born girls: Daisy, the prettiest little thing you've ever seen, and her sister Gwen. Tom's too proud to take charity, so the children suffer. They carry that little feller around on a pillow like he's a prince. He can crawl, but that's about it. You going to heal that child, too?"

"Mary Louise healed herself," Noah said.

Aunt Em chuckled. "God bless you," she said.

"The doctor wants you to come by shortly for supper. He likes what he's heard about you."

Noah left the emporium and crossed the street to the newspaper office. He had in his coat pocket a third commentary for the *Hub* to print concerning the healing of Mary Louise. It was a commentary he hoped would make clear to everyone that it was not the doll that had healed Mary Louise, but her faith.

Sam the editor's follow-up story about the "miracle" had been even more sensational than his first one, and, regretfully for Noah, out-of-town papers had picked up the piece. Noah glanced in the direction of the Bon Marché, eager for a glimpse of Abby. "What are you trying to do, get me run out of town?" Noah said, greeting the editor and shoving the news article into his hands. "I thought we were friends."

"We are friends," Sam said. "I'm trying to make you famous and Abby rich. I hear people are clamoring to buy the dolls."

Noah groaned and struck his forehead with his palm. "Oh no."

"The gossip is you're a covert Catholic who's secretly trying to put something over on your congregation, but I won't print that."

Noah was still smiting his forehead when Abby came through the door, a troubled look on her face. "Customers are asking to buy the figurines. What shall I do?"

"Sell them," Sam answered. "You're a businesswoman, Abby. Give the customers what they want. If you don't, someone else will."

"Sell them," Noah said, nodding his head in agreement. "It's the only way I know to let them discover for themselves that the doll doesn't hold some kind of mystical power."

"What if someone is healed?" Abby asked worriedly.

"More power to them," Noah said. "Then they can go into the healing business."

"Oh!" Abby said in dismay.

"By the way," Sam said, chiding the young preacher, "where do you keep all those graven images? I'd like to see them some time."

Noah grimaced.

"You know, this could turn into a gold mine," the editor said. "Manufacture bottles made in the shape of the woman, and sell miracle water." He turned to Abby and said, "Dresses? I saw the kid in the dress. You could whip up a whole line of clothes. Oh! I see all kinds of possibilities. Why, I'd even buy stock in your enterprise."

When Abby and Noah left the newspaper office, Sam was still laughing and rubbing his hands together like a villain in a melodrama.

Noah told his housekeeper, Rosie, to pack a food box to take to the Browns on Sunday after church. Rosie reminded him that the Browns would not accept charity.

"Then we'll have a picnic: you and me and Abby and the Browns."

Having been made aware of the gossip about him and Abby, he made sure they were always seen in the company of others.

The yard in front of the Browns' unpainted house had been swept clean, and Abby, Rosie, and Noah sat beneath a large tree on chairs brought from the house. A table made of roughhewn boards was set with a snowy-white cloth and mismatched plates, water glasses for the guests, and mason jars for the children. Mrs. Brown, in constant motion, did not join them at the table.

To impress Noah, Abby had worn a full-skirted dress made of yellow-dotted Swiss fabric and a large-brimmed white hat. She regretted the vanity of her act as soon as she saw the shabbiness of the girls' dresses.

The sisters—beautiful, raven-haired Daisy and brown-haired Gwen, both in their late teens—wistfully observed Abby's every move and, whenever their mother wasn't watching, touched the skirt or sleeve of her gown.

Noah brought a camera to take pictures of the family. He made a portrait of each one before grouping them together. The girls hid their shoes, with holes worn through the soles, beneath their dresses, posing as prettily as they could in their old clothes. Often the pictures Noah snapped at family gatherings were the only pictorial records a family would ever have. He sent the camera and negatives to the Kodak Camera Company in New Jersey for developing, and the pictures were returned to him in paper frames or printed on postcards.

Except for the two oldest girls, none of the children moved with agility, and the crippled boy, Joey, an angelic-looking child with long dark hair and mischievous eyes, did not walk: he crawled, or pulled himself about by holding onto things, seemingly content with his fate. His small bowed legs gave him the mobility and stature of a two-year-old, not a boy of five.

Noah told Mr. Brown he had ordered a figurine for Joey. The news made everyone in the family ecstatic. Noah thought, concerning the healing powers of the figurine, *I'll cross that bridge when I come to it.*

Returning home, Noah dropped Rosie and the picnic basket at the ark then turned the horse toward Abby's house. Away from Rosie and the Browns, Noah became a different person. He placed a robe over Abby's lap and later searched for her hand, holding it unseen beneath the blanket as they drove alone up Main Street.

He saw her to her front door. "You know I can't come in," he said, "but I would like to give you a good-night kiss."

Abby's smile was reserved, but there was an affectionate look in her eyes that hadn't been there before.

Pulling her into the cover of the honeysuckle vine, he kissed her. Abby entwined her arms around his neck. He placed his hands on her cheeks and, angling his head, made the kiss deeper and longer. She liked the way he kissed her and the manly smell of him.

CHAPTER 42

June 1907

A WEEK AFTER THE PICNIC, the Browns were at the ark's Sunday morning service, seated on the long bench built into the back wall. Tom sat in the center of his family holding Joey on his lap, ensconced on his princely pillow.

It was a glorious day. The interior of the chapel was dancing with rainbow prisms of light glowing through the stained-glass windows and the clear panes of the open transoms located close to the ceiling. Noah, reveling in the playful nature of the light, was preaching a sermon on the joy of giving when he became acutely aware of someone standing near him.

Thinking someone from the congregation was on the podium, he glanced to his left. No one was there. Still, he was definitely aware of a presence near him. And something was delighting Joey; the boy's face was alive with a look of intense happiness.

Noah's eyes swept the congregation and saw no one except Pie Face, hiding in a corner, and Joey, looking amused. The crippled lad pointed his forefinger toward the pulpit before slipping from the pillow on his father's lap and beginning a lopsided tottering up the aisle, touching the ends of the pews for balance as we went. Tom's long arms reached out for his son but froze—*what's to be will be,* he thought.

From Noah's vantage point, he could tell Joey was not pointing at him, but to his left. When Joey reached the pulpit and could go no farther, he looked up; when he saw Noah, the smile faded from his face. Noah did a one-handed vault from the pulpit and, picking up the boy, embraced him. "Good boy, Joey. Good boy."

Joey was looking over his shoulder, his eyes grown large. Noah could feel the presence standing with them. He felt it when the spirit entered Joey, and in the burning heat surrounding himself. The boy's head fell onto Noah's shoulder, and Noah cradled him in his arms. Everyone was still; they all felt the change and the static charge in the atmosphere. Eventually Joey turned his head, looked up at Noah, and smiled.

Noah placed the boy back on his feet, and Joey, realizing he had walked there by himself, stood wavering on legs that felt as if they had sprouted wings.

"Go to your father, Joey," Noah whispered, and Joey, bouncing on the balls of his feet, covered the dreamlike distance back to his dad.

The congregation was astounded, but none more so than Noah. Their reverent handshakes, and eyes timid with awe, communicated a new respect for their minister as he bade them good day at the door of the church.

Tom kept up the shaking of Noah's hand. He repeated, "I knowed you could do it, I just knowed it." The mother and sisters, too overcome with joy to stop their weeping, were unable to thank him. Joey was enjoying his newfound notoriety but clung to his father's neck and refused to be put down.

After everyone was gone, Noah drew Abby aside. "I'm sorry," he said in a voice thick with emotion, "but I can't see you today. I need to be alone."

Abby's voice, also shaking from the drama of the morning, told him she understood. "I believe we all need time alone."

He held her hand, and they gazed at each other, her eyes showing the same reverence his parishioners had.

The "new miracle" was duly reported in the *Hub*, and Noah's congregation and his reputation as a healer grew anew.

Among the many strangers present in the congregation on the following Sunday was a woman with painfully pleading eyes sunken in a sickly-yellow face. Noah wanted to heal her—he wanted to heal all of them—but the presence that he'd felt on the pulpit with him the day Joey was healed never manifested itself. The next

Sunday, the woman returned with an even greater number of strangers.

Two weeks went by without a healing, and the pain-racked face of the woman haunted Noah's dreams. He went alone into the forest, where he found comfort in the simplicity of nature and the feeling of oneness with the universe. He prayed for understanding and courage.

On the third Sunday, he again felt the presence, stronger than before, which gave him the necessary incentive to try again. "Lord, there is someone among us today who desperately needs a healing," he said. He quickly descended the two steps from the pulpit and held out his hands to the woman of the beseeching eyes.

Lars was immediately on his feet, helping her from the pew and into the aisle.

"Can you kneel with me?" Noah asked. Without answering, the woman dropped to her knees. Noah placed a hand on either side of her head and silently prayed. Warmth flooded over him, and he felt the energy transposed into his body by the presence passing into the woman. She tumbled over onto her side and curled into a fetal position. Noah sat with her on the floor, stroking her head until the heat had faded from her. Lars and Orion were there to help her to her feet.

"The pain is gone!" she cried, tears streaming down her face as she clutched Noah to her. "Thank you. Oh, thank you!"

Others pressed around him, all clamoring for a cure.

The presence was not always with him, but when it was, Noah conducted a healing service. As the number of people who came to the Chapel of the Ark for a healing grew, the Sunday services were forced into overly long, exhausting hours—hours that left him drained.

On Sundays the ark was filled to capacity. People gathered outside the church, and a few townspeople from other denominations attended Noah's services. Nonmembers began to drop in to the church on days other than the Sabbath, and reporters from out-of-town newspapers requested interviews.

The Unholy Seven from Old Church also showed up. Noah, recognizing who they were, greeted them warmly and invited them to look around. He told them he would answer any questions they might have. He shook hands with each of the men and smiled at the women. When he clasped Hyrum Dinwoody's hand, he felt a wave of heat pass from him to Mr. Dinwoody and knew, by the startled look on the man's face and the sudden straightening of his arthritic posture, that he had received a healing. No one said anything, but as they were leaving, Noah noticed that the man was no longer dependent upon his cane.

If the seven had come looking for graven images, they must have been sorely disappointed. Only the beautiful polished wooden cross Els Olsen had carved hung from the aft wall back of the altar; no tortured Jesus drooped from its simple lines.

A week later, Mr. Dinwoody, with his wife and children, attended Sunday services at the ark. Their son

Lester, seated with the Langleys, shyly greeted his apologetic parents. He had not seen them in a while, given that his father had told him he could never come home if he was going to play ball. Lester's family seemed surprised by how much their son had matured in the short time he had been away from them.

Noah and Abby were seated in the swing on his front porch. Abby, like the rest of Noah's congregation, was in awe of him, and this made them shy when they were in each other's company, which these days occurred less and less frequently. Tonight, however, was one of the rare occasions when they were alone.

Noah sat with his arm across her shoulder, holding her close to him as though seeking warmth. He looked tired, and in the twilight she could see a touch of silver in the hair at his temples.

"Don't let this healing thing change what we have," he said to her.

"I'll never change, and I'm very proud of what you're doing."

"And don't let me change!" he begged, crushing her to him and capturing her mouth in a hungry, searching kiss.

CHAPTER 43

August 1907

"Aunt Em is sick! Aunt Em is bad sick!"

The disturbing news spread rapidly over the town. Upon first hearing it, people felt their hearts skip a beat. Remembering how healthy Aunt Em had always been, they quickly recovered and went about their business. But when the warm spring days moved toward summer without Aunt Em leaving her house, the distraught women of the town did the only thing they knew how to do to show their concern—they cooked.

Soups, broths, and casseroles; roasted young spring hens; pies, cakes, and puddings—all prepared from good, nourishing homegrown foods and served up in their best dishes—were lovingly toted to Aunt Em's, where they reposed with other bowls, platters, and their best dishes of healthful foods, all left untouched.

The women came away troubled by how thin and poorly Aunt Em looked. Still, she blessed them, her raspy voice weak and deeper than ever, no boisterous laughter in it now. Finally, in late spring, she took to her bed and never left it.

After Sunday morning services, men, women, and children had begun to congregate at the doctor's house. Knowing Aunt Em was too sick for callers, they stood about in groups in the front yard, reminiscing. They found comfort in telling their favorite Aunt Em stories, which often raised a chuckle. But mostly they were quiet and spoke in whispers as they stared at the windows of the room where she lay. On one occasion, the doctor came out on the porch and said to the crowd, "Aunt Em says, 'God bless you.'"

Another time, on one of her good days, the doctor and the nurse propped her up in a chair by the window so she could see all the people assembled there. She waved a feeble, emaciated arm, and her weak smile exposed her healthy white teeth looking far too big in a face gone gaunt and eyes sunken in dark circles of pain, all of which gave her a skeletal look. The people gathered on the lawn waved and smiled back, then quickly hid their faces, not wanting her to see what they all knew. They were losing their beloved Aunt Em.

A ripple of "Why Aunt Em?" could be heard like a muffled cry weaving through the crowd. "Why should a woman who's devoted her whole life to caring for others be so ill?" Mrs. Oberlander asked Pastor Gillian of New Church. "Why her? Of all the people in the world, why our Aunt Em?"

With no answer for her question, the pastor lamely quoted scripture. "God moves in mysterious ways."

People wrung their hands and gave up long sighs, feeling powerless. They could do nothing for her when she needed them.

The doctor's son Adam arrived with his wife, Lillian. Adam, a Johns Hopkins medical school graduate, had been in Europe taking advanced studies when he received the news that Aunt Em was sick.

By summer, she was too ill to sit by the window, but on Sundays the crowds still came, mutely standing and staring at the blind-drawn windows of the room where she lay ill. The doctor acknowledged them by coming out onto the veranda now and then. "Aunt Em knows you're here," he would say.

July came, and still she clung to the depleted thread of her life, slipping in and out of consciousness and always in pain. She watched the two people she loved most in the world prepare a pain mixture for her, and when her husband held the draught to her lips, she refused, gasping, "Let God do His work."

Her husband set the cup down and held her hand. "You've been so busy all these years walking in His footsteps that you never questioned Him, did you?"

Aunt Em placed her hand over the doctor's, the love she had for him reflecting in her pain-filled eyes. She looked at his son standing back of his father's chair. She had lived with this man, raised his child, shared his bed, but had never called him by his first name, knowing his heart and affections belonged to his first wife. No word of love had passed between them, and yet she loved him, plain and simple. Her eyes implored him, but he could not say what she wanted to hear.

"Thank you, Emma, for everything," he said.

Aunt Em gave the doctor's hand a frail squeeze. "Send for that new preacher," she said.

Even in the heat of an August Sunday afternoon, the people were there, as they were every Sunday, showing by their numbers their love for the woman who was their beloved. Not everyone in Rockville was there, but the large crowd made it seem so. People were milling about and coming and going. The sick and the elderly sat on a garden bench that encircled the large shade tree, or on chairs brought from the house for their comfort by Meiko Toma and the nurse whom the doctor had hired from a nursing school in the city.

Mario Brocoloni, Flora Maria's father—music teacher and spokesman for the Italian immigrants who populated the quaint village of Saint Margaret's—was there, as were the gardeners who maintained the grounds for the doctor.

Chance Collins was there with his nearly blind mother. Mr. Oberlander the banker mingled with the farmers, and Mr. Parlett conversed with the Italian grocer. The Tuesday Benevolent Society of Old Church shared their sorrow with the Thursday Social Guild of New Church.

Redheaded Velvet Preston, wearing a blue satin gown with a small black ruffled straw hat perched on her head decorated with three bobbing doodads made of blue feathers in parasol shapes, darted and glided through the sea of funereally dressed mourners like an exotic fish in murky waters. Her presence provided the assemblage a temporary respite from their mourning.

The widow McCoy was in attendance with her eldest son, Ben Franklin, a dark-haired young man with a mustache, and daughter Willa Mae, who had the physical distinction of having one blue eye and one brown one. Everyone called the widow "the widow McCoy," as if she were the title of a book. They were a handsome family in a different, mysterious sort of way. The gossip was that her husband had been a member of the infamous McCoy family who had been killed by the feuding Hatfields. No one knew, and no one asked. Some said Chance Collins knew, since he had called on the supposed widow for the better part of a year. But if he knew, he wasn't sharing.

Abby found her uncle Joe's family and joined them. The gregarious group did not remain together long. Aunt Rose left the family circle to look for her sisters. Uncle Joe, who wanted to be the town's new mayor, moved through the crowd, backslapping as he went. Jennie Jeanne Oberlander, with her friend Susan, found Orion, and the three of them walked down the slope of the spacious lawn to the gazebo, away from Jennie Jeanne's mother's prying eyes. Leo, with Flora Maria Brocoloni possessively holding onto his arm, strolled about, and Sags was off looking for girls to tease. Corvus and Cetus, the towheaded Langley twins, left alone with their cousin Abby, were soon in pursuit of Illa May and Twilla June, the flaxen-haired Davis twins, with little brother Percy at their heels.

After their departure, Abby stood alone on the fringe of the crowd. Not a group nor a person she could join would welcome her. She was aware that Chance Collins had been staring at her, and she watched helplessly as he left the assemblage of old people seated on the iron bench encircling the oak tree and began what looked to be an aimless meandering.

Not wanting to appear to be running from him, she didn't stir. Maybe he wasn't moving in her direction, but the knot in the pit of her stomach told her otherwise.

Chance now stood before her and pulled on the brim of his hat, giving her a polite nod. "Good afternoon," he said.

Not wanting to embarrass him by looking at his face with the angry scar, or the green and gold teeth of his leering smile, Abby lowered her head and repeated his greeting. "Good afternoon," she said in a barely audible whisper.

The long lashes of her lowered lids and the heightened color in her cheeks brought a quickening of his breath. *God, she's beautiful,* he thought. "I wonder if you would be so kind as to come by and say hello to my mother," he said. "I'm certain she would appreciate it."

Abby couldn't refuse to greet his mother, but she didn't answer him, just numbly moved in the direction of the big tree where the elderly woman was seated. Once they were in the crush of the crowd, Chance placed a hand on her elbow to steer her around a group, but she quickly straightened her arm, and he dropped his hand.

Leaning over his mother, Chance said, "Mum, this is Ronald Langley's daughter, Abigail."

"He died from yellow fever," Mrs. Collins said, smiling sweetly in the direction of Abby's voice without any recognition showing in her milky eyes. She inquired of her son, "Is she a bonnie lass, laddie?"

Chance, observing the curves of Abby's body as she bent to greet his mother, answered in a slow drawl, "Yes, Mum, she's a very bonnie lass indeed."

Abby tolerated the old woman clasping her hands and pulling her closer, but a faded, sweet odor emanating from the elderly woman's powdered skin, mingled with old perspiration and Chance's appraising leer sliding over her, gave Abby an uneasy queasiness.

"Can I give you a ride home, Miss Langley?" Chance asked in a fawning tone.

"Oh, thank you, but no," she answered, breathless from the surprise of his invitation. "I'm riding with my cousins." Quickly dropping Mrs. Collins's hands, she went in search of any one of them. She saw Leo and, rushing up to him, claimed his other arm, receiving an astonished look from him and a withering glare from Flora Maria as she fell in step with them.

Brother Griggsby and Pastor Gillian moved through the crowd offering words of encouragement and consolation. "If love alone can make her well, it's here in abundance," Pastor Gillian said.

"Our prayers will see her through," Brother Griggsby said.

Noah arrived, escorted by Meiko Toma, and the crowd parted and made way for them. Everyone wondered why the new minister was being admitted to the house but remembered he had been endowed with the healing powers of the Holy Ghost.

"She'll git bedder now," Lars Larson whispered.

"He'll show those college doctors a thing or two," someone else added.

In the living room, which had been turned into a hospital room, Dr. Townsend introduced Noah to Adam and Lillian. "This is a fine young man who has come to us by his own consent. He's a preacher, but no matter—he shows signs of intelligence."

Noah knelt by Aunt Em's bedside. "Bless you," she said, trying to laugh, but she only managed a long, depleting cough. Holding her hands, Noah silently prayed for the Holy Spirit to intercede. But the Spirit remained absent. No lightning transformation passed between Noah and Aunt Em. *I'm not the healer, only the means of expression,* he reminded himself.

After a half hour of silent prayer, he looked to the doctor and shook his head. "Nothing's happening; maybe we need to be at the ark."

"She's too weak to move," the doctor replied.

Aunt Em spoke. Noah bent his head closer to catch her words. "I'm ready to go."

Outside, in the midst of the mourners, Pastor Gillian of New Church in his fine tenor voice began singing "God Be with You Till We Meet Again."

Flora Maria Brocoloni, moving toward him like a homing pigeon, picked up the song, and soon everyone was singing the hymn. The song was all they had to give Aunt Em, and they gave with heart, soul, and voice.

Aunt Em's head turned on the pillow toward the sound. "Lordy, I love them. God bless you all," she whispered.

"I'm sorry," Noah said to the doctor. "I'm not the one who chooses who's to be healed. If I could, I would heal them all."

Dr. Townsend, with his hand on Noah's shoulder, said, "I know, I know. I'm well aware of the feeling. During an extended illness, the time comes when death is the savior, and release is the blessing. Pray for her release."

Lillian knelt with Noah at the bedside, with father and son standing behind them.

"Go in peace, Aunt Em," Noah said in a quiet voice. "Jesus will take you there. We'll be all right. We've been made strong just by knowing you. We will look after ourselves and each other. And we will forever keep the blessing of having you in our lives in our hearts."

Noah began his prayer of supplication. "Dear benevolent Father, we give our most heartfelt thanks to you for sharing this beloved woman with us. She taught us, through her service to the sick and needy, that we are all Your children. Through her we have learned love and sacrifice and unselfish devotion to others. Now we ask that she be allowed to return home, to find succor from her pain and suffering, and in her passing alleviate the pain and suffering her family and her extended family have endured. If her calling in this life is over, then may it be Thy will that she not dwell further with us but be allowed to enter her heavenly home and find peace and compassion in Your goodness. We ask this in Thy name and in the name of Jesus, in which all things are possible. Amen." The doctors, Lillian, and the nurse together uttered, "Amen."

Aunt Em, her eyes closed, looked to be at peace. The doctor felt for a pulse from her wrist and her neck.

The melancholy sound of the tolling of the church bell in the wee hours of the morning struck terror into the hearts of the people. Some slept through the first peal; others awakened, thinking maybe they had dreamed it. Then the bell from the school and the carillon from New Church began to toll. Was there a fire? No. The bells would be clanging furiously for a fire. The ringing was slow and mournful.

The people knew. Knew their Aunt Em was gone from them forever, and they held each other in their beds and wept.

CHAPTER 44

God Bless You, Aunt Em, read the headline on the front page of the white sheet, bordered in the blackest of ink.

> It is with the greatest sadness of my job as editor-in-chief of this newspaper that I must report the passing of our beloved Aunt Em...

In the days that followed Aunt Em's passing, men, embarrassed by their own emotions, avoided one another's eyes. Women openly embraced when they met; they wept on one another's shoulders and cried, "Whatever will we do?"

Brother Griggsby called on Dr. Townsend about holding the funeral service at Old Church, seeing as it was the largest congregation in town, and promptly received a resounding no. "Aunt Em, to my knowledge, was never baptized and belonged to no single faith," the doctor informed him. Pastor Gillian also called on

Dr. Townsend to voice his request for a service; because the doctor considered him in kindlier terms, he received a gentler no.

Aunt Em had crossed the barriers of the different faiths in town, knitting them together and teaching them tolerance in her service to all. Her death, however, had a disturbing effect on the religious zeal of the town. A crack was forming that threatened to become a gulf.

Dr. Townsend, with his deeply embedded disdain for religious doctrines, had refused a funeral service. He told the townspeople they could call at the house and pay their last respects, but the burial would be a simple graveside service for members of the family only.

This was a burden the sorrowing people could not bear. Their grief demanded its hour of lament. Noah, out of concern for his grieving parishioners, especially the younger ones, consulted with Dr. Townsend. "She belongs to the people," he said. "They need to have a service for her. They need healing, and a funeral is the only way they know in which to alleviate their grief."

The doctor finally consented, but he made it clear that he and his family would not attend the spectacle.

When Aunt Em had come to Rockville as a young, practical nurse fresh from the six-month required training (but with a natural gift of her own for the healing of the sick) to work for Dr. Townsend, she had never taken the time to join a church, nor had she felt the need for one. She had on occasion attended both Old and New Church—had even attended services at the Catholic church in Saint Margaret's and the one-room building that served as church and school for the Seventh-Day Adventists and home-teaching base for Presbyterians—and was known to every family in town.

Every denomination, each with its own ministers and representatives, held a meeting for the planning of Aunt Em's funeral in the neutrality of the town hall. The two largest of these religious factions were clearly divided by the center aisle: Old Church on one side and New Church on the other, with all other denominations seated in the rear.

Noah attended. The people expressed their resentment of his presence when he explained that he was there to represent the Townsend family. "They have asked me to join you this evening and be of service in any way I can."

"They must think he can walk on water," Perthy Prettyman whispered.

Brother Griggsby, speaking to them in morbid tones, opened the meeting. "What I have to say to you this evening is very difficult," he said. "Oh, very, very difficult indeed." There was a long pause, with the brother looking upward, as though calling on heavenly strength, then back to his audience. "It seems that Aunt Em"—he took a deep breath, looking heavenward again and back—"was never baptized." A loud communal gasp filled the town hall, followed by a moment of utter silence, then a crying and babbling of voices.

Without knowing it, Dr. Townsend had let loose a snake in the henhouse when he had inadvertently let slip to Brother Griggsby the fact that Aunt Em had never been baptized. This knowledge had fired up the ardent brother with the fanaticism of a religious zealot. "Not baptized? Aunt Em not baptized!"

"Will she go to heaven?" Hyrum Dinwoody asked.

Mrs. Dinwoody, seated beside her husband, began to wail. "No! Oh no! Do you mean our Aunt Em can't go to heaven?"

"This can't be!" Mr. Dinwoody said, embracing his distressed wife.

"Brother, what can we do?" Will Stanton, the dairyman, asked of the preacher. "Is there some way she can be baptized?"

"Even if there were, the doctor would never allow us to do such a thing," Mr. White, a member of the Unholy Seven, said.

"Would he have to know?"

The question hung suspended in the air, like a delicate bubble, before slowly, cautiously descending.

They sat back in their seats, mulling it over. *Would he have to know?*

"And if she can be baptized, which church?" Mr. Dinwoody warily asked.

"You can't immerse a corpse," Mr. Oberlander from New Church said, speaking with authority. "She would have to be sprinkled."

The immersion side of the aisle was on its feet.

"Never!" Mr. Dinwoody shouted. "She'll never go to heaven if she's only sprinkled."

"It would be better to do nothing at all," Mr. Stanton said, agreeing with him.

Now the baptism-by-sprinkling side was on its feet. Yelling and angry accusations, mingled with words like "heretic" and "infidel," peppered the arguments on both sides of the aisle. Brother Griggsby was shouting but could not make himself heard above the din.

"Shut. Up!" Noah shouted as he rose to his feet. It was the raw anguish in his voice that brought them up short. "Have you listened to yourselves? You sound like a pack of dogs fighting over a bone. We need not be concerned about Aunt Em's immortal soul. Her soul has already departed her body, and it would be of no avail to baptize a corpse. Your place in heaven is earned through your humanity to others, and your humility of spirit. Aunt Em has more than earned her place in the hereafter. May I suggest that you hold two services?"

Subdued, the opposing sides gave this some thought, not quite sure what to believe but also not wanting to be hoodwinked by the interloper. And why had he, someone outside of the family, been the last person to see her alive?

After much discussion, those gathered decided that because Aunt Em had not belonged to any denomination, they would indeed hold two services: the first service to be held at New Church, followed by a second and final one at Old Church, both services open to one and all.

Noah said he would encourage his parishioners to attend one or the other, and at a later date he would hold a memorial ceremony at the ark to honor her life, and not her death.

Aunt Em's passing had left Abby bereft, and the churches' fighting over her funeral only made things worse. She spent time in her rose garden, the only place she could find solace, to grieve for the Aunt Em she had known: her friend, her soul mother. She wanted the roses for her funeral to be the most beautiful ever.

The facts that Aunt Em had never been baptized and that her soul could very well burn in hell weighed heavily upon the town's collective conscience. She was also the first person in Rockville to be embalmed, and this made them nervous. Could an embalmed person go to heaven?

Whenever and wherever two or more people met, Aunt Em's immortal soul became the topic of conversation. Members of all faiths, in private and in groups, called on their spiritual leaders to do something. The ministers and church elders busily thumbed through their Bibles and sifted through church literature, seeking a precedent with which to solve their dilemma. Never had so many technical points on theology been argued. Could you baptize a dead person? When does the soul reach heaven—or hell? They shuddered. Could one, after death, be baptized by proxy?

Dr. Townsend had advocated embalming for quite some time, but Brother Griggsby had emphatically preached against it, declaring that the soul would be denied entrance to heaven if it were embalmed. Hence, anyone who died in Rockville was usually kept on ice and laid out by family members, or Aunt Em, sometimes with the help of Mr. Tibbits, the aspiring undertaker.

They had heard stories of mutilation being done to corpses during this newfangled embalming procedure, and they grimaced in pain for poor Aunt Em. They had always thought of Dr. Townsend as an odd stick, but now they were beginning to think of him as some kind of ghoul.

Late on the evening before the funeral, Brother Griggsby met with the chosen seven and the elders of Old Church in a secret meeting in the small study at the rear of the church to discuss Aunt Em's soul, whereupon it was decided, had Aunt Em lived long enough, she most surely would have joined their church, the one and only true church. This she had not done because she was unselfishly tending to others' earthly ills while neglecting her own, everlasting one. Therefore, the blame lay with them. They would now do in death what they had failed to do in life: baptize Aunt Em.

That same evening, and at the very same time, a similar meeting was taking place at New Church, and, given that their belief in baptism was by sprinkling, their dilemma was not as great. And since theirs was the one true church, there wasn't any doubt that it was the one Aunt Em would have wished to have belonged to. They hoped and prayed that Aunt Em's unbaptized soul had not yet reached the pearly gates but, if it had, that Saint Peter would understand the tardiness of the baptism.

On the day of the double funeral, when the cortege of mourners from the solemn ceremony that had been performed at New Church delivered the coffin holding Aunt Em's sprinkled remains to Old Church, the elders of Old Church received it and with haste carried it into the small back-room office.

With doors firmly bolted, they quickly removed the dress and layers of white petticoats from Aunt Em's body and were more than a little surprised to find plain Aunt Em clad in silk underwear, which they did not remove. Because they hadn't figured out how they could immerse a corpse, they washed whatever parts of Aunt Em were not covered by her silken undies, prayed over her, and, in the name of Jesus, offered her up to the one true God, begging Him to understand and forgive them the omission of full immersion. With Aunt Em dressed and rearranged in the coffin, they triumphantly carried her remains to the nave of the church and to a service that tried the townspeople's souls in agonizing pathos.

The rains began the night of Aunt Em's funerals. The showers poured forth from the heavens for most of a week. Thunder stalked the surrounding mountains like a marauding animal. Night and day, lightning streaked across angry skies, and, for the first time in living memory,

Stony Creek overflowed its banks. Water ran in streams down streets and sidewalks. Pools of muddy water stood in every front yard, and backyards were turned into ponds. The downpour washed away the planks on the cross corners of the downtown streets and sent them skittering along like rafts. Water inundated the town as if by baptism and, in place of salvation, left behind *mud.*

Late on the afternoon of the fifth day, the sky lightened in the west, and in the east a rainbow appeared in its fairy-tale splendor. The pastel colors arched from north to south, with the ends seeming to touch down at the quarry and reach across the sky to the forest. Children, barefoot and laughing, padded about in the mud, while adults left the safety of their homes to come outside and stand on their drenched porches and stoops, there to revel in the beauty of God's promise of a new day.

CHAPTER 45

THE SECRET WAS OUT AND had finally reached the ears of Dr. Townsend: Aunt Em had been baptized—not once—but twice. Sprinkled at New Church and bathed at Old Church. The doctor had shown up at the Benevolent Society's Tuesday meeting, walked into the house without benefit of knocking, and startled everyone present. Brother Griggsby, mouth open to receive a forkful of cake with fluffy white icing and a generous sprinkling of coconut, froze in surprise.

Dr. Townsend stood in the middle of the room, surrounded by the ladies of the society. "It has reached my ears," he said, "what took place prior to my wife's burial, and I am here to tell you"—his voice rose as he pointed an index finger heavenward—"that if there is a heaven, Aunt Em is there now, seated on the right hand of God, and she didn't need your confounded sprinkling and washing and bathing to get her there. And furthermore, if there is a hell, may you and all your heathen superstitions burn there for all eternity."

He delivered the same message to the Thursday Social Guild at New Church and proceeded on to the ark. To Noah he said, "Did you, in any way, sprinkle, bathe, or baptize Aunt Em?"

"No, sir, I did not."

"The Catholics?"

"Not to my knowledge."

"What's the matter? Wasn't she good enough for the Catholics?"

The doctor returned home. He kicked thick layers of mud picked up from the sidewalks and streets from his boots and viciously raked them over the iron shoe scraper on the stoop before entering the kitchen. "I am leaving Rockville," he announced to his son as he removed his boots and flung them into a corner. "I've told them all what I think of them, and now I'm going to leave this mudhole of creation to the religious bigots. Let them sink in it."

"Aunt Em would forgive them, you know that," Adam said to his father.

"Yes, she would laugh and bless them. They were her children, and she forgave them their sins and their silliness, but I cannot." Then he coughed and said, "Son, I'm making arrangements to go to Canada. I'll set you up in practice anywhere you want in the States, or—and this is what I would like you to do—come to Canada with me. I'm interested in ore, and there's plenty of it up there. I've sold my proprietary drug company lock, stock, and barrel to my fiercest competitor. I'm not sure if you've heard, but since the Pure Food and Drug Act went into effect and forced all of us to cut the alcohol content of our tonics, Survivall is not the big seller it used to be. Once those holier-than-thou do-gooders and crusaders against devil rum found out that the very tonics they were imbibing so freely contained alcohol—the very thing the teetotalers were so dead set against—they deserted us in droves."

The doctor laughed good-heartedly. "My tonics never contained opiates," he said, shaking his head in disgust, "but I will always affirm that a good nip of liquor never hurt anyone."

Adam liked his father's sense of humor. Most people never saw this side of the doctor and knew him only as a serious man devoid of amusement. "If I go into business, it will be a small sanitarium for tuberculosis patients," Adam said.

"But you know, most consumptives don't have the money for an extended hospital stay," his father said.

"Then the recompense from the haves will have to cover the have-nots," Adam replied. "By the way, what happened to the blueprints for that king's palace of a health spa you planned to build at Indian Springs back when I was a kid? A spa for the very rich, I believe."

"The young dream big," his father said with a wry smile.

Adam said, "A hospital with clean, simple lines—not all the folderol that's so dear to the hearts of architects and doctors today—could be done on the same spot. What I would like to do is remain here and take over your practice."

"Aunt Em's practice, you mean," the doctor said, standing at the kitchen sink and scrubbing his hands. "And what about Lillian; what does she think of this?"

Adam handed his father a clean towel. "She feels the same as you do about me remaining in Rockville, but she's willing to give it a try. God knows the people here will need someone. There's a boy waiting in your office right now with a broken arm, and word arrived that Louella Bradley's been in labor for two days."

"I didn't educate you, or endure being separated from you all these years, just to have you become a country doctor."

"I like Rockville. No matter where I go, Rockville has always been home."

"You'll be paid in chickens and apples, or, like Aunt Em, in love."

"Rockville's growing, and I'd like to grow with it," Adam said.

"The practice of medicine will not make you rich—but patent medicine will."

His father's medicine made people feel good, but Adam wanted to make them well, especially those who had consumption. His plan was to live in the small town, without the pressures of a big-city practice, where he would set up a laboratory and continue his search for a cure for tuberculosis.

The doctor sighed resignedly. "If you've made up your mind, go ahead and give it a trial. I'll leave you the Indian Springs bottling plant and Meiko Toma to run it.

You've done well with investing your money, son; maybe you should think about the banking business. As for me, baptizing Aunt Em was the last straw. I can no longer endure the townspeople's ignorance or their obstinate conformity."

As Dr. Townsend and Adam entered his office, the doctor said brightly, displaying a genuine concern for his young patient, "Well now, what do we have here?"

CHAPTER 46

After the deluge worthy of biblical distinction rained down on Rockville and left streets and sidewalks covered with mud, the people demanded that the town council "do something" about the streets. Petitions were circulated, and the council voted to pave Main Street from the depot to the cemetery. The mayor declared it a "street for Aunt Em," and the town's sorrow was turned into a frenzy of brick paving.

The work was to be done by subscription, and every male from age twelve and up was required to devote one ten-hour day per week to road work. A brigade of men in black armbands had found a way to honor their cherished Aunt Em.

Abigail Langley attended one of the council meetings and made the suggestion that the bricks for the sidewalks in the business district be laid in a zigzag pattern. Her proposal elicited stares from the councilmen, who hoped she was not going to be another cocklebur sticking to their coattails like "Ol' Selmy." Selma Ward, who attended any and all council meetings concerning the beautification of Rockville, found herself in complete accordance with Abby's suggestion for the bricks on the downtown sidewalks.

Abby had found herself an ally and a friend. "It's the first time I've had a good look at her since her fall from grace," Mrs. Ward reported to her husband. "She's the prettiest woman I've ever laid eyes on, and she's every inch a lady."

Noah, surprised to see Abigail at a council meeting, asked if he could walk her home.

Sitting down beside her on the porch glider, he reached for her hand. "I've been appointed to the celebration committee," he said. "Your uncle Joe is talking about an ox roast. Do you know anything about roasting an ox?"

"No, but Uncle Joe does—and pig and deer and bear," she added, laughing.

"You have a wonderful laugh," he said. "It's catching."

Swinging in the glider and holding hands, they talked about Aunt Em, the new street, baseball, and women's hats. They watched silently as a lone rider, coming from the direction of Stony Creek Bridge, rode past the Langley residence at a leisurely pace.

Noah knew it was Chance Collins from the way he sat his horse, even before the streetlight confirmed it. *Now,* he thought, *what would Chance Collins be doing in this end of town at this time of night?*

The laying of the brick road was moving along in an orderly fashion until startling news arrived by wireless at the train depot: the barnstorming Pittsburgh Pirates baseball team, with the great shortstop Honus Wagner, was coming to town in a fortnight and had requested an exhibition game against the Rockville Rockets. Rockville was now a baseball town; even the women had heard of Honus Wagner. Now the town had a new incentive for completing the street.

It was generally agreed that the team needed to practice for the big game and therefore would not be required to lay brick. The men in charge of the ox roast would also be excused from roadwork in order to prepare the pit for the ox. All males twelve and older agreed to work in round-the-clock shifts, laboring at night by generator and lantern light to have the street finished in time for the ball game; a few women, and boys younger than twelve, also pitched in.

When Joe Langley told his mother-in-law that the Pittsburgh Pirates were coming to town, she did a little jig and said, "Oh my, they'll be a-dancing in the streets!"

Joe thought for a minute. "Well, heck yes," he said, "why not dancing in the streets? Aunt Em said she wanted us to have a good time, and what better way is there to have a good time than dancing? We've brought baseball back, so why not bring dancing back?"

That evening at the council meeting, Joe made his pitch for holding a street dance to celebrate the new street. To show their approval of the idea, the council, the celebration committee, and whoever else happened to be in the town hall that evening voted unanimously in favor of the proposal.

Anyone who stood on the town's new and sparkling brick road and looked east to the depot, where the last of the street was being laid down, all put in place by their own hands, wanted to dance—needed to dance—in the streets. They had earned it, and they were ready to celebrate. Some did worry aloud about Brother Griggsby.

All Joe said about it was: "Let the chips fall where they may."

"Abby, it's Noah," he said from the salesroom of the Bon Marché. Abby went to greet him. "Are you all right?" he asked with concern.

"Oh, I'm just tired. It seems every woman in town wants a new hat for the celebration."

"Well, you better get some rest," he said, removing his hat and bowing in a courtly fashion, "because I've come to ask you to save the first dance for me—and the last one."

"What? What do you mean? I don't understand," she said, noticeably confused.

"We're going to celebrate the new street with a street dance," Noah said with boyish enthusiasm.

"Oh, I don't believe you." Her eyes glistened, and the dimples in her cheeks deepened. "When did this happen?"

"We voted on it at tonight's council meeting."

"What about Brother Griggsby?"

"We haven't told him," Noah said in a whisper, "but this time, I think we've put one over on him." And, taking her into his arms, he led her into a dance step.

Their festive mood ended when a stranger wearing an ill-fitting black suit, so old it had a green veneer to it, entered the shop and approached Noah. "Are you Dr. Edwards?" he asked, not pausing long enough for Noah to answer. "I'm Colonel Wango," the man said, extending his hand. "They call me the 'Prophet of the Old West.'" His left arm was supported by a black scarf tied around his neck, from which a small, baby-pink hand, incapable of movement or grasp, hung inert.

The man briefly raised his black, broad-brimmed, flat-top hat in the style worn by "Wild Bill" Hickok. He further emulated the famous Indian fighter by wearing his hair long and sporting a Hickokian-style mustache. The stranger's facial hair, however, was too sparse to be effective, and the mustache drooping from either side of his small, resentful mouth made him look more Manchurian than western.

"I've heard of the gift that God has so kindly bestowed upon one of his servants, and I wanted to meet that man. Sir, you have been called upon by God to heal the masses," he said in a rhetorical tone. "A man who has received such a bountiful gift should toil night and day in the name of the Lord, and never cease."

Noah was at a loss for words, but the muscles near the corners of his mouth had tightened.

"Toil without cease," the man repeated and, with a tip of his hat to Abby and a salute to Noah, he left.

Noah and Abby stared at each other. Then the smiles appeared, and then laughter, and, like children, they escaped to the workroom, where they laughed until tears wet their cheeks.

The day of the street dedication dawned crisp and cool, with the tang and snap of a newly ripe winesap apple. The entire town was up early to attend the dedication. The ceremony was to take place at the entrance to the depot and the beginning of Main Street.

When the ceremonious last brick and a marker inscribed with the words DEDICATED TO EMMA TOWNSEND, OUR AUNT EM was put in place, the ever-expanding town band led the parade of people on their resplendent new brick road to the ballpark.

Selma Ward, who was sitting with her husband, Eldon, motioned Abigail and Frieda to seats in the grandstand. Abby sat next to Mrs. Ward, and each time the home team made a good play, she patted Abby's hand. Once she whispered to her, "Young Dr. Townsend is seated in the bleachers near third base and is wearing his black armband."

Abby tenderly touched her own band. They all wore black armbands and would continue to wear them until their year of mourning for Aunt Em had come to an end.

"Mrs. Townsend is not with her husband," Selma said, referring to Lillian. "I do hope she isn't going to be uppity toward the town." Abby and Frieda exchanged glances, because it was Mrs. Ward whom the townspeople always referred to as being uppity.

The much-anticipated baseball game took place in the early afternoon before the ox roast. The famous Honus Wagner was there, although he didn't play due to broken bones in his left hand. Still, he was the main attraction. He held court, greeted people—especially the kids—and rooted for the Rockets. The Pirates, always scouting for new players, were in Rockville to look over the Rockets. As Wagner entertained the kids by showing them how he held his bat or threw the ball, he watched each individual Rocket player. Sagittarius, who was now on third and ready to run, was a fearless player, and his teammate Lester, the base stealer, was at bat. Wagner noticed that the two men had an interesting rapport. Lester drew a base on balls and was trotting slowly to first, but about halfway there, he took off like a blue streak, touching first base and running to second, with Sag streaking for home plate. Wagner jumped up and, ripping his ball cap off, cheered the Rockets' play.

The Rockets lost 5–3, but just knowing that they had put up a reasonable contest against a big-league team, met the famous Honus Wagner, and competed in a game they could be proud of were all good enough for them.

Two long lines of people snaked their way to the barbecue pit, where the ox was being carved and where tables laden with food waited. The players were served first, which gave the Pirates the opportunity to invite any member of the home team to come to Florida for the winter tryouts—and a chance to play in the minors. It was Orion and his explosive fastball that interested them the most, and he was the first one they approached. For Orion, leaving Rockville and Jennie Jeanne was unthinkable. Each player was interviewed, all except Harlan; because the big leagues were not integrated, Harlan Jones was never considered.

Many strangers were in town for the festivities, among them Colonel Wango, the Wild Bill imitator. Six or more families appeared to be traveling with the Prophet of the Old West in a small religious cult known as the Foot Soldiers for Jesus, even though they had ridden into town in covered wagons drawn by pitifully thin animals. The group ambled about the ballpark, Colonel Wango in the lead, the useless, angry-red hand dangling from the black silk scarf tied around his neck bouncing against the dingy whiteness of his shirtfront with each step. He held the crippled arm pressed tightly to the side of his chest, where he secured a crudely painted sign attached to a pole that on one side proclaimed JESUS SAVES! and on the other THE END IS NIGH.

"Have you been saved?" he asked of the townspeople as the group slowly paraded past them. "Get right with Jesus before it's too late. Let me baptize you in the name of Jesus into the true faith!"

The women and children parading with him carried tin cups, with which they pleaded for alms. "Help us support our missionary work," they begged, not showing much enthusiasm. Grown-ups in the crowd, otherwise indifferent to them, sometimes paused and listened for a few minutes or lingered longer if the group members had knelt in prayer and were beseeching God to save the world. Only the young boys of the town remained focused on the cult, and, after several minutes of preaching to an audience of kids mesmerized by his infirmity, Colonel Wango used his sign pole to push them out of his way. "This isn't no sideshow, you dirty little scalawags," he snarled, poking them in the ribs with the pole. "Be off with you. Move! Move!"

The colonel approached Noah, where he was waiting at the head of the food line with the other ballplayers. Dark circles around the colonel's deep-set eyes disguised their color, but the glow of the fanatic gleamed from their depths like gold nuggets in a muddy stream. With his black hat at a cocky tilt, he once again rebuked Noah for not availing himself to the people at all times.

"Sir, you are obliged to heal," he said to Noah. "You have been called upon by God to heal the masses. It is your Christian duty to toil in the fields of the Lord from dawn to dusk." In a loud, theatrical voice, he announced, "Your gift, sir, is not yours. It is God's. You are only the keeper of His bounty. Your gift belongs to all of us," he said, waving his good hand back and forth as he expansively indicated everyone within the range of his voice.

Joe Langley, overhearing the tirade, stepped in and said to the man, "Religion is a business, and, like any other business, it has business hours. You, sir, can attend a healing service any Sunday morning of the month. Good day." And with those words, Joe turned the man around and steered him toward the end of the food line.

At the close of the daylong celebration, two ballplayers were missing, Lester Dinwoody and Sagittarius Langley, both men aboard the four o'clock train headed for Florida.

It was a magical night; the clear sky was filled with stars, and the country air with music. A platform erected on the sidewalk in front of Fountain Park provided a stage for the bands, and ropes tied to sawhorses outlined the space set aside for dancing, with smooth wooden planks covering the bricks.

The evening of dancing and music began with members of the Langley family band—Rose, Leo, and Aries—and three members from the town's marching band, including Noah Edwards on coronet. They were followed by the Italian string band from Saint Margaret's playing waltzes; the night ended with the McCoy family band playing bluegrass.

And dance they did! Couples who had enjoyed dancing before Brother Griggsby had come to town were trying it again. Some of them were recapturing their skills enough to show off their long-forgotten expertise on the temporary dance floor. The waltzes, almost unknown in Rockville, were performed by the Langleys and the Italians and a few couples from New Church. Mr. and Mrs. Parlett proved wonderfully graceful in their execution of the waltz.

Donald and Dovie Vaughn, of the Music Arcade, knew all the steps and danced every dance. Their group of friends, the progressive newlyweds in town (who no longer attended Old Church), took part in the dancing whether they knew the steps or not.

Noah left the orchestra long enough to dance with Abby as the band played "Casey Would Waltz with a Strawberry Blonde." She was surprised at his mastery of the dance; he was equally impressed by her skill and wondered where she had learned to waltz.

When the widow McCoy, her two older sons, and daughter Willa Mae took to the bandstand to play mountain music on fiddle, banjo, washboard, and jug, no one danced; instead they clapped and stomped, keeping time to the lively music.

But when the band played "Put Your Little Foot Right There," many couples took to the floor, including Abby and Noah. Men and women pointed their toes, and the women's skirts swirled above their ankles as they twirled beneath the arms of their partners.

The Langley clan finally seized the space reserved for dancers and clogged to the upbeat music. Grandpa Mosley pulled a reluctant Abigail onto the dance floor, and almost immediately she was caught up in the spirit of the music and was beaming with excitement. Abby loved to dance, and she especially liked clogging with the old man.

Old Church members stood apart from the participants and felt a tremor of fear as they listened to the strangeness of the mountain music and saw, with unbelieving eyes, the totally decadent abandonment of the dancers. Should they be dancing and listening to devil music? Were they really on a direct path to hell and damnation, as Brother Griggsby had predicted they would be if they participated in the festivities? He had said it was all right for them to partake of the food, but were they about to suffer dire consequences for their all-out enjoyment of the day?

It was that night when Lottie Oberlander was made aware of the attraction that existed between her daughter and Orion Langley. It was by chance that she had seen them kissing in the light emanating from the bonfire burning in the middle of the park.

Lottie's world ebbed, and returned. *When had this happened?* she thought. Jennie Jeanne was too young to have a boyfriend; she was still a baby. "And," Lottie quietly fumed, "she's made a spectacle of herself being seen kissing in public." She would have to talk to Jennie Jeanne, and Mr. Oberlander to the boy.

At the close of the festivities, Noah walked Abigail the short distance to her house. They sat on the veranda watching fireflies and the last of the celebrants leaving the park. Noah seemed unusually quiet after his exuberance of the evening. Abby stole uneasy glances at him. "Is something bothering you?" she asked.

"Well, yes. Colonel Wango's bothering me. He approached me at the town park this afternoon to tell me again that I should never stop 'toiling in the fields of the Lord.'" They smiled at the memory of the colonel in her shop.

"I saw him talking to you," she said. "He is such an unsavory little man."

"I want things back the way they were," Noah said. "God forgive me, but I don't want to be a healer, and that makes me feel guilty as sin. I want my church back. I want my anonymity back. I want my girl back," he said, hugging her shoulders.

"I'm here. I never left," she said.

He turned and, taking her in his arms, drew her gently to him. The kiss was mixed with the tantalizing sweetness of desire. Overcome with happiness, Abby let her head rest on his shoulder.

"By the way," Noah whispered against her cheek, "where did you learn to waltz?"

"A boy," she said. "A boy I used to know."

"Should I be jealous?"

"No," she said with a sigh. "It was a long time ago."

CHAPTER 47

September 1907

As HE STOOD AT THE bow of the ark, Noah looked out on the Sabbath-morning crowd. Each Sunday the number of strangers had been increasing, and today, after the street dedication and the free food the day before, many new people were waiting to be admitted to the ark, including Colonel Wango and his Foot Soldiers for Jesus. Wagons were caravanned on the opposite side of the street, and the new brick road between the campers and the ark was filled with the sick, the lame, and the curious, all waiting to crowd into the ark.

The Prophet of the Old West's little clan had formed a prayer circle, and one of the foot soldiers was beating on a drum: a slow, steady measure that sounded like a funeral dirge. When the prayer ended, they spread through the assembly, proselytizing for converts. They exhorted the people to join them in believing that doomsday was near, and they invited people who were waiting for the healing service at the ark to join them at Stony Creek Bridge afterward to be baptized into "the one and only true church" and to become foot soldiers for Christ.

People who had traveled quite a distance to receive a healing were camped out on what was once Old Church property but was now zoned for business. Breakfast preparations were taking place over individual fires, and recently washed clothes were spread out to dry on clusters of bushes. Children, screaming, laughing, and calling out to one another, raced through the temporary camp. Women stood about in groups, gossiping. Dogs ran loose, and bartering for rabbits penned in a wire cage was soon underway.

Noah understood how Jesus must have felt in the temple amid the money changers. Clenching his jaw, the muscles tightening, he turned his back on the scene. Each Sunday had taken on more of a carnival atmosphere, and he found the sacrilege disturbing. *What has happened to the sweetness and dignity of Sunday morning?* he asked himself. *And to my own dignity?*

Abby joined Noah on the deck. "It's going to be a long afternoon," he said apologetically.

"I'll wait," she replied, her voice gentle.

Shifting the Bible he was holding to his left hand and turning her toward him, he caressed her cheek. "You're like sunshine to me," he said, stroking the line of her jaw with his thumb and briefly resting his fingertips on her lips. Hungry for affection, she closed her eyes and let her cheek rest against his hand. "And moonlight," he added, kissing her temple. She straightened his tie, and he caught her hands, pressing them to his chest. She was aware of his desire for her, and deep inside her body she felt a reciprocating response.

"You'll stay?" he asked, his voice husky.

"I'll wait, no matter how long it takes," she said, smiling up at him, her eyes full of promise.

The afternoon healing service followed the Sunday morning church service, with an hour's break in between. During that time, Noah fasted, and the men assisting him were served Sunday dinner prepared by Rosie and Abigail. Lars had had a change of heart about the propriety of Abigail being a mate for Noah and had made friends with her, especially once he tasted her cooking.

At one o'clock, the doors to the ark opened for the healing service, and Lars and the Olsen brothers, escorting the pilgrims to seats in the pews, scrambled to find room for everyone. When it was a petitioner's turn to receive a healing, the escorts delivered them to Noah, who waited in front of the stage below the pulpit. The Langley men acted as "catchers" for those who fell backward after receiving Noah's electrifying touch on their foreheads.

Aries played the organ as the church filled with sojourners in an air heavy with the anticipation of deliverance from their torment. As quietness settled around them, a blissful peace descended on the chapel. Noah, seated on the pulpit, head bowed, deep in prayer, quietly waited to enter a state of grace and to have a visitation from the Holy Ghost.

Just before Noah would feel the presence at his side, Pie Face would begin to wave, and little Joey Brown would beam and point at something only he could see. *Unless ye believe as a child,* Noah reminded himself. He requested that Pie Face and Joey be in the chapel for every healing service.

Today, Dr. Adam Townsend was in attendance, and he remained through the long afternoon observing the many healings. The doctor's attitude was one of respect and professional interest. Colonel Wango and his followers, seated on the long bench in the rear of the ark, were the last seekers to be brought forward at the end of the long day. The group didn't look so much like zealots as castoffs washed up from life's seamier shores. The colonel secured his hat by pressing it beneath his crippled arm, with the wasted hand tucked into a coat pocket.

The pseudo-colonel was the last one waiting for a blessing. He received a touch from Noah that so paralyzed him that he slipped through the hands of the two Langley men acting as catchers and dropped to the floor. Once fully recovered, he sat upright and had the look of shock on his face that had become familiar to Noah. He knew instantly that the man had received a divine blessing.

The colonel pulled the tingling, awakening hand from his pocket, and it plopped into his lap, an entity unto itself. So startled was he by the hand's resemblance to a newly born piglet that he recoiled from the red, wriggling, squirming mass. Gaining control of his senses, he turned it over, staring in awe while he tested its strength.

After recovering from the shock of his healing, the colonel bounded to his feet and, making his way to the lectern, picked up the Bible that was kept there. He grasped the book with his still-flopping hand, turned to Noah, and, with an unstable wrist, shook the Bible in Noah's direction. "Hallelujah, brother!" he shouted. "Praise be to God. I've been healed!"

Why him? a tired, overwrought Noah inwardly raged. *Why him, God? Why not others more beneficial to society than a pumped-up, pompous, counterfeit colonel? Why not Aunt Em?* He wanted to scream it aloud and was close to weeping. *If I were you, God, I would heal the worthy.*

"Thank heavens it's over," Noah said to himself. He was tired, his head ached; in fact, he ached all over and was weary beyond words.

Lars, looking at him with concern, said, "It's too hard on you, son—you can't keep this up." He grunted in disgust and showed his disdain for the strangers by shaking a fist toward the street and the camp. "They want too much." Lars, like many people in the town, where very few had availed themselves of the healing services, felt their town had been overrun with riffraff.

Frieda waited with Abby on the deck for Noah's return from the chapel; once he appeared, she slipped quietly away.

Abby and Noah moved toward each other with arms outstretched. When Abby saw Noah's dejected posture and slumping shoulders, she felt a wave of panic; as his body sagged against her, she had a glimpse of the terrible torment in his eyes. They sat down at the rail bench, and as his head dropped onto her shoulder, she shielded him as she would a child. After a long wait, she felt the tenseness leave his body.

"I dared to question God's wisdom," he said, a frayed weariness to his voice. "I'm not worthy of my calling."

"Shhh! Shhh!" she said, and with the deep affection she felt for him, held him tighter and gently rocked as she comforted him. "You're very worthy, Noah. You're the most worthy man I know. You're just worn out." As she listened to the heartbreak in his voice, a shiver passed through her. *Please, God, don't take him away from me,* she silently pleaded.

The late Sunday afternoon had turned cold, and Colonel Wango, coatless, shoeless, and wearing shrunken white pants, tested the creek water with the toes of one foot. "Damn," he said under his breath, "that's cold." Pie Face, dressed in what looked to be a nightgown—grimy and in need of mending, supplied by the Foot Soldiers for Jesus—stood waiting at the water's edge, a smile on his round blank face. He was seemingly amused by the colonel's dipping his foot in the cold water and cussing.

The restoration of the colonel's hand that afternoon had been the most profound healing of the day. Many had borne witness to the hand turning from new-baby pink, to the waxy yellow color of fat, before taking on the color of normal skin. A small group of the witnesses, seeking healing or redemption, had followed the Prophet of the Old West, receiver of this divine miracle, to Stony Creek Bridge, where he hoped to conduct a baptism for new converts to his Foot Soldiers for Jesus ministry.

Never before in his insignificant life had Colonel Wango felt such power, such exhilaration, or such joy. He wanted his own messianic gift. He wanted to heal the sick! And baptize new souls for Jesus.

The colonel stretched forth his miracle hand to the knot of people standing on the bridge, most of whom seemed unsure about joining his Foot Soldiers, and motioned for them to unite with him at the water's edge. "I have been touched by God!" he declared. Reaching forth his blessed hand, he touched the forehead of the man nearest him. The receiver of this distinction did not fall down. The colonel tried again, touching another, and another. All remained upright. The Prophet of the Old West quickly reverted to his old mission of saving souls through baptism, and he began to proselytize.

A cold gust of wind blew across the rounded shoulders of the small group of people, ruffling the water in the creek. They backed away, looking toward the town, and, quickly deciding against joining the Foot Soldiers for Jesus, crossed over the bridge, leaving the colonel with his only convert—Pie Face—and a choir of shivering, hungry, dispirited followers singing "Bringing in the Sheaves."

Colonel Wango, the Prophet of the Old West, disappeared into the bushes and upon his return revealed to his followers that he had received a heavenly message: he was to baptize Pie Face in the watering trough at the campground. This way, he rationalized, he wouldn't have to stand in cold water up to his waist while he dunked the town idiot.

Upon returning to the campground, the little band was confronted by Marshal McCombs. McCombs, seeing Pie Face all got up in the white gown, knew what was about to take place. "And just where do you intend to baptize him?" he asked. The colonel nodded to the horse trough.

Marshal McCombs lowered his head, staring up at the man from beneath the brim of his Rough Riders hat. "This young man..." he intoned, pausing and searching his memory for the boy's given name, and, when he couldn't come up with it, reminding himself to someday find out what in hell's tarnation the kid's name was, anyhow. Then he continued. "No one in the history of Rockville has been saved as many times as Pie. He gets saved every time there's a revival, he gets baptized and graduated and married," the marshal said, hammering out each phrase. "At every wedding, he's standing right up there with the groom saying, 'I do.' Half the time the bride don't know who she's married to: Tom, Dick,

Harry, or Pie Face. Hell, we have to watch him, or he'll get buried!"

His tone softened. "But he's our cross to bear, and we try to suffer it with grace and humility." Raising his voice, he said, "And we're not about to let some stranger come to town and make a—a—a—a *fool* out of him." The marshal harrumphed, sputtered, and spat. He knew what he meant, even if it hadn't come out right. "And I suggest very strongly that, no later than tomorrow noon, you and your followers shake the dust of our town from your heels and rid yourselves of us and our charity."

After the dramatic healing of the colonel's wasted hand, Noah did not leave the ark. He remained in his study, or paced the deck. The colonel's withered, waiflike hand filled Noah's waking hours and haunted his dreams. He saw it as a symbol of what was crippled inside him; God had tested him and had found him undeserving of His gift.

The crowd was larger than ever the Sunday following the healing-hand service. But Noah knew without trying that the presence had forsaken him. Pie Face did not wave, and Joey did not point and beam.

Noah looked out on the sea of faces—sad faces, and hopeful faces, pained, hurt, and expectant faces—and knew he could not heal them. In turn, each of the afflicted was brought forth, but no one fell; no one received a miracle.

What tormented Noah was that, in his egotistical audacity, he had dared to question God about whom He healed. *I deemed one of His chosen as being unworthy to receive His blessing; now, whoever comes to me is denied. I chose Mary Louise to be healed; now it is God who is choosing, and I've been contemptuously disgruntled with His choices. Did I think I could play God and pick and choose whom I thought should be healed? Did I think that I, in my small, earthly experience, could in any way comprehend His ways? Have I grown so arrogant that I assumed I could challenge the Divine Healer? Is He saying, "Behold! I am God?"*

The pain in his soul was unendurable.

"Father," he prayed over and over, "teach me humility. Teach me to graciously accept Your gifts, even the most humble ones. Teach me not to doubt Your ways, to be thankful, and to receive Your blessings with gratitude. I have grown disdainful and willful and impassioned by the weakness of my flesh and have put another before You in my thoughts, and for this I am truly repentant."

Abby's beautiful face and sad eyes floated before him.

Frieda and Rosie sat in the kitchen, Rosie's eyes red and swollen from crying. Frieda, an elbow cupped in one hand, tugged with nervous fingers at the skin on her neck and commiserated with Rosie by silently weeping; they didn't know why they wept.

Noah led Abby to the deck. The early-fall evening had turned cold, and she was wearing his black varsity sweater with the white H on a field of crimson. Noah walked her to a seat at the rail bench, his hand lingering briefly on her shoulder. No rush to each other's arms this time; no kindred magnetism flowed between them.

Noah stood at the rail. The ruby clouds of sunset reflecting on the faded steeple of Old Church turned it a bright and cheerful red, flamed the mullioned windows of the Townsend mansion to fiery molten glass, and brushed the Rock House with a deep terra-cotta wash. After the splendor of sunset had faded, he sat down beside Abby and, taking both her hands in his, examined her ringless fingers.

Abby's heart ached. She had not seen Noah for two weeks, and during that time he had visibly aged. He had lost weight, and his eyes revealed a sickness of soul.

"The first time I saw you, soaking wet and dripping muddy water," he said, "I believe I was already in love with you." He looked up at her. "I'm going away. I can't ask you to go with me. It's a personal journey."

Her hands, like wounded birds, fluttered in the unresponsive cage of his grasp, then grew as still as death. "Let me take care of you," Abby said in a voice breathless with fright. "I can make you well. I can. I love you, Noah."

Noah caught his breath, but still he shook his head. "I questioned the omnipotence of God, and for a man of

God to do so is an unforgivable sin. I was taking the credit for His miracles, forgetting that I am not the healer, only the servant. I became arrogant."

"You could never be arrogant, Noah, never," she said, almost crying.

"In my heart, and soul, I have fallen from grace. I am no longer worthy of spreading the teachings of Jesus. I no longer feel His love, hear His words, or feel His presence." He released her hands into her lap. "It's my spirit that's sick, Abby, and only God can heal me." He gave her hands a fatherly pat. "I feel confident in leaving you. You've become a very strong and desirable woman."

The suffering in his eyes deepened. They remained silent, sitting side by side and not touching.

"You won't do anything foolish?" she finally asked him. "I mean—you won't take any midnight swims or anything like that?"

He managed a weak laugh. "No, that would only compound my sins." Remembering her near-drowning and the day after that fateful night, he said, "I promised I would never forsake you."

"Yes, you did, and on bended knee," she reminded him, managing a smile. She was trying for humor but was afraid it had sounded like she was hinting for a proposal. She stood. "You're right—I am strong." She removed his sweater and handed it to him. "Don't worry about me. Go. Do what you have to do. I'll be fine."

And he never asked, "Will you wait?"

CHAPTER 48

PERTHY PRETTYMAN AND LUCINDA HIGGINS were on their way home from the Tuesday Society meeting, the one where Brother Griggsby had demanded of them the names of every member who'd been seen dancing at the street dedication. "And how close were they dancing?" he insisted, as if this were an inquisition. Because every member of the Tuesday Benevolent Society had been there, they were chastised as a group.

"Sometimes I get good and tired of being told it's a sin to have fun," Perthy said. They had paused on the sidewalk in front of the ark, and both of them stood looking at the imposing edifice.

"You know," Lucinda said, "I've lived next door to the Chapel of the Ark all this time, and I've never once looked inside."

"I'm game if you are!" Perthy declared with a nod of her head.

They walked to the entrance of the ark, opened the door, and peeked inside. What they saw, and heard, made perfect wreaths of their open, wrinkled mouths and surprised circles of their dumbfounded eyes.

They sucked in air, let it out in a noisy puff, and collided with each other in their hasty retreat. They did not speak. They did not look at each other but marched with fixed intent to the residence of Brother Griggsby.

The Chapel of the Ark was a popular meeting place for the young people of Rockville, and adolescents from churches other than the ark could be found there almost any day. Band-practice days were especially popular, and days when the band was rehearsing their marching formations in the street brought girls to the church.

Susan and Jennie Jeanne were at the ark because Jennie Jeanne was waiting for Orion, and Susan had a crush on Noah—as did most of the girls, although no one had seen him for quite some time. Noah's attention to Abigail Langley had not lessened Susan's girlish infatuation for the pastor. Just having Noah smile, or speak to her, gave her butterflies and goose bumps and was worth the trip to the ark.

Today the band, without Noah, was in the backyard of the church practicing marching maneuvers, while the two best of friends sat in a pew near the center of the church talking about boys. "Have you ever been kissed?" a blushing Jennie Jeanne asked Susan.

"Not as many times as you have!" was Susan's coy reply.

"I know," said Jennie Jeanne, blushing again. "Mother is having a conniption fit. She's even forbidden me from seeing Orion. She saw us kissing at the ox roast. You'd think it was the end of the world. I told her we were betrothed, and she was horrified."

"Are you betrothed? Are you spoken for?" an excited Susan asked.

"No, but everyone knows we will be, someday," Jennie Jeanne said, a worldly, grown-up expression on her face. "Now, I'm serious, have you been kissed before?" Jennie Jeanne said, narrowing her eyes. "You know, really kissed?"

"Well, yes," Susan answered. "As a matter of fact, Teddy White kissed me when we played spin the bottle at Sara's birthday party last month. It was a long kiss, and he kind of felt me, too."

They both giggled, Jennie Jeanne's eyes slanting upward in her pixie face and Susan covering her mouth in embarrassment.

"When Orion kisses me, I don't know what to do with my lips," Jennie Jeanne confessed in all sincerity. "I don't know if I should pucker up or let my mouth be natural." She parted her lips, affecting an engaging little pose, and further expressed her dilemma by delicately patting her face on either side. "Or if I should press against his mouth, or what?" Throwing her hands up in dismay, she said with a little pout, "I don't know how it's supposed to feel."

"Let's kiss, then we can tell each other how it feels," Susan suggested.

"Oh," Jennie Jeanne said, doubt wavering in her voice. "OK."

After a few uneasy moments interspersed with giggles, they closed their eyes and strained toward each other. This set off another spate of laugher when they bumped heads.

"No, no, no," Jennie Jeanne protested, "don't laugh. We have to be serious."

She rose, bending over the seated Susan, and in a deep, dramatic voice said, "I love you, Susan." Eyes tightly shut and feeling with their lips, they found each other's mouths, and kissed—each one thinking: *Did I just hear something?*

Breaking apart in an explosion of giggles, they laughed until tears streamed down their cheeks. Finally, drying their eyes and straightening their hair ribbons, they solemnly critiqued the kiss.

"It felt fine. I guess," Susan said, suddenly embarrassed.

"You were puckering, Suzy," Jennie Jeanne, the more experienced of the two, said, "and it made your lips feel firm."

"Well! I'm not going to kiss you again," Susan said in exasperation.

"Me neither, ever!" Jennie Jeanne agreed, and together they erupted into another spasm of innocent laughter.

CHAPTER 49

At the pealing of the half-hour school bell, children from all over town began their daily trudge to classes and their first day of school. The girls eagerly pushed ahead of the malingering boys—young men whose white necks, exposed by too-short haircuts glistening palely next to their farmwork tans—who wanted neither haircuts nor school.

The boys wore homemade overalls, or Brownie-brand overalls if their school clothes had been purchased from Parlett's Emporium. Several of them went barefoot, saving their shoes for cold weather. The girls wore cotton dresses. The twelfth-grade girls wore long skirts for the first time, and showed their delight in doing so, but the young men were behaving as though it was nothing out of the ordinary for them to be wearing long pants.

The beginning of the new school year revived the "girls seen kissing in the ark" story, first started by Perthy Prettyman and Lucinda Higgins, and by October the gossip had moved from the women's sewing circles to the school's playground. Jennie Jeanne and Susan Ann, the two most popular girls in school, were being ignored by the other students, which was hard for them to accept or understand. No one had told them the stories that were being spread about them. Their friends were too embarrassed to repeat the stories, and their families did their utmost to keep the gossip from them.

When Corvus and Cetus, the Langley twins, returned home from school, they dropped like sacks of flour onto the bench by the kitchen sink, where their mother sat on a stool peeling a pail of potatoes.

"We want to talk to Leo," Corvus said.

"About what?" their mother asked without looking up.

"It's private business," Cetus said, throwing his shoulders back in a show of bravado.

"It's 'cause Leo knows everything," Corvus added, assuming his brother's stance.

This time Rose looked up, causing the twins to lower their heads and roll their eyes at each other. "Knock on the door and ask Leo if you can come in," she said, eyeing them suspiciously. "And behave yourselves!" she said, raising her voice to be heard above their scramble from the bench.

It was Leo's claim that, between the two boys, they shared one brain. "What's on your one mind?" he asked as the twins entered the business office, a room on the first floor of the house away from the dust and noise of the lumberyard.

The twins looked at each other before asking in unison, "What's a 'morphadite'?"

Leo's eyebrows shot up. His unwavering stare made them uneasy, and they moved closer to each other, touching shoulders and finding the other's hand.

Placing his fists on his knees and leaning forward in his chair, Leo said, "In the first place, 'morphadite' is not a word—the word is 'hermaphrodite'—and where did you hear it?"

"At school," they said.

"From your teacher?"

"No!" they said, their eyes wide. "From the kids."

"Who are they saying it about—you?"

"Heck no! Jennie Jeanne."

"What? Jennie Jeanne? Well, it's a damn cruel thing to say about anyone."

"Yeah? So what does it mean?" Cetus asked.

"Why are they saying it about Jennie Jeanne?" Leo wondered aloud. "And who in the hell in this town of ignoramuses would know about mor-pha-dites?" he said, mockingly mispronouncing the word.

The twins shrugged and waited, not taking their vigilant eyes from his face. "Well, is her a her-ma-phro-dite?" Corvus asked at last, struggling with the pronunciation.

Leo knuckle rapped him on the head. "I very much doubt it," he said. Then, jumping up so fast his wheeled swivel chair scooted backward across the hardwood floor, he exploded. "No! No! Of course not, and don't you let anyone say she is. And not one word of this to Orion, understand? Are you listening?"

"Well?" Corvus demanded, ignoring his question and standing his ground, although he was still smarting from the knuckle rapping.

Leo finally relented. "It means a person who's born with both male and female sex organs, and he—or she—is both a man and a woman."

The twins stood stiff with panic, their eyes unnaturally large, their chests expanding from holding their breaths.

"Scat!" Leo said.

They ran from the room, hands clasped over their mouths, not wanting this new unheard-of knowledge to come spilling from their lips.

"Oh, and find Dad and tell him I want to see him!" Leo called after them.

The twins escaped to the two-hole outhouse, the place where they discussed man-woman stuff.

Today's discussion was a big one.

"How do they do their business?" they wondered. "Do they sit or stand? How do they dress, half like a man and half like a woman?"

Their interest soon shifted to their favorite outhouse pastime: looking at a torn-off page from last year's Sears, Roebuck and Company catalogue—the section advertising women's undergarments. They held the page up to the daylight coming through the quarter-moon-shaped ventilation opening near the ceiling and tried to make out the naked bodies of the women beneath the clothing they wore in the drawings.

The rumor about Jennie Jeanne had turned sinister. It was no longer about two girls kissing but that Jennie Jeanne was a "morphadite" and that she liked both girls and boys. Old gossip about Lottie and the baby was resurrected. People recalled how, at the time of Jennie Jeanne's birth, Lottie Oberlander had not wanted anything to do with her premature newborn and, as in the case of Jennie Jeanne, it wasn't the first time a fully formed, robust baby had been declared premature. But Jennie Jeanne, from the beginning, had demanded that she be noticed, made over, petted, and adored.

The fact that Mrs. Oberlander "possessed a nature too delicate to nurse" meant that the baby needed a wet nurse. The widow McCoy was called on, she being the only mother with a nursing infant available at the time.

"Well! That explains it! That's enough right there to make someone funny," waggish tongues declared.

As a result of the whispered scandal, the twins were in a fight every day at school.

Jennie Jeanne had been branded the aggressor. It was she who was seen standing over the other girl, declaring her love for her and speaking in a masculine tone. At school, someone printed with chalk on the boy's outhouse, "Jennie Jeanne is a boy." And a crude drawing appeared in her desk of a girl, presumably she, with both male and female genitalia showing between her legs.

"I never looked back," Perthy Prettyman would say when describing the kissing scene. "I knew if I did, I would be turned into a pillar of salt."

CHAPTER 50

JOE LANGLEY WAS IN THE Rockville Repository chatting at the window with the teller when Mr. Oberlander appeared at his side. He patted him on the back and asked him to stop by his office before leaving the bank.

Mr. Oberlander's demeanor and the gentlemanly furnishings of his office always made people feel good about having entrusted their money to his bank. He motioned for Joe to take a seat in the big leather chair.

"Joe," he began, "can we talk about our children, Orion and Jennie Jeanne? Orion's a fine young man, the best, but can't we separate them for a while, give them a cooling-off period, so to speak? Mrs. Oberlander, bless her heart, is a typical mother, and she wants her little girl to experience life a little before settling down, maybe go east to a finishing school." He took a deep breath. "In fact, she is dead set against a marriage—or even a betrothal—anytime soon."

"You mean, ever?"

"No, no, but a good time," he said. Then he added thoughtfully, "And I personally think the engagement should be postponed, at least for the time being."

"Well, an engagement is certainly news to me," Joe said.

"Jennie Jeanne told Mrs. Oberlander they were betrothed."

"I didn't know they were talking marriage, and if they are, then yes, I agree they're too young to be thinking about marriage. I'll talk to Orion." Joe rose from the chair, and they shook hands.

"We want what is best for our young people," Mr. Oberlander said. "And above all, to put the mothers' minds at ease."

Orion had come into town with his dad, and while Joe was in the bank, he had crossed the street from the livery to the Bon Marché.

"Hi, cuz," he said on entering the hat store. "How's my favorite cousin?" Orion had worried about Abby ever since Noah's departure, but she seemed to be in good spirits.

"I had a postcard from Noah from New York City," she said. "He wrote that he was on his way to London on the RMS *Lusitania*."

"Wow!" Orion exclaimed. "All the way to London, England. I'd like to go there myself someday, maybe on a honeymoon."

Orion's enthusiasm made her laugh. "You're too young for a honeymoon," she said teasingly, and she told him about the gift she had received from Noah.

Joe Langley entered the shop, greeting Abby and tipping his hat to Frieda, who was in the store as well. But he seemed preoccupied with something other than inquiring about his niece's welfare—which, it's true, he was always concerned about. Learning that Abby was not in need of anything, he said to Orion, "Let's get started for home, then."

"Dad, Dr. Edwards left his horse and buggy for Abby to use, and she needs that old shed in her backyard fixed up for a stable."

"Is that so?" Joe said, his voice brightening. He turned to Abby. "That was mighty nice of him. Orion, you and your brothers get on it right away."

Abby remained at the door, looking out on the graying day. She imagined the shape of the wind as it tumbled a sheet of newspaper across the street, where it caught on the trunk of the Poster Tree and remained there, unchanging, from the steadfastness of the wind.

"I thought he would marry you," Frieda said.

"I wasn't good enough for him," Abby said. Remembering Frieda was hard of hearing and needed to see the speaker's face, she closed the shop door and crossed the room to the display case, where her friend was standing. "I wasn't good enough for him," she repeated.

Frieda bristled and in her anger struggled to express herself, the mushy, half-formed words maneuvering around in her mouth as they fought to get out. "You are good enough for any man, Abigail Langley, even a king—or a president."

"I meant 'good enough to be a minister's wife.'"

"And a minister's wife, too," Frieda declared. "He was a coward."

With an ache in her heart, Abby said, "No, Frieda. No, oh, never. Not a coward."

"Yes," Frieda said, defiantly bobbing her head up and down. Large teardrops clung to her sparse lashes before splashing onto her dress front.

"He didn't love me enough to stay," Abby said with a sigh. "They never do." She gave Frieda a hug and returned to gazing from the window at the empty street and the deepening September sky. "I can't bargain with God," she said. "I've tried it before."

Abby watched Orion and her uncle drive away. Looking to the livery stable where Miss Molly was stabled, she wondered, as she often did, if it had been her questionable suitability to serve as a minister's wife that had driven Noah away.

She sighed, a long, wavering sigh, certain in the knowledge that she would never have another chance for love and marriage. Her little hat business was all she had. *I shouldn't look out of the window,* she thought, chastising herself. *It always makes me think of Noah.* Then, with a glance at the window of the hotel lobby: *And my mother.*

CHAPTER 51

ROBERT MAYNARD, THE NEW PASTOR of the ark, was a young man, but because of his size—just under six feet—and his well-trimmed beard, he appeared older. He was handsome, in a robust kind of way, with thick, dark-red hair, a short nose, and a generous mouth. His good black worsted-wool coat draped well from his broad shoulders, and his dark-blue eyes were charmingly affable. He had a booming baritone voice and, like Noah, taught band music; when asked if he played baseball, he had bellowed, "Yes, indeed. Yes, I do indeed play ball."

The young belles of the town and their mothers were all dancing in attendance. Since the departure of Dr. Edwards, the women of the town seemed to harbor less ill will toward Abby, given that the "big catch," as they put it, had eluded her. But this time, they were determined that the new and unmarried preacher would not be ensnared by an unfit, albeit beautiful, old maid.

Noah had handpicked Reverend Bob, as he was soon known, and had sent him to Rockville to be the new pastor of the ark. His first task as the new minister was an unpleasant one: the report of two girls seen kissing in the Chapel of the Ark had to be dealt with immediately, the rumor stopped, and the reputations of the girls and the church saved.

At first it remained just two anonymous girls seen kissing.

"Kissing who?" Amelia Tibbits asked in her sharp little voice, her needle poised above a quilt block of the "Crown of Thomas" quilt the Tuesday Society was working on that day.

"Each other," Lucinda answered her.

"Lord have mercy!" old Mrs. Wallace said, dropping her thimble; with the ping of the thimble on the hardwood floor, the society dissolved into a gossip forum. The truth became more bizarre with each rotation of the kissing story until eventually, through gossip and insinuation, the girls' names became known.

The Reverend Robert Maynard, in his first test as a minister, met with Jennie Jeanne Oberlander and Susan Leffler and their parents in the Oberlander home. He sat with military posture on a deep-rose velvet chair in the very formal Oberlander parlor.

"I'm not saying it's normal for girls to kiss each other, but it is understandable, and they did it in all innocence," Reverend Bob said.

"It wasn't anything," Susan said through tears. "We just wanted to know if we were good kissers."

"It's all my fault," Jennie Jeanne blurted out, twisting and untwisting the damp white handkerchief bunched up in her fingers. Teary eyes downcast, she added, almost inaudibly, "I wanted to know how kissing me felt to Orion," she said, stealing a sidewise glance at her mother.

Mrs. Oberlander turned toward the fireplace so that she was not speaking directly to Jennie Jeanne and whispered, "Do you know what they're saying about you? They're saying that you like girls."

Jennie Jeanne's lips trembled, her face wrinkled into an agitated expression, and, shaking her head in confusion, she looked to her father. "I don't understand," she said.

The mother turned on her daughter, looking directly at her for the first time that evening. She hissed the repulsive words, "They're saying you love girls."

"But I love Orion and I want to marry him," Jennie Jeanne said.

"Oh, you do not," Lottie Oberlander said, huffing.

"I do. I do!" Jennie Jeanne said, weeping.

Mr. Oberlander rose and patted his daughter's shoulder. "What they're saying, angel, is just malicious gossip, and it'll soon blow over." Removing a handkerchief from his breast pocket, he wiped at his eyes and blew his nose. The very thought of anything even the least bit unpleasant happening to his cherished daughter caused him almost unbearable pain.

Robert Maynard wanted desperately to wipe his damp brow and place his fingers between his neck and his high, stiff white collar, which felt to be strangling him, but he remained stoic. "I assure you that nothing untoward is going on in the ark. Everything we do there, we do with the highest degree of ethical propriety. We supervise our young people with the utmost care. We're committed to our youth. They are our foundation and our hope for a better tomorrow."

Mr. Leffler, having been quiet all evening, spoke for the first time; like Mrs. Oberlander, he addressed his remarks to the cold fireplace. The matter they were discussing was of a nature too delicate and too personal for one to look at another person. "I think that, for the time being, those two girls should not be in each other's company."

"Or the company of boys," Mrs. Oberlander said, breaking in, her usually musical words jangled like breaking glass. She was holding herself so rigidly upright and pressing her hands into her abdomen with eyes so bright that she looked as if she might have a fever.

Pastor Maynard cleared his throat and verbally stepped into the strained silence. "These are frightening years for parents as well as for their maturing children," he said. "The young ones are peeking out of the nest, straining to see their future, searching for new identities, new knowledge, and new experiences. They are trying to understand their desires, understand what it is they're feeling, and they're looking to us for guidance, and, with our love and understanding, they will come to know that they are healthy, moral, normal human beings."

Cupping his hands together and extending his arms, the minister said, "We, as parents and teachers, must keep in mind that if we strive to hold things with wings too closely, they will perish." He sat nodding his head up and down several times before opening his nested palms; with a little boosting motion of his hands, he sent an imaginary bird on its way.

CHAPTER 52

February 1908

FROM THE WALL TELEPHONE IN her workroom—the town of Rockville now had telephone services—Abby rang the operator. "Margie, this is Abigail. Will you get Judge Andrews on the telephone for me, please?"

Later, while Abby waited in Judge Andrews's office for him to return from lunch and her friend Selma Ward to meet her there, she studied the town from the judge's office window and was reminded of how much it had changed in a year's time.

Before the summer heat is upon us, she thought, *our year of mourning the passing of Aunt Em will have come to an end. We'll put away our black armbands, and the older women, who covetously obey the rules of mourning etiquette, their funereal attire. Aunt Em hadn't wanted us to mourn, but mourn we did.*

During the year of bereavement, any celebrations had been kept to a minimum, and holidays had been quiet. But the new people moving into town who had never heard of Aunt Em, and the opening of new businesses with tempting offerings, made it hard to remain grief-stricken for long.

From the window, Abby had a bird's-eye view of the Bon Marché and her new business, the Drapery Shop. The *Hub* newspaper had moved into one of the new and larger buildings on Main Street, so she had expanded into the vacated building and had hired pretty, bright, and capable Daisy Brown to work for her: her first employee.

With the passing of Aunt Em and the departure of Dr. John Townsend from the town, along with the terrible snows and whooping cough of the winter of two years past, the building of the opera house had come to a halt. Now, Dr. Adam Townsend had taken over the project, and the edifice was no longer an opera house but a memorial to Aunt Em: a two-story building with a library occupying the first floor and an up-to-date, acoustically perfect auditorium on the second. His wife, Lillian Townsend, had said that she would not live nor raise her children in a place that had no library.

The mansion was being worked on, and the rumor was that it was being turned into a hospital. Dr. and Mrs. Townsend had taken several trips out of town and at one time had been gone for a period of two months.

Abby's business adventures had taken over her life, which left her little time for personal regrets. New houses going up and old homes undergoing a renaissance in styles and colors had kept her busy. She had become the town's authority on décor.

Abby was teaching Daisy to make draperies and to trim hats, and it hadn't taken much persuasion on her part to get Daisy to move into her home with her. Now Abby had a companion to share her home, the household chores, and the care of Miss Molly. The ark had a new minister, and Noah's letters to her had come to an end.

The judge, along with Selma Ward, whom he had met in the lobby, entered the room after his lunch break was over. Judge Andrews rushed about arranging seating. "It's not often I get lady clients," he said by way of apologizing.

"It's quite all right," Abby said. "I was enjoying reminiscing from your window."

"I know what you mean," the judge said. "I, too, enjoy reminiscing from there."

"I miss the trees," Selma said from the window, "Those new telephone poles are no replacement for the trees."

"Judge Andrews," Abby began, "every morning when I come to work and leave Miss Molly at the livery stable, where she stands idle most of the day, it makes me think about the lack of transportation in town. Could I hire out the buggy, complete with a driver?"

"Whom do you have in mind for a driver?"

"Horace Brown, Daisy's brother."

"I see no reason why you couldn't. I'll take it up with the town council." He glanced to the window and to Selma.

Abby said, after a quick look to Selma, "I also want the school board's ban on teachers going to the Bon Marché rescinded."

Selma returned from the window and quickly seated herself before the judge could rise to the occasion. Bouncing her tapestry bag from her arm to her lap, Selma said, "Not allowing schoolteachers to shop in the Bon Marché, or even be seen in the store, is interfering with her rights as a storekeeper and with women's rights in general."

The judge now understood why Selma had joined Abby in his office: Abby's new friend and ally was tutoring Abby in what Selma called "the fight for women's rights." Selma, Rockville's only suffragist and women's rights activist, had made Abby's rights as a businesswoman her fight, too. Selma displayed a suffragette sign on her front lawn that read GRANT WOMEN EQUAL RIGHTS. Every night the sign was knocked over, and every morning Selma righted it.

On their way out, Selma dropped a suffragist pamphlet on the judge's desk.

The men in the barbershop watched the two women as they left Parlett's and crossed the street to the drugstore. "Selmy must be making a suffragette out of Abby Langley," the barber said.

"Well, women ain't never going to get the vote, no matter how many suffragettes they get," Chance Collins said.

“Women don’t have sense enough to vote,” Whoop Peterson said, scoffing.

“Yeah, and besides that, you got to have a dick,” the barber said.

With that said, Whoop Peterson did his “whoop” thing, slapping, cursing, and jumping.

“Goddammit, Whoop,” Chance swore. “Do you have to do that?”

Chance no longer held court from the barber chair when he was in the shop but sat on the bench by the window, where he said he was “watching the town grow.” But what Chance was really doing, like a lovestruck boy, was keeping an eye out for Abigail Langley and waiting for her to appear outside. She was always fussing over the flowers in her window box or crossing the street to the post office or the emporium.

That preacher man’s been gone thereabouts a year, he was thinking as he stroked the scar on the side of his face. Abby had been burned into his consciousness like an itch needing to be scratched ever since the day the town had gathered in Dr. Townsend’s yard and had said their farewells to Aunt Em. That’s when he’d had his first really good look at her, all grown up and as classy as a thoroughbred. Trips to the pleasure houses in the city had not quelled his carnal craving for her, and today he made up his mind to do something about it.

CHAPTER 53

March 1908

MEIKO TOMA, IN DR. TOWNSEND'S handsome carriage drawn by a team of black geldings with white noses and black chary eyes, reined in the team at the Bon Marché. Lithely dropping to the street, the nimble-footed Gypsy helped his passenger, Lillian Townsend, from the carriage and onto the stepping-stone block and to the sidewalk.

Meiko removed a coin from his vest pocket and gallantly flipped it toward Pie Face, who, with his red wagon at his side and shovel in hand, stood waiting well back of the horse.

To keep the young lad out of mischief, and from wandering into people's homes whenever it pleased him, scaring the wits out of the housewives, Marshal McCombs had created a job for the simpleminded young man. The immature misfit was guaranteed a nickel a day and tips to keep the streets in Rockville's downtown business section clean of animal droppings. Pie Face took his job seriously, working from sunrise till dusk and never missing a day.

Abby stood in the shadow of the showcase window inside her store and got her first look at Mrs. Adam Townsend. She was indeed beautiful, as had been reported by the few people in town who had seen her.

"She's a tony one," someone had said in describing her.

"Oh, she's as fine as a starched lace doily," Perthy Prettyman had declared.

Mrs. Townsend's blond hair, fair skin, blue-green eyes, and fine-boned facial features suggested a cool demeanor, but when she introduced herself to Abby inside the Bon Marché, Lillian's cultured voice was warm with finesse, something Abby had strived for. "I've been told you make draperies," she said.

"Yes, I do," Abby said. "With so many customers requesting draperies, I've taken on a whole new venture and have just opened a drapery shop." Smiling, Abby added, "I'm Abigail Langley. The drapery shop is next door."

Very stylish for a country girl, Lillian thought, *and very pretty—perhaps a bit too pretty.* "Ummm," Lillian simply said aloud. Mrs. Townsend had a habit of producing a little humming sound each time she made a decision or solved a problem to her satisfaction.

An open house was to be held in the stately, newly refurbished Townsend mansion, the purpose of which was to stock the new library and to establish Lillian Townsend as the leader of the hierarchy of Rockville society. The charge for attending the event was twenty-five cents, or one book. Not everyone thought the cost to attend the event was worth the price, but most people went along with it just to get a glimpse of the fabled house.

Lillian Townsend informed Abby that all the rooms of the mansion were being renovated. She said she had been told of Abby's sewing skills and wished her to make the draperies for the parlor and the living and dining rooms. And they must be ready and hung by the completion of the new Emma Townsend Library and Auditorium, named for the town's beloved Aunt Em.

The prospect of being a part of the decorating of the mansion excited Abby. Ideas were already forming in her head. It seemed the Townsends were always her first customers.

Mrs. Townsend didn't appear to be in any hurry to look over the fabrics in the drapery shop. She had become interested in the hats. Choosing one in a deep shade of aqua, she sat down at the vanity table and removed her black mourning hat.

Abby, standing behind her, placed the hat she had designed and made on the head of the very sophisticated Mrs. Townsend. The two women, their eyes meeting in the mirror, openly evaluated each other. The elegant hat dramatized the extravagant color of Lillian Townsend's imperious blue-green eyes.

“The new hats are so small, almost jaunty,” Mrs. Townsend said, turning her head back and forth as she studied her reflected image. “Ummm,” she hummed. “Put the old one in the hatbox; I’ll wear this one. Black is so tiresome.”

An alarming, unrecognizable noise interrupted the hat show, drawing Abby and her customer to the window, and then to the sidewalk.

“Oh, it’s an Oldsmobile,” Mrs. Townsend said, lightly clapping her hands together. Lillian was seemingly delighted by the sight of Oliver Johnson, a successful farmer and sheepman, in the front seat of an automobile, with two of his grandchildren riding in the back seat and a pack of barking dogs running after them. He was driving down Main Street, sounding the car’s Klaxon as a warning, while stiffly moving his head from side to side, on the lookout for people, farm animals, and dogs.

Upon reaching the center of town, Mr. Johnson made a large arc and steered the car toward the Farmers Co-op, but rather than slowing down, the auto gained speed and commenced going around in circles, with the circles becoming smaller and smaller. It was as if an alien beast had been dropped into their midst and gone berserk, with the vortex of its madness moving closer and closer to the Poster Tree. Stray dogs ran after the unfamiliar thing, barking and snapping at the revolving wheels, and the horses secured at the post office’s hitching rail whinnied and stomped, all of which added to the confusion.

Mr. Johnson, his hat slipped to one side of his head, was reared back into the seat of the touring car, his arms ramrod stiff, his white-knuckled hands gripping the steering wheel as he yelled, "Vhoa! Vhoa!" And finally, "Gottdammitt, vhoa!"

And with that, the automobile ran smack into the big maple tree and came to a stop. The engine spluttered twice and died, a little plume of black smoke issuing forth from beneath its hood.

It always amazed Abby how quickly a crowd of people could form. It seemed they always did so from out of nowhere when something unusual was happening downtown. Today was no exception. Men in the crowd of sidewalk spectators ran toward the halted machine, one of them carrying a pail of water. Abby, truly embarrassed by the town's lack of sophistication, cast a sidelong glance at Mrs. Townsend, who seemed to be enjoying the fiasco.

Meiko Toma, one of the men who had surrounded the new automobile, had to be summoned from the scene of Rockville's first car accident to drive Mrs. Townsend, accompanied by Abby, back to the mansion.

Abby was astonished by the changes to the mansion. The magnificence of the grand staircase when one entered the foyer through the double doors, with their panels of glistening, diamond-shaped glass, was breathtaking. The golden oak of the woodwork reflected the incandescent lights of the crystal chandeliers hanging in the long hall. The lights had been purchased in Bohemia and installed by Bohemian artisans who had traveled to

America to do the job. On the first floor, the doors to the formal dining, living, music, and morning rooms to the left of the stairs opened onto the great marble hallway, allowing one to appreciate the opulence of each room. The kitchen and informal dining room were to the right of the stairs, as was Adam's study. The Townsend Clinic was in a separate wing.

Sharing the experience of the splendor of the house gave reason for the women to exchange warm smiles. "I had hoped to live my married life in a cosmopolitan city," Lillian Townsend confided to Abby as her eyes boldly swept the expanse of her domain. "But the house almost makes up for relinquishing a life in the city for the tedium of living in a small town." Quickly recovering from her denigrating remark, Lillian smiled gratuitously at Abby. "You have an occupation to keep you busy, of course. Two of them," she said, emphasizing her words cheerfully.

As Abby measured the stately windows of the parlor for draperies, she admired the white-gilded French furniture already in place. The pastel colors of the walls and Oriental carpets admirably complemented the mansion, and its new mistress.

The King Louis XIV style was definitely not Aunt Em.

CHAPTER 54

It was late afternoon, and Abby was tired and still in her workshop sewing on Mrs. Townsend's draperies when the door chime sounded. "I'll be right there!" she called out, after removing straight pins from her mouth. But before she could move, the domineering figure of Chance Collins, ignoring the obvious exclusivity of her workroom, pushed the curtains aside and entered.

Wearing a well-cut black suit, a snowy-white shirt with stiffly starched collar and cuffs, the scarred side of his face turned away from her, he cut a rather handsome figure. When he drew near and raised his hand to remove his hat, however, the coarse black hairs on his knuckles reminded her of a daddy longlegs. He stood so close to her that she could smell his aftershave lotion and the oily brilliantine on his freshly cut hair. With her senses nervously alert, she also detected, despite the disguise of anise-flavored Sen-Sens, the biting aroma of liquor. Chance's presence in her workroom so upset her that at first she wasn't aware that he was talking. After regaining her composure, she tried to make sense of what he was saying.

His awareness of her vulnerability brought a quickening to his groin. Holding his hat between the thumb and forefinger of one hand, he twirled it around with the other. "I give you my word—I'll stay away from the city."

What in heaven's name is he talking about? she wondered with growing desperation.

"And, as a married woman, you'll have the respect of the town and my good name."

She managed to stammer, "I—I beg your pardon?"

"I'm asking you to marry me." His face turned a darker shade of red.

With her hands behind her, Abby pushed her back against the large worktable, her skin gone goose-prickly cold, legs swaying like willow branches, deathly afraid she would lose control of her body and, for a brief, wild second, her bladder. She gripped the table's edge as she struggled to remain upright.

"I'm asking you to marry me. I know we haven't courted, but I figured we could get acquainted, so to speak, after we're married. I promise I'll bide my time. I'll be patient with you for as long as you want." He looked down at his hat and brushed something from its brim with his coat sleeve. He had seen the fearful look in her eyes. *It's like breaking a horse*, he thought to himself exultantly, and he became further aroused. *Don't see that often in the women I meet in the city.*

Abby was horror-struck, and when Chance looked up from the brushing of his hat and saw the look on her face, rage, from a bottomless pit of real and imagined rejections, swept over him. The purple scar on his face twitched, twisting into a smirking snarl and sparking his eyes into sudden hatred. He recognized in her face the curse that was always there when he saw himself through another's eyes—the ugliness of his own damaged face. And something else was there: the shock of him, Chance Collins, asking her, Abigail Langley, to marry him.

"Miz Abby, Miz Parlett wants to know if her new bonnet's ready yet."

Neither had heard the ringing of the doorbell, and a man's voice coming from the other side of the curtain startled them both. Chance stiffened, and his eyes filled with malevolence.

Harlan Jones's dark hand pulled back the curtain, and he stood looking over the situation before stepping into it.

"Not yet," Abby answered him. "It needs another bow."

Chance grabbed her wrist and, jerking her toward him, hissed, "That man of God's not coming back and marrying you. Ain't nobody going to marry you. Ever."

Abby, wrenching her hand free of his grasp, snatched up a hat from a hatstand and swept boldly between the curtains Harlan was holding open for her and out into the salesroom.

Chance strode through the room past them both and out to the sidewalk, where he stood muttering to himself. "That goddamn little slut thinks she's too good for me. The goddamn harlot. Who does she think she is?"

When Harlan made his appearance on the sidewalk, Chance confronted him. Jutting his face into Harlan's, he growled, "You keep your goddamn black nose out of white folks' business, or I'll fix it so you don't have a nose—or a neck." Their bitterness almost exploded into a fight right then and there, but they both knew they'd better control their tempers, especially Harlan. Being the only black man in an all-white community, Harlan knew he needed to be affable and, above all, in control of his temper.

Abby retreated to the farthest corner of the workshop and sat down next to the potbellied stove, jumped up, and immediately sat down again. Chance's loathsome presence still permeated the room and clung to her like viscid webs of poisonous spiders. Infuriated, she made scrubbing motions with her hands across her bodice and down the skirt of her dress. "I hate his eyes on me," she said aloud. "I hate the way he makes my flesh crawl. I hate him—I hate him. I hate all of them. I hate their eyes on me. Ugh!" she cried in disgust, flinging imaginary cobwebs from her hands.

Chance had timed his proposal to Abigail so that, if need be, he could catch the 4:00 to the capital. He retrieved Demon from the hitching rail between the emporium and the pool hall and rode to the station.

Before boarding the train, he gave the horse a stinging slap on his hindquarters to send him home, knowing that Ross, the live-in handyman, would take care of both horse and Mum.

He stayed in the city for a week, drinking and laying with prostitutes. A vicious bar brawl in which he almost killed a man landed him in jail; when he was released, a police officer escorted him to the train depot, where he held him in custody until the train to Rockville pulled out of the station.

Chance, on his return to Rockville, stayed away from Ma's. He hung out instead with two old drinking buddies, "Hardhead" Hudnutt and "Beaver" Rasmussen, at the blacksmith shop. Hardhead and Beaver never went into Ma's, both preferring the scabrous frontier atmosphere of the smithy instead.

The town never knew why Chance Collins had gone into the Bon Marché that day, and no one speculated on it—not out loud, anyway. They didn't want the knowledge that they even knew about the Bon Marché incident getting back to Chance. They knew he was more hateful than other men, his practical jokes crueler, his temper shorter; even the men who knew him well became more vigilant when in his presence.

Part 2

CHAPTER 55

April 1908

Abby was standing on a stool in the Townsends' parlor with one of the heavy pink-peony-brocaded draperies carefully hanging from her outstretched arms. Meiko Toma, on the ladder, was waiting for her to hand the drapery up to him. Lillian Townsend, near the ladder, was looking up at Meiko, and Abby was facing the door, when Dr. Adam Townsend entered the parlor. Abby was the first person he saw.

"Eve," he said. The word sounded like the wind being knocked out of him more than it did a name, or perhaps a polite cough in which to make his presence known.

At the sight of him, Abby wanted to rush into his arms, fall at his feet, cry out her monstrous pain. Instead, the room receded, shifted, tilted, her boneless body drifting downward until stopped by the footstool. She sat there—*foolish woman,* she thought—in a field of pink peonies, within a poof of blue silk, and wanted to die.

Lillian turned toward Adam then, looking back at Abby, scolded her. “Oh, look what you’ve done to the draperies!”

Meiko, glancing down and seeing the deathly pallor of Abby’s skin, rapidly descended the ladder. “Hey, are you all right?” he asked.

Dr. Townsend also rushed forward, and both men assisted her in getting up from the stool.

“I’m s-sorry,” she said, stammering. “I had a moment of dizziness. I’m fine,” she said, assuring them. “Really, I am.”

The doctor reached for her wrist, but she quickly rebuffed his offer by bending over and picking up the bundle of wrinkled drapery.

“I’ll have to press it in my shop,” she said apologetically, holding the crumpled drapery in her arms as she rushed from the house.

“Maybe she’s in a family way again, getting faint like that,” Lillian said later that morning as she served Adam his breakfast.

“Who?”

“That woman,” Lillian said in a whisper, with a nod toward the living room. “She’s already had one child out of wedlock.”

“‘That woman,’” Adam said pointedly, “has a name: it’s Abigail, or Abby, or Miss Langley.”

"Miss Langley," Mrs. Townsend said, acidly addressing her husband's back, "had an illegitimate child, a boy, and gave him up for adoption. And," she said, sitting down beside him and resuming her whispering, "they think the father was a married man."

Adam felt the beating of his heart in his temples. "When did all this happen?"

"Ummm, I assume a few years ago."

Somewhere between a bite of egg and a sip of scalding coffee, Adam Townsend learned he was a father. *My God, I have a son.* He knew the child was his, for Abby would have no other. She was, after all, his Eve.

Abby stumbled into her house and, dumping the silk peony-covered drapery onto the floor, slumped into a kitchen chair and sat there gazing out of the window toward the Rock House, crying out names from a broken heart. "Adam, Ronnie, my loves, my darlings!" And, remembering, she again felt faint.

Like a watchman at a prison tower, a part of her since her rebirth had stood guard over the darkness of her life, never allowing a chink of memory in all its tormented light to enter her consciousness. Now she was seated in her chair at the kitchen window where, each day in her sorrowing past, she had looked at the Rock House, the bed of her agony.

Here, at this window, she had watched the subtle turning of the seasons, along with the stagnant pool of passing years that had once been her life—a life without love, or her child.

"Eve," he had said. She had been the Eve of his boyhood passion, their passion an obsession too extravagant for anyone so young.

In the summertime, when Dr. Townsend was in the city tending to his mammoth medicine empire, Aunt Em was tending to the town's ills, and her mother was working at the hotel, she had spent hours with Adam in his classes in the dormer room at the end of a long corridor at the mansion. It was just the two of them and Adam's tutor, the myopic Professor Wells, who, through thick lenses, conspiratorially read love poems to them. Although the professor was only four years older than Adam, he seemed far older and wiser.

Professor Wells was a romantic sentimentalist who required his students to memorize Poe's "Annabel Lee," which they loved and called "their" poem, as well as the work of English poets whom they did not love. They would recite, "I was a child and she was a child, In this kingdom by the sea, But we loved with a love that was more than love—I and my Annabel Lee."

They listened to records on the phonograph—classical, ragtime, show tunes—and had a weakness for Strauss waltzes. Professor Wells taught them to waltz. He was adept at dancing both the male and female roles. Adam needed to be proficient at dancing when he attended the college dances. Abby went home when Adam had Latin and science studies, where she cleaned house, washed and ironed clothes, and prepared dinner for herself and her mother.

On days when their youth demanded they get out of the house and do something physical, they climbed to the Rock House: "their house." She was his Eve, his "Abigail Lee," his anyone he wanted her to be. And, as God molded the first man from dust unto His liking, so Adam molded her to his.

The fierceness of their feelings for each other, and their covert time together, were not to be shared by any other person—except the romantic co-conspirator—not by look, word, or deed, not even a letter for the postmaster's eyes to acknowledge during the occasions when Adam was away from Rockville. The secret of their love was theirs alone.

One day, Adam nobly presented her with a fragrant red rose from the mansion's garden. She planted the stem and rose and the following spring was more than a little amazed that it had taken root and survived. This was the beginning of her rose garden.

"Roses become you," he had said. "It will be our flower."

And, the last day at the Rock House, his last day home before he went east to university, how she had pleaded with him not to leave her. "Take me with you; put me in your trunk." Unashamedly, she had clung to him, begged, wept. She didn't want them to be two people anymore. She wanted them to be one. She arched her back and pushed against him so that his tears fell onto her face.

He said reassuringly, "I know, I know. I want us to be one, too."

And both of them pulled at her skirt.

Later, Adam covered the nakedness of his Eve with her tossed-aside garments, and she, tracing her fingers over his bare torso, searched for the empty space left by his missing rib, the rib that she alone, in the entire universe, had been carved from. She was Adam's rib.

"Abigail Lee," he had whispered into her hair there at the Rock House, "my bride to be."

"You never call me by my name, do you, just plain old Abigail?"

"Just plain old Abigail is too tame for my love, too timid; it lacks fire. My Eve conspires with serpents and feasts on forbidden fruits. She eats the apple," he said, smiling wickedly, "and loves me."

He had pushed her hair away from her forehead, cupped her face within both his hands, and, looking deeply into her eyes, declared, "You are my Eve, my rib, my Abigail Lee, my woman forever and ever."

And she, believing it to be true, snuggled closer.

A wrenching sob now erupted from her throat. "His lump of clay!" she said out loud, deriding herself. That he could still move her to the point of fainting was a shameful and wicked humiliation. She felt accursed and she shivered, as with grippe. She remembered the cold and the falling snow on that terrible Christmas Eve when Aunt Em had told her, "Adam won't be coming home for Christmas—he has a sweetheart."

And I carried his child, she thought—*known only to me.*

CHAPTER 56

THE RINGING OF THE DOORBELL sent chills through her. Expecting to see Chance Collins, she picked up a pair of scissors from the worktable and, hiding them in a fold of her skirt, drew back the curtain. But it was Adam Townsend standing there, just inside the door, hat in hand.

He opened the door of her little hat shop and stepped back into her life, seemingly oblivious to all the years and all the pain she had endured since last they had been together. Upon seeing him, she had the distinct feeling that all her blood had drained from her body and had pooled at her feet, and she was left with an overwhelming curiosity to look at the floor.

"You need to put your head down," he said while looking around. Taking her hand, the one holding the scissors, he led her to the vanity. Placing his hands on her shoulders, he gently pushed her onto the bench. He slid his hand down her arm and pried the scissors from her grasp. He placed them on the vanity table.

"I thought you were someone else," she said in a voice gone weak.

He unbuttoned the cuff of her shirtwaist, exposing a scratch on the inside of her wrist. "Roses?"

Overcome with the actuality of seeing him again, and so soon after the drapery fiasco at the mansion, she replied in a voice raspy with emotion, "You remember?"

He looked toward the curtained door of the workroom and asked, "Is there water back there?" Unable to control her breathing, and not trusting her voice, she nodded. Adam returned with a glass of water and held it to her lips while she sipped. "You have to stop fainting on me," he said in a scolding voice as he continued his evaluation with a gaze that made her uncomfortable.

In the years since she had last seen him, he had grown into his maturity and was now an incredibly handsome man. *Does he look at every woman this way*, she wondered, *or is it just the professional, clinical stare of a doctor?*

Feeling her resistance ebb and her pulse stabilize, he relaxed his hold on her arm. "Of course I remember," he said. "Every time I see a rose or smell one, I remember."

She did not withdraw her hand but let it lie loosely in his. Adam covered her hand with his and gently asked, "Where is my son?"

She quailed, but he would not let her pull her hand from his and again took her pulse. He could tell by her racing heartbeat how profoundly emotional the question was for her. He kept talking, and he rubbed her cold hands between his own.

"You know?" she said in a whisper.

"Yes."

The remembered pain made her cry out. "I had no one to turn to!"

The anguish in her voice stabbed at his very soul. "My God, Abby, I am sorry—truly sorry. I just found out. Why didn't you let me know? Dad never said anything in his letters, and Aunt Em was always too busy to write." His hand tightened on hers, and his expressive brown eyes searched her face. "You know I would never knowingly hurt you."

"I thought you would be home for Christmas, and I could tell you then." She wanted him to feel some of the pain and humiliation she had suffered through the years. She wanted to hurt him. She rose from the bench, trying to rid herself of him, but he wrapped his arms around her waist and would not let her go. "Ronnie needed a father," she said. Recalling Ronnie, her resolve collapsed, and she sank back down onto the seat and became still, knowing that if she spoke of her lost child, she would go to pieces.

They sat crowded together on the little bench holding hands.

"Someone might come in," she said in a whisper.

"Let them," he said, louder.

She struggled with her need to cry and, once she was sure it had passed, tugged on the chain she always wore around her neck and tucked it inside her bodice. Producing the golden locket, she opened the gift her father had given her (by way of Mr. Oberlander) and held it out for him to see: a picture of Ronnie and a curl of his dark, silky baby hair.

"He was sixth months old. Frieda took the photograph."

Adam looked at the picture for a long time before snapping the locket shut, but he still held it in his grasp. With his clenched hand resting on her bosom, he lowered his head, taking in several deep breaths and letting them out slowly. At last, when he looked up, his eyes were tinged with red.

She handed him the glass of water, and they smiled weakly over the shimmering rim at each other. The intimacy of being together was so familiar to them that soon the awkwardness of the long separation fell away, and they were at ease.

"Do you remember when we both had chickenpox?" he asked.

"Of course" she said, pushing back the hair from her brow and exposing a pox scar. "And you sprinkled me with cornstarch to keep me from scratching."

"One of Aunt Em's remedies. Your mother almost fainted when she saw you," he said with a laugh.

"I could never stand for you to have something and not me," she said. "And you had everything!" she said teasingly.

"Dad believed in the natural order of things. If I was going to be a doctor, then I should get the childhood diseases over with while I was a child."

"And so, that went for both of us," Abby said.

"Who were you going after with the scissors just now?" he asked, changing the subject.

"Chance Collins. He wants to marry me."

"Oh God," he said, rubbing the fingers of one hand across his forehead.

Mother-of-pearl twilight filtered into the room. Still they sat on in companionable silence, holding hands—friends, lovers, parents, strangers, quiet in their reveries. The amber glow of the gaslights in the street slowly replaced the gray of the interior.

When Daisy entered the millinery from the drapery shop, she was more than a little surprised to find Abby alone in the semidarkness with a gentleman customer.

CHAPTER 57

DRESSED IN FORMAL EVENING ATTIRE, Dr. and Mrs. Adam Townsend stood in the marble entrance hall of their home and greeted their guests for the charity event to benefit the Emma Townsend Library. They had positioned themselves by the grand staircase near the intricately carved cherrywood banister post, topped with a bronze statue of a scantily clad maiden holding a metallic grapevine of lights curving in an arc over her head.

When Adam introduced gruff, deep-voiced Hans Rasmussen to Lillian, Hans asked, "Are you called Eve to your husband's Adam?"

Adam quickly answered for her, as he always did when Lillian was asked if she were his Eve, by assuring Hans, "Now, Hans, you know there's only one Eve."

Two tables were set up in the foyer, with school principal Otis Leonard and his wife, Mary Lou, seated at one table accepting the monetary collections for the new library. The three women teachers, all of whom boarded at Frieda's, and all a-twitter and a-flutter, were in charge of the second table, collecting and stacking the donated books.

Abby and Frieda met on the veranda in a crush of guests arriving at the same time. Adam, looking toward the door, saw the two women as they entered the hall; escaping from the knot of people surrounding him and Lillian, he moved toward them.

Drawing the two donated books from Abby's gloved hands, Adam looked at the titles; then, opening the Edgar Allan Poe book, he read from "Annabel Lee" in a voice meant for her: "*I* was a child and *she* was a child, in this kingdom by the sea: But we loved with a love that was more than love—I and my Abigail Lee."

Abby felt her face become pale and her hands tense. *Have I always grown weak in his presence?*

"A good choice of books," he said to Abby before turning his attention to Frieda, who, as she handed her donation to him, was also behaving like a tongue-tied schoolgirl.

"Thank you very much, ladies," Adam said. "In appreciation of your contribution, I will personally escort you to the punch bowl." After procuring cups of punch for Abby and Frieda in the dining room and showing them the tables laden with dainty tea sandwiches and cake served up on small plates with dessert forks, Adam returned to the entrance hall.

Abby sipped her punch while appreciating the dainty foods and the loveliness of the room, now packed with guests made uncomfortable by the lavishness of the place.

She looked at the beautiful brocaded draperies hanging at the windows and knew, unfortunately, that they would always remind her of the loathsome Chance Collins, who had burst into her shop while she was working on them. She wondered if he were present at the gathering.

Abby and Frieda left the dining room for the music room, where Aries was playing classical selections on the grand piano. Although the house was intended for large gatherings of people, the evening was very subdued. Aries begged Abby to sing, and she was in the middle of declining when Adam arrived with Orion. "Liven this place up, will you? It's like a morgue in here," Adam said. It didn't take long for a crowd to gather around the piano and for Orion's mother, Rose, and her sisters to join Abby and Orion in singing "Beautiful Dreamer."

After the duet with Orion, Abby excused herself; she and Frieda stood on the fringe of the singers, who were now performing Stephen Foster melodies.

"That awful Chance Collins is staring at you," Frieda said in a whisper.

"Where?" Abby asked, trying to remain calm.

"Back of you."

Adam's eyes were on Chance as he lingered in the doorway of the music room, and, by using another entrance, Adam entered the same room. Approaching Abby and Frieda, Adam said, "Let's get you ladies another drink of punch." He hooked his arms through theirs and led them from the room.

"Chance can't have you," he said to Abby with a mischievous grin.

Late that night in their bedroom, Lillian, tight-lipped and silent, removed her jewelry. Exasperated with the entire evening, she was not speaking to him.

"This isn't Baltimore, Lillian," Adam said, "or New York. For heaven's sakes—it's Rockville. We took in a lot of money tonight for the library, and plenty of books were donated, although their literary merit may be questionable."

"Oh, their grammar!" Lillian burst out, shuddering and shaking her head. "And did you see the way they held their punch cups? Like children, and they had not the slightest notion what to do with a tea napkin. And the little hat maker's singing voice leaves much to be desired, don't you think?" she said in a mocking tone.

"She did it as a favor to me."

"Maybe favors are what she does best. Ummm."

"Pardon me?" Adam said.

"Never mind," Lillian replied, putting an end to the conversation.

"Lillian, you have to learn to laugh with them and not at them."

"This insufferable little backwoods town is not where I want to raise my children."

Her children, Adam thought. *Not ours?* Smiling and radiating his most charming self, Adam spread his arms wide in an expansive gesture and said, "Look at it this way, sweetheart: I grew up here, and I turned out all right."

Her answer was a withering, disparaging stare. Eventually she said, "And who was that Johnny Appleseed character with the baritone voice whom everyone was kowtowing?"

"Hans Rasmussen? Why, he's the poet laureate of Rockville, brother of the famous trapper 'Beaver' Rasmussen. Hans's poems are published in our very own *Hub* newspaper. It was a downright honor to have him among us'n tonight," Adam said in an attempt to win her over with humor. "When Hans recites 'The Shooting of Dan McGrew' down at Ma's Pool Hall, it sends chills down your spine. He's better than any Broadway actor. Old Tate Morgan gets so excited when he hears him, he gets to wheezing; the boys lay him out on a pool table, sometimes clapping a hand over the old man's mouth so he won't interrupt the recitation. They damn near smother him to death. I tell you, it's high dramer," he said, exaggerating the rural accent for her benefit.

Then he began to recite, imitating Hans's deep voice as he untied his black silk bowtie and removed the gold studs from his shirt: "'A bunch of the boys were whooping it up in the Malamute saloon; The kid that handles the music-box was hitting a jag-time tune; Back of the bar, in a solo game, sat Dangerous Dan McGrew; And watching his luck was his light-o-love, the lady that's known as Lou.'"

Adam winked theatrically at Lillian.

Lillian, with elegant thumb and forefinger in a fastidious circle, held her pearl necklace by its diamond clasp and, swinging it back and forth, gave Adam another one of her withering looks before disdainfully dropping the lustrous, perfectly matched strand of pearls into the red velvet–lined jewelry box.

Her unspoken reference to the biblical admonition "Cast not thy pearls before swine" was not lost on him. As he observed his beautiful wife, Adam was thinking, *What have I done to her? She belongs in salons and soirees, among her own kind.* He knew, after tonight, that Lillian would never be, could never be, happy in Rockville.

CHAPTER 58

May 1908

THE WIDOW MCCOY, ALONG WITH three other patients, sat in the waiting room of the Townsend Clinic, located in the north wing of the mansion, all waiting their turn to see the doctor. The clinic had its own private entrance on the end of the veranda.

Oliver Johnson, who had been laid low with nervous tremors since becoming the owner of the first automobile in Rockville shortly before running it into the Poster Tree, was waiting a bit impatiently. Upon his departure from the office, clutching a bottle of Adam's father's medicine, Survivall, prudently wrapped in newspaper, it was the widow's turn to enter Dr. Adam Townsend's consultation office.

Once the widow was admitted and seated in a side chair next to his desk, she informed the doctor that she had not come for herself, but for her son, Sherman Jackson McCoy. "He's dying," she said.

Adam, alarmed, said, "Mrs. McCoy, I will have to see your son and conduct a thorough examination before I can prescribe anything for him. What symptoms is he displaying?"

"Mortification," the widow McCoy said.

"Excuse me?" Adam said.

Ramona McCoy's coal-black eyes blazed. "Sherman is dying from mortification because he is in the finals for the county spelling bee competition and he don't have a suit, or shoes, fit to wear." She said this in one breath, her proud eyes never wavering from the doctor's.

At the end of office hours that day, Adam, writing in his personal journal for "Diseases, and the Cures Thereof," listed the symptoms: "Mortification—cure: One new suit. One pair new shoes. Cost to doctor: $5.00. Accounts Receivable: $0.00."

Each spring, before school was suspended for the summer, grade schools across America were deep into spelling bees. The competitive nature of spelling bees and the prizes that were given to the winners brought great excitement to small towns. This bee, however, would be the first time Rockville had played host to the district competition, and the event would take place in the new Emma Townsend Auditorium. The building was being dedicated to the town in memory of their beloved Aunt

Em on the same evening, which made this event especially important to the people of Rockville.

Pride shown from the faces of the townspeople as they assembled in their new auditorium and sat in upholstered seats facing a sumptuous red velvet curtain. Abby and Frieda sat together in two of the red velvet chairs in a hall abuzz with excitement.

The lights lowered, and the mayor approached the lectern. He delivered the welcoming address and introduced Dr. Adam Townsend. Adam, elegant in both dress and bearing, entered from the right side of the stage. His sleek black hair, brushed to a patent-leather sheen, reflected the bright overhead lights as he strode front and center of the proscenium.

"I am truly honored tonight to share in the dedication of this building, donated by my father, Dr. John Townsend, in the memory of a great woman, his wife, Emma Townsend, our beloved Aunt Em, and to the people of Rockville—her children. And what more fitting dedication could we have than a program by and for the young people of our community and the county? Ladies and gentlemen, I am proud to present to you, on this auspicious evening, the contestants of the 1908 county spelling bee championship."

The dimming of the houselights was accompanied by oohs and aahs from the audience as the velvet curtains parted and the lights shone down on the students seated on the stage. The standing room only audience welcomed them, and the gift of the wondrous building, with thunderous applause.

"Ladies and gentlemen," Adam said, this time addressing the contestants, "welcome, and good luck."

Adam took his seat in the audience beside Lillian and waited for the appearance of Sherman Jackson McCoy. Because he had a vested interest in the young contestant, Adam wanted him to place well.

The acoustics in the new building were so perfect that every letter of the winning word—terpsichorean—that the young Sherman McCoy pronounced at the end of the long and sometimes excruciating contest was plainly heard by all.

The following Friday, the *Rockville Hub* reported on the dedication of the Emma Townsend Auditorium and Library with a detailed description of the building. The newspaper also presented a list of the winners of the spelling bee contest and the prizes donated by the merchants and various town organizations. The top winner in the county was Sherman McCoy, who would now progress to the state spelling bee. The county school board presented Sherman with a dictionary, along with the top monetary prize of the evening: twenty-five dollars, donated by Dr. Adam Townsend. Also of note in the week's newspaper was the announcement of Dr. Townsend's appointment to the newly formed post of county health commissioner.

The Rockville Hub
May 15, 1908

Dr. Townsend's first undertaking in his capacity as Commissioner of Health is to rid the town of Rockville of its pest house and the stigma of being the only town left in the county that still condones a place for a person with a communicable disease to be housed.

The pest house has been in use since the founding of the town, although it has not been occupied by an infected person for quite some time.

Dr. Townsend reports, "The thinking in the past of imprisoning a sick person in a pest house was that it was the only way to control the spread of a virulent disease. That thinking is now obsolete and generally considered inhumane. Any patient who has a communicable disease, with the proper hygiene, can be taken care of at home and need not be subjected to the indignities and cruelties of confinement, in solitude, to a place of neglect at a time when he or she is most in need of care and understanding."

Dr. Townsend's main interest as a physician is in finding a cure for tuberculosis, also known as consumption, a dreaded disease that affects the lungs and has no known cure.

The pest house, purchased by Ramona McCoy, has been converted into a covered bridge and now sets on a low spot on Stony Creek at a place between the McCoy property and the town.

Floods occur in this location whenever there is a heavy rain, which makes for impassable conditions. It is especially inconvenient for farmers who live in town with farms on the south side of the creek or for families in the country who wish to come into town.

The old pest house is now a toll bridge. A wooden box is attached to the bridge for the collection of the fare of one dime (or barter) and will be conducted on the honor system. Your donation is good for the day.

> The term “barter” does not mean you can put just anything in the box; let’s be fair and honorable about this dealing.

“Once a pest, always a pest,” was Perthy Prettyman’s noteworthy opinion on the subject.

CHAPTER 59

August 1908

PRECIOUS AMY AND HER BROTHERS were not allowed to stay in the house when Velvet Preston took her bath. But they had to get it ready for her. Amy watched her older brothers wrestle the big round tin tub into the house and fill it with water. Once again, since Velvet's arrival, the kitchen had running water. Her stepmother had a way of getting things her mama never had.

Workmen from around town did jobs for Velvet, and when their pa asked her where she got the money to pay them, she always said real sweet-like, "Why, Bobby Lee, honey, I still got a little bit put aside."

In order to strain the water, which was piped into the house from a well in the backyard, Velvet kept a rag tied around the spigot. Amy and her brothers liked to untie the little square of cloth and spread it out on the kitchen table to see what had gotten caught in it—always sand and tiny pebbles, and sometimes hideous little squiggly bugs.

In the wintertime, when Velvet took her bath in front of the kitchen stove, she sent the boys up to the attic. BJ would sneak downstairs and spy on her and would get into fights with Jeff for peeking at his mother while she was bathing. In the summer months, she sent them outside.

Today, while Velvet was taking her bath, Amy, along with BJ and Jeff—who took turns pulling the wagon and the little ones, Billy and Sammy, who rode in the wagon along with an empty bucket—were on their way to Chance Collins's orchard to gather apples. They could have all they wanted of the fallen fruit as long as they gave the best of it to Chance's mum.

The "yellow transparent" apples got mushy within a few days of ripening and were good only for eating or making applesauce. Amy and her brothers had taken a bucket of the best ones up to the house to Mum and had their bucket full again and setting in the wagon to take home with them.

Amy lay stretched out on a towel she had brought with her, along with a bar of homemade soap, in case they went to Chance's pond, where she could bathe. She was eating an apple and watching the boys yelling and pelting one another with the overripe fruit. The apple fight would mean extra work on washday, but she didn't boss them; they got enough of that from Velvet.

From his granary not far from the orchard, Chance could hear the sound of children's voices. "Goddamn kids," he mumbled. He drunkenly rummaged through the pile of gunnysacks he was sitting on and found another bottle of whiskey. Pulling out the cork with his teeth, he took a good long pull from the long, slender neck of the bottle, welcoming the bear-clawing burn that furrowed his throat. He couldn't get Abby out of his mind any more than he could let go of the humiliation he had brought on himself. Getting drunk had become an everyday occurrence.

Chance spent his days in his granary, drinking and ruminating about his life. Slights, like bad wounds, festered in him; until he got his revenge, he never let them go. He still harbored a raw ache of desire in his gut for Abigail Langley. "Goddammit, I wanted that woman!" he mumbled aloud. "Still want her."

He scraped at the stubble of whiskers irritating the scar on his face and recalled the early days of his youth, when his mother would say in her Cockney accent that he "was such a handsome little fellow, and so sweet." He hated the leering scar. In secret he examined it, cursed it, cursed the mirror, and cursed the day it happened. Recalling the memory made him strike out viciously at anything within his reach. He blamed Harlan for his humiliation, and he wanted to get even with him. He hated him as much as he hated the mule that had kicked him. "Got even with that son-of-a-bitchin' critter, though, didn't I?" he yelled out loud.

"I hated that mule from the minute Mum took the bandages off and I saw my face for the first time." He said to himself, gloating, "I got even with him, though, killed the son of a bitch. Got my revenge, even if it was on a poor dumb son-of-a-bitch mule."

He shook his head and, laughing out loud, took another swig from the bottle. "Put blinders on him and led him by a rope tied to the saddle horn on my pony to the quarry canyon, untied the rope, and moved my horse away, leaving the mule alone on the cliff edge, then sicced my dog on him. 'Sic 'em, Sandy,' I said. Ol' Sandy barked and nipped at the mule's legs, and that ol' mule just jumped forward into the canyon. Screamed once. One looooong scream."

He continued his rambling to no one in particular. "Pa figured what had happened, and he made me shoot my dog. Kill old Sandy just to punish me. I still miss that ol' hound. Don't miss that old man of mine. He'd just as soon punch you as look at you. The old son of a bitch blew his head off. 'Good riddance,' is what I said. I was a man then, graduated from eighth grade and ready to take over the ranch. I celebrated his passing by taking my first trip to the big city. Goddammit, I want that woman. I would've been good to her. She could've had my good name, and Mum's. Mum liked her."

He stopped for a moment, struggled to his feet, and shouted, "Goddammit! What in the hell is that ruckus out there?" Chance tore at the thorny branches of the tall, brambly gooseberry bushes that separated the house from the orchard, clearing a space big enough to look through. Chance saw Bobby Lee's kids at play. The boys were having an apple fight, and the girl was lying on a towel chewing on an apple, her head propped on her hand and one elbow. She looked so damn sweet and innocent. The faded cotton dress hiked up well above her bent knees, and her spindly little bare legs treading back and forth made him want to touch her.

Chance approached them, hands in pockets, pushing his pants away from his "peep," as Mum called it when he was a boy. "You play with your peep, Chancellor, and you'll go blind," she would warn him.

"Ho and hell," he said out loud, "and I still worry about going blind." Removing his hand from his right pocket, he brought out some change and gave a quarter to the biggest boy. "Take your little brothers and go to the store and buy yourselves some candy," he said. "Precious Amy's staying here with me. I got a job for her," he said, trying to control the slurring of his words.

Amy backed away from him like she would from a quarry snake. No one ever called her "Precious" except her ma. "I've got to go with my brothers," she said, rolling up the towel with the bar of soap wrapped inside. She was fearful of the big man and didn't want to be left alone with him.

"Ah, Precious," Chance said, wheedling, his words slurring. "I got a job for you."

The boys were already moving away, each telling the other what kind of candy he was going to get. Amy wished she was going with them. *I'd like some candy*, she thought; *maybe he'll give me a quarter, and I can spend it just for me.* Billy and Sammy waved to her from the wagon as they rolled away.

"You like apples?" Chance asked her.

She didn't answer him, just looked at the ground.

"Cat got your tongue?" he asked with a short whiskey laugh. "Sit down. Sit down. You don't have to be in no hurry." Chance, almost falling himself, sat down and patted the ground as an invitation for her to sit beside him.

She turned her body without moving her feet, undecided whether to remain or leave. The awkward movement caused her to drop the towel on the grass. It completely unrolled, exposing the large hole in the center of the towel, with the chunk of homemade soap lying exactly in the middle of it and the earth showing through.

Chance gave a hooting laugh. "Bet you couldn't do that again, even if you tried!"

The worn-out towel embarrassed her. Her mother had kept the holes mended until they were too big to patch. Keeping it for rags, she had hung it on the far side of the house so that on washdays, passersby wouldn't see it. Wearily Amy sat down.

"Your pa got work yet?" he asked.

"Sometimes."

He moved closer. "You could use a little egg money, then?"

The money women got from their egg-laying chickens was theirs to spend any way they pleased. She became wistful. They never had egg money; they always ate the eggs their chickens laid. For the first time, she looked directly at him.

The look of expectation in her eyes made him bold. “I’ve got a job that a nice little girl like you can do, and I’ll pay you for it.” He got up from the ground, lurched about while brushing at the seat of his black trousers, took a few steps, and waited. She rolled the soap up in the towel and tagged along after him.

Every few steps, Chance looked back to see if she was still following along. He wanted to keep her with him as long as possible and was trying to think of a job he could have her do. From the open door of the granary, he spied a straw broom just inside the door. Ducking into the shed, Chance motioned for her to follow.

“This here’s the job I want done, this here floor swept.” He held the broom out to her. “The floor’s got to be cleaned up and made ready for the new wheat.” The floor was already clean; some grain had spilled from buckets as they had been lifted in and out of the bin made of boards, and some had seeped out from the corners. Otherwise the floor was clean.

Amy swept the kernels into a pile and used her hands to carefully scoop up the few small handfuls, throwing them back into the bin. The large room was quite dark; after she swept the floor, golden dust motes, reflecting the brilliant sunshine of the day, sliced into the granary from the narrow gaps between the boards, striping Amy’s back as she bent to her task.

He wanted in the worst way to touch her but didn't know how to proceed without scaring her off. Through the thin material of her dress, he could see the stubborn little rise of her nipples, and he had an overwhelming desire to pinch them. He tried to think of another chore she could do.

"That was a good job, Amy," he said huskily, clearing phlegm from his throat and patting her shoulder.

"I have to go," she said. Still, she hung back, afraid he had forgotten about the money he had promised to pay her.

Behind the fear in her eyes, he knew, was a plaintive plea of "Like me."

"Give me a little kiss, then you can go." He put his face close to hers—so close she could smell the sourness of his breath. She began backing away from him toward the door. The scar and his leering mouth frightened her.

Chance put his hands on her shoulders to stop her. "Just one little kiss," he begged.

"On my cheek," she said in a whisper, placing the tips of her fingers to her face.

He kissed her cheek and worked his mouth around to hers. She kept jerking her head away. Exasperated, he straightened up and, shoving his hands deep into his pockets, again pushed his pants away from his "peep."

She was near the door. "Now, don't you run off, Amy, I ain't paid you yet." He withdrew his hand from his pants pocket with a silver dollar pinched between his fingers. She remained by the door, unsure. "Now, we're gonna play a game here, Amy: hide and seek. You close your eyes and try to find which pocket I hid the dollar in. When you find it, it's yours."

Amy trembled as, with eyes closed, she felt about his person. The first pocket she put her hand in, she could feel a pocketknife and some string, but no dollar. She found the next pocket—still nothing.

"Keep your eyes closed," he said. Taking hold of her wrist, he guided her hand into an opening, and she felt bare skin. Skin so thin and smooth and vulnerable to her touch that it repelled her. She struggled to pull her hand away. She knew from tending to her baby brothers what she was feeling, but this one was much bigger.

Chance tightened his grip on her wrist. "Squeeze," he said. She spread her fingers apart in an effort not to touch it. Grabbing a handful of her hair, he jerked her head back. She was staring straight up at him, her hair pulled so tight her eyes were slanted. *That's funny*, he thought, *she's crying, but she ain't makin' no sound.*

He let go of her hair and, taking her arm, twisted it in back of her. "Squeeze," he demanded. Working his free hand under her dress, he pinched her nipples. Giving her arm another sharp twist, he let his hand slide down her body while he fumbled with her bloomers. "Squeeze it hard!" he demanded.

Feeling the silky fuzz of her pubic hair, he lifted her off the floor and pressed her small body against his. He unbuckled his belt while breathing hard and making convulsive movements. The big silver buckle made a loud metallic *clump* as it hit the floorboards.

He held her close to his side and tore at the waist button on his pants and in one swift motion skinned off her bloomers. Throwing them across the room, he stood her on her feet. Amy quickly retaliated by swinging at him with both hands, hitting him in the abdomen. He took a step back, trying to regain his balance, but with his pants around his knees, he fell onto the floor in a sitting position. She turned to run, but he lunged forward and caught her around her ankles and brought her down. Rolling onto his back, he pulled her on top of him, cradling her legs over his hips. With one arm he gripped her waist, and, holding his penis in his other hand, he probed the area between her legs. This left one of her hands free, and she pushed against his chest with all her frightened strength.

"Hold still!" he hissed, grabbing both her hands in his. She dropped her feet to the floor and pushed herself up and away from him. Chance gave an exasperated howl and, like an angry bear, batted her back in place. Catching her again around the waist, he gave a vicious jab between her legs—and found his mark.

The uncomfortable position, along with his pants binding his legs, was making penetration difficult. Arching his back, he pushed steadily until his big mouth fell open. "Ahhh."

Her whole body stiffened, and for the first time she cried out. "Mama! Mama!"

The cries rose and fell with the heat waves across the fields and went begging at the white puffy clouds of heaven that today billowed softly like lacy curtains full of gentle breezes.

CHAPTER 60

AMY UNTIED THE GRIMY RAG and handed Mrs. Parlett her silver dollar. Her knees almost buckled when she thought of where it had come from. "I want to buy cloth for a school dress," she said, barely above a whisper. "And I promised my brothers they could each have a penny." She raised her shoulders close to her ears in an attempt to hide her face.

Mrs. Parlett studied the pinched, unhappy face of the girl; *she's too young to take over the responsibility of a family*, she thought. *Her mother couldn't handle it, and neither can this child. Agnes, I wonder if you know what you've done to your precious girl.* She said aloud, "Has your dad found work yet, Amy?"

"I-I found the dollar in the house; Mama must've hid it away." Her face blanched white with the telling of the lie.

While Mrs. Parlett helped Amy make a selection for a school dress from the many bolts of cloth stacked on the shelves reserved for dry goods, the boys knelt in agony before the tall candy case. Their fingers tapped and scraped on the glass as they pointed out the individual candies. Should it be the big jawbreaker, or a black-licorice pipe, or an "all day" sucker, because that would last longer? Or, should they take a chance on the chocolate-covered vanilla patty? If they were lucky, they knew, and picked one with a pink center, they would get a free one.

From time to time, Amy sneaked a glance at the case as well.

Mrs. Parlett placed the blue-checked gingham fabric she had helped Amy choose, along with thread, and a McCall's pattern for a girl's box-pleated dress on the brown square of paper she had torn from the big roll at the end of the counter. She told Amy to remind her grandmother that the pattern didn't have seam allowances. Thinking it over, she wrote it on the wrapping paper. Paper and string were valued commodities that housewives carefully preserved.

She tied the bundle together with white string that spun out from its cone-shaped core, tallied the purchases on a notepad, and, when finished, dropped the slip into a basket beneath the counter on which the cash register sat. She told Amy she had a dime left over for candy.

Amy sent her brothers home. She was going to her grandmother's house in the hope that her grandma would help her make the dress. She didn't want the boys tagging along, because they got on their grandma's nerves, and that made her out of sorts.

Amy cut through the alley that separated the store from the barbershop and livery stable. When she neared the hitching post, the Gypsy she had seen around town, who had ridden into the alley, jumped down from the big cream-colored horse he was riding; the quickness of his athletic action scared her into dropping her package.

Smiling broadly and making an exaggerated bow, Meiko Toma bent over to retrieve the bundle. His face came so close to Amy's that she could see the tiny holes in his earlobes and the space between his very white front teeth. And, from the open collar of his white shirt, hidden in the thick, black, curly hair that grew high on his chest, she could see a gold chain. The man, so different from the men she knew, held the package out to her.

Whimpering, she backed away from him, arms straight out and her hands up in a "stay away" gesture. Seeing that he had frightened her, he thrust the bundle into her arms, which terrified her even more. Nowadays, all men terrified her.

The following week, members of the Thursday Social Guild of New Church, of which Mrs. Parlett was a member, showed up at Bobby Lee's with food and clothes for the family. They had no use for Velvet and not much for Bobby Lee, but they were not going to let children go hungry or work themselves into an early grave, regardless of which faith Bobby Lee believed in.

Stunned into action when the guild from New Church had turned up at Bobby Lee's house with assistance, Bobby Lee's mother emerged with the completed school dress for Amy. And, not to be undone, the Benevolent Society of Old Church came calling with clothes and food. For a while, the Preston household was well cared for.

CHAPTER 61

September 1908

DR. ADAM TOWNSEND AND HIS wife were seated on the veranda, enjoying a view of the town, made beautiful by the incredible colors and cloud formations of the late-afternoon autumn sky. Lillian sipped tea, and Adam drank a highball as he told her about his busy day in the clinic.

"Mr. Oliver has a case of boils, and he told me that Aunt Em used to use bacon fat to draw out the pus." Lillian made a face. "And I have my first maternity case: a new bride who's new to the town. She's never experienced the ministrations of Aunt Em and so comes to me without prejudice. And I'm still having a hard time convincing patients who live out in the country that fresh cow manure is not the best treatment for burns." Lillian made another face.

From their wicker chairs, they watched Meiko Toma riding toward the house on the path from the Indian Springs Mineral Water bottling plant. The Gypsy cut a dashing figure as he reined in the palomino and walked him the rest of the way to the veranda. The impatient Apollo, head high, tail arched, kicking and prancing and ready for a run, stomped at the earth.

Adam jumped from the porch and went to the horse. Holding Apollo's bridle close to the bit, he petted and stroked the pale-amber nose and creamy mane, all the time gently talking to him. "Meiko, I'll take Apollo for a ride. Why don't you join Mrs. Townsend on the porch and have a drink?"

Meiko, climbing the steps to the veranda, smiled tentatively at Lillian as together they watched Adam mount and ride toward the creek. Meiko sat down on the balustrade facing her.

"May I get you something to drink, Mr. Toma?" Lillian asked.

"No, thank you. I had water at the plant."

The mention of water at a water-bottling plant caused them both to smile.

They watched Adam as he rode Apollo along Stony Creek, then both commented on the extraordinary beauty of the sunset and after that couldn't think of anything to say.

Later in the month, Lillian Townsend stood at the kitchen sink sipping from a glass of water and peering from the window into the backyard at Meiko's covered wagon. In the beginning, it had disturbed her having a Gypsy living so near the house. But seeing him daily as he went about his work, cooked over a campfire, or tended his flowers and herbs that grew in a circle around his caravan, she had become accustomed to his presence. Adam had remarked that his father had probably put him in the backyard so he could keep an eye on him.

Once a week, Meiko came into the house to confer with Adam about business at the bottling plant, where he was the supervisor. They went over any problems or concerns with the plant or the horses and wagons they used to haul the cases of the medicinal water to the train depot.

Meiko waited just inside the kitchen door until Adam came for him; whenever Lillian glanced in his direction, he seemed to be taking her measure. He looked very foreign to Lillian, standing there in her immaculate kitchen, a red bandana wrapped around his head, gold chain and a mat of black hair showing in the open collar of his shirt, and a gold earring—really!

One morning, while he waited in the kitchen for Adam, Lillian offered him a cup of tea. Not wishing to appear snobbish or uneasy, she joined him at the table. He was wearing the red silk scarf knotted about his head, and when he slipped the scarf to his neck, his curly black hair sprang to life. Meiko, ill at ease, nervously moved his cup around in its delicate saucer. He took a deep breath; *find yourself*, he commanded from within.

"Stir some leaves into your cup," he said to her, his European-accented voice flowing easily. "When you're finished drinking the tea, I'll read the leaves for you."

"You tell fortunes?" she asked in astonishment.

"All Gypsies tell fortunes," he said, puffing out his chest with feigned pride. Lillian finished her tea and handed him the cup. He looked into the white porcelain of the cup and studiously deliberated the story of the leaves; then, raising his eyes to hers, he reached for her hand. It was Lillian's first physical contact with him, and the gesture sent a little shimmer rushing through her body.

He turned her hand over, and it lay in his own hand, cool ivory against sun-darkened amber. With the little finger of his right hand, he traced the delicate lines exposed to him in her open palm. "You will have a son."

Lillian quickly looked up at him. The impassioned desire in her gaze was unsettling, causing him to catch his breath and turning his eyes a deeper shade of blue.

"Two sons," he added with great solemnity.

After the promising reading of the tea leaves, Lillian became comfortable in his company. She often asked him to join her for a morning cup of tea or coffee, no longer in the kitchen but in the sunny breakfast room. This left the kitchen to Mrs. Sheridan, the housekeeper/cook, Adam to his patients, and the maid to her upstairs duties.

Lillian began to look forward to their morning ritual. Meiko brought excitement and, because a few women worked in the plant, he also brought the town gossip.

She had been unable to find common ground with the women her age in town, because the two subjects they knew best and discussed most often—religion and babies—left her out of their conversations. Her need for his friendship made her realize how bereft she was of friends. Meiko talked about Europe and of his upbringing in Hungary, where he was born.

"In Hungary, we were accepted. Gypsies did not grow up separated from the rest of society, or denounced." He told her of his strict training by his aristocratic aunts, who demanded elegant manners from him. From them he learned the charming etiquette all women adored: the kissing of the hand and the art of flattering compliments. He entertained Lillian with accounts of his travels on the continent and in England, and of the rich and artistic people he had met. He told her that if he had been born in America, his name would have been Michael.

On another day, Lillian related to him stories of her travels in Europe: of her honeymoon there and about living in Germany while Adam trained at the Heidelberg Medical School. She told of her tours of the galleries, dining in little out-of-the-way cafés, and shopping in the many boutiques. "And then Aunt Em died, and we came home for the funeral, and remained here. She was the only mother Adam ever knew."

"Do you like it here?" Meiko asked.

Lillian hummed, was still for a long time, then, spreading her hands palm down on the tabletop, slowly and cautiously said, "No."

He reached across the table, expressing sympathy by pressing the tips of her fingers. "Everyone loved Aunt Em," he said. "I was here all through the year of her sickness. When she passed on, everyone mourned." He hunched his shoulders and extended his hands. "The whole town, the whole county," he said, throwing his arms wide. "Did you know," he said, leaning across the table and rapping his knuckles lightly on Lillian's arm to make his point, "that after the big rain, an old woman from Roseville who had heard about Aunt Em's death and wanted to attend her funeral was found dead in a ditch?"

"No," she said, expressing alarm. "No one ever told me."

"Her family didn't know where she was. They only knew she was gone. She dressed in her best Sunday dress, black silk with a white lace collar, and just disappeared. The marshal organized the men here and in Johnstown. He had us spread out in two long rows and walk toward each other, searching for her. It was mean work because of all the mud. Trees were down, and bushes and sticks and trash washed into piles." He moved his hands back and forth, indicating heaps and mounds.

"I was with the men who found her body." He turned up his palms. "Her good dress was almost torn from her body, she was caked in mud, and she had cuts and bruises all over her. Her long gray hair was tangled all around her head. It was a terrible sight." He shuddered, making a convulsive movement with his shoulders. "I hate death."

“Michael—that’s a nice name,” Lillian said, bringing the morbid subject to an end. “I don’t believe I’ve ever known anyone named Michael.”

She watched with fascination as he looked into her eyes, and his turned a smoky, opaque blue.

CHAPTER 62

October 1908

THE ROCKVILLE HUB
October 9, 1908

Announcements:
A meeting to discuss the formation of a Merchants' Association will be held at 7:00 p.m. in the Annex room of the Parlett Hotel, Friday next.

All Rockville merchants are encouraged to attend.

Richard Stevens, druggist
Stevens Drugstore

THE ANNOUNCEMENT APPEARED IN THE weekly paper, which was delivered to everyone's doorstep on Fridays after school. The notice gave the merchants, as well as the townspeople, a week in which to speculate as to the manner of the meeting. People were suspicious as well as curious.

"What's going on?" they asked.

"Does the town need a merchants' association?"

"Probably looking for new ways to gouge us," some grumbled.

Abby left the Bon Marché to consult with Dovie in the Music Arcade. The tune "You Tell Me Your Dream, I'll Tell You Mine" was playing on an eighteen-cent wax-cylinder record.

"Does the meeting mean women, too?" Abby inquired of Dovie.

Dovie, singing and moving to the music, led Abby to the sidewalk and into the drugstore, where they confronted Mr. Stevens with their question.

"Are women invited to the meeting?"

"Of course it means women, too!" he exclaimed. "You have two businesses, Miss Langley," he said with an ingratiating smile, "and that makes you one of our leading merchants."

Abby blushed. The druggist's ever-forthright gaze always made her want to check the buttons on her shirtwaist.

Back on the sidewalk, Dovie asked Abby, "Will you come to the meeting with me and Donald?"

"I'll go with Frieda," Abby said.

"Your chaperone," Dovie said teasingly while making a wry face.

"I'll never need a chaperone," Abby said with a sigh. "Not in the real sense."

"Don't say that," Dovie said, scolding her friend. "You're young and beautiful, and someday, Prince Charming will come along and sweep you off your feet. You shouldn't always be in the company of Frieda. I've seen the way men look at you—Richard's eyes almost popped out of their sockets just now," she said, motioning her head toward the drugstore.

"Frieda and I need each other. And she is a businesswoman. She needs to know that she counts as a person—that she belongs. We both need to know that we belong."

Eyebrows were raised as to the inclusion of Frieda as a merchant, but the townspeople had learned that Abigail Langley could not, and would not, appear in public alone; consequently, Frieda had been Abby's companion and escort for the past year. Perthy Prettyman called her Abby's "chaperone-in-waiting."

"You're a good person, Abby," Dovie said. She hugged her friend and added, "Any new postcards from exotic places?"

"Not recently," Abby said, avoiding her eyes.

All the owners of the downtown stores were present at the Friday night meeting that had been set up to discuss the formation of a merchants' association. Carl Offerman, the overweight and foot-sore baker, who never attended any of the town's functions, was there, looking like he'd been dusted with flour. Carl didn't talk much; he preferred grunting to talking. Bob Rinehart of the Farmers Co-op, another businessman never seen outside his store, was there. Bob was more at ease in the presence of farmers.

Four women were in attendance: Dovie, with her husband, Donald; Francoise Parlett, with Mr. Parlett; and Abigail and Frieda. The women were dressed in tailored suits, their hats purchased from the Bon Marché. The "pouter pigeon" look of the latest dress styles exaggerated the smallness of the women's already-small waists.

Abby, prim but fashionable, wore a navy-blue suit. Her hat was in the newest French sailor style, with a wide brim, narrower in the front, and covered in navy silk taffeta. A large bow, of the same fabric and wired to hold its shape, was attached to the headband. A small, tailored navy bow was fastened to the collar of her white shirtwaist. The townswomen always paid careful attention to Abby's attire, knowing she was dressed in the latest style.

Sam Morris, editor and owner of the newspaper, was in attendance and taking notes. At seven o'clock sharp, Richard Stevens, the druggist, addressed the group.

"Rockville," he began, "is becoming a good-size town with an enviable business segment. When I visit other towns in this and surrounding counties, I do not see merchants in any of them doing the business that I see carried on right here in Rockville." Several of the men nodded in agreement. "I think we could benefit even more by blowing our own horns, so to speak, loud enough to be heard in other parts of the county. This alone could generate more business for ourselves and, in so doing, attract more new businesses to our town."

He took a sip of water and continued. "The Langley lumber mill is expanding their furniture shop into a factory, and that means newcomers to the town and a payroll to be spent right here, if we play our cards right. I was hoping Joe and Leo would be with us tonight, but they are two very busy men. But for those of you who *are* here this evening, are you interested in forming an association that could benefit all of us and be good for the town as a whole?"

They looked around at one another, seeing who approved, then looked again at the speaker. They all nodded in agreement, still unsure as to what exactly the meeting was about.

"Well, with all of us in agreement in forming a business association, our next step will have to be the election of officers. I think first we should decide on a president. Would you like to do this by written vote, or from the floor?"

Mr. Parlett rose. "Because most of us are new at this or forgetful of parliamentary procedure, and because the idea of the association is yours, I move to nominate you as president."

"Hear, hear!" some of them responded, and Donald Vaughn said, "I second the motion," amid unanimous murmurs of "Aye, aye."

"It has been moved and seconded that I become the first president. Given that I proposed the formation of the association and want to see it come to fruition, I accept your nomination as president."

Other officers were elected next. Mr. Parlett was elected vice president, which everyone believed was as it should be, he being the most successful and trustworthy businessperson in the community. The very likable Donald Vaughn from the Music Arcade was elected secretary treasurer, with Dovie Vaughn as recording secretary.

"Tonight gets us off to a very good start," Stevens said in closing the meeting. "As president, I want to propose, as our first project, the electrification of the whole community, and not just our business area. John Miller's generator can only do so much, and to the stores downtown, it's been a godsend. The city council is getting nowhere on this. I believe, with the credibility of our newly formed merchants' association behind us, we can force their hand. We won't discuss it tonight, but let's all mull it over. We'll bring it up for discussion at our next meeting, which will be held two weeks from tonight. If this is agreeable with everyone, may I see a show of hands?"

The newspaper editor stood. "Mr. President, may I take the floor?"

"The chair recognizes Mr. Sam Morris."

"I'm very impressed with what I've seen and heard here tonight. May I suggest that you take into consideration the suppliers of services in Rockville as members of your association? I, for one, would be honored to join your organization."

"Thank you, Sam. Merchants, this gives you something else to give thought to before our next meeting."

Everyone applauded, showing the druggist they approved of his stewardship of the meeting and of his bringing them together.

Abby looked with excitement toward Frieda. Seeing the strain on the face of her friend from trying to comprehend what was going on, she clasped Frieda's hands where they lay clenched in her lap. Smiling with understanding and holding up one hand, Abby pantomimed pulling on a string and turning on a light. Frieda smiled faintly while nervously pinching the skin on her neck. The group milled about, congratulating the officers and showing a new amiability toward their business neighbors.

At the second meeting of the association, Leo Langley was present, representing the Langley enterprises. Also in attendance was Dr. Adam Townsend. Given that the association had voted on accepting professional men into the newly formed organization, they had invited Dr. Townsend to join, along with the newest resident to Rockville, the no-longer-itinerant dentist, Dr. Thomas Veering.

The dentist, a tall man with sandy-colored hair cut short and combed straight back, had an earnest, open look in his hazel eyes that made people trust him. Upon his arrival at the meeting, he found an empty chair next to the always eager to please Mr. Fontell, who jumped up from his seat and extended a hand toward the chair. "Please," the little suit maker said in way of greeting.

The druggist began the meeting by introducing the newest resident to Rockville, Dr. Veering, and by welcoming Dr. Townsend. All those present were inscribed in the minutes as charter members; the roll included purveyors of services as well as goods. A mission statement was voted on: "Building a better community through service."

"Another element that is brought to mind in building a better community," the new president said, "is the promotion of goodwill by fostering good deeds in the way of charity. How many of you are familiar with the charity-collection boxes that Miss Langley makes at Christmas time? They're fashioned to look like a brick chimney with Santa Claus putting one leg inside? She placed them in some of the stores last year in an appeal for charitable donations. Her message on the base of the box is: 'A Christmas for every child.'" There was a small showing of hands. "I, too, believe every kid deserves to wake up on Christmas morning to a toy from Santa. And I propose we adopt this project for the association to take on as our first charitable endeavor.

"We all know of children and adults here in Rockville who need charity, and it has to be made available to them without them feeling put down. We need to convey to the public that we have not formed this association for our own financial betterment; we are dedicated to what our motto stands for: building a better community.

"Would you be willing, Miss Langley, to give up your project as an individual, and become chairman—I mean, chairwoman"—the members laughed—"of the undertaking?"

Abigail nodded her agreement, too overwhelmed to speak.

"Doc," he said, addressing Adam, "this might be a good place for you to get your feet wet. If you will accept, we'll make you co-chairman of our charity-collection event."

Abby's heart jumped into her throat. "Oh no," she breathed.

Adam Townsend rose from his chair, an easygoing smile spreading across his handsome features. His dark eyes sparkled in a friendly way as he nodded in affirmation.

"I gladly accept," he said, taking note of Abby's surprised look.

"Thank you, Miss Langley, Dr. Townsend."

"Now," Sam said, energetically rubbing his hands together, "let's move on to the really important things. Our association is not just about good business and good work: it's also about having a good time." Everyone applauded. "Donald, let's make you, along with the help of your charming wife, our chairman."

CHAPTER 63

LILLIAN SWEPT INTO ADAM'S STUDY, the dark-blue velvet skirt of her at-home dressing gown swirling about her slim ankles as she joined her husband for a before-dinner drink. Lillian had not acquired a taste for alcoholic beverages, but she did enjoy the feeling of well-being that came from having a cocktail—or two.

The couple still chose to have dinner in the evening and not at noon, as did the townspeople. And Lillian insisted upon a formal meal, which was a hardship on the housekeeper. But, after she got the food on the table, they encouraged Mrs. Sheridan to leave. The Townsends preferred that their conversations and customs not become a topic of discussion for others.

Adam was entertaining Lillian with an account of the meeting he had attended the night before. "It's an association for the business and professional people of Rockville. They're going to have social functions as well, and that'll give us something to do together."

"Ummm," Lillian hummed doubtfully. "I had a letter from Father today," she said. "He says a chair is opening up at the university, and it's yours if you want it."

"I thought we'd settled all that. I don't want to walk in your father's footsteps. I want to make my own path. And I like living in Rockville. It'll get better now that the house is finished and we're settled in."

Lillian held out her empty glass to him, shaking it impatiently. "He says all the facilities at the school would be open to you for your little experiments, and an experienced staff would be there to help you. And there'd be faculty parties and people we could relate to."

"You make my work sound like a game. Now that I've set up my laboratory, I have everything I want right here." He leaned over the chair and, taking her empty glass, held her hand. "We'll have children, then you'll have plenty to do. And if we don't have a child of our own, we can adopt one." His voice caught. The manifestation of his son was a picture in a locket.

Lillian pulled away from him.

Always away, never toward, he reflected.

"Oh, I could never raise another woman's child," she said.

But someone else is raising mine, he thought.

Lillian had come to resent her husband's obstinate refusal to leave Rockville. Her dream of a social life in Baltimore, or New York, as the wife of a brilliant and handsome surgeon, was becoming just that—a dream.

After replenishing their drinks, Adam sat down in the red leather recliner. The fingers of his left hand absently traced the face of a lion carved into the curve of the walnut arm as he observed his wife. *Could she raise a child? Lillian doesn't like messes, and a child can be messy. To her, even the making of a child is messy. Lillian likes orderliness: beautiful and inanimate objects, a well-run household, and adoration from afar.*

He held his drink up to the light, a distorted image of Lillian appearing in the bell curve of the glass. *I wonder what she and her father are cooking up now?* he thought to himself. *The first time they ganged up on me, I was too young and too impressed by the famous doctor and his beautiful daughter and ended up married. A month after the wedding, there came a very convenient miscarriage and, according to her, one since then.* He sighed a very audible sigh. "Let's take the train and go into the city for a few days," he said. "See a show and dine on cuisine other than Rockville suppers."

"Ummm, yes, let's do that," Lillian said, suddenly sounding happy.

The first morning back from the trip to the city, Lillian fussed over the breakfast table setting. Among the purchases she had made in the city were a new blue-and-yellow-striped tablecloth and yellow napkins. Mrs. Sheridan, the housekeeper, had received a gift of yellow mums as thanks from the Italian farmer who went from house to house in his horse and cart selling the fresh produce he raised in his home garden.

Lillian loved flowers. *Maybe I'll take up gardening*, she thought as she arranged the yellow flowers in a silver bowl. She hoped Meiko Toma would come by for tea. She needed to interact with someone, to enjoy some playful banter. She had not seen Meiko recently, and today she would have the details of her trip to the capital to share with him.

Sure enough, Meiko soon arrived, tapping on the kitchen door before he entered; he seemed genuinely pleased to see her. She was wearing his favorite morning dress, a fluid, silky robe in pale blue, her hair loose and flowing, and she appeared to be in a good mood.

Lillian poured tea, and Meiko commented on the flowers. She told him about the association's meeting, but he already knew about that. Then she told him about their trip and the musical stage show they'd seen, and the food. He was always interested in the food, especially if they had dined in a continental restaurant.

"Why did you come to America, Michael?" she asked suddenly, using his American name.

He smiled, then grew serious, a look of determination on his face. "I want to act in moving picture shows. They are very big in Europe. Not yet in America. But they will be. I'm here in this place," he said, nodding his head and indicating the town, "because I need the money the doctor pays me—and for the love of a horse." His eyes went to hers, and he shrugged, turning his mouth down in a disparaging frown.

Inwardly she cringed. The subject of money was never discussed in polite company, and certainly not in the presence of a woman. He leaned back in his chair, flashing her one of his most flamboyant smiles, his eyes challenging what her opinion of him might be.

"What will you do in the movies?" she asked coolly.

"Dance, make love..." he said, searching for a word. His eyes passed over her face, lingering on her mouth. He finished boldly: "Make love to beautiful women like you."

She was instantly annoyed. She resented his sudden familiarity toward her, and she resented the bold statement he'd made about women while in her company. He was overstepping the bounds of propriety and sending their friendship down a path she certainly had no intention of following. She became angry with herself for encouraging his friendship. What was she thinking? He was a servant, a stableman, an inferior human being.

She stood. "You will have to excuse me. I have things I must attend to."

He also stood, automatically reaching for her hand, but, quickly picked up her teacup, she walked away.

Meiko, not noticing the change in her disposition, called after her. "I have a surprise for you! You will find out later, at Christmastime."

Lillian did not look back. She withdrew, leaving him standing alone in the sunlit room.

CHAPTER 64

November 1908

DOWNTOWN WAS UNUSUALLY LIVELY THIS holiday season. People had heard of the new business association and were curious about what was going on. They were making purchases and, feeling generous, dropping coins into the Christmas charity boxes.

Abby was busy making hats for customers as well as her own and Frieda's dresses for the association's first event, a Christmas ball. She kept her gown on her wire dress form in the workroom and worked on it whenever possible. During one of her many errands away from the store, she returned in time to see Velvet Preston and Precious Amy leaving. When she entered the shop, Daisy was in a snit of exasperation.

"What happened?" Abby asked, alarmed.

"Oh, that Velvet makes me so mad! She just walks into the workroom—uninvited, mind you—just to look at your gown. She's going to have it worn out just from looking at it, and dirty from fingering it. And her eyes—I hate looking into her face. The envy in her eyes is smothering. And that Amy winds around you like a homeless cat," she said with a shudder, rubbing at her upper arms.

Laughing, Abby placed her hands on Daisy's quivering shoulders. "My goodness, such a tirade. Do you feel better?"

"I'm sorry; I guess I'm tired," Daisy said apologetically before joining Abby in laughing at herself.

"Well, Velvet and Bobby Lee are among the families on the association's Christmas list. Maybe I'll slip some fabric into their basket. Velvet must really love Bobby to put up with him the way she has."

Velvet was in a terrible temper and walking too fast for Precious Amy to keep up with her. Amy, stumbling along behind Velvet in the rutted, icy road, was freezing in her little jacket and coughing from the cold air burning her throat. Velvet paid her no mind. She heard a buggy approaching and, without looking up, belligerently moved aside to let it pass.

"Whoa!" a man's voice said. "Good evening, ladies, could I give you a lift somewhere?"

Smoldering inwardly, Velvet lifted her raging eyes to the man in the rig, sizing him up. She had seen him before; he was one of the drummers who came to town regularly. One time last summer she had attracted his attention when strolling past Ma's dressed in her finery, and he had left the pool hall and tried to tease her into taking a ride with him. She had also observed him on occasion in a rig driving by her house. She'd never found an appropriate time to speak to him, but now, she didn't care. Tossing her head backward and gesturing toward Amy, she said, "She can walk."

At her gate, the drummer helped Velvet from his carriage and suggested that she meet him the next day at the depot. Before today, she would not have taken him up on his invitation. Now, out of desperation and the hatred she bore for the detestable life she was forced to live in Rockville, she agreed to meet him.

Velvet entered the house and yelled to the boys to get the tub ready. She was taking a bath. She changed into her black Chinese robe with the large embroidered red flower on the back of it and looked with disgust at the stained and shabby little embroidered bedroom slippers as she slipped her feet into them.

She thought of Abby's new party dress, and anger roiled inside her. *I hate this town. I hate the people. I hate this shanty, and above all I hate being poor.* "Is that bathwater ready yet?" she yelled, causing Timothy, who was afraid of his stepmother, to burst into loud crying.

Living here, all of them piled into one tiny house, was driving her crazy. In the winter, the kids were always underfoot, with no outdoor chores to do and nowhere to go. Even their own grandparents didn't want them. And her son worried her. Jeff, always thin, had lost more weight since moving to Rockville. The family kept rabbits—which sometimes they sold, but mostly they ate—and Jeff, growing up in the city without pets as he had, loved the rabbits and could not abide eating them. On the days they had rabbit for supper, which was often, he became physically ill.

Money had been easy for Velvet to come by in the city, but not here. She knew only too well the wrath of a small town, because she had run away from one.

She watched from the window as the man in the buggy, returning from the end of the dirt road, drove by again, slowly. He was good-looking in a way, with dark hair and mustache, the ends of which were turned up and waxed. Underneath his dark topcoat, with its black curly lamb collar, he wore a green and black plaid suit and sported a bowler hat.

She knew his type: big spender. If you were a lively woman and a looker and showed promise of a hot time, well then, the really big sports took you to dinner at a nice restaurant.

Velvet peeled the crispy white paper from the last bar of her Jergens Buttermilk Soap, saving the box and the wrapper, before stepping into the tub. She sat cross-legged in the round tin tub, slowly rubbing the bar across her bosom and shoulders, then raising her arms high to let the soapy water trickle down her body and into the tub.

Velvet was scheming. *That drummer could be my ticket out of here. But what can I wear to meet him? What do I have that isn't old and soiled?* Again she thought of Abby's beautiful green silk dress, and the bitter bile of envy rose in her throat.

When Velvet finished with her bath and stepped from the alcove beneath the stairs, cordoned off for privacy with an old faded curtain that Bobby Lee's mother had presented to her as if it had belonged to the Queen of Sheba, she saw Amy, her head drooping and her shoulders slumped, sitting on a chair by the stove. Two bright spots from the cold night air flamed brightly on her pale cheeks. She did not look well, and in a moment of regret, Velvet felt sorry for the girl.

"Amy, before you empty the tub, why don't you add some hot water from the stove reservoir and take a bath yourself? I put some French bath salts in the water, and it smells real good. Tomorrow morning, you can get my black suit out of my trunk for me." She knew Amy liked going through her trunk. "I'm going to need it," she said with an air of importance.

Velvet sat on the cot gently massaging her face and throat with thick cream that she kept in a jar. Cream she skimmed from the pail of milk the kids' grandmother sent home with them every other day. With no way of keeping the milk cool, it quickly soured and turned into clabber, a thick, pudding-like dish that, when they had enough milk left over to sour, they ate for supper.

From a slit in the drawn curtains, Velvet caught a glimpse of Amy standing in the tin tub scratching at purplish ribbed lines on her roundly extended abdomen. When Amy saw Velvet watching her, she turned away.

"Just one minute, missy," Velvet said with an intimidating slowness. "I want to get a better look at you!" Striding across the room, she jerked back the flimsy drape. Amy stepped out of the tub and into the corner of the alcove, trying to hide her nakedness. Velvet grabbed Amy's thin little arms and pulled her into the room. "Stand up!" she demanded.

Amy, cowering all the more, reached for her clothes, neatly folded on a nearby chair. Velvet gave the girl an ear-ringing slap to the side of her head that caused her to cry out. Placing her hands under Amy's elbows, she forced her to stand erect. Velvet's green eyes narrowed as she studied the enlarged, purple-streaked belly, and in another instant they were wide open.

"Are you—oh my God—are you—are you pregnant?" She had whispered the words. Now she was yelling them. "Are you pregnant? You little tramp, you dirty little whore, are you pregnant?" Velvet beat at her with both hands, the blows falling wherever she could land them. "What kind of a house is this?" she screamed.

Yelling and cursing, Velvet dragged and pushed a sobbing Amy about the room. Because of her nakedness, Amy could not run from the house, and she didn't try to ward off the blows. Around and around the room they went, bumping into chairs, the dresser, until she finally fell to the floor at the foot of the attic steps. The boys, sitting at the top of the stairs, too afraid of Velvet's fury to interfere, looked on in horror. Velvet, agile as a cat, sprang to her feet and gave Amy one last vicious kick to her bare bottom as she lay helpless and weeping.

Velvet continued her rampage about the room, kicking the already tipped over chairs out of her way and throwing a glass mason jar filled with water against the wall, sending water and shards of glass flying about the room. The ironing board, wrapped with an old blanket and balanced on the backs of two chairs, with a cold flatiron setting upright on the wide end of the board, was the only movable object in the room not in shambles.

Velvet stood back and, as one long, shapely leg swept forward into a high kick, her black silk robe fell open, revealing a flat, white stomach with a little triangular pillow of bright-red hair. Her bare foot caught the underside of the ironing board, sending it sailing into the air before it fell to the floor with a dull thud. Velvet screamed as the cold, cumbersome iron, free of its perch, hurtled downward, striking the top of her foot.

Velvet hopped about on one leg, holding her injured foot in both hands, a stream of oaths pouring forth from her mouth and scalding the air.

For the first time, Velvet saw the boys, having forgotten about them during the course of her tantrum. The brothers had sneaked down the stairs and were trying to aid their battered sister. "You little bastards!" she yelled, and she picked up the stove poker and went after them. The two older boys escaped to the outdoors with Velvet in pursuit. She threw the poker at them, and it landed with a clunk in the dirt yard. Chickens that had gone to roost for the night were set to cackling and running around.

Returning to the house, her pent-up anger spent, Velvet wearily limped about righting the chairs. She placed her foot on the seat of one and examined her injury. A hard red knot from the heavy iron was already forming on the top of her foot. She looked around for Amy. She was back in the curtained alcove, still nude and still standing very straight, too afraid of Velvet to do anything else. Her little-girl abdomen stretched taut, the waist thickening, the developing young breasts swollen and rock hard, all hurting and itching.

Velvet went to the girl and, hugging her savagely, said, "I'm sorry, Amy. It's not you I'm mad at; it's me, and everyone else in this stinking, rotten world." She found a gown in a basket of washed, yet-to-be ironed clothes and, gently pulling it over Amy's head, sat down with her on the cot and wrapped the two of them in a quilt.

"Amy, you're going to have a baby."

Not comprehending what Velvet was saying, Precious Amy's dark eyes, still wild with fright, stared out from her white face.

"You don't even know what I'm talking about, do you?" Velvet threw back her head. As she rolled it from side to side, a tormented wail escaped her throat so impassioned it encompassed all womanhood. "You're—going—to—have—a—baby," she repeated, with agonizing emphasis.

"Like Mama?" Amy said, and she began to cry.

"Yes, like Mama."

"Am I going to die like Mama?" Shaking with fright, Amy squeezed the words out in a tight, childish voice.

"No," Velvet said. "You'll wish you could, but you won't. Who did it to you, anyway?"

The girl's face remained blank.

"Amy, some guy opened up his pants and took out his wang and stuck it in you."

Amy chewed at her fingertips.

Velvet made the vulgar motion of poking the forefinger of her right hand into the fist of her left.

A light dawned on Amy's face, and her expression quickly turned to one of terror. She pushed herself away from Velvet. "He said if I ever told he would cut my tongue out!"

"Well, you're going to tell me, missy," Velvet said in a threatening voice, "or I'm going to cut your tongue out. Right now," she said, bouncing off the couch and moving quickly in the direction of the kitchen.

"Chance Collins!" Amy screamed. "He said if I swept out his granary, he would give me a dollar, and, and then he hurt me," she said, wailing.

Woman and child wept, Velvet cuddling Amy and rocking her.

The boys crept back into the room, testing Velvet's disposition.

"You may come in if you'll be quiet. First sweep up the floor and, Jeffy, bring me a wet washrag and a towel."

She washed Amy's face and hands. The boys brought quilts from upstairs and, making pallets of them, lay down on the floor near the stove.

Velvet was sitting on the cot and leaning against the wall with a pillow supporting her back, Amy's head resting in her lap, her thumb in her mouth. With the smooth, creamy-scented palm of her hand, Velvet stroked the girl's forehead and brushed at her hair with her fingers. "You're still a baby," she said. "I was born in a little town just like this one," Velvet said, looking down into the face of the girl, "with all the do-gooders and busybodies in it trying to save me from hell's damnation, and all because I was born with red hair. Ha! My mother hid the color by rubbing stove black on it. The old biddies of the town were always snickering at me from behind their wrinkled old hands, hiding their mean, wrinkled old mouths.

"Every time a revival was going on, I was trotted out and prayed over and my sins made clean. I didn't even know what my sins were, but I knew they must be terrible. In the minds of the people in Glen Oaks, I didn't even have a childhood; I just went from a baby to a full-grown harlot. And like you, Amy, I didn't even know how babies were made.

"Then, one day, I just walked out of that town—walked for two days until I reached the city. I got a job washing dishes in a café. The owner said I could stay there and bed down in the storage room if he could come and visit me once in a while. I said I'd be much obliged if he'd visit me, thinking it would be nice to have someone to talk to in a big city full of strangers. I thought he was a real kind man, giving me a job and a place to live and all, a little room back of the kitchen where the restaurant supplies was kept.

"The first thing I did that night, after everyone was gone and the dishes all washed and stacked, was wash my hair. I about used up all the dishwashing soap, but I got all that stove black out of my hair, and it was curly and shiny and red, just like it is now." She beamed with pride.

"The next morning, when the owner, Mr. Pergola, saw me, he looked mighty pleased and said he thought he would pay me a visit that very night." Velvet laughed ruefully. "Well, he came to the storage room that night after he'd closed up and everyone was gone. He locked the door and told me to get undressed and onto the cot and be quick about it, 'cause he didn't have all night. I was scared and didn't know what was going on. He yelled at me and said that if he couldn't get some, then I couldn't get out. So I hurried and got undressed and onto a rickety old cot covered with a ratty old army blanket. He didn't take off his clothes, not even his shoes, just got on top of me and did his business. None of the men I was ever with, except for your pa, took off their clothes, but after I moved from the café, I made them take off their shoes at least. It was over so fast I hardly knew what happened. I never did like it—maybe for a little while, with your pa. But I didn't like it then, and I don't like it now. But I sure learned fast that men like it—like it enough to pay you for it."

She stopped talking; her long story had put everyone to sleep.

Amy, her head still in Velvet's lap, had inherited her father's long, dark lashes. They fanned out on her cheeks, partially hiding the violet shadows beneath them.

"Poor innocent baby, your nightmare is coming, and soon."

While the children slept, Velvet went on rummaging through her beat-up trunk of memories. "One afternoon when the owner was gone, the cook told me he'd give me a quarter if he could get into bed with me. After that, he gave me a quarter a couple of times a week. Some of the waiters began coming to the storage room, and they always left two bits. Finally, Mr. Pergola fixed me up a room down in the basement. It was real nice, with a bed instead of a cot, and he said I didn't have to wash dishes no more, just stay in my room and he would send some of his very best customers down to visit me. I found out later they were paying Mr. Pergola two dollars a visit and leaving me a quarter. Then I got pregnant.

"It was a long time before I knew why I was throwing up every morning. It was Mr. Pergola who had to tell me. He gave me some money and found me a room in a house down by the railroad station. I only left the room long enough to eat. I just laid there on the bed, 'cause I thought the baby would just drop out and fall on the floor and get hurt.

"Then one night, I got so sick and was in so much pain I was screaming and hollering, and another woman, Amour, who had a room there in the same building, came into my room and stayed with me, and when it was all over, I had Jeff there." She looked in the direction of her sleeping son. "Amour wrapped the baby in one of her old petticoats, 'cause I sure didn't have anything. She was the best friend I ever had. She had red hair about the color of mine, only hers wasn't natural. She helped me take care of the baby and, when I got my strength back, taught me to be an honest-to-God prostitute. Told me to charge two bucks, but I knew the men had paid Mr. Pergola two bucks and me a quarter, so I figured that's what I was worth: two dollars and twenty-five cents." She looked around with a measure of pride. "So that's what I charged. Amour had it fixed up with someone so's that only the women who lived in that building by the station could ply their trade at the depot, and for that, we paid her five dollars a month.

"When we went into the 'profession,' as Amour called it, we gave ourselves a new name, and all the girls who lived there had a party for you—just like a birthday party, with cake and presents."

Velvet named all the girls, counting them off on her long smooth fingers. "There was Floret and Lacy and Orchid and Sara Beth—she was a real pretty little thing, with blond curls and the biggest, bluest eyes you ever saw. She was so little, we all mothered her, and, oh, how the men loved her." Velvet rolled her eyes upward. "I chose Velvet for my new name. I always liked the feel and look of velvet. I liked the way the word felt on my tongue when I said it, all soft and smooth." She pronounced the name, letting it roll slowly across her tongue: "Vel-vet."

"Every time a train pulled into the depot, we would walk around or through the station. We liked it when we got a man who was just getting off the train to stretch his legs and maybe only had a half hour to kill; he usually paid you more than what you asked for. In the evening we would stroll about in pairs, all dressed up in our best dresses, hair curled, and all of us smelling of real, honest-to-God French perfume.

"Men from town would come by the apartment building, older men with tired wives and younger men looking for their first one, all red faced and ashamed and never looking at you. The farmers stopped in after selling their wares in the big city, once they had some spending money. Anyone looking for sin and wickedness and satisfaction found their way to that flatiron-shaped building by the railroad track. But I soon found out you couldn't just lay there like a stick; they had paid their money and wanted their money's worth.

"Three of us had kids, and an older woman who lived there had a spare room set up like a nursery and took care of our kids while we worked. Amour taught us how to take care of ourselves and not get pregnant, and if we did, a doctor in town would fix us up and treat us for other things, too.

"I was there five years when your pa came along, and with his new suit and fresh haircut, he looked like money. He was one of the best-looking men I'd ever seen. He was the first man I had who took all his clothes off. It sure was funny seeing a naked man for the first time in my life. And when he was finished, he just curled up and went to sleep.

"He was the first man to spend the night, too. I liked seeing a man there in the bed, undressed and sleeping; it was like being married. After taking care of myself, I got back into bed with him and crawled into the curve of his body. He wrapped his arms around me, a hand on each breast. He was the only man I ever knew who wasn't ashamed, or in a hurry to get it over with, and he talked to me. Told me I was pretty and that I had the most beautiful hair he'd ever seen. It was the first time I realized that loving a man was like loving a baby: warm and cozy and satisfying. And Bobby Lee was like a big baby. I used to sit up in bed, leaning against the headboard, and I'd cuddle him in my arms, and he would kiss my breasts. I never knew a man could like a woman's breasts the way he did.

"It was nice going to bed with a man because you wanted to, and not because you was getting paid to do it. It was wonderful kissing a man. That's one thing you don't do in the whore business—you don't kiss them, and they sure as heck don't want to kiss you.

"The next morning, I fixed breakfast for us, then he got dressed and said he was going out and look for a job—that he wanted to live in the city and not on a farm. When he came back that night, I was honest to God glad to see him. Jeff liked him, too.

"He told me his wife had died and he had a couple of kids." She looked about the room at all the sleeping bodies and thought, *Yeah, some "couple" of kids.* "I kept thinking about his farm. In my daydreams, it was a big farm with a good house, and I could see Jeffy living there, happy and healthy. He was getting too big to live in a whorehouse, with the railroad tracks the only place to play. A man wasn't allowed to stay there, so we moved into a little two-room place. I stopped working, 'cause I didn't want to go to bed with any other man; I had some money saved, and Bobby Lee kept looking for a job."

A deep sigh escaped her when she thought about a room of her own. "Bobby Lee was also the only man I knew who wasn't upset with a child in the room; he would go right on sleeping, or making love—it didn't disturb him one bit. I should have known right then and there that there was more than a 'couple of kids' at home. And I should've known he was lazy when days went by and he didn't look for work, but I was in love, and when he asked me to marry him, I said yes.

"I paid for the train fare for the three of us to come to Rockville, and for the first time in my life, I was excited and happy. When he said we were getting near home and the train rolled by all those nice farms, I kept asking him which farm was his, and when we got off the train, and I smelled that long-forgotten country smell, I wanted to cry, it smelled that good to me. Not anymore!

"We walked across town, staying close to the tracks, past the neat little houses, right back to what I'd left years before, and when we stopped before this dilapidated old shack and all the kids come running out, love just up and died."

CHAPTER 65

Bobby Lee returned home from his day's work in the Rockville coal mine to a strangely peaceful house: Amy asleep on the couch, her head turned to the wall, and two-year-old Billy curled up and asleep at her feet. The older boys seated on the floor were quietly playing a game they called "Farm." It was long past suppertime, so Velvet knew he had stopped off at Ma's.

In the kitchen, Bobby Lee stripped down to his waist and washed his arms, face, and hands in the enamel washbasin.

"When you get all that black stuff off of you, you can get in the tub," Velvet said. "There's enough hot water in the stove reservoir to heat it up real good. I'll keep your dinner warm."

Bobby Lee grew suspicious. Velvet was being awfully sweet, for Velvet, and bathing in her perfumed, leftover bathwater was about as close as he got to her anymore.

Velvet brought Bobby Lee's dinner to him where he sat waiting at the kitchen table in clean long johns. His hair glistening and curly from the bath, his skin glowing from the harsh scrubbing with the brush reserved for removing coal dust, he looked down at the bland plate. Having been kept in the warming oven too long, grease had congealed on the fried potatoes, and the chunk of fatback pork and the boiled green beans lay pale and soggy in a puddle of green water. His good mood deserted him.

"Velvet, can't you warm this up some?"

"Bobby Lee, hurry up and eat. I've got to talk to you."

The urgency in her voice made him attack the unappetizing dinner without further complaint.

Velvet couldn't sit still. She went limping around the room, stopping several times to look at his plate. She would open her mouth as if to speak but then change her mind.

"Why are you limping?" Bobby Lee asked, his mouth stuffed with food. She waved a hand back and forth, indicating it was of no importance. Once he finished with his supper, she started up the stairs.

Bobby Lee hung back. "I don't know, Velvet, my stomach don't feel so good."

"It isn't that!" she said in exasperation.

Upstairs and sitting side by side on the edge of the bed, they were suddenly overcome with shyness. Velvet turned to face him. Her green cat eyes blazing, she blurted out, "Amy's pregnant."

Looking at her numbly, Bobby Lee swallowed. "Amy?"

Velvet moved closer to him, her voice a deep whisper. "She was raped."

"Amy?"

"She was raped by Chance Collins."

"Chance Collins," Bobby Lee said in the same flat tone.

Velvet told him the story, just as Amy had told it to her, and when she finished, Bobby Lee said Chance Collins's name again in the same vacant voice.

"Bobby Lee," she said, "you've got to do something."

"Me? What can I do?" he said, a whine creeping into his voice.

"Who is this Chance Collins, anyway?" Velvet asked. "What does he do?"

"Well, he's a rancher," Bobby Lee said. "He's got a big cattle farm and lives due south of here. He rides by sometimes, on a big black horse."

"Oh, yeah, I know who you mean: the guy with the big ugly scar on his face. I know his kind—mean. Is he married? Has he got money?"

No longer uncomfortable, they sat looking at each other, each wondering what the other had in mind.

"Yes," he said with a nod of his head. "Chance is pretty well off, and he's single. Do you think I should go to the marshal?"

Velvet jumped up and stood in front of him, her hands on her hips, rocking her head from shoulder to shoulder. "No. I think you should go see Mr. Chance Collins and ask him what he's going to do about his bastard kid he dumped into your daughter's belly. That's what I think you should do."

Bobby Lee turned down the covers and crawled into bed. "Geez, Velvet, keep it down."

"What are you doing?"

"I'm going to bed."

"The hell you are!" Velvet snatched the quilt from his hand. "You are going to see Chance Collins right now."

"Jeez, Velvet, Chance will be in bed, and besides, I'm done tuckered out." Sighing, he sat up and reached under the bed for his shoes. The look on Velvet's face told him he was going to Chance's place, or else he'd be listening to her going on a tirade for the next hour or so. He really missed Agnes at times.

The long walk after a hard day's work, the unpalatable supper, the cold, the shock of his little girl pregnant, Velvet's temper tantrum, and the drink of whiskey at Ma's, long worn off, all had left Bobby Lee tired and irritable. All told, he was pretty riled up by the time he got to Chance's farm.

The place was pitch black when he banged on the kitchen door, and it took a few minutes before a light came on in the kitchen. Chance called out, "Who is it?" in a loud, hostile voice.

"It's me—Bobby Lee."

Chance opened the door. He was wearing knee-length underpants and had slipped into a pair of work shoes, the laces untied and dragging on the floor. "Bobby Lee," Chance said, surprised. "What's goin' on?" He looked past Bobby Lee into the night.

"I got to talk to you, Chance."

"Well, hell, Bobby Lee, whatever it is, can't it wait till tomorrow?"

"No, it can't!"

"Well, come on in, then."

Bobby Lee blinked into the harsh brightness coming from the electric bulb hanging from the middle of the ceiling. He was nervous, but Chance standing there in his underwear looked more comical than dangerous. "Chance—you—my little girl…" he rubbed the back of his hand across his mouth. "Amy's pregnant," he blurted out. "You got her that way, and I want to know what you aim on doing about it."

Chance strode to an inner door, closed it, and pulled on the knob to make sure it was tight. When he turned around, he bumped into Bobby Lee, who had followed him across the room.

"Now, don't you go trying to lie your way out of it, Chance. Amy told me and Velvet the whole story about how you raped her."

Chance moved his finger rapidly back and forth across his mouth. "Shhh! Not so loud," he said, glancing around at the closed door. "Come over here and sit down."

Bobby Lee dropped into a kitchen chair, propped his elbows on the table, his head in his hands, and began to cry.

Fear and disgust ripped through Chance Collins. He hated weakness in man or beast, but Bobby Lee's weakness could be his downfall. *There's no telling who he'll go bawling to,* he thought. Chance brought a bottle and two glasses from a cupboard and sat down across the table from Bobby Lee.

"I'm not going to deny it, Bobby Lee—I wronged you and that pretty little girl of yours. But, I tell you, if it wasn't me, it would've been some other man. Bobby Lee, you're gonna have to watch that little girl of yours, or you'll have a full-blown little whore on your hands. Why, she would come over here when you was away and tag me around. Always teasing me and putting her hands on me. She'd put her hands right in my pants pockets and feel around."

Bobby Lee sat sniffling through Chance's recital and said, "Amy?" in a tight, bewildered voice. How many times during this strange night had he said her name? Saying it as if he were trying to fit the name to the face, or maybe the face to the deed, and he began crying again. Chance quickly refilled Bobby Lee's glass and pushed it between his elbows; the acrid smell made Bobby Lee's head jerk up, and he looked sidewise at Chance, a faint smile on his face.

Chance immediately reached across the table and shook Bobby Lee's shoulder.

"Hell, Bobby Lee, we're both alike, you and me, we're men of the world. We get out of this hick town now and then, and we both know what kind of a woman we want in bed. We want one a-pushing and a-shoving and taking as good as she's giving."

Bobby Lee sat taller, swiped his coat sleeve across his nose, and took another long drink of the whiskey.

"Hell, boy," Chance said, "ever since you brought that little filly of a wife home, you got all us men running 'round like stud horses, you old rascal, you." He gave Bobby Lee's shoulder another good-natured shaking. "This is all your fault," he said, slapping him on the back. "You sly old fox."

Chance laughed heartily, and Bobby Lee, in a feeble, half-hearted attempt at jocularity, laughed with him. "Chance, I've had a hard time—everybody knows I've had a hard time—and if there's one thing we don't need, it's another kid. I can't feed my own, let alone somebody else's. And what am I going to tell people about Amy?"

"Now, Bobby Lee, you know I'm not going to marry Amy, but I am going to do right by you. Now, suppose every month I give you a sack of flour, and every harvest a wagonload of potatoes and a wagonload of coal? And every fall, when I slaughter, I'll see to it that you get some prime meat for your table. See, you'll be better off with another kid than you was before."

Bobby Lee slowly nodded his head in agreement. "But people are still going to ask questions, and what am I going to tell them?"

Chance left the room, and when he returned, he held out his hand to Bobby Lee. Resting on his big callused palm were five gold coins glowing richly in the glare of the naked light bulb. "Them's double eagles, Bobby Lee: twenty-dollar gold pieces. You and Velvet can say the kid's yours, and nobody ever needs to know any different. A hundred dollars, Bobby Lee, if you never tell anybody it's mine." Chance bartered by lightly bouncing the coins up and down on his open palm.

Bobby Lee wiped his hands on his pant legs before reverently picking up the five twenty-dollar pieces. He had never held gold coins before.

Bobby Lee walked tall, his hand loosely holding a rope tied around the neck of the milk cow plodding along behind him. Now and then he broke into song: "She'll be coming 'round the mountain when she comes."

Velvet, waiting up for him, ran to the stoop when she heard him at the gate. The light from the open door dimly illuminated the man and animal.

"Whatcha got?" she said in a loud whisper.

"A cow. A milk cow." He patted the jersey's flanks.

"Do you mean to tell me a man raped your daughter, forced his bastard child on us to take care of, and expects to get away with it by giving you a cow?"

"Jeez, Velvet, don't yell like that."

"Yell? I haven't even started to yell. You are the weakest, most namby-pamby man I ever met. You don't know beans when the bag's open, and anybody can talk you into anything." She turned to go into the house.

"Velvet, wait. I haven't told you all of it yet."

She turned back, eyeing him suspiciously. "There's more?" she asked, squinting into the darkness.

"There's a whole lot more." He untied the rope from around the cow's neck and, swatting the animal with it, turned it loose.

They went into the house and into the kitchen. Velvet fixed him a bowl of bread and milk, and when he had finished eating, they went upstairs, stepping over sleeping bodies in the living room as they went. In the attic, they prepared for bed. Once Velvet moved in, the attic had become the property of the adults.

"Well?" Velvet said.

"Well, he won't marry her."

"Of course he won't marry her. Who wants to marry a baby?"

"Well, he gave us a cow."

"I know he gave us a cow," Velvet said in frustration.

"And flour and potatoes and meat whenever he slaughters." Bobby Lee's eyes were shining, and his face courted a boyish grin. He was clearly pleased with himself.

Velvet rolled her eyes heavenward and dropped down on the bed, letting her hands dangle between her bare legs. She stared at the lump on her foot already turning black. *I expect too much,* she thought. *If I expected nothing, then when I got nothing, it wouldn't hurt so much.*

"Sweetheart," Bobby Lee said, causing Velvet to wince, "close your eyes and hold out your hand."

Dully she did so, and he placed something on her palm. She opened her eyes and brought her hand closer to her face. "What is it?"

“It’s five double eagles,” he said, pointing to them with unaccustomed pride.

“He gave you these?”

“Yes, but Velvet, it’s for us to keep quiet. It’s a hundred dollars in gold if we never tell a living soul that Chance is the father of Amy’s baby.”

Velvet stroked the shiny pieces, turning each one over and over on her palm. Bobby Lee made a move for the coins. “No. Let me keep them,” she said. “I’ll take care of them.”

“Jeez, Velvet, think what we can do with a hundred dollars. We could have electricity put in, a new dress and shoes for you, boots for me—maybe something for Amy and the baby.”

Velvet was up early the next morning preparing a hot breakfast for everyone. Bobby Lee wanted to stay home from work, but she wouldn’t hear of it. She packed a lunch for him in the lard pail he carried. She was happy and sweet to everyone. Even the oatmeal, which she rarely cooked, was not as lumpy as usual, but the children watched her more warily than they did when she was in a temper.

All the kids except Jeffery went out to take turns milking the cow before they left for school. Velvet, placing a hand on her son’s forehead, declared him to be sick. After much scrounging around for writing paper until finally being reduced to writing her message on a scrap of wrapping paper, she handed the note to her son. "I want you to take this to a Mr. Bowman—he's one of them drummer guys," she told Jeff. "He'll be at the emporium, or Ma's."

The following morning, Velvet was sweeter than ever, and even Bobby Lee, growing wary, left for work without grumbling. Jeffery again remained at home.

"I'm going away, Jeffy," Velvet told him when the others were gone and they were upstairs in the attic room. "And as soon as I'm settled, I'll send for you. I just can't stand living in this house and this town any longer. Not—one—more—day," she said as, with each word, she tossed another piece of clothing into her trunk. Taking up a red feather boa from the trunk, she teased her two youngest stepsons with it, tickling their faces, and left it for them to play with.

A sniffling Jeffery sat on the bed, tears trickling down his face as he watched his mother take clothes and personal articles from where they hung on wooden pegs and in makeshift cupboards. "I have a chance to make it out of here, Jeffy. Please don't be sad, and please don't cry. Everything's going to be just fine—you'll see."

At three o'clock, the drummer arrived. Jeff watched the big man drag his mother's trunk down the stairs and out to the road, where he had a buggy waiting. His mother looked very pretty—the prettiest and happiest he had seen her in a long time. And she smelled good, a scent he had not smelled on her before.

"As soon as I'm settled, I'll send for you," she kept reminding him as he dashed tears from his eyes. She bent over him, placing a hand on each of his thin shoulders, and looked into his face. "Honest, Jeffy, honey, here, look at me." With a finger she made a cross over her heart. "Cross my heart and hope to die."

This made him feel better, along with the promise that she would send for him, and soon.

After helping Velvet into the buggy, the man gave Jeff a silver dollar. "Take care, kid," he said.

Jeff watched the wagon all the way down the dirt road, his mother turned around in the seat and waving to him, until it disappeared onto Main Street and headed toward the depot. Jeffy ran into the house and up the stairs, the attic strangely empty now with all his mother's belongings gone, and watched from the tiny attic window, the cracks around the wooden frame stuffed with rags, as the train snaked its way across the flat farmland until he could see it no more.

The train conductor accepted tickets from the handsome man with the black mustache, the ends waxed and curled. The woman traveling with him had the reddest hair he'd ever seen; she sat next to the window looking back in the direction from which they had come.

One of Velvet's white-gloved hands rested on her breast, where, nestled in her bodice between the soft mounds of her bosom, lay a hundred dollars in gold coins tied into a corner of a white lace-trimmed handkerchief securely pinned to her corset cover.

CHAPTER 66

December 1908

DONALD AND DOVIE VAUGHN HAD chosen a buffet dinner-dance for Rockville's newly formed merchants' association's first "Good Time" event. The formal dance took place on the night of the twenty-third of December at the Parlett Hotel.

That evening, every window in the hotel shown with candlelight, and, in Mr. and Mrs. Parlett's private quarters, green wreaths with red bows hung in the windows, with candles aglow.

A fir tree with small colored electric lights had been set up in the hotel lobby. It was the first time anyone in Rockville had seen decorative lights on a tree. Garlands of greens hung from the lobby-stair banister, and in the place of honor, beneath the mounted elk's head, its horns bedecked with red bows, was a holiday arrangement of flowers.

Streams of association members, most of them seeing the second floor of the hotel for the first time, crowded the stairs. Early arriving guests coming down the stairs, and new arrivals making their way up, had everyone coming to a halt when jovial greetings and handshakes broke out between the two passing lines. The party was off to a good start.

Perthy Prettyman, who just happened to be downtown at eight o' clock on that particular Saturday night and just happened to look in the window of the hotel lobby, reported to the Benevolent Society the next Tuesday that the association's members were in "fine feather and fettle."

Two rooms had been set aside for the guests' wraps: one for ladies' outerwear, with a townswoman in attendance, and Harlan Jones attending the men's room. A room next to the two bathrooms at the end of the long corridor had been turned into a women's vanity for the evening.

Abby wore the chinchilla cape and carried the muff Aunt Em had bequeathed to her in her will.

"I'm glad she willed it to you," Frieda said, stroking the luxurious fur. "No one else in Rockville could look as good in it as you."

Abby removed the cape from her shoulders and draped it around Frieda. What had been meant as a light moment soon became overshadowed by the memory of Aunt Em.

Dressed in an emerald-green peau de soie silk gown that turned her eyes a vivid green, gave her a modest showing of décolletage, and displayed her beautiful bare shoulders, Abby critically appraised her reflection in the tall easel mirror set up in the women's cloakroom. She had swept her shining dark auburn hair up into a large pompadour and adorned it with a black plume. The gold locket she always wore tucked away tonight hung from her neck on a black velvet ribbon, her only jewelry.

Frieda peeked into the mirror. She didn't like looking at herself and was astonished to see that she looked almost pretty in her party dress of carnation-pink silk, chosen by Abby to lend color to her pale complexion. Abby used all her skills as a seamstress to disguise Frieda's sharp shoulder blades, too-long neck, and meager bosom.

Outside on the sidewalk, another flow of traffic was taking place as the curious sauntered by, trying to catch a glimpse of the members of the merchants' association and the "blowout" taking place inside.

The young boys of the town, noses pressed to the lobby windows, leering and poking fun at the partygoers, were chased away by Deputy Hansen, dressed as Santa Claus, only to return as soon as the deputy could be seen at his post in the Annex, playing Santa Claus in "Santa's Workshop," as the room had been dubbed for the evening.

Abby and Frieda descended the stairs together and pushed their way into the Annex. Earlier in the day, Abby had been one of the members who'd helped arrange the collection of toys for children for the families who'd been chosen to receive the association's bounty. All gifts had been purchased with coins from the collection boxes as well as donations from association members. The toys were on display along with a crate of oranges, one for the toe of each stocking. One of the members, upon reviewing the gifts, jovially announced, "My own kids should be so lucky."

Abby went into the kitchen to speak to her mother, but when she saw the stress on her mother's face, she did not remain. Mr. Parlett had hired a chef from the capital for the evening. The man was barking orders in a thick foreign accent while continually pushing the tall chef's toque back from his sweaty forehead. All of them—her mother, the chef, the young assistant he had brought with him, and the two waitresses who worked in the hotel dining room—appeared anxious.

Dr. and Mrs. Adam Townsend arrived later than the other partygoers; when they entered the festively decorated room, all heads turned in their direction. They made an extraordinarily handsome couple. Adam, dressed in a black tuxedo that accentuated his dashing good looks, was in striking contrast to his wife's golden goddess appearance.

The exceedingly beautiful Lillian Townsend wore a dazzling gold satin gown with a modified bustle that allowed for careful sitting; in a velvet bag she carried her dancing shoes, dyed the same shade of gold, which she changed into in the cloakroom. (This being the custom in Baltimore, it prompted a second look in Rockville.) A diamond-and-aquamarine necklace adorned her neck, a wedding present from her father-in-law. Ill at ease with the provinciality of the townspeople, Lillian found it difficult to smile or show warmth toward them. "Cool" was always the first word that came to mind when anyone greeted Lillian Townsend. Adam sensed his wife's tenseness and placed a reassuring arm around her waist.

Abby, witnessing the husbandly gesture, felt a stab of pain and was reminded of that long-ago Christmas Eve when she had learned from Aunt Em that her lover loved another and would not be coming home for the holidays. *And I carried your child, Adam.*

The first exquisite notes from the violins stilled the room, hung achingly in the air, rare and poignant, and trembled and mystified before falling gracefully from the high ceiling and gliding into a Strauss waltz. The orchestra for the occasion consisted of four musicians from Saint Margaret's (three playing violins and one a cello), with Aries on piano and, astonishingly, the Gypsy Meiko Toma playing the fourth violin.

Oberlander the banker was the first to get to his feet. Placing one arm across his waist, he bowed and extended a white-gloved hand to his wife. Lottie rapped his hand sharply with her closed fan before smiling and rising. Mr. Oberlander, upon hearing entertainment would be provided, had enthusiastically endorsed, and joined, the new association. The still-girlish Mrs. Oberlander was dressed in a royal-blue ball gown—very décolleté—with a bejeweled necklace and feathers and ribbons adorning her hair. The Townsends joined the other dancers on the now-crowded floor, moving with graceful skill among them.

Members of the association who were members of Old Church and against dancing were, in general, dressed in their dark Sunday best. They sat stiffly upon straight-backed chairs placed in a row along the wall separating the Annex and lobby from the dining room, their darting, overly bright eyes taking it all in. Dancing was considered one of the "evils of the day," and the waltz the most wicked dance of them all. Some of the wives wondered what den of iniquity their merchant husbands had lured them into.

Lillian surveyed the crowd and thought the hotel looked rather splendid and the people in attendance quite presentable. *I'll have something to write home about when I next correspond with Father,* she thought. *I can regale him with a tale of the small-town merchants and their countrified Christmas party taking place in the only hotel in their bucolic little town.* He loved her stories; they always gave him a good laugh.

Bob Williams, one of the churchgoers seated on one of the stiff-backed chairs, after tapping his toes to the music and recalling the good times of his bachelorhood, could no longer contain himself. He pulled his wife from her seat and waltzed her around the floor, much to the astonishment of their fellow parishioners.

Lillian, looking in the direction of the music—and this time, she had to agree that the orchestra was quite commendable—was almost startled into faintness when she saw Meiko Toma beaming at her. She forced her eyes to sweep past him, without a hint of recognition. He had said he had a surprise for her. Was this it? Thereafter she looked at the ensemble as little as possible, thus avoiding eye contact with him. She did not want anyone present to suspect she even knew him. He had donned a black suit and proper white shirt and black tie for the evening, but he was still a Gypsy. Lillian didn't want consorting with Gypsies added to the list of grievances the townspeople held against her.

Abby, meanwhile, was partaking of the dessert buffet—some of the items several times. Then, during the hubbub of moving tables and chairs out of the way to make more room for the dancers, she took the opportunity to further examine the centerpiece on the refreshment table. She was impressed with the tiered arrangement of greenery, fruits, ribbons, and Christmas flowers, including red and white roses.

She heard a man's voice in her ear. "I'm jealous. I believe I was the only person in town who knew you had dimples in your shoulders; now they all know."

Reacting to a chilling moment of being entirely exposed, Abby spun around, white faced and panicky, and looked into Adam Townsend's vibrantly affectionate eyes. "God help me, Abby, but I'm still in love with you." And, having said it, he knew it was true, had always been true.

Hastily averting her eyes from his and trying to catch her breath, Abby turned back to the centerpiece. "I'm thinking it would make a lovely chapeau," she said, trying for light banter while Adam very casually served himself a cup of punch.

He loves me! Her heart was racing. A declaration of love from him was more than she had ever dared hope for.

Lillian, left alone, was coolly witnessing the little drama being played out at the buffet table between her husband and the very alluring Abigail Langley. Adam had failed to inform her that the beautiful Miss Langley was a member of the association. Of course she would be. The fact that Lillian was older than her husband had never been revealed, and she didn't wish for comparisons to be made with a younger woman. The intensity of her observation stiffened her posture and narrowed her eyes. A new, never-thought-of revelation entered her mind. "Ummm," she purred.

Cousin Leo, at the party alone and causing all kinds of speculations as to what had happened between him and the Italian nightingale, joined Abby and Adam at the buffet table. After kissing Abby on the cheek, he greeted Adam with a handshake and said, "May I ask Mrs. Townsend to join me in a dance?"

"Only if I may have the honor of a dance with your beautiful cousin," Adam replied.

Together they approached Lillian, and Adam introduced them. Lillian seemed pleased by the request, and Leo led her onto the floor.

"You won't faint on me, will you?" Adam inquired of Abby as he took her in his arms and they moved onto the floor.

Abby was feeling so many emotions that she could not look at him, the other dancers, or the seated guests. Her first sensible thought after quelling the tumultuous feeling in her heart from the touch of his arms around her, and the stirring of memories, good and bad, was her mother's oft-repeated lament: "What will people think?" She wondered if her mother were watching from the kitchen.

Adam, content though not fulfilled in his marriage, had put Abby out of his thoughts over the years he'd been away from Rockville, but now, seeing her, touching her, old feelings were awakened in him. *My God, she is a beauty*, he thought as he looked down at her. He was reminded of what the newspaper editor had said about her: "It's her calendar-girl beauty that sets her apart and causes tongues to wag, not having a child out of wedlock."

After the dance set, Leo returned Lillian to her seat, accepted Abby from Adam, and led her onto the floor. Noting Abby's trembling hands and the paleness of her lips, he asked, "Are you OK?"

"It's been a long day," she breathlessly replied.

Abby, still dressed in her ball gown, opened her bedroom door and stepped out onto her balcony. Tossing back her head, she took in a deep, invigorating breath of the brisk night air. Experiencing a wonderful aliveness, she wrapped her arms across her body and hugged herself. Snowflakes caught in her hair and melted on her warm bosom.

"Adam loves me," she said to the starry night. She could still feel the pressure of his arms around her, could hear his words, the sound of his voice, and see the affection in his eyes.

Tonight there was a terrible rebelliousness in her, a need to find fulfillment.

She wanted to be touched, held, hugged, and kissed till she swooned. *I wasn't suitable for a preacher,* she thought, *but maybe I'm suitable for someone else. Perhaps I could find a husband.* Admiring looks from the men tonight had proven to her that she was still desirable. *Maybe someone will want me for a wife. But would he not be put off by my past mistake? Ronnie was never a mistake,* she thought, censuring herself. *With the new year, I'll begin looking. I'll make it my New Year's resolution.*

CHAPTER 67

January 1909

FROM THE DINING ROOM WINDOW, Lillian watched the long shadows of late afternoon stretch across the town as she waited for Meiko Toma to appear on the trail coming from the bottling plant. When, in the distance, she saw the palomino and its rider, she left the house and, walking briskly, was inside the stable when man and horse entered the dusky interior.

Meiko, his eyes not registering emotion, jumped lightly to the ground, remaining indifferent to Lillian's presence.

They stood on either side of the palomino, coolly contemplating each other; his hand lay on the horse's neck, on which he loosely held the reins. She wrinkled her nose at the acrid smell of the sweating horse.

"His smell is heroic, like his royal blood," Meiko said, disdain blanching his dark-blue eyes to a chilly coolness. She placed her gloved hand over his.

"I'm sorry about the Christmas ball. I was rude."

"Don't be sorry. I understand." He jerked his head upward, a look of contempt on his face. "You *gadjes* are all alike. I know the feeling only too well. I've had lots of practice at being ignored."

"I would like very much for you to return to the house and take tea with me again in the mornings." Her pale Nordic cheeks colored vividly from the humiliation of pleading with him.

He removed his hand from beneath hers and pulled the saddle from the horse.

"I miss you," she said to his retreating back.

Meiko's amorous, unfulfilled frustrations exploded in his blood. Throwing the saddle to the floor, he grabbed her, pushing her against the rough boards of the stalls. He pinned her there and kissed her. He gave to the kiss all the pent-up passion that was lacking in hers. Forcing her lips apart, he probed with his tongue the startled interior of her mouth. She struggled with him, and he freed her arms, only to drop his hands to her posterior and press her against his hardness. When Lillian finally succeeded in ending the kiss, they both were gasping for air.

The dimness of the stable and Lillian's fear had dilated her pupils to blackness, rimmed by the narrowest of aquamarine irises. Her face filled with loathing, she punched at his shoulders and slapped at his face as she tried to free herself from his grasp.

Meiko threw back his head and exploded with laughter. "Whoa, you are a little tigress!" he said.

"Beast!" she hissed, viciously scrubbing her gloved hand across her mouth. Peasant. Gypsy." Her face grew ugly in her attempt to demean him. Stumbling from the stable, she almost ran to the house.

Lillian entered the house. Bypassing the dining room, where the table was set for dinner, she went straight to the library and was absurdly irritated to find her husband already there.

"Lillian," he said, looking surprised. "Come in. Come in." Rising from his chair, he held out a chair for her near the fire.

"I feel like a drink," she said.

"I'm delighted. I like it when you join me. I don't like drinking alone. What'll it be? I know—I'll make you an old-fashioned."

They drank in silence. Lillian, visibly upset, avoided Adam's eyes by watching the flames in the fireplace.

"Why don't I ask Mrs. Sheridan to serve us dinner in here tonight, in front of the fire?" Adam said, closely observing her. "It would be a nice way to spend a cold winter evening."

"That would be lovely," she said in a clipped voice. "And I'll have another drink."

He thought the second drink would loosen her up, but she still seemed overly tense. *Why?* "What have you been doing today?" he asked.

She seemed to have to think about his question. "Oh, nothing interesting," she said brightly, lifting one shoulder as if her day wasn't of any consequence. "I took inventory of the linens, and then I walked to the stable. I wonder if I might ride Apollo?" she asked.

"It's been a while since you've ridden. Apollo may be too spirited for you. Ask Meiko to fix you up with a tamer horse."

Adam was still observing her. Her composure was normal, but her breathing and color were not. He wondered if she could be developing hypertension. He studied her by looking over the rim of his glass.

They capped off dinner with an after-dinner drink before retiring to the bedroom. He was feeling enjoyably amorous and hoped Lillian would respond in kind. She appeared acquiescent when she went into her dressing room to change. "Leave that Mother Hubbard gown of yours off for tonight, will you?" he called to her. "Break out something seductive."

He groaned when she returned wearing a long-sleeved, high-necked gown, yet she had left the bodice unbuttoned. "Can't we get rid of this?" he said, and he helped a willing Lillian wriggle out of it.

"Nudity makes me feel dirty" she said, pulling the covers up to her chin.

"Lillian, please," he teased, trying hard not to sound exasperated. "Naked is not dirty. For once in your life, can't you just let yourself go?"

Lillian, wanting to be a good wife, was always submissive to him, but in a condescending way.

Adam tenderly kissed her, stroked her small firm breasts, and gently massaged her shoulders, trying to relax her. "If I enter you now, when you're not ready, it won't be a pleasant experience for you, and intercourse is something we should both enjoy."

He could feel her body trying to reciprocate, but when his tongue glided across her tightly pressed lips, she stiffened, and a shudder passed over her unclothed body. *They're all alike,* she thought. *Nothing is sacred; nothing is off limits to them, not even our mouths.*

Behind her closed lids, Lillian saw Meiko and was sickened by the image of them together in the stable. Covering her face, she began to moan into her hands.

Adam, interpreting her action as a rejection of him, slid out of bed. In his erectness, he stood looking down at her, a cold fury building inside him. "If you want children, Lillian, you're going to have to accept fucking as the due process."

She cringed.

"Oh, I know, Lillian Elizabeth Victoria," he said, bitterly repeating a litany of her Christian names, "you hate the word as much as you do the act. Well, guess what, Lillian? Fucking is what makes babies." He slammed his way out of their bedroom and into another one, slamming that door as well.

"Abigail Langley's bastard is yours, isn't it, you bastard!" Lillian screamed at the closed door.

THE ROCKVILLE HUB
February 8, 1909

Dr. Adam Townsend has proved a godsend to the people of Rockville in treating the many sicknesses brought about by the inclement January weather.

Dr. Townsend has taken care of numerous cases of grippe complicated by serious ear, throat, and chest infections and two cases of diphtheria. Sadly, both of those cases succumbed to pneumonia.

Last summer, Dr. Townsend sent to Germany for the new diphtheria antitoxin and at the time strongly expressed to parents the need to have their children inoculated against the debilitating disease.

With so many of our citizens laid low by illness, Dr. Townsend requested, and received, the services of dentist Dr. Thomas Veering to help him in the vaccination of those who are not yet infected.

Next month, Dr. Townsend will attend a symposium in St. Louis on infantile maladies, including the crippling and dreaded poliomyelitis.

Mrs. Townsend is to accompany her husband to St. Louis, where she will visit a sorority sister and attend a luncheon, at which she will be the guest of honor.

CHAPTER 68

March 1909

ONE OF THE MANY WAYS in which Abby compensated Frieda for accompanying her on buying junkets to Saint Louis or Chicago was by giving her the window seat on the train. The schoolteachers who boarded with Frieda showed their appreciation in practicing their homemaking skills by way of cleaning Frieda's house and doing their own cooking, in the event that someday, they would be blessed with the good fortune of cleaning and cooking for a man of their own.

Once aboard the train, Frieda removed her heavy winter coat, complaining that she was too warm, and with a sigh of weary relief sank into the upholstered seat, only to say minutes later that she was cold; she put her coat back on. She lacked the usual enthusiasm she had for traveling, and to Abby she looked peaked.

Once they were settled in their hotel room, Abby called the desk to request housekeeping services and ordered a hot water bottle and a pot of hot tea and soup delivered to their room.

Later in the evening, Abby left a sleeping Frieda and went downstairs to the dining room for dinner. Being a guest of the hotel, but a single woman, she was placed near the swinging kitchen doors, out of sight and partially hidden by a potted palm.

Wishing she could go outside for a walk, Abby strolled about the lobby after dinner. She could feel the eyes of the men following her. She thought it was only in Rockville where the men stared but soon realized they were not hostile stares; they were admiring glances. She stood taller, taking pride in what she was: a successful businesswoman on a business trip.

During her second turn about the lobby, she was startled to see a man with the familiar posture of Dr. Adam Townsend making a purchase at the tobacco counter. She had momentarily frozen, trying to decide in which direction to flee, when he turned and saw her.

Adam's brown eyes filled with amazement as he raised a black eyebrow. Reaching out, he walked toward her and took her hands in his. "What a delightful surprise," he said, looking over her shoulder. "Where's the chaperone?"

"Sick," Abby squeaked, and clearing her tightened throat muscles, she said in a normal voice, "Frieda isn't feeling well. I think she may have a cold."

Right away, Adam's expression became serious. "Does she need a doctor?"

"I don't believe so. Not yet, anyway."

"I'll have a look at her. Have you had dinner?" he asked. She nodded her head. "Too bad. We could have dined together. If you're free this evening, we could take in the entertainment at one of the clubs. Saint Louis has a lot of fine, respectable places. You can't spend the whole evening locked up in a room with Frieda."

"Where is your wife?" Abby asked, a ruffle of pique in her voice.

"Home," he said, his nostrils flaring. "Indisposed. Let me have a look at Frieda, then you can decide if you want to join me." Drawing her hand through the crook of his arm, he led her toward the elevator, aware of the faint rose scent that was so much a part of her.

"It'll be harmless entertainment, and something to rescue both of us from an evening of boredom. Say yes." Humor colored the persuasiveness of his eyes.

They soon arrived at a small and elegant club filled with smartly dressed patrons, where a combo was playing for listening and dancing. Adam ordered drinks for them: a pink creamy concoction in a stemmed glass for Abby, and scotch over ice with seltzer for himself.

"It tastes like ice cream," Abby said to make conversation.

"After you're feeling relaxed, we'll try dancing."

"Oh dear," Abby said, pushing herself into the corner of the plush banquette and placing her hands, fingers splayed, across her chest. "Oh, I couldn't. I'm not dressed for it."

"Now, don't you go getting provincial on me, Abigail Langley. Look around you. You are the most beautiful woman in the room. You would be in *any* room," he added. He stood and held out his hand. "Miss Langley, may I have the pleasure of this dance?"

They danced. They talked. They laughed. They forgot time. They were just an ordinary couple enjoying an evening in each other's company.

At the hotel, Adam entered Abby's room with her to check on Frieda, whom he woke enough to take her temperature. He had left his doctor's bag there and, removing a bottle of medicine from it, gave his patient two more tablespoons.

"When are you going home?" he inquired of Abby.

"Tomorrow," she replied, a worried look on her face.

"That's impossible. Frieda should remain in bed for two, even three more days." He placed the bottle in Abby's hand.

"It's Aunt Em's medicine," she said. She read the label, which said AUNT EM'S FAMILY MEDICINE, along with a picture of her.

"I haven't found anything better; I've even had it patented. Give her two teaspoons every four hours, and if there's any change, call me. Call me anyway. I like to hear your voice. Room ten fifteen."

Abby saw him to the door, where he pulled her into the hall. With his arms tight around her, he kissed her. It was a long passionate kiss on both their parts, and when it was over, he nestled his face into her shoulder and whispered, "My Eve."

Her reaction to the name was immediate and violent. Placing her hands on his chest, she pushed him away. "Don't call me your Eve. Don't you ever call me your Eve," she said, hurling the words at him, her fury shocking them both. "You left me!"

"But I'm back."

"And married! And where is our son?" Bursting into tears, she rushed into her hotel room, leaving him standing, bewildered, in the empty corridor.

The following morning, a dozen yellow roses were delivered to the room with a card that read, "Whatever I said, or did, last night—I'm sorry." A half hour later, Abby answered a knock on the door.

"I want to check on my patient," Adam said, "and to collect my bag."

She let him in. He said to a still-groggy Frieda, "You need to spend another two days in bed. It won't be safe for you to travel, not yet. For today, drink plenty of fluids and try to eat something light: say, soup and custard."

At the door he said to Abby, "Whatever I did last night that upset you so much, I am profoundly sorry. Please have dinner with me tonight or, at the very least, see me. Meet me in the lobby at seven."

Abby looked away without answering; she didn't trust her voice. Since the previous night, her mind and emotions had been in turmoil, and her heart wouldn't behave.

When she looked up at him, the naked flash of yearning in her eyes left him stunned. *My God, she does still care,* he thought.

Abby spent the day touring the shops, where she looked at the latest hats and discovered what was new this year in Easter bonnets. Then she shopped the supply stores, trying to keep her mind on the newest millinery fashions, only to have her thoughts drift away to Adam and her predicament.

When she returned to their hotel room, she found Frieda sitting in a chair by the window. Some of the color had come back to her cheeks.

"Where did the roses come from?" Frieda asked.

Abby hesitated before answering. "I thought they'd cheer you up," she said, not exactly telling a lie. "I bought a new dress today, and a hat. They're very chic. I have no idea where I'll wear them in Rockville, but I couldn't resist."

"Oh, put them on!" Frieda urged in a breathless, croaking voice. "I want to see you in them."

It was close to seven when Adam knocked on their door. His right eyebrow shot up when he saw Abigail in her newly purchased ensemble. "You look marvelous," he said.

He himself was handsomely attired in an elegant suit tailored in the latest style, with a cravat of iridescent silk and a vest of handsome navy-and-green scotch plaid with pearl buttons.

He examined Frieda, speaking in her ear confidentially while looking at Abby. "Frieda, doesn't Miss Langley look lovely? Don't you think she should join me for dinner this evening? It would be a shame to waste a beautiful new dress dining by oneself."

Frieda, clapping her hot, dry hands together, hoarsely rasped, "Oh, I do, I do. She never has any fun." Turning to Abby and struggling to talk without coughing, she said, "Please go; it would do you good."

Abby and Adam dined at a hotel other than the one in which they were guests and later stopped at a club featuring the new ragtime music. Wherever they went, heads turned in their direction. Abby had never felt so special, nor had she ever felt beautiful until this night.

Back at their hotel, Adam persuaded her to come to his room for a nightcap. "I won't touch you," he said. "You will be as safe as in your mother's arms."

This unfortunately reminded Abby of her mother's oft-repeated admonition: "What will people think?"

When Abby entered the lavish hotel suite, she felt every bit the country girl she was.

Aware of her hesitation, Adam said by way of explanation, "I made the reservations"—his jaw muscles tightened—"before my wife became indisposed."

Abby realized for the first time that he never spoke his wife's name.

Removing Abby's wrap, he placed it on a chair and walked with her to the bar. Cut-glass bottles of colorful liquids were displayed along a wall of glass shelves, and on the mahogany bar was fresh ice in a silver bucket. "What would you like to drink?" he asked.

"Nothing. I shouldn't be here." She was very uncomfortable; every appointment in the room lent itself to intimacy. She moved toward the chair where her coat lay.

At once he was at her side with his arms around her; then, remembering his promise, he released her. "Stay long enough for me to tell you how much this time with you has meant to me. I don't know when we'll ever have the chance again, or the privacy. Please, Abby, we need to talk."

She sat on the edge of the couch while he went to the bar. He returned with a lime-green drink poured over cracked ice. "It's peppermint schnapps—an after-dinner drink. Please sit back and relax. I won't touch you, I promise, although it's hard not to. You are a very lovely and desirable woman, Abigail."

Her hands felt cold. "Desire is wicked," she said, her breathing tenuous.

"Desire is not wicked. Wicked is what you were taught by your mother, and some archaic religion—you and all the other women in this country."

Abby took a sip of her drink. His assessment of women made her nervous.

He moved closer and, removing the glass from her hand, set it down on a side table. He took her hands in his and said, "I have to know what I did, or said, last night that made you so angry with me."

She met his eyes and, lowering her head, looked down at their entwined hands. "Because, at one time, Adam, I was foolish enough to believe that I was really made from one of your ribs." Her voice quivered. "That I truly was your Eve. And when you fell in love with someone else, I almost died. I—I tried to die."

"Why didn't you write and tell me?" he asked, distraught.

"I couldn't write—there was the postmaster—everyone in town would have known we were corresponding. I thought you would be home for Christmas and I could tell you then—tell you that I was pregnant. On Christmas Eve, Aunt Em told me you wouldn't be coming home because you had a sweetheart. Hearing you call me Eve just brings it all back—all the pain and humiliation. It hurt so much." She caught her lower lip between her teeth to keep it from trembling.

He wanted to hold her, protect her, cry with her, get down on his knees and beg her forgiveness.

Tears rolled down her face. He put his arms around her, and she let him hold her.

"I didn't know how I could be your rib if you didn't want me," she cried into his shoulder.

"I wish to God I had come home. It was my selfishness that kept me away, and my naïveté. When I left Rockville and went east to Baltimore, everything was so unbelievably worldly; a life I had never imagined was opened up to me. And of course there was my father's fame and pocketbook opening all the right doors. Until I went to Johns Hopkins, I never knew my father was famous, or just how prosperous he was. And there was Lillian and her doctor father, opening even more doors." He sounded bitter. "But something in my memory always pulled me back to Rockville. I know now it was my longing for you, for my rib," he said with a smile.

"I thought we would grow old together," she said, sighing.

"Believe me, I never meant for us to be separated. Never." He kissed her cheek. "I love you, Abby."

"The first time you said that, I—"

"We," he said, holding a finger to her lips.

"We made love—and a baby."

"Abby, my Abby, my Abigail Lee," he said, taking her by the shoulders and lightly shaking her. "You are my rib, my flesh, my blood, my very soul. I love you, Abby. I have always loved you. Even after death do us part, I will love you." He placed his fingers beneath her chin and, lifting her head, looked into her eyes. "My Eve."

With these words, she collapsed into his arms, all flesh and blood, and desire. He carried her into the bedroom.

"Please forget everything you've ever learned, or heard," he said. "For this moment in time, nothing else in the world exists but the two of us."

With each piece of clothing he removed from her body, he kissed the newly bared, reciprocating flesh. "I want to see all of you—naked as Eve in her garden. You've grown curves since I last saw you—luscious ones."

She moaned as Adam, kissing her mouth, separated her lips, and his tongue entered and entwined with hers. His hands caressed her arms, molded her shoulders and bosom, and stroked the length of her legs. His tongue savored the essence of her skin and found hidden places to kiss, pleasing her body with sensations she had never known existed.

He loved the scent of her. Most women he came in contact with smelled of moth balls, lye soap, sour breast milk, cooking grease—anything but femininity.

"Your skin feels and smells like rose petals," he whispered.

And it's mine, she thought dreamily. *My skin belongs to me, I belong to me, and Adam belongs to me.*

The room and time itself faded away until there was just her and the sensate desire pulsing through her veins. Her entire body was alert and ready for the moment, open and quivering, soft and fluid, her every limb and muscle begging to be fulfilled. Adam's strong hands slid beneath her buttocks as he raised her to meet him.

Taut now, like a tightrope walker, she moved with him to the ancient rhythm. Rolled and swayed, rocked and crooned, and when she felt the tumultuous explosion of his seed deep within her, she convulsed into the final thrusting of her own maddened tempo before catapulting from the heights.

They lay silent, spent, satisfied.

Smoothing back her hair and drinking in the wonder of her, Adam kissed her eyes open. "I don't want you to go," he said. "Ever."

"I shouldn't have to go—ever," she said archly.

God help me, I love them both. The feelings he had for Lillian he could explain—she was his wife—but his passionate, undying devotion to Abby he could not explain, not even to himself.

CHAPTER 69

"Damn it, Bobby Lee," Chance Collins swore at the man sitting across the kitchen table from him. "I give you that money in good faith to keep your mouth shut and keep my name out of it."

"Jeez, Chance, that hundred dollars was what Velvet left town on."

"Well, can I help it if your wife ran off with a sleazy drummer man and left you empty-handed?" He said with a sneer, "Now, I ask you, can I?"

"But what am I going to tell people?" Bobby Lee said in a whining voice. "Brother Griggsby's already been to my house asking questions that I rightly can't answer, and you know what that means? It means that the next thing I know, the Unholy Seven will be there grilling me and Amy, too."

"Tell them you don't know a damn thing about it." Chance was murderously upset, so much so that the scar on his face was throbbing like some living organ. "Tell the religious, pointy-nosed bastards to go to hell."

"That's easy for you to say. What if they ask Amy?"

Slowly and with exaggerated calmness, Chance said, "Bobby Lee, I give you that money in good faith, and you give me your word."

Bobby Lee, replying in the same slow cadence, said, "And I aim to keep my word, Chance, but in the meantime, what am I going to tell people?"

"What about your boys?" Chance said. "Ain't they big enough to be foolin' 'round with their sister?"

"Hell, Chance, they ain't that big."

Chance brought out the whiskey bottle from a high shelf in the kitchen cupboard, high enough that his mother would never feel her way to it. "That ain't a good idea anyway," he said. "We got to pin this on somebody people will believe did it—somebody they don't trust."

Immediately his mind settled on Harlan. He chuckled to himself, but then he sobered. The kid would have to be black to name him as the father. "Shit."

Wonder what the little bastard will look like? he wondered. *Maybe it'll be a boy and look like me—before the accident.* He felt a twinge of pride. He was sure he had fathered a kid somewhere along the way, but this was the first one he knew about.

"Now, Bobby Lee, we're going to cook us up a story for Amy to tell to anyone who asks her, and it's up to you to see that she tells it right. You hear, old buddy?" he said, squeezing Bobby Lee's shoulder. "Will you shake on that?"

"Yes, sir, I will," Bobby Lee said as his hand was swallowed up in Chance's vise grip. He knew what was in store for him if Amy didn't stick to the story.

Chance sat with his chair tipped back against the kitchen wall, his face darkening as he deliberated on the situation. *Drummers? The town ain't never trusted traveling salesmen.* Maybe they could pin it on the one Velvet ran off with. No, the little brat was pregnant a long time before Velvet left town. Who then? Who could they make the fall guy?

Brother Griggsby knocked on the door. The black-clad figures stood on the frozen earthen sidewalk huddled together for protection from the stinging wind. The brother had already rapped several times on the rough wooden door, each time louder, but still no one answered.

Cautiously, he opened the door and looked in and pushed the door open wide enough to allow the seven of them to step into the small living room. No one was about, yet the stove lid, wired like a sliced pie, seemingly on its own accord, rose from the stove and moved to one side. He heard a rumble in the stovepipe coming from the attic; from the pipe's open end, hovering over the exposed fire in the stove, a lump of coal dropped into the stove. Then, magically, the wired lid slipped back into place on top of the stove.

The uninvited guests crowded against the still-open door and stared at the stove and at one another in disbelief, undecided whether to stay or to leave.

Amy peeked into the room from behind the faded cretonne curtain that separated the lean-to kitchen from the living room. Her eyes, large with fright, met Hyrum Dinwoody's.

"Where's your pa, Amy?" Mr. Dinwoody demanded. Amy stopped chewing on her fingertips long enough to point toward the upstairs room. "You go tell him there are folks down here calling on him," Mr. Dinwoody said, closing the door.

They all watched the clumsy, visibly pregnant little girl climb the rickety steps, two-year old Billy hanging onto her skirt. The two women in the group looked knowingly at each other.

The seven men and women gawked about. Where to sit? The two women gingerly turned up the bedclothes on the cot and spread what looked to be a bed cover over it before sitting down.

There were three chairs in the room, but the men remained standing. Mr. Dinwoody and Brother Johnson inspected the coal-delivery contraption. The wires, wrapped in wedge shapes across the stove lid, had been brought together in the center and twisted into a metal rope that disappeared into a hole in the ceiling along, with a second stove pipe that was used as a coal chute to feed the potbellied stove from the bed in the attic, allowing Bobby Lee to remain in bed for the night and still stoke the fire.

"This must be the invention that Bobby Lee says is going to make him rich," Mr. Dinwoody said in a mocking tone. Mr. Johnson, with a belittling smirk, nodded in agreement.

After hurriedly pulling on rumpled clothes and running his fingers through his uncombed hair, Bobby Lee appeared, rubbing at a week-old beard on his chin. He dragged two chairs from the kitchen into the front room and returned for a three-legged milk stool, on which he sat.

"We'll need Amy down here, too, Bobby Lee," Brother Griggsby said in a full-of-himself tone.

Bobby Lee, his voice shaking, called upward toward the ceiling. "Amy, come on down here."

Amy appeared; she had changed the patched nightgown for a faded dress that her oft-pregnant mother clearly must have worn. The two women seated on the couch parted and, patting the empty space between them, indicated to Amy that she should sit there.

"Bobby Lee, as your pastor and guide in moral matters, I have to ask you. Is Amy in a family way?" The brother's forehead glistened, and his voice grew husky.

"Yes, she is," Bobby Lee answered, his voice shaking. He was deathly afraid of what Amy might tell them.

Brother Griggsby turned his lacerating gaze on Amy. "Amy, are you going to have a baby?"

She looked at her father, and Bobby Lee nodded for her to answer. Yes," she answered in a timid voice.

"And do you know who the father is?"

"The Gypsy," Amy whispered, desperately trying to keep her thumb out of her mouth.

The Unholy Seven reacted with stiff little jolts, all of them sitting straighter. But no trace of surprise showed on their faces, for they had readily accepted the accused as the perpetrator of the dastardly deed.

"He raped her," Bobby Lee said, hanging his head and crying. The two women pressed their handkerchiefs to their mouths; Mrs. White, of the *Mayflower* Whites, clutched at the buttons on the front of her dress, and Mrs. Dinwoody dug through her purse and extracted a vial of smelling salts.

"He caught her coming home from my parents' house one night after dark and forced himself on her," Bobby Lee said. "He threatened to cut out her tongue if she ever told us about it." The two women, gasping, placed their dry, reddened fingers over their mouths. "So she never told us anything. It was a long time before we knew. She told Velvet first." He looked at Amy, a look of warning in his eyes.

The women's mouths turned down, and they lowered their chins. What could they expect from a young girl who lived with the likes of that woman? And where was the hussy, anyway?

"When is her confinement?" Mrs. White delicately inquired of Bobby Lee.

"As close as we can figure," he said with authority, "about April. I'm thinking about taking her to see the doctor."

Brother Griggsby scowled. He knew he would never be allowed to see the birth of the child's child if Dr. Townsend was her doctor.

The seven did not ask further questions. They were anxious to be gone. The news must be shared at once, with friends, with neighbors, over back fences and cups of tea, at church meetings and socials, at the pool hall and the blacksmith shop.

"Hang the son of a bitch!" the regulars at Ma's said upon hearing the news.

"Hanging's too good for him. We ought to brand the bastard, and then hang him!"

"I heard the scoundrel beat her first. Left her black and blue."

And the news had to be shared in the dark with one's own mate, because this embarrassing, shocking subject could not be dealt with between a man and a woman in broad daylight but whispered in evasive language late at night, under the cover of darkness.

"He tore off her clothes before he did his dirty act."

By the end of January, the rumor was no longer whispered but talked about openly and with heated discussion. After the Unholy Seven were seen on the doorstep of Bobby Lee's house, everyone knew that the gossip was true: little Precious Amy was with child.

Perthy Prettyman, at the next Tuesday Benevolent Society meeting, summed up the whole indecent episode in one short proverb: "Early ripe, early rotten."

The town had never encountered a known case of rape before, so the townspeople were unsure how the legal and moral aspects of it should be handled. The Unholy Seven had for many years solved the moral problems of the citizenry, but this seemed to be more the case of a crime being committed than a moral issue. Furthermore, the town was growing; it was no longer just a one-horse town governed by Old Church. Hell! The town even had two automobiles.

The marshal called on Bobby Lee. "Bobby Lee, my hands are tied until you have a warrant sworn out for the man's arrest; then we'll have to hear Amy's story, and—I'm guessing—go to court."

Chance Collins could not rest until the Gypsy, as the accused rapist, was run out of town. He wasn't about to wait for a trial. He grew meaner and his irritation more perverse as the worry of being found out gnawed at him.

"Damn, Bobby Lee, I didn't expect it to come to this. I thought the li'l varmint would get wind of it and be long gone by now."

Dr. Adam Townsend, Lillian, and Meiko Toma were unaware of what was going on. The gossip had yet to reach their ears.

CHAPTER 70

April 1909

For the first time in her life, Lillian was experiencing desire. She had an awakening of feelings in her she had never acknowledged before. Meiko Toma had excited her. Even Adam had never caused her heart to race as it did when she thought of the adulterous kiss in the stable. *When you give yourself to a man*, she thought, *what should it really feel like?* To her, "the giving" had always been a humiliating act, and one to get over with as quickly as possible.

Among the books donated at the open house for the benefit of the library, and now stored in an unused room at the mansion, were some that the ladies of the library board had rejected as being "objectionable." The ladies of the literary committee had termed the few books "racy" and "trashy." Similarly rejected were digests featuring pictures of naked natives. No one knew who had donated the undesirable books and quarterlies, but the women on the board, which included teachers and ministers' wives, had contemptuously, and with an air of superiority, commented on each one before quickly tossing it into the "burn box."

Lillian had retrieved the racy books from the stored boxes; while reading them, she was experiencing daydreams and fantasies that made her blush.

Now that Adam had moved into another bedroom and she occupied the master bedroom alone, she was at last, after a lifetime of chaste modesty, able to view her nude reflection in the long oval mirror that stood in a wooden stand in a corner of the room. She felt free to admire the whiteness of her skin and the slender, graceful curves of her body.

She spent a great deal of time brushing her hair—not pinning it up into her usual intricate pompadour style but wearing it loosely, enjoying the softness of her hair when it brushed against her face and shoulders. She also reveled in wearing the luxurious silk gowns and peignoirs she had packed away after the first month of their honeymoon.

What have I done to you, Adam? Lillian asked herself. *What have I done to you all these years? Are these the same feelings men experience? I want to come to your bed, Adam, not as a wife, but as a woman who wants to be loved.*

Lillian saw very little of Adam after he returned from his medical conference in Saint Louis. His attitude toward her remained aloof and indifferently polite. She wanted to make things right between them, to prove that she could respond to his overtures. That she could—she thought of the vile word he had flung at her—yes, do that, too.

Adam's waiting room nowadays had enough patients to keep him busy. "Going to the doctor" was something new for the people of Rockville. And yet, most evenings he still had to make house calls, returning late at night and eating a dinner left for him in the warming oven by Mrs. Sheridan.

Lillian was lonely. In the late afternoon of a day when she had seen no one, she stood at the kitchen window watching the first snow fall. She saw Meiko Toma come from the stable and enter his wagon. Throwing a black shawl that had belonged to Aunt Em (and still hung back of the kitchen door) over her head and shoulders, she walked to his wagon. Not knowing how to reach the door to knock, she called his name.

Meiko's head and shoulders appeared in the upper half of the Dutch door. He peered down at her before swinging open both doors and reaching for her hands. He helped her into the caravan and closed and bolted the double door.

Lillian's eyes were slow in adjusting to the dimness of the vardo. When she could finally see, her eyes swiftly swept over the small space. Meiko pulled her deeper into the room. The smell of tobacco and rich cooking spices hung in the air. He was breathless and making nervous, unnecessary gestures.

"Welcome home," he said, adding quickly, "my home."

Looking at her, he brought her hands to his lips, kissing the back of each one. The wonder of her coming to him shone in his eyes.

Still holding one of her hands, he guided her about the room. Lillian expressed womanly curiosity over the cupboards and drawers, the ornate samovar for heating water displayed on a tiny wooden fold-up table, the built-in bed that occupied one side of the room, with drawers beneath it for storage. He pulled out one of the drawers, revealing brightly colored shirts and handsomely decorated boleros.

"Do you wear these?" she asked, her voice holding a touch of incredulity.

He laughed nervously. "Only when I meet up with a caravan of Gypsies, and we have a festival, or I'm hired to entertain."

"Entertain? What do you do, other than play violin?"

Dropping her hand, he threw his arms above his head, snapping his fingers and clicking his Cuban-heeled boots on the floor. "I dance."

They laughed, both feeling more at ease.

"Would you like some tea?" he asked as he moved toward the samovar.

"I can't stay."

He reached for her and took one of her hands, and with his other hand he tilted her chin up. They gazed with candor into each other's eyes. "Lil-ly," he said, his tongue caressing each syllable, making of her name a lullaby. A passionate, opaque wave of emotion washed over the color of his eyes, leaving them a darker, deeper blue. Bringing her palm to his mouth, he kissed it with longing before holding it against his cheek.

"I love you, Lil-ly," he said in a whisper.

He sat on the bed and pulled her down beside him. She couldn't look at him. Instead she studied his hands, noting the fine black hairs that grew close to his knuckles and considering his palms and the many lines crisscrossing them.

"I always judge men by their hands," she said, "and I like yours." She dared a look at his face, then back to his hands. "They're good hands, masculine and yet tender and honest, too."

"Hey, you tell fortunes, too," he said.

She looked at him and grew embarrassed. His eyes glistened with moisture, and she was afraid he might cry. "I really must leave."

"Take something with you," he said. He placed a small cloth bag in her hand. "It's cooking herbs."

Adam, coming in from making his round of house calls, wondered why Meiko wasn't at the stable to care for his horse. Then, looking in the direction of the caravan, he saw Lillian walking away from it toward the house.

At dinner that evening, the first time they had dined together formally since his return from Saint Louis, Adam admired the beauty of his wife. Seated at the lace-covered dining room table, candles glowing in crystal holders, a fire burning in the fireplace, she looked lovely, and very seductive. He wished their married life had been better. If it had, perhaps he wouldn't be in the turmoil in which he now found himself.

But he had never really trusted her, not since her timely miscarriage so soon after they were married. He knew after spending those few days with Abby that an intimate relationship was something he could not, and would not, live without. It would be wonderful, he thought, if he could enjoy a passionate relationship with his wife. He wanted his wife to respond to him the way Abby had. Remembering Lillian's agonizing rejection of him, he vowed that he would never intimidate her again with his sexual desires.

Lillian said she wanted children, and they did nothing to prevent the conceiving of a child, but she lacked passion, the carnal, bodily need for emotional closeness.

He would have to choose.

Is it me? he wondered. *Am I in some way to blame for her lack of passion?* He knew intimacy was a problem for many women. He had heard the complaint often enough from his male patients during his intern days, and sometimes, more surprisingly, from their wives. He had also heard the complaints from his peers at the hospital where he had interned. He recalled the robust association he had enjoyed with a nurse at the hospital in Germany. European women had a different outlook on intimacy. Thank God Abby was unspoiled.

As always, Adam, like his father, blamed the lunacy of the world on religion. *How far,* he thought, *the pendulum has swung from the sex-oriented pagan religions of the past to the puritanical zealots of today.*

Tonight there was an appealing glow to his wife's skin and a sparkle in her eyes he had not seen in a long time.

"You should get out more; the walk in the fresh air today did you good. It's becoming," he said, toasting her with his wine glass.

"The walk?" Lillian said uneasily.

"Yes. I saw you coming from the direction of Meiko's wagon."

"Oh, I went there to borrow some herbs Meiko had spoken about," she said nervously. "I'll show them to you." She began to rise.

"For God's sake, Lillian, sit down. You don't have to show me anything."

"He has medicinal herbs as well, for all kinds of ailments," she said, indignant that he had placed her on the defensive. "Aunt Em used them."

"Yes, well, I'm sure he and Aunt Em got along famously."

Her face paled. "Meiko liked Aunt Em. He likes to talk about her," she said, her demeanor still defensive.

Adam reached for the wine decanter, his romantic mood slipping away. He did not want to spend this promising evening discussing Aunt Em, or the Gypsy, and wondered again why he had married her.

"Adam. Adam." Lillian stood near the foot of her husband's bed, whispering his name.

Adam's professional anticipation of emergencies had him immediately awake. Rising on his elbows, he asked, "What is it?"

Untying the ivory satin ribbons at the throat of her peignoir, Lillian let it fall to the floor. Slipping the delicate straps of the nightgown from her shoulders, she let the gown glide down her body to her feet and stepped out of the luxuriant pile. The soft breeze coming through an open window carried the promise of lilacs with it as it caressed her nude body.

She rose on tiptoe with the grace of a ballerina and unfolded her arms, raising them high over her head; holding the pose, she stood perfectly still. The pale-cerulescent moonlight filtering through the trees etched their midnight shadows upon the translucent surface of her body.

Slowly, seductively, she came alive and, approaching the bed where Adam lay, sat down on the edge of its moon-washed smoothness and stretched her body full length alongside his.

Lying intimately beside the naked form of his wife, Adam did not experience desire. Within him nothing happened. He waited a few minutes, thinking, and with inevitability, turned his back to her and in minutes gave every indication of being asleep.

Lillian, reeling from the rejection, her face burning, stomach lurching, too ashamed to move or even to cover herself, at last fell asleep.

Hours later, she awoke with a start, her eyes flying open, her heart racing, positive that Meiko was bending over her. So sure was she that he was there in their bedroom, with Adam lying asleep beside her, that she peered about in the partially darkened room, squinting to see into the corners, her blood pounding furiously in her ears.

It was the scent of him that had awakened her. She had smelled him, his aroma: tobacco, alcohol, leather, wood smoke, and his personal body odor that was like no other's. In the dream state of her sleep, she had recalled his essence more completely than she ever could awake.

Once she was convinced that Meiko was not in the room, she rose from the bed and, retrieving her gown and robe from the floor, quietly left the room. Making her way to the kitchen, she gazed from the window over the sink at the vardo, glowing silver in the light from the stars.

All Lillian could see in the darkness was the burning end of his cigarillo, but she heard the quick intake of his breath. She made her way toward the glow. Grasping both her arms, Meiko pulled her on top of him, removing her robe as they embraced. She rubbed her hands over his chest. The coarse hair curling between her fingers left a prickling sensation. The skin on his back was surprisingly smooth, his spine deeply indented. He tested her acceptance of him by quickly sliding his tongue over her lips, and her mouth willingly opened to him. With hands and mouths they explored each other's bodies, testing, trying, discovering the other's demands and desires. His hands and mouth found her breasts, and she felt a delicious reciprocating response in her groin. She found a delectable agony in prolonging the consummation, yet delaying what he was offering was almost painful.

He pushed his aroused organ against the channel of her being—and she froze.

"Am I hurting you?"

Deep inside her, Lillian's inviolate ancestral blood, like water seeking its own level, coursed through the ages and pulsated in her veins, beat in her ears, and erupted in her throat. "No! I can't! Meiko, I can't! It's wrong." And she knew she neither wanted this man—nor his bloodline.

"Lil-ly," he said, crooning. "Please, you are ready." His tongue coaxed at her closed lips.

"You must give me more time," she said, begging.

"If you leave now, there won't be another time."

He watched her go.

Adam did not see Lillian again until dinner the following evening. When he greeted her in the dining room, her cheeks were colored, and her eyes had a defiant radiance to them. He held the French provincial gilt-trimmed chair for her and, after she was seated, placed his hands on her shoulders and kissed her cheek. "You were sensational last night," he said. "I'm sorry I couldn't respond. I was bushed."

Without responding to his touch, Lillian dipped her head forward, pulling away from him.

Adam sighed. Last night, for the first time, he was made aware of a wanting in her, a need, that had never been there before.

The pain of his emotional entanglement with two women only deepened.

CHAPTER 71

SEVERAL TIMES THIS DAY, THE women of Rockville had stopped whatever it was they had been doing and listened. Maybe they walked through the house to see if anything was amiss, stepped off their shady front porches into the sun and felt a chill run through them, even though it was a warm day, warm for April. They went about their work quietly, swept floors without the swoosh of the broom, gently kneaded the bread dough so as not to burst trapped bubbles; today, even a little pop made them jump. They were listening, always listening, while the day without hours secretly fermented like new wine.

A farmer walked by, not working his farm, but walking like a man with a purpose—downtown. From all parts of town they came, men with that same purposeful walk descending on the blacksmith shop. The big double doors that stood open most of the time today were closed tight as a drum and bolted from within. Each man, upon reaching the smithy, knocked on the doors and, when identified, was let in and the heavy double doors bolted anew.

The usual group of boys who hung around the shop were turned away—and, later, chased away—when one of them found a ladder and was caught peering through the loft's dirty windows. But not before seeing the men standing in a circle and passing a jug of liquor around. And some who never drank took a pull on that jug today. From the cherry-red coals in the forge, a long, slim branding iron protruded, ash-white from the intense heat. Silence, a day pregnant with silence.

Women talking over back fences mentioned the peculiarity of the day.

"Maybe there's a storm brewin'," one said, looking to the sky, a vast canopy of blue with nary a cloud in sight. They discussed the strange behavior of their husbands.

"Jess didn't even go to the field today, and that's not like him."

Businesses felt it, too. Parlett's was quiet, as were the co-op and Stevens Drugstore, with few women customers coming in; those who did speak spoke in hushed tones. No one stopped to chat, just purchased their goods or picked up their mail and hurried home. Even the talkative postmaster, Lars Larson, hardly had a greeting for them.

After supper, men who had worked that day quickly changed into clean work clothes and admonished their wives and children. "Go to bed early, and don't wait up."

They made their way to the smithy. By dusk, the streets were strangely empty of women and children.

As each man entered the overheated room—reeking of animals, leather, manure, male sweat, and liquor, with the added pungency of malignant justice—he made his way to the workbench. Laid out there on a horse blanket, like a rare stone in a jeweler's case, was a branding iron, twisted, hammered, and tortured into the letter R.

With nightfall came an urgent rapping on the door. Marshal McCombs, there to see that justice was not trod upon, entered with Bobby Lee and Precious Amy.

Amy's eyes bulged with fright, her young body with child. Bobby Lee led her through a path cleared by the assembled men. She hugged to her chest a sock doll given to her by the members of the Tuesday Benevolent Society.

"Good God almighty," a man uttered in righteous indignation upon seeing the pregnant child.

"This is a crime against God and nature," Hardhead Hudnutt said, railing. "An eye for an eye and a tooth for a tooth is what we need here today," he said, even though he had impregnated his child bride when she was fourteen.

Amy clung to her dad, hiding her face against his sleeve. He comforted her by holding her close to him as he walked her to the raised platform put together for the occasion. He helped her, awkward and heavy, up the crude steps to the chair placed there for her to sit on.

Hardhead, with white, unruly hair and beard, the mesmerizing, self-proclaimed leader of a cult settlement twenty miles outside Rockville, quoted Bible verses from the good book as he marched from man to man. The biblical words, together with the excessively bright gleam in the self-anointed preacher's eyes, were strangely hypnotic to the men in their present mood.

"Who did this to you, Amy?" a man called out as they crowded around the platform.

The marshal, sharing the stage with Amy, raised his hands and called for quiet. "Get back! Don't crowd her—give her some breathing room."

The crowd moved back a pace. The marshal held out his hands and pushed them downward. "Now all of you, just simmer down. We'll get to the bottom of this thing. Let's not put the horse before the cart. We'll find the guilty one." Turning around, he faced the girl and gently asked, "Are you all right, Amy?"

She nodded.

"Can you answer some questions for us?"

She nodded again.

"Amy, a man did a very bad thing to you. He hurt you. Can you tell us his name?"

"Meiko, the Gypsy," she said in a whisper.

Bobby Lee reached for his daughter's hand, removing the tips of her fingers from her mouth. "Speak up, Amy. They can't hear you."

Drawing her shoulders up to her ears, but speaking louder, she said, "Meiko, the Gypsy."

"Are you telling us the truth, Amy?" Marshal McCombs asked.

"Yes," she said timorously. Upon seeing the menacing look on her father's face, she yelled, "Yes! It was the Gypsy who hurt me." Then she added, wailing, "He hurt me real bad."

"Let's burn the son of a bitch!" someone in the crowd said.

"Let's hang him," Ralph Cox said. He threw a hangman's noose he had brought with him over a rafter above his head, where it remained hanging and swinging.

The men, restless and wanting action, moved about in disorder.

Chance Collins, the main instigator in blaming the Gypsy, remained strangely subdued. He stayed in the background while the cause for justice was taken up by his drinking buddy, the frenetic Old Testament zealot Hardhead Hudnutt.

"Just a minute now," Marshal McCombs called from the platform. "Hold on. There will be no frontier justice taking place here tonight." He pointed in the direction of the dangling rope. "I agreed to this meeting to get a confession, and that's the only reason we're here—to get a confession. Teach him a lesson, and maybe give him a good scare. Nothing more," he said, raising his voice in warning.

"We'll teach him a lesson," Beaver Rasmussen yelled. "Don't fool around with our women and children!"

"And give him a good scare, to boot!" someone else shouted.

"He deserves whatever we give him!" a man shouted from the back of the room.

Hardhead Hudnutt's preacher's voice overpowered that of the marshal's as he took to the platform and assumed command of the meeting by quoting scripture. "'The same shall drink of the wine of the wrath of God, which is poured out without mixture into the cup of his indignation; and he shall be tormented with fire and brimstone in the presence of the holy angels, and in the presence of the Lamb.'"

His eyes, full of righteous vengeance, fell upon Amy as he repeated the words "the Lamb" in remorseful incantation. "I tell you men, we're not pissin' around here; we know who the culprit is. We know we have the guilty party. The little lamb told us the truth. Go forth in groups of twos and threes and find the scoundrel," Hudnutt said in a commanding voice. "Take different routes to get there; that way you won't attract attention. Lon, you take a couple of men with you and scout the town. Beaver, you and some of the others go to that wagon he lives in, and be quiet about it. Don't alarm the doctor, or that wife of his. Some of you other men go to that dago joint in I-taly Town and see if the bastard's there. Round him up like the dirty dog he is, and bring him back here. We will meet back here."

The crowd voiced the aroused excitement of their mission as they streamed from the building and into the bracing vigor of the night air.

"He could be innocent!" the marshal shouted after them, straining to be heard above the noise.

"Not a chance!" the men replied.

"No violence!" the marshal bellowed after their retreating backs.

He had a mob on his hands. What could he and one deputy do with a mob? It never occurred to him that reasonable men might get out of hand. Removing his knife from his pants pocket, he angrily jerked the rope from the rafter. He viciously sliced off the noose with its thirteen wraparounds and slammed it into the fire. Looking toward the workbench, the marshal said to his deputy, "Where's the iron?"

Just three of them remained in the building. The marshal, with his hand on his still-holstered gun, confronted the blacksmith. "Where's the damn branding iron?"

The big Swede, tending the fire in his forge, shrugged his massive shoulders and pushed the noose into the hot coals. His bald head glistened, and his pale eyes lacked compassion. Looking at the marshal, he hawked and spat into the fire before scornfully answering, "I only do vhat I vas told."

CHAPTER 72

MEIKO TOMA SAT IN THE bruise-blue dusk by the side of his van, his back resting against a wheel of his wagon as he watched the colors fade from the western sky and, with them, the meager warmth of the day. He was exquisitely sensitive, to the point of superstition. Nature's moods were his moods. The gentlest breeze caressing his skin moved him to sensuality. The feel and smell of the earth; the mutable moon and eternal sun; warmth, cold, rain, snow, golden days, and days when earth and heaven's rage all were felt within him; all were absolute.

The deep-purple shadow from the rapidly setting sun slid down the slope of the mountain, engulfing him and besmirching the blue-velvet sky of late day. He shivered instinctively at the sight of a late homing bird silhouetted against the thin pale disk of the moon—a bad omen for a Gypsy. Still he sat.

His animal instincts told him to seek shelter. The big house? No. The danger could be there. He had not seen Lillian since she came to him; maybe she had told her husband. He groaned with guilt for his betrayal of the doctor and also with the terrible physical ache of wanting her. With body and mind he craved her: craved her beauty, her chasteness, the very scent of her. He had perceived the awakening in her and yearned to ignite the coldness of her with his own fire.

Take flight! The barbershop? Friendly people would be there; at least they seemed friendly. He entered the van and with a moan stretched out on the cot. *I've been alone too long*, he reflected. *It's not the Gypsy way*. Pinching out the candle by his bedside, he fell into a restless sleep.

With one kick from a farmer's heavy boot, the intricately carved wooden doors shattered, and in the dark, Meiko sensed the van filling with inebriated men. A lantern was passed to the men inside, and the wagon sprang to light. When three of the men lunged at him, Meiko let loose a high, piercing wail like that of a trapped animal. A fist smashed into his mouth, and he tasted his own blood.

Amid the sounds of hitting, shoving, and the breaking of earthly possessions, Meiko was dragged from the van. Outside the confines of the wagon, the men hurled him to the ground, where they kicked him, one of them giving him a vicious kick to his groin. In agony, he rolled into a ball with his knees to his chin and his arms wrapped around his head, protecting his face.

A light appeared in an upstairs room of the mansion.

"Hurry up!" the men said in urgent whispers. "Let's get him out of here."

Two men grabbed Meiko's arms, dragging him through a trail of his own vomit to horses waiting near the stable. Throwing him over the back of a saddled horse and quickly tying him to it, they disappeared into the night, avoiding Main Street and the telltale sound of hooves chinking on brick.

At the blacksmith shop, Meiko was unceremoniously dropped to the floor in front of the platform, where he lay encircled by a crowd of angry men, the brims of their hats turned low to hide their eyes. He looked up, numb with pain, at the platform, where he saw a girl seated, hugging a doll. By the appearance of her, she was pregnant. The presence of the girl, and the fact that he had a faint remembrance of seeing her somewhere before, disturbed him even more.

Forced to his feet by Hardhead Hudnutt and Beaver Rasmussen, Meiko was pushed and shoved to the forge, where he watched in horror as Hardhead pulled a branding iron from the burning coals. The branding head was in the shape of the letter R.

"This is what we do to rapists," Hudnutt said. "We brand them."

Meiko, too terrified to cry out, made stifled choking noises. Urine, visible on the front of his pants, stung the cuts made from being dragged from his van to the stables; one cheek was bruised and an eye swollen, his bloodied upper lip split open and distended.

"Rapist. Defiler of innocence!" Hudnutt said, accusing him in his most godlike voice and shaking the red-hot iron in his face.

For the first time, Meiko understood: they were accusing him of rape.

"Not me! I didn't do it," he said, panting. "I never touched her. I don't know her. Gypsies would never force themselves on a woman. It's against our laws."

The men within earshot of him guffawed: "Against their laws."

Meiko was led back to the platform, where he stood mutely staring up at the young girl.

"Is this him? Is this the man?" Hardhead demanded of her.

Meiko in his present condition resembled a bogeyman, the red glare of the fire playing over his person and his black, unruly hair standing in kinky spikes. Sweat poured over his bruised and swollen face, and his olive skin was blanched to a sickly yellow. His open shirt, bloodied and nearly torn from his body, exposed the thick matted hair on his chest, and the gold chain around his neck glinted in the firelight.

His terrified eyes cast about for someone he knew. The butcher, the milkman, the barber, storekeepers, the men from the pool hall—all looked at him with contempt and loathing.

"Is this him?" Hudnutt asked Amy again in his deep, awe-inspiring voice. "Is this the man who hurt you?

A new jug was brought out and passed around.

"You'll burn in hell for what you did to her!" a man called from the crowd.

"Yeah! Yeah!" The other men's vehement agreements echoed through the room.

Amy, whimpering and hugging the sock doll to her little-girl bosom, shrank into the chair. The room was stifling, the smell nauseating. Chewing on her fingernails, she swallowed the saliva that kept erupting into her throat and dribbling onto her chin; she rubbed it away with the sock doll.

Her eyes had grown too heavy for her to control, and her head bobbed in all directions, up and down and from side to side. Dreamily, she looked at the men standing around the platform; they looked very far off. As she watched, they took on the appearance of tadpoles and squiggled backward into the skulking blackness.

"Amy. Amy." At the sound of her name, Amy struggled to open her eyes. The smithy doors were open, and the smell of fresh, cool air rushed into the stifling stable. Someone was rubbing her face with a wet cloth and calling her name.

She opened her eyes, thinking it was over, but she could tell by the stirred-up look on their faces that they were still waiting to hear her story. Her father, looking scared, was kneeling by the side of her chair. She didn't know why her father wanted her to fib, but she knew from the fearful look in his eyes that she'd better do it.

Hardhead Hudnutt had assumed command of the crowd and had taken over the interrogation of her. "Now, little girl, don't be scared. We're all friends here, and friends of your dad's." He gave Bobby Lee a brotherly pat on his shoulder. "And we want to hear your story in your own words."

"Just tell the story the way we rehearsed it, Amy, then it will all be over with," Bobby Lee whispered nervously into her ear.

For the first time, Amy looked at Meiko, tied to a chair with his red silk kerchief stuffed into his mouth, and she closed her eyes.

"That's a'right," Hudnutt said, "close your eyes if you cain't stand to look at 'im; we cain hardly stand to look at 'im ourselves."

It was during the telling of her story that Marshal McCombs and his deputy left for the depot to send a wire to the police department at the county seat.

In a monotonous little-girl voice, Amy dutifully told her rehearsed story. "I found a dollar in Mama's chest of drawers. I took my brothers to Parlett's and promised them each a penny for candy if they behaved, while I bought cloth for a new school dress. Then I sent my brothers home, and I went to my grandma's house to show her the cloth and ask her if she would help me make the dress. When I left for home, it was dark. I walked past the pool hall and took the shortcut to Old Church, and that's where someone grabbed me. It was too dark to tell who it was. He made me kiss him." Amy felt her face burning. "I hit him and pulled his hair. It was very curly."

The men nodded to one another: we've got the right man, they all knew.

"Then he took that red handkerchief from around his neck and tied it across my mouth and pushed me to the ground, and then he took off my underpants." She squeezed her eyes shut, speaking faster. "I got away from him once, but he grabbed my legs, and I fell back down on the ground."

The jug was making the rounds again.

"He pulled my legs apart and—and laid down on top of me, and—and he hurt me. After a while, he got up and sit down by me and took a little cigar out of a box, and when he struck the match, I could see it was the Gypsy. He took a knife from his pocket and held it across my mouth and said if I ever told anybody what he did to me, he would cut my tongue out."

During the telling of the story, the crowd of men had shifted, and Chance, knowing Amy's eyes were closed, had moved closer to hear her better. Discernible by the light from the forge, he now stood in back of the chair Meiko was tied to; Amy opened her eyes and for the first time since her rape saw her nightmare come to life.

At the sight of Chance Collins, she became hysterical, pointing and screaming, "It's him. It's him!" Scrambling out of her chair, she fell to her knees behind it, pleading, "Don't cut my tongue out!" over and over.

Amy's actions and hysterical shrieks of terror, and the absence of the marshal, spurred the men to action. The crowd, believing it was the sight of the Gypsy that had sent her into a frenzied outburst, dragged Meiko to the workbench and tied him, spread-eagled, to the top of it.

"Brand the son of a bitch!" someone shouted.

"Cut his tongue out!"

"Where's Bobby Lee?"

Beaver found Bobby Lee in the alley, with both arms wrapped around one of the posts that supported the hitching rail.

"Come on, Bobby Lee, we're going to brand him—the bastard's as good as confessed. It's your little girl, and you get to do the honors."

"I can't. I can't," Bobby Lee said, blubbering. "He's not...it's all been too much."

Beaver returned to the smithy and told the men, "Bobby Lee can't do it. He wants to take Amy and go home." He motioned for Amy to come down from the platform. "Come on, Amy, your pa's taking you home."

Some of the men, looking to see what was going on, followed Beaver and Amy outside to the hitching post. Chance, watching everyone's enthusiasm wane, pushed his way through the crowd of men to Bobby Lee; the sight of the sniveling man had him worried.

"Bobby Lee," he said, "you know that dirty, curly-haired, earring-wearin' little freak raped this little girl of yours, and he's got to be punished." The alley was filling up with men who were ready to call it quits. Chance appealed to them. "Why, a nice clean little town like ours can't have Gypsies runnin' loose in it, ruinin' our women and rapin' our children, and stealin'. Hell, everybody knows Gypsies are the biggest thieves there is. And liars! You'll see, he'll try to lie his way out of this. Come on! Let's get it over with. If Bobby Lee won't do it, then we'll do it for him. Don't back down now. Let's get a confession out of him."

He marched back inside and waved his arm for the others to follow. They stood around the forge frozen in their indecision, some backing away; no one made a move for the abhorrent branding iron resting in the fire.

"Chance, I think he's been taught his lesson," someone said.

"Yeah, he's had his punishment. He won't be raping any more children."

"Not after this. Not in our town."

"Not for a while, anyway," someone said with a laugh.

"That's right, we wuz to scare him into confessing."

Chance glanced toward the chair vacated by the girl. Amy had him right out worried. He knew it was him she was pointing at when she'd become hysterical.

"Then make him confess, goddammit!" Chance demanded. Picking up the hot iron from the coals, he menaced the Gypsy with it. "Fess up. You know it was you who raped that little girl!"

"I never touched her!" The Gypsy's frantic denial bubbled up from his swollen and bloodied mouth.

Moving the iron very deliberately toward Meiko's face, Chance said, "You know it was you who raped that little girl." Then Chance saw—saw with startling clarity the truth dawn in the Gypsy's eyes.

"You did it," Meiko whispered in surprise. "You're the one who did it." Trusting in truth, he hoarsely called out, "He did it! Chance did it!"

Scared and infuriated, Chance touched the tip of the iron to Meiko's cheek.

"Shut your trap, you lyin' freak, and confess to it, you bastard."

When Meiko felt the heat of the flaming R against his face, he tried to escape by straining against the ropes. "No!"

In the orange light of the forge, Chance looked like a deranged devil tending the fires of hell. As he raised the crimson iron high above his head, a mighty bellow escaped from his lungs in concert with the fiery arc as it descended toward the Gypsy.

"I did it!" Meiko shrieked, trying to save himself from the branding by confessing to the lie. His confession was accompanied by a horrified scream and the smell of burning hair and flesh, followed by an uncanny moment of deathlike silence before the clamorous sound that a stampede of men makes upon leaving the place of their shame.

When Marshal McCombs and his deputy returned from the depot, where they had cabled the county seat for help, they found the place empty, even of the big Swede, and the Gypsy unconscious.

"Good God almighty," the marshal said, his eyes transfixed on the blackened R oozing blood, fluid, and scorched flesh from the brand burned onto the chest of Meiko Toma.

The blacksmith appeared from the shadows, looking belligerently defiant. "I only did vhat I vas told."

"'Vell now,' damn you, 'do vat you are told,'" the marshal mimicked, biting off each word. "Hitch up a wagon, and let's get this man to the doctor."

The continuous sound of the buzzer, relayed from his office door to his bedroom upstairs, startled Adam. It was the first time he had heard it at this time of night since setting up practice in Rockville. Slipping into a robe and slippers, he ran down the grand staircase to the front door.

Marshal McCombs was at the door, trying his best to remain calm while giving the doctor the bare facts of what had happened. He asked him where he wanted the Gypsy.

Adam said, "Before he's moved, I'll need to have a look at him."

Meiko regained consciousness long enough to recognize the doctor and make a feeble attempt to reach out to him.

Adam caught his hand. "It's all right, Meiko. You're safe. You're going to be fine."

Lillian, from the top of the stairs, watched the men carry in someone who was hurt. A momentary glimpse of the person as they carried him inside told her it was Meiko, and deep inside her woman's soul she felt an aching response.

The sullen smithy, after carrying Meiko into the clinic and placing him on the operating table, disappeared from the premises. Dr. Townsend gave Meiko a cursory going over before administering morphine. Upon examining the swollen, secreting, and burned flesh on the man's chest, he said, "Who in the hell did this?"

"I have to take full responsibility for everything that happened tonight," McCombs said. While the doctor worked on the sedated man, McCombs related the whole story to him. "The branding iron was done as a threat to scare him into confessing. It was never meant to be used on his person."

"Do you believe the girl's story?" Adam asked.

"To tell the truth, Doc, her story's been scratching at me like a dog with fleas. I think this whole fracas was a setup, elaborately and deliberately planned. I think she was coached and threatened into telling a lie."

"Did she actually stand before Meiko and point a finger?" Adam asked.

"No, near as I can tell, she stood before a bunch of besotted men hell-bent on justice, and she became hysterical. You know this man," McCombs said, nodding to Meiko. "What do you think?"

"I think the wrong man was branded. How in the hell could one man do this to another?" Adam asked, the tone of his voice expressing his disgust.

"It was hatched up by that gang of men who hang out at the blacksmith shop—Hardhead, Beaver, 'Stump' Miller, that mongrel bunch of humanity—and you can bet that damn Chance Collins was the ringleader. I swear that man is a disciple of the devil."

"Somebody should shoot the bastard," Adam said.

"Hell, he ain't worth the bullet," the marshal said.

Meiko was moved to a bedroom in the clinic wing of the mansion.

Dr. Townsend, not wanting any men in the Gypsy's presence, fearing that the sight of a man could send him into shock, recruited an able band of women volunteers to nurse him back to health: Rose Langley, her mother and sisters, and her son Aries; being a friend of Meiko's, Aries was the only male in the nursing brigade. They took turns with round-the-clock care of the sedated Gypsy.

Three days later, when Meiko regained wakefulness, he saw, in the dimness of his strange surroundings, the serene beauty of Lillian Townsend seated in a chair near the bed he was lying on. The terror-stricken man, not knowing where he was or what had happened to him, tried to rise, only to fall back in agony.

Lillian was instantly on her feet, her hands on his bare waist. "No, no," she said soothingly, "you mustn't turn over. You have to lie on your back. You've been—wounded." She faltered in her choice of words, not wishing to remind him of the branding.

Scenes of his degradation came rushing into Meiko's consciousness. He did not want to look at her. He did not want her looking at him. In complete humiliation, he turned his head toward the wall and, with an arm thrown across his face, covered his eyes and began a low moaning. "Get me something red," he begged. "Get my red scarf."

The doctor, on his hourly visit to his burn patient, was surprised to see a red silk scarf tied around his patient's neck.

"He believes red protects him from evil spirits," Lillian explained.

"Well, it can't hurt. Just keep it away from the wound. You don't have to do this, Lillian. You don't have to sit with him. Others here can do it."

"Don't shut me out, Adam."

"I am not shutting you out. I'm trying to protect you. I know how repulsive all of this is to you."

"I sometimes think you don't know anything about me, Adam. I want to help. I don't mind. I really don't."

Lillian was suffering from feelings of guilt; she believed that somehow she was to blame for what had happened to Meiko.

"He's a nice person, and he's always been courteous to me, and I feel sorry for what happened to him. In a way, we're his family—the only family he has. He does live here and work here, and if we don't care what happens to him, then who will? It was a horrible injustice to happen to anyone."

She had avoided looking directly at Adam, and when she did, her eyes were full of distress. This was a side of Lillian that Adam had never seen before.

CHAPTER 73

THE PROS AND CONS OF the branding were discussed wherever and whenever a group of men got together.

"Oh, we got the right man all right," the initiators of the fateful event would say.

"When he came face to face with a hot iron, he soon fessed up. Livin' here all that time without a woman, a man like 'at cain't do without." Knowingly, they laughed, winked, and nudged.

The week after the branding, Aunt Henny, the midwife, dispatched Bobby Lee Jr. to bring the doctor. Precious Amy was in labor, had been since the night of the branding, and Aunt Henny, who was in attendance, was unable to deliver the baby.

Adam drove to the medical emergency in his buggy and returned to the clinic with Amy and Bobby Lee aboard and Aunt Henny to assist him in the delivery. Adam, very much aware that he had to keep his burn patient ignorant of any knowledge of his accusers being in the same surroundings, moved the Gypsy back to his vardo, something Meiko had begged him to do after regaining full consciousness and getting most of his strength back.

Adam performed his first caesarean section operation since graduating from medical school. He delivered Amy of a male child and again recruited his volunteer nursing force for the care of his recovering child patient and her baby.

Visiting the new mother and child provided members of the Tuesday Benevolent Society with an excuse to see the clinic, and they came by twos and fours and sixes to call on Amy. The ladies were very much surprised by the white, sterile, efficient atmosphere of the place. Adam explained the operation to them, and the need to keep Amy and her baby in the clinic, where he could monitor their progress. When Adam left the room, the gossip began, some of them repeating to one another what he had said.

"And he cut the baby right out of her abdomen? And what will our good brother think of that?"

"The little fellow sure has straight hair for being sired by that Gypsy man," old Mrs. Wallace said after looking the baby over.

Mrs. White grimaced. "We mustn't even think about those things," she said from the wellspring of her *Mayflower* upbringing.

"Marshal McCombs is certainly insistent upon the Gypsy's innocence," Ethel whispered to Mabel with a tongue-in-cheek expression.

"Do you believe him?"

"We must be charitable," Mrs. White said in a scolding voice when she overheard the comment.

"Who else in Rockville would do such a terrible thing?" asked the naive Mrs. Griggsby, her rosacea-flushed face turning rosier.

"Where there's smoke, there's fire," said Perthy Prettyman.

This reminded the ladies of the Gypsy's branded chest. They shuddered and, full of hope, stole surreptitious glances down the long corridor of closed doors in the wing reserved for patients. Feverishly yearning for a glimpse of the "madman," as their husbands had described the Gypsy to them on the night justice had been meted out, they kept on hoping.

Adam found time during his busy schedule to write to the *American Medical Journal* and the *Capital Call* newspaper in the capital and to place a boxed ad in each: "Wanted: Experienced nurse to assist doctor in small clinic."

Two weeks later, Althea Boggins, a nursing-school graduate and practicing nurse for the past seven years, walked into the Townsend Clinic, looked around, removed her no-nonsense black hat to reveal frizzled peach-colored hair, and jabbed the long hatpin back into its straw crown. She opened her valise and, pulling a nurse's white apron from it, gave the heavily starched garment a good brisk snap, which sounded like the cracking of a horsewhip, before tying the sash into a precise bow and pinning the bib to the front of her sensible black dress.

With the jab of the hatpin, Dr. Townsend felt the bond. "I never hired her," Adam would later say of Althea Boggins. "She just walked in and took over."

He was incredibly handsome-bodied, she would later reminisce. A look in his eyes said "Life is an adventure and can be worth the trip." Althea's calling was nursing, but her devotion, forever after, was to Dr. Adam Townsend.

He was her religion.

CHAPTER 74

It was close to daybreak when Lillian, leaving her room, made her way to the kitchen by means of the back stairs. She was standing at the sink gazing from the window, sipping from a glass of water, when she was suddenly struck with a seizure of wheezing and gasping. The tumbler she was holding slipped from her hands and shattered in the sink.

The vardo was gone!

She ran outside and, standing in the middle of the forsaken spot, still encircled with brown stubs from last summer's herbs and flowers, turned around and around repeating over and over, "No! No! No!"

Back in the house, a dazed and unfeeling Lillian walked through the formal rooms of the first floor, numbly touching various objects. "This is a chair. This is a table. This is a dish. That is a painting," and, at last, seeing herself in the hall mirror, "and that is what I'll look like when I'm a very old woman."

Meiko Toma and the vardo were gone and so, too, was the doctor's golden palomino.

"With this new covering of snow, we could track him," Marshal McCombs suggested.

"No, let the poor bastard go," the doctor said. "As for the horse, he's earned it."

"That Italian woman over in Saint Margaret's has turned up missing, too—the singer, Flora Maria Brocoloni, I believe her name is."

Days turned into weeks, and people were forgetting the disappearance of the singer and the Gypsy, but Lillian could not let it go.

She returned to the window above the kitchen sink several times a day, eventually covering it over with a dish towel and using the excuse, "The light hurts my eyes." Her red-rimmed eyes, blurred with torment, lost their luster. She took to wearing dark glasses inside the house—small round ones meant for the bright out of doors—and spending long hours alone in her darkened room. She could not forget the branding. The sadistic brutality of the act sickened her, and in nightmares she saw Meiko with a flaming, bloody R covering the whole of his torso. She blamed the "uneducated and bigoted" people of Rockville for what had happened to him, and she hated them and the town all the more. She implored Adam to move back to Baltimore, insisting she would never raise a family in a barbaric place like Rockville. She wanted to go home.

Lillian avoided everyone in the household and required that Mrs. Sheridan serve her meals in her room. She especially avoided Adam and, when she did see him, looked at him with contempt, which Adam could not understand.

She had come to him again in the late night seeking fulfillment, a disquieted, sterile presence of her all-too-briefly awakened self mewling, "Make love to me; I can't sleep." And Adam, perfunctorily performing his husbandly duty, tried to satisfy her obsessed desire. During the union, she had cried out in torment, feverishly thrusting; then, crazed with her failure to achieve satisfaction, she wept with rage.

The memory of their lovemaking of that night repulsed Adam. It left him even more discontented and with a heightened longing for Abby. He wanted her in his life as well as in his bed, and he swore he would not resign himself to a sexless, childless marriage.

Lillian's abandonment from the genesis of her passion, Meiko's brutal and unconscionable treatment at the hands of the town, and her isolation combined to rob her of the amorous desire she had found so late in life. And Adam felt robbed, too, of the love of a wife and of the offspring he wanted, and he resented more than ever having another man raise his only child.

Adam was concerned with Lillian's mental and physical well-being; her vision especially disturbed him. He finally persuaded her to take a trip to Baltimore, have a long and much-needed visit with her parents, and make an appointment with the city's leading eye specialist while she was there. He would go east with her, remain for as long as was necessary, and take over her care himself, but he made it clear that he meant to return to Rockville with or without her. He had become established in Rockville and wanted to remain there, to grow with the expanding town, but Lillian's health and happiness must be the deciding factor.

Six weeks later Adam returned to Rockville without Lillian. Their differences were still unresolved, and Lillian was exuberantly happy in everyone's presence, except her husband's.

Seeing the young Dr. Townsend making his rounds was becoming a common sight for the people of Rockville. Still, they didn't especially trust a doctor with just fancy school learning. Nor did his nurse bring a soupbone and make soup, as Aunt Em had done. But "Doc" had his good side and was showing signs of good old common horse sense. They went along with him when "No spitting" signs appeared everywhere. They thought differently about him, however, when it concerned their livelihoods. Now he wanted them tested for tuberculosis and the milk tested, and anyone who sold milk for others' consumption was required by law to have the milk tested. As the new county health commissioner, the doctor had seen this made into an ordinance, and a felony if ignored. He talked about the prevention of tuberculosis with the zeal of a preacher. The dreaded disease was generally looked upon as one of life's miseries that had to be dealt with stoically, and who had ever heard of milk making you sick? Nevertheless, he was slowly gaining their confidence.

Nurse Boggins, who was settled in for the long haul, entered the clinic office with a little girl who looked to be about four or five years of age and guided her toward Adam, seated at his desk. "This is Dr. Townsend," the nurse said to her. "Can you give the doctor your message?"

"Daddy says you're to come at once," the girl said, looking at the floor. "Mama's sick."

"All right," Adam said. "And what is your name?"

"Gertie," she said in a whisper, twisting at the skirt of her dress.

Adam smoothed her dress. "And Gertie, what is your daddy's name?"

"Will."

"Does he have a last name?"

She shrugged and again twisted her dress.

Taking Gertie by the hand, Adam went to the kitchen in search of Mrs. Sheridan.

"Well now, I don't rightly know who she is," Mrs. Sheridan said, studying the girl's face. "There's Will Stanton, the dairyman, and Will Sorensen, and I believe I do recall the Sorensens naming a baby Gertrude. Anyway, Will Stanton would have come himself."

When Dr. Townsend entered the Sorensen home, he could smell the illness. Mrs. Sorensen was in bed in a hot, dimly lit, smelly room, her eyes burning bright with fever and fear. "I know what it is," she said with patient endurance, "but it's my back that's killing me. The pain is terrible." She tried to move and broke into a fierce sweat.

"Lie still. I don't want you to move." Adam pulled up a chair and sat down by her bedside. "Mrs. Sorensen, I'm going to loosen your gown so I can better examine you." He could see genuine humiliation in her eyes; patients were reluctant to remove their clothes, even the men. After undoing her gown, he lifted the bandage covering her bosom, and his heart wrenched in his chest. Slices from a slab of fatback pork lay neatly beribboned across her right breast.

"I'm going to take a look," he said. Recovering his poise, he gently removed the strips of bacon to reveal a dark, swollen, weeping, asymmetrical, and deeply dimpled breast. After applying a fresh dressing and buttoning her gown, he said, "I'm going to give you something to ease the pain."

The fear came back into her eyes. She shook her head.

"Brother Griggsby says—" she began.

"Virginia, you don't have to bear intolerable pain just to prove you're a good Christian. You are a good Christian. God doesn't want you to suffer. God is not a cruel and vindictive God, no matter what they teach you in church."

"But I'm a God-fearin' woman," she said feebly.

"Maybe you should try loving Him instead," Adam said gently.

She was still looking at him with a show of doubt in her wavering eyes when she swallowed the liquid savior he held out to her in a spoon.

Adam later sat at the kitchen table with the sorrowing husband and joined him in drinking a mug of coffee. "You know your wife has cancer."

"We've knowed that for quite a spell, but what's wrong with her back?"

"Cancer," Adam said. "The cancer has spread to her bones."

Gertie came into the room and, smiling shyly at the doctor, climbed onto her dad's lap. "How long has she got?" the man asked, hugging the little girl.

"Two, three months at the most. I'm going to leave you a bottle of medicine, and you give her a spoonful every time her pain is unbearable. You'll have to keep her in bed and see to it that she doesn't try to be brave. There's no need for that. Do you have someone to help you?"

"She has two sisters who ain't sick with it yet, and there's neighbors, and the church ladies," he said, his voice breaking. "Her ma died from cancer a few years back; it runs in the family."

"Then you have someone to help you. That's good. Keep her quiet, or her bones are going to break." Adam rose from the table, gripped the shoulder of the bewildered farmer, and patted his back. "I'll be by every day, and you send for me if you need me, day or night. Day or night," Adam repeated, looking at the man and making sure he understood his sincerity.

The townspeople argued the right or wrong of taking something for pain or of "bearing it like a good Christian as God metes it out to us." And good Brother Griggsby, in his Sunday sermon, exalted sin and Christian pain and the glorious heavenly rewards awaiting one in the next life in exchange for the denials practiced in this one.

Lillian was packing what looked to be all of her belongings. On her last night at home before she left for Baltimore, she joined Adam in the library for a cocktail before dinner. She sat erect, distant in her demeanor; the pale blue of her gown, worn with a single strand of pearls, enhanced her glacial Nordic beauty.

After Lillian finished her drink, Adam was relieved to see a heightened color come into her cheeks and a restored sparkle to her eyes. He prepared a second one, trusting it would not lead to another attempted copulation. He cared for her but no longer felt desire toward her.

Twirling her glass while observing the movements of its contents, Lillian, without raising her head or her voice, said, "When I leave here, Adam, I am not returning. I want a divorce."

The scandalous word lay between them, ugly and alien. Respectable people did not divorce, Adam thought. Could failure in his marriage mean failure as a doctor as well?

"You are not the same man I married, and I find us no longer compatible." Lillian raised her head, her expression candid. "I've tried for your sake to fit in, but it isn't working. There is a certain style of life I need, a style of living that is as necessary to me as being a doctor is to you, and I will never acquire it living here in Rockville." She took several quick swallows of her drink. "I want to be with my own kind, live with my own kind, socialize with my own kind. I want to be with you, Adam, but not here. Never here." Her face colored with the passion of her feelings. "I hate Rockville. I hate the people—they're so common!" Her voice broke, and a shudder passed over her.

"Did you ever love me, Lillian?

"I wanted you for a husband," she said as a matter of fact.

"Wanting is not the same as loving."

"Yes, of course I love you, but not enough to live in Rockville for the rest of my life, or to sacrifice my own happiness. I certainly didn't marry you with the intention of becoming the wife of a small-town doctor. Now, I find I no longer care that you insist on remaining among them, and that leaves me with one alternative—divorce." She leaned toward him, her face mirroring the intensity of her feelings. "You could have a brilliant practice in a big city, and we could take our place in society, where we belong."

Adam felt a deep sorrow and at the same time an enormous sense of relief. He had done her a great injustice in marrying her and in bringing her to Rockville. She was right: she belonged in salons and soirees, summer homes and grand tours on the continent. But he wanted to create his own destiny, be a pioneer in his chosen field, and on his own terms. Not on her terms, or her father's. "I agree with you about a separation," he said. "Time spent apart would be good for both of us. It'll give us time to think things through and know what it is we really want. I'll take you home, Lillian."

CHAPTER 75

The Rockville Hub
May 10, 1909

The wedding of Miss Wilma Mae McCoy to Theodore Leslie White took place in the law office of Judge William J. Andrews on Friday the 15th, followed by a reception at the residence of the mother of the bride, Mrs. Ramona McCoy.

The bride wore a white dress and hat with a short veil and carried a bouquet of lavender gladiolas. The mother of the bride wore a flowered gown with a wide-brimmed hat embellished with multicolored flowers. The mother of the groom, Mrs. Ethel White, wore a stylish black gown and black hat.

The reception, following the wedding ceremony, was held in the lovely backyard garden of the McCoy home, with the grape arbor providing the backdrop for the festive occasion. A dance followed the cutting of the cake and toasts saluting the newlyweds.

Family and friends of the happy couple attended the celebration, and a good time was had by all.

"Teddy" and "Willy Mae" are a splendid young couple who deserve a generous piece of happiness and prosperity.

The bride composed a song for the bridegroom in honor of their nuptial day, one that she sang during the reception. The song is reprinted here in its entirety.

TILL I WALKED BESIDE YOU

Never saw your hand reach out
Never felt your touch,
Never heard the song you sang,
Never cared that much.
Never cared enough, love

Never cared enough,
Till I walked beside you,
I never cared enough.

Never saw your smiling face
In the morning sun,
Never heard your evening's grace,
When the day was done,
Never cared enough, love
Never cared enough,
Till I walked beside you,
I never cared enough.

Never known love before
My heart was like a stone,
Till I felt your sweet embrace
I always walked alone.
Never cared enough, love
Never cared enough,
Till I walked beside you
I never cared enough.

Ted White knew the town was laughing and calling it a shotgun wedding—and his mother would never forgive him for marrying a McCoy, to the point where she wore her black mourning dress to his wedding—but in his heart, he loved Willy Mae. He especially loved her songs and thought her beautiful of face and body. He still found her eyes charming, even if one was blue and the other one brown. What's more, the widow McCoy had not held a gun to his head, as the town was implying.

After the complimentary article announcing the marriage appeared in the *Hub*, the townspeople laughed. They knew the bridal bouquet was nothing but crepe-paper flowers, the grape arbor a weed patch, and the widow McCoy's gown at least twenty years old. This time they said the widow McCoy must have held a shotgun to the head of the newspaper editor for him to write such a glowing report.

CHAPTER 76

June 1909

THE TELEGRAM TO ABIGAIL LANGLEY was dispatched from Chicago: "Room reservation for LaSalle Hotel confirmed. Stop. June 6 through 10. Stop. Signed, P. Wells, reservations."

Abigail smiled, recognizing that the telegram had been sent by Adam. He had used the name of his old tutor, the romantic, myopic Professor Wells, as the pseudonym for the reservation clerk. Abby stood at the desk in the elegant walnut-paneled lobby of the LaSalle Hotel, the man at the desk making her, as a single lady traveling alone, feel decidedly welcome as he signaled for a bellhop and handed him the key to her room. Today's hotels were increasingly catering to women guests as well as men. The new prosperity of the working-class woman, along with comfortable transportation, afforded them trips to major cities for shopping and entertainment without suffering the stigma attached to a woman traveling without an escort.

Roses in rainbow colors arranged in cut-glass vases greeted her as she entered the suite. After the departure of the bellhop, the adjoining door between the two suites opened, and Adam entered.

No words were spoken; she just walked into his open arms. He kissed her mouth, her cheeks, her forehead, her neck, clasped her head, her shoulders, her waist, both of them wildly impatient to make love.

Abby delicately complained about grime from the train.

Adam, meanwhile, was helping her shed her clothes and kissing away her apologies as they moved toward the bed. "Go where your body takes you," he whispered, picking her up and laying her on the bed. His eyes feasted on the lush feminine curves, the satin hollows; gone the tomboy body of the fifteen-year-old girl he had first loved. Spread out before him now was the bounty of a ravishing woman at the apex of her womanly loveliness.

An almost-tangible heat of desire emanated from her. Her hair had come loose from its combs and pins and tumbled about her face; impatiently she brushed it away. She wanted nothing between them. His mouth found hers, and she opened hers to his searching tongue and the demands of his kiss. She would never get enough of him; it had been too long coming.

He rubbed his thumbs across her nipples, arousing them to hardness, and watched them tighten into little puppy faces. He pressed his thumb against her lips until her mouth opened, then carried the wetness to the small, swollen bud cloistered between her legs, massaging it. Fighting to get her breath, she grabbed his hands, stilling his movements. When he again began the caressing strokes, she convulsed into a spasm of undulating motions of unendurable delight. And when she parted her legs to him, he pushed his manhood into her deep and far, entering her sacred place and pillaging the sacraments of her secret self.

She rode with him, a Viking queen, fierce and wonderful. Rode the wave, swelled and receded and swelled again, rocked and swayed, forgot him, forgot her. There was just the wave, higher and higher, and when she crested the wave, she screamed her triumph. She returned to him with serene little gasps and sighs vibrating in her throat, celebrating her victory.

Abby covered her face to hide her embarrassment; Adam pulled her hands away.

"Please, don't." She was his Eve, his mate, the only woman to sublimate his desires.

The first evening, they remained in the elaborate suite, dined, drank champagne, and made love again. Late in the evening, Abby left the bed and, standing facing him, proudly announced without shame or remorse, "I'm pregnant."

"Since noon?"

"No, since February."

Adam's mouth fell open.

"And you waited until now to tell me? Darling, it's been two months!"

Abby, assuming the pose of a gunslinger, hands on hips, forefingers pointing at him, said with a western drawl, "I aims to hev this kid, mistuh."

"Then I aims to hev it, too," he said. "You little minx, you're like a barnyard cat. I'll be afraid to touch you for fear you'll have a litter."

"As long as it's your litter, mistuh," she said with mock toughness.

"I'll ask for a divorce," Adam said. She joined him on the bed, snuggling into his arms.

"Are you sure?" she asked, her eyes dancing about his face searching for recriminations.

"I want this child, Abby, and this time I mean to raise my son," he said, holding her tight, one hand possessively caressing her abdomen, "and to marry his mother. At long last to marry my Eve," he said, kissing her stomach. "Lillian's already told me she wants a divorce. I'll return to Baltimore and break it to her as gently as I can. Not about us, but to let her know that I'm in agreement with her about the divorce. I won't tell her about you. She's had three miscarriages, and it would be a terrible blow to her womanhood, and her sexuality." He said the word cautiously, and still she blushed, "sex" being a lewd word that no one with proper manners used. He kissed the tip of her nose.

"As for us, we'll work out the details later. For the next few days, let's just be a newly engaged couple who are madly in love with each other."

“I’ve always been madly in love with you, Adam, for as long as I can remember.”

After eating lunch in the beautiful Blue Fountain Room at the LaSalle, they shopped for a ring, choosing an emerald with a flange of diamonds on either side.

“Isn’t it rather too spectacular?” Abby hesitatingly asked, already in love with the ring.

“Nothing is too spectacular for my Abigail Lee, my bride to be.”

Back in the suite of rooms at the hotel, Adam tried again to place a call to Lillian to let her know he was returning to Baltimore, but he did not receive an answer.

He and Abby celebrated their engagement with dinner and dancing on the rooftop-garden dining room. Adam toasted her with champagne: “To my Eve, my bride, my love.”

Abby’s hand left her lap, rose to the table, to his shoulder; cupping his cheek in the palm of her hand, she pressed her cheek to his. “My Adam,” she whispered.

There was a sharp intake of his breath as he grasped her hand and moved it to his lips. The exquisite sensation of his lips on her palm left her weak.

To regain their composure, they sipped their champagne. Her slender fingers slowly twirled the stem of her glass, and the bejeweled ring sparkled and flashed from a hand that for too many years had remained virginal.

The next time Adam called Lillian at her parents' home, the housekeeper answered the phone. She informed Adam that Mrs. Townsend, along with her parents, had set sail for Europe on the RMS *Lusitania* on a two-month trip to the continent.

"It's a setback," Adam said, "especially when time is crucial. But we'll be OK, and our baby will be as well," he said with a grin.

CHAPTER 77

August 1909

"DAD?" THE FIRST WORD OF any conversation spoken on the recently installed telephones at River's Bend always began as a question.

"Hello?" Joe Langley yelled into the telephone from inside the furniture shop, making sure he was heard. He startled Leo enough that he dropped the receiver.

Recovering the swinging earpiece, Leo answered, almost whispering. "Dad, Mrs. Oberlander is here in my office and would like to have a word with you." This further convinced his father that the newfangled hearing thing was a damned nuisance.

"A feller could holler and get the same results," Joe mumbled, and did so. "Well, send her out here!"

Lottie Oberlander genteelly raised her bluebonnet-blue flounced skirt up to her ankles and stepped over the plank threshold and into the noisy, dusty furniture shop. To avoid making eye contact with the workmen while awaiting the appearance of Joe, Lottie gave her complete attention to the signs nailed to the wall above the machine across the aisle from where she stood: WHEN THE BUZZ SAW HUMS, LOOK OUT FOR YOUR THUMBS and ANYONE CAUGHT SPITTING WILL BE FINED $1.00.

Joe Langley showed gentlemanly restraint in greeting Lottie Oberlander. He lifted the brim of his hat and cleared his throat before leaning forward in an attempt to better hear her.

"I need to speak to you in private, Mr. Langley."

Turning his head and looking into her face, Joe saw the look of desperation in her eyes. "Is it about Orion and Jennie Jeanne?" he asked. His expression grew grim, and his jaw muscles tightened as he motioned her outside.

"Yes, and about us, too, Joe."

Seeing her horse and buggy tied to the railing, he said, "Let's take a ride." Handling the reins, he drove the buggy into a stand of trees outside the entrance to his property and stopped, waiting for her to speak.

She spoke rapidly in a soft, controlled voice. "Joe, can't you put a stop to our children seeing each other? Mr. Oberlander and I think they're too young to be so serious. It's our wish that Jennie Jeanne attend the music academy in Saint Louis; she has a wonderful singing voice—much better than I ever had. We have plans for Jennie Jeanne, and we don't wish for her to marry."

"Just like your parents had for you," Joe said. "Is there another bank president in the offing, Lottie?" he asked with sarcasm. "Because I will not stand in their way. Yes, I agree they're too young, and I think they know that, but darn it, they're in love, and I refuse to be the one who throws the ashes on the fire."

"You have to. We have to," she said.

Her desperate insistence fueled Joe's own emotions. "Your father called me a bum when he told me I wasn't good enough for his daughter," Joe said heatedly. "Well, my sons are not bums. They're the best kids around."

"I know, Joseph, I know they're the best, but can't you just send Orion away to school? I'll pay for it."

"Tarnations, woman, you're trying my patience. All my boys will go away to school when the time comes, beginning with Orion. And I won't need your confounded money to send him." His voice rose, causing her face to blanch. "And if my son wants to marry your daughter," he said, "then he can do it. With or without your blessings, they'll have mine."

He jumped from the wagon and turned to face her. She sat slumped on the seat, disconsolate and deathly pale. "I'm sorry I lost my temper, Lottie. My sons mean a great deal to me."

"She's your daughter." She said the words without feeling or inflection.

"What are you saying?"

"Jennifer Jeanne is your daughter and Orion's half sister." The words gushed forth in a rush of years of dammed-up silence.

Joe Langley braced himself against the wagon wheel, not thinking about the paternity of an unknown daughter, only the pain he would have to inflict on a son, and the thought was making him sick.

"How?" was all he said.

"I was pregnant when I married Leon."

"You mean you married another man when you knew you were carrying my child?"

"You were gone for the summer," she said, "off barnstorming." Ridicule crept into her voice, "And I didn't know how to reach you. I wanted to come to you. Neither my parents nor Leon knew I was pregnant. Finally, it was easier just to give in to my parents' wishes, to forget about you, and either go away to school or marry Leon. Being pregnant, I chose marriage. I was desperate, Joe. I couldn't wait any longer. Leon must never know. He worships Jennie Jeanne. I cannot and will not cause them pain. I love them both too much."

So Orion has to be the one to suffer the sins of his father. My beloved son pays for my transgressions. God, he silently pled, *don't do this to me.*

"I thought no one would ever know, but now something has to be done," Lottie said, and she began sobbing. Joe reached across the buggy seat and patted her knee. "All of these years, I've been the one to carry this burden," she said. "Now some of the responsibility has to be yours. I will not tell Jennie Jeanne—I can't, I just can't—or anyone else." Her sobs grew louder, and she covered her face with her hands.

Woodenly, Joe continued patting her knee, his movements frozen and his mouth dry as dirt. "I'm sorry, Lottie. What do you want me to do?"

"Tell Orion the truth. Let him…be the one to break it off." She looked down at Joe, her face tortured. "No one else, please. Please, I beg you, don't tell anyone else." She clutched at his hand, still resting on her knee. "And Orion can't tell her."

"I'm sorry, Lottie, for all the grief I've caused you. Don't worry. I'll take care of everything. Jennie Jeanne is a fine girl—a beautiful girl."

"And mine," she said fiercely.

"Yes, yes," Joe said, rapidly patting her knee.

"You know they're saying terrible things about her, and they're not true." Lottie moved about on the buggy seat in a state of panic. Confronting him again, she said, "She is my life!"

"You can rest easy. I'll take care of it. I give you my word."

Relaxing, she sighed with relief. "I watched you in the park with your three children that first summer after your wife passed away. They would sit there on a bench—Leo, Andy, and little redheaded Sags—and watch you play ball. When the game was over, oh, how they would run out onto the field and cling to your legs. It was such a dear sight that I fell in love with all of you."

"But your dad soon put a stop to that, didn't he?" he asked. "Especially after the set-to I had with him about wanting to marry you. So I left those 'dear little boys' with my mother and took off, like the hothead I was in those days. I knew you deserved better, Lottie: a young, unencumbered man your own age. But I had to have you." His face contorted with the memory. Removing his hat, he beat it on the carriage wheel to remove the dust and try to beat away his shame. "I was sick with wanting you, but I swear to you, the thought never crossed my mind that I was leaving you in a family way. And when I did come back, you were married. Married to another man when you knew you were carrying my child."

Lottie's tormented eyes looked into his, her child her only concern.

Joe put his hat back on his head, patted Lottie's knee again, and, raising his eyebrows, made little sucking noises from a corner of his mouth.

CHAPTER 78

A WEEK HAD PASSED SINCE Joe's meeting with Lottie and her confession of her daughter's paternity. During that time, Joe had devised a plan to separate Orion from the girl, and he decided the sooner the better. He felt optimistic that if, given time away from Jennie Jeanne, his son would soon discover that there were other girls in the world besides the one in Rockville and would never have to be told that Jennie Jeanne was his half sister.

Orion was throwing a baseball at a knot in the big ash tree in the front yard when his father called to him from the lumber wagon. "Rion, I need you to give me a hand."

"Where are we going?" Orion asked, climbing into the seat beside his father.

"I need a load of lumber from the west side stacks."

Orion showed surprise; the same lumber was in stacks much nearer.

Joe drove in silence to the end of the yard, where a mountain of discarded lumber was piled. He sat quietly twisting the leather reins in his hands before letting them drop to the seat beside him. "Son, I've been giving some serious consideration to your education. I want you to go away to school—leave early, and don't wait until fall. We'll find you a tutor when you get there, and you'll have a head start on everyone else."

"I can't do that, Dad. I don't want to leave here. I don't want to leave you and Mom, and my brothers, and I won't leave Jennie Jeanne."

"Orion, just how serious is this friendship between you and…" He found he couldn't say her name. "And this girl?"

Orion's blue eyes calmed, and his face became serious. Looking into his father's eyes, he said, "I mean to marry her."

Joe gripped the wooden armrest and for the second time in a week thought he was going to be sick.

"You all right, Pop?"

"Riney, you can't marry her—not now, not ever."

Orion jumped to his feet so fast the horses shied, causing both men to grab for the reins and shout, "Whoa!"

Orion, still standing, demanded, "What do you mean? Has old man Oberlander been talking to you? Well, I don't care what he says. And if Mrs. Oberlander thinks I'm not good enough for Jennie Jeanne, well—I am, and I intend to marry her."

"Sit down, son, please." Orion, defiant, remained standing while making his point. "You can't marry her,

Rion," Joe said, defeated. "She's your sister. I'm Jennie Jeanne's father."

Orion dropped to the seat, grasping for meaning to the words he had just heard from his father. "What? What?" He could not make sense of the words, or of his world that was now spinning out of control. "I don't know what you're talking about," he said numbly. "How? Why?" he stammered, facing his father, anger and the meaning of the words escalating in his head. "You're the one who's always taught us to be good, obey the rules, be gentlemen. Obey the Ten Commandments." He sneered at the significance of the words.

"For God's sake, Orion, you would be fornicating with your own sister."

"How about fornicating with thy neighbor's wife? Sir."

Joe Langley grabbed his son by the shoulders and shook him, his face dark with anger. "It wasn't like that. She was a kid, just like you, and her parents thought I wasn't good enough for her, either. Her dad didn't like ballplayers; to him we were all no-account bums. I was a widower, ten years older, with three little boys in need of a mother. I left you kids with your grandmother and took off. I went off to prove them all wrong. I said my goodbye to her, and when I returned, she was married. I didn't know until last week that I had left her pregnant." The fight had gone out of him. "Oh God, Orion, I'm sorry; I'm sorry, son." Joe jerked a bandanna from his back pocket, wiped his eyes, and noisily blew his nose.

Orion sat slouched in the seat, elbows on knees, holding his head in his hands, taking knuckle swipes at his face. Tears rolled down his cheeks, leaving dark, wet circles on the knees of his trousers as his father's infidelity tore him to the quick.

Joe put an arm across his son's shoulders. "Without my sin there wouldn't be a Jennifer Jeanne," Joe said, gently reminding him.

With an intense shrug, Orion rejected the proffered excuse. "I thought you and mom loved each other."

"And we do. Your mother and I have always felt blessed, like fate smiled on us; blessed us with each other, with you boys, with a good home. It isn't the end of the world, son, even if it seems that way right now.

"The first time I noticed your mother was in the ballpark that very same year. Over the summer, Rose had blossomed into adulthood. I threw a ball to her—at her, really, a low ball—and she just scooped it up off the ground and threw it back. Threw it like a man," he said, smiling at the memory. "She was beautiful: black curly hair and that milk-white skin and a big friendly smile. Just like yours," he said to Orion, a sob catching in his throat.

Orion straightened up, wiped his face on his shirtsleeve, and, jumping to the ground, looked back at his dad. "It's OK, Pop. Everything will be OK," he said, touching his father's arm before disappearing into the stacks of lumber.

Joe Langley remained in the wagon until dark, waiting for Orion, but he did not return.

The next few days, Orion was intensely busy. He avoided his father and had little to say to his brothers. He lost his healthy appetite, which concerned his mother. "Are you sick?" she asked one evening at supper, reaching out her hand to touch his forehead. Orion pulled back from her, and for the first time Rose saw the soul sickness in her son's eyes.

"Yeah," the brothers said, teasing. "He's love sick."

"That's enough, boys." The sharpness of their father's voice quieted them. Their father had always let them settle their own tormenting without interference from him. They looked away from their dad, wondering if he had heard the gossip about Jennie Jeanne. Their father having knowledge of such a mortifying story caused them an uneasy embarrassment. They also worried that Orion had heard the malicious rumor, and it made them afraid to look at either Orion or their father.

CHAPTER 79

Rose Langley and her sisters rode into town on horseback, long wool gabardine riding skirts discreetly covering their legs, Rose's sister Iris the only one riding sidesaddle.

Rose met Orion at Fontell Clothiers, where he was being measured for his first custom-tailored suit. Afterward, on their way to the Bon Marché, they walked past the Music Arcade, where Rose could hear her sisters singing from the latest sheet music. Glancing in the window, she could see Donald Vaughn playing piano and singing with them: "I wonder who's kissing him now…"

Abby was outside tending to the summer plants in the window boxes, a watering can close by. Rose greeted her niece with a kiss on each cheek. "I have never seen you looking happier," she said.

"I've never been happier," Abby replied, wishing she could confide her engagement to her aunt and show her the emerald-and-diamond engagement ring. She had added the ring to the chain that held the gold locket her father had given her, both now concealed beneath her shirtwaist. She liked to think the locket embraced the tiny portrait of Ronnie like loving hands.

"Orion's going away to college," Rose said, patting her son's arm with pride. "He will be the first one in our family to do so."

When Abby saw the torment in Orion's eyes, her heart turned over. She took his hand in hers and squeezed it reassuringly. He did not return the gesture. "That's wonderful, Riney," Abby said. "Is Jennie Jeanne going to wait for you?"

She could see his heartache sting his eyes, and he dropped his head. *So Jennie Jeanne is the thorn,* Abby thought. *But why? The pain of separation?* Abby knew that pain all too well, and she looked at him with sympathy.

Orion declined his mother's invitation to join her and his aunts in the music store. At one time he would have been the lead singer and the biggest cutup.

Abby watched him as he crossed the street to the hitching post where his horse was tethered. He walked with his shoulders slumped like those of an old man, the natural buoyancy gone from his step. She wondered what had happened between him and Jennie Jeanne to cause him so much unhappiness.

Abby picked up the watering can and turned to wave to Horace Brown, Daisy's brother, coming from the direction of the depot with a lone passenger in the buggy for hire: a smiling Lillian Townsend, waving and calling out a greeting.

Abby was unaware of dropping the watering can until a cool dampness coming through the soles of her shoes reminded her.

"I wonder who's kissing him now…" the sisters sang to Donald from the new sheet music while flirting and making goo-goo eyes at him as he accompanied them. The melancholy words and the plaintive voices of the women singing the newest waltz floated out to Abby, where she stood immobile on the sidewalk: "…I wonder who's teaching him how. I wonder if he ever tells her of me, I wonder who's kissing him now."

Horace Brown reined in the horses before the steps of the mansion. He helped his passenger alight from the buggy, unloaded her baggage, and opened the door for her. He waited on the veranda until Mrs. Townsend entered the clinic door before driving away.

Inside the office, Lillian coyly seated herself and quickly placed a finger to her lips when Althea Boggins appeared in the waiting room to call the next patient into his doctor's office.

"It's a surprise," Lillian whispered to her with a beseeching look at the waiting Mr. Johnson, he of the nervous tremors. The happy look she gave him coaxed him into the conspiracy.

"Oh, not a word from me, ma'am," the man said with a brisk affirming nod of his head as he went in to see the doctor.

"And none from me," said the efficient Nurse Boggins, with as much starch in her voice as there was in her stiff white apron.

After the last patient had left for the day, the nurse opened the door to the doctor's office for Mrs. Townsend and discreetly disappeared.

The sight of Lillian in his office left Adam too stunned to raise his arms as Lillian wrapped hers around him.

"Oh, sweetheart, if you could see your face! I've imagined your surprise, but it never compared to this." A laughing, coquettish Lillian stood on tiptoe to kiss the unfeeling cheek of her husband. She removed her hat and gloves.

"I need an examination, doctor," she said, cooing. "Shall I undress?" she said, fluttering her eyelashes at him. "I've had one doctor's opinion, and now I want my husband's." She sat on the side of his desk looking up at him from her lowered head. "The doctor on the ship said he'd never seen a healthier or prettier pregnant woman."

Adam felt himself actually stagger as he looked up at the half circle of sky visible through the rounded window of the open transom. He stood there without sensation, staring at nothing and inanely thinking, *The air must be very dry today to make the sky so blue.*

"I think you better sit down, Doctor," Lillian said, concern affecting her good humor. She sat on his desk with her ankles crossed, watching him. Her demeanor grew serious. "Adam, this baby has to live." Taking his hands, she placed them on her abdomen. "I don't think I could bear the torment of losing another one. I want more than anything in the world to give you a son. Please, you must safeguard our precious gift."

"What about the divorce?"

"Adam, I could never leave you, and divorce is so gauche."

Adam raised her hands to his numb lips. "I promise you, I will do everything I can to keep you from having another miscarriage." His voice sounded unfamiliar to his own ears. Adam sat down at his desk. In his observation of her, she seemed to be in good health, but very thin for a pregnant woman. "What doctor did you see?"

"The ship's doctor. I thought I was seasick, and the funniest thing happened as soon as he pronounced me pregnant—I was no longer sick. And I have felt absolutely peachy ever since," she said, sliding from his desk. "Oh, darling, darling Adam, isn't it wonderful news? I'm going upstairs now to our bedroom to rest. I'll join you tonight for dinner and cocktails," said a very changed Lillian. "My doctor recommended I have one glass of wine with dinner," she said, playfully wiggling her fingers in a farewell gesture after blowing him a parting kiss. "Will you tell Mrs. Sheridan your wife is home?"

Adam paced the room, his hands on either side of his head; he squeezed his temples so hard his brow furrowed. "God, God," he murmured, and after a while, "Abby, my God, Abby." *What jokester of a deity is making these two women conceive at the same time?* He stopped his pacing. *To which woman do I legally and morally owe my allegiance? How can I say to Abby, "Of course I owe my allegiance to my wife?" And dammit! What allegiance do I owe myself? What do I want?*

"What I want doesn't matter," he said aloud, jerking the stethoscope from his neck and flinging it across the room. "What I want isn't worth a hill of beans." Adam opened his father's old medicine cabinet and removed a flask of gin from it. *I could move to Utah, join the Mormon Church, and have all the wives and kids a man could want.*

"Now there's a fine idea," he said aloud, raising the flask in a toast before pouring himself a very generous drink.

CHAPTER 80

ADAM ENTERED THE BON MARCHÉ and was immediately commandeered by Mrs. Higgins, the town's leading gossip, and her toothy daughter, Erlina Mae. They responded to Adam's manly good looks and urbane manners like schoolgirls: giggling, batting their eyes, and slyly touching his coat sleeves. Abby couldn't help but smile at Adam's obvious discomfort.

"We hear there'll soon be a blessed event at your house, Doctor," Mrs. Higgins said in a simpering voice. Adam's eyes darted to Abby and back to the ladies.

In the sobriety of comprehending what the women were hinting to Adam, Abby's smile froze on her lips, and her hand dropped from fingering the ring hidden beneath her shirtwaist to the unborn child asleep in her womb. Adam saw the protective gesture, and the pain of it wrenched at his gut.

The gossipy women finished fawning over him and the "blessed event," then blessedly, they were gone.

Alone in the shop, Abby and Adam faced each other, Abby's face stricken, her eyes wide with shock. "Adam." His name leaped from her mouth like a cry for help. "Is it true?"

"Yes."

She could tell by his eyes that happiness had been snatched from her again. She grasped his hands. "What can we do? There must be something we can do." Her old feeling of abandonment flooded over her.

"I've been racking my brain for an answer. My ethical and moral obligation is to my wife. But I have to protect you, Abby. Above everything, darling, I have to protect you and our child. My wife is already protected."

"Of course. She has a husband."

"I will take care of you, Eve, and my child—always. I love you both." He sat on the bench and pulled her to him. "This has to go," he said, pinching a fold of the unbecoming apron and making a ratcheting movement. "It looks suspicious."

Abby shrugged out of the apron, and he wrapped his arms around her waist, pressing his lips to her abdomen and his unborn child.

She felt the warmth of his breath on her skin through the fabric of her dress, and her body betrayed her with a passionate stirring. Shame prickled her skin like cocklebururs.

"God will punish us, Adam."

Looking up at her, he said pleadingly, "Dearest, we have not been visited with a chastisement from God. If there is a deity, He will not punish us. Only the people who made up the God myth will punish us with gossip and rejection and showering us with shame. My shame is that I want both of my women, and all of my children."

Abby had a fleeting picture of Lillian miscarrying, and she pulled away from him. She hated herself for the dark thought, but in the weeks to come, she would do penance many times for her repetition of the thought by praying for Lillian. "This time I will have to move," she said. She paced the room nervously. "I'll have to pose as a widow, or the wife of a traveling man."

"I cannot live without you," he said. "I won't." They clung to each other.

Out of necessity, Abby entrusted her secret—the fact that she was "in a family way," not the name of the father—to two people: her grandmother, and her assistant, Daisy. At work, because her eighteen-inch waist was rapidly expanding, she wore the unbecoming black cover-up and remained hidden away in the workroom. "And the time will come," she confided to Daisy, "when I will have to stay at home."

"What will you do?" a teary-eyed Daisy asked, upset for the friend she cared for like a sister.

"I don't know, but I'll know the path when I come to it," she answered with a self-confidence she wasn't at all sure about.

Grandma Langley came to live with Abby. It was Grandma's need to care for someone, given the fact that Uncle Pete had died that year, that brought her to this decision.

Her grandma's piercingly blue eyes bore into Abby's. "The same man?" she testily inquired.

"He isn't available to marry," Abby said, brusquely answering her grandmother's unasked question.

"Then he is a married man, just like they've been whispering about you all these years!" She slapped the dish towel onto the table and sank down into the kitchen rocker. "Not one of the darn fools in this town is good enough for you, be they married or single." Out of nowhere, the handsome, smiling face of Dr. Townsend swam into her consciousness. "Of course," she said, sitting upright. "Now, why did it take me all these years to figure it out? Adam Townsend!"

With the pronouncement of his name, Abby burst into tears. Dropping to her knees, she buried her face in her grandmother's lap and wept for shame, for relief, for the sharing of her burden, and most of all because someone cared about her.

"His wife went home to Baltimore to get a divorce, and this time he promised to marry me. He gave me a ring." Abby fumbled with the chain around her neck, and when she pulled forth the impressive emerald-and-diamond ring, her grandmother's eyes widened.

"Mrs. Townsend didn't know she was pregnant when she left here, and now she's back, and pregnant. Anyway, she's had three miscarriages in the past, and she could again." She sat back on her heels looking up at her grandmother. "Couldn't she? Oh, Grandma, couldn't she? If she miscarries again, there will be nothing holding him to her, except his honor."

"Hush," Grandmother cautioned, "don't wish bad luck on another; it has a way of coming home to roost. Besides, people in Rockville don't get divorced. That preacher should have stayed in Rockville and married you. Never could figure out what that man had against healing the sick."

"Noah rejected God's gift," Abby wearily replied. "That's what drove him away. But it has always been Adam I've loved. Ever since I was a little girl, he's been the one, and, for as long as I can remember, I believed I would be his wife." Abby stood up. "I'll move away. I'll take Daisy with me and open up another hat shop somewhere far away, where no one knows me."

Grandmother Langley, rocking slowly, dolefully considered what kind of future her granddaughter would have. Pulling a handkerchief from her sleeve, she wiped her eyes.

"This time I am keeping my child," Abby said, regaining her confidence.

CHAPTER 81

September 1909

After the shameful branding of the Gypsy, the town seemed to withdraw into itself. Church attendance was on the rise, especially at the fundamentalist Old Church, and the most unlikely harbinger of bad luck had occurred: the Rockville Rockets were on a losing streak.

The popular, confident Orion had become a loner—alone within a crowd, that is. Orion tried to behave as usual, but it wasn't working, and no matter how hard he tried, he could not pitch a winning ball game—or forget Jennie Jeanne. The whole town knew Orion and Jennie Jeanne had broken up.

"They were far too serious for people their age," was the reason the Women's Thursday Social Guild of New Church, where Lottie was a member, put forth. Faces burned when repeating this excuse, inasmuch as everyone knew the real reason: the kissing incident that had taken place inside the ark and had left Jennie Jeanne Oberlander branded as "funny."

Jennie Jeanne and Susan Leann Leffler were not allowed to see each other. That was fine for Susan, but it left Jennie Jeanne without her best friend, or any friends, for that matter. Out of desperation, she became cunning, disappearing from the house, or yard, in broad daylight, and she became especially adept at vanishing after dark, when concealed by the camouflage of night.

"I didn't know what to do with the Oberlander girl," Rosie Kandel said apologetically to Reverend Bob, "so she's waiting in the living room."

"You did the right thing, Rosie. Keep supper warm; I believe I can smell apple pie."

"Apple dumplings," the housekeeper said, beaming.

Reverend Bob, pausing in the doorway before he entered the room, observed the downhearted girl. In the weeks since Jennie Jeanne's fall from grace, her happy elfin face had taken on a lean, hungry appearance, and her twinkling eyes had become sly and secretive. They blinked nervously now into Reverend Bob's concerned gaze.

"It isn't true, you know. I don't want to kiss girls." Jennie Jeanne's head shook uncontrollably as she drew closer to him, squinting up into his face. "I want you to tell Orion, Reverend Bob. He'll listen to you."

"I think Orion is trying to protect you."

"No. No. He won't talk to me," she said in a whisper. "He won't touch me. He won't look at me. He's heard the story they're spreading about me, and he hates me." She began to pinch and twist the skin on her forearm.

"Mrs. Kandel?" a nervous Reverend Bob called out. Rosie appeared at once. "I'm inviting Jennie Jeanne to have supper with us. Go with Mrs. Kandel, Jennie Jeanne, while I wash up."

A few minutes later, standing alone, Rosie looked at the reverend as he returned to the room. She said, "I only turned my back on her for a second, and she was gone, just like that."

Reverend Bob patted Mrs. Kandel's shoulder in complete understanding.

"I called Mr. Oberlander from my office and expressed to him that, in my opinion, Jennie Jeanne needs medical help."

"I think she knew you were calling her father," Rosie said. "That's why she skipped out. Oh, she's turned into a foxy one."

Jennie Jeanne walked west on Pine Street, cutting through the alley and past the blacksmith shop to the hitching rail. All the young Langley men's horses were tied there, including Orion's.

She hid in the shadows, achingly listening to the harmonious voices of the teenagers gathered on the steps of Parlett's Emporium.

Keeping to the shadows, she made her way to the ballpark and sat on a bench beneath a tree in Fountain Park. She saw her father drive by in his buggy and knew where he was headed; she had overheard the minister's conversation. She sat alone, waiting until the light from the gas lamps revealed the girls and boys who used to be her friends walking home in a group. They were laughing and calling out to one another. And, as the brothers, leading their horses, passed by the park, she herself called out to Orion.

"You don't have to talk to her, Rion," Aries said, offering his brother protection.

"I want to. You go on. I'll catch up with you later."

Orion tied his horse near the turnstile gate and entered the park. They conversed quietly for a minute by the fountain before moving into the seclusion of the stadium.

"Don't leave me, Riney. You're my true north. Without you, I'm lost." Her never-still fingers plucked at his shirt-front. "I did it for you," she explained. "You know—the kiss? I just wanted to please you. It was an experiment. I wanted to know how kissing me felt to you. I love you, Riney."

"Shhh, Jenny, don't say that! We can't say that to each other anymore," he said, whispering.

"Let's run away, Riney. Let's run away and get married. Then they can't separate us, ever." She clutched at his collar, trying to pull his head down to hers.

He had thought about the same thing but knew it still wouldn't be right. Her arms winding around his neck aroused old feelings, and he remembered with nauseated aversion that she was his half sister. He recalled his Sunday school teachings and knew that what he felt was an abomination unto the eyes of the Lord, and he jerked away from her. "Don't do that, Jennie Jeanne," he said, as she tried again to put her arms around him. "We can't feel this way about each other anymore. It's wrong!" He stood up.

"I don't love girls, honest I don't, Riney. I don't want to do things to them. I don't even know what things I'm supposed to do." She began to cry.

"It's not that, Jennie!" Orion said, grimacing in discomfort.

"Then tell me what it is!"

"It's not you. It's me. It's you *and* me. It's us, Jennie." Struggling with his emotions, Orion juggled the air with his hands in search of the right words. "It's us! We're all wrong for each other." He dropped his hands to his sides in a show of finality. "We can't ever be together again, Jennie, and I can't tell you why," he said, his voice breaking. "It's just the way it has to be."

Jennie Jeanne followed him to the turnstile gate. And when he rode away, her pleading voice trailed behind him.

Early the following morning, Dr. Townsend received a phone call from Mr. Oberlander. "Could you come over right away, Dr. Townsend? Ah, Jennie Jeanne's acting up." The banker sounded distraught.

Adam took Nurse Boggins with him, thinking she might be better at dealing with a hysterical young woman, but he was totally unprepared for the tragedy he found: a bed soaked with blood from self-inflicted wounds on Jennie Jeanne's wrists, neck, and arms, the partially coagulating cuts barely keeping her alive.

After treating and stabilizing his patient and reassuring the parents, Adam received an unconventional request from Mr. Oberlander.

"Doctor, have you heard the rumor about our daughter?"

Baffled, Adam looked to Nurse Boggins, who, averting her eyes from his and those of the parents, whispered the gossip to him.

Mr. Oberlander said, "While our little girl is sleeping, could you tell us..." He paused, trying to find the right words. "If she—well, if she is a real girl, and not what they say she is?" He spoke in a rush of embarrassment, inclining his head toward the town.

"Yes," Lottie said, pleading. "She spends hours in her room"—she pressed a handkerchief to her mouth, stifling a cry—"standing naked before a mirror, looking at herself. I've taken to locking her in her room for fear the household help might see her. More gossip," she added bitterly, wringing her hands in dismay.

Together the doctor and nurse removed the pillow from behind Jennie Jeanne's head and lay her flat on the bed, being especially careful of her bandaged arms. Her parents modestly retreated to a corner of the room, not wishing to be witness to the intimate intrusion upon the virginal body of their daughter.

Rolling the nightgown above her hips, revealing the smooth, taut stomach and youthful waist of the teenager, Adam gently separated Jennie Jeanne's legs, and with sympathetic gentleness parted the maturing labia and performed the requested examination.

When the exam was over, Nurse Boggins, after quickly pulling the girl's nightgown down and covering her with the white sheet monogrammed in blue embroidery with the girl's initials, was the first to make a statement. "Why, she's just as normal as any lady, and that includes you and me, Mrs. Oberlander."

The Oberlanders looked to the doctor. He finished washing his hands in the flowered porcelain bowl on the washstand before smiling broadly at them.

"That's right. You have nothing to worry about. Physically, she's as normal as they come," he said, drying his hands on the linen towel the nurse handed him. Adam shook hands with Mr. Oberlander and comforted Mrs. Oberlander with a hug.

The parents' noisy rejoicing disturbed the patient. Adam, returning to the bedside, placed his fingers alongside Jennie Jeanne's neck. She moaned, and a sigh fluttered from her lips in response to the intimate pressure of the doctor's hands on her throat.

CHAPTER 82

"SON, YOU'VE LOST YOUR SHOE." Joe Langley knelt on the hard-packed earth clutching a shoe to his chest. From the open barn door behind him, a lazily curling plume of smoke could be seen in the distance—a farmer burning off his field, with the lingering haze disappearing into the blue sky of autumn. He could faintly hear the chiming of a cowbell.

Andy entered the barn. "Pop, have you seen Orion?" He followed his father's gaze to the rafters in the center of the barn and to the gently moving body rotating in one direction, slowly reversing, then turning in the other.

Andy, mouth agape, stood staring upward, trying to grasp the magnitude of what he was seeing before exploding in a shout of anger. "You stupid kid!" he screamed, scooping up a handful of straw from the floor and uselessly throwing it at the lifeless form of his brother. "You stupid kid, how could you do such a stupid thing?" He kicked and stomped at the loose straw on the barn floor and, falling to his knees beside his father, rocked back and forth, sobbing. "No, Rion, not you! Oh God, no, not you, Riney."

"Bring him down, son, bring him down. Don't let his mother see him." Joe clasped the shoulder of his tormented son.

Andy's first thought was to ring the bell, but the old farm bell had been silenced, the rope put to another use. He ran to the barn door barking out the names of his brothers.

The morning of Orion's funeral, the twins Corvus and Cetus, with Percy not far behind, went to the family burial plot to examine, again, the frightening hole in the earth where their favorite brother would be placed.

From the house they could see what looked like a many-branched tree, the limbs stripped bare of their leaves, protruding from the grave. They raced to the site, belly flopping onto the excavated mound of earth, only to come face to face with an enormous buck. The great animal stood trapped in Orion's grave, its giant antlers extending beyond the unearthed hole. The ensnared beast, its frightened eyes darting about, was trying in vain to escape from the sounds of the excited hoots and yells and the ominous smell of danger.

The twins ran whooping all the way to the house. Grandma Mosley, sitting on the porch peeling potatoes, grabbed at them as they raced by, catching little Percy by the seat of his pants, but not for long.

"You wild little Indians, what's all the ruckus about?" she called after them. The boys tumbled into the kitchen and onto the floor, receiving warning stares from the Langley men eating breakfast at the big dining table.

"Dad, Dad!" Corvus said, wheezing, out of breath, and panting. "There's—there's a big old buck in Riney's grave." There was an instant of startled surprise, then a thudding and scraping of shoes on hardwood as the men sprang into action.

"Orion would have loved this," Leo said as the brothers worked to free the animal.

"It's like he's returned to us in the body of a deer," the poetic Aries said. The others, holding back tears, thought so, too.

"Bring me some red paint from the furniture shop," Joe said to the twins.

After the men dug and graded a path from the grave to several feet beyond the pit, and with prodding by the boys and pulling by a team of horses, the animal—with a big red X on each flank encircled with a ring of paint, meaning off-limits to hunters—was released to freedom. The twins would spend many boyhood hours searching for the paint-branded buck, but, like Orion, it was never to be seen again.

The funeral was private and held out of doors at River's Bend. Suicides were not permitted to be buried in the consecrated ground in the town cemetery.

"He was the best damn kid who ever lived" was what his father had to say about that. Orion was buried in the heart of the Langley cemetery surrounded by a grove of pine trees.

Although the funeral was announced as private, many nonfamily members were in attendance. They came out of respect for Joe and his family and the love they'd had for Orion, remaining a respectful distance from the family and the service. The baseball team was there as well, dressed in their uniforms.

The tall trees surrounding the plot lent a chapel-like reverence to the solemn occasion, and a northerly breeze gently sweeping over the mourners cooled the warm day. Standing on the steps of the veranda, where the family was seated, Reverend Bob Maynard offered up the eulogy. "Today, a much-beloved tree is missing from our familiar landscape, laid to rest in the prime of its life."

A dry, violent sob from the innermost recesses of Joe's soul tore from his throat. Rose, persevering through her strength and willing herself to silence, placed a calming hand over Joe's clenched ones.

"We are gathered here today, united in our sorrow, to honor the memory of Orion. For God so loved the world that He gave us His only begotten Son, and God so loved Joe and Rose that He gave them many sons, sons to love, sons to carry on, sons to stand by them in this their hour of need, sons to close ranks when a beloved brother and comrade falls. May Orion's memory be a gift of valor.

May it bring us succor, quiet our pain, and dwell in our hearts all the days of our lives.

"Many times in the past few days, I have been asked if Orion will enter the kingdom of heaven. Does God turn His back on His children? Does He bar us from the heavenly kingdom? No! No, I say to you, a thousand times no. He does not! The cold night of hopelessness fell swiftly and tragically upon our brother, and only in that black night of agony was his soul overcome with despair. Orion's only sin was the sin of despair.

"And to you, my brothers and sisters, whose spirits are broken from the sorrow of Orion's parting, Jesus is waiting to heal your own despair. Seek Him in enlightenment, and He will find you in your darkest hour. The glory of paradise that is promised by Jesus leads us to embrace His eternal light.

"Jesus is always present and waiting with open arms. He may condemn our deed, but He does not condemn our soul. To Him, we are all precious, and our sins are not the sum of us. Orion had accepted Jesus into his heart, and He has already healed and forgiven this wounded brother and taken him to His bosom. God has loaned us to this earth, and when our time is over, He calls us home. Home is where Orion is today. Home in paradise—still your good son, still the good brother, the good friend, the good and devout Christian. No. God will not turn His back on one of His own. Orion is as precious to Him as he is to us, and so, today, Orion is at home in the greater spirit of the universe."

While the brothers bore the casket, followed by family and friends, to the waiting earth, Abby, accompanied by Aries, playing his violin, sang "Oh Promise Me" ("that someday you and I will take our love together to some sky...") and remembered her favorite cousin and the many duets they had sung together. She thought of Ronnie, and Aunt Em, of her father, all of them gone, and of her fatherless baby yet to be born.

Her voice caught. *Someday my heart will surely break*, she thought.

The mourners turned away from the wound in the earth, now bandaged with flowers, to the house, where food was being served. In the living room, Leo and his fiancée, Eloise Saunders, playing piano, sang the popular heartfelt song that had been sung at President McKinley's funeral, "Beautiful Isle of Somewhere": "Somewhere the sun is shining, somewhere the songbirds dwell; Hush, then, thy sad repining, God lives, and all is well..."

Leo and Eloise were active members of New Church, her church, and belonged to the engaged and young married couples' circle. The town had forgiven Leo his straying, inasmuch as, when he had decided to marry, he had come to his senses and chosen a woman from town to be his betrothed: "a good Christian all-American girl."

"Leo certainly sowed his wild oats before he settled down," Perthy Prettyman whispered to Ethel White.

"Well, he's a Langley. What can you expect?" Ethel whispered back, darting a glance at Abby.

Nonfamily mourners soon departed after the burial, leaving the relatives to heal their sorrow by coping in familiar ways: the women in the kitchen serving up food, and the men relaxing on the veranda. Joe saddled up his horse and rode away, leaving a rift in the solidarity of the family, the twins running behind the horse and crying, "Dad, don't you leave us, too!" Rose, as usual, took care of everyone.

"There's more going on here than just that Oberlander girl's funny business," Grandma Langley said to her daughter-in-law as she watched Joe ride off.

"I know," Rose replied with a somewhat overly energetic replacing of a stove lid. "And when Joe feels it's time for me to know, he'll tell me." Just then, unexpected laughter coming from the porch alarmed her.

Sags, on leave from his ball club and home for the first time since Christmas, was dispensing healing in his own way by telling baseball stories about the team's experiences on the road. The women in the kitchen knew from the raucous bursts of hilarity following periods of enraptured silence that Sags was telling stories meant for men only.

"Where's the boys?" Rose asked, meaning the twins and Percy.

"They need the company of men today, Rose," Grandma Langley said, gently placing an arm around her daughter-in-law's shoulders and giving her a hug. "They won't understand the jokes, but they understand the need to be with their own."

During the burial, Abby's mother had surprised her daughter by joining her where the family group stood surrounding the grave; she waited beside her until it was time for the dirt to be shoveled back into the hollow space. Nita Langley knew her nephew had been as close to her daughter as a brother. And now, inside the house, she was sitting beside Abby on the long kitchen bench.

Is my mother trying to make amends? Abby wondered. *Well, when she hears of my present condition, it will be short-lived.* She could hear her now: "What will people think?"

Dr. Adam Townsend entered the kitchen. Removing his hat, he looked around the large room filled with women, charming them with his charismatic smile before moving among them with ease and self-assurance. He offered his condolences and inquired if he could be of service.

Abby sniffed into her handkerchief, which allowed her to cover her burning cheeks while she marveled anew at the effect Adam had on women. Even in their time of grief, the women still played the coquette in his presence.

THE ROCKVILLE HUB
September 17, 1909

Miss Jennie Jeanne Oberlander, daughter of Mr. and Mrs. Leon Oberlander, has departed our town for the state capital.

> Miss Oberlander will be attending music school, as well as receiving private voice lessons. She will be living with relatives in the capital city.
>
> Our good wishes go with her.

The week after the funeral, a sedated Jennie Jeanne, without knowledge of Orion's suicide or his body being laid to rest, was placed in a private sanitarium for the mentally disturbed in a town not far from the state capital. Nonetheless, gossip that Jennie Jeanne had been committed to the state lunatic asylum spread over the town. Now the word "crazy" was added to the vocabulary of the town's misconceptions about her. To the people of Rockville, "sanitarium" meant a crazy house for crazy people.

CHAPTER 83

THE NIGHT OF ORION'S FUNERAL, Adam made a house call on Abigail and Grandma, and later he and Abby sat alone in the parlor. "Are you all right?" he inquired, reaching out to her.

Abby pushed him away. "No, I am not all right! How dare you even ask me such a question? No, Adam! I am not all right!" Fury burned in her eyes, and her voice shook with rage. In her present circumstances, she felt clumsy, ugly, and forsaken. "And don't you dare call me your Eve," she said through clenched teeth.

Adam rose and spoke to her in a voice gone cold. "My father is coming from Canada for a visit. I think he may have a solution for us." He wanted to say more, to comfort her, but her hostility kept him at a distance. He left her in the parlor and, mounting his horse, rode off toward home, leaving her alone with her anger.

Sitting inside the gazebo and thinking about the pain he had caused to the woman he loved, Adam wept. He wept for Abby, and for Lillian, for Joe and Rose and their lost son, for his own lost child and his children to come, and, yes, for himself.

Abby had been brave up until Orion's suicide. Orion had been a friend when no one else was. Now the old feeling of abandonment and loss of joy was reclaiming her. She was incapable of making the decisions she knew had to be made. That night in bed, Abby found herself wishing for Noah. "I'm drowning again, Noah," she whispered into the black silence.

Adam and his father, both on horseback, rifles slung from their saddle holsters, rode across their property and into the forest. His father had grown older since Adam had last seen him: the handsome face thinner, the nose and cheekbones sharper. Adam felt a stab of remorse, knowing that someday he would be deprived of his father's presence.

"I guess if there's a place I can call home, it's Rockville," John Townsend said.

"It's always been home to me," Adam replied, "and even though I never really belonged to the town, deep down it belonged to me. I want my children, all of them," he said, smiling at his father, his eyes twinkling as he spoke, "to belong to the town and go to school here. Things in Rockville are improving, and in six years the school should be bigger and better."

"Then you better settle down to one woman," his father said. "I do not condone adultery. A man loses his capacity to love wholeheartedly when he dilutes his affections with infidelity. It inhibits his potential for contentment. It isn't too late for you to have a lifelong, meaningful relationship with your wife. What is Abby to you, anyway?" he said, looking directly at his son.

Adam grew painfully emotional, and when he answered, his voice was husky. "I don't breathe easy without her. It's as if the air has been sucked out of my lungs. If the Bible stories were true, sir, then Abby would have been made from my rib. If I've committed adultery, then it's with my wife, not with Abby. I feel calm and complete when I'm with her, which I've never felt with Lillian."

"Then God help you, son. Life loses its bliss when you spend it with a woman you're not totally committed to."

Adam, taking in a deep breath and sitting taller in the saddle, said, "Still, it was Lillian I chose for my mate. When I first met her and her father, I was blindsided by what prosperity can achieve. In spite of your wealth—which I'm sure is considerably more than Lillian's father ever dreamed of having—you never exploited yours, and at that period in my life and the life I envisioned for myself, I believed Lillian would be the perfect mate for me. I chose with my head, and not my heart. And it probably would have worked out if I hadn't learned that Abigail had borne my child."

His father said, "I blame myself for this tragedy and the part I knowingly played in it. When I delivered Abby's son, and he looked so shockingly like you when you were born, I think I knew, but I wanted my dream for you more than I wanted the truth, so I ignored what I suspected—and for that, son, I am eternally sorry. If I had acted on my suspicion that you might have been the father, you would've had your Abigail."

They rode on in silence, each man looking away from the other. It was some time before either one of them spoke.

"I'm being too hard on you, Adam," John Townsend said. "There is an equation of the male animal that we are ignoring here: the law of nature. Some conditions go beyond our emotions. It's the natural forces of human nature that dictate our conduct. If you strip us of the civilities of our modern society, you will find at our core the primeval force to reproduce. It stands to reason that it is stronger in some than in others, and that is the reason why the strongest of any species survives and propagates."

"I'm doing my best, Dad."

They laughed, regaining the easy companionship they had shared earlier in the day.

CHAPTER 84

October 1909

NOW THAT ABBY HAD MADE up her mind to leave Rockville, she felt energized, renewed. Dr. John Townsend had called on her, and she felt comfortable in meeting him as an equal, unashamed and unabashed. They discussed her living in Toronto in a house near him until the birth of her baby; after that, she could decide which path her life would take.

"I am not altogether satisfied that this is the right strategy," the doctor had said, "but at the present time, I think getting you out of town is of the utmost concern and must be done first. None of us want to lose another child. I will make it as pleasant for you in Canada as I possibly can," he promised her.

The doctor admired Abby's astuteness and her good looks, robust good health, and resolute independence; most of all he admired her ability to rise above adversity. If adversity is an invitation to opportunity, then she had accepted hers with courage and backbone. He was sorry that she, too, was not a daughter-in-law. He sighed. He had wanted a large family, a dynasty; now here was another Townsend without the Townsend name and Lillian already confined to bed rest.

While Abby waited for Judge Andrews to come into his office, she passed the time sitting on the window ledge and looking down on Main Street. Across the street, a crowd of men had gathered on the sidewalk next to the drugstore to watch a crew of workmen painting a large red-and-white sign on the west wall of the brick building advertising Coca-Cola. The tall figure of Dr. John Townsend was among them.

Farther down the street, a workman was attaching a discreet bronze plaque that read GENTLEMEN'S CLUB—MEMBERS ONLY next to the door of a private club on the first floor of the new commercial office building. A center hall separated the exclusive club from the jewelry store that occupied the other half of the ground-level space.

A four-faced clock on a ten-foot pole had been erected on the sidewalk to advertise the new jewelry store. The name, Dennison Jewelers, inscribed with a flourish of black-and-gold lettering, appeared on each clock face. Every Monday morning, Mr. Dennison, standing on a ladder, unlocked the glass cover and rewound and reset the new landmark clock. The store carried Elgin and

Hamilton pocket watches, along with a stock of fine jewelry for men and women. Homer Dennison had attended horology school and could make a timepiece, or any part of one.

All along Main Street, new buildings were going up; above her, Abby could hear pounding sounds coming from the addition of a third floor to the hotel, which was to be Mr. Parlett's spacious new ballroom.

As she continued to watch the people in the street below, Daisy came into view, presumably coming from the emporium, and upon crossing the street and reaching the door of the Bon Marché, she turned and waved meaningfully to someone.

Who? Abigail wondered. *I no longer know everyone in town,* she thought with surprise. She did, however, recognize Chance Collins, who still made her flesh crawl. He and Bobby Lee stood facing each other, a little apart from the group of men watching the painters. The two of them seemed to be in a disagreement over something.

Arriving at his office, the judge paused in the doorway to admire the charming scene presented to him: that of a beautiful woman in a large black hat against a window curtain of white lace. She held the drapery aside with a gloved hand so as not to obstruct her view.

The judge, coughing politely, interrupted his guest's observation. She turned toward him; the play of light and shadow on the perfection of her face was baffling to him. He was a circumspect and venerable man of the law, but still he felt something for this woman. With vivacious gallantry, he held a chair for her. In appreciation of her beauty and the pleasant aroma of roses emanating from her, he found himself quoting from a favorite Lord Byron poem: "'She walks in beauty, like the night of cloudless climes of starry skies; and all that's best of dark and bright meet in her aspect and her eyes...'"

Abby, both flattered and flustered, quickly proclaimed to the judge, "I'm leaving Rockville."

The judge looked confused, and for a moment wondered if it was the compliment he had just paid her by reciting poetry.

Aware of his confusion, Abby smiled kindly; a little bit flirtatiously, she said, "It's one of my favorite poems, too," then, taking a deep breath, she got down to business. "I wish to give to my friend and employee, Daisy Brown, half interest in the Bon Marché, making it a fifty-fifty partnership. Daisy is to remain here and operate the Rockville store, while I establish another business in a larger city—a city I have not as yet chosen," she added, smiling pleasantly to soften the rebuff of not disclosing her destination, or any further plans, to him.

"But, Miss Langley, you would be sorely missed in Rockville; your very presence would be sorely missed, and Rockville is growing!" he added, with fervor.

"Yes, it is," Abby replied. "The view from your window made me appreciate how fully it has grown. For myself, however, I feel the need for change, for new experiences, to grow and expand." She lowered her chin, her eyes dropping to her lap, and she immediately regretted her choice of words. Judiciously she rearranged the fur cape across her expanding abdomen.

The argument between Bobby Lee and Chance continued as the two left the scene of the sign painting and crossed the street to Ma's.

"I'd like to see him, Bobby, just one little peek. Hell, he is my kid, you know. Does he look like me?"

This startled Bobby Lee. He and Amy had lied about the rightful father for so long that he had almost forgotten it was Chance who had fathered her baby and not the Gypsy. "You can't see her, Chance," a perturbed Bobby Lee answered. "The shock of seeing you might sour her milk."

"Is she nursing him?"

"Of course she's nursing him. Amy's a good little mother."

Dr. John Townsend was watching the painters, but his mind was on his daughter-in-law. He never wanted Lillian to know his duplicity in the cover-up of his son having a child—a second out-of-wedlock child, the mother of whom happened to be the town beauty. *How am I going to accomplish this?* he wondered. He cast the situation from his mind. *Plenty of time for that later.* He went back to watching the progress of painting the Coca-Cola sign.

Afterward, in the fan-cooled drugstore, the doctor tried a glass of the new beverage. The first cold sip of the cola brought him up short. He immediately liked the strong, bold, satisfying taste of the drink. He later reported to his son that he was going to look into investing in the soda-fountain drink.

"In my opinion," he prognosticated to Adam, "it will be a bigger seller than Survivall."

CHAPTER 85

Grandma Langley, with her usual impatience for slowness, did not wait for Horace Brown to assist her in stepping down from the carriage and, missing the stepping stone in front of Parlett's Emporium, promptly fell to the street. With a cry of anguish, she reached for her leg, wedged at an awkward angle at the base of the stepping stone. Horace ran across the street to get Abby as shoppers and clerks coming from the stores gathered around the injured woman.

"Oh, I'm just a clumsy old woman," Grandma said in exasperation. "Too clumsy to stay upright."

"Someone telephone the doctor," said the postmaster.

"I have already," said Pierre Parlett.

Abby ran across the street from the Bon Marché and, dropping to the ground, placed her grandmother's head in her lap but was too distraught to speak.

"You'll get your dress dirty," Grandma scolded her, giving herself an excuse to cry.

The concerned gathering could see the doctor on horseback racing toward them. Upon reaching the group, the doctor threw the reins to Horace before alighting. After examining the elderly woman's leg through the many layers of clothing she was wearing, Adam said, "I'm afraid you have a broken leg, Mrs. Langley." He turned to Horace. "Would you go to the livery stable and tell them to bring us a wagon, one in which we can lay Grandma down?"

Mrs. Parlett brought blankets and pillows from the hotel, and the men lifted Grandma onto a makeshift stretcher and into the bed of the wagon and rode along to the clinic to help carry her inside. The white-capped, stiff-aproned Nurse Boggins awaited them at the door. Grandma, released from pain by a narcotic, lay in a bed in one of the clinic's rooms, her broken leg in a cast and the nurse in attendance.

"I'll drive you home, Abby," Adam said. "Grandma will be out for the night, and you need your rest. You've had quite a shock."

Once in the carriage, they were free to talk. "Poor Grandma; I can't leave her now!"

"Yes, you can. You can wait until we know how this will affect her, then we'll get you out of town. I want you safe, sweetheart. I don't want them demeaning you, or my child," he said, his voice tense. "I want both of you safe from the gossip, and from the exclusion that will follow." He placed an arm around her, drawing her nearer to him.

Gratefully, she leaned her head on his shoulder, and it reminded her of the night she had given Ronnie away: the Nelsons' tender comforting of each other and her epiphany as she watched the couple—an insight into what her little boy's future would hold for him and how his life, and hers, had changed forever.

If only there had been someone there for me, she wondered. *Will this time be any different?* She raised her head and peered up at Adam. *What do I want from him? What can I expect from him?* And, like the epiphany of that terrible night, she knew she had only herself to decide the path her life would take.

With Grandma released from the clinic and ensconced in the downstairs bedroom, she at last had a legitimate excuse to stay home from the Bon Marché.

"I can't leave you now, Grandma," Abby told her.

"You mean you can't leave *him*, and he's not going to leave his wife," was Grandma's curt reply. Abby had not purged her mind of the wicked thoughts she sometimes had of Lillian having a miscarriage, and she quickly said a little prayer for her.

Everyone knew she was leaving town and moving away, so when friends and neighbors made a sick call on Grandma, she could forgo entertaining them by leaving Grandma in the hands of old friends, with the excuse that she had packing to do.

Chance delivered blind Mrs. Collins to the house for a visit with Grandma. His clay-cold eyes slid over her when she opened the door to them, leaving her with goose bumps.

Frieda also came to call on Grandma, using the kitchen door instead of the front one, which gave Abby the chance to explain to her friend why she had been ignoring her. Taking Frieda's hand, she placed it on her rounded stomach, sharing with her that she was with child; and, touching fingers to lips, she indicated it was a secret. Frieda's round birdlike eyes darted away, only to return, fast as hummingbird wings, to peek wide eyed again at Abby's swelling abdomen.

After each new visitor arrived and duly reported the gossip of the town to Grandma, she, in turn, told them about the coming marriage of Leo and Eloise and the progress of the house being built for the newlyweds on the now-extended Stony Creek Road. She would tell them of Leo's office that was being readied into a bedroom for her to move into at Joe and Rose's house on River's Bend.

After gossip and refreshments, and after the wayfarer sun was on its infallible march toward the mountain, the talk would slow, the creaking of rockers cease, and the elderly visitors and the visited would nod off, sometimes one or two of them snoring. Abby could relax at the kitchen window and look to the Rock House and the Townsend mansion, both celestially golden in the sun of a late-October day, and think about her future.

CHAPTER 86

Leaning on his elbows on the stone balustrade of the second-floor balcony, Adam looked out on the early-winter darkness: only five o'clock, and the streetlights were already aglow. Snow was piled high around lampposts and shoveled from sidewalks onto the streets. Two strings of colored lights crisscrossed Main Street in the downtown business section, one red and one green, twinkling cheerfully through the falling snow.

Celebrants who were observing the holiday by attending private parties or the gala at Parlett's new Dance Emporium (added to the hotel during the summer), or just out for a ride, would have to travel by sleigh on this New Year's Eve. The coming year of 1910 would see him the father of two children: Abby's baby, due early in the year, and Lillian's in March. His plans for New Year's Eve were to join his wife for a quiet supper. He trusted she would feel up to joining him in a champagne toast at midnight to welcome in the new year. Adam hadn't liked the pallor of Lillian's skin when he'd seen her earlier;

her heartbeat was fine, and the baby's pulse was slow as usual. The few movements he had felt from the child during its gestation period were always languid, not nearly vigorous enough for a seven-month-old fetus—and what a long seven months they had been.

A tap on the bedroom door aroused him, and when he called out "Come in," Nurse Boggins entered. She was got up for a New Year's Eve party, the excitement of it making her almost pretty. She wore a gold clip in her hair, of a crescent moon with little jeweled stars dangling from it. This was a stylish accessory for the holiday season; anything related to Halley's comet, due in May, was popular this year. The nurse was spending the evening at Frieda's. Frieda and the two unattached schoolteachers who boarded with her had planned a little festivity for earlier in the evening. Close to midnight, they intended to leave Frieda's home and join others gathered on the street in front of the hotel. Partygoers, whether attending the celebration in Parlett's new ballroom, dancing in the street, or crowding onto the balcony and throwing confetti and paper ribbons into the crowd gathered below, would all join together at the stroke of midnight in the singing of "Auld Lang Syne."

"Now, don't you women get rowdy and make me have to bail you out of jail," Adam said, teasing her. He embraced Boggins, kissing each cheek. Holding her hands, he spread her arms wide so he could get a better look at her. "Happy new year, Althea," he said, taking her in his arms. His kindhearted embrace was too much for

Boggins, and she couldn't answer him. Tears sprang to her eyes, and she blindly left the room, unable to wish him a happy new year in return.

Bruce Sorensen, a middle-aged farmer who had given up farming to take over Meiko Toma's duties, drove Althea downtown and would be there to pick her up sometime after midnight.

After Boggins's departure, Adam returned to the balcony and to the snowy view of the town. Rockville was certainly a different place compared with when he was a boy, he reflected. Back then, Old Church had put a damper on everything. But the town was growing up, literally squeezing the old-timers and their old-time "it was good for my father, and it's good enough for me" brand of religion out of the running of the town. And none too soon. He wanted to call Abby and wish her a happy new year, and although he had a private telephone line, he could never be sure if Marjorie, the telephone operator, might be listening in.

Thinking of Abby filled him with pleasure. She was the perfect picture of an expectant mother. For the rest of her time in Rockville, however, she would have to play the role of a woman remaining at home to care for an ailing grandmother. Grandma was mostly recovered but for an arthritic leg that required the use of a cane. Adam wondered again how to save Abby and his child from the contempt that would surely come if she were to remain in Rockville.

The town had forgiven her the out-of-wedlock child from years before, but would they forgive her a second one? *And the child, my child, what will he be, another bastard without his father's name? I don't want to just be in Abby's life. I want to be her life. Somehow I have to get her out of town.* She would have to go to his father in Canada, as he and Abby and his father had planned to do before her grandmother's accident.

On New Year's Day, the snow was still coming down in earnest, keeping most well-wishers at home. Marjorie phoned the doctor, relaying a message to him that he was needed at the Owenses' farm. "There's been some kind of an accident," she informed him.

"Do you need anything, Marjorie?" Adam inquired. She had been at the telephone office for twenty-four hours, and although there was a cot and a stove in the tiny room, he knew she could be in need of assistance.

"No, thanks, Dr. Townsend, I'm fine. Ma's is open, and John's been over here to look in on me. He brought a bucket of coal, and Mrs. Parlett sent a basket of food. You be careful, now, driving out to the Owenses' farm."

Adam left instructions with Bruce Sorensen to watch Mrs. Townsend's bedroom window for a white flag, which would be an indication that he was needed at the house. Ordinarily the flag was used to signal Adam not to take his horse to the stable and that another patient awaited him. Adam set off in the cutter with the big bay hitched to it, first making a quick stop to check in on Abby and Grandma. On parting, he held Abby wrapped in his arms for a long time, getting as close to her as possible, which was difficult to do, given her protruding abdomen. Kissing her tenderly, he wished her a happy new year, and they laughed at each other when the baby reacted with a good healthy kick.

"Whoa, a football player!" Adam said with pride, grinning down into her face. These days they didn't speak of love. For the time being, speaking of love didn't seem a decently proper thing to do. She saw him to the kitchen door and out onto the stoop. She didn't want him to leave; her arm trailed down his coat sleeve, and their fingers entwined. He kissed her cheek.

Abby watched from the living room window until the gray day swallowed Adam, horse, and sleigh from sight, and she tried not to think about what would happen to her and her child. "'Don't open that kettle of fish until it smells,'" she said aloud, quoting Aunt Em. How very, very much she missed her.

Adam returned home after dark and related to the waiting Lillian and Nurse Boggins the catastrophe at the Owenses' farm. Melburn Owens's horse had slipped on ice hidden by a cover of snow, and both man and horse had broken a leg. "I had to shoot him—the horse, not the patient." The nurse laughed, and Lillian managed a faint smile at his attempt to entertain them. Lillian's overly bright, questioning eyes followed Adam's every movement about the room. "Will you please see if you can round up something for me to eat, and a drink?" he said to Nurse Boggins.

He helped Lillian to a sitting position and began massaging her back. "Do you feel at all queasy?" he asked.

"No," she said, rolling her head and purring with the calming relief that came with the self-confidence she felt in Adam's surgeon's hands.

"Good," he said, "then I'll dine in here with you."

Lillian's pains subsided for a week then began in earnest early on the morning of the seventh of January and soon ceased altogether. At noontime, Adam was called out to attend a sick baby; he left instructions with Althea not to leave Lillian alone.

Nurse Boggins sat in a rocking chair at Lillian's bedside crocheting a pink-and-blue-patterned baby coverlet. As the crotchet needles crossed and clicked and jabbed, she observed her patient. *She's a fidgety one,* the nurse decided, not so cool as a cucumber now. Two spots of color burned high on Lillian's cheeks. When the nurse gave her a glass of water to sip, Lillian's hands were hot to the touch. She was as restless as a defiant child confined to its bed.

"What time is it? Can you see the doctor? Is he on his way home? I need a drink. I can't get enough to drink. Is the baby all right? Check its pulse again. Read to me."

Not until the following morning did the pains begin again, hard and fast, and not building steadily or in a timely manner as they should. Lillian's face was drawn, and an alarming look of panic became visible in her eyes. When they moved her into the clinic, she became plainly terrified.

"Don't cut me, Adam. Promise you won't cut me!" Lillian said, panting while trying to raise herself from the table. "I don't want to be cut open. Promise me!" she pleaded. "I didn't know it would hurt so much. I'm going to die. I know I'm going to die." She took turns biting her lips and screaming, her face red and contorted. "I don't want a baby. I really don't. I don't care what happens to it. Just don't cut me. I want my father."

"Lillian, sweetheart, you're doing just fine, and you're not going to die. It'll be over soon." But it was not over soon. Through the long, weary evening, she rested, sleeping fitfully, then the contractions began anew. Adam encouraged his wife to push, rest, and push again. "Hard, Lillian, bear down hard. Let's get that baby out of there." Nurse Boggins was taking the fetal heartbeat, and fright was building inside her. Shaking her head and looking into Adam's eyes, she whispered, "Thirty."

The weakened placenta, already detached from its wall, was aborting. But still the baby would not deliver.

"Lillian, I have to take the baby. I'll put you out, and you won't feel a thing."

"No! No!" she screamed, wide eyed. "You promised!"

Adam climbed onto the table beside her and, kneeling, placed his knees to one side of her unwieldy body; with both hands, he pushed down hard on her abdomen, just below her rib cage. "Spread her legs!" he shouted to the nurse. An alarming amount of blood gushed forth, covering Lillian's thighs and staining the padding beneath her like violently spilled wine.

Lillian's wail was long and shrill, like a train approaching a tunnel, with the whistle terminating precisely upon its entrance. And that was Lillian's experience: of being brutally pushed into a dark tunnel where she couldn't breathe. "Let me go. Let me go!" she begged. "Get me out of here. It's caving in on me!"

The baby shot out. There was no other explanation; one second it wasn't there, and the next second it was, hopelessly entangled in its own lifeline. The room turned as quiet as the stillborn's silence. The child, without a heartbeat, was a dark, smoky blue. The umbilical cord had wrapped around the baby's head, crossed over its face and sealed off its eyes, and twisted tightly around the tiny infant neck. Nurse Boggins attended to the baby while Adam worked over his wife. With the appearance of the afterbirth, the loss of blood stopped, and a heavily sedated Lillian was returned to her bed. She remembered nothing.

CHAPTER 87

January 1910

Two days later, Adam stood on the same balcony where he had stood on New Year's Eve, again watching the falling snow. There must have been four feet by now, he reckoned. He was grabbing a break from his wife's bedside vigil, where he and Althea were taking turns sitting with the heavily sedated Lillian. Behind him in the frigid bedroom lay his son, a diminutive, perfectly formed three-pound baby boy wrapped in the pink-and-blue coverlet Nurse Boggins had made for him. The infant lay on a container containing a block of ice covered over with oilcloth and blankets, waiting for a casket and the frozen, unyielding earth to become ready to accept his tiny remains.

He heard a tapping on the door leading to the balcony, and Miss Boggins appeared in the doorway.

"Dr. Townsend, there's a call from Daisy Brown. I told her you weren't taking calls, but she said to tell you Abigail Langley is not feeling well."

Adam, listening to Daisy's report on Abby's condition, was concerned with the timing of her contractions. "Get her ready, Daisy. I'll come for her. It's necessary that I remain at the clinic, so I'm bringing her back here."

He gave no explanation as to why he had to remain at the clinic, nor did he recount the tragedy that had taken place there two nights before.

Bruce Sorensen, who was waiting beneath the portico for them, helped to lift Abby from the sleigh before driving it away.

A crosscurrent of air tugged at Abby's loose hair, tumbling it around her head, and the bright lights in the ceiling of the veranda caught her in an aura of splendor, turning the dark-auburn hair a blazing red and making her naturally beautiful skin radiant.

At the door to the office, she was gripped with a contraction that had her bending over; she clutched Adam's hands with both her mittened ones while he steadied her. When it passed, she laughed breathlessly. "Oh my," she said.

The shock of a pregnant Abigail Langley entering the confines of the clinic was etched on Nurse Boggins's face. Her jaw dropped, her mouth fell open, and she was, without a doubt, speechless. Abby tensed. Her eyes never wavered from the nurse's, for she clearly expected the nurse to challenge her right to be there. Although Dr. Townsend was exhibiting an ethical manner toward his patient, the nurse was openly scowling disapproval at the familiarity displayed between the two of them.

Sniffing through her nose in short snorts, mouth turned down and jaws clenched, Nurse Boggins recited to herself, "Salt rubbed into wounds. Dirt kicked in the face." She punched the pillows on the bed she was preparing for Abby in the clinic bedroom. "I wasn't born yesterday." Punch. "I can add two and two." Punch. Punch.

She loathed the very ripeness of Abigail Langley—the swollen abdomen, the silken breasts glistening with perspiration—and she deeply resented Abby's seemingly earthy enjoyment of the very act of childbearing. But, most of all, she found fault with the woman's brazen lack of shame. She seethed inwardly at the deep attachment the doctor was showing toward the hussy. The way he stroked her long thighs and slender ankles, massaged her feet, and caressed her stomach when he felt for fetal movements, while his own legitimate wee one lay alone in the cold, silent room above them. Oh, the sin of it!

Throughout the long night, as a respite, and to ease Abby's contractions and back pain, Adam helped her from the bed and walked with her around the room and out into the marble foyer. During the times when Nurse Boggins checked on Mrs. Townsend, mental images of what the two of them were up to while she was not present became burned into the nurse's mind like lye on silk.

Shortly after midnight, and a wearying pushing session, Adam covered Abby's abdomen and with one hand reached beneath the sheet to feel into the birth canal and announced that he could feel the baby's head. Soon after, Abby screamed, desperately trying to sit up on the clinic table. "Adam, I'm sorry, but I really need to go to the bathroom."

"Sweetheart, that's the nicest thing you've said to me all night. It's the baby coming down."

With the urgency of the need to push, she did so with all her strength, Adam coaxing and cheering her on: "Atta girl! Good girl!"

The baby's head emerged, displaying a cap of black hair; two shoulders, one then the other; torso, legs, and feet, followed by the umbilical cord; and finally the whole baby—a boy. Adam separated child from mother and, lifting his son high by his ankles, gave him a smart slap on his blessedly pink bottom and was rewarded with an angry squalling.

The nurse whisked the baby away, and Adam administered a deep breath of ether to Abby.

"What does he look like?" she asked.

"Handsome," he answered.

"Like his father," she giddily replied.

Adam lovingly washed and cared for Abby as he would a child. He professionally stripped the soiled covers and pads from the bed and replaced them with clean ones. After washing his face and hands, he leaned over the bed and gently massaged the uterine mass just under Abby's navel, passing his thumbs over the stretched skin while his fingers kneaded her abdomen. "This will have you back in shape in no time at all."

Nurse Boggins came into the room and, observing the ritual between doctor and patient, remarked, "I'll bring the baby in for you to nurse. He won't have the knack of it yet, but it will be good for him. And," she emphasized sourly, her Irish brogue slipping out, "nursing will stimulate your contractions better than massaging, any time." That said, she flipped her head toward the doctor.

The nurse left the clinic, and Adam carried Abby to the lying-in room, where he tucked her into bed and kissed her cheek. "Get some rest, sweetheart. You've earned it."

She smiled smugly, like a schoolgirl who's just won a coveted prize.

He administered another whiff of ether to her before leaving to check on his newest patient—his stillborn child, and his still-sedated wife—after which he went to the library for rest and a brandy.

Adam had attended parturitions with Aunt Em, not because he'd wanted to, but because his father had insisted upon it. "You'll practice medicine in a civilized place," his father had told him, "where most births will be in hospitals, but you'll need to know the joys and pitfalls of obstetrics, and there's no better teacher than Emma."

What Adam was recalling now was the coming together of loved ones who were present at home lay-ins: mothers and grandmothers, aunts and married sisters. It was a happy time, a communion of sisterhood, after which came a two-week period with the mother and baby confined to bed rest and cared for by relatives and neighbors. He normally encouraged the attendance of relatives for his childbearing mothers. The two women under his roof tonight, however, were alone. In the room next to Abby's, her baby slept, and in the room above, a child slept the eternal sleep.

Nurse Boggins, attending to Mrs. Townsend in the upstairs bedroom, adjusted the bedclothes and took the pulse of her patient. Lillian struggled to open her eyes.

"Baby cry?"

"No, dear. No. A baby did not cry. Hush now, hush," she said soothingly, stroking Lillian's forehead. The nurse settled into the large rocking chair by Lillian's bed and fell into a deep sleep of overwhelming exhaustion. The house grew quiet, and for a while everyone in it slumbered.

Adam, making the early-morning rounds of the patients in his keep, quietly entered Abby's room. The sweet hypnotic smell of ether still clung to the air. Adam adjusted the transom and welcomed the invigorating sting of fresh air into the room.

Abby was curled into the sheets, fully awake and smiling. She made a request for him to sit down by moving to the center of the bed and tossing back the covers.

The nearly naked sensuousness of the woman he loved and cared about so deeply stirred his senses. Her hair covered her white shoulders, and her lovely breasts were swollen to magnificence.

Supporting herself on one elbow, she leaned forward; holding a breast in her hand, she said, "They ache. I need to nurse my baby."

"Your baby's sleeping, and you need to rest," he said, his voice grave.

Mother Eve, in an age-old gesture, her hand cupping a tantalizing breast, had proffered the apple. Adam, groaning, sank onto the bed and, pushing back her hair, buried his head in her shoulder. "My Eve, my wonderful, beautiful Eve." He kissed her lips with a fierce tenderness before reverently carrying the full breast to his love-parched mouth, and when, with his lips and tongue, he drew her nipple into his mouth, she gasped, making little crying sounds.

Her breath was hot on his cheek as he held her in his arms.

Lillian awoke at some point during the early morning. In the dim light, she could just make out Nurse Boggins asleep in the rocker, her head resting on one shoulder, legs spread apart; her feet, removed from her shoes, were turned outward; her stiff white cap of authority, rakishly tilted, masked one eye. Gazing at her, Lillian was trying to recall something as ephemeral as specters seen through smoke.

Mirages crowded Lillian's memory, illusive as fading dreams. Deeper and darker, hidden from all light, she sensed an apocalyptic nightmare of pure madness. She ran her hands across the breadth of her abdomen, back and forth from hipbone to hipbone. Laboriously raising her head, she beheld the flatness of her stomach. The baby? She struggled to a sitting position. *Where is my baby?*

CHAPTER 88

THE SCREAM TORE THROUGH THE dark, penetrated skin and pierced bones, stunned the brain, echoed through empty rooms, and cooled the blood. His mouth froze on paralyzed breast, startled seed arrowed into bedclothes, and benumbed legs found floorboards.

"Stay here," Adam said.

Abby grabbed at the sheet, hiding her nakedness.

"Bring me my baby," she cried.

"Just stay here!" he commanded.

With his analytical mind in control, Adam stoically moved up the clinic's staircase to the bedrooms above, and the sound of terror.

Lillian stood in the cold room staring down at the diminutive blue baby she had uncovered, vulnerable in its size and quietness, desperately trying to understand the meaning of it.

Gently taking her shoulders, Adam turned her around. Upon seeing her glazed eyes and slack mouth, he was immediately moved into lifesaving action. Lifting her, he brutally kicked at the partially closed door, slamming it into the wall, and carried Lillian back to her bed while shouting orders to Nurse Boggins. In the bedroom he jerked the pillows from the head of the bed and threw them to the foot.

"Get her legs up." All the time, he talked to his wife and rubbed her cold, clammy hands. "Stay with me, Lillian. Don't leave me." Her eyes rolled back in her head, and her faint pulse grew fainter.

The nurse covered the woman with a quilt, dampened a cloth with spirits of ammonia, and waved it beneath her nose.

"Talk to me, Lillian. Talk to me," he ordered. "What's my name? Who am I?" Her eyes couldn't stay focused on him. "Don't leave me, Lillian." Adam clutched her jaw, forcing her to attention. "Look at me, Lillian. Lillian! Listen to me, Lillian. Listen—to—me! There were two babies, Lillian. Twins, and one baby is still alive." Gently he shook her shoulders. "Do you hear me, Lillian? There were two babies. One baby—is—alive. Your baby is alive."

From deep within their sockets, her eyes focused on him.

"Listen to me, Lillian: you have a baby boy. I'll show you. I'll bring the baby to you." Panic showed on her face. "It's a live baby, Lillian, a real live baby," he said with growing intensity. "Keep talking to her," he told the nurse, flinging the words over his shoulder as he strode from the room.

Abby listened to the sound of running footsteps down the length of the long upstairs hall, heard them clatter down the steps to the clinic. She heard a shuffling sound in the room next to the one she was in, followed by a series of muffled steps fading away.

Leaving her bed, she stealthily opened the door connecting her room to an adjoining one. She entered the room and saw an empty bassinet. Placing her hand on the padding in the baby bed, she could feel warmth coming from it and knew someone had taken the baby.

Adam stood by Lillian's bedside holding his child. She looked up at him with enlivened eyes. Nurse Boggins scrambled to recover the pillows that had been flung to the foot of the bed and helped Lillian to a sitting position secured with the pillows. Adam uncovered the newborn baby and laid it in his wife's lap; immediately its arms shot out, and it began an angry wailing.

Lillian looked down at the squirming infant dressed in a fine white muslin gown as if she weren't sure what it was she held.

Remaining in the shadows and groping the wall for support, Abby climbed the hall stairs to the second floor. The current of cold air attacking her body through her flimsy nightgown was coming from a wide-open door. Cautiously approaching the door, she paused, looking around before stepping inside the balconied bedroom.

In the dim light from the only lamp burning in the darkened room, she saw what looked like an altar. Attracted to the pink-and-blue cover draping the stand, she drew nearer and gasped in horror at the sight of an obviously dead baby. She clenched her arms across her stomach and staggered backward as if from a blow; then she forced herself to creep forward again. *This dead little thing can't be mine!* She peered down at it. The blue baby, too tiny for clothes, lay naked in a fetal position. *Is it mine? I saw my baby alive. I heard him cry.* Trembling with fear and misgivings, she dropped the coverlet over it and left the room.

Still supporting herself by touching the wall with one hand, Abby made her way down the long hall to a partially opened door with light streaming from it. She peeked into the elegantly furnished bedroom and saw Lillian sitting upright in the massive bed, exposing an inadequate breast to a crying child. The baby's hungry cries brought painful constrictions to Abby's breasts and breath-stopping contractions to her womb.

Adam was standing near the bed rubbing at the back of his neck, watching the nurse as she assisted Lillian in the nursing process. Boggins, glancing toward the door, saw Abby shrink into the shadows, and with her eyes she signaled Abby's presence to Adam by darting her head toward the hall door.

Abby, rushing ahead of him, was there to confront Adam as he entered the balconied bedroom at the front end of the hall. "Don't you lie to me, Adam, don't you dare lie to me. That poor dead thing is not my baby," she said, pointing toward the pink-and-blue-covered basket.

Adam looked down on the child no one wanted but him. *My son.* Dark little brows furrowed his forehead;

black silken hair hugged his scalp. Tiny nails on tiny, perfectly formed fingers and toes forever stilled. He wanted to comfort him, to warm him, hold him, breathe life into him. He wanted to weep, to mourn, to cry out his pain and his loss. He rearranged the pink-and-blue cover over the child, covering his face and shielding him from the world. *Will I be able to remember all of what has happened this night and put it clearly into perspective?*

Abby crossed the room and stood facing the cold fireplace. "Did the cock crow three times, Adam?" She turned to him, eyes blazing. "Flesh answers flesh, Adam. Blood calls to blood, Adam."

He crossed the room to her. Crying hysterically, she pounced on him, pounding on his chest and slapping at his face. "That child is not my flesh, or my blood. Why are you doing this to me? What am I, Adam, a walking orphanage, a brood mare for any woman in Rockville who can't make a baby of her own? I want my baby, Adam. My baby! Don't you try to pawn another woman's dead baby off on me, you Judas." She spat at his shirt-front. "You never wanted me. You only want what I can give you—what you can take from me!" she said, slapping at him again.

"Abby, please." He jerked her around, clasping her arms behind her back and pressing her against him. Still she kicked at his shins and jabbed at his ribs with her elbows.

"You Judas!"

"Good God, you're hemorrhaging!"

Adam carried a fighting Abby in a bloodstained gown down the stairs and into the clinic. He laid her on the examining table, but she immediately slipped to her feet in an attempt to escape. With his body he pinned her to the table, holding her there with his hip while he reached across to the oak medicine cabinet and clumsily prepared a needle as she continued to beat on his back. In one swift movement, he spun her around and, bending her over the table, deftly injected the needle into her posterior.

All willpower left her, and she crumpled to the floor, clutching her arms around his knees and crying. "You never choose me, Adam. You never choose me."

He sat on the edge of the bed where a drug-induced Abby slept, holding one of her hands and gazing at her beautiful face, calm in its dreamless state. The woman he was indelibly linked to, his childhood love, his grown-man love, as much a part of him as his own breath, his own flesh—and yet, because of him, two innocent children had been lost to her forever.

After taking her pulse and kissing her forehead, he went into the library, poured brandy into a snifter glass, and sat down before the fireplace in his big leather chair. The bottle handily within reach, he sipped and meditated upon his actions of that night.

Who owns a child? Who is truly the proprietor of a child: The man, the woman, the womb, the seed? Who can lay claim to him? Man or woman? Who is the rightful owner: The sower of the seed, or the cultivator of the fruit? And, when born, to whom does the nameless entity, free of its lifeline, belong to? Which parent, when not legally united, can lay claim to a child? To whom does the fruit belong? If I chose the garden, and, when my seed matures, can I not take up that which I put down and claim it as my own? Without man, woman is naught, only fallow ground—waiting. Who owns the fruit? Mother? Father? The sower of the seed, or the caretaker of the seed?

Was man meant to love one woman, live with one woman, be loyal to one woman, and plant his seed in one woman? And, if he chooses not the mother, is he not to have a say in his child's life? Who raises him? How is he raised? Who decides his schooling, his religion? Who instills in a male child the value of self, his sense of importance? Will he have value and self-esteem as the son of an unwed mother?

A daughter bakes a cherry pie. A son builds a cathedral, sets sail to unknown continents, conquers new worlds. Woman weeps in the night: the sheep, the martyr, and, yes, the mother of kings. She is the past, the constant. But a son—a son is the future. King of kings. Man among men. He is the seeker, the doer, the wayfarer, the preserver and the plunderer, the changer and the changing. He is the now and the tomorrow.

Can the planter of the seed claim possession of the fruit? How would our biblical fathers have answered the question of who owned the Christ child—God—or Mary?

"Or the philanderer?" Adam said aloud, flinging with savage contempt his brandy glass into the dying fire. A kaleidoscope of fireflies burst from the splashes of alcohol and shards of exploding glass fell on the dying embers, dazzling briefly before disappearing.

Abby awoke in a hospital bed in the clinic, everything around her white, sterile, and impersonal. She saw the door open a crack, but no one entered. Soon afterward Adam came into the room and sat down on the bed beside her.

"What have you done?" she asked, looking at him through pain-seared eyes. He took her hands in his, his repentant tears falling onto the emptiness of hers. "Oh, Adam," she said with a weary sigh. "The deed is done; don't look back." She touched his hair, her hand gliding across its smooth surface. He would always move her. "Don't cry over spilt milk," she said, her voice wavering. "We're both to blame, and I'm too tired to fight you anymore."

Taking a deep breath and clearing his throat, Adam stood, all business. "Miss Johnson was here soliciting hospital news for the paper," he said. "Althea told her that Mrs. Townsend had borne twin boys, only one of whom survived. And it will be reported in the paper that Miss Abigail Langley was operated on for an emergency appendectomy in the hospital clinic. That's why we moved you in here—on the chance someone might pay you a call."

"I doubt anyone would do that," she said wryly. "Daisy, maybe, but she knows why I'm here."

"You're forgetting that we live in Rockville," Adam reminded her.

"Oh. Yes," she said, emitting a long sigh.

"As your doctor, I want you to remain here for a few days, then I'll take you home."

"I want to go home now, Adam."

"I can't allow you to move. Having a baby is a serious business, and you've lost a lot of blood, and it won't look right. You've supposedly had a complicated operation, and in reality, you are still in a fragile way."

"Adam, as long as I am in this house, I will never get better. I want my grandmother." Her voice began to crack. "And I will leave here on my own."

Adam drove her home and, over her objections, carried her into the house and into the downstairs bedroom Grandma had prepared for her. Grandma did not ask questions. She had read the account in the newspaper, and for now that explanation would suffice.

"She needs absolute bed rest, Mrs. Langley," Adam said.

After receiving a vial of medicine and instructions on Abby's care, Grandma discreetly left the room.

"I'll check up on you tomorrow," Adam said.

"There's no need for that," Abby answered dismissively.

"I'll see you tomorrow," he said, his eyes narrowing.

"Please, Adam, don't come back. I don't want to see you again. I can't. You bring too much pain with you. Seeing you uncovers terrible wounds, and right now I don't want to care. I don't want to feel. Just let me heal in my own way, in my own time. Let it be over. Please, Adam, let it be over between us. Grandma can take care of me. After all—it was only a baby." Saying it like that, she again felt the utter despair of her aloneness.

"I'll never again let another man raise a child of mine," Adam replied.

"I have nothing left to give you."

"Was there a dead baby?" Grandma asked as soon as the door closed on Adam.

"Yes."

"Whose?"

"Mine," Abby said hesitantly. Adam had never flat-out admitted that it was her child he had given to Lillian, and his omission left her with a nagging doubt.

"Nonsense," Grandma said in a huff. "You're as healthy as a horse; you couldn't birth a dead baby."

"I don't believe it was mine," Abby said with a frown. She wrinkled her brow. "I saw mine when he was born; I heard him cry. He was a normal-size baby, I think. The other one was so tiny."

"Tell me what happened." Grandma sat down heavily in the rocking chair that still awaited mother and babe, her stiffly healing leg robbing her of grace. Clearly distressed, she sat rocking and drumming her fingers on the wooden arms while Abby told her the story.

"And he gave it to her," Abby said when she finished.

Grandma was incredulous. "Adam gave your baby to his wife?"

"I'm not really sure," Abby said, "And it is his child," she said in his defense.

After much deliberation and taking care in choosing her words, Grandma rendered her verdict. "I think Dr. Townsend did the right thing. I think he did the best that could be done under the circumstances. He saved your reputation and, it sounds like, his wife's sanity, and maybe even her life. The baby will be cared for, and without the controversy of his birthright hanging over him for the rest of his life. I'm sure Mrs. Townsend will be a good mother, and the boy will grow up with a father—his own."

Abby hung her head to hide her anguish, her pain, and her enduring sorrow.

"It's entirely my fault. Every day, I wished a dead baby on her."

CHAPTER 89

NURSE BOGGINS BROUGHT THE BABY, bathed and dressed in a long white gown, with lace-and-satin bows decorating the scalloped hem and a satin-and-lace baby cap on his head, to the waiting Mrs. Townsend. Lillian reached out for him, still full of wonder that at last she had a child, but she winced with pain as he clamped his hungry mouth onto her tender breast. Modestly covering her bared bosom, she asked, "Were there really two babies, Miss Boggins?"

"Yes, two of them," Althea said, her Irish voice lilting.

"I wish I could remember."

"Oh no, it's better that you don't," the nurse said, her brogue deepening.

"It's all such a jumble," Lillian confessed, a deep furrow burrowing between her brows.

"And Dr. Townsend has his baby," the nurse singsonged with pleasure.

"And mine, too," Lillian added testily.

"Oh, yes, by all means—and yours, too, Mrs. Townsend."

Nurse Boggins busily straightened bedclothes and rearranged items on the nightstand before withdrawing. At the door she met Dr. Townsend coming in. "Might I have a word with you, sir?" she whispered. They retreated into the hall. She stood, head high, her face candid, boldly looking him in the eye. "I think you did the right thing about the wee ones, and that's all I have to say, and that's all I'll ever have to say, to you, or to anyone—about the whole affair."

"Thank you, Althea. Your opinion, and being in your good graces, means a great deal to me. I hope you won't judge me too harshly."

She bristled. "I would never judge you." She was proud that Dr. Townsend's child was under his roof and in her care.

Adam smiled his warm, ingratiating smile, his eyes merry again, and he was still smiling when he entered the bedroom. Leaning over the rocking chair, he kissed Lillian's cheek and the crown of his son's head. He sat in a chair near the bed and watched his wife nurse Abby's baby. "Your milk seems to be adequate," he remarked. With motherhood, her youthfully small breasts had matured.

"He's always hungry, and my nipples are quite sore."

"They'll toughen up."

"Nurse Boggins seems to think so."

"Why don't you call her Althea? I think we're going to be living together for a very long time."

"Oh, she's so starchy, it's hard to remember she has a first name," Lillian said, wrinkling her nose and smiling up at him.

Adam watched, enjoying the tableau of mother and child, and recalled Abby's breasts. Remembered how the proud nipples had felt in his mouth, pebbled like tender young raspberries. He stirred, rubbing a hand across his eyes to shut out the memory.

The baby dozed, and Lillian, grimacing, pinched the baby's cheeks together and released her breast. "He's a little glutton," she said with relief.

Adam crossed one long leg over the other and straightened the crease in his pants leg. "I think it's time we named the babies, Lillian," he said. "It's been ten days. Have you thought about names?"

"Names?" she said, seeming puzzled. "Oh, yes. Well—I had been thinking about Michael." She said the name hesitantly. "Do you think it would be a proper name for our son? Michael Adam Townsend."

So it was the Gypsy man who bestowed the awakening kiss on our sleeping beauty. Adam felt a pang of jealousy, yet he felt gratitude that she had been awakened to her womanhood by whatever means. Otherwise, it may never have happened, and how barren her life would have been without her ever experiencing sensuality. He knew the baby Lillian had borne was his. Lillian could never be unfaithful—it wasn't in her character—and yet he knew she had been psychologically altered to feel something for someone else.

"I think it would be a fine name," he answered at last. "It's a good Irish name." *Abby should approve,* he thought. "If you've chosen a name for one of our children, may I have the privilege of naming the other?"

"Of course, and what will you name him—the other one?"

"Absalom."

"Absalom! You're not serious," she said. "That's a frightful name for a tiny baby."

"Well, he'll never know, and it is the name I have chosen for him."

"It's biblical, isn't it? I can't think what book," she said.

"Second Samuel. He was the favorite son of King David."

"I wonder if anyone has ever counted all the names in the Bible, beginning with Adam," she said. And, smiling brightly at her husband, she asked, "Is there a Michael in the Bible?"

"Yes, Archangel Michael. He slew a dragon after doing battle with it."

Lillian cooed at the sleeping baby in her arms and, working her finger into the tight little knot of his fist, whispered, "You slew a dragon, darling."

Adam raised an eyebrow.

"Michael: it's a lovely name. Do you really like the name, Adam?"

Adam felt his jaw muscles tighten. "Yes, Lillian, yes," he said resignedly.

"You know so much about the Bible, and yet you're an atheist."

"Agnostic. The Bible is our history. It's the foundation of our beliefs, our music, our art, our literature. The Bible is what shaped us and educated us and made us who and what we are. My father believes that to know yourself, and your fellow man, you have to know the Bible. 'Know what a man believes, and you'll know the man,' he used to say. He held that knowing the Bible was a prerequisite of an educated man. Myself, I prefer Shakespeare." He paused. "Lillian," he said gently, "it's time to bury our other son; would you like to see him—say goodbye?"

She recoiled. "No, it might mark the good baby," she said, holding her child closer to her.

The "good baby." Does dying make you bad? he wondered.

Lillian did not seem to countenance the finality of his request. The nurse came into the room. "It's time for you to get back into bed, Mrs. Townsend," she said, cheerfully taking the baby from her.

"Let me have him," Adam said, sitting down in the rocking chair Lillian had vacated. He crossed his knees, and Althea draped a blanket across his lap and handed his son to him. Adam untied the blue satin bow from beneath the baby's chin and, removing the lacy cap, smoothed his hair. Baby Michael opened his eyes and studiously contemplated the person holding him as though he were grading him. Adam felt the infant's warmth enter his own flesh, meld with it, honor it; inhaled the baby sweetness of him; admired the shape of his head and the handsomeness of his facial features; and thought pleasantly of all the years he would look upon this face. He placed two fingers on the baby's sternum, thumped the tiny chest, felt the steady heartbeat, depressed the sturdy flesh of the baby arm, and noticed, when he removed his finger, how quickly the color returned. Marveled at the baby's strength, the way he grasped his fingers and tried to rise, and the remarkable quickness of his reflexes; he admired the length and heft and color of the "good baby." The child's eyes never wavered from his. "What do you think, young man, did I pass muster? Did I get a good grade?"

The January thaw came, and Rockville was able to bury its dead: old John Palmer, Aunt Sadie Cunningham, and baby Absalom. Water from the melting snow mixed with rain, slicking the unpaved side streets and walks with mud.

There had been time during the waiting period for the Italian stonecutter in Saint Margaret's to carve a tombstone for the infant, one with a tiny lamb gracing the top and the biblical epitaph:

O MY SON ABSALOM, MY SON, MY SON ABSALOM.
WOULD GOD I HAD DIED FOR THEE, MY SON.
ABSALOM JOHN TOWNSEND.

Son born to Adam and Lillian Townsend
b. January 8, 1910
d. January 8, 1910
Sleep in peace, beloved son.

Adam looked down at the raw earth disturbed from its winter slumber and, patting the head of the little marble lamb, said, "Someday, son, your mother will come to visit you."

CHAPTER 90

March 1910

JUPITER HUNG LOW AND BRIGHT in the early-morning sky. Fifteen-year-old Illa May Davis sat huddled on the cushioned window seat in her upstairs bedroom, her arms wrapped around her knees. She was following the progress of the barely discernible figure of a lone man as he walked down the deserted sidewalk, entered the churchyard, and paused at the chapel door before disappearing inside. Twilla June, Illa May's twin, was still peacefully asleep in the bed shared by the sisters. Twilla June's otherworldly and ashen hair, escaped from the confinement of her beribboned night bonnet, framed her angelic face and created an iridescent halo on the pillow.

Twilla was the younger of the twins, born after midnight on the first of June; Illa May, the older, was born before midnight on the thirty-first of May. Their birth dates and names were the only tangible evidence that distinguished the girls. Otherwise, they were as alike as the proverbial peas in a pod. They were sometimes called "dolls" because of their delicate skin, pink cheeks, white hair, and China doll–blue eyes.

Illa May was yearning to discover the oneness of self. She had a passionate need for separation from the other. She hoped for an act her twin could not share and a secret that would belong to her alone, never to be shared by the one from whom there was no apart.

Across the street, a light in the back room of the church flowered into life, a beacon in the dark. Illa May slid her feet into her slippers, covered her nightgown with a wool cape, and, quietly letting herself out of the house, found her way across the dark street to the church.

She stood out of view of the amber light cast by the office window and could see Brother Griggsby. He appeared to be pacing the floor, sometimes stopping to raise his arms toward the ceiling, and when he did, she would hear a faint rumble of sound coming from inside the small office. Creeping beneath the window and rising on tiptoes, she listened intently, but the words he uttered were indiscernible to her. She watched and listened until she grew bored and, turning about, she faced the garden.

New young plants were bravely putting forth tender green shoots near the warmth of the old frame building. The dry soil within the circle of the small flower bed, however, outlined with rocks and spread out before the window of the office, remained as yet unbroken by new spring growth.

She chose the largest stone from the circle of rocks and pushed the flat-topped, peach-colored rock—which bore a remarkable resemblance to the Rock House—into the center of the patch of bare ground. Kneeling down before it, she scooped up a handful of the black earth. She made a funnel of her fist and began to form letters and numbers. "Illa May Davis, May 31, 1897," she wrote on the rock. Her name and her birth date: the only possessions she had that belonged to her alone and were not shared by her sister.

The yellow square of lamplight crisscrossed with dark lines formed by the window grids suddenly disappeared from the ground. Fearing that Brother Griggsby would see her, Illa May sprang up, hesitant as what to do; in her state of indecision, her feet scrunching this way and that, she laid waste to her name and the numbers 31 and 97, leaving behind a legacy: May 18. She raced for home, highly exhilarated that she had accomplished something without Twilla June and now had a secret of her very own: she had spied on Brother Griggsby at his prayers.

Sneaking back into their bedroom and stealthily lying down beside the still-sleeping Twilla June, she closed her eyes and instantly fell into a deep, gratifying sleep.

When she awakened late in the morning, Illa May was not sure if she had dreamed that she had inscribed her name and birth date beneath the window of the church office. Upon inspection later that afternoon, the inscription was gone—or had a nighttime drama taken place that she couldn't remember?

The first rays of the sun, like a mystical goddess unfolding her robes, rose over the eastern horizon, bathing the town in a palette of sunrise colors and turning the windows of Old Church into a glowing, primeval red.

Inside the church office, Brother Griggsby had extinguished the kerosene lamp and was fervently beseeching God to interpret the dream he had experienced that very night. He begged the Almighty to give him a sign that He was hearing him; that God knew that he, Brother Griggsby, existed. "Lead them to me, oh God, so I can lead them back to You," he said, pleading.

Upon the completion of his lengthy prayer, Brother Griggsby opened his eyes to a supernatural glow filling the room. Getting to his feet, he looked out from his window into the breaking dawn; when he lowered his head, he saw there before him a rock, a rock that had the fiery mark of the Maker's light upon it—and a shape strangely suggestive of the Rock House. But, most important, writ upon the rock was his sign from God: May 18.

While Brother Griggsby stared in wonder, meekness, and disbelief, the first gusts of a windy March day swooped around the corner of the church, churned up winter debris and loose dirt, and swept clean the area beneath the window, causing the nocturnal secret to disappear as if by the very breath of the Almighty Himself. Trembling with awe, Brother Griggsby did as he always did when he wanted a direct word with God: he went to the source—the holy Bible.

He stood before the podium on which rested the large leather-bound book, the cover inscribed in gold lettering; Brother Griggsby closed his eyes and opened the Bible. Separating the delicate pages, he chose a page. He placed his forefinger on the spot and read his message from God: *And they heard a great voice from heaven saying unto them, "Come up hither." And they ascended up to heaven in a cloud; and their enemies beheld them.*

When Brother Griggsby had a direct message from the Lord, he stayed within that book, and again he closed his eyes, chose a new page, and read:

> And white robes were given to every one of them...And the kings of the earth, and the great men, and the rich men, hid themselves in the dens and in the rocks of the mountains: And said to the mountains and rocks, "Fall on us, and hide us from the face of Him that sitteth on the throne: For the great day of His wrath is come and who shall be able to stand."

And again he chose and pointed, so excited with exaltation that his hands shook.

> And I went unto the angel, and said unto him, "Give me the little book." And He said unto me, "Take it, and eat it up; and it shall make thy belly

> bitter, but it shall be in thy mouth sweet as honey." And I took the little book out of the angel's hand, and ate it up; and it was in my mouth sweet as honey and as soon as I had eaten it, my belly was bitter. And He said unto me, "Thou must prophesy again before many peoples, and nations, and tongues, and kings."

Brother Griggsby was so overcome with gratitude that he tore the page from the Bible and, methodically chewing and swallowing, consumed it. Sinking to his knees, he proclaimed in a loud voice of thanksgiving, "Oh, Lord, I am thy prophet! I am thy mouthpiece. I am thy trumpet." After which a long, rumbling belch issued forth from him, and the words were indeed bitter upon his belly.

But his mouth was as sweet as honey because God, on this day, had delivered unto him, Erasmus Griggsby, a divine prophecy: the date of the end of the world!

CHAPTER 91

At the whimsy of the chaotic winds of March, the flag at the post office snapped, snarled, and stood at attention. At Old Church the wind rattled windows and, stealing through cracks, assaulted wintered bones, reminding the faithful that nature is treacherous.

Brother Griggsby stood at the pulpit quietly gazing over his congregation and, after a lengthy silence, said, "I have had a vision—a terrible, prophetic vision." With his shoulders convulsing in a shudder, he covered his eyes and lowered his head, leaving his congregation to tremble in anticipation.

When he spoke again, his voice was thick and teary with emotion. "You were there, all of you, burning in a fiery pit."

In unison, the newly damned gasped, and the cold day grew colder.

"I could hear your pitiful cries and smell your burning flesh. And then I saw that it was not just the fires of damnation, but the whole of the earth. Our great cities were burning, the ships at sea were burning, our fields and animals were burning, our stores and homes, and, yea, our very own church and town were all aflame, even unto our hearths and our children." He wiped tears from his cheeks, his voice quivering with emotion.

"And because God had turned a deaf ear to you, you stretched out your arms, pleading to me." His voice broke. "I knelt there on the brink of that dastardly place and, with my knees burning, I prayed, 'God, let my people go! These are my people, and their sins are my sins. Grant me the power to lead them away from the fires of hell. They are a good and obedient people, Lord, and they will follow me.' Out of the clouds, the Lord's voice, like the sound of a glorious trumpet, spoke to me: 'Bring your people to me,' he said, 'and I will save them as I saved Noah and his family. I will gather you unto me before I destroy the earth by fire.' And when I looked into that fiery pit again, it was full of black sheep, and I said, 'All who believe in God the Father, the Son, and the Holy Ghost, follow me.' And the black sheep who believed jumped out of that fiery pit and turned as white as snow and followed me to a mountaintop, and there, amid the destruction of the world, we ascended on a cloud unto heaven.

"When I awakened from this dream, I left my house and came here, and in my humble office I prayed for an answer to my dream, and when I opened my eyes, I was enveloped in an orange cloud. In my agitation I thought the church was on fire, but slowly the vision faded away as in a morning mist. I arose from my knees and, looking out from my office window, I saw the first rays of light shining on that little bare garden just below the study window." Brother Griggsby's voice rose dramatically as he said, "And I saw written there by the finger of God"—people leaned forward on the edge of their seats, straining to hear the words even before he spoke them—"the date of the end of the world: the eighteenth of May. And, as I looked, the message turned to dust right before my very eyes, scattered as if blown by a mighty breath to the four corners of the earth." His hand flicked back and forth to imaginary corners.

Stunned, bloodless of face, weak of body, the parishioners turned to one another.

"So soon?" they gasped. "So soon?"

Somewhere amid the wails and weeping, the sound of retching could be heard.

Other voices in the congregation were whispering, "It's the comet. It's the comet that's coming to destroy the earth!"

"And I tell you, brothers and sisters, Judgment Day is here. Will your soul be saved or condemned to hell?" He pounded the lectern, restoring order. "Before that day arrives, however, we shall purge ourselves of our sins, big and small. We will prepare ourselves to ascend unto heaven as pure as the angels, before the wholesale destruction of the world touches us. This—I—promise—you!"

He gave the benediction and marched to the vestibule of the church, where he was mobbed by his flock, crying, sobbing, and demanding to be heard, everyone asking questions and begging answers.

But there was one thing that was certain: the tail of Halley's comet was expected to hit the earth on May 18, 1910, and so, too, apparently, was the hand of a riled-up God.

The unwavering belief by the members of Old Church, and their enthusiasm about ascending to heaven, were being felt by members of the other denominations, some of whom began a stampede to become members of Old Church. What had begun as a fire in someone's backyard was now jumping fences and setting flame to the neighbors' yards. If the world was coming to an end, and Brother Griggsby could save them, then they did not want to be left behind. Others, wavering in their beliefs, demanded the truth from their spiritual leaders.

"It is not the end of the world," Pastor Bob Murphy at the Chapel of the Ark said to assure his parishioners. "People are experiencing a religious renewal," he said, "and this is good. We are returning to a deep and abiding love in the Almighty, with a new respect for His laws: the Ten Commandments."

Murphy had a feeling of suffocation, as if he were preaching in a vacuum. "It is not the end of the world," he emphatically announced over and over. Still, both

New Church and the ark, as well as the smaller churches, lost members to Old Church.

I suppose, in times of calamity, people need fire and brimstone, Reverend Bob surmised.

Adam sent word for Bob to join him for dinner. The note read: "I feel a sermon ready to spew forth from your lips that would best be delivered to a sympathetic ear: mine."

During dinner at the Townsend mansion, and while Lillian was present, Bob and Adam made small talk. But later, alone in the study, over a bottle of brandy, the men talked long into the night. Bob, pacing back and forth, was releasing the annoyance he felt for Brother Griggsby and his old-time religion. At last, exhausted, he fell into a chair.

"I take it, then," Adam said, "you don't believe the end of the world is going to befall us on the eighteenth of May?"

"Good God, no."

They both laughed heartily, Bob wiping his eyes.

"I believe this will be the best thing that has ever happened to this town," Adam said. "Rockville is about to take a giant step forward into the twentieth century, and the God-fearing, righteous Brother Griggsby is about to nail himself to a cross of his own making."

"But what will happen to people's faith when this is over?" Bob asked.

"Maybe, at last, people will start to think for themselves," Adam said. "You can't control ignorance, but you can control intelligence."

Catching Adam's enthusiasm, Bob said, "You're right; I can see it now. Progress is on its way to Rockville. I'll even drink to that."

Adam poured them each a nightcap, and he offered a toast: "To progress."

"To progress," agreed Pastor Bob, raising his glass.

CHAPTER 92

April 1910

It was the spring of 1910, and many things were coming to Rockville: progress, Judgment Day, and a religious revival the likes of which even old-timers couldn't recall. The doomsday fires started by Old Church were now spreading over county and state lines, and news items of Brother Griggsby's revelation from the Almighty appeared in out-of-town papers, which added more fuel to the flames.

Each day, the 4:10 train brought an influx of new people to town: newspapermen, salesmen, hucksters, the curious, and those who had come to be saved. Religious emissaries arrived to investigate the cause of the alarm. And, day and night, newspapermen from around the country, there to investigate the revelation, sent their findings back over the wireless at the train station. Pictures of Brother Griggsby pointing to the spot of earth where he had seen the message from God appeared in big-city newspapers. The hotel and the boardinghouses were full.

People opened up their homes and rented out rooms. Travelers were camped at the ballpark. Temporary stalls were set up along Main Street, with vendors hawking their wares: religious items, Halley's comet charms, end-of-the-world trinkets, and Bibles with gold engraving on imitation-leather covers.

Adam, driving down Main Street on his way to a sick call, thought, *This is not the progress I envisioned.*

On Saturday, when the 4:10 pulled in, a wiry little man wearing a green plaid suit with a red flower stuck in the lapel, a black derby hat, and a face resembling that of a monkey's bounced onto the platform. The little man's darting, quicker-than-the-eye hands flashed pinkie rings. A crowd was gathered at the depot, as it was every day, to see what new curiosity the train had deposited. After looking over the newcomers and dismissing them as nobodies, the crowd of spectators gave its attention to the gaudy little man in the derby.

"Brothers and sisters, Saint John is coming," the little man said. A hushed silence fell over the gathering. "Saint John is coming to Rockville to give you his blessing."

"Saint John!" they whispered excitedly. Soon the whole town was whispering the famous name: "Saint John, the great evangelist, is coming here, to Rockville, to bless us!"

On Sunday, a good many townspeople, as well as the newly arrived, were at the train depot. Saint John did not appear, although a bevy of women the likes of whom the town had not seen since the departure of Velvet exited the train: six painted and perfumed Jezebels who had spent the night in jail for the lack of a room to be had anywhere. The next day, Marshal McCombs escorted the women from the jail back to the train.

The good women of the town averted their eyes and did not look at the fallen women as they boarded the train. But the men looked—stretched their necks to look, stood on the divided half-circle brick wall separating the depot from the street to look. The ladies winked and flounced their harlot skirts and called to the men as the train pulled away from the station: "We'll come back when you've got room for us at the inn!"

"Are you ready for Judgment Day?" people asked one another. Brother Griggsby, the new latter-day prophet, was ready, and he was wasting no time in saving as many souls for Jesus as humanly possible before that day arrived.

The scriptures said he must prophesy again before many peoples and nations, and tongues and kings. Brother Griggsby sent a letter in which he recounted his vision, his sermon, and God's disclosure to him that the world would end on the eighteenth of May to President William Howard Taft and King George of Great Britain. With this done, the brother turned his full attention to his own flock.

Brother Griggsby's followers would have two months in which to prepare to meet their Maker. The times demanded a return to the old-time religion of their forefathers, and to their old-time customs. In preparation for the rising to heaven, Brother Griggsby decided to begin the ritual of the purging of sins with an old-time foot washing. Those participating prayed they would be among the chosen few on that heavenly ride.

Willa Mae McCoy-White composed a song about the heavenly ride, set to the tune of "Turkey in the Straw," and the words appeared on the front page of the *Hub*: "And get your tickets for that heavenly ride."

On Sunday evening, people had filed into the church long before the half-hour bell sounded, all wanting to get a good seat for the foot washing. It had been quite some time since a washing had taken place. Once people had stopped taking part, the custom had been dropped. Now, during these trying times, it was being revived. Those who held grudges or hatred in their hearts against their neighbors or family members, and those who uttered impieties against them, were to wash their feet in an act of servitude and humility and seek their forgiveness as a sign of reconciliation.

Frank and Lizzie Doyle could be seen coming down Oak Street on their way to church. Lizzie, walking a few paces behind her dour-faced husband, carried a blue and white enamel basin and towel. Frank and Lizzie had been married for thirty years, and for the last fifteen of those years had not spoken to each other. They did not eat together. They did not sleep together. They did not even sleep in the same room together.

But they did attend church together (she walking a few paces behind his unbending back), sat on the hard wooden benches, and sang with stiff lips from their hymn books, never looking across the aisle. Still, they were pious and devout in their religious beliefs and firm believers in the Old Testament, in damnation, and in the coming battle of Armageddon and Judgment Day.

The evening service began with a prayer and the singing of "Bringing in the Sheaves." Brother Griggsby delivered another fire-and-brimstone sermon. Now that the end of the world was near, his audience was attentive and alert during his long discourses. He ended with, "Oh, ye men. Oh, ye women. Oh, ye sinners. Awake! Come. Wash away your sins and beg forgiveness from those you have sinned against, in the name of Jesus, amen." Then he added, "Now, all of you who are participating in the foot washings, bring your basins and your sins and find yourselves seats up here on the pulpit."

A tub filled with water and a dipper floating in it was carried in and placed near the altar. As Mrs. Doyle followed her husband up the aisle, the audience held its collective breath: Lizzie and Frank, after not speaking for fifteen years, were about to wash each other's feet!

She filled her blue and white basin from the tub of water and carried it to where Frank was waiting. She was about to set it down when Frank took the bowl from her, slopping the water as he did so. "I'll wash your feet first, woman," he said.

Lizzie, fierce as a warrior in her determination to be first, snatched the bowl back, spilling more water. "No, Mr. Doyle, I am washing your feet."

Frank turned a deep red. "A man is head of his house and first before his woman. Give me the basin."

Lizzie turned a lively geranium pink but clung to the curved rim of the enamel basin as both pulled on it.

Brother Griggsby rushed forward, waving his hands and chastising them. "Sister Elizabeth! Brother Doyle!" His hands were stilled, and he made a pushing-away motion toward the woman with an exasperated, "Please, Sister Elizabeth! Brother Doyle, as patriarch of the family, will wash your feet first."

Lizzie, with a little sigh of exhaustion, fell onto the seat, only to bounce up again, turn the chair about, and remove her button shoes and rolled-up black stockings away from prying eyes. When she placed her naked feet into the cold water, she reacted with a little start. Frank, on bended knee, looking her in the eye while at the same time rubbing her feet with his bare hands. He said, "Elizabeth Ann Doyle, I forgive you for being a sharp-tongued, flibbertigibbeted old woman."

"Oh!" said an infuriated Elizabeth, again turning a bright pink. Breathing hard and biting her tongue, she reminded herself that Atonement Day was nigh. Jumping up, she gave Mr. Doyle a little push into the chair. She replenished the water in the basin and, returning to

Frank, helped him off with his shoes and socks before plopping his feet into the water. "I've been a mean and spiteful woman and a poor wife, but if you can find it in your heart to forgive me, I promise to once again honor and obey." *Two months*, she thought: *surely I can keep a civil tongue in my head for two months.*

Ignoring the towel, Lizzie Doyle slowly sat back on her heels and removed her hat; she placed it on a chair seat and began to pull the tortoiseshell pins from the bun at the nape of her neck. Like a sinuous pink serpent, the released coil of strawberry-blond hair slid from neck, to shoulder, to waist. Lizzie undid the braid of her long thick hair, shaking it out into a curtain. Everyone was agog, Frank perhaps most of all, as Lizzie, removing one of his feet from the basin, dried the long and thin white foot—first one, then the other—with the mantilla of her own hair.

"Amen and amen!" shouted Brother Griggsby.

"Hallelujah!" shouted the congregation. Everyone burst into another chorus of "Bringing in the Sheaves."

All in all, fifteen foot washings took place, old hatreds and scores were washed away, and the foot washers were forthwith ensured of their place on that heavenly ride.

CHAPTER 93

John Murphy sat in one of his barber chairs reading aloud the lead story from the *Hub*: "'Harlan Jones has purchased, from the heirs of the late Mr. John Fuller, the Fuller family's old homestead. The heirs to the homestead reside in the Ozarks, from whence Mr. Fuller came. Harlan Jones, who is in the employ of Henri Parlett, is moving his wife and three children to Rockville from Illinois. Harlan, affectionately known as Bla—'"

A fist came crashing through the newspaper, stopping just short of the barber's nose. "What in the hell?" John swore, dropping the paper and pushing back into his chair.

Chance Collins was glowering at him, his purple scar pulsating. "I give that black bastard the name 'Blackie,' and I did not do so 'affectionately,' as the paper says. That subversive nigger's diggin' in. I ask you, do we want niggers livin' here, bringin' in their little black piccaninnies and whore wives? Hell, they're worse than Gypsies! And that damn editor is no better," he said, jabbing a finger in the direction of the newspaper office across the street. "He's a nigger-lovin' rabble-rouser," he finished, viciously spitting tobacco juice into the brass spittoon.

An agonizing, guttural howl shattered the early-morning Sabbath; a few seconds later, another anguished, tortured cry born of the ages followed. A cry of unrestrained pain and years of mind-withering humiliation assailed the ears of the town's early risers, numbed their senses, prickled their unscarred white backs, and called into accountability the very morality of their sacred morn.

Mr. Parlett, in the midst of his Sunday morning toiletry, hearing the scream, jousted with a stuck window frame and hit his head on the raised sash in his rush to look outside his second-story hotel residence. Down on the street, in front of the barbershop, swinging from a rope on the arc of the streetlamp, hung the body of a man.

After hastily putting on his Sunday-morning clothes, Henri Parlett was the first to arrive on the scene. As he neared the post, he saw the configuration of a man hung in effigy. Black socks made up the face and hands of the scarecrow figure; white buttons, the teeth; red paint, the lips. The tormented soul at the foot of the lamppost was Harlan.

Mr. Parlett glanced up at the swinging figure and read the hand-printed sign attached to the back of it:

No niggers. Humbled by Harlan's pain, he placed a hand on his shoulder. "I'm sorry, Harlan," he said. "I'm sorry. I should have seen it coming. I apologize for all of us. Come on now; get up," he said, rocking Harlan's shoulder. "It's only someone's idea of a joke—one person, no doubt," he said with irritation.

Harlan didn't seem to be listening. He had lifted his head, and his bloodshot eyes were staring up mournfully at the grotesque figure, which prompted Mr. Parlett to take another look. This time he saw the reason for the man's agony: hanging from the neck of the straw-stuffed effigy, its head at an unnatural angle, was Harlan's little white dog, Princess.

Churchgoers within hearing distance of the commotion hurriedly donned their Sunday clothes; rushing downtown, they soon approached the figure of a scarecrow with crudely painted red lips on a black face, a little white dog suspended by a rope resting on its chest. Their pace slowed, some people stopping altogether, and they recoiled from the raw misery of the man who had his arms wrapped around the lamppost, sobbing and moaning and beating his head against the hard metal of the pole.

"We didn't do this, Harlan," someone in the growing crowd said.

"We don't feel this way," another voice added. They moved closer. "You and your family—you're welcome here—anytime."

"Our dog Sylvie just had pups. You can have one of them, mister," a boy with a teary voice offered.

Marshal McCombs rode up and, touching the brim of his hat to the crowd in general, surveyed the situation. "Now this here's one sorrowful sight," he announced before riding to the hitching rail, tethering his horse, and returning to the scene.

Everyone present began to talk at once, demanding of the marshal that he do something. And for a while, it looked like they were going to turn on him.

"Quiet!" Marshal McCombs bellowed.

"You know who did this!" a local farmer said, speaking for all of them.

But no one uttered the name, each waiting for the other to be brave enough to say it.

Old Church's half-hour bell sounded just then, and in the quiet that followed, the carillons at New Church could be heard as well as the soft little bell from the ark. No one moved, and the crowd swelled as others joined the gathering.

"We all know who he is," another said. "We all know that every dastardly deed that happens in this town can be laid at the feet of one man."

Still, no one even whispered the name.

"Yes, I know who you mean, but I can't arrest a man without proof," the marshal said.

At the far end of Main Street, a rider on a black horse could be seen. Someone pointed him out, and they all watched as the black-clad rider advanced. As he drew nearer, an angry hum emanated from the crowd, and someone shouted, "You did this, Chance!"

The big man, making his scarred smirk obvious, nosed his horse into the crowd until he was beside the lamppost and, casually looking up at the ragged effigy, said, "Looks like somebody had a necktie party."

"You had the party!" a man's angry voice said.

"What y'all so fired up about? That's just a bunch of rags hangin' up there."

"And a dog!" a man shouted.

"Yeah, you killed this man's dog!"

His laughter mocked them. "Hell, it's jist a little old potlicker."

Harlan, absorbed by the mass of people, broke away from them and, running toward his provoker, yelled, "Get off that horse, Chance, 'cause I'm going to kill you!"

"Ain't no damn nigger gonna call me by my first name and live to tell it," Chance yelled back, drawing his right leg across the saddle, with his left foot in the stirrup.

Harlan was wildly jumping about, his fists punching the air, when he bellowed, "You killed her. You killed my dog. You killed Princess!"

The big black horse, now skittish, reared up on its hind legs and, backing away, caused Chance to lose his tight hold on the reins and plunge headfirst to the ground with his left foot still jammed into the stirrup. The frightened horse, its eyes showing white and ears pointed, looked around at the thing dangling at his side. It reared again and tried to shake free before breaking into a full gallop.

"Whoa, boy!" Chance yelled as he bumped along the ground. The men in the crowd began yelling the same command: "Whoa! Whoa!"

Chance did not call out for help. He knew none was coming, but his hands, sliding along the bricks, palms up, stretched out imploringly.

The marshal bolted for his horse and called back, "You men, get your horses and go after him. Hell, he'll be drug to death."

The church bell tolled its final call.

The men in the crowd scattered and headed for their horses, wherever they might be. The women tried to collect their children for Sunday services, but the children were running helter-skelter down Main Street in the direction of the runaway horse, now out of sight.

"Come back here!" mothers called. "You come back here and go to Sunday school. You're going to get hurt. You're going to get dirty. Did you hear me?"

Not long after, Chance's horse, the once-haughty animal, stood at the gate of Collins's farm waiting for admittance. Chance's foreman, Ross, came to the gate and peered without concern between the posts at the riderless horse until he saw the apparition hanging from the empty saddle. "Whoa, now," he said, gentling the horse and reaching for the dragging bridle.

The arriving posse, dismounting quietly so as not to startle the big black horse, silently approached the wearied animal. The horse, no longer snorting and prancing, didn't move; it just turned its head in the direction of the men, submission showing in its docile black eyes and lowered ears.

The end result of the tragedy had a hypnotic affect upon the men. They stood in a semicircle, hats in hand, staring.

A grotesquely twisted leg protruded from the boot, still caught fast in the stirrup, extending into a bloody, dirt-caked mass of ragged flesh, bone, and shredded clothes. The eye sockets were pools of coagulating blood; the lids, no longer with the support of eyeballs, were sunken into the head; flies had already gathered about their lifeless rims. The torn flesh of the leg exposed shreds of muscle, and resilient white tendons jutted from the disjointed knee like broken violin strings. Most of the hair from his head was missing, exposing the shattered skull. The nose was gone. Arms, with shirtsleeves and skin worn away, stretched forth from the inhuman bulk; the mangled fingers still clutched bits of brush and roots imprisoned in the death grip of the huge raw hands.

But what held the men spellbound was the mouth: a cavity surrounded by tufts of skin displaying the few remaining teeth, swampy green, with the gold inlays reflecting the sun. The men looked and waited, expecting a last mighty howl—furious in defiance of death, gurgling and spluttering blood—to come blasting forth from that gaping, lipless hole.

"He lived mean, and he died mean," the marshal commented to the newspaper editor upon reporting the particulars of Chance's death.

When the last will and testament of Chancellor Collins was read, the townspeople were stunned, but they quickly recovered to hash and rehash the terms of the will. Precious Amy Preston, among the poorest of the poor, with the bucking of a horse and the stroke of a pen, had become a young woman of property.

The stipulations of Precious Amy's good fortune were that, with her baby, she was to move into Chance Collins's house and take care of his blind mother until such a time as the demise of Mrs. Collins should take place. And, upon said demise, the house and the five acres on which it stood would pass on to Amy. The balance of Chancellor Collins's substantial estate was to be divided between Amy's baby boy and Chance's foreman, Ross.

"Oh, he had a good heart after all," said the ladies at the Tuesday Society meeting, commiserating with one another.

"He got what he had coming," said the men at the pool hall.

"Beneath that wickedness was a heart of gold," said a woman at the Thursday Social Guild.

"He was the meanest man what ever lived," said the men at the smithy.

"Showed char-tee to a poor fatherless child, he did," Tate Morgan said.

"He was such a 'andsome wee laddie 'afore the haccident," his mother said, weeping.

Perthy Prettyman added that "handsome is as handsome does."

"Well, it was the least the bastard could do, after branding the kid's pa," Marshal McCombs said. Everyone still believed the Gypsy man was the progenitor of Amy's child.

CHAPTER 94

A TIGHT LITTLE KNOT OF people was gathered in front of the *Hub*'s office window, as they were every day now that the end of the world was near. They earnestly ranged over the diagram displayed on the lower half of the office window detailing the daily positions of earth and comet. The illustration, shown on a field of dark-blue watercolor paint, showed fifteen white spheres with long tails, portraying Halley's comet, and fifteen brown balls, representing the earth. The caption read: "The diagram depicts how earth and comet will pass, both going 23 miles a second."

Small triangular flags of white paper with dates printed on them were posted next to the brown orbs. They disclosed where earth and comet would be juxtaposed with each other daily from May fifth to the twentieth, and they showed their paths crossing on the eighteenth.

The Rockville Hub
April 15, 1910

Is it the end of the world?

Are we living in the last days? Our own mellifluous prophet, Brother Griggsby, tells us we are.

The Brother's prophecy coincides with that of many religious leaders throughout the world, who are predicting that the sweeping tail of the comet will annihilate all evil things on the planet, thereby purifying the world for the Second Coming of Christ.

Brother Griggsby has been as sensational and frightful in oratory as our expected celestial visitor will presumably be when it appears in our sky.

Others say we are not to fear; that the Comet may quite possibly heal us of our aches and pains and cure us of our ills, if we but expose ourselves nightly to its light.

Professor David Todd of Amherst College says, "When the earth passes through the comet's tail, the experience will be no more startling than putting your finger through the beam of a searchlight."

Most experts agree we are in no danger, because the comet will be 15,000,000 miles away at its nearest point to us.

Doctor of divinity Noah Edwards is back in town after living the past two years in Europe, India, and the Far East, where he has been expanding his knowledge of other cultures and religions. When asked his view on Halley's Comet, he commented, "It will be an awesome sight, but nothing to fear."

And my message to you as your editor-in-chief is: enjoy Halley's Comet for what it is, a grand show that comes to town once every 75 years. The Comet is only a small part of our wondrous universe.

When the sun rises on the morning of the 19th, as it will—the same as yesterday, today, and tomorrow—maybe, it just might cure man of some of his hypocrisies and superstitions and remind us to celebrate who we are, and what we have been given.

The Hub Travel News

Mr. and Mrs. Joseph Langley are taking an ocean cruise to Hawaii, on the week of the 19th, there to view Halley's Comet, as Hawaii is reported to be the best place to see it.

They will travel by train to the West Coast and board the Canard cruise ship in Los Angeles.

Mr. Langley, an avid amateur astronomer, says he cannot let this opportunity of a lifetime pass him by.

"That towheaded preacher is back in town," Grandma Langley said to Abigail, folding the newspaper and removing her spectacles.

Abigail stared at her grandmother in disbelief before dropping into a chair, visibly shaken. "What did you say?"

"Says so right here in the *Hub*," Grandma said, tapping the newspaper. "And Joe and Rose are going on a cruise to Hawaii. Things must be lying easier between them. Joe took Orion's death too personal, I think. He plum fell apart after that boy died; somehow he blames himself. Lordy, if we blamed ourselves for our children's transgressions, we would all end up in the state lunatic asylum."

Goose bumps rose on Abby's arms, and she wondered if someday she might be a reason for her own mother to end up there.

With the heady wine of success flowing through his veins, Brother Griggsby had caught fire and ignited everyone within his rarefied universe. The people looked to him for guidance, for assurance of life after death, and especially for a guarantee of their place in heaven.

The nearer Halley's comet drew, the greater grew the hysteria. The fame of Brother Griggsby, after his personal message from God had appeared in the out-of-town newspaper, had grown to the extent that strangers were now crowding out the local churchgoers at his Sunday services.

The elders of the church, convinced that it was their mission to convert as many people to Christ in these last days as was in their power, decided to hold a revival, with their own Brother Griggsby as the evangelist. If ever a town was ready for redemption, and a revival, it was Rockville. As a people, they were ready to admit their transgressions and be saved in the name of Jesus. The three-day revival meeting was to culminate on a Sunday evening in the coming forward of "angels for Jesus."

Threatened by the fires of damnation, the congregation of Old Church had at last grown generous. "You can't take it with you," they reasoned. And, concerned with the overflow crowds the church was attracting, they decided, in their newly found philanthropy, to purchase a revival tent large enough to accommodate everyone who wished to be saved.

Inquiries were sent out, and a tent was found at a good price from a retired evangelist, Frank Miller, in a neighboring state. The tent was shipped by train to Rockville, and the seller of the tent, for an additional remuneration, came along as overseer. With permission from the town council and manpower from the males of the church, the tent was soon hoisted on the grounds of the ballpark.

During the raising of the tent, a long, narrow tarp-wrapped bundle piqued the interest of the men; unwrapping it, they found two posts, one six feet long and the other twelve, both six inches square and painted a garish gold color. The shorter bar was attached to the length of the taller post by a large screw bolt.

While the posts lay on the ground, the former evangelist demonstrated their function. Loosening the screw that was inserted into the center of the short post, and matching it to the hole three-quarters of the way up on the length of the tall one, he pushed on the short crossbar until it came to rest horizontally on a small block of wood attached to the larger post, creating the shape of a cross. Either way—single pole or cross—it was the center support for the black curtain at the back of the stage that hid from view the stacks of material necessary for the shipping and raising of the tent.

The ex-evangelist explained that in his evangelical meetings, the gold cross provided a dramatic background for his sermons. "With the spotlight on the cross and the tent lights dimmed, the black curtain fades to nothingness, and the speaker is revealed to the crowd as the servant of God standing beneath a cross of gold—something akin to Gethsemane."

Brother Griggsby and the elders debated using the cross for their revival meeting and at last decided against it, their reason being that the material symbol of the cross belonged to the Catholics and those "painted-window Protestants." Brother Griggsby did, however, accept the offer of a white satin robe that flaunted a rainbow lining of colorful stripes.

CHAPTER 95

May 1910

ON OPENING NIGHT OF THE revival meeting, the large evangelical tent was filled to overflowing; those who were unable to get into the tent were crowded together on the grounds of the ballpark. Without hope of finding seats (or even standing room) inside, the outsiders felt set apart, abandoned, unprotected, and they looked uneasily to the skies, from whence the comet, Jesus, and hell's fires were all expected.

Meanwhile, within the stifling tent, the lights dimmed, the buzz of people stilled, and there in the spotlight, wearing a lustrous white robe, stood Brother Griggsby. He stood assuredly, arms relaxed at his side, waiting, exalting. A hush fell over the crowd, the spotlight vanished, and a string of overhead lights beamed down on a man in his finest hour.

Once silence reigned absolute, he began: "Dogs—hanged in our streets. Innocent little girls—raped in our streets. Men killed in heinous ways—in our streets. A man, a human being, branded like an animal. Children begetting children. A beloved son, a symbol of splendid manhood—hanged by his own hand. A beautiful, much-beloved daughter—attempting suicide by her own hand. Girls kissing girls." His voice rose to describe this last act. "This is not a natural act, but an unnatural act, and an abomination unto the sight of God, and it took place in one of our very own churches."

Brother Griggsby shook his head in woeful despair. "I weep. My heart weeps. God's heart weeps for our little town. God looked down on us and saw wickedness as depraved as in the days of Lot, in the book of Genesis. The sin cities of Sodom and Gomorrah were cities of virtue compared to our little town. The place where we worship, work, and raise our children is as depraved as the Cities of the Plain. God is going to act," he said, solemnly rocking his head up and down to bring home his point.

"We are facing the end of the world; the very end that the Bible has warned us about for decades is here. We need God to enter our lives. We need Him in our hearts, our souls, and our minds. Are we a wicked and stiff-necked people, too afraid to admit Christ into our lives? Is it too late to be saved? I don't know," he said, his voice booming. "But what I do know is God's word to me, personally."

He placed his hand on his chest and experienced an exquisite feeling of sensual delight in the smoothness of the satin material. "God's promise to me is that on the night of May eighteenth," he said, still rubbing his chest, "if we have accepted Jesus as our Savior, we will rise up bodily to heaven on a cloud as pure and white as the snow, thus escaping the agony of death. One moment you'll be here, and the next you'll be gone," he said, flicking his hand heavenward. "Have we kept His Ten Commandments?" He sipped from a glass of water and rephrased the question: "Have *you* kept His Ten Commandments?"

People looked at one another, as if their neighbors might know the answer.

"Commandment one: 'Thou shalt have no other gods before me.' One God. One good old Christian God. No other God, and if you are not singing the praises of God morning, noon, and night, then you are singing the praises of the devil. As much as we hate the devil, the devil hates goodness. Either we are good—or we are bad. We cannot serve two masters. The devil needs you to fall from the path of righteousness." Brother Griggsby pointed his finger at the crowd. "He needs *you* to stoke the fires of hell. He needs *you* to worship him, and not the evils of sin. God hates sin. He hates liquor, card playing, and lying. He hates cursing and dancing, and prancing about in harlot bonnets. We cannot practice evil and love God. We can serve only one God, and we can have no other God before us."

Abby nervously fingered the bow at the neck of her shirtwaist. She had an uneasy feeling and wondered if her decision to attend the revival meeting had been a wise one.

"Commandment two: 'Thou shalt not make unto thee craven images.' We are Christians; we have been spared heathen worship. When I visit our great American cities, all around me I hear foreign tongues. I see skin unlike ours. I see people of heathen faiths worshiping their statues and practicing their strange rituals, which lay our good old American beliefs under siege. Right now, today, unknowns are infiltrating our little town: yellow-skinned, swarthy-skinned, black-skinned unknowns. Are we to mix our precious God-given red American blood with that of different colors? Are we to tolerate their heathen gods? We are Christians, our good names spelled from God's alphabet, not foreign names from some godless alphabet. Not hieroglyphics, not squiggles and upside-down letters, not unpronounceable names that tangle the tongue."

In his audience, the Nelsons, the Larsons, and the Jensens; the Adamses, Whites, and Clarks—the proud inheritors of names from God's own Christian alphabet—gently smiled. The women smugly affirmed their namesakes by smiling prim smiles at one another, the men by self-consciously stroking the length of their thighs and brushing away lint from lintless pants.

"Right now, at this very moment, high-minded scientists in their ivory towers are scrutinizing our sacred Bible. They are ridiculing those of us who believe that the stories in the Bible are true. They say we should not accept them as the truth, that they are only fables. I say God's laws will always be greater than scientific laws. At this very moment, those so-called professors are teaching the abomination of evolution. They are proselytizing the notion that we all sprang from monkeys. Yes, all of us: you, me, our forefathers." He shook his finger at the audience. "If we believe that man was once a monkey, then we must believe that God, too, was once a monkey!" A disruptive, negative rumbling came from the audience.

"Not my God!" he thundered, pounding his chest. "Not my Father, who art in heaven. Not my holy Father. Never!"

Shouts of "hallelujah!" and murmured amens rang throughout the tent.

"Thou shalt have no other God before ye!"

He paused to take a drink of water and lovingly stroked the Bible prominently displayed on the lectern. He looked with shrewd eyes into the crowd. "Commandment number three: 'Thou shalt not take the name of the Lord in vain.' Oh, ladies and gentlemen, the number of times I have heard the name of our dear Lord and Savior taken in vain are too many to be counted. Yea, and we have right here, in our very own little town, a den of iniquity. I need not name the place; you all know the vile den of which I speak. The language heard in passing leaves their mouths like fumes of black smoke deadlier than the fires of hell. Daily, hourly, they are breaking one of God's precious commandments.

"How many times have we let His holy name slip from our own tongues, thinking if no one hears us, it's all right? It's not all right! His name is sacred, and it is one of His commandments: 'Thou shalt not take the name of the Lord in vain.'"

He paused to measure the degree of angst in the audience. A woman, overcome with heat and anxiety, was helped from the tent.

"Commandment number four: 'Remember the Sabbath day to keep it holy.' Have we kept His day holy? Can you, in all honesty, say you have not broken the fourth commandment? Have you sinned on this day of days? Have you danced, sang, drank, played cards, listened to music, read the big-city Sunday paper, told a joke, played ball, and not gone to church and worshipped Him on His day?"

Inhaling deeply, he paused, sipped water, and looked out at them from beneath a brow furrowed in condemnation. "Our God is a jealous God; he does not forget, nor does He forgive. I remember a few years ago, right here in Rockville, when a man defied God and raised a 'Sunday Crop,' as he called it. Bragged about it. Blazoned it across his fence in big red letters. Worked it only on Sundays. Was going to harvest it on a Sunday."

He raised his brows, wisely nodding his head. "Dearly beloved, a fire doesn't just start out of nowhere. It doesn't just spring up and destroy a man's labor. No. It was God's wrath that started that fire and burned that Sunday Crop right down to the ground and scorched the very earth that grew it. Sunday belongs to the Lord!" he boomed, pounding the lectern.

As a whole, the audience had grown somber, sweaty, and uncomfortable, some silently counting out the remaining commandments on their fingers. The ladies fanned themselves to move the dead air about, to no avail.

"Commandment number five: 'Honor thy father and thy mother.' How many times, in the years since you laid them to rest in that cold, still earth, have you wished you could say to a dearly departed mother, a dearly departed father, 'I'm sorry, Mother; I'm sorry, Father. I wish I had been a better son, a better daughter, kinder to you. Helped you more, taken the time to listen to you.' Instead, you believed that you knew better, were better, than those dear, precious, long-ago parents."

Pulling a handkerchief from a pocket, he wiped his eyes. "Honor them now, this day, and the ones still with us, before it is too late." He paused again, wiping his eyes and blowing his nose.

His gift for reaching people swelled inside him, stinging his skin and reverberating along his spine. He loved the powerful persuasion of his own words.

"Commandment number six: 'Thou shalt not kill.' Thou shalt not kill, not even dumb animals, or for the sake of vengeance. Thou shalt not kill another, or thyself," he said ominously. "It is too late for that young man who hanged himself to reach the glory of heaven."

"That's a godforsaken, bald-faced lie!" an angry voice shouted from near the back of the tent. Joe Langley, stepping on toes and bumping knees, pried himself free from the crowded row of seats. People in his immediate area thought he was headed for the preacher, but Joe just wanted to be out of sight and earshot of the preacher.

"'Thou shalt not kill,' sayeth the Lord."

There was another disturbance, this time near the front. Poor little Mary Louise Richards had fainted. Adam, seated two rows behind her, saw her tumble forward onto the floor, and, pushing his way through the row of seats, picked up the girl and removed her to the aisle. Placing her on the ground, he worked his breast-pocket handkerchief into her mouth, hoping she had just fainted and was not in the throes of an epileptic fit. In a short time, Mary Louise opened her eyes, seemingly in good health, and Adam, with Grandma Richards at his side, carried the revived girl out of the tent.

The mesmerized crowd, unaware that anything was amiss, had begun swaying, some with their arms raised and eyes closed. A recitation of muted prayers blanketed the canvas tent. Some were crying the praises of Jesus, while others hollered them. Some were stricken and fell to the floor, only to jump up again, shouting and praying. The air was charged as before an electrical storm, heralding great drama and destruction.

Adam was deeply concerned about the effects of Brother Griggsby's hellfire message upon the more excitable members of the audience, Mary Louise being the first to justify his fear. The tent was airless; the lack of oxygen alone could lead to emergencies.

He looked to his wife. Lillian was sitting as if in a trance, head bowed, her lips silently moving. He touched her shoulder, and she looked up at him, her eyes calm, and it was apparent that she was not succumbing to the near–mass hysteria.

Damn this whole mess, he thought. Yet he and Lillian were in attendance because of his contempt for the preacher and his fundamentalist's teachings, and, closer to the truth, for Adam's own egotistical religious views. In all honesty, he had relished seeing Brother Griggsby in action. He watched the man, now sipping from a glass of water while skillfully surveying the crowd.

Suddenly, eerily, a wave of silence rolled over the audience as one person then another pointed to the stage. The short crossbar attached to the tall golden post, which had been set up as the main support of the black background curtain, had come loose from its bolt and, slowly and inexorably turning on the tall post, had come to rest in the shape of a cross. In the hush that ensued, the man controlling the spotlight shone it upon the radiantly majestic Christian symbol.

"How in the hell did he do that?" Adam marveled aloud.

Brother Griggsby, as surprised as his audience but with impeccable timing, had chosen that moment to spread his arms wide, revealing the inner lining of the white robe, with stripes every bit as splendiferous as the coat of Joseph in the Old Testament.

"Ooh! Aah!" The congregation was enraptured as currents of excitement raced through the tent.

His mighty preacher's voice thundered out the sin of the seventh commandment: "'Thou shalt not commit adultery'!"

Adam's head jerked up, his scalp tingling. *Is she here?* He was overwhelmingly alarmed as Brother Griggsby's voice boomed again: "'Thou shalt not commit adultery'! We have sanctioned harlots right here on our Main Street and in our homes. They have brought dishonor to us and to the names of their good husbands and good mothers. They are as thorns in the eyes of our innocent children: women flaunting themselves before men other than their husbands, dancing with men other than their husbands, lying like bitches with men other than their husbands, having babies out of wedlock by men other than a husband.

"We have harlots bedecking themselves in their Jezebel gowns, with their pomaded mouths dripping promises, enticing upright, God-fearing men and bringing them to their knees, right here in Rockville. We have harlot bonnets besmirching our saintly senses, made and sold in our stores by the hands of harlots. Repent," he bellowed, "or burn in hell's everlasting fires for all eternity!"

The dire threat of his words rumbled in the stifling tent like faraway thunder. Brother Griggsby rested a beat before again shouting, "Repent!"

He raised his arms into the air and shook his fists.

"She's here! The harlot's back here!" a voice in the rear cried. At first it was one voice, the shriek of an overzealous woman—then a man's voice—then many voices all shouting, "She's here! The harlot's back here. Repent! Repent!" The people all chanted in a disharmony of madness.

The new disturbance was great enough to be heard by everyone. People stood, pushed into the aisles, or climbed onto chairs and craned their necks to see what was happening. The brimstone-fevered hysteria of the crowd demanded a victim, and the hungry animal, no longer in abeyance, leaped at its prey.

Abby sat erect, her hands gripping the purse in her lap, her mind a vacuum. She knew she should have left when Brother Griggsby had started in on the commandments, but, too afraid of drawing attention to herself, she had remained. When he had shouted "adultery," the blood had left her extremities and all sounds had ceased. Now they came roaring back.

Rough hands grasped and tugged at her body. Her hat was knocked from her head; the auburn-burnished hair, now set free of the bone pins and its neat coiffure, flowed around her shoulders. She was lifted bodily and dragged across people seated in the same aisle. The button popped off her single-button jacket, and her shirtwaist of thin white cotton, hiked above her skirt band, provided a peek at her undergarments.

Abby found herself imprisoned in a knot of humanity, all chanting, "Confess! Repent!" Helplessly entrapped in its maniacal center, she surged with them toward the podium.

Adam, battling the tide, was frantically pushing and pulling people from the aisle in his desperate attempt to reach her. Through the sea of faces, Abby glimpsed him and could see the terrible rage upon his face.

From behind her, someone wrapped his arms around her in a possessive grip. She punched her elbows backward, determined to fight back.

"Abby, it's me, Noah."

"Noah?" Abby gasped, trying to turn her head to look at him.

Adam reached her seconds later, and her strength and the will to fight left her body, and she collapsed in his arms.

With their arms encircled around her, the two men maneuvered her to the side of the tent, where a flap had been lifted. The crazed mob, seeing Abby's head lolling about and the doctor in attendance, backed off, some of its martyr-lust satisfied.

Others, who were on the periphery and not part of the little drama, were still shouting "Confess!" as the three reached the cool, revitalizing evening air. Brother Griggsby, from the podium, his voice like a cannon, boomed again: "'Thou shalt not commit adultery'!"

"I'd like to commit murder," Adam said, lifting Abby into his arms and carrying her, with Noah following, across the street to her house.

Inside the living room, Adam laid her on the couch, unbuttoned the neck of her bodice, and rubbed her hands in an effort to revive her.

"Dr. Edwards," Adam said to Noah, "Grandma keeps a jar of her fruit brandy in a cupboard above the kitchen sink. Would you pour us a glass, please?"

Kneeling on the floor beside her, Adam lifted Abby's head and put the glass Noah had brought to her lips. She gulped at the liquid. Her nose wrinkled, her eyelids fluttered, and, as she coughed and sputtered, color returned to her cheeks.

"It's these damn tight corsets you women wear that make you faint," Adam said, railing.

This time her blush was genuine. Looking into the concerned faces of both men, she felt confused and foolish.

"Why were you there?" Adam demanded.

"Because I loathe him," she said in a squeaking voice. "I wanted him to make a fool of himself, and instead he made a fool of me. He's hated me ever since the night Ronnie was born." Doubling her hands into fists and placing them on her temples, she drummed the floor with her feet, releasing her pent-up anger in a mewing, squealing cry.

Adam gathered her into his arms, where she continued to twist and squirm like a captured kitten. "Abigail, it's all right. It's all right. It's over," he said, gently shaking her. When he took her again into his arms, she let her head fall onto his shoulder. "Just promise me you won't go back to the revival," he said, stroking her hair, "that you won't get involved in any more of this end-of-the-world bunk." He said it like a loving father.

Still breathless from her angry outburst, Abby offered her acquiescence by nodding her head up and down on his shoulder.

Adam let her cry before gently lifting her chin with his thumb and forefinger. Looking into her wet-little-girl face, he said, "I'm sorry, Abigail, but I have to get back to the meeting."

Her eyes filled with blame.

"Don't do this, Abby," Adam said. "Not now; this is not a matter of choosing."

"I'll stay with her," Noah said.

He was standing by the fireplace, one elbow resting on the mantel, a silent observer of the intimate drama being played out by the man and woman seated on the couch, and apparently forgotten by them.

Adam, quickly recovering, said to Noah, "Step out on the porch with me for a minute, will you, Doctor?"

Outside, the faint sounds of singing and amens borne on the cool night air drifted toward the two men. "This is insane nonsense," Adam said in a voice bitter with disgust. "How much longer do you think it'll go on?"

"He's wound up," Noah said, "and drunk with power. It could go on all night. My guess is it will end when he gets through the Ten Commandments and saves all the sinners who are begging for redemption."

"I have to get back to my wife. You will watch after Abby?" Adam said, nodding toward the house. The men shook hands and parted.

Noah entered the house and resumed his position at the fireplace. Abby was sitting primly upright on the couch, her bodice buttoned, her slender white hands chastely folded in her lap.

"Marry me," Noah said.

The only sound between the two of them in the room was the sharp intake of her breath.

She studied the man. After a long silence, she said, "It's too late for us, Noah."

"No, it isn't. It isn't too late for us."

"You're two years too late, Noah," she said, her eyes glistening.

"Is he the father of your child?" Noah abruptly asked.

"Children," Abby said, at once on the defensive. "I had another child while you were away." Noah said nothing. Abby said, "He died."

Noah turned his back to her, and when he turned around again, the muscles near his mouth had tightened to whiteness and his brilliant blue eyes to ice. When he spoke, there was a cold fury in his voice. "Why do you give yourself away?"

Abby answered in a voice smoldering with anger. "It's my right as a woman to give myself away." She rose from the couch, confronting him. "It's my birthright. It's every woman's birthright to give herself away, for love, for money, for sanctuary, for our children, for food in our mouths and clothes on our backs, and just to be wanted and needed by someone, even for a few minutes. It's our birthright—and our history."

"Leave here, Abigail." Noah took a step toward her, but the look on her face stopped him. "You will be persecuted in this town, all the days of your life."

"Are you going to save me, Noah? Keep me from drowning again?"

Who am I saving her from, Noah wondered: *Adam, herself, me? And how does she feel—can she feel?* "I'll do whatever it takes," he said. "I was a coward before. I loved you too much."

Abby raised a skeptical eyebrow.

"I put you before God, so I ran, but I could never run far enough. I alone am to blame for your debasement." Slamming his hand on the mantelpiece, he said, "Those should have been my babies you bore, not his."

He stepped forward, this time taking her by her shoulders. She remained haughty, her eyes cynical. "Forgive me, Abigail. Please forgive me. If I had been an honorable man, followed my heart instead of running off, you would not have had to bear the loss of another child or suffered tonight's humiliation, and how many other affronts I cannot imagine." Humbly dropping his arms at his sides, he said, "Abby, I'm begging you: leave here."

"With you?" she asked with disdain.

"Yes, as my wife—unless you can't leave him."

Her resolve wilted. "Is it that obvious?"

"It is to me."

"And you still want to marry me?"

"Yes."

CHAPTER 96

MONDAY MORNING DAWNED BRIGHT AND peaceful upon a tired town. The good people, for the most part, had survived the religious revival with a righteous sense of saintly accomplishment. The women went about their Monday clothes-washing chores with a full heart, often breaking into song, even though they knew it could very well be their last one. During the fateful week ahead of them, the people as a whole performed their daily duties in the usual manner, yet they performed each act with that dreadful last day in mind.

On Tuesday, the sisters of the Tuesday Benevolent Society met at the home of Frank and Lizzie Doyle to begin the onerous task of stitching the ascension robes. They were long and white, of course: one for each member of their family.

Lizzie Doyle, who was presiding over the group today, had blushed like a new bride each time anyone had looked at her since the foot washing, which caused

Perthy Prettyman to sniff to her neighbor, "Lizzie Doyle's behaving like an angel with a new halo."

Brother Griggsby, omnipotent in his divine calling, joined them at refreshment time. Lizzie, blushing, blissfully asked, "Is it still the end of the world, Brother Griggsby?"

"Yes, ladies, it is the end of the world, but you have nothing to fear. God will be with you, and I will be with you, leading you to heaven like the children of Israel, there to become virgin angels." Rapturously they looked to him and, overcome with joy, knelt at his feet in prayer.

Perthy Prettyman later remarked that she thought Brother Griggsby believed heaven would be made up of him, God, and virgin angels.

The days were a fever of sewing, praying, worshipping, and proselytizing. Parlett's Emporium ran out of white yard goods three times, and the good ladies were forced to buy luxurious sateen fabric used for lining draperies from the "harlot store," the Bon Marché.

On Wednesday, Adam and Lillian, with their son Michael, sat in the wicker chairs on the wide veranda contentedly enjoying the warm weather and the baby's first outing. Lillian fretted that the spring air would not be healthy for Michael, but Adam convinced her otherwise.

Adam had one ankle crossed over his opposite knee, and the baby, propped on his folded leg, was observing him. Pride filled Adam's chest as he again rejoiced in the magnificent child he had sired.

"Is it the end of the world?" Lillian suddenly asked.

"Lillian, please," he said, gently chiding her. "You know better than that. But because you ask, recently I've been giving a lot of thought to religious doctrines, and I've come to the conclusion that people need to believe in heaven and hell; in a loving God, and a jealous God, and the devil; in love and hate and forgiveness. It's what gives order to our world. It's the belief in a higher being that makes our laws and gives them power. Sometimes we need to bend a knee to something greater than our own puny selves, to sing the praises of something we love with all our heart and all our might." Pulling on Michael's arms, he drew the baby to him and kissed his forehead. "The sincere belief in a deity rights a flawed world and, with any luck, will prevent us from committing mayhem against one another. We need the Griggsbys of the world, God bless them, to keep us on the path of righteousness in our quest for a better life, even if it is in the next one. In fact, I envy the true believers their uncompromising faith."

"What would you do differently if you were God?" Lillian asked.

"Well, to steal words out of the mouth of the agnostic Robert Ingersoll, I would make health catching, instead of disease."

"Ummm," Lillian responded as she reached out her hands for the baby's feet, shod in embroidered white satin shoes, and wiggled his toes. "For that act alone, I would grant you godship. Will baby Michael go to Sunday school?" she asked.

"Of course, baby Michael will go to Sunday school," Adam said. "I want him to be just like all the other little boys, like Johnny and Georgie and Tommy, because civilization depends on Michael's going to Sunday school. To preserve civilization, we must conform."

He handed Michael to her, and she put him to her breast. He studied mother and child, the baby noisily nuzzling as his fingers kneaded the smooth white skin of her bosom. "The hunger to worship begins at our mother's breast, along with an inborn determination to survive. And, if there is a God, he should come down here and smite us all for the ungodly acts we have committed in his name. Like my father, I'm a freethinker, and I form my religious opinions from my own reasoning powers, but in order to have a sane world, I believe we need to conform. We need religion, and rituals, and rites of passage. They're important; they keep us grounded."

He looked at Lillian and continued. "I believe nonbelievers are philosophically charged with the sacred responsibility of upholding the inalienable right of people to worship as they see fit. Believing in God, and the devil, is what keeps us obedient. Without fear of the devil, we will not fear God, and it's easier to control people's actions if we all believe in a heaven and a hell. But, in the end, it will all come down to the quality of our offspring. In each generation, our children will be our salvation—or our ruin."

"Where is God?" Lillian asked.

"Well, He's not up there," Adam said, pointing to the sky. "God exists in our minds. Where else could that elaborate myth find nurturing? Let me burp him," he said, quitting his pacing of the porch and stopping before her.

Lillian relinquished the baby and excused herself to go to the house. "I'll be right back," she said. "He needs another blanket."

"Take your time. My son and I are going to have a man-to-man talk."

"He's too young for man-talk," she warned him as she walked away.

"Beware of women, son," Adam whispered into the baby's ear. "Their honeyed lips and scented skin can bring strong men to their knees with the gnashing of teeth and cries in the night." From the veranda, he could see the roof of Abby's house. *Let her go,* he thought. *For the sake of all of us, let her go.*

On Thursday, Noah parked his sleek new cream-colored Cadillac convertible on the street in front of Abby's house. Opening the gate, he went up the walk, the same way he had the first time he called on her, after saving her from drowning all those years ago. And now, as then, Abby stepped outside onto the porch and greeted him. She felt apprehensive, not having seen him since he had proposed marriage to her, and she didn't know how she should act, or what to expect.

She sat in the glider, and Noah sat on the railing. The haunted look that had been in his eyes when he left Rockville was gone. He looked like a man at peace with himself.

"How are you?" he asked.

"Much better, thank you," she said. "I believe I survived the revival; now I just have to stay the course."

Noah chuckled. He removed a red velvet case from his inside coat pocket and, opening the lid, revealed a gold charm bracelet with multicolored stones, bangles of dancing Siamese figures, and fat-bellied gods.

It reminded Abby of the times her father had returned from his travels with exotic gifts. Remembering him made her eyes fill with tears. She looked toward Noah.

When he saw her tears, he went to her and took her in his arms. "Dearest Abby, there is a second chance for us."

She did not tell him that the tears were for her father. *That was then,* she reminded herself, *and this is now. This is about a man I once cared for deeply, and regaining those feelings.* She smiled up at him.

Noah lifted the bracelet from the box and fastened it around her wrist. "I found it in a bazaar in Calcutta. The women of India reminded me of you. As a matter of fact, every woman, each new place I traveled to, everything I saw, reminded me of you. Someday I'd like to show you the Sphinx and the Pyramids, the Taj Mahal by moonlight. I wanted you with me."

Abby looked away. *Although Noah left me, during the time he was away, he was remembering me. And yet, when Adam came back into my life, I completely forgot about Noah.* Her eyes glistened. He pulled her behind the honeysuckle vines and, wrapping his arms around her, kissed her.

On Friday, Mrs. Lizzie Doyle held her annual "demon rum drive." She was not waiting for the day after the Fourth of July—because this year, there wouldn't be a Fourth of July—but just in case…

After touring Main Street and chanting at each place of commerce, she excused this year's group of ten-year-old boys and felt it to the quick when she saw their utter delight upon being dismissed. *If they would perform with that same gusto when they chanted their slogans to the town's drunkards,* she inwardly fumed, *it might do some good.*

We hate whiskey,
We hate rum,
You can put them on the run.
Do it now!

The noisy boys chanted to one another in a mocking tone as they raced toward the emporium window. Lizzie departed for the doctor's office, where she patiently explained to

Dr. Adam Townsend what medication his father had given her for her weariness after a laborious day of proselytizing against drinking. "It's in that cupboard," she said, pointing a finger to the cabinet with etched glass containing bottles, vials, and boxes. "It's that square-shaped bottle right there," she said. "And then he had that Gypsy man drive me home in the doctor's carriage."

Adam picked up the bottle containing a golden liquid and, removing the cork, smelled the contents. Rum! *Why, that sly old scalawag,* he said to himself. He left the office and returned with a small bell-shaped glass for after-dinner drinks. He filled it and said, "I'll have Bruce give you a ride home, Mrs. Doyle."

Later he recorded in his journal, "Diseases, and the Cures Thereof": "Patient's complaint: stress. Cure: a good belt of rum."

The ten-year-old boys, now free, ran to the window of Parlett's Emporium where items marketed to cash in on the popularity of Halley's comet were on display.

Among the many items were cloth masks designed to cover the mouth and nose the moment one smelled the cyanogen gas from the comet. Most of the men, women, and children of Rockville, however, were depending on plain handkerchiefs to spare them from the deadly fumes. They went about with the kerchiefs tied loosely around their necks in preparation for the gas attack that would likely come when the tail of the comet swept the earth, killing them like the gas did gophers when farmers shot the deadly substance into the pests' tunnels.

Hyrum Dinwoody, dressed in his white ascension robe, was being ejected for the second time that day from the barbershop for preaching hellfire and damnation to the regulars in Ma's. Booted out onto the sidewalk, he met up with another of his brother Ascensionists, and they stood facing each other, their arms crisscrossed and hands grasping each other's shoulders in prayer.

"I'd like to douse them with a bucket of water," someone in the barbershop said.

"Water's too good for 'em; douse 'em with horse piss," was the response.

The coming of the comet, although they would not admit it, had the regulars in Ma's uneasy, so the ribald remark, and subsequent laughter, received more hearty guffaws than it warranted.

The Ascensionists had not planted their spring crops and gardens. They had turned loose their livestock and chickens or given them to neighbors; families were divided, as in the days of the Civil War, as to who was right or wrong. The old beliefs in God, the Bible, and the end of the world were sorely tested.

CHAPTER 97

EARLY AFTERNOON ON THE EIGHTEENTH day of May, after the main meal of the day was over—some housewives leaving the dirty dishes on their kitchen tables, and others, out of habit, readying up the house; some men locking their doors, and others not—the believers, white robed and steadfast in their conviction that it was their last day on earth, began their exodus to paradise by way of the cemetery and the Rock House.

A large number of the members carried Bibles, while others carried babies. Walking by twos or threes, in groups or in families, neighbors, relatives, and friends migrated from the town. The graveyard soon filled with ghostlike souls walking among the tombstones.

The soon-to-be raptured spoke affectionately to the mounds of earth, tenderly touching the cold headstones or speaking with great elation to departed loved ones.

"I'm coming, husband."

"I'll hold you soon, little one."

"Be ready to welcome us."

"Be waiting, Dad, Mother; we'll see you before long."

"I'll see you in the great yonder," one nervous little man said to the graves of the two wives he had buried in years past. He wondered what his dearly departed would think of the young wife he had brought with him.

"That first Monday in heaven is going to have a lot of dirty linen hanging on the clothesline," Perthy Prettyman prognosticated.

"Today, Lord, today, I will look upon Thy face," said Brother Griggsby.

The brother called his flock to him, and together they filed across the shaky old timber-and-rope bridge that spanned Stony Creek at the site of the cemetery and began their ascent to the Rock House.

Like great white beetles, they scaled the slope of the mountain, singing, climbing, and stopping often to rest and to pray. The rise was steep, and the Ascensionists, encumbered by their long robes entangling their feet or snaring on rocks and bushes, tired easily.

"How much longer, Lord?" they asked themselves, looking up at the treacherous slope of the mountain. Young boys already atop the Rock House called down to the people below.

"Hey, Dad, Mom, look at me!"

"I haven't been up here since eighth grade," one man huffed to his companion.

"Me neither," his companion huffed back.

Upon reaching the Rock House, now in the shadow of the mountain, the hot, tired climbers cooled off fast and looked with envy to the town below, still basking in warm sunlight.

Later in the evening, with the flimsy ascension robes their only wraps, they huddled together. The faithful servants of Jesus were prepared for heaven but not for the unexpected cold. No one had thought to bring matches, and the rubbing of sticks together to build a fire proved a dismal failure. To keep up their spirits, they began to sing, looking first to Brother Griggsby for his approval. It was the singing and not the promise of paradise that sustained them through that long, cold vigil.

During the never-ending day, the ones left behind who had witnessed the mass migration looked often to the mountain and wondered if they had done the right thing by remaining down below with the doubters. The merchants closed their places of business early and went home, only to return later with their families. No one wanted to be alone on this unpredictable night. They opened their stores, turning on lights and chatting with people either inside the store or out on the sidewalk.

The earth was scheduled to enter the tail of the comet, and its toxic gases, at 11:20 p.m. By nine o'clock, most of the townspeople who were not on the mountain were downtown. People leisurely strolled about looking in store windows, enjoying ice cream cones from the drugstore or licorice sticks and peppermint candies from Parlett's. They called out greetings to one another and moved from one group to the next, but always with an eye to the sky.

The door at Ma's was propped open for easy access, and the hilarity within, along with the raucous music of the player piano, spilled out onto the sidewalk. This tempted teetotalers and the merely curious to sneak a quick look inside as they sauntered by, and for that bit of daring, they were accosted with bits of rowdy conversation.

"Did the damn fools take anything with them to eat?"

"Hell no! They're going to feast on that heavenly banquet up in the sky: eat on gold plates and drink out of gold goblets."

"Well, they'll eat crow pie tomorrow."

The moon—a great white globe lighting earth and sky, faded stars, and Milky Way alike with a noonday brightness—heartlessly exposed the hidden fear they saw in one another's eyes.

At 2:00 p.m. on the eighteenth, Adam stood and, removing his coat, rolled his shirtsleeves to his elbows. He placed his hands on the small of his back and bent backward as far as he could before sitting again. "It's getting harder to crank," he said to Bruce Sorensen, who was taking his turn at churning the cream-and-sugar concoction in the metal container of the four-quart White Mountain Ice Cream Maker set in a wooden tub of ice and salt into ice cream.

"What do you make of all of this comet stuff?" Bruce asked Adam. His blue work shirt, like that of all farmers—no matter how hot the day—was buttoned at his wrists and tucked into his bib overalls.

"We'll all be here tomorrow," Adam replied matter-of-factly.

"Listening to you explain the reason why the comet isn't going to destroy the world to Eric Thompson yesterday, while you set his broken leg, I decided right then and there I'd take your word on anything."

"You were a big help to me yesterday," Adam said.

"I rode over to the Thompsons' place early this morning. Eric's leg is coming along fine, they said, but he's still fretting about missing that heavenly ride."

Adam, seated on the ornate iron-and-wood bench encircling the oak tree, could see his wife in the gazebo. Lillian was showing the new Italian maid a piece of silverware before placing it on the table. Lillian was instructing the woman on the finer points of setting a proper dinner table. The young woman was helping Lillian prepare the gazebo for the comet party the Townsends were giving that evening.

Adam was looking forward to one of nature's many phenomena, but Lillian was suffering from feelings of trepidation. Her eyes often wandered to the mountain and to the covering of white robes, like a blanket of foreboding, spread on and around the big rock.

"My wife and kids are at the Rock House. I may go up there later tonight, just to make sure they're all right," Bruce said.

"Let's take a look in the telescope," Adam said. "You may be able to pick them out." Earlier in the day, Adam had set up the telescope at a place on the lawn that would afford him an unhampered view of the sky. "It's one of the most exciting events to happen in years," he said to Bruce as he focused the scope on the Rock House. "Someone's going to get hurt, and I don't want them to come crying to me to climb up there to save them. Let Jesus do it."

At dusk, Adam and Lillian's guests began arriving for the comet party: Leo and Eloise Langley; Reverend Bob Maynard and his fiancée, the very pretty and lively Emily Adams; the school principal, Otis Leonard, and his wife, Mary Lou; druggist Dick Stevens and wife, Barbara; attorney Mark Davis and his wife, Maxine; Dr. Veering and wife, Faye; and the match-up that still surprised everyone: Daisy Brown and Pierre Parlett.

The women lingered at the house to ooh and aah over Lillian's baby before joining the men on the lawn. Eloise Langley, blushing, confided to the women that she would soon have to remain at home—given that it was the custom for a woman in a family way not to be seen in public until after her confinement.

In honor of the comet, Lillian had decorated the gazebo with blue and white balloons tied with silver streamers. She set the table with a white linen and lace tablecloth set with white porcelain china, gleaming silverware, and white candles in silver candlestick holders. A centerpiece of white peonies and snowballs, cut from the bush that grew near the kitchen door, was arranged in a blue chinoiserie vase, completing the blue and white color theme for the dinner party.

The men drank whiskey and soda. Reverend Bob, the school principal, and the women, wearing wraps on this cool, clear evening, sipped on sherry. Supper consisted of picnic foods Mrs. Sheridan had prepared earlier in the day: fried chicken, potato salad, carrot-and-raisin slaw, vegetables in cream sauce, lemon cake, and homemade ice cream.

After preparing the picnic food in the early afternoon and cleaning up the kitchen, Mrs. Sheridan had donned her white robe and joined the believers at the Rock House.

Following supper, when all the guests' minds seemed to be elsewhere, the men stood in a cluster around the telescope, talking, while the women remained in the gazebo.

If the comet was there, the gleaming moonlight made the sky too bright to see it. Adam, striking a match, regardless of the brightness of the night, looked at his gold pocket watch and informed the men, "It's eleven fifteen."

"Eleven fifteen," Brother Griggsby announced, looking up from his Sears, Roebuck's pocket watch. He was standing in his long white robe on the Rock House surrounded by his family and the disciples of the church, which included the Unholy Seven. Clustered close to the big rock and beyond, surrounding it on three sides, were his white-robed followers.

"I have to pee-pee, Mama," a little boy said.

"Hush, you can go when we get to heaven."

"Is there an outhouse in heaven, Mama?"

For an answer, his mother jerked his arm, and she herself wondered if heaven had an outhouse.

"Everyone face east," Brother Griggsby commanded. And they did so. "Now, remember, no stampeding. There will be room for everyone: children first, then women, and the men last."

"You go first, Brother Griggsby," a woman's solemn voice urged.

"Where's the cloud, Daddy?" a six-year-old boy asked.

"Jesus will make one."

"Will the cloud hold us up? Won't we fall through it?"

"Shhh, son, Shhh!"

"Hey, everybody, look back here at the mountain!" an excited voice from the rear of the crowd exclaimed. High above them, against the black backdrop of the mountain, a glowing apparition, awesomely beautiful, hovered in the night sky before descending toward them.

"What is it?" people whispered.

"It's Him!" intoned the sonorous voice of Brother Griggsby. "We are here, precious Lord Jesus, waiting to rise with You to heaven." Reaching out his arms, he cried, "Christ is risen. Glory be to His name!"

Little shreds of light, glowing like dying stars, fell earthward from the gleaming specter.

"It's not Jesus!" shouted an excited male voice. "It's the comet!"

At that precise moment, and with a deafening explosion, the world was torn asunder! The earth shook, rocked, and reeled. Colors in the shapes of pinwheels and globes erupted in the sky, booming over and over. The calamitous sound coming from the mountain echoed in the valley below and was joined there with another detonation coming from the town. Fire erupted in the heavens, accompanied with lightning and thunderbolts, as rocks loosened from the blasts tumbled down the mountainside.

Because he was sore afraid, the good brother fell forward and tried to bury his face in the hard rock of the Rock House. People crumpled to the ground, crying and shrieking, for there was no place for them to hide; they were trapped on the mountain at the mercy—of what?

Gradually, the pleading prayers of men, the sobbing of women, the crying of children, the pounding of blood, the ringing of ears, and the chaotic movements of people half scared out of their wits ceased—and there was nothing. Nothing!

Where is the cloud? Where is their savior? Where are the pearly gates and the streets of gold? They waited, and they waited, before cautiously rising to bended knee, some sniffing at the air for the smell of the deadly gas before clamoring to their feet. They were not in heaven! They were on earth! Their lives had been spared from the comet. But the glorious dream of the coming of Jesus was gone, and so was hope—and faith.

The people looked toward the town, tranquil in the moonlight, their homes, their church, the school—everything as it had always been.

"First thing in the morning, we go home!" someone shouted.

"Yeah! Yeah!"

In their gullibility, they could not look at one another; they made what preparations they could to spend the rest of the night on and near the Rock House. For survival, they huddled together with friends and neighbors, closer than they had ever been, or wanted to be. Many of the young men began the descent to town, but most of the Ascensionists, out of necessity, remained on the mountain to wait out the night.

"What in the hell is that?" Leo exclaimed, pointing to the bright-orange light floating near the top of the mountain.

Adam was trying to find the flaming ball in the telescope before it disappeared from sight, and just as he located the glowing image, the night detonated into a thunderous boom. The sky above them, tranquil a second before, was now alive with celestial fireworks and horrific noises. The world appeared to have come to its end after all.

For what seemed like an eternity, no one moved, then the men raced toward the gazebo and the women.

Lillian, looking into Adam's startled eyes, thought, *Do our brains go on thinking after we die?*

Adam shook his head like a man coming out of a trance. For one terrible moment, the thought—is this the end?—had flashed through his mind and had become immobilized in the marrow of his bones. He said, "What the..." and stopped.

The noise from the chaos had ceased, and everything was as still as death; absent were the familiar sounds of a summer's night; sky and earth were at peace. Floating on the awful silence ever so faintly from the direction of the town park, the heinous sound of the laughter of grown men could be heard.

"Chance Collins, you demonic bastard!" Leo bellowed from the gazebo and into the night before he remembered the man was dead and that ladies were present.

"It was my first thought, too," Adam said.

"A forceful, dynamic man, whether he stands for good or evil, will always have converts to carry on his work," said Reverend Bob, knowing he sounded stiff and pretentious, but darn it, he was still visibly shaken from the horrendous scare they had all suffered.

Pierre was valiantly trying to reassure Daisy, who was weeping on his shoulder, that it was not the end of the world and that they were all safe and sound.

Nurse Boggins, with the baby in her arms, came rushing toward them from across the lawn, Adam and Lillian running to meet her. "Dear Jesus, Mary, and Joseph," the nurse said, her carefully controlled American English now richly thick with her lilting Irish brogue. "What happened?"

Adam and Lillian gathered nurse and baby into their arms.

At the gazebo, the men were laughing and shaking hands all around, and the women hugged one another and cried.

They were alive!

Out of the night, a voice called to them from the bridge, and Marshal McCombs approached on horseback. "Everyone all right here?"

"What happened?" they all asked at once.

"It's those so-called friends of Chance's carrying on his pranks. I got wind of what they was up to tonight, but by then it was too late to stop them. It was a few sticks of dynamite and some fireworks. You folks got the full repercussion, being situated between the two dynamite blasts. They set one off in the ballpark, for the benefit of the townspeople, and the other one close to the Rock House, along with the fireworks. The floating orange light was a fireball—one of those things you make with paper and cotton and set on fire, and it floats," the marshal said by way of explanation.

"They went to a heck of a lot of work to scare the wits out of people just for a belly laugh," Leo said, still fuming.

"Oh, they'll talk about this one for a long time to come. This'n'll be better than wagons on top of barns on Halloween," the marshal declared.

"The darn fools could've given someone a heart attack," Adam said.

"I'm on my way to the Rock House now, to see if anyone needs help," the marshal said.

"I'll go with you," Adam volunteered.

The Townsends' guests made their way to the house. The friendly chirps, rustles, and croaks of a spring night had returned. The couples, walking arm in arm to their buggies, knew that somewhere in the sky over their heads hurtled the mysterious visitor as yet unseen, and they appreciated more than ever the solid feel of the everlasting earth beneath their feet.

Through the late afternoon and evening, Abby sat alone on her front porch. She had watched almost everyone in town either disperse to the mountain or downtown. Except for some unusual activity taking place at the ballpark—where three or four men were doing something with sticks—everything was normal.

Noah rode up about 11:00 p.m. and, after tying his horse to the side gate, came around the sidewalk to join her. Abby, with a pale-blue shawl draped across her shoulders, was easily visible in the moonlight. She wore Noah's gift of the charm bracelet on her wrist, which pleased him. He greeted her with a kiss on the cheek. "I've been with Grandma Richards and Mary Louise," he said. "I was concerned about Mary Louise, but I don't believe all the excitement is going to affect her."

"I've spent the evening searching the skies," Abby said, "and I haven't seen any sign of a comet." Together they walk to the front lawn, away from the two large maple trees in the front yard, for a better view of the sky and the mountain.

"Look at that!" Noah said, excitedly pointing to a bright flame of light in the direction of the Rock House.

With the same ferocity as the ensuing blast that had assailed their world, Abby flung herself into Noah's arms. "Oh, Adam, darling," she cried. "What's happening?"

Adam? I called Noah Adam! How can I take it back?

And Noah, as he held her through the reign of terror surrounding them, wondered: *Will he always be there, between us?* Was calling out to Adam in a time of peril a slip of her tongue—or a slip of her heart? "Shhh, listen," he said to her, holding her at arm's length.

In the dreadful heart-stopping silence, they could hear the rollicking laughter of men emanating from the ballpark.

By dawn's early light, a chain of men organized by the marshal could be seen extending from the Rock House to the base of the mountain, bringing the Ascensionists back to reality. Cold, hungry, miserable, and too embarrassed to look at one another, they began their descent assisted, or lifted, from man to man: mothers with babies first, then toddlers and older children. "We're glad you're still with us," the rescuers said soothingly, easing the Ascensionists' self-consciousness. "Welcome back."

Awaiting them at the Townsends' gazebo, still decorated with last night's party decorations, was Lillian Townsend, along with women from the various churches, ready to disperse coats and blankets, hot coffee and soup, and freshly baked breads. A line of wagons and buggies waiting on the curving driveway in front of the mansion was set to take the tired wayfarers to their earthly homes.

Brother Griggsby was the last one to descend the mountain. He didn't partake in any of the welcoming services; instead he hurriedly departed with his wife and children, not looking or speaking to the members of his church—or anyone, for that matter.

The procession of wagons drove past the park, where a group of boys encircled the depression that the exploding dynamite of the night before had made in the earth. The boys were shooting their arms skyward and making booming and hissing noises.

"A little stick of dynamite sure put the kibosh on that flapdoodle," was Perthy Prettyman's summary of the end-of-the-world prediction, even though she, too, had endured the night of agony on the mountain along with the others.

Brother Griggsby did not appear on Sunday for the early church service. In place of a religious service, a committee made up of disgruntled and embarrassed church members had assembled for a grievance meeting.

"How did we let ourselves believe it was the end of the world?" Hyrum Dinwoody asked. "What kind of naive fools are we, anyway?"

Members of the congregation were making known their demands for changes in the dictates of the church.

"We want our church back," said Ralph Cox.

"We want our choir back," said Mrs. Stanton.

"We want our music back," Will Stanton said as he strode to the organ and, whipping off the patchwork quilt, exposed the instrument to the view of the members for the first time in a dozen years. A few members of the congregation were taken aback, as if they were laying eyes on something obscene.

"Where's our old organist?" Will asked, his voice pulsating with excitement. Seeing her seated near the back of the church, he called out, "Come on up here, Kate."

Hugging her purse to her bosom and looking about for sanctioning, the tall, rail-thin Kate Johnson let herself be led to the organ. With hearty assurances from Will Stanton, Kate was helped to a seat at the organ, where Will, opening the hymn book with exaggerated aplomb, placed it on the music rack before her. Inadvertently he had selected the hymn "Come Climb the Mount with Me, O Lord." Kate's eyes, again, helplessly appealed to the congregation for guidance.

"Play, Sister Kate," Will Stanton urged. "Play."

Quivering music, due to shaking fingers as much as to the neglect of the instrument, humbly filled the church. Tremulously, the contrite end-of-the world believers began to sing, building with confidence, and finally with jubilance, as they were filled with the joy of once again singing with accompaniment.

Brother Griggsby, ousted from the church by the newly organized church committee, with his wife and five children, impatiently waited at the station for the 4:10 train.

His children strutted about in new shoes, and atop Mrs. Griggsby's head rested the infamous hat from the Bon Marché: the very hat her husband had branded sinful.

No one showed up at the station to bid them adieu.

Brother Griggsby didn't mind; he had found a new calling: evangelism. He was in possession of a tent of commodious proportions, and a manager. He had a tent crew and a choirmaster. He had been persuaded that an evangelist needed, above all else, a choir. He had a new suit and three new shirts. He had a cross of gold—and he had a calling. He had also found that money in his pocket soothed him like nothing before.

The former evangelist, Frank Miller—who liked to refer to Brother Griggsby in public as the "golden-throated bird" and, to himself, one who was going to lay golden eggs—had convinced a group of well-heeled businessmen to look upon Brother Griggsby as an investment.

Another traveler was waiting at the station for the next train. Velvet, at long last, had sent for her son. The boy was seated alone in a far corner of the room. A cardboard placard with his name and destination printed on it hung from his neck by a string.

Bobby Lee had brought the boy to the station but had not remained to see him off. He was glad to be rid of the responsibility of one who was not his own, especially now, when he needed the extra room. Having been granted a divorce from Velvet, Bobby Lee had posthaste married the plump, matronly, and already in a family way Lucy White. To Bobby Lee, and his mother, Lucy had many fine qualities in her favor, one of them being that she had entered into the marriage with a dowry that included money and a horse and buggy. And, furthermore, she got along well with her mother-in-law; in fact, they were very much alike, especially in their solicitous concern for Bobby Lee's welfare. In the eyes of mother and bride, he was the perfect catch.

CHAPTER 98

June 1910

ANOTHER UNASSUMING WOMAN HAD FOUND her good fortune, Precious Amy having been the first. Abby's friend and business partner, Daisy Brown, was to marry the county's most eligible, indeed most desirable, bachelor, the moneyed and handsome Pierre Parlett, heir to the Parlett enterprises.

"She rose to the top like cream in a milk pan," Perthy Prettyman was heard to say.

This brought Abby once more into the Bon Marché, this time with the job of planning and supervising everything required for Daisy's summer nuptials: the gown, the bedecking of the hotel ballroom for a wedding reception, and decorating the cake. Surprisingly, she discovered that something she had dreaded doing turned out to be pleasurable as well as challenging: the designing and making of the wedding gown.

The day of the wedding, Abby, wearing an apple-green gown with the new short sleeves and sweetheart neckline, was at home and sewing on her own dress, for a change. She was rushing because she expected Noah at any minute. Daisy's wedding was to be their first date without a chaperone. They'd been seen at various events together, and, as in years past, in the company of Frieda Johnson. The townspeople, still recovering from their own folly, were hardly free to point accusing fingers at Abby, who had been publicly ridiculed and embarrassed beyond words at the revival and who was, after all, just another hapless victim of the end-of-the-world fiasco. She watched from the window as Noah parked his new convertible at her front gate. As usual, she met him halfway down her front walk.

"You look like a bride," he said, grinning. "I'll have to take a picture of you." He raised his camera and pointed it at her; she made a face and posed, smiling at him. Noah, like her father, had the latest in cameras and took pictures of everything.

They drove in style to the wedding at New Church, where the Parletts were members and Pastor Gillian was performing the wedding ceremony. She prepared for the open car by wearing a motoring scarf of sheer rose-colored chiffon, which covered her picture hat, head, and face. It was the very scarf that she had used in her first window display at the Bon Marché.

Pretty, petite Daisy was a radiant bride, her black hair and milk-white skin made stunning in a bridal gown strewn with seed pearls and inlaid lace. Abby, admiring her own handiwork, found herself wishing she had a business that would cater to weddings only. She had spent a good deal of her precious time sketching wedding gowns; she didn't know if it was the possibility of a new business venture that drew her to the dress or if it was the desire to be a bride herself. She could picture herself as a bride, but the groom by her side always had a blank face.

The Brown family all took part in the elaborate ceremony, and Timmy, not so small anymore and walking as well as anyone, was the ring bearer. Mr. Brown had given up farming and taken a job in the Langley furniture factory. Now with a steady income, he had moved his family into town, where they occupied half of a two-family flat with a small patch of lawn on either side of a walk leading to their front door.

At the reception, held in the Parlett ballroom, Abby drew as much attention as the bride. Members of the merchants' association greeted her with enthusiasm, telling her how much they missed her. Mr. Fontell, the little French tailor, his brown eyes melting when he looked at her, ceremoniously kissed her hand. "You are as beautiful as a bride," he said in his enchanting French accent. "Do please come back to our meetings." Others at the reception, however, still looked askance at her, causing her neck to grow warm. *I'll never get used to being stared at,* she thought.

In the crush of people, she saw Adam and Lillian Townsend enter the hall. The two couples, when they inevitably met, formed a polite little foursome, but they all greeted one another with restraint. Abby admired Adam's grooming; *the small-town doctor still has big-city taste,* she thought.

While Lillian chatted, Abby studied her. She was very thin and her skin oddly moist, with a mist of perspiration on her upper lip and mauve circles beneath her eyes. The pale-blue summer dress she wore to the event was ill fitting and her hat an old one.

"I never thought I would have a baby," she was saying, gushing, "and now I want to share him with the entire world. He is truly the most wonderful child." Laughing with delight, she put her arm through Adam's, hugging him to her in a wifely gesture.

Adam, looking at Abby, said, "Yes, we have a wonderful child." In a brief, perilous moment, Abby met his gaze.

"Let's dance," Noah said to Abby. "Better still, let's have some punch. I hear one of the bowls is spiked," he said sotto voce over his shoulder to Adam.

In the throng of people at the refreshment table, Abby became separated from Noah. As she moved away from the mob, Becky, once her best friend, approached her. When they spoke to each other, Abby was shocked to see wrinkles near Becky's mouth and others radiating from the corners of her eyes and onto her cheeks. *Is that how I look?* she wondered. *Old? An old maid?*

Her eyes scanned the room for Noah. She saw Daisy surrounded by her family, Pierre's arm around her waist; Lillian, fanning herself while seated at a small table with Lottie Oberlander, their husbands not with them. At last she saw Noah, a punch cup in each hand, conversing with the young and beautiful Marylyn Adams. The crowd in the room forced the two to stand close together, and Marylyn's cheeks were flushed with the virginal blush of innocence as she stood smiling up at him.

When Noah saw Abby watching him, he apologetically telegraphed his excuse to her by raising the punch cups, demonstrating to her that he had the punch. But what Abby saw in Marylyn's young eyes, when she deigned to look her way, was a curt look of dismissal. She was surprised by the blatant attention the young women were paying to Noah and disappointed in how much he seemed to be enjoying it.

Overcome by a sudden feeling of suffocation, she sought fresh air and privacy. She made her way to the balcony, where she was met with another crunch of people, and Adam Townsend. Together they made their way to the railing and stood looking down into the street, where a group of men were gathered around Noah's Cadillac. She was surprised to see that Noah was one of them. He was indicating something on the steering wheel to Oberlander, who was seated in the driver's seat.

"I hate you, Adam," she said, not looking at him.

"I know, and I'm sorry."

She wiped at her eyes.

"Please don't cry," he said. "You'll have me crying, and then people will have something to talk about."

"What did you name him, the baby?" she asked, keeping her eyes on the men below.

"Michael," he said, placing his hand over one of hers where it rested on the railing.

They continued to look down into the street, and she did not withdraw her hand from the old familiar feel of his.

"It was Ronnie's birthday on Monday," she said, her voice catching in her throat. "He was five."

Leaning sideways and shielding her with his shoulders, he carried her hand to his lips, kissing her fingers where they curled over his, and threaded them between his. "I hear you have a steady companion," he said.

She locked eyes with him and didn't answer. He gazed into the depths of her hazel-green ones and knew she was still his Eve. But knowing she was still in love with him, and not someone else, was not enough. It would never be enough.

CHAPTER 99

Abby and Noah sat side by side on the glider on the front porch of her house. She felt content when she was with him. His easygoing personality made for good company, and she believed he would make a good husband, and a good father.

"Do you love me, Noah?" Abby unexpectedly asked him.

He looked surprised. "I believe I've loved you since my first night in Rockville, when I heard the story of an innocent young woman giving birth to a blameless child." Abby hung her head, and Noah put his arm around her. "I wish I could erase the part I played in your unhappiness. I wish I could take back my actions, erase them like chalk on a slate board, and start over. Yes, I love you, and I want to marry you. It can be a winter wedding, a spring wedding, in a church, or by Judge Andrews—whatever you want. I'm ready to settle down, be an ordinary citizen—have children." He felt her stiffen.

Adam is the father of my children.

"I would like for you to set a wedding date and choose an engagement ring. You can design it yourself," he said, ending on a happy note.

Her hand clutched at the fabric of her bodice, where lay, close to her heart, the engagement ring Adam had given her the day she had told him she was pregnant with their second child.

Noah saw her consternation and wondered why the mention of a ring could cause such obvious anxiety.

"Will you remain a minister?" she asked, changing the subject.

"No. I haven't made my amends with God. Truth be known, I've lost my religious convictions. After my travels to other parts of the world, mixing with other cultures, and seeing the inhumanities committed against man and nature in God's name, I'm not sure God deserves our devotion, our obedience, our love. I found we each, with or without religion, do what is right by our own internal moral code, and not because it's a commandment, or because of the promises of the rewards that await us in heaven, or the fear of damnation when God scares us into doing the right thing. We do the right thing out of respect for ourselves and our fellow man, and I don't think we need a preacher to tell us what's right or wrong. Man must seek God within himself, and make himself as great as he's capable of doing."

"But virtuous men make us feel good," Abby said. Then, thinking of Brother Griggsby, she added, "Some of them do."

"What about Adam Townsend? Where does he fit into your life?" he quietly asked her.

She remembered the wedding reception and Adam's touch. "It's over," she said. "You replaced Adam in my heart once before, Noah, and I believe you're still there—in my heart."

He took her hands in his. "I should never have left you."

"You had to leave. After the extraordinary experience you had in healing people, and your spiritual crisis, a completely different venue was necessary for you. You never would have been whole again if you'd remained here."

"Yes, but in leaving, I hurt both of us."

Noah's last official act as a minister had been to conduct the service at the Chapel of the Ark for Lars, the builder, the dreamer of the dream. The construction of the ark had been Lars's journey; to Noah, looking anew at the edifice, he saw that for him, it had been a tribute to his own ego.

"Religion doesn't belong on Main Street," Noah said to Reverend Bob Maynard as they strolled along Main Street, tipping their hats when people greeted them. Both were relative newcomers to the town, yet everyone appeared to know them.

Bob was chagrined. "Has religion become something so derelict that we need to hide it in alleys and on back streets?"

Noah laughed. "Commerce belongs on Main Street." They were standing on the street facing the ark. "I plan on dismantling the ark," Noah said quietly. Bob showed his surprise. "Together we'll build a handsome new stone church around the corner on Sunrise Street. I'm donating the land, and I'll be your biggest booster and fund-raiser," Noah said. "And here, in place of the ark, I'm erecting an apartment building with storerooms on the ground level. You know Rockville's a little boom town."

"Well, I hope the boom isn't going to bust religion," Bob said.

"We'll always have religion, and good men and bad men and fools and saints—and preachers," Noah said, cheerfully ending the discussion with a spirited clap on Bob's shoulder.

"And commerce," Bob said wryly. He didn't mind. The ark had outgrown its attraction. Attendance at his church was expanding, along with the town, and he was in need of a larger building with classrooms and a band room. And, more important, Emily, his betrothed, had made it very clear to him that she did not wish to live in an ark.

CHAPTER 100

NOAH KNEW HE COULD NOT rush Abby into a romantic relationship; she still had too many painful memories to put to rest. And Abby, assuming that, if she accepted his marriage proposal, they would leave Rockville, went on with her preparations to move—plans she had begun negotiating long before Noah's return.

Her mother had at last grown weary of the demands of the hotel, and Abby was preparing the house for her mother to once again occupy. When she entered her mother's bedroom, she felt strange, as an intruder must feel. Raising the window shades in the stark, sunless north bedroom, she looked about and decided to brighten it up; she'd bring it back to life with new wallpaper and paint.

During the cleaning process, she removed the brown wrapping paper her mother had used to line the top drawer of the chifforobe. Beneath it she found the marriage certificate of her mother and father, and she discovered that her mother's maiden name was Juanita Sanchez

Driggs. Abby had known her mother only as Nita Driggs Langley.

A letter written on lavender stationery in faded purple ink and addressed to her father was also hidden beneath the paper liner. She found many handwritten forwarding addresses on the envelope; the original cancelled stamp was postmarked Dallas, Texas. There was also a photograph. Abby cautiously peeled back the folds of fragile paper and uncovered a studio photograph, done in soft sepia tones, of a woman. A deep scratch crisscrossed the image and extended from corner to corner, marring the beauty. She placed the photograph back in its wrapping and unfolded the delicate pages of a love letter written to her father. The author ended the letter by saying that she was terribly worried about him, to please let her know if he was well, and to hurry back.

Abby didn't know she was crying until she saw the wet stains mingling with the pale ink. *Was it my mother's tears that first faded the purple ink to lavender?* she wondered. She looked again at the postmarks; the last one was from a month after her father had died. Was this the cause of her mother's bitterness and unhappiness? And what about the author of the letter, this Marcie—was she still waiting for a reply?

Not long after, they sat, mother and daughter, in two rocking chairs on the front porch, not on the glider, for they had forgotten how to be close. After an uncomfortable silence, Abby's mother went into the house to approve, or disapprove, of the decorating Abby had completed in her bedroom. When she returned to the porch, she stood back of Abby's rocker with her hand on her shoulder.

Abby wanted to cover it with hers, to clasp it, kiss it, clutch it through all eternity, never to lose it again. But she could not. She and her mother had been alienated for so long that Abby knew if they touched, she would disintegrate—layer upon layer of her would unravel, crack, peel, and fall apart. How many years had it been in which she had yearned for an act of motherly love?

Soon her mother relinquished her sacrificial offering, and they sat as prisoners in their familiar silence glacially formed over an eon of time without light or touch, prisms of glass without rainbows; brittle, breakable.

Abby stroked the letter in her pocket, its delicate pages yellowing in the amber of time, but she could not bring to light the sorrow buried inside its lavender folds. *Maybe someday I'll unravel the enigma that is my mother,* she thought, *and maybe, I will forgive her for being my mother.*

Abby found the empty house depressing. Grandma had lived at River's Bend with Uncle Joe and his family since spring; now Daisy was married and in a home of her own, a fashionable house on Stony Creek Road; her mother was not yet wholly committed to retiring from the hotel. She was cheerless. Her relationship with Noah didn't seem right, not like before. She felt numb inside, as if she were sleepwalking through life. She hadn't announced her engagement to Noah to anyone.

I wonder where we will live, here, with my mother. The thought of living with her mother again, after all these years, gave her an uneasy feeling. Noah had suggested they live in one of the apartments in his new commercial building until they could build a home of their own. But she had spent her whole life in this house. It was her home, her rock, her solace, her family. She sat up straight, shaking her head; she was a businesswoman, with dreams of her own, not a homemaker.

Daisy had retired from working at the Bon Marché. Alice Sizemore, a schoolteacher who resided at Frieda's boardinghouse, had given up teaching—and the many restrictions required of a woman schoolteacher—and was not one bit sorry to work at the Bon Marché. Abby was teaching her the art of creating a desirable hat as well as the business end of running a retail shop. Alice didn't have Daisy's daintiness or Abby's style, but she had refinement and possessed levelheadedness. Her figure was standard, and she wasn't too pretty, which Abby knew would appeal to the women customers.

THE ROCKVILLE HUB
August 1, 1910

Noah Edwards will be his own first tenant in a storeroom on the ground floor of the new Edwards Building on Main Street.

Mr. Edwards opened his car dealership before completion of the other offices on the first floor of the commercial building. Apartments will occupy the second and third floors of the new Edwards Building.

"My grandfather made his fortune in buggies," Mr. Edwards says. "I'm going to make mine in horseless buggies." Mr. Edwards, who is the regional dealer for both Cadillac and Oldsmobile, informs us he is interested in the designing and manufacturing of his own line of autos.

The town has been quick to accept the new mode of travel, and Mr. Edwards says the men of the town and the county have purchased, or shown interest in owning, automobiles from his dealership.

To make travel by automobile even more attractive, a macadam road is being put down between Rockville and the county seat, seven miles away.
Mr. Edwards says, "It will take only one hour to drive by automobile to the county seat on the new road, whereas driving a

horse and buggy, that distance would take two hours."

Miss Perthy Prettyman was almost run down last week when crossing Main Street from Stevens Drugstore to the Emporium by one of the "new disturbances," as Miss Prettyman likes to call the new automobiles.

"What is the world coming to when a woman can't even cross the street in her own hometown without getting run over?" Miss Prettyman asked Marshal McCombs, when he rescued her from the middle of Main Street.

Marshal McCombs says times are changing, and we must change with them. He emphasized that we must learn to look both ways before crossing the streets.

Miss Prettyman is resting at home, where she is welcoming visitors.

CHAPTER 101

September 1910

NOAH KNOCKED ON THE SCREEN door and waited for Abby to answer. Leaving the mason jars to soak in a dishpan filled with soapy water, she made a bracelet of her fingers and slipped the soap suds from her forearms before picking up a dish towel and answering the knock on the kitchen door.

"Noah? Come in," she said, surprised, flicking the damp towel at the top of the screen door to scare away the flies that had gathered there, waiting for a chance to get inside.

"Ah. I have news—bad news," he said, still standing on the wooden stoop. No shirt cuffs showed on his long, bare arms. *What has he done,* she wondered, *just donned a coat over his rolled-up sleeves?*

"Lillian Townsend passed away last night. Heart attack."

Abby said nothing. She felt rooted to the spot where she stood stalk still, the dish towel slipping from her fingers.

"Do you want me to come in?"

She studied him for a time through the screen. The flies again settled on the door, no doubt drawn by the sweetness of the apricot jam cooking on the stove. She picked up the dish towel from the floor and stood pulling it back and forth through her hands. "Thank you, Noah. I believe not—if you don't mind. I believe I would like to finish making my jam." She glanced behind her as if to verify what she had said.

He lifted the latch on the gate before looking back. She had vanished from the doorway.

When the ebb and flow of her body returned to her, Abby walked to the kitchen chair, the place where her father had sat—when he was a father—before it had become her place. How often had he been home to be a father? Through the kitchen window, she looked idly to the Rock House, gray in the mountain shadow of late day, then to the Townsend mansion, recalling how, years ago, Adam had hoisted a red flag from the balcony, signaling to her that he was free from his studies.

They buried Lillian in the heart of fall, the season of death and goodbyes. Lillian's father had come from Baltimore for the funeral. The service was held at Sunrise Chapel, the new church on Sunrise Street, with interment in the town cemetery. Backyard leaf burnings scented the day with the incense of fall. Amid the dying leaves, bursts of brilliant colors of late-blooming purple asters and yellow chrysanthemums boasted the life spirit, while the fallen crimson, gold, and russet leaves crumbled beneath the boots and wagon wheels of the mourners—rust to dust.

Abby watched from her front porch as the hearse, its black plumes motionless in the still day, drove by. Adam sat in the seat beside the driver, while Miss Boggins (holding the infant) and Lillian's father rode in the cab.

The autumn scenery would soon be monotonous shades of brown, but today Rockville was wrapped in the brilliant hues of fall. Flying overhead in a V formation was a flock of black double-breasted cormorants headed south for the winter. Abby wished she could take wing and fly away with them.

Since Lillian's death, Abby had rarely been seen in Noah's company. She had become drawn more and more to isolation and to gazing from the kitchen window at the Rock House, or the mansion, more than she listened for Noah's footsteps. Was she marrying Noah to punish Adam?

By Thanksgiving, the gossip of a possible engagement between Abby and Noah had died down; when the holidays came, she released him from his impetuous proposal of marriage. She said to him, "You're still a knight in shining armor, waiting to save the damsel, but I'm no longer the damsel in distress. When we first met, you were not ready to settle down, and I was. Now you're ready, and I'm not. We're not in harmony. I think I've been a working woman for too long. My mind is on business—the latest styles and colors—not home and children."

"I crossed four continents and the Atlantic Ocean to come back to you."

"But when you returned, I was no longer waiting." Deep inside she felt a pang akin to anger as she remembered the heartache she had suffered when Noah had left her to seek the forgiveness he needed from his God.

"I'll wait," he countered.

But Abby concluded that he was content with her decision to break off the engagement.

Arriving home from the Bon Marché on the day of Michael's first birthday, Abby found a wrapped parcel leaning against the kitchen door—obviously a book, from the shape of it. She waited until she had removed her winter coat and hat, built up the fire in the cookstove, and put on the teakettle before she sat down at the kitchen table to unwrap a handsomely bound copy of *India's Love Lyrics*, by Laurence Hope.

A sheet of notepaper with just the letter A written on it was tucked inside the book, next to a poem with the title "Till I Wake":

When I am dying, lean over me tenderly, softly,
Stoop as the yellow roses droop in the wind from the south.
So, I may, when I wake, if there be an Awakening,
Keep, what lulled me to sleep,
The touch of your lips on my mouth.

As long as I remain true, she thought, *there's a chance that Adam will come for me.* The day passed. The season passed.

Dressed in a suit of black silk gabardine and wearing a large black hat, Abby assessed herself in the dresser mirror. Removing the hatpin, she replaced the large hat with a small, beguilingly flirtatious one with a stem of bright-red artificial cherries attached to the crown. The hat's short black veil, sprinkled with black velvet polka dots, tickled the tip of her nose.

Her eyes sparkled conspiratorially back at her from the dresser mirror as, with her forefinger, she rubbed a red rose on the bedroom wallpaper and rouged her already-glowing cheeks; a stylish reflection smiled back at her.

Not long after Abby had shown up in Dr. Townsend's waiting room, Nurse Boggins led Abby to the doctor's office and stoically remained in the room with her. Adam, upon seeing Abby, rose from his desk. A tremor of excitement rushed through him, and a look of delight spread across his face with the beginning of one of his dynamic smiles.

"I have come for my son," she said, her strength of mind showing in her face and posture.

A spasm of grief replaced the pleasure in his eyes. With a shock of déjà vu, he recalled his own childhood: a string of nurses, cooks, and housekeepers before Aunt Em had come into their lives.

Lillian had never been strong enough after the birth of the stillborn child to care for Michael—love him, yes, beyond all reason, but physically care for him? No, that had fallen to the nurse. Adam searched her face while summarizing the facts in his mind. He turned to the nurse. "Althea, my child's mother has come for her son. Will you please get him ready?"

Neither one spoke. Adam busied himself at his desk, and Abby looked from the window into the garden while they waited.

She had stopped shaking, and there for the first time she came face to face with her woman power: her Eve power. The seductive power of a woman's Eve-ness learned at that first mother's knee. She felt acutely the awakening in her soul. Felt the great cleansing pull of the tidal wave that forever prepares woman anew for her wondrous journey, shapes her completeness, and presses the core of her being into diamond hardness. She knew in that moment that she didn't need anyone: just her child and herself.

Miss Boggins returned with the baby and a valise and gave the baby to Adam. He held his son to his chest, stroking his head and kissing each cheek, before delivering his heir to another.

For a moment they stood, mother, father, child, a family portrait captured in tragic strokes. The child, turning his body away from Abby, imploringly extended his arms toward the nurse—then the bright baubles of color on a capricious hat bobbed and clicked and drew his attention back to her. Dimpled hands reached toward the ornament and in so doing touched Abby's cheeks, and son and mother, touching each other, bonded soul to soul.

Adam gave the baby's valise to Horace Brown to store in the buggy, already loaded with Abby's traveling cases. He leaned into the open carriage to speak with her. "After a decent period of mourning, I was coming for you."

"And if I had married another in the meantime?"

"Abigail, I trusted that you would never marry another."

She looked away from the pain in his eyes. "We'll be in Chicago," she said.

"Thanks for telling me. Take care of our child," he said in a whisper, "and yourself and"—touching the top of Michael's head—"our son."

The buggy set off down Main Street, Abby holding her son for the whole town to see. Rockville was in the season of its rebirth, picturesque and fragrant in a cloud of pink and white blossoms. They drove past her childhood home, the only home she had ever known, the honeysuckle vines with their pale lemon-green leaves already climbing the porch railing; they passed the town suffragette, Selma Ward, sweeping her sidewalk and stopping to wave at them.

They passed Pie Face, the town's solitary tycoon, negotiating with a ten-year-old over the price of a ride on the bicycle Pie had purchased with nickels from his street-cleaning business; lacking the mind-body skills to operate it himself, he was left to making money. Offered a dime or a nickel, Pie Face still chose the bigger of the two coins. The yellow-brick schoolhouse, with afternoon recess in full swing, the kids running, hopscotching, and playing snap-the-whip. Frieda, working in her garden, waved to her with both hands and, when she saw the baby, covered her mouth with her apron. Abby could make out a customer in the Bon Marché. And there, on the emporium steps, was Letty Peacock and her daughter Maureen, both of them frankly gawking. In Abby's memory, they would forever be standing on the steps of the Parlett store; she wondered, *What name will Letty call this little boy?* There was her mother, gazing out from the lobby window of the hotel. *What will people think, Mother?* Lyrics and the melody of "Down by the Old Mill Stream" ("where I first met you...") floated out to the street from the Music Arcade. And Noah, his back to the street, directing the placement of a sign across his new storefront, glanced over his shoulder and turned all the way around, staring in disbelief.

Abby waved the baby's hand to him.

She watched from the train window until the town was gone, the Rock House gone, the mountain gone, and lastly the sun was gone. The evening star came into view; no wish tonight—she had her wish. From around her neck, she withdrew the locket with the baby picture of Ronnie in it. Saying a final farewell to her lost son, she closed the locket and dropped it into a yellow silk coin purse; then, removing the emerald ring from the gold chain, she dropped it into the purse as well and snapped it shut. "Some things belong to the past," she said to Michael, who had been observing her little ritual. His brown eyes turned merry. "You look like your daddy," she told him.

"Da-da," he said in a squeal, bouncing up and down, clapping his baby hands together, and looking around expectantly, painfully reminding her of the baby who was only a picture in a locket.

The amethyst dusk turned black, and the sky filled with stars; far into the night she sat, her son asleep on the seat beside her, her only companions her reflection in the train window and long-ago memories. When Michael awoke, she changed him and again held him on her lap; the conductor brought her tea and scones and a baby bottle filled with warm milk. "And what do you want, Abby?" she could almost hear Noah's voice asking her, as he had during that first encounter with him back on the bank of the Stony.

What did she want? Michael finished the bottle, and she held her son to her shoulder, close to her heart, to burp him. "How would you like to go all the way to Canada, young man, and visit your granddaddy Townsend?" Abby said, laughter filling her voice.

From the little yellow silk bag, she retrieved the ring of intent to marry, the one Adam had placed on her finger so long ago—the ring, their love, and their child no longer forbidden

THE END

Dedicated to the memory of:

my mother, Mabel Duzett Jensen
my father, Daniel Homer Jensen
my husband, Dean Purdy Close
to the best brother a girl ever had, Randall Duzett Jensen
to "Aunt Maney" Maxfield, who, through many a red-flag winter, nursed me back to health and was the model for Aunt Em in the book.

ACKNOWLEDGMENTS, WITH DEEPEST GRATITUDE:

To my literary editor, Diane Raintree, my love and my thanks. It was a good trip.

To my beautiful and talented daughters Deborah and Michelle Close, my heartfelt gratitude for your word and art editing and most of all for being my daughters and for listening to my stories all of these years. To my son Daniel Jensen Close, thank you, Danny, for just being you.

To Joanne Haydock, for her editing and very personal love of the story.

To my "Birthday Angels," for their love and encouragement.

To my friend Jack Brown, for keeping the home fires burning.

To another friend, Darko Perovseks, who kept my computer up and rolling and knocked on my door one afternoon and said, "Let's get your novel published." Without his encouragement and prodding, my novel

The Rock House, I fear, would never have seen the light of day.

To all of you, my thanks and my love.

Finally, thank you to Lawrence S. Ritter, author of *The Glory of Their Times*, for giving me the courage to write about baseball, a sport I knew little about. The humorous story of the baseball player who runs from second base back to first was brought to my attention in the reading of his remarkable book.

ABOUT THE AUTHOR

DELANA "JACKIE" JENSEN CLOSE WAS born and raised in the tiny town of Emery, Utah. She graduated from Snow College and did her part for the war effort in the 1940s as a regular "Rosie the Riveter," spending years working on 155 mm Howitzers.

Later moving to Columbus, Ohio, Close pursued her entrepreneurial dreams and opened several restaurants and art galleries. She also met her husband in Columbus, where she settled down and started a family of her own.

Close now lives in Dublin, Ohio, where she continues to happily dream up historical romances and other dramatic tales.

Made in the USA
Lexington, KY
14 March 2019